NAMELESS SOVEREIGN

BOOK 1

A CULTIVATION EPIC

NAMELESS AUTHOR

Timeless
Wind

First published by Timeless Wind Publishing LLC 2024

This novel is entirely a work of fiction. The names, characters and incidents portrayed in it are the work of the author's imagination. Any resemblance to actual persons, living or dead, events or localities is entirely coincidental.

First edition

Editing by J. Massat and Silas Sontag.

Beta read by Sol and Morcant.

Cover art by Macarious. Typography by Lorne Ryburn.

CHAPTER 1

WAKE UP

"PROTECT THE GROVE! Don't let a single one of them through!" a grave voice rumbled over the battlefield, overwhelming even the deafening sounds of conflict.

The screams woke Red from his stupor. Sensation gradually returned to his body, and his eyes took in his surroundings. What had once been a beautiful palace had been leveled to fine powder by all the explosions, the sole exception being a white temple. His vision was blurry, but even then, he could still make out the motionless figures around him. Countless bodies lay on the ground, clad in shining armor.

My allies.

He knew they were trying to hold off an invader, but a sudden pain in his stomach made recalling the details difficult. Red looked down. There was a large hole going through his belly, large enough to see out the other side. He was surprised and rather glad that he was still alive.

Loud thumps followed. He turned his attention away from his injury and looked up just in time to see more bodies falling from the sky. These men were dead before they even hit the ground. He followed the path they had taken, looking up above. Far above in the sky was a sight his mind could hardly wrap around.

An enormous vortex spanned the heavenly horizon as far as the eye could see, rotating as more and more golden beings poured out from it. Each had an additional eye on their forehead, wings on their back, and two sets of arms. The invaders. They rushed down and soon clashed against the defending human forces, blinding spells and huge explosions bombarding the senses without end. Though Red's allies outnumbered the invaders, he saw more and more of his comrades pushed back and killed as the seconds ticked by.

Amongst them, one figure held firm against the swarming tide of enemies. Wielding a single glowing blade in his hand, this single man clashed against multiple invaders, holding the line almost on his own. Red instinctively recognized the man as his leader, whose voice had rumbled through the battlefield. He didn't know why, but the sight lit a burning spark within his spirit and forced him to his feet. Despite his wound, he was ready to rejoin the battle.

However, a flash of light came from the vortex, blinding everyone on the battlefield and bringing the fight to a momentary stop. When everyone's eyes could see again, they noticed that in the place where that human warrior once stood was only a figure wrapped in burning white flames.

"Don't... let them..."

The general struggled to let any words out. The flames burned his body until nothing was left. It was as if the man had never been there.

The invaders roared, seeing their biggest obstacle reduced to ashes, and pushed the defenders back with renewed vigor. Casualties mounting, Red's allies began to flee and scatter into a rout.

Red looked up as a gigantic, rune-covered golden arm emerged from the vortex. It pointed down with its index finger at the last standing temple down below, and a beam of condensed white flames shot towards it at dizzying speed. A cloud of fire expanded from where it hit, slowly consuming everything in its path until it reached the very heavens itself, with no sign of stopping. It was the end of the world.

How bright...

That was the last thing Red thought before the flames consumed him, too.

"Red."

A loud voice woke him up.

"Wake up, your food is here," it said.

Just as suddenly as the dream had started, it ended. When Red opened his eyes, what greeted him wasn't the sky lit up by a war between gods, but the rock ceiling of a cave dimly lit by torches.

"Had another dream?" the same voice asked.

Red sat up and saw a middle-aged man staring at him while holding up a piece of bread in his direction. A bushy graying beard covered his battle-worn face, where a scar crossed over his nose.

Red nodded before grabbing the bread from the man's hand and unceremoniously taking a bite.

"What was it about?" the man asked.

"White fire..." Red said.

All around him he could see other slaves in ragged clothing, eating their own pieces of bread just as eagerly, while a handful of the burlier slaves distributed the food from a basket.

"Is that so..."

After seeing that Red wasn't interested in elaborating, the man let the matter go. He sat down nearby and started eating his bread too, a far larger piece than the one he had given to Red.

His name was Viran, and he was the self-designated leader of the slaves in the cave. A former soldier, his strength became evident soon after his arrival, as he had beat everyone who questioned his authority, setting his own rules in this almost lawless land.

All the slaves down here were assigned to gathering precious ores. At the end of every three days, they could exchange what they had gathered for food and some other goods with the guards near the cave's entrance.

The overseers of the mine really didn't care about how the guards handled things, as long as they got what they wanted. The exchange rates were horrible and there was barely enough food to live on. Before Viran arrived, slaves would backstab each other over a piece of bread, and sometimes even resort to cannibalism. Now, Viran had made the gathering of slaves into a semi-functioning society that mined the ores more efficiently to exchange all at once. He distributed the food according to each person's contribution, all while outlawing murder and fighting.

Even if in the end their new leader got a bigger portion of the food than he deserved, the situation was beneficial to the barely ten-year-old Red. He didn't have the strength to contend with the older slaves. Before Viran arrived, he had often given a big part of his food to other people, even if he gathered more ores, just so they wouldn't beat him to death. Now, instead of living in a perpetually starving state, he was full enough to get by in the cave tunnels.

That would have been ideal if it weren't for another thing he now had to worry about.

"How many acupoints have you opened since the last time?"

Viran interrupted his meal once again with a question.

"... One," Red said before stuffing what was left of the bread in an improvised pants pocket.

Viran frowned. "That's not enough."

"I'm doing my best," Red insisted.

"It's still not enough." Viran went silent for a few seconds. "I've been speaking with the guards... I might get a Vein Opening Pill from them soon enough, but you'll have to have reached the third vein by then—"

Suddenly, a scream interrupted their conversation.

Not far away from them, the slaves had formed a circle around two men. One of them bled profusely from his head, where a large rock had made a clear indentation. His skull was fractured. The other one stood above him, with the rock in hand, ready to deal the final blow. Before the man could act, he was tackled to the ground by the slave that had been distributing the food. He tried to fight back, but another two slaves piled on and immobilized him.

Red barely had the time to register what was happening before Viran took off. He looked furious. He crouched down and examined the other slave's wound before shaking his head. His skull was already crushed, and his gaze wandered aimlessly while his mouth babbled incomprehensible words. It made for a rather disturbing scene, but Red was already accustomed to the mine's brutality.

With practiced movements, Viran put his hands around the man's neck before twisting it with a crack, putting him out of his misery. All the slaves watched in fear as their leader stood up and walked towards the aggressor. Suddenly, the bloodlust-filled state left the killer. As two other slaves put him on his knees, he stared at Viran with fear.

"He lied to me! He went into our stash and ate everything—"

Before he could finish, another crack sounded as Viran twisted the man's

4

neck as he had the neck of his victim. Complete silence filled the large cave chamber.

The slaves stared at the two bodies, too afraid to speak.

"Put both of them near the hunting room. It seems we finally have some new bait," Viran said. "What are you staring for? If you're done eating, go do your job!"

The rest of them started spreading out and leaving the chamber like startled ants.

Viran shook his head and turned to where he had been talking to Red. The boy, however, was nowhere to be seen.

He sighed. "Goddamn rat."

Red retraced his steps, as he did so often, through a narrow tunnel. The twisting corridors and passages of the caves seemed endless. Some slaves said they went miles deep into the ground, but of course, none of them were stupid enough to see for themselves. It was extremely easy for anyone to get lost in a place like this.

The red-haired boy, however, was already used to wandering these tunnels from an early age. He'd made his own markings to recognize the paths, as well as his preferred routes to search for minerals and avoid other slaves. Remaining inconspicuous and unnoticed was critical for someone as young as him to survive.

So, like a ghost, he walked barefoot across the rocky ground, the only source of illumination being a bright-green rock he held in his hand. It was a moonstone, one of the more common ores down in the cave that the slaves were tasked with gathering. It was abundant enough that it was one of the major materials they used as a makeshift currency. The stone glowed relatively brightly in the dark, making it easy to find and offering illumination when torches were in short order.

With the green stone brightening the way forward, Red finally arrived at a small intersection. This path led deeper into the less explored areas of the caves, areas full of danger. He looked around and found a small mound of rocks that blended in with the cave wall.

He threw the rocks out of the way, revealing a narrow path, one that no adult could ever fit through. Thankfully, if there was any advantage to being a young kid in such an inhospitable environment, it was that he could get into places no one else could.

Without hesitation, Red got on all fours and started crawling through the small passage. His arms and knees scraped against the rough ground, but he barely registered the pain.

Soon the passage narrowed and even Red had to lie prone on the ground to continue. This was the longest part of the journey. It took him twenty minutes of breathing rarefied air and scraping his chest against pebbles and rocks before the passage started widening enough to crawl again.

Soon it broadened enough to allow him to stand up. Ahead, he could see faint purple light from around the corner. Red walked further in and finally arrived at his destination.

The passage grew into an enormous chamber, far bigger than the one the slaves gathered in to eat. Huge black-purple tentacles sprawled across the walls, thicker than several humans placed side-by-side before tapering off at their ends. They emitted a purple light just bright enough that one could distinguish their shapes.

If you followed the tentacles to their root, you would find a strange and bulbous circular shape near the ground. Roughly the size of a grown adult, it was riddled with veins and pulsated a purple glow which spread into its tentacles, feeding them with its light like a heart.

As Red approached, an oversized human mouth formed on the "heart's" surface.

"Human, is that you?"

He heard a voice that seemed to belong to a child. Although the mouth formed the words, the voice sounded only inside Red's head.

"Yeah..." Red said, unfazed by the situation. He fiddled around with his pouch and pulled out a piece of bread. "Here, I brought you food."

CHAPTER 2

SPIRITUAL VEINS

"Is it meat?" the strange blob asked, its voice full of expectation.

"No, it's bread."

"Oh..."

Without standing on ceremony, Red threw the piece of bread in the blob's general direction. Even after they'd spent so much time together, he still didn't dare to get close to it.

A pink lizard-like tongue emerged from the mouth, flicking through the air and snatching the piece of bread with such speed that it was hard to follow with the naked eye. Quiet chewing sounds were heard as the being ate the food with undisguised excitement, despite how disappointed it had seemed before.

At that point, Red had already stopped paying attention to it. Turning around, he headed to the center of the room and took on a sort of combat stance, his legs slightly bent and his fists by his waist.

Soon enough, Red started punching the air in front of him in a slow and deliberate manner, alternating his hands, taking care to time it with his breathing. After repeating the same slow motions for thirty seconds, he changed his movements slightly, bringing his feet forward along with his punches. Then low kicks got mixed in. Slowly but surely, the speed of his repetitions grew faster, moves chaining into each other to form a complex routine.

The force in Red's punches left much to be desired, even for someone of his age, but his form was still good. At least, that was what Viran had told him when he taught him these specific moves. All he could do was exert his body as the old soldier had instructed him to, and sure enough, after less than two minutes of the high-intensity training routine, Red felt his muscles ache as sweat gathered on his body.

He never considered himself to be strong, much less so down in these caves where one barely found enough food to stay alive. However, the exercises seemed to take more out of his body than seemed logical. This was the intent, Red had learned. The routine was meant to push the body to near-exhaustion, the optimal state to absorb Spiritual Energy.

The routine continued for thirty more seconds, which seemed like an eternity for him, until eventually, beneath his aching muscles, another feeling appeared. It started like a dull spark, but before long it intensified into an electric numbness that covered his spine before spreading to his upper arms. Red knew this was his cue.

"Hey!" he called out to the blob.

The creature was still chewing on the single piece of bread, but it stopped at Red's voice.

"Do it now," he said.

The chewing stopped as the dark blob pulsed slightly, swallowing the bread. Suddenly, the purple lights flowed in reverse along its tentacles and gathered in the central "heart," making it glow with intensity. The mouth opened again and expelled a purple mist, which quickly dissolved into the chamber's air.

Although Red couldn't see the purple mist anymore, he could feel it. It was very pure Spiritual Energy. The numbing feeling in his arms intensified as he sat down cross-legged, grabbed two moonstones from his pouch, and holding one in each hand, concentrated on the sensation.

He was trying to open his Spiritual Veins according to the method Viran had taught him. As the man had explained, everything in the world contained Spiritual Energy, even the air they breathed. It was a wondrous type of invisible matter that could be used to control the elements and shape the world at your will. Red was skeptical at first, but by following the instructions given to him, he could really sense this energy and unlock organs he hadn't even known existed.

Opening the Spiritual Veins was the first step towards being able to control this energy. From what he'd been told, Red knew that there were twelve individual Spiritual Veins in the human body: two in his arms, two in his legs, four in his torso, three in his head, and one that connected them all together through his spine. Together, they formed a perfect circuit through which Spiritual Energy could flow freely. To open each of them, he needed to absorb the energy and slowly force the acupoints in each vein open. This was an extremely dangerous and delicate process. Any deviation could cripple his Spiritual Veins in the best-case scenario—and explode his entire body with excess Spiritual Energy in the worst.

Most human beings weren't born with any sensitivity to Spiritual Energy, either, and opening their Veins was much harder for them. Those people had little to no talent for manipulating the energy. Red was one such individual. However, while the path was more difficult for him, it wasn't impossible.

Viran happened to know a set of special exercises and breathing techniques that could help him open his Spiritual Veins. He seemed to be experienced in the matter, too. Everything Red had come to know about Spiritual Energy was from Viran. No other slave could talk about Spiritual Energy in nearly as much detail as the old soldier. Not to mention, his unnatural strength seemed to back up his knowledge, as the man could beat any other slave in these caves with the same ease, no matter how big or strong they were. Not to mention the many monsters that had fallen at his hands.

The effects of opening his Spiritual Veins were showing themselves to Red, too. Previously he had opened the Spinal Vein, and he had never felt as energetic as he had that day. Even though he ate the same amount of food, he now felt he could run twice as long, and the acupoint-opening exercises were becoming less draining on his stamina. This much had only been accomplished with Viran's help and close guidance. If Red had tried to go at it alone from the start, he knew that his practice would have gone wrong.

Still, either Red was a quick learner or he had an excellent teacher, because since the opening of the Spinal Vein he had done the exercises and breathing techniques by himself. Viran even encouraged him to practice on his own, mentioning that he wouldn't be able to guide him every step of the way. Right now, Red was focused on opening his second Spiritual Vein. This one was in his upper arms and shoulders, which connected to the central Spinal Vein.

This was, however, proving itself to be much harder than he initially thought. Viran had warned him of this, too. The task was much like climbing a mountain, getting harder and harder the higher you ascended. But Red had never thought it would be this difficult this early on. Even opening the first acupoint on this second vein had taken him close to a week, whereas the first few ones he had opened in a matter of days. The old soldier had been bothering him to be quicker, but it was to no avail. It seemed all his potential was already being tapped.

It was lucky, then, that in his time of need, Red had met this *thing*.

As soon as the purple mist completely dissipated into the air, he concentrated on his right arm. He felt a strong torrent of Spiritual Energy pouring into it, far more than the caves normally held. Thanks to his already opened vein, Red had some degree of control over the energy that entered his body. Of course, he didn't exactly control the Spiritual Energy; rather, he directed it towards the closed acupoint before it could damage his body.

A sharp pain spread in his upper arm as the invisible energy battered against his closed vein. It tried to open a path that it knew was there, but that had been sealed tight.

A few minutes passed by. It took all of Red's attention not to let himself pass out from the sheer pain and exhaustion that wracked his body. It was an arduous process for someone his age, but it was one that he'd both expected and his hostile upbringing had trained him for.

His efforts eventually paid off, as he felt the acupoint give way and let in the Spiritual Energy. This was the sixth acupoint he'd opened in this second vein—around halfway through it.

Even after having progressed, Red didn't feel the Spiritual Energy around him dissipate much. However, he knew any further practice would have to wait. His body was near the limits of what it could handle, and if he continued, he would suffer from some very nasty side effects.

The same childish voice resounded in his mind. "You know, you could be doing this much faster."

Red turned his gaze towards the blob, seeing its mouth moving in conjunction with the words.

"How?" Although he indulged the creature, he had a bad feeling about where this was going.

"Bring me *meat!*" it said. "It would make the energy around here purer, and you could open those channels in your body much more easily."

Red shook his head. This wasn't the first time the blob had brought up the matter.

"I would bring you meat if I could, but it's difficult to come by."

He wasn't lying. What meat they got from hunting monsters was divided, cooked, and eaten on the spot, most of it going to Viran. Red received some of it too, more than a child deserved according to the grumbles of some slaves, but he would never give that nutrition up. It was one of the few things that kept his body in functioning shape. What use would it be to increase the speed of opening his Spiritual Veins if he was too weak to defend himself?

"Well... the deal still stands whenever you get some meat."

Once more, the blob sounded disappointed. Red knew the next time he came by, it would probably bring up the matter again.

"I'm leaving." Red patted the dust off his pants and turned around, heading towards the exit.

"Farewell—and bring some meat next time!" the voice said, the blob's mouth retracting into its body.

His body aching, Red made his way back through the twists and turns of the narrow passages leading to his hidden training room. He didn't dare to spend one second more than was necessary in that place. Even if that shadowy being was intelligent and not intent on hurting him, there was no telling what sort of things could happen if he stuck around too long, especially considering its hunger for meat.

Crawling through the narrow tunnel, Red couldn't help but wonder how long he could fit through here. It would be an unfortunate day when he could no longer partake in trading food for pure Spiritual Energy with the strange creature. Still, that was a matter for another time.

He exited through the opening and hid the small tunnel entrance with a pile of rocks. As he got ready to return to Viran, though, he heard faint but quick steps approaching from a connecting corridor.

Red's tired muscles tensed. A threat?

CHAPTER 3

MENTOR

THE FIRST THING Red did when the footsteps approached was to hide in an adjacent corridor, crouching behind a piece of the protruding rock wall that perfectly concealed his slight frame in the dark and tight space. This was a place he had picked beforehand when he started visiting the room. One of many.

One thing that had kept him alive for many years inside the caverns was his extreme amount of caution and planning against things that could kill him. It was far more consideration than even the average slave would put into their survival, let alone someone his age.

The steps approached. Red heard them reach the small opening, where they stopped. Faintly, he could see a green light emanating from that direction. A few seconds of complete silence went by before the individual spoke up.

"You little shit, are you here?!"

The rough male voice echoed in the cave.

Red recognized the voice. This was Gruff, a strong, burly slave and one of Viran's direct "assistants."

He didn't respond.

"Fine!" the man barked. "If you're not gonna come out, I'll drag you myself!"

Red heard the shifting of steps around the cavern. Gruff seemed intent on finding him at all costs, but that part didn't worry him. He could hide from the man all day in these tunnels if the need arose.

A few minutes went by as Gruff paced around the nearby tunnels, turning over almost every rock in sight.

"Damn it!" the man shouted in frustration. "Listen, Viran wants something from you. If you're not gonna come out, then I'll just tell him that you didn't want to meet him!"

This was enough to give Red some pause. He could hide and avoid other slaves, but there was no escaping from Viran. Still, he didn't trust Gruff enough to take his words at face value either.

He left his hiding place and made his steps loud enough to draw the man's attention, while still keeping a prudent distance between them. Gruff was a large bald man who always carried a frown on his face, the poor diet doing little to diminish his menacing figure and the power behind it.

Gruff strode in his direction. "Finally gonna show your face, huh?"

"What does Viran want?" Red asked in an impassive voice, even as the bumbling giant made his way towards him.

He showed no fear despite his aching body.

This made Gruff stop in his tracks. If his earlier words held true, Red was fairly certain he wouldn't try to kill or hurt him out of fear of their leader's retaliation. Still, Red was ready to run if his reminder wasn't enough to dissuade the goon. Many people in the caves weren't always prone to acting logically.

"... Hmph, like I would know why he wants to waste his time with a useless brat. Just follow me!" Gruff said, his frustration mounting.

"After you." Red wouldn't follow orders that easily. There was no way he was going to give him that satisfaction.

Gruff, fed up and not wanting to waste any more of his time, sneered before making his way back through the tunnel. Red waited until he was almost out of view before following him.

Throughout the whole walk back, Red was busy with his thoughts. Usually Viran just gave his orders while they ate. If he had something important to tell him, why didn't he do it back then?

And then there was the more worrying problem. How had Gruff known where he was?

If there was one thing Red prided himself on, it was his ability to traverse the tunnels undetected. It was what had kept him alive all these years while other slaves fought and killed each other over breadcrumbs.

Having checked many times, he had been certain that he had never been followed while going to meet the strange creature. But now, he was not so certain anymore.

Red wasn't worried they would discover his secret partner, since the tunnel was barely wide enough for a child to fit through, but the mere thought that someone had followed him without his knowledge unsettled him.

It was unlikely someone as stupid as Gruff could have tracked him down. None of the other slaves seemed skilled or smart enough to do so, which left only one answer in his mind.

Viran.

To everyone else around him, the relationship between Viran and Red seemed to be that of a mentor and a student. To them, the old soldier had pitied the young boy who had been cursed to live a miserable life in these caves and taken him under his wing, keeping him fed and training him to become self-sufficient.

Red knew this was not the case. After Viran had taken over as the leader of the slaves, he proposed to him a simple deal.

Red would be protected and fed under Viran's authority. In exchange, he would need to practice the Spiritual Vein opening technique that the older man was going to teach him.

It had seemed too good to be true. After all, it was a win-win situation where Red was not only protected by the leader of the slaves, but also able to get stronger by practicing whatever magical method Viran had in mind. Nothing about the man had showed him to be the softhearted type, so there must have been something he gained from this.

Red just couldn't see it.

However, he had been left with little choice but to accept the deal, knowing better than to test the man's patience like many others had before him. So it was that he took on his role as an apprentice under Viran. Much to his surprise, after months of practice under his new mentor, nothing bad had happened to Red. Perhaps he was truly overthinking the matter, and the man didn't have any bad intentions towards him. He wasn't about to put his life in the hands of someone he couldn't fully trust, though.

That was why Red hadn't told him about his deal with the dark creature, and why he'd lied about how much progress he'd made in opening his Spiritual Veins.

Even though no one besides Red could make their way through the tunnel, he worried Viran had somehow found out about it.

If that was the case, what would happen? Would the creature make a deal with the clearly stronger and more capable man instead? Would Viran think that Red had outlived his usefulness now that he had a Spiritual-Energy-spewing fountain at his disposal? Would he just freak out and kill the monster—or get himself killed by it?

Red wasn't too sure, but clearly, none of the options meant anything good for him. That was why he couldn't afford for Gruff to snoop around this place and get anywhere near the hidden tunnel.

Before long, the sounds of talking and shuffling feet could be heard over their steps. Soon enough, he could see yellow light coming from a bend in the tunnel ahead, just over the big man's shoulder.

As he approached the clearing, Red saw scores of slaves shuffling around, messing with all kinds of equipment. Ropes, stone spears, bone spikes, and even some knives made of a black, shiny material. He knew it wasn't metal, but pieces of the carapaces of the monstrous insects found further down in the caves. None made for very good weapons, but it was better than going barehanded into what they were about to do.

There were about twenty slaves here, most of them men, still in good enough physical condition to help Viran. They gathered in circles and talked while checking their equipment. Around them were boxes full of torches, torn clothes, and a copious amount of moonstones. Some improvised bedding was also strewn throughout the cavern, a kind of luxury only the slaves that worked under Viran were afforded.

Off to the side, Red also saw the bodies of the two people he'd seen Viran kill earlier. Their corpses were being prepared for transportation by other slaves.

Gruff stopped near the middle of the chamber before pointing towards a large tent made of old and patched leather set up towards the back of the cave. A shadowy silhouette could be seen inside, backlit by a bright light.

"He's waiting for you," Gruff said before turning around and walking away, paying no more attention to him.

Red stood in place, staring at the entrance of the tent. After what felt like an eternity of consideration, he shook his head and walked in, lifting the flap over his head. What greeted him was an environment that seemed entirely foreign to the caves.

Two torches tied to upright sticks illuminated an improvised desk, comprised of a large, flat rock covered by a piece of leather, with a smaller flat rock serving as a seat. On the desk were yellowed papers and a small stone bowl filled with whatever Viran used to write. Red didn't know how to write or read, so he had no idea about its contents.

Occupying the adjacent wall was the man's bedding, made of pitch-black fur and even some kind of stuffed sack that passed for a pillow—an extravagance only the leader of the slaves could afford. Viran must've gotten it in a trade with the surface guards for rare minerals and monster parts he had gathered. Even though it was far from ideal, Viran could still afford to live far more comfortably than anyone else. Those who tried to challenge his privilege or steal from him, by force or otherwise, were no longer around to tell their story.

On the other side of the spacious tent, Red saw the man himself sitting on the ground and sharpening his iron knife against a smooth rock, an acute noise resounding in the shelter. The knife was the only metal weapon down here, and it had seen the blood of no small amount of people. Viran always kept it on him, and it was clearly more precious to him than any of his other possessions.

He lifted his head towards Red, who stood by the entrance waiting patiently. His rough and stern-looking features formed what the boy thought was a smile for a second before he returned his attention to sharpening his knife.

"You're coming to hunt with us," Viran said. It was an order, not a request.

Red felt alarmed that this matter had been brought up out of nowhere, but he didn't let it show in his voice or expression.

"... I've never hunted before."

"I'll teach you," Viran said. "You won't need to take an active role, anyway. Any of those things could tear you apart with ease, so you can take this as a learning experience. Just listen to what I say, hang back, and don't get yourself killed."

Red didn't know what had compelled Viran to invite him on such a risky venture out of nowhere, but like always, he didn't think of complaining. He had always been eager to learn how to hunt those horrible monsters, and he didn't think Viran would go to such lengths just to dispose of a child. He could snap his neck in front of everyone in the camp and no one would say a word.

"I'll need a weapon," Red said.

"Hah!" Viran snorted and stopped sharpening his blade. He brought the knife close to his face and ran a finger over its edge, examining the sharpness. Finally, after a nod of satisfaction, he threw it towards Red.

He caught it by reflex, taking care to grip the handle lest he cut himself. Although Red's expression remained impassive, a glint could be seen in his eyes as he examined the weapon, imitating Viran by running his thumb over the edge. A small cut opened on his skin, and a drop of blood slid down the blade.

"You can use that for the hunt," Viran said. "Now, let's get the rest of the hunting party ready."

As he got up, a dangerous smile grew on his face. "We have some big bugs to kill."

CHAPTER 4
HUNTING

THE SLAVES MARCHED in an orderly line, advancing in pairs through the tunnels. Viran took the lead, carrying a stone spear in one hand and a black chitin knife in the other, while Red stayed more towards the middle of the pack. The twenty people in the hunting party were all armed with improvised weapons. Five of them carried torches, lighting the surroundings as they passed. Two of them carried the wrapped bodies of the slaves that had died earlier in the day.

The bait.

Viran had managed to beat some discipline into the group of slaves, and they carried themselves with a degree confidence, even though their clothing and equipment left much to be desired. This wasn't the first time they'd done this. Once they had feared and avoided the monstrous insects at all costs, but under their new leader's guidance and strength, they could now kill them for another source of food.

That was why some were unhappy when they heard they would be taking a child along.

"Don't know what he's thinking."

Red recognized Gruff's voice speaking from further back. He carried one of the two wrapped bodies and didn't even attempt to keep his voice down.

"Kid's just gonna get in the way, and we have to share our meat with him?" The man scoffed. "Not fair, I tell you. If the little shit gets in danger, I'm not helping him, no matter what Viran tells me."

"Shut up!" someone else said. "Do you want him to hear us and tell the boss?"

"Hmph, like I care..."

Still, Gruff didn't continue the conversation.

None of the other slaves berated him for his complaints, though. Red knew they all felt the same way, even though most of them were not brave enough to speak up about it in Viran's presence. He could see the glares they cast his way and how they chose their words carefully around him. They had never liked the privileged treatment Red got from Viran, but now that he was about to take a share of their meat, their loathing for him grew stronger.

He knew some of them wouldn't mind killing him off when their boss wasn't around just to sate their anger. They'd tried that before, too, but Red was too good at hiding for them to catch him.

Every slave knew the importance of meat, even meat that came from insects. It was essential if they wanted to keep themselves fit enough to survive another day. The guards up top rarely traded for any kind of food that wasn't bread—that by itself was rarely enough.

Before the old soldier arrived, they'd stolen from each other or scavenged the nooks and crannies of the caves for the rare edible mushroom. Since Viran had come around, and proven he could hunt down and kill the monsters that dwelled further in the mines, all the slaves had been excited to get their share of meat.

It became a sacred activity for them, and even though it wasn't uncommon for one or two slaves to die every other hunt, all of them were more than willing to put their lives on the line for the chance at a full stomach.

Of course, what they were hunted weren't just any animals. They were giant insects larger than the average human. They didn't stay near the surface like the slaves, but it wasn't uncommon for a few to make their way up in search of food. The slaves, who wouldn't be able to fight back even in their best condition, made for easy prey.

That was also why Viran had started using the bodies of dead slaves as bait. In the past, one reason the beasts reached their dwellings so often was because dead bodies would simply be left nearby. The insects, who relied heavily on smell to interact with the world around them, could detect the scent of blood on a breeze blowing down the cave tunnels from very far away. By using the corpses of these unfortunate slaves as bait, Viran was both removing a danger and also getting them meat. He got a bigger share than everyone else, of course, but none of them dared to complain after they'd seen him fight.

"Should be getting near the clearing." Viran looked back at them. "We'll set up the bait and then kill our torches. After that, get in position behind cover and stop fucking yapping your mouths."

All the slaves nodded. Red himself didn't know what he was supposed to do here, as Viran had neglected to explain anything to him. He decided he would just hang off to the side and watch as the other slaves worked.

He touched the knife hidden at his waist. Red couldn't help but feel excited. All he had done for his entire life down in these caves was avoid combat due to how small and weak he was, but now that he'd started opening his Spiritual Veins, he could feel his body becoming more durable as he advanced. Red was quite certain that it wasn't enough to fight against someone like Gruff, who could still easily twist his neck with one hand, but he was confident the difference between them was shrinking.

Naturally, he still didn't let his guard down. Viran had never taught him anything about combat, and Red doubted he'd invited him to this hunting party out of the goodness of his heart. Even now, he worried about what would happen once the confrontation with the monsters went down. Perhaps Viran would use him as additional bait? It didn't seem like his style, not after giving away his knife. He did not bother tricking people when he wanted to kill them. Still, Red would be foolish not to be a little suspicious.

All kinds of thoughts ran through his mind as the group walked for another half an hour through the twisting tunnels. The passage finally widened up ahead of them. Red guessed this was where they would be hunting.

The space was very wide, even wider than their gathering area near the surface. The ceiling was easily five meters high, and the room opened into a wide circle measuring over fifty meters across. It was an enormous space, but what caught his attention was located towards the back of the expanse.

A small pond lay near the wall, the clear water reflecting the light from the torches, signs of dripping moisture decorating the rock behind it.

Pure water.

What they usually drank, they gathered from cracks in the ceiling, collecting the dripping water in pots—but it was just barely enough for the slaves to survive. These kinds of ponds were rare, let alone one of this size. Red swallowed, not noticing how dry his mouth was until now. It hadn't been a short walk, after all.

He wasn't the only one who thought so. Many of the slaves looked towards Viran as they spread around the room's entrance, waiting for permission to walk forward and approach the pond.

"Everyone will have their turn," Viran said. He looked towards the people carrying ropes and the human bait. "You guys help me set up the bait. The rest of you can go drink."

With that, Red felt relief. At least he could cross off being used as live bait for giant insects from his list of concerns. Many other slaves rushed past him, eager to be the first to drink from the pond. Red wisely decided to hang back until they were done.

He looked around and noticed two additional passages that led into the cavern. They extended down, deeper into the caves. He supposed the insects would come from those tunnels. Perhaps they frequented this place to drink. For now, Red couldn't see any signs of them.

Around the walls of the openings, he noticed a faint green glow shining from various points. They were moonstones embedded in the rock surface, giving off some illumination but not nearly enough to light up the room. No one had gathered them yet, not to mention they would need a pickaxe to pry them from the wall—something none of them had brought down here.

Red had always been fascinated by the thought of those stones. Not only were they abundant, but they seemed to grow out of nowhere in the cave walls. If you collected a moonstone from a certain vein and then waited for several weeks, it would sprout back in the same area where it had been extracted. It was an unnatural phenomenon, but at the very least, it meant the slaves didn't have to descend further into caves to the monsters' lairs to gather more stones for their survival.

Red himself had his own secret moonstone-gathering spots. Although he didn't have the equipment to mine the stones in huge chunks, he could still grind them down into smaller pieces with the help of some sharp rocks. That yielded him enough moonstones to exchange for food.

While he waited for his own turn to drink, his gaze wandered to the ceiling, where he saw more of the weak, green spots of light. They truly did grow everywhere in this cave. As he observed them, however, Red felt something shift.

He blinked, and a section of the green light disappeared for a brief second, as if something had passed over it and blocked its light.

A moving shadow.

Red's eyes narrowed. "There's something there—"

"AAAAH!"

His voice had barely spoken before deafening screams drowned it out.

His gaze lowered, following the sounds. An enormous set of insect jaws had pierced a man's torso, each pincer larger than an adult's head. The giant creature, which Red could only partially see, raised the man into the air. Its body was segmented in many parts, each with their own sets of legs, and covered by a pitch-black carapace. On its head a pair of meter-long antennae swiveled, sensing the prey that had gathered here just for it.

The man who had been caught by the creature's jaws howled, struggling against its grip.

"Help me!"

This was the last coherent thing that Red heard before screams erupted all around him.

CHAPTER 5
CENTIPEDE ATTACKS

As THE CENTIPEDE-BEAST claimed its first kill, bloodcurdling shrieks were also reverberating from a different corner of the room. Red could see another one of the creatures by the pond, another slave grasped in its mandibles. But he didn't have the time to worry about his allies, as the first centipede-beast dropped from the ceiling just in front of him. Now it wrapped itself around its victim, and the man's screams died down as his lungs were crushed. Looking through a shifting crowd of slaves, Red could finally witness the full appearance of the monster.

From head to toe, he guessed it was about five meters long with the width of a human torso. Its segmented legs wriggled, and its mandibles held firm, not releasing their grip until it was certain the man had died. Red wasn't sure, but he swore he could see a smaller set of inner mandibles concealed by the bigger ones nibbling at the victim's shoulder.

At that point, the people around the room panicked. Some of the braver slaves lifted their weapons towards the two monsters while others were already running away. As much as they were used to hunting down the creatures, being hunted instead still came as quite a surprise.

"Stop fucking screaming!" Viran's voice drowned out all the other panicked shouting, snapping the slaves out of their terror. "Tie the ropes around them and stab them where you can!" he ordered.

Red turned to stare at their leader. Viran himself was about to face another two of the giant, hissing centipedes. Six other slaves stood behind him, ready to help but not courageous enough to step forward. Gruff was among them.

It was clear that Viran was too occupied with himself to come to the aid of the other slaves. The rest separated into groups. The first positioned themselves by the human bait near the center of the room, facing the two centipedes. A larger group by the pond faced another centipede, and the final group at the side of the room confronted yet another monster. This last group was composed of Red and one other slave that was nearby.

It was only now, as he sized up the horrendous creature in front of him, that Red realized the situation he found himself in. He hesitated for a few seconds. He felt a sense of dread rise over his body, but he didn't let panic take over his mind. He ignored the sounds of clashing weapons and screams coming from around him.

The centipede hadn't noticed him yet. It seemed content with feasting upon its victim. Red took advantage of this opportunity to regroup with the other slaves. His feet slid backward, trying not to draw the attention of the monster.

The other slave behind him didn't think to do the same, though.

"H-HELP!"

He ran in a panic towards Viran's group.

At that, the monster lifted its head in Red's direction. Its small beady eyes stared at him, assuming the child to be the source of the hurried steps. Red froze, but the centipede did not hesitate. With a loud hiss, the creature unwrapped itself from its meal and slithered towards him with impressive speed.

Red could only try to run from the rapidly approaching legs. It took him but a second to realize he couldn't outpace the nightmarishly fast creature. He looked back and saw the monster rear up its upper body as it lunged in his direction. In a desperate reaction, Red threw himself to the side, feeling the wind blow against his back as he barely dodged the mandibles of the beast. He rolled a few times and felt his body bruise against the hard rock, but he didn't have time to register the pain.

Another hiss came from behind him. The centipede was apparently quite mad that its prey had escaped, but it didn't give up the pursuit. Red hurriedly got to his feet and started running again, taking just a moment to orient himself in the cavern. The monster had unintentionally put itself between him and the rest of the group, cutting off his only route towards a safe retreat.

Red thought he could hide instead. However, he was too far from the connecting tunnels, and the cave itself didn't have anything he could use for cover.

While he struggled to make a decision, he could already hear the centipede's feet quickly approaching, the possibility of death becoming clearer and clearer. As he looked for a way out, his eyes came upon the body of the slave the monster had been eating.

A plan formed in his mind.

With a dive, Red reached the body and pulled at its clothes with an effort one could only muster in the face of death. In the same movement, he covered himself with the body.

It was not a moment too soon.

He felt a weight crash down on top of him, taking the air out of his lungs. He twisted his head under the tremendous weight and saw the centipede's legs wriggling above him. Its pounce had been stopped by his improvised shield.

Red gathered his courage and shifted up his body with some effort, looking over the shoulder of the corpse. The centipede had sunk its large mandibles deep into the dead man's torso again, and now it stood still, waiting to drain the life of its victim.

It took a few seconds for Red to understand what had happened. The centipede must have thought that it bit the victim it had just been chasing, unable to differentiate one human from another. Still, the situation for Red wasn't that much better. If he tried to move from under the body, he was certain the centipede would just chase him again, and from this close distance, it was unlikely to miss. Not to mention, Red wasn't sure he could escape the heavy weight piled on top of him.

He heard the sounds of chewing, as after a few seconds the centipede had started munching on its prey again. With little choice, Red fumbled around with his right hand, reaching for his waist. He felt around until he managed to grip a wooden handle.

The iron knife.

Of course, Red himself wasn't sure that attacking the centipede was the best course of action, but he would rather take his chances than wait for the monster to notice the presence of his still-living body.

From his position, there was not much Red could reach with his short arms, not to mention he wasn't sure he could pierce the sturdy-looking carapace of the centipede. Examining his options, his gaze wandered to the centipede's head. He held his breath. Still, the creature seemed too occupied with its food to notice his squirming, perhaps confusing his movements for the last death throes of its prey.

Red then saw hope. What he had thought was a single pair of eyes were actually multiple small sets of circular eyes clustered closely together on each side of its head. An idea took shape in his mind. Thankfully for him, the creature had to lower its head close to its food so its inner jaws could tear and gorge on the food. This proved to be the perfect opportunity.

With a deep breath, Red focused on the movement of his arm, freeing it from under the corpse of the other slave. Just as the centipede noticed the stray limb moving right in front of his eyes, he stabbed down with all the strength he could muster.

With a far louder hiss than Red had thought the monster capable of, it freed its mandibles from the corpse of the slave, its upper body arching back in pain. The iron knife had lodged itself in the centipede's eyes, up to the hilt.

Red pushed the corpse off him once the centipede backed off, twisting around several a few meters away from him. As he got up, he felt a sharp pain in his torso that made him stumble. The impact from earlier might have broken his ribs. Red struggled for air and turned around to run back towards the group of slaves—when a shadow darted out from the corner of his eye.

He barely had enough time to avoid a direct collision. The strong carapace of the centipede struck a glancing blow against the side of his body with enough force to send him flying. All Red could think at the moment was that if he didn't have a broken rib before, then surely he would have one now.

His vision blurred from the pain, but he still struggled to pull himself up and faced the centipede. It wasn't targeting him, continuing to thrash around in a blind rage. Red was just unlucky to have been caught in the way. Still, he could see that some sort of sense was returning to the monster, its flailing subsiding as it leveled its head.

Red didn't have enough time to get up and run back to his allies. He was also struggling to breathe through the sharp pain running up his chest.

He had nowhere to hide or escape to.

Red, however, was no stranger to pain or the threat of death. He had been hurt multiple times, either by other slaves or by accidents while exploring by himself, and yet he had lived to tell the tale.

Under even the most dangerous situations, Red maintained a calm and analytical mind, and that was his strength.

He still was afraid of dying, perhaps even more than most people would think under his emotionless visage. However, he had always pushed past his fears to act with the utmost serenity and logic. Or at least as much that he could muster in the moment.

He ran over the possibilities in his mind. If he tried to run, the centipede would quickly detect his movement and attack him, so that wasn't a feasible plan. The only thing left for him was to hide. But where?

His eyes darted around.

The body he had been using for cover had been thrown far away during the monster's rage, and there were no other hiding places in his sight that he could use.

It was then, as he searched for a way out, that he saw it. The centipede turned its back to him as it calmed down, and a plan came to Red.

Still struggling through pain, Red stealthily moved forward. Not towards his allies, but towards the centipede instead. Just as the beast had stilled and could finally hear his approach, Red gathered his remaining strength for one last jump.

He gripped the black-carapaced back of the monster and wrapped his arms around it.

Another deafening shriek echoed in the cave.

CHAPTER 6
FINISHING BLOW

THE CENTIPEDE REACTED as Red expected. It squirmed in anger at the prey latched onto its back. Its mandibles clicked together as it tried to twist its upper body to reach Red.

Unfortunately for it, this was something he had accounted for. He climbed further up the creature's body and closer to its head so that it wouldn't be able to touch him with its deadly mandibles. The centipede realized its struggling wouldn't work, and its fit of anger turned into a berserk state. It lifted its upper body and started swinging it around in wide and erratic movements.

Red had to reach around its underbelly and clasp his hands together so he wouldn't be thrown off. His ribs still screamed in pain from the effort, but Red managed to shrug it off with the adrenaline coursing through his veins. He knew the discomfort he was feeling now was preferable to being killed by the monster throwing him off.

The centipede's panic only mounted. Suddenly, with a lurch, it threw itself on the ground and started rolling around. Red felt his vision blur and spin as the monster repeatedly twisted itself against the rock floor. His back scraped and banged against the floor, adding more bruises to his already beaten body, and for a moment he felt his grip slip from the carapace.

Unwilling to let go, Red instead latched onto the monster's legs for support, rattling around like a rag doll.

Just as he couldn't hold on any longer, the centipede slowed down. It appeared that the effort was also disorienting the creature and draining its energy. His vision slowly came back, and Red felt like vomiting out the contents of his almost empty stomach.

"Between the eyes, right on top of its head!" a loud voice said. "STAB IT!"

It took him a few seconds to recognize the owner of the cry—Viran. It took him another second to even register that the man was speaking to him. Almost out of instinct, Red followed his instructions. The centipede was still recovering from its panicked state, head low to the ground, the knife still lodged into its compound eyes.

Red took the opportunity and reached up with his right hand, grasping the handle of the knife before pulling. But the knife was stuck tight, and the centipede once more reared its upper body with a painful hiss. He held on to his position with his right hand as the left struggled to pull out the knife. With a great effort, he yanked it free, and greenish blood spurted out from the centipede's eyes.

The monster twisted in the air, and Red lost his grip and slid back, his hands raised above his head from the momentum. His legs, though, wrapped around the monster's body, keeping him from being thrown off. The beast was about to re-enter its berserker state, and Red doubted he could hold on for another round of twists.

Suddenly, he focused on the spot Viran mentioned—between the eyes of the centipede. At that moment, he had no time to consider whether he had enough strength to pierce through the thick carapace. Strength Red didn't know he had welled up in his arms and, with a grunt, he stabbed the knife down into the target.

A spurt of green blood hit him in his face as the weapon lodged itself to the hilt, the carapace cracking around the wound. The centipede wailed and suddenly jerked its body back. This time, Red's efforts weren't enough, and he was thrown off.

He fell on his back and the wind got knocked out of his lungs. All the wounds and exhaustion he had accrued during the fight finally caught up to him, and it was a struggle to keep his eyes open. He looked to the side, making out the silhouette of the centipede frantically twisting and curling its body on the ground. Not even being stabbed in its head was enough to kill the monster right away. Red, however, couldn't muster any more strength to finish it off.

From behind him, he could hear the slaves approaching the centipede.

Viran was among them, barking orders. "Throw the ropes around it and hold it down!" Red thought he saw him look in his general direction. "And someone make sure the boy's not dead!"

He didn't know if it was the comfort of knowing the centipede was dealt with or the fact that Viran wouldn't leave him to die, but as soon as those words were spoken, all the strength left Red's body and his vision went black.

Pain. That was the first thing Red felt when he woke up. His entire body ached. It reminded him of the first time he'd practiced the training routine Viran had taught him. Except this time, his situation was much worse. As he took a deep breath, a sharp pang shot through his chest, and he almost felt his consciousness slip once more. His hand couldn't help but shoot up towards his ribs as an agonized groan escaped his mouth.

"Hmm, alive and well, then?"

A voice came from his side, but Red didn't register it.

"Don't worry," it said. "Pain is good—means you can still feel."

Red ignored the voice. He felt around his body, discovering more and more newly bruised spots as he squirmed. Not making the same mistake of breathing too quickly again, he calmed himself, taking short and slow breaths as his eyes adapted to the light.

He inspected his surroundings.

A warm orange light illuminated the place, and it didn't take long for him to recognize the leathery ceiling above him. He was in Viran's tent. He turned his head and saw the man sitting on his stone bench, munching ravenously on some kind of food. Right by his side, Red could also see the man's bed covered in black fur. Even now, Viran was too stingy to let a wounded child rest in comfort.

"Take your time getting up," Viran said in between bites, unconcerned. "A broken rib is no joke."

It seemed like the assessment of his injuries was on point. Red noticed some bandages wrapped around his chest, a luxury very few slaves could afford. He decided then to gather his strength and sit up. It took a very long and painful half-minute before he accomplished the task. Once he was done, he dragged himself to the tent wall to support his back.

He looked up and saw that Viran's attention had returned to the food in his stone bowl. Whatever he was eating had an unappetizing, brown color and a rather unpleasant smell that pervaded the tent. He figured it must've been the centipede they had fought earlier.

After a long silence, Red finally spoke up. "What happened?"

He didn't remember much from his confrontation with the insect, everything still a blur in his mind. Adrenaline and instinct had taken control of him during the ambush.

"You killed it," Viran said, a smile growing on his face. "Well, you didn't really kill it. It would still have taken a long time for it to die even after having its brain stabbed, but you made it easier for us."

Red didn't feel any pride, even with what he had accomplished. If Viran hadn't been there to rescue him, he would have died from his wounds all the same, so he felt it was a loss on his end.

"Did we get all of them?"

"Three. The fourth one ran away." Viran paused and threw another piece of cooked centipede in his mouth. "Never seen that many together this close to the surface. We usually only get one or two, and that's after setting the bait to attract them. Those were just waiting there." Viran frowned. "It's not a good sign, Red. Either they've been breeding way too much and don't have enough space to share, or a stronger monster has been pushing them out of their territory. Either way, it's not good news for us up here..."

He let his words trail off and started eating his food again.

Red agreed—that definitely wasn't good. He had seen his fair share of monsters that came wandering near where the slaves lived, and a pile of corpses was always left in their wake. Things had gotten better after Viran had arrived, but if even he was worried about these monsters, how could Red find any hope in this new information?

"How many people died?" he asked.

He remembered that before he'd passed out, there were at least two people that had fallen victim to the centipedes' bites.

"Seven," Viran answered. "Most killed on the spot." He didn't seem bothered by their deaths, his voice casual.

Red was ready to continue their conversation, but as he slowly got accustomed to the pain, the smell of cooked insect meat registered to his senses.

Even as unpleasant as it was, it still brought attention to his now-empty stomach. Red had neglected to ask how long he had been out, but after all the energy he'd spent, it was no wonder he felt like he was starving. His attention settled on the bowl of meat in the old soldier's hand.

"I'm hungry," Red said.

"Hmm?" Viran stopped chewing and stared at Red with a confused expression.

"I... helped you hunt and kill a centipede," he replied, his tone indifferent. "I deserve my share of the meat, too."

A few seconds of complete silence went by before the man suddenly burst into laughter.

"Hah! Of course, you need to eat something! I sometimes forget you're still just a child, you know."

Viran grabbed another bowl full of cooked centipede parts. He got up and approached the boy, crouching down to his level.

"Here, take it."

Red was about to grab it before Viran pulled it out of his reach. "Ah, yes, I forgot. First, I need you to answer me something..."

His carefree expression changed into one Red was all too familiar with.

The killing face.

Red suddenly felt an immense sense of danger, and a cold shiver ran down his spine.

"How many acupoints have you opened?"

CHAPTER 7

THE TRUTH

A HEAVY SILENCE settled in the air. Viran kept his eyes trained on him, and Red felt the pressure of the whole world fall onto his shoulders. It took a few seconds that felt like an eternity for him to gather his thoughts. His life was not in his own hands anymore. There was no wriggling himself out of this situation, so why even hesitate?

On the surface, no sign of Red's agitation could be seen. His mind finally calmed down as he accepted the position he had found himself in.

"How did you know?" he asked, not breaking eye contact with the man.

"It's not easy," Viran said. His expression relaxed, and he placed the bowl back on his desk. "You already know that the more acupoints we open in each Spiritual Vein, the stronger our bodies get. Someone who has opened three or four Spiritual Veins would be completely capable of taking on several normal people in a fight."

Red hadn't had the chance to witness it before, but he was aware of how the process worked. There were ninety-nine acupoints divided amongst all twelve Spiritual Veins in the human body, and for someone to fully wield Spiritual Energy, they needed to open them all. Viran had told him in the past that the more acupoints you opened, the stronger you would become. This was not only in the physical aspect, but your senses and your mind would also improve substantially. And someone who had only opened one

Spiritual Vein, for instance, would be hard-pressed to match someone who had opened four.

"The difference between having or not having a few Spiritual Veins completely opened is quite clear," Viran went on. "But it's harder to notice it when you get to the acupoints themselves. There probably won't be much of a difference in strength between an adult who has opened two of his upper arm acupoints and another who has four." A mocking smile grew on his face. "That's probably what you were thinking when you tried to hide your progress from me, right? And well, you weren't entirely wrong. But unfortunately, you forgot you are dealing with a genius here." He tapped the side of his head with his finger.

At that point, Red had an idea about how he'd been found out.

"Was that why you invited me for the hunt?"

Viran nodded. "More or less, but things went far more smoothly than I thought. It would've taken weeks of observation normally, but thanks to those centipedes, all your secrets were laid bare before me." He took an iron knife from his waist, the same one he had let Red borrow earlier. "I measured how deep you managed to stab that damned thing. To the average person, this wouldn't tell them much, not to mention as a kid your body is still in development—but I've done my research."

He demonstrated his point by making a stabbing motion with the weapon.

"Although I can't be sure of the specific number, the strength needed to get the knife that deep into the centipede's head was more than a kid who'd just started opening his second Spiritual Vein could muster."

Having said his piece, the man lay back against the stone seat and continued to stare at Red.

"... This seems unfair."

It was all Red could say at that moment. This was all new information he obviously wasn't privy to, and even if he'd known about it while fighting the centipede, there was no way he would've been able to hold back when his life was on the line.

Viran smiled. "Of course it's unfair! Look, you're smart, smarter than anyone your age should be. That much was clear from the beginning. But you were always outmatched against me, kid. I'm smarter, stronger, and have far more experience in life than you. You may meet some people during your journey who are just superior to you in every way, and at that point, you can only blame your own luck." He flipped the knife in his hand before tossing it onto the desk behind him. "I've answered your question. Now you have to answer mine. How many?"

"Six," Red said with resignation. The man already knew he was lying, so he saw no point in hiding the truth from him any longer.

"Hmmm..." Viran turned away and scratched his chin. "That's not a bad speed. Far faster than someone with your talents should have..."

A terrible feeling came over Red, far worse than how he'd felt when the centipede had almost killed him. Back then, he could have died on his own terms. Right now, Red had no agency over what would happen to him. Whether he lived or died, it would all depend on what Viran wanted to do. Such was the difference in strength between them. This feeling of hopelessness pervaded every part of his body, and there was nothing he could do about it. Red felt like it was about to consume him if he let it, but even so he refused to lose himself to the feeling. There was a natural pride ingrained in his being, allowing him to maintain his composure.

Renewed silence came over the room. Red knew what question would come next. He would be forced to reveal how he had opened so many acupoints so quickly, and who knew what Viran would do then? Still, he remained silent. Although he was more or less resigned to his fate, he wouldn't spew everything he knew without prompting.

Finally, Viran sighed loudly and returned his attention to Red. "Do you know the history of these mines, kid?"

Red felt surprised by the question. What he was expecting hadn't come. Even Viran's tone had changed, becoming heavier, more tired. He paid attention—Viran wasn't the kind to speak without a purpose.

"No."

"To be truthful, neither do I. It's the kind of legend that was spread throughout the ages and has changed so much that no one really knows the true origin of this place anymore." The old soldier reached back, grabbing a moonstone that was on his desk. "They always involve the moon, though... have you ever seen it?"

Red shook his head. "No."

He had heard it described before by other slaves, this celestial body that floated in the night sky, but he had a hard time visualizing it.

"It's a beautiful thing, but also very terrifying if you look at it too much," Viran said with a smile on his face. "They say these moonstones contain traces of its power, borne from a fragment that fell down to this world a long time ago. I never believed it, and when I was sent here and could see one of them up close, I only had my doubts confirmed. They only glow with soft green light and contain a meager amount of spiritual power, completely useless, and yet those fools up top created a whole mining operation of slaves to gather them..." He shook his head. "Turns out I was the fool all along."

Red felt lost. Viran seemed to be talking to himself more than he was to him. The image of his mentor as a stalwart warrior diminished into one of a weary and bitter old man, spewing his grievances into the air.

"You know no one has ever managed to escape these mines?" Viran said. "This was what I heard all the time while I was rotting away in prison, and yet I was still confident. Perhaps they were right, but the only types of people they ever sent here were the lowest of the low, peasants and criminals they couldn't even be bothered with killing themselves. Of course, they wouldn't be able to escape, but these caves never faced someone like me..."

Suddenly, loud laughter came out of his mouth.

"What an idiot! All these stories about how arrogant heroes met their downfall I read when I was a kid, and yet look at me now, destined to rot in these caves."

Red couldn't help but feel a sense of curiosity well up in his mind. Escape. The word had sounded so foreign before Viran taught him how to open his Spiritual Veins. Now, it instead seemed to be a possibility in his future. And yet even the seasoned soldier in front of him laughed at the idea.

"Is it that hard to escape?" Red asked.

"Hard? It is extremely hard, but not impossible. No, escaping is not the real problem. It's what comes after you leave this place that's the issue..." Viran's voice drifted off as his attention returned to Red. "You know, I asked one of the guards up top—since when did they start putting kids in these caves? Do you know what he said?"

Red didn't know why, but he felt this was not something he wanted to learn.

"He said they never put any child in these mines, that even they weren't cruel enough to let a child suffer such a fate." The man studied Red's expression closely. "How did you end up here?"

"... I don't know."

Red did not lie. He truly didn't know. Ever since he became aware of

36

himself, of his first memory, he had been in these caves. That was little over two years ago.

"You truly don't remember." Viran shook his head. "This place, the more I try to understand it, the farther the answers seem to evade me. I'll give you a piece of advice, kid, something I had to learn for myself when I took my first step into this unknown world." His expression became more serious. "Some things you see in this place... it's best to just pretend that they aren't there. Do you understand?"

At that point, Red's mind recalled an image. A purple glow. After a few seconds of silence, he simply nodded.

"Good." With a smile, Viran took the bowl of food once again and offered it to Red. "Here, eat. You're gonna need it if you want to recover."

"That's it?" He grabbed the bowl, still confused about the entire conversation.

"For now, yes. What, you think I'm gonna kill you just like that?" The man returned to his old self. "You are my investment, kid, I can't just get rid of you like this."

Viran patted his ragged pants before getting up and walking towards the tent's entrance.

"Eat, rest, and get used to the pain. Tomorrow, I'm gonna start to teach you some things."

With that, he lifted the flap and left the tent.

Red didn't move, silent in thought for a good minute before the hunger got the best of him, and he scarfed down the centipede meat.

CHAPTER 8
TRAINING BEGINS

RED DIDN'T SLEEP VERY WELL. In fact, he didn't sleep at all. The stinging pain in his ribs and the strange environment of Viran's tent didn't grant him any rest during the next few hours. He didn't know how long he lay there, staring at the ceiling and reflecting on his encounter with the man. Soon, even the light of the torches inside the tent burned out and Red was left in absolute darkness, except for a faint green glow coming from the desk.

It wasn't until he heard approaching steps outside the tent that he snapped out of his reverie. He looked up. Rays of light flooded his view, and Red saw Viran standing by the entrance, looking down at him.

"Did you get some rest?" the man asked. "Actually, don't answer that. Get up. I'll be waiting for you outside." He was about to leave, but stopped in his tracks and looked back. "Don't forget to bring the knife."

With that, Red saw the tent flap fall down as darkness was restored. He hadn't tried to move much during the past few hours, so he wasn't sure what sort of state his body was in. If he had to guess, it wasn't anything good, but lying down here was not likely to help him much further.

Red took deep and slow breaths. He gathered his strength as he sat himself up. Just as he had confirmed last night, his arms were in working condition, capable of supporting his upper body weight, albeit with some difficulty. Next were his legs. They hadn't recovered nearly as well, a dull pain spreading through them as Red straightened his knees. They felt weak, and he didn't know how well they could support his body.

Red didn't feel like waiting around to see them fully healed, though. Returning to the ground, he looked for a means to pull himself up. He crawled over to Viran's desk, grabbed the edge of the improvised furniture, and tried to lift up his body in one go. The simple task took a huge amount of his energy, and his arms eventually failed him, sending him tumbling bottom-first to the ground.

His situation was worse than he had thought. Red had been hurt before, but nowhere near as badly as he was right now. The unfamiliar feeling of weakness mixed with the pain that came with his every breath was a difficult opponent to contend with, but he wouldn't let himself be defeated.

After regaining his composure, Red grabbed the desk once more, this time intent on working at the task in segments. First, a single pulling motion of his hands lifted him enough to put his knees beneath himself. Then, a pause for breath. On the second pull, Red got his feet beneath him, staying crouched even as his legs protested under the effort. Finally, the last pull.

He almost fell down once again, but by throwing his body weight against the stone desk, Red managed to stay up. The muscles in his limbs protested in pain, but now at least he was standing up on his own two feet. Looking around, his eyes found the shining reflection of the iron knife on the stone surface. He grabbed it and stowed it at his waist.

Next came the hardest part—walking. Gathering his breath once more, Red made a tentative step forward with his right foot, gradually putting the full weight of his body onto his legs. This was a mistake.

His legs buckled under him, and his vision went dark for a second. Thankfully, Red managed to latch onto the desk and avoid falling down. The sudden movement made him breathe deeply in surprise, at which point extreme pain shot through his chest, and his consciousness almost faded again.

It took one more minute for the pain to subside, and Red could have sworn that he'd been at the task for the last hour. Viran seemed understanding enough not to press him, though, as Red had never heard from him during the whole ordeal.

This time, instead of stepping forward, he flexed his legs by bending them ever so slightly before extending them again, letting the strength and sensation of his muscles return to him. After repeating the movement a few times, he finally felt capable enough to take another stab at walking.

First, it was one step. A success. Then came the second one, and one of his hands let go of his support. This one was a bit trickier, but Red retained his balance, and his confidence rose. A few more steps later, he tried to let go of the support entirely to stand on his own.

Another sharp jolt of pain shot up his legs, but this time he didn't fall. With slow and steady steps, he approached the tent's entrance and lifted the flap before moving outside.

Many slaves were sleeping in the cavern, some of them covered in injuries like him. The hunting party, Red realized. He'd almost forgotten that he wasn't the only one that had fought the centipede monsters. If it wasn't for Viran, he truly didn't know if any of them would have made it back alive.

Much to his dismay, Gruff was among the survivors, sound asleep atop some rags with not one visible injury. He looked at the center of the camp and saw the smoldering remains of a bonfire, as well as the leftover carapace pieces of the centipedes stacked to the side. They would be used to craft simple tools later. Up ahead, Viran was leaning back against the cave's entrance, holding a torch in his hand.

As Red approached him, the old soldier's brow furrowed.

"What took you so long?" Viran seemed quite serious. He didn't let Red answer, though. "Make sure to pick up your pace and keep up with me."

With that, he walked off into the dark corridors beyond.

Red didn't even have time to take a breather. Although Viran didn't rush his steps, he kept a steady adult pace, the young Red obviously struggling to keep up in his condition. They passed through various caverns packed full of slaves whose eyes squinted as the torch broke the darkness of their rest. Some of the braver ones even started to complain, before they noticed who was holding the light.

Red had rarely visited these parts of the caves before. He tried to keep away from crowds, and they tended to gather in larger groups towards the surface. This kept him away from certain parts of the mine, but he survived by finding moonstones in the darker regions where monsters were more likely to wander.

Soon enough, they entered a tunnel Red was entirely unfamiliar with. It wound and stretched, and just when he feared he couldn't keep up with

Viran's pace much longer, they found themselves facing a dead end. Or at least so it would seem.

"We're here."

Viran shined the light in front of them, and Red could see that what blocked their way wasn't a rock wall, but a stone the size of an adult that obstructed the passage.

"Hold this for me, will you?" Viran held the torch in his direction, and Red grabbed it from him.

The old soldier approached the stone and crouched down. He then put his two hands beneath the boulder and lifted it with a grunt. Red saw him raise the rock up little by little. Eventually, the stone hit the ceiling. Still, Viran didn't seem particularly pressed holding the weight, even in his awkward half-crouched position, and started to move the boulder from the previously blocked passage.

Looking on, Red saw a cavern open up before his eyes. Eventually, Viran set down the stone to the side with a heavy thud before patting the dust off his shoulders. Then Red could see the area fully.

The space was fairly large and had a smooth floor. A handful of large wooden boxes lined the walls, and in them, Red saw all sorts of things. Insect parts, improvised weapons, torches, glass bottles full of water and food, paper, and moonstones—heaps of them. In fact, it wasn't just the boxes that held them; they were spread all over the floor. There was also an improvised stone desk and seat near the back wall. As the torch illuminated the environment, Red could see what was on the walls too.

There was a picture of a rough human silhouette. In the empty shape of the figure, Red saw interconnected lines that traveled all over its body, as well as dots interspersed along these lines. He didn't need to count all ninety-nine points to recognize this was a depiction of the Spiritual Veins and their acupoints.

Viran walked over to a box while Red stared at everything in wonder. The man fetched some torches and firesteel, lighting up the room as he set them in sconces along the wall. Red put his torch in a sconce and walked over to the large drawing on the wall.

"Is this where you keep your stash?" he asked.

He knew someone like Viran would keep supplies and other things he found in the cave to himself, more than what he had in his tent.

"One of them," the man said. He pointed to the huge rock that had been blocking the passage before. "It was a pain to find a safe hiding spot, not to mention it wouldn't necessarily fit everything that I wanted. So rather than looking for one, I decided to block off one of the clearings and make it my hideout."

It was a smart plan and something that only someone with Viran's strength could do. Red was sure that no other slave could push the rock out of the way, not even if several worked together.

"What are we doing here?" he asked.

"Right. I think we need to make something clear, kid." Viran walked over to his desk. "You are an investment, Red. Something I decided to use to escape this place. At first, I wasn't too confident it would pay off. Your talent is mediocre at best, and in an environment this lacking in Spiritual Energy, your training speed was gonna suffer no matter how hard you worked. Not to mention, the training method wasn't guaranteed to work either." He looked at the drawing on the wall. "Still, you surprised me. Some way or another, you managed to train far faster down here than you should have been able to, and your survival instincts have proven to be much stronger than they appeared at first glance. You've shown to me that you're worth further investments..."

He trailed off, picking up another knife from his desk. As the weapon was brought into view, Red could see the glint of metal reflecting the torchlight.

"Now, I'm gonna make sure you don't die before you can pay me back for all my efforts."

CHAPTER 9

ACUPOINTS

"IT'S NOT GONNA BE anything complicated at first." Viran, now armed, moved towards the center of the room. "First thing you need to learn is footwork. Let me tell you, you're not gonna want to clash against any monsters head-on even after you've opened a few Spiritual Veins, so the best way to avoid getting yourself killed is by dodging their attacks."

"What about against another person?" Red asked.

"In your case, it's best that you don't get hit by anyone. You're still just a kid, so don't expect to overpower a fully grown adult just yet. What I'm gonna teach you are the basics of hand-to-hand combat that I learned in the army... or, well, something like it, anyway. Most of these teachings go out the window when you're fighting against giant monsters whose teeth are bigger than your head, but the principle of the matter still stands."

Viran entered a combat stance, his left foot forward and his knees slightly bent. He gripped the knife in his right hand.

"Every move when you're fighting starts with your feet. Whether you're about to attack and need to push off the ground for momentum or you just need to avoid getting yourself killed, it all starts from the base of your stance."

Viran displayed as much with some demonstrations. With a slight impulse from his back foot, he pushed himself farther than most could jump, clearing nearly the entire room in one go. Afterwards, he dove back, returning perfectly to his starting position.

"Even if you've started to open your Spiritual Veins, the importance of footwork doesn't diminish. For your own sake, and so you don't end up with more broken ribs, we're gonna focus on dodging right now." Viran relaxed his stance, turning back to stare at Red. He smiled. "Now, I'm not a good mentor by any means, kid. Never had to teach a ten-year-old how to fight, and I very much subscribe to the idea that experience is the best teacher. Do you understand what I'm getting at?"

At that question, Viran ran his thumb slowly over the knife's edge.

Red couldn't help but feel that something bad was about to happen.

Red felt like he was about to collapse from exhaustion before Viran finally told him their training session was done. His breathing was labored and painful, and he had new bruises all over his body to add to his collection.

The training had felt more like a one-sided beating. Red knew that even if he had been in better condition, he still wouldn't have lasted much longer against Viran's unrelenting attacks. Every blow carried monstrous strength and perfect precision behind it, and Red felt like the man could see through his every move. Not to mention that he was clearly holding back, pulling his blows at the last second just enough so they wouldn't crack any bones. They still hurt, of course, but thankfully the man never used the sharp side of the knife in his attacks either.

Red had needed to use every fiber of his being just to stay afloat in their sparring session, and after it was over, he couldn't say whether he had learned anything.

He sat on the ground covered in sweat, as the adrenaline left his body. The pain that he had ignored returned. At that point, Red felt like he'd just fought another centipede and couldn't gather an ounce of strength.

"Here, catch." Viran threw something.

Red only saw a small circular object flying towards him. He made no effort to catch it, letting it bounce off his chest. He grabbed it off the floor and brought it to his eyes. It was some kind of wooden container with a round lid and a strange smell.

"It's paste," Viran said, noticing Red's inquisitive gaze. "I managed to make it using monster body parts after some experimentation. Apply it to your ribs every day and you should be good in a week."

"Really?" He was skeptical. Even minor injuries took a long time to heal down here, and in some cases, they could become infected and lead to death. A paste that could make a severe injury heal in one week instead of a month was too good to be true.

Viran looked offended by the question. "No need to doubt me. This is truly nothing compared to what I could cook up on the surface. If I had the materials and equipment to make proper Spiritual Medicine, then your cracked ribs would heal in less than a day."

Red didn't push the matter, simply storing the small box in his pouch.

"What now?" he asked. Although he already felt spent, the training session had barely lasted five minutes.

"Right—I suppose I need to clarify some things about Spiritual Veins." Viran walked over to the seat, plopping himself down. He looked at the drawing on the wall. "I told you before that you needed to open ninety-nine acupoints split between twelve veins to allow Spiritual Energy to flow freely through your body, but... that's not entirely true."

"What do you mean?" Red's face remained emotionless, but he was alarmed. He didn't know why Viran would need to lie about something like this.

"Well, it's hard to explain without first going in-depth about this matter." The man pointed towards the drawing. "Do you see what it says?"

"I can't read."

"... Right." He scratched his beard. "The function of opening the Spiritual Veins is to allow the Spiritual Energy to flow freely through your body, as you should know, but that alone doesn't allow you to accomplish the most important thing. That is, you can't manipulate Spiritual Energy with your veins alone."

Red had gathered as much from his practice. He could gather and stimulate the energy within his Spiritual Veins, forcing them to open his acupoints, but he couldn't exert any finer control over it. He had guessed that perhaps once all Spiritual Veins and acupoints were opened could one manipulate the energy, but now it seemed like this wasn't the case.

"Opening these acupoints is merely the first step towards controlling Spiritual Energy—and not even the most important one. Even a peasant with no talent could open quite a few veins during their whole life if they got

their hands on the right method, but that's the easy part. The hard part"—
He pointed towards the center of the figure at a large circle—"is opening
that. The Spiritual Sea."

Red tried to connect the name to the characters written on the wall next
to the circle. His eyes narrowed in doubt. "You mean to say that something
that big is inside our bodies?"

"... No, it's not that big. Well, at least not entirely." Viran seemed to
struggle to explain things. "The Spiritual Sea is an organ that every person
has, but in normal situations, it's not fully formed, existing in a half-real,
half-illusory state. The specifics about what it is are not important. You
should focus on what it does, which is enable a person to manipulate and
store Spiritual Energy in their body. Opening the Spiritual Sea is the hardest
obstacle, keeping millions of ordinary people from truly elevating themselves..." Viran's eyes became unfocused for a second before he continued.

"Spiritual Energy is a wonderful thing. It both affects and is affected by
its surroundings. It can be shaped and used to accomplish extraordinary
things, but wielding it is no simple task. From ancient times, humans have
studied it and discovered the necessary tools within themselves to absorb
that energy, namely the Spiritual Sea. But you see, they had the means but
not the method. They could store the energy, but how would they transform
it and use it? It would simply remain static if you absorbed it into your Spiritual Sea, and expelling it out of your body wouldn't necessarily result in
anything magical..."

Viran trailed off, looking at Red as if waiting for something.

"This is where the acupoints and Spiritual Veins come in?" Red asked.

Viran nodded. "Exactly. Once they absorbed the energy and cycled it
through their veins and acupoints, they noticed its properties would change
just slightly. Running it through different patterns and paths would result in
different transformations. It was this discovery that led to the development
of the Spiritual Arts, and allowed people to truly rise beyond the ordinary.
That's something you will only need to concern yourself with when and if
you ever open your Spiritual Sea, though. The experts noticed that to wield
the most simple of Spiritual Arts, you need to have opened all twelve of your
Spiritual Veins and the ninety-nine basic acupoints contained within
them..."

Red frowned. "Ninety-nine?" Viran had just implied that number wasn't
the true amount.

"Indeed, but that's just the bare minimum. The human body itself is a magical wonder, kid, and even today no one dares claim to know all its secrets. Those same experts noticed that there were other special acupoints hidden within the Spiritual Veins, and opening them would allow for even more wondrous transformations and manipulations of Spiritual Energy. At that point, stronger Spiritual Arts could be performed and one could reach even higher peaks of strength. Most of these special acupoints, however, required unique methods and resources to open. In fact, some of them didn't even exist in some people, and those that did carry them were sought after to be trained as great talents."

"So, the method for opening the acupoints in my Spiritual Veins you taught me is a special one?"

A normal person would've been elated to consider that possibility, but Red was not happy. The man had told him again and again that his talent was mediocre, so how could opening these special acupoints be anything simple?

"More or less, but you don't need to do anything hard," Viran said. "Merely practicing down here is enough to meet all the conditions for opening them."

He got up and walked to the picture on the wall, pointing at thirteen dots spread throughout the figure's body. On top of the ninety-nine standard ones, it all added up to 112 acupoints.

"Although I must tell you, this is just something I've developed in the last few months after being thrown in here. It's possible that further down the line, other acupoints may also need to be opened to form a perfect cycle. But with these"—He grabbed a moonstone off the table, the soft green light shining against his face—"it shouldn't be a problem."

It was a lot of information for Red to digest. Obviously more was left unsaid by the man, but at the very least, this proved one thing to him. By revealing this much, Viran was seeking some sort of honest collaboration.

"And what kinds of Spiritual Arts do these special acupoints allow me to practice?" Red asked. It was something that had been on his mind from the start of their conversation.

"What kinds? Ha! None that I know of, but they will allow you to do something much better," Viran said. "They will allow you to escape this place alive."

CHAPTER 10
TALENT

Escape?

"How?" Red asked.

"I can't tell you."

Viran shattered his curiosity before it had even begun to sprout.

"Trust me, it's not that I don't want to," he said. "But anything you learn about this could be detrimental to your current training. When you manage to leave this place, you'll understand what I mean."

Red didn't know why Viran wanted to keep it a secret, but he gave him the benefit of the doubt. It didn't matter either way. As long as he continued opening his Spiritual Veins, one day he would be strong enough to fight his way out of these tunnels by himself.

"Do I need to open all those acupoints before leaving?" Red asked.

"No. If that was the case, who knows how many years you would still be stuck down here? Three should be enough for what I have planned," Viran said. "Look, I don't mean to dishearten you, kid, but when I said your talent is just average, I really meant it. Without any external support, even on the surface it could take well into your twenties before you can open all your Spiritual Veins. Not to mention being down here where the Spiritual Energy is so sparse."

It was the first time that Red had heard such a specific number from Viran's mouth. From when he had first learned about the Spiritual Veins and their acupoints, he knew the difficulty in opening them varied depending on the vein. Convention had it that one should go from the easiest veins to the hardest ones, and this was also what Red had been doing per Viran's instructions.

Accounting for all acupoints, the order from easiest to hardest was:

The Spinal Vein, with twelve normal acupoints and thirteen including the special acupoint. Red had already completely opened this vein.

The Upper Arm Vein, with ten normal acupoints and twelve in all. Red had opened six already and was currently in the process of opening the rest.

The Upper Leg Vein, with eight normal acupoints and ten in all.

The Lower Arm Vein, with fourteen standard acupoints.

The Lower Leg Vein, with twelve standard acupoints.

The Lung Vein, with ten standard acupoints and eleven in all.

The Stomach Vein, with eight standard acupoints and nine in all.

The Liver Vein, with four standard acupoints and five in all

The Heart Vein, with six standard acupoints and seven in all.

The Five Senses Vein, with seven standard acupoints and eight in all.

The Brain Vein, with seven standard acupoints and nine in all.

And finally, the last and hardest vein to open—the Third Eye Vein, which had a single normal acupoint and two altogether.

Those numbers added up to ninety-nine standard acupoints and 112 with Viran's special method. Red might've appeared to have been making good progress, opening nineteen already in just a few months, but the truth was that he could clearly feel the difficulty increasing as he progressed. Back when he had focused on the Spinal Vein, he could open one acupoint himself in a single good day, but now with the Upper Arm Vein, a single acupoint would've taken an entire week to open if not for the help of the strange blob creature.

Red could only imagine how the time necessary would increase exponentially the further he went.

"What makes someone more talented at manipulating Spiritual Energy?" he asked. Even if Red knew his talent was poor, he still liked to have a frame of reference so he could dedicate himself further.

"Simple. It's based on their Spiritual Energy sensitivity," Viran said. "No one really knows why, but some people can feel that energy far more easily than others. They have an easier time opening their veins than someone like you."

"And how long do they take?"

"It depends. Even someone with good talent would take a lot longer if they only started opening their veins after reaching adulthood. It's why I chose you, being a kid and everything." Viran exposed the reason for their collaboration without a second thought. "However, if we're talking about the talented children that get recruited by the big organizations up top, they can do it in a few years if they start around your age, which is the best time for opening your veins. Of course, even then some rare talents can do it even faster.

"For instance, some people are so sensitive to Spiritual Energy that their veins open naturally as they grow up. If they put some genuine effort into opening them, then they could accomplish the task in a few weeks. Opening their veins would be as easy as tearing paper."

"Is there a way to increase your talent?" Red asked, not dissuaded.

"What? No!" Viran snorted. "Why do you think it's called talent? It's something you're born with, not something you can change or acquire. Stories on the surface would tell you about peasants having some lucky encounter that transformed them into geniuses overnight, but those are all false and created to give people like you hope. Don't be fooled by them."

The old soldier had never been one to mince words, and he didn't hesitate to crush any such thoughts in Red's mind.

"You can increase your training speed with the help of external items, like special medicines and concoctions, but talent doesn't only increase your development speed... Either way, you're getting too far ahead of yourself, kid. Trust me, I know how interesting it is to think about the future and the possibilities that await us, but for your own benefit, you should focus on the now and not let yourself be distracted by your dreams."

With that said, Viran got up and started messing around with his storage boxes, shuffling around all sorts of things.

"If you're done recovering, you should leave and go get some sleep," he said. "These training sessions will be a daily thing, so come find me by the tent around this time, after everyone else has fallen asleep."

Red had been so absorbed in their conversation that he'd forgotten about the state of his own body. He could feel his limbs protest in pain, but after a few seconds catching his breath, he stood up.

"Then I'll be leaving," Red said.

Viran only grunted in response.

Most of their interactions ended unceremoniously like that. In fact, most were even more abrupt, and they had never spoken with each other as much as they had today. In a certain way, the slight return to normalcy made Red feel relieved. It indicated Viran's interest in their partnership and that he was unlikely to have other hidden intentions. It wasn't a normal relationship between a student and his teacher, but Red much preferred it this way.

Red grabbed a moonstone off the ground and walked out of the chamber. His body throbbed in pain, and he had to support himself against the wall as he went along.

Suddenly, an uncomfortable realization dawned on him, and he paused. He was in an unknown part of the mines, and to reach his usual hideout, he would need to pass through many other caverns where the slaves slept. He wouldn't be able to do anything in his condition if they tried to attack him.

Red considered returning to Viran's hideout and asking to sleep there, but he decided against it. He chose instead to explore the tunnel for a sleeping spot.

It took the better part of an hour before he found a good hiding place lodged in between the cave walls. He looked around to make sure there were no monsters or other hostile creatures lurking in the small chamber. Only after confirming it was safe did Red sit inside and take the medicinal paste Viran had given him out of his pocket.

After taking off his bandages, he smeared the brown substance over his bruised ribs. An uncomfortable stinging feeling spread through his chest, but compared to the aches he had felt today, it barely bothered him. He lay down on the hard rock floor and scooted over to hide his body from view. Many thoughts about today coursed through his mind, but it didn't take long for his body to give out and for sleep to overtake his consciousness.

"Heed your most holy God-Emperor's decree!"

A booming voice woke Red up. He looked around and found himself in a completely foreign environment. He stood on top of a wall made out of the most pristine white bricks decorated with symbols and figures that he found incomprehensible. Red was close to the edge of the ramparts, and from here he could see the ground below. Or so he thought.

A wave of nausea came over him as he noticed that the ground seemed impossibly far away from him. The wall ran so far down that it eventually receded into an unfathomable and blurry mess. To his sides, the noble structure extended far beyond his view in a straight line, cutting the world in half. The sky above flowed with golden light that seemed to come from nowhere and everywhere at the same time. The ground on the other side of the wall, however, was a desolate waste of pale sand as far as the eye could see. Red didn't know why, but he felt the smell of death rising from deep within the earth.

His mind couldn't take it, and he felt as if he were about to collapse as he closed his eyes. Suddenly, the same booming, deafening voice echoed again, the sound reaching deep into his consciousness.

"The White Temple is commanded thus to surrender its False Idols to our God-Emperor. Your Holy Priest and his Ministers are commanded to offer themselves to our God-Emperor and bear his judgment. The territories under your protection are also commanded to submit to occupation by our God-Emperor's holy armies. Every cultivator inside your territory must..."

The voice spoke in a foreign language, but Red comprehended it at first. However, his consciousness threatened to break apart, and the words soon became incomprehensible. At long last, he dared to open his eyes once more and look towards the source of the voice.

A light as blinding as the sun was all he could identify at first, bearing down on him with all its sacred glory. His eyes slowly adapted, and in the middle of it, a shape took form. A disembodied eye. Then another. Then one more. Soon enough, there were thousands of them of varying sizes, and their numbers were only increasing.

Suddenly, all of them turned to stare at him. Red felt terror. And then he felt nothing.

Only darkness.

CHAPTER II

TRUE NATURE

RED WOKE UP. This time, however, he wasn't panicking. His eyes were greeted by the cold, familiar cave wall faintly illuminated by the green light of the moonstone. The first thing he noticed when he sat up was that the pain in his chest had substantially lessened. It still hurt, but at least it didn't feel like he was going to die with every breath he took.

The rest of his muscles ached, but Red was used to moving around with this sort of discomfort already. As he finished examining his body, his thoughts returned to the dream he'd just had. He did not want to think back on that memory, and especially not on those spectral eyes, but even without reflection, one thing was crystal clear to him. He had died again.

This was a theme in his dreams, and he didn't know what to make of it. Since he had found himself in the caves two years ago, they would happen every few weeks, each one realistic and scary enough for Red to wake in a cold sweat. But something had changed since he'd started to open his Spiritual Veins, and these dreams now came to him far more frequently.

Red wasn't sure what that meant, but for now, it didn't seem to have any effect on his body. Either way, he didn't know what to do about it. The best strategy he'd found was to ignore the vivid images that flashed in his mind, since thinking too much about them had the result of giving him a sharp headache. It was not a problem he would like to have right now.

Red peeked out of his hiding place to make sure no ambushes were waiting for him. After confirming it was safe, he got up and patted the dust off himself, checking if all his possessions were still there. To his surprise, he found the iron knife still strapped to his waist. He had almost forgotten the weapon had remained with him after the training session. This was a powerful tool down here, and it was something Red would keep well-hidden.

He gathered himself up and grabbed the moonstone to light the way. As he took a step forward into a tunnel, however, a chilly breeze blew against his back, rustling his clothes and red hair.

He froze in place.

Red looked over his shoulder and found, much to his relief, that nothing was waiting behind him, just an empty tunnel leading in a completely different direction. Still, he couldn't shake the uneasy feeling that had come over him.

He could have sworn he'd heard something, a sound carried by the wind from deep within the cave, too soft to make out. That put him on alert. But he knew better than to investigate every noise in this place, so he chose to walk back to the path leading to the other slaves.

Along the way, he passed by many people who had just woken up. From afar, Red even saw the figures of a few slaves from the previous day's hunting party who glared at him as they prepared to go gather moonstones. Gruff was among them, but Red escaped into the tunnels before the giant man could get any ideas.

Soon enough, Red found himself in front of a familiar path, where a small hidden passage lay buried beneath a pile of pebbles.

"Bread again?"

"You guessed it."

Red could hear some childish frustration in the dark blob's voice. Still, the thing opened its large mouth and snatched the piece of food out of the air with its long tongue, chewing it with gusto. He had considered bringing it some centipede meat but had ended up eating it all himself after some consideration.

First of all, there was simply no way to store that kind of food down here. It had to be eaten soon after being cooked, or else it would quickly spoil.

This was also one of the first times Red had eaten so much meat, and every morsel he consumed would benefit his training. He didn't need the extra Spiritual Energy from the blob as much as he needed physical strength. There was also the fact that Red simply didn't trust his strange companion. Who knew what would happen once the thing ate flesh?

As the dark being focused on the bread, Red prepared for his training routine. This time around, he only kept at it for a few repetitions, lest his body collapse from exhaustion once again. Sitting down cross-legged, he looked expectantly at the dark blob.

"Now!" Red said.

"One shecond." The blob spoke into his mind as if its mouth were full.

Red sighed but found no option other than waiting.

Loud, annoying chewing sounds echoed in the space.

Red frowned. "Chew with your mouth closed."

"Whash that?"

"Keep your mouth closed while you chew your food. No one wants to hear you eat."

"Oh, okay."

Despite what he said, the being shortly went back to its loud chewing noises. Red could only shake his head. A good half-minute passed before the dark blob spoke again.

"Okay, here it is!"

It spewed out a purple mist that soon dispersed. Red felt his skin tingle as the concentration of Spiritual Energy in the cavern increased. He directed it towards his second vein and began the laborious task of forcing his energy against the next acupoint in his upper arm.

The attempt lasted for a few minutes, but unlike the last time, the acupoint didn't give way and Red had to let the Spiritual Energy disperse into the air to avoid any serious injuries. This was the usual process. Opening an acupoint was a forceful but cumulative process, so if you strained your Spiritual Veins too much in a single attempt, it was likely you would cripple yourself as the energy exploded inside your body.

Red knew that, so he stopped as soon as an aching feeling radiated from his upper arms. It was a sign that he had done enough for the time being— at least that was what Viran claimed. Red couldn't accurately judge that, but he felt that perhaps with two more sessions of practice with the dark blob, he could open another acupoint.

After finishing his training, Red didn't stand up. Instead, his eyes wandered over to his strange companion. He examined the creature as if he were seeing it for the first time. An aberration, clearly not human, but also more intelligent than any monster or animal that Red had ever seen.

He knew nothing about it.

Suddenly, Viran's advice came to mind. The strangeness of the mine, and his warning to ignore strange things in this place. What was the blob, if not the strangest thing Red had come across?

For the first time ever, Red asked the blob a question out of simple curiosity. "What are you doing here?"

"Hmm, me?" it said, surprised. "I thought you'd never ask! Well, I got trapped here when I was running away from some idiots who were pursuing me while I was injured... Oh yeah, did I tell you how I got injured? Basically, when I first entered this world, a big bolt of lightning appeared in the sky out of nowhere and hit me, almost frying me alive. And then those three-eyed freaks started to chase me... I seriously almost died! Those guys were no joke. One of them had a seriously disgusting blue face, and another glowed with a golden light. I mean, what kind of monster glows? And then the other one—"

"Please," Red interrupted. None of its words made much sense to him, and if he let it talk its mouth off, how long would he be here? "Just get to the point. How did you end up here?"

"Oh, right..." The creature seemed disappointed, but it kept on talking. "Well, I fled here while those guys were chasing me, and imagine my surprise when they refused to enter the caves... And imagine my surprise again when I discovered I couldn't leave this place! Not to mention, my energy was constantly leaking from me! I spent so long looking for different exits, but every time I tried to leave, this place pulled me back. I thought about going further down, but some scary folks lived there and there was no way I was beating them in my current state, so I could only find a cozy place down here and hibernate while trying to find ways to recover my energy!"

"Is that why you want food?"

"Yes! Exactly! I can't absorb the energy from the air around me, but food is another story. I can convert it directly into Spiritual Energy, like the kind you use in your body!" The blob seemed quite happy to be having this conversation, but its tone soon deflated again. "Of course, food down here is very rare! Not to mention that I can't move, so I can only wait for it to make its way into my mouth... Oh, all those times I spent without a single piece of food, for who knows how long! You have no idea how much I've suffered."

"Then you decided to make a deal with me." The whole situation was becoming clearer to Red, even though many questions remained unanswered.

"Yes! It was my brilliant idea! I can't hunt for food, but someone else can do it for me." Its voice swelled with pride. "I was so dumb back then. If I had thought of this plan sooner, then I wouldn't be in this condition. There was another human who found me in the past, but I was so hungry that I ate him whole without even trying to talk to him! Then I spent much longer without any food... So stupid!"

A shiver ran down Red's spine. A few seconds of complete silence went by before he got up and headed for the exit.

"Are you already going? There's so much more we can talk about!" The blob seemed to be quite eager to continue their conversation.

For a moment, Red stopped. "Yes, there are some things I need to take care of." He kept his voice as emotionless as ever.

"Ah, I see. Goodbye then!"

He started walking again, leaving the cave before the blob had even finished speaking. After that, Red picked up his pace, crawling through the small tunnel back towards the main section of the caves. When he finally arrived at the exit, he collapsed to the floor, as if he had snapped out of a frenzy. Cold sweat dampened his body, and his heart nearly burst from of his chest.

Why had he made a deal with the being in the first place? Why had Red so easily trusted such a strange creature to keep its end of the bargain when he barely trusted Viran despite knowing much more about the man? All the questions Red had never dared ask himself before came to his mind in a flood, and he feared he would collapse from the sheer mental effort. The brief interaction with the blob had taken more out of him than any training session.

Struggling to catch his breath, Red once more remembered Viran's advice. There were some things down here that you should just pretend you couldn't see.

CHAPTER 12

HOLLOW

A MONTH PASSED.

"Faster!"

Viran's voice struck his ears, but Red didn't register what he said. The man had a habit of providing obvious advice when it was least actionable. Naturally, he needed to go faster, but how would he achieve that when his body was already being squeezed for all it had?

Another stab came his way, which Red tried to parry as he'd been taught. It was to no avail, though; Viran's knife slipped through his defenses and cut into his cheek. The man followed up by charging forward, and Red could only throw himself to the ground to evade his attack in a desperate dodge. It was clear by that point, however, that he had already conceded too much initiative to his opponent.

A merciless kick came his way, which Red desperately blocked with his arms, the impact sending him skidding across the room. Before he could recover, Viran rushed up and pinned his knife hand to the ground with a swift stomp.

He stared down at the struggling boy with a disappointed expression. When Viran made no further moves, Red realized the training session was already over.

"Not good enough." Viran shook his head. "You're not fighting a centipede here. Any trained fighter would take advantage of such a sloppy move."

After that, he stepped away, walking to the other side of the room.

Red massaged his sore arms as he got up. This had become a familiar scene in their training sessions. Viran would push him to his absolute physical limit every sparring match, and when Red couldn't keep up his defenses any longer and was forced to make a desperate move, Viran would press him into defeat and chastise him about how it had been a bad decision. Red didn't know if this was supposed to teach him anything or if the man was just venting his anger on him.

Over the previous month, his footwork and general endurance had greatly improved. While he could only hold out for less than a minute against Viran at first, he was adapting to the man's rhythm, lasting longer and longer. His movements and reflexes became more efficient. But as one would expect, just as Red was getting used to that level of difficulty, Viran increased the pressure.

The soldier's strikes became stronger and more ferocious, and after a few weeks, they started sparring with the iron knives. He didn't hold back his blows either, slashing Red just hard enough to draw a fine line of blood every time he failed to dodge or block an attack. The only proper technique Viran taught him was the correct combat stance in their very first training session. Other than that, he was left to his own devices, learning by trial and error and by copying his opponent's movements.

Red's progress was obvious after a short month of training, but he couldn't help but think he would've improved even further if Viran offered useful advice rather than just screaming at him to be faster or stronger. When he brought up the matter, he was told that "experience was the best teacher." Red wasn't sure how much he believed that, but it was clear the old soldier was set in his ways.

Red sheathed the knife and made his way to a corner of the hideout where he had stored his possessions.

"How's your progress?" Viran asked from behind him.

It was immediately clear to Red what he was referring to.

"I'm trying to open the ninth Upper Arm one," Red said.

"You've slowed down."

The man's tone was one Red recognized very well.

Annoyance.

He was right, though. Over the last month, Red had only opened two additional acupoints. His training speed had slowed for one reason: he refused to visit the dark creature since their last encounter. Red felt as if he had woken up from a long nightmare that day, and the unknown danger the being presented made him afraid of taking even one step into that chamber.

However, without the aid of the blob's concentrated Spiritual Energy, he could feel the mounting difficulty each new acupoint presented to him, and it was clear it would only get even harder. At this rate, it would take him at least another month to open the entirety of his Upper Arm Vein, and he wouldn't be surprised if the vein following that took him half a year. And what about the ones following that? Would they take years? Would one of them take a decade?

The speed was excruciatingly slow, and Red had never felt the limitations of his talent this clearly, much more so now with the dire situation down in the mines.

"Another slave disappeared overnight," Viran said, as if talking to himself.

"Did you discover anything?" Red asked.

"Nothing. No footprints, no blood, fucking nothing." Viran gritted his teeth and threw his knife at the stone desk. "I told these morons not to walk alone out there, but they're too stupid and greedy to listen to me!"

Red remained unaffected by the man's angry tirade, having seen them grow more and more common over the past few weeks.

"Where did it happen?"

"A few hundred meters away from our meeting chamber. Whatever it is, it's growing bolder, and it didn't get caught on the other side of the tunnels."

Over the past month, the number of monstrous insects that appeared near the slave's living quarters had grown. Gigantic centipedes, spiders, beetles, and other ungodly creatures kept wandering into their camps, and casualties mounted faster than new slaves could be thrown into the caves. Viran had suspended the hunts once their party suffered another ambush like the fight with the centipedes, and he'd ordered several tunnels leading into the depths to be blocked by as many rocks as the slaves could find.

Although these measures kept them alive, they reduced the number of moonstones the slaves could collect, and in turn, the amount of food they could exchange with the guards on the surface. Many of slaves already complained about hunger, and their attitude towards Viran, their supposed leader, soured as his authority over them slipped away. Red, however, knew that the man was not bothered by this. If need be, he could kill half of the slaves, and then there would be food for all of them. No, it was those insects that worried him, on top of the mysterious disappearances that happened right under his nose.

"Have you ever heard of a creature that could do this?" Red asked.

"What, one that can hunt humans one by one without leaving a trace?" Viran snorted. "Certainly heard of them, but those that can do it are all so strong they wouldn't bother hiding from a bunch of ragtag slaves. No, whatever or *whoever* is doing this is quite good at hiding their tracks. Two times might have been a coincidence, but five disappearances without leaving a single clue? This is the work of a clever creature. Even when I use myself as bait, it never attacks me!"

Red more or less understood what Viran was experiencing at the moment. It was something he had become familiar with ever since working with the soldier—helplessness. Viran was extremely strong and intelligent, but even he was not capable of tracking the thing that was kidnapping these people. The entire social structure he had built inside this mine and—more importantly, his plans to escape—were now in jeopardy, and there was nothing the man could do about it.

"Have you talked to the guards about this?"

"What use would those idiots be?" Viran asked, brushing off the notion. "They don't care about what happens down here and refuse to come into the caves. The only way this creature becomes their problem is if it tries to leave the mine. No, we'll have to deal with it ourselves."

"So, what can we do?" Red asked.

The situation also concerned him. If something happened to Viran or his plans, Red didn't believe he would fare well with whatever would be left of the mine and its inhabitants. Not to mention the risk that he would be targeted next, considering he mostly kept to himself in the caves.

Silence settled in the room as Viran stood in deep thought.

"I have a plan," he said, "but we'll talk about it later. We'll need the help of the others, too." The man picked up his knife and sheathed it at his waist. "Come, I need to check up on those idiots."

Red exited the hideout, and Viran once again blocked the entrance with the giant rock. Soon, they were walking side by side through the tunnel.

After a long journey back to the slaves' area, they heard panicked conversation echoing from far away.

Viran frowned. "Hurry."

It was the only word he said before he picked up his pace.

Red followed and soon was greeted by a well-lit chamber, where a bunch of agitated slaves were gathered in a circle around something. His vision was obstructed, so he struggled to see what they had found.

"What the fuck is going on here?" Viran's loud voice drowned out all the others, and the slaves went quiet.

Soon the circle parted, and a slave passed through it. It was Gruff, who had survived all the perilous situations over the past month virtually unscathed.

"They... they found something, boss." The big man was out of breath. "Said they found it in one of the deeper tunnels connected to our meeting chamber." For some reason, Gruff stole a quick glance at Red as he said this. "It's Bertel, boss. I'm sure of it. It's just..."

He hesitated, a look of fear crossing his face.

Red recognized the name. It was one of the people who had disappeared not so long ago.

"Enough, let me see it." Viran pushed the big man out of his way and the rest of the slaves parted to give him space.

Red followed from farther away as Gruff glared at him.

In the center of the gathering, a cloth had been spread and a round, dark object rested on top. It was not until Viran carefully rolled it over with his foot that Red could recognize it. A human head—or what had been one, at least.

The head looked completely desiccated, taking on a strange gray shade, like all the moisture and blood had been sucked out of it. The eye sockets were empty and only small tufts of hair remained on its scalp. A clean hole had been made in the middle of the forehead, roughly half the size of a fist. Viran crouched down and examined the incision, shining a moonstone light inside of it.

Red could see even from afar as the green glow reflected off the inside of the skull.

The brain was missing, and the head was hollow.

CHAPTER 13
UNREST

"WELL, *SHIT,*" Viran cursed under his breath as he saw the empty skull.

"What... what is it?" one of the nearby slaves asked in fear.

"He's dead." Viran got up. "Get this head out of here!"

"Wait, what?! Where should we—"

"I don't know, throw it to the guards for all I care!" He turned towards Gruff. "Gather your group and bring them to the meeting chamber. The rest of you"—Viran turned to the others—"Go tell whoever's still alive to go there too. Immediately!"

With that, the old soldier walked past the circle of people and into the tunnel beyond. Red followed shortly after, catching up with a quick sprint.

"What did you find out?" he asked.

"Bertel was his name, right?" Viran answered his question with one of his own. "Wasn't he the first to disappear?"

"The first one." Red nodded. "He liked to dive deeper than the others to search for moonstones."

"Makes sense. It was one of the first times it hunted us, so it was bound to make a mistake."

"Do you know what it is?"

"No," Viran shook his head. "This place is full of unknown creatures that have never been seen on the surface. No person wants to explore these caves, and these monsters rarely make their way out of here, so our information on what lives in these depths is very limited."

"But you do know something."

"Yes." The man sighed. "I don't know what it is, but from that head back there, I know what it can do. It was sucked dry but none of the flesh itself was eaten, meaning it's something that feeds off the blood essence of other creatures. It's not unheard of, but that's not what makes it special." Viran tapped the center of his forehead.

Red understood the gesture. "The brain." He considered a thought he had ignored at first glance. "How did it disappear from inside the head through such a small hole?"

"You're getting to the crux of the matter. There are several ways that could happen. Some insects digest food outside their body and then consume it later in liquid form. However, none of the flesh in the head had signs of acid damage. The creature may also have a protruding tongue that it used to pierce the forehead and eat the brain. But the main question is why only the brain was eaten."

Red tried to think of an explanation. "Could it not have a selective diet?"

"Possibly, but it's a rare trait to find in a monster, especially down here where food is so scarce. The fact of the matter is it sucked out all the blood from its prey and didn't bother eating any flesh except for the brain..."

"You mean it may have another use for the brain besides food." Red frowned. "What makes you so sure?"

"Its behavior," Viran said. "In the end, you may be right, and it may turn out to be just a picky monster. But even then, what monster down here would be so thorough with hiding its tracks and intentionally going after vulnerable and isolated prey while constantly avoiding the ones it can't kill?" He pointed to himself. "Besides, I've never seen them, but I've heard of such things on the surface. Monsters that can absorb memories and knowledge from their victims by messing with their brains."

"You mean to say it knew not to fight you because it absorbed the other slave's memories?" Red asked.

"Maybe. It might also be capable of judging my strength based on instinct. That's not unusual among stronger monsters either."

"So, if I have this right, we have an undetectable monster that can perfectly hide its presence while hunting and can absorb a person's knowledge by eating their brain, becoming smarter as a result?"

"Definitely matches the behavior we've seen. It was sloppy on its first hunt, which is why we were able to get some clues about it, but eventually it got smarter and started to cover its tracks even better than before. Not to mention, the appearance of such a monster in these caves would also explain why the insects have been moving up into our territory." Viran scratched at his beard, his mind working furiously. "Stronger monsters have a commanding influence over the weaker ones, and they can give them certain orders..."

They had first thought the centipedes had ambushed them because they'd been pushed out of their home territory by overpopulation or a stronger creature, but it seemed like this was not the case. Instead, a possibly sentient monster was ordering them to move up and attack the slaves. At one point, Red wondered whether the blob was behind this, but he felt certain the creature was still stuck inside its chamber.

The problem of the situation, as the two of them saw it, wasn't so much this hidden monster's strength. Since it was afraid of Viran, its strength wasn't beyond them and they could probably still kill it. The actual issue was that it could potentially control masses of insects and lay siege to the slaves, who would either die against the flood of monsters or starve to death isolated inside the mine.

The pair had walked for quite a distance. Red noticed this wasn't the way to the meeting chamber, and he hadn't seen many slaves cross their path. Most of them had gathered near the entrance of the dungeon after the monsters began pouring out from the depths.

"So, it all comes down to killing a creature we haven't even seen yet," Red said. "What's the plan you mentioned earlier?"

"We're gonna ambush it."

"How?"

"It's quite simple. The monster knows how strong I am and that it can't fight me, but it doesn't know even half of the things I'm capable of. You might not be able to manipulate Spiritual Energy without your Spiritual Sea, but you can still store energy inside your body and activate certain innate abilities." Viran pointed towards his chest. "If you stimulate the right acupoints in your Lung Vein, for instance, you can go without breathing for quite a while. It's useful for swimming underwater..."

"... And to keep yourself hidden," Red finished the thought.

"Indeed. It's just one example of how opening your Spiritual Veins and their acupoints grants you more than just pure strength. However, it's extremely dangerous to keep Spiritual Energy inside your veins for too long without the help of a Spiritual Sea. It can explode and cripple you if you let it go out of control—you'll learn more about it if you survive this whole affair."

Viran concluded as they finally arrived back at the chamber where his tent was located. No one was around, and Red saw the whole place had much fewer beds and possessions than before. Another sign of the number of casualties Viran's goons had suffered and the fact that many survivors didn't want to follow him anymore. The man walked into his tent while Red waited outside.

His angry voice erupted from inside the tent. "These motherfuckers really have some balls!"

A few seconds later, Viran walked out with a heavy leather bag.

"What happened?" Red asked.

"They stole from me! I thought killing a few food thieves would have been enough to teach them all a lesson, but it seems their desperation has overpowered their fear."

Viran laughed, but Red could easily tell that the man was fuming beneath the surface.

"Did they take anything important?"

"No, nothing here is important, but I guess some of them will have to fight with their bare hands."

Viran walked past him, and Red followed.

This time, the path they took led to the meeting chamber. As they walked past the blocked tunnels, Red couldn't help but notice an unsettling feeling. A strange expression also came over Viran's face as they got closer to their destination.

"There should be more people around here," Red said.

The man only grunted in response, and soon enough they arrived in the meeting chamber. What they saw there was only a handful of slaves sitting around, most of those being Viran's direct subordinates, including Gruff. It was far fewer than they had been expecting, and the old soldier wasn't pleased.

"What the fuck is this?" Viran's voice snapped many of the slaves out of their daze.

"Boss!" Gruff got up, a look of worry on his face as he ran over. "I told them to come here, but they're all stupid! They wouldn't listen to reason! You need to—"

"Calm yourself, idiot!" Viran grabbed his shoulder and held the giant still. "Tell me what happened."

"They didn't want to come here, boss, not even when I told them it was an order," Gruff said, calming down. "A bunch of them started making a fuss, saying how you wanted to use them as meat shields and get them killed just so you could keep all the food for yourself. More people joined them, and they decided to go towards the entrance, saying that they would negotiate with the guards. I told them it was a stupid idea, that they didn't care about us, but—"

"Fucking morons!" Viran gritted his teeth and pushed Gruff aside. "Idiots, all of them! They're gonna come back here right now even if I have to break every single limb in their bodies. You lot!" He pointed at the rest of the slaves and threw the leather sack on the ground. "Pick your weapons and follow me! Gruff, Red, you're with me! Today I'm gonna remind them why I rule this place."

Viran marched down the tunnel towards the cave entrance as the other slaves picked up whatever weapons they could and obeyed. Red had never considered himself one of the man's subordinates, doing his bidding and helping him keep the order amongst the more unruly slaves, but at that moment he felt it was better if he just followed along.

As he watched the slaves get ready to leave, Red felt someone staring at him. He looked over and saw Gruff.

"It's your fault. It all started after you went hunting with us," he said with his rough voice. "I can't wait for you to get eaten by one of those things."

After that, the giant stormed away, and Red found himself alone in the chamber.

CHAPTER 14

INSECT BATTLE

IT DIDN'T TAKE LONG before Red and their party discovered the tracks of the other slaves. Up here, only one tunnel led to the surface, so it wasn't too hard to chase after them. However, this path extended for a long stretch, and it was unlikely that they could catch the other group before they made it to the guard post at the entrance of the mine.

"How many were there?" Viran asked Gruff, who walked alongside him.

This was a commonly traveled tunnel, so it was hard to determine the number of people who were in the slave group by the footprints left in the dust.

"Sixty, maybe more," Gruff said. "Most of them were the weaklings, but quite a few of our own were with them, too. They were armed with some of our weapons."

Viran grunted. To Red, those people were insane if they thought they could defeat the old soldier with that cheap equipment. In fact, he didn't think they could kill him at all, even if they were fully outfitted with iron weapons. It wasn't a matter of weaponry as much as it was a matter of skill.

Most of the slaves in the runaway group weren't in the mines half a year ago, so even if they witnessed the occasional display of authority by Viran, they had never truly seen what he was capable of. The worst massacre was on the first day after he had announced he was going to be the ruler of this place. Some of the slaves hadn't tolerated that and tried to shut the mouth of the crazed man.

Viran slaughtered them all, barehanded. It was the most brutal display of violence Red had ever seen, made worse because most of his victims didn't immediately die from their injuries. He could still remember their haunting screams echoing through the cave tunnels, but no slave dared to approach them to help. Still, for as many people who died that day, the body count kept increasing over the following week.

Multiple assassination and poisoning attempts were made against Viran. He saw through and survived them all. The people responsible were tortured and gave up their accomplices. Another massacre took place, this one slower and more deliberate. All sense of defiance was crushed in the hearts of the slaves when more than half of them ended up dead after the man's arrival. The survivors chose to follow Viran's rule wholeheartedly.

Red, having observed these events in person, knew that there was no chance these slaves would survive what was coming for them if Viran decided to be merciless. He had about twenty people following him, so the other slaves technically outnumbered them three to one, but even if he were alone, his enemies would still have no hope of victory.

"Stop!"

Viran's shout made the entire group freeze in place.

Red approached the front of the line, where he saw the man crouched down, examining the ground in front of him. When Red got close enough, he saw what had caught Viran's attention. A large hole, about two meters in diameter, had been dug into the wide tunnel floor, and it certainly hadn't been there the last time they'd passed through here. One slave illuminated it with a torch, and Red realized he couldn't see how deep it went.

"Insect tunnel," Viran said in a solemn tone.

"That's not possible, the ground is too tough up here." Gruff said.

Burrowing insects were relatively common, but the slaves lived in an area full of ores and rock walls, so digging through would be no easy task, even for a giant insect.

"It's centipedes!" one slave said, pointing towards the footprints of a creature with far too many legs. They led away from the hole, towards the cave's entrance.

"Not just that," Red said after inspecting the dusty ground. "There's more than one type of footprints too. Probably horned beetles, but some of them I don't ever remember seeing before."

He hadn't fought these creatures, but he had lived long enough in the mines to recognize these kinds of tracks and avoid them at all costs.

"But these things don't just walk around together," the same slave said, seemingly more to convince himself than to disprove Red.

It was true. The monsters were just as hostile to each other as they were to humans. Many of them would even engage in cannibalism if they got too hungry, proving once more how brutal the environment down here was. The idea of them walking around together without tearing each other apart was ridiculous. Not to mention there were quite a few of them here, judging by the footprints.

That is, unless someone was compelling them to do so.

As Red remembered his conversation from earlier, he looked towards Viran, but the man had already stood up.

"There's no time to waste here," he said. "We'll close this hole later. For now, we need to kill whatever damn monsters have made their way into my territory!"

At that, Viran started walking up the tunnel again.

The slaves looked at each other, gripping the weapons in their hands tighter, but they followed their leader. As much as they feared the monsters, they knew he was their best chance at making it out alive.

The tunnel leading up to the surface was very large, more so than most chambers down in the mine. In some areas, all twenty of them could have walked through side by side.

As their group went along, they saw that the monster footprints took no detours, simply following the main tunnel path. Tension mounted amid the slaves as they realized they were on a collision course with the creatures. Sure enough, it didn't take long for the sounds of battle to reach their ears.

It was faint at first, but Viran had picked up on it before anyone else, and his steps suddenly became faster. The entire group was surprised by the change, but they hurried their pace, and soon they could hear the sounds too. Screams, and the hissing of insects.

The first thing they spotted was a bloodied slave running towards them. His expression brightened when he saw Viran and the other slaves, but suddenly his body was hoisted into the air as a large spike impaled him through his chest. Behind him, they could see the hulking figure of a horned beetle. It shook itself, throwing the slave against the wall with a sickening thud. No further movement came from the body.

For the first time, Red could see a beetle in its entirety. It was about two meters long and over a meter tall. It had a very bulky body covered by a brown carapace, with a single straight horn protruding from the top of its head. The projecting spike was around a meter and a half in length, ending in an unnaturally sharp tip that dripped blood. The menacing sight of the monster gave pause to a few of the slaves, but Viran didn't slow his pace.

The monster noticed the man running in its direction, and it likewise charged at him, its horn pointed forward to stab its new target. It seemed like Viran was about to impale himself on the spike, but abruptly he took a light step to the right, twisting as the horn missed him by what looked like centimeters.

Red didn't notice when Viran had grabbed his knife, but it was already in his hand as he stabbed down into the creature's eye. He used the momentum of the monster's charge and dragged the knife along the rest of its body, making a long cut that went from the head all the way to the end of its shell.

The beast didn't even register the extent of its wound, as the knife was not long enough to reach its organs. Still, when it saw its target had suddenly disappeared, it twisted angrily around, almost toppling over from the sudden shift in direction. Viran saw his opportunity and approached the monster from its now-blinded side.

He jumped onto its head and stabbed his knife down right between its eyes.

The anguished beetle reared up on its hind legs, trying to throw its opponent off, but Viran didn't lose his balance for a second. He dislodged his knife and jabbed it down again, cracking the carapace around the area of impact. Even his hand seemed to go inside the monster's head along with his weapon.

Viran repeated the same attack a few times in quick succession while the creature tried its best to throw him off, but its movements became weaker and weaker. With a thud, the beetle crashed down and stopped moving.

Red didn't know if even ten seconds had passed before the battle was over, as he and the other slaves could only stare in wonder. Viran turned towards them, his face and clothes covered in green blood.

"We don't have time to waste, you morons! Stop gawking and follow me!"

They all obeyed and rushed after him. Soon, they arrived on the battlefield.

Bodies were scattered around the cave tunnel, most of them missing limbs or chopped in half. Blood pooled on the floor as the battle still raged. The slaves, clearly on the back foot, were scattered around the tunnel with their improvised weapons, struggling to keep the monsters at bay. Red counted four giant centipedes, two horned beetles—and something much bigger.

This monster had a very long body, about four meters, with a thin thorax and a bulkier abdomen. Its triangular head held two large, oversized eyes that scanned the limb-strewn ground, two antennae twitching on top. The creature had six limbs, standing on four high enough to easily reach the ceiling.

That wasn't the most frightening part, though.

Its two front legs resembled curved, glistening scythes, sharper than any weapon Red had ever seen. He had the feeling these same scythes were responsible for the cleanly bisected bodies scattered around the monster.

At that point, even Viran stopped to take in the scene in front of him. The creature stood in the center of the wide tunnel, and everyone, including the other monsters, gave it a wide berth. Uninterested in the battle happening around it, it busied itself by shoving pieces of flesh into its relatively small mouth. Red himself had never seen this kind of creature before—he didn't even know its name—but he knew that if he were to face it head-on, the only fate awaiting him was death.

"Listen well!" Viran's shout rang through the tunnel. Even the people who had run away from him were relieved to see him assume command.

"Remember your training! Immobilize the bastards and stab them in between the eyes!" He turned and looked at Gruff. "Go ahead and gather the stragglers together so they don't get picked apart. I'll deal with the big one."

Gruff nodded before ordering the people behind him to move. Red was just about to follow before Viran grabbed his shoulder.

"Not you," he said. "You'll help me with that *thing*."

CHAPTER 15
SCYTHES

"I'm gonna need you to distract it," Viran said.

"I don't even know how fast that thing is," Red protested. "It's going to kill me."

"No, it won't," he shot back, unaffected by Red's complaints. "Listen, it may be stronger and faster than you, but it's still just a dumb monster. We're gonna take advantage of that. You'll attract its attention first so I can strike it while it's distracted. If it's still alive after that, we'll change our strategy, but I need you to do this."

Red didn't immediately respond. He looked over at the monster, examining its scythe-like arms that reflected the light of torches in the wide tunnel. Fighting against it, he wouldn't have as much room for error as he'd had against the centipede. One mistake and those arms would chop him in half. Red considered running away, but if the monsters killed every single slave down here, including Viran, he didn't like his chances of surviving alone.

Not to mention, he and the old soldier had a deal to help each other escape this place, and Red didn't feel comfortable simply walking away.

He took a deep breath. "How should I do this?"

"I've seen this type of monster before," Viran said. "It attacks in snaps. Its pounce is extremely fast, but if you can predict it, then dodging is easy. Keep your attention on its upper body." After saying that, Viran inverted the grip on his knife. "Now, go! Who knows how long that thing is gonna just keep eating."

Red didn't need any further incentive. He tried to calm his nerves, preparing his body for what he was about to do. He reached down and picked up a stone axe from the ground with his left hand, while his right held the iron knife Viran had given him.

As Red got within eight meters of the monster, it finally seemed to notice his approach. Its large beady eyes stared unblinkingly at him while the rest of its body remained completely still. Red felt a shiver run down his spine. If the tunnel had been darker, it would've been possible to miss the enormous insect standing in wait for its prey, the dark carapace blending perfectly with the cave walls.

When Red finally got within range of his target, he hurled the axe with all his strength in the monster's direction. The weapon spun in the air and reached the beast in a split second, striking true. However, it harmlessly clunked against the tough carapace. The beast didn't even flinch, taking a second to register that the small child in front of it had just tried to attack.

The monster slowly reared up, retracting its scythe arms close to its thorax. Red stood five meters away, where he assumed he was outside of its range of attack, but suddenly, a premonition of danger washed over his mind. He saw a flash of movement, and all Red could do was throw his entire weight to the side in a desperate dodge.

The sharp sound of rushing air passed over his left ear. He tumbled to the floor in a roll, splintered stones peppering painfully against his back. A second later, he could see what had happened.

The monster's upper body had stretched unnaturally as it leaned forward, its extended scythe arms closing the rest of the distance between them. Its natural blades were buried in the cave floor. Not even solid rock could stop the sheer cutting power of its arms.

Viran had failed to mention the creature could double its attacking range by stretching its body. Or perhaps he simply hadn't known. Red was certain of one thing, however—the distance between him and the creature made no discernable difference if it could still strike from so far away.

He hurried to his feet and put some distance between the creature's arms and himself, circling it with as much speed as he could muster. The monster's eyes followed his movements as it pulled its sharp limbs from the ground. This time it didn't stay still, moving forward with impressive speed.

The fact that such a gigantic monster could run so fast rattled him, but he didn't have time to dwell on the thought.

The beast closed on him and prepared for another pounce, this time much closer to its target. Red, however, was aware of the force behind its attacks, so he didn't stop moving. He wouldn't give it a chance to take aim at a stationary target.

He remembered Viran's advice and paid attention to its upper body as it prepared to attack.

Now!

With a quick thrust of his back foot, Red imitated his mentor's movements and pushed his entire frame to the side with as much strength as he could muster in his legs. Sure enough, a fraction of a second later, the monster attacked. More pieces of rock flew into the air from the impact, but Red had successfully avoided certain death once again.

He rolled across the ground from the sheer momentum of his dodge, stopping in a crouched position as he looked back at the monster. Suddenly, his eyes narrowed.

In the ground where he'd once stood, the beast had lodged its scythe arm into the floor as he'd expected. However, it had only used one of its limbs to attack. The other remained retracted against its body, primed and ready to attack.

The creature's eyes had followed Red's figure all along. Now, it moved.

He didn't have time to think and pushed himself off the ground with all his power. Another blade flashed through the air. But this time, a misty explosion of dust and blood came with it.

Red rolled sideways to escape the blow, but his back flared in pain. It took a second to register before he felt the blood trickling down his side.

At that moment, he couldn't stop to assess his injury. All that he knew was that he was still alive. Tentatively shifting his body, Red found he could still move without difficulty if he ignored the flaring pain. He'd grown more than used to it by that point.

He looked up and felt his blood run cold. The creature hovered over him, just a few meters away. During his dodge, Red had ended up between the monster's arms, which were stuck into the ground on either side of him.

The giant insect freed its arms again, and this time there was no preparation. It brought them down on its prey in a flash.

The attack was slower than its pounce, but Red was also not in a good position to dodge. In a split-second decision, he tried to avoid the blow by moving forward and towards the beast rather than away from it. He successfully evaded the blow even as small rock splinters hit his already injured back. But this time, Red found himself beneath the creature's body.

For a moment, the monster seemed to have lost sight of him, and Red took full advantage of the opportunity. He grabbed his knife with both hands and stabbed up.

A shower of sparks flew from the monster's carapace, the knife skidding across the tough surface forming a faint line. Much to his surprise, he had failed to penetrate the beast's sturdy exoskeleton. Even the centipede's defenses hadn't managed to block the knife's stab, but this monster's hide was much tougher than those of its fellow insects.

While Red's attack failed, he had also revealed his position to his opponent. The bug suddenly leaned over and peered beneath its body. A scythe arm shot forward with no hesitation, aiming to impale him. Thankfully, its awkward position afforded Red time to hide between its hind legs.

After dodging, he tried to slash its abdomen with his knife. Another shower of sparks and yet another failure followed. Red was about to get some distance when the monster suddenly spun in place, its blades extended. He crouched down in a hurry, and a powerful gust of wind passed over his head as the beast's scythe missed by a thin margin. He almost swore a few strands of his hair were cut during the attack.

Where's Viran?

Red started to think he'd been left to die.

The creature became enraged by its slippery prey, and its attacks rained down in quick succession. Another one-armed overhead slash came Red's way, and he cursed Viran for telling him the creature only attacked in bursts. His training was paying off, though, and he once more pushed off his back foot to avoid being cut in half.

Red was doing far better in this fight than he would've thought, although he could only barely keep himself alive. This kind of battle, where a single mistake meant death, was thrilling, and it pushed him to improve and perform far past his limits. His awareness neared its peak, and Red dodged another slash while increasing his distance from the beast.

As he stepped away, however, his back suddenly hit something. Turning around, Red saw a rock wall. He had run out of space, but the monster didn't stop. It raised both of its scythe arms in the air, ready to bring them down upon its prey. Just as Red wondered whether he would lose an arm, he saw a shadow moving from the corner of his eye.

With a sudden shower of green blood, one of the monster's hind legs was cut clean off its body. The loss of balance tipped the creature to one side, allowing Red to dodge its attack. He then saw Viran retreating a safe distance away from the monster as it angrily slashed at where the soldier had once stood.

"The joints are its weak points!" he shouted, continuing to dodge the monster's now desperate attacks.

That was all Red needed to hear to snap into action. He took advantage of his opponent's sudden change of focus and dashed forward, aiming for one of its front legs. The slender leg had four segments including its spiked foot, and three joints he could target. Most of them were far too high for Red to reach without jumping, and so he aimed for the lowest one.

With a quick dive, he arrived by the monster's limb. He grabbed onto it for support, and his right hand stabbed his knife into the joint connecting the foot to the rest of the leg. Red felt a strong resistance, but his weapon dug in nonetheless.

The monster hissed in pain, and it was just about to turn around before Viran advanced and distracted it once more. Red took this opportunity to twist his knife and drag it across the joint with both hands. It was a strenuous task, but with the effort that came from his life on the line, he succeeded.

The monster buckled as its foot was severed from its leg, having lost its support on both sides of its body. Suddenly cornered, it flew into a rage and targeted the opponent who had injured it last—Red. It was a mistake it wouldn't have much time to regret, however.

Viran dashed forward as the giant insect turned its back on him and grabbed onto one of its scythe arms. The monster tried to shake him off, to no avail. He brought down his knife, and with one clean motion, the beast's main weapon was severed from its body.

Viran didn't stop there.

Before the limb could even hit the floor, Viran had already grabbed it with his free hand. With a heave, he cleaved down, cutting the monster's head in half with its own scythe. It fell to the ground, still alive but in great pain.

The man didn't stop. He pulled the scythe free from the monster's head before striking down again.

Red could only stare in wonder as the creature's twitches slowly faded under Viran's assault. Before long, the man stood victorious on top of his kill, covered in green blood.

A god of death.

CHAPTER 16
NEW WEAPON

THE BATTLE still raged on around them. Although the surviving slaves from the first group had received reinforcements, dealing with the monsters was no simple task. Gruff and his goons enforced some semblance of discipline on the panicking group, and they had already managed to trap and slay one centipede. Yet casualties were mounting on the slaves' side.

Red estimated that thirty people had died in the tunnel already. At least he and Viran had managed to take out the biggest threat. The man was currently occupied with sawing away at the other scythe arm of the giant monster.

"Here, kid, take it!" Viran threw the severed limb in his direction.

Red didn't move to catch it, avoiding the object as it clattered to the ground. The arm segment was longer than he was tall, about a meter and a half in length. After sheathing his knife and taking care not to hurt himself, Red tried to pick up the scythe near the cut-off joint where he could find some grip without cutting his hand.

Even using both hands, he could barely lift the massive blade, resting it over his shoulder after much effort. He looked over at Viran and shook his head. There was no way Red could move around swiftly while handling something this heavy.

Viran laughed. "Bah, stop complaining! That's even better than an iron weapon. Just get used to its weight!"

Red decided to ask about something that had been on his mind for a while. "Was that the leader?"

Viran didn't respond, silently scanning the battlefield. He didn't seem to be in a hurry to help the rest of the slaves.

"Maybe... I doubt it." He shook his head. "Either way, we need to get rid of these things first. Follow behind me, and pay attention."

With that, he was off.

Red followed him to the best of his ability, carrying the polearm-like insect limb atop his shoulders. Viran soon found a target, a centipede too preoccupied with the other humans to notice its impending doom.

All it took was a massive one-handed swing with the scythe limb to bisect the monster before it had even detected Viran's approach. The slaves cheered as their savior took to the field.

"Finish it off!" Viran barked at them, pointing with his unoccupied hand at the two wriggling halves. He ran past them before they could even reply. The slaves threw confused looks at Red as he struggled to keep up.

Their next target was a giant horned beetle, but this one saw their approach. While it charged in Viran's direction, the soldier didn't stray from his path. As they were about to crash, he held his weapon sideways, blocking the creature's horn with a loud collision.

The impact did not send him flying. His feet slid backwards for a few steps, but Viran held firm against the powerful monster. The beetle, however, looked fairly stunned by the impact.

"Now it's your turn, kid!"

Instead of arguing with the man, Red did as he was told. He flanked the beast and hoisted the scythe arm above his head with both hands. Before the weapon weighed him down, Red brought it to bear against the monster.

With a sickening crunch, the improvised blade found purchase, cutting halfway into its neck. The beast roared in pain and to his dismay, Red found that his weapon was stuck in its carapace. Before he could try to take it away, however, Viran stomped on the blade and forced it the rest of the way down. The creature's head was severed from its body, and Red almost fell backwards as his weapon was freed.

"It was a nice idea, kid, but beetles' necks are quite thick." Viran patted Red's shoulder. "Unless you're confident that you can cut through it in one strike, you should just go for the limbs."

Red was already surprised he'd managed to cut the beast so deeply with his new weapon, but he still took the advice to heart. When it came to fighting, Red could never claim to know as much as Viran.

Over the next few minutes, the duo killed most of the monsters, dispatching them one by one with the help of the other slaves. Viran did most of the work, but Red was there to learn, attacking the insects as he was told. His body felt tired and his back burned, but at the very least he felt more capable of wielding his new weapon.

The group of survivors stared in wonder at Viran as he stood amidst the corpses of the monsters. He had long since shown he was far stronger than what any of them thought possible, but today he had gone even further. Even Red felt surprised by the ease with which he had dispatched the monsters.

"Don't be shocked," Viran said, able to guess what he was thinking. "This is the difference a good weapon makes. When you open your Spiritual Sea, you'll have your magical arts to contend against these monsters, but until then"—He patted his scythe—"you're gonna have to rely pretty heavily on these things."

With that understanding, Red looked at the weapon he held over his shoulder with fresh eyes. He didn't know if he could keep it, but just wielding it had given him a new feeling of power.

"Gruff!" Viran looked over at the big man.

"Y-yes, boss?" Gruff seemed to have a puncture wound on his shoulder, presumably from one of the beetles.

"How many did we lose?"

"We... we have some fifty people left, boss," Gruff said after some hesitation. "Only lost seven of the ones who were with us."

Viran's face soured in anger as he looked at the survivors. Now that their lives were saved, the slaves were suddenly reminded of the conflict that had brought them to this tunnel.

"Fucking morons... Fuck!" Viran glared at them. He pointed at the bodies of the dead slaves. "Look at this mess! How are we even gonna clean this shit now? It's all your damn fucking fault for thinking you could disobey me!"

No one dared to argue against him, either out of fear or shame.

"You think I haven't talked to those idiots up top already? You think the guys who barely give us enough to eat would care whether some insects eat us? Who was the genius that came up with this? Give him up, right now!"

"He... he's dead," one slave said, pointing at a nearby corpse, its skin completely darkened from centipede venom. Red recognized him as one of Viran's direct subordinates.

"What?" Instead of feeling any satisfaction, the man seemed to get even angrier. "The bastard didn't even have the balls to stay alive so I could kill him myself! So much for your grand escape plan, huh?"

He walked over and kicked the corpse, sending it flying against the wall.

It took him another minute of screaming and venting at the slaves to calm down. Truthfully, Red thought it was merciful on his part. The Viran he knew would have likely killed or tortured every single member of the rebel group. Right now, though, they lacked manpower, and he assumed this was why Viran stayed his hand.

"Gather the equipment and prepare to drag the corpses," he said. "These monsters dug a tunnel right into our territory, so we're gonna throw these corpses down there before closing it." Viran seemed ready to say something else, but the words died in his mouth. "Gruff, skin the monsters and strip whatever you can carry from their carcasses. We are not leaving anything behind."

"Yes, boss..."

The giant, however, didn't immediately attend to his task, his face full of hesitation.

"What is it?" Viran asked, irritated.

"Was that... that big thing, the one that was making our boys disappear?"

"We'll talk about it when we get back to the meeting room." With that, Viran turned around and walked towards Red.

The boy was sitting on the ground, quietly watching the proceedings. His new weapon rested against the wall, and he was in the process of wrapping pieces of cloth around the cut on his back.

"What do you think?" Viran asked, pointing at the scythe arm.

"Too big..." Red said, after some thought. "Too heavy. Hard to walk around unnoticed with that."

"Hm." The man picked up the bladed limb and weighed it in his hand. After some consideration, he used his own scythe and swung it against Red's weapon. The blade snapped in half against the blow.

Viran examined the weapon before handing it over. "What about now?"

Red stood up and grabbed the blade. The weapon had lost nearly half its length, becoming about eighty centimeters long. It resembled a long cleaver and felt far easier to wield. With a few test swings, Red discovered that using it with one hand was still hard, but would become possible as he grew and got stronger.

The more important part was, he could now carry it without feeling weighed down.

"Better," Red said.

Viran smiled. "Good." He picked up the other part of the blade and strapped it to his waist. "Go help the others skin those monsters. We need to talk when we get back—we'll probably need to speed up our plans."

He walked towards the center of the room and started to speak with some other slaves.

Red had guessed this would be the case. If the mastermind behind the wave of giant insects was still alive, then it was possible that another hole and more monsters could emerge at any moment. They had been taken by surprise, but the slaves had still nearly lost half their numbers in this battle alone. Red didn't believe they could defend themselves against further attacks.

He looked at Viran's countenance from afar, thinking about their next move.

However, something else caught his attention. A wounded slave in ragged clothing was walking towards his leader. Red didn't know why, but something felt familiar about the man's expression.

Suddenly, it hit him. The image of the decapitated head they had found earlier flashed through his mind. Memories of past encounters with the dead man came to him. The ragged figure and the images in his head overlapped.

It was Bertel—who was supposed to be dead.

"WATCH OUT!" Red screamed, but it was too late.

The figure shot forward with incredible speed. Viran, perhaps feeling the danger himself, turned around and was about to put up his arms in defense. "Bertel," however, was already upon him.

An arm pierced straight through Viran's stomach, creating a shower of blood.

CHAPTER 17

THE ENEMY REVEALED

SILENCE DESCENDED OVER THE ROOM, seeming to stretch for an eternity as the carnage etched itself in the observers' eyes. Then came a thunderous sound that shook the slaves out of their stupor. The assailant was pushed back a considerable distance, his momentum coming to a stop after sliding some ten meters away.

Viran carried his new weapon in one hand and gripped his stomach with the other. Blood streamed through his fingers, the wound too serious to ignore. Still, he didn't collapse or buckle under the injury, which would've easily killed anyone else in his place.

His eyes narrowed, and he glared at his attacker.

Neither of them moved.

He and "Bertel" stood staring at each other, and Red couldn't help but feel as if an invisible confrontation was being fought between them. Whoever moved first might decide the winner of the battle.

The slaves were slowly realizing what had just happened.

"It... it's Bertel, but he— We saw his body earlier!"

Murmurs of panic ran through the crowd. Even those who had missed the attack connected the dots after seeing Viran's wounds and the odd scene that had unfolded in the tunnel.

And yet, everyone was too apprehensive to make any sudden movements, the tension in the air so palpable it could be cut with a knife.

"B-boss, are you okay?" Gruff asked.

He tried to approach his leader, but Viran raised his weapon hand to stop him, his gaze trained on "Bertel" all the while. The stout subordinate seemed unsure of what to do before finally looking at the attacker.

His eyes widened in fear.

"There's no way..." Gruff said. "Boss, you need to believe me. The head we saw earlier was definitely Bertel. He wasn't even here during the fight. There's—"

Viran cut him off. "That's not Bertel."

His voice carried a solemnity that Red had never heard from the old soldier.

Red took the time to inspect the assailant. The man's expression was abnormal, completely devoid of emotion or movement, and his eyes remained unblinking. This revelation made Red to pay close attention to the rest of his body, specifically his bare chest. It was unmoving.

"Bertel" wasn't breathing.

As Viran's blood dripped from Bertel's arm, Red inspected the limb. Initially, he thought he saw an armored glove, which he assumed had been the weapon used to pierce the old soldier's stomach. But that wasn't the case.

As seconds passed, the glove slowly expanded. The human skin-coat fell away, and the true form of the weapon was revealed. What Red had thought were fingers more resembled sharp claws, like those of a bear. What he'd assumed was armor now looked more like a dark exoskeleton covering the hand and the rest of the limb.

In the joint, a purple pulsing musculature connected the plates of the exoskeleton to form a humanoid arm. The process continued, as the peeling skin gradually reached the thing's shoulder.

"We need to attack it before it completely transforms!" Viran pointed at the monster. "This is what's been killing us one by one. If we let it go, there's no way any of us are getting out of here alive!"

The insectoid creature remained still. The slaves were hesitant to move, much more so given the state their previously invulnerable leader. However, at that point, Gruff's voice suddenly rose.

"You heard the boss!" he said, seeming to recover his courage. "None of us can escape right now. If Viran dies here, what do you think awaits the rest of us?"

At that, some slaves stepped forward, still fearful, but intent on joining the incoming fight.

"Are we just going to let ourselves be killed by this bug?" Gruff asked.

Shouts of agreement echoed through the tunnel. The slaves surrounded the unresponsive humanoid creature, brandishing their weapons in the thing's general direction. At that point, part of its neck and chitinous chest had been revealed.

"Wait for my command!" Viran screamed, uncharacteristically hanging back behind the other slaves.

Red didn't step forward either, instead staring at his mentor. Viran looked over and waved for him to come closer. He walked over, and when he arrived, his expression grew concerned.

He crouched down and whispered in Red's ear. "You need to follow me when I tell you to. Do you understand?"

This close, Red could see the man's hand tremble, and his voice took on a tone of concern.

"Do you understand me, kid?" This time, Viran didn't bother whispering.

Red nodded his head.

"Boss, it's getting faster!" Gruff called out.

The transformation had reached the insectoid's face and lower body. A bony pair of legs were revealed, as well as a large set of serrated mandibles where Bertel's mouth used to be. Unarmed slaves grabbed whatever makeshift weapons they could find and stood on the sidelines, while the more capable fighters squared up to their opponent. After giving Red a grave look, Viran got up and turned towards the rest of the slaves.

"On my mark!" He raised his weapon above his head, his other hand still holding tight to his wound. Seconds went by as the others waited with bated breath for his signal.

Viran's arm swung down. "Now!"

First came the throwing weapons—no one was eager enough to engage the monster in melee. Stones, axes, and spears flew forward. A few of them missed, but from a short distance, even the most unpracticed slave had an easy time hitting the creature.

Weapons clattered against the humanoid monstrosity, all bouncing off its exoskeleton. The insectoid didn't so much as flinch, remaining fixed in the same position. At that, some slaves hesitated.

Viran gritted his teeth. "What are you waiting for?! Don't let it rest!"

Finally, a brave slave charged the creature from behind. He heaved a heavy stone mace against its head.

And that was when it moved.

It was too fast. Red barely followed its movements as the insectoid's arm swung back. A green light traced its afterimage, remaining visible in the air for a few seconds before dissipating. The head of the slave exploded in a fine mist of blood, and the weapon he once held clattered to the ground, cut in half.

They all froze as the corpse of the slave toppled over lifelessly. The insectoid lifted its head, the right half of its face already transformed into what looked like part of a triangular skull.

Three narrow, green eyes stared impassively at them. Suddenly, the glow within them intensified. The creature bent back.

Viran looked over at Red. "Cover your ears!"

Red didn't hesitate. His hands had just reached his ears when a shrill, deafening sound reverberated from the insectoid.

As much as Red tried to block it, the noise seemed to penetrate every inch of his body. He felt his consciousness slipping, but before his vision went black, the sound stopped. All around him, slaves collapsed to the ground, their eyes completely white and foaming at the mouth.

A few fortunate ones still stood, but they could only groan in pain. Red was about to get up before something pulled on his shirt and he was dragged off his feet. He crossed fifty meters before he noticed Viran was the one dashing away, hauling him along.

After a few more seconds of running, the man suddenly dove down a branching path. He continued to run and weave through the tunnels for the better part of a minute before coming to a stop. Red felt dizzy. He was certain he would've vomited if there was anything in his stomach.

His feet touched the ground again, and he immediately fell down. Viran leaned against the cave wall, breathing heavily while still clutching his wound.

"Get... get up!" the man said in between gasps. "I can't carry you the rest of the way. We need to run."

Red felt some semblance of balance return to him and, using a rock as support, got to his feet. However, when he noticed his empty hands, he looked around in alarm.

"My... my weapon."

"Here, I took it," Viran said, handing over the cleaver.

Red accepted the blade, and relief washed over him.

"Hold it close. You're gonna need it. "

"Shouldn't we hide?" Red asked.

"There's no hiding from that... We need to—ugh!" He gripped his wound tighter and his legs buckled under him, threatening to fall.

Red frowned. "... You're not gonna make it like this."

He could see that the attack had pierced the side of Viran's abdomen rather than the center. The soldier had avoided having his spine broken in half, either by luck or by his swift reactions. But it was still enough damage to kill a person, even one as strong as him.

"I know my condition better than you, you fucking bastard!" Viran glared at him. "We need to go to my hideout, get some of the paste I have left. Won't do shit for my crushed organ, but it should stop the bleeding... We need to kill it."

"It managed to cripple you in a single strike. If we fight it, we'll both die."

Even in this situation, Red tried to remain calm and analyze their situation logically.

It wasn't because he wasn't afraid of dying. That was still a constant worry in the back of his mind, eating away at him. Rather, he had confronted death time after time over the past few years, and much more since he had met Viran. He had learned from experience that panicking or letting fear drive your decisions wasn't helpful, even if the situation seemed hopeless.

"You don't understand," Viran said. "That fucking thing will track every single human in this place and hunt them down."

"But it'll focus on you, right?" Red said.

Viran gave him a bitter smile.

It seemed he'd hit the nail on the head. The ambush earlier had proven the insectoid could judge the strength of all the slaves fairly well, as it had targeted the strongest among them. It had observed them from the shadows while they fought the other monsters, waiting for the opportunity to strike.

"If it kills me, you'll not be far behind."

"I know," Red said. "I don't intend to run. We have a deal, you and me. You still need to help me escape."

Viran laughed, spitting blood.

"Haha! And I thought it was the other way around... Let's go, before it catches up." With that, Viran took a deep breath and started running down the tunnels.

Even with a hole in his stomach, the old soldier was still fast. Red had to push his shorter legs hard to keep up, but the effort barely registered amid the concentration he kept on his task.

As they sped through the tunnel, Red asked something that had been on his mind for a while. Something he'd noticed when the insectoid had killed the slave. "What was that green line?"

"Spiritual Energy," Viran said.

Red had a hunch this was the case. It would have surprised him if humans were the only ones capable of harnessing that power.

But if that's the case...

"It looked like it manifested outside of its body..."

"Yeah. That thing has opened its Spiritual Sea."

Somehow, their odds got even worse.

CHAPTER 18

INSECTOID

"Do all monsters have Spiritual Seas?" Red asked as they ran.

"They do. Every living being has a Spiritual Sea," Viran said. "Besides, that thing is not a normal monster. It's got more Spiritual Energy than even your average monster."

"How did it disguise itself as Bertel? By using that energy?"

"Most likely. It was waiting for the right opportunity to attack me after all this time killing other slaves, and it wore the face of one of them to get close enough. Monsters in this world have all kinds of abilities you can't even fathom..."

Red remained silent at that.

"Ha, I know what you're thinking!" He looked at Red. "If that thing was fighting a normal person, it would win for sure, but it chose to face me. It is in for a rude awakening if it thinks it can just kill me."

Red thought those were some brave words for someone who had already been stabbed by the monster, but he refrained from commenting.

Soon the two of them arrived in front of Viran's hideout, and the man did his best to move the huge stone out of their way. It was an arduous task in his state, but Red knew that the help of a stronger-than-average ten-year-old would make no difference.

After some effort, Viran finally opened the entrance to his chamber. His ragged clothes clung to his body with sweat, and Red could see that his wound still hadn't stopped bleeding. It was a wonder the man could still move.

"Get some bandages for me. I'll look for the rest."

Viran lit a torch and started to search through the wooden boxes.

Red asked himself how bandages were supposed to help heal a hole in his stomach but didn't say anything out loud. After rummaging through some crates, he found what he was looking for. Some white wound dressing, at least as white as you could find down here, that Viran had probably exchanged with the guards.

Viran already sat on the stone bench and removed his shirt, quickly covering his wound in a brown paste. Red recognized it as the same he'd used for his broken ribs.

Viran handed the ointment to him with a grimace.

"Hurry, help me put it on my back."

Red didn't complain and moved over to examine the injury. Seeing the injury up close, he swore he could see some of Viran's organs pulsing. Raw flesh squirmed to the rhythm of his breath, and a small trickle of blood flowed from the fist-wide hole that had been punched through his abdomen.

"You should be dead," Red said.

He applied the paste around the puncture, his hands inevitably getting smeared with blood. It wasn't the gory sight that bothered him, but more so the fact that someone could still live in this condition.

"Good thing for you I'm not." Feeling the sting of the medicine, the soldier drew in a sharp breath. "That's enough. Now press the bandage against it. Hard."

Red did as he was told and pressed the dressing against the wound. Viran tore a strip of cloth from his ruined shirt and wrapped it around his pierced abdomen a few times. After making sure it was tight enough, he tied it into a knot and stood up.

"Should be enough to keep me alive for the next hour," he said.

Finally having both of his hands free to use, he started taking a few additional items out of the boxes.

Red watched him line them up on the table. A few tiny narrow stone containers and a small, glassy white rock, its surface too foggy to see through. The unremarkable mineral, however, invoked a familiar feeling inside Red's body.

"Is that...?"

"Spiritual Stone. Energy condensed into physical form. Unfortunately, it's not for you," Viran said, pocketing the rock. After that, he picked up one of the stone vials, uncorking it and downing its contents in one go. "That's for my pain, and this one"—The man picked up the other flask, tossing it to Red—" is for you."

Red examined the bottle. It fit in the palm of his hand, and he could hear liquid sloshing inside when he shook it.

"What is this?" he asked.

"A drug made from Spiritual Stone dust and various insect parts. It'll fill your body with power and increase your strength for a few seconds."

"Seconds?"

"That's right," Viran said. "That's why you only use it if you need to save yourself. There are some side effects, but if you don't make it through the fight, you won't be feeling anything at all."

Red nodded, storing it in his pouch. Suddenly, a faint screeching noise reached the chamber, echoing from far away.

"... It's coming," Viran said. "Listen, boy, I haven't taught you much about fighting, but I'm gonna need you to pay attention. In combat, you must seize the initiative and finish the battle as soon as you can."

He started going over his plan.

"That thing uses smell to track its prey, so you'll carry this to confuse it." He threw his bloody shirt at Red. "You'll run through the tunnels and act as bait, while I'll stay hidden, following behind you. It might smell me too, but it'll have a hard time differentiating me from the shirt. The moment it tries to attack you is when I'll ambush it and give it a taste of its own medicine."

"What if it sees you?" Red asked. The man had bragged about his stealth abilities before, but there was no way to be sure the plan would work.

"Then we adapt!" Viran spat a glob of blood. "There's no such thing as a perfect plan, much less one made up on the fly like this. After the battle starts, I want you to stay out of the way and only attack when I tell you to. Do you understand?"

Red frowned. "Do you just want me to stand aside and watch?"

Viran nodded. "Look, this isn't something you can handle. One hit from that thing and you'll die for sure. You'll still play your part with that drug I gave you, but you must wait until I give the order."

"And what if you die?"

Viran smiled. "Then you run and pray for your life."

Red wasn't too confident in this plan. He didn't know how the warrior was so sure that the insectoid used smell to track its prey and wouldn't notice him. The first assumption was a solid conclusion based on the behavior of the monsters down here, but the second one seemed more like a guess. Still, Red didn't think Viran would go to such lengths just to trick him.

"How will you deal with those abilities it has?" he asked.

"I suspect the screech is not something it can use repeatedly based on how much Spiritual Energy was behind the attack. As for the green light..." Viran shook his head. "It's simple. Just don't get hit."

That didn't seem like a good plan either, but Red was past the point of arguing.

"Remember this, kid." Viran touched his temple. "There are many situations where you don't know all of an enemy's strengths before fighting them. At that point, quick thinking and the ability to adapt will be your most important weapons." With that, he pointed at the chamber's exit. "Go on, head towards the main tunnel, and don't look back. You might not see me, but I'll be behind you."

Red didn't understand what that meant, but he walked out all the same. He held a moonstone with one hand and his cleaver with the other, while the bloodied shirt was tied around his neck. At first, he could hear Viran's steps following behind him. However, as the tunnel widened and they passed through a few chambers, the sound vanished.

Red had to fight his instincts to not look back and, most of all, to continue moving towards an enemy that could kill him in a single blow. After a brief moment of hesitation, he strode forward.

His silent walk continued, with the only sounds he could hear being the rhythm of his breathing and the muted shuffle of his steps against the rocky ground. For a few minutes, he almost jumped at every shadow, before he finally arrived at a larger chamber still lit by a few waning torches. Red was quick to recognize it as their meeting room, where they had gathered earlier that day.

He was just about to continue when he heard faint steps coming from another tunnel in front of him.

Red froze.

The approaching sounds were more akin to metal striking softly against stone than footsteps.

The source of the noise slowly revealed itself under the torchlight. A humanoid creature, wearing what resembled a suit of shining, segmented black armor as its exoskeleton. The insectoid was over one and a half meters tall, and it had a thin humanlike figure. Purple ligaments connected the various parts of the monster's body, bridging the joints and rare areas not concealed by the dark carapace. Its hands resembled those of a human, except for the fact that in place of fingers, five sharp-looking claws would greet whoever was foolish enough to receive a punch from the creature. The insectoid's feet were composed of three large talons each, one at the heel and two at the front. Its head was triangular and flat at the top, with two large, serrated mandibles jutting downwards from where its jaw should have been. It had six round eyes, three on each side of its face, glowing with bright, green light.

Red felt an indescribable pressure in his mind when the monster stared at him. It was like his own body and psyche naturally recognized the creature as his superior in every possible way. He made some effort to maintain his composure, but it was to no avail. Even moving or thinking straight was difficult under its gaze.

The insectoid stopped when it noticed Red on the other side of the chamber. The green glow in its eyes seemed to intensify. Much to Red's surprise, some manner of sounds started to come from its mouth. When he paid attention to it, the creature almost seemed to be forming words, with a strange and buzzing intonation befitting an insect language.

At that moment, Red knew it was trying to communicate, but he didn't know how to respond. When the monster noticed that the small human in front of him wouldn't answer, it stopped talking. It raised its right arm, and a small green light formed at the sharp tip of its claw.

Lowering its arm, it walked forward in slow and steady steps, the glow remaining in its hand. Red took a step back, feeling the Spiritual Energy building in the air. He knew that if he moved, that beam of light would immediately shoot at him.

Right as the creature made it halfway through the room, it suddenly jerked its head in a different direction. However, the monster didn't have time to react.

Viran finally attacked.

CHAPTER 19

LIFE OR DEATH

THE WARRIOR'S scythe-blade struck the insectoid in the chest.

A thunderous sound of metal clashing against metal echoed through the chamber as the creature was sent flying against the cave wall. Broken rock and dust erupted upon the monster's impact, but from what Red could see, there was no damage to its chest.

Just as it sought to recover, Viran was already upon it. His blade pounded the insectoid's body, making the air scream with each swing. His opponent was hammered against the wall after every blow, sparks flying off its exoskeleton. It was disoriented under the storm of attacks, but Red saw no cracks emerging in its carapace.

Finally, the insectoid managed to raise its hands to block Viran's weapon more effectively. His swings no longer connected with the creature's torso, but he kept up the pressure. With its back pressed against a wall, however, the monster finally found an opportunity.

It dove under one of the soldier's slashes, its hand glowing green as it thrust forward into a punch under its opponent's guard. But Viran reacted just as quickly. He moved aside to dodge the blow, and his free hand grasped the striking arm of the insectoid.

He hurled the creature across the room like a rag doll.

As the battle moved towards him, Red retreated to a safe corner of the chamber. He was glad to see Viran maintain his advantage against the monster, but not even his new sword could damage its thick carapace.

The insectoid crashed against a stone pillar, the green glow dissipating from its hand. When the monster tried to pick itself up, it saw a shadow thrusting down towards its head. The creature threw a punch against the scythe, shifting its trajectory so it stabbed the ground beside the insectoid instead.

It didn't have any time to strike back, though, as a fierce kick to the gut sent it soaring towards the cave wall once again.

The same scene repeated itself a few times, Viran throwing the insectoid around the room while the creature desperately tried to defend itself. Red thought back to the old soldier's words before the battle started. Viran showed the importance of seizing initiative as he relegated the monster to a punching bag. Still, there was no evident damage to its carapace.

The insectoid protected its vital areas with its shielded limbs, and even those Viran could only scratch. Such a high level of combat expertise wasn't something you typically found in a normal monster. Red felt the old soldier's situation had to be more pressing than what one might think from watching the combat so far.

Even if you hit something a thousand times, what did it matter if you couldn't leave a mark?

Sure enough, his worries were soon validated.

The insectoid was sent flying once more, and Viran's figure followed a few meters behind. Suddenly, however, green Spiritual Energy exploded from the monster's body. Its momentum was arrested as the force allowed the monster to reposition and land on its feet.

Viran didn't stop his charge, but this time, the creature was ready for him. It dove under its opponent's weapon and whipped around, delivering a vicious kick to the man's stomach. Now it was the soldier's turn to be launched back.

His feet slid back across the ground, but despite the pain, Viran kept his balance. He took up his combat posture once again, expecting the monster to charge and follow up on its attack. However, when he looked up, he only saw a green light.

"Fuck!"

Viran jerked his body sideways, barely avoiding a direct hit as the Spiritual Bolt grazed his chest. Though blood spilled across the ground, he was safe.

But once the insectoid had the initiative, it wasn't keen on losing it. After seeing that its attack drew blood, it circled to Viran's back, Spiritual Energy covering its hand. The creature swung its arm forward, as if to deliver a chop, and a large green blade of light shot towards Viran.

Red had never seen so much Spiritual Energy gathered in one place, and his entire body shivered, sensing the danger. Viran's expression darkened, but this time he threw himself entirely out of the way before the blade of light cut him in half.

The manifested energy crashed against the wall of the cave, and a deafening boom rang out as the attack shattered the rock in an explosion. Red felt the cavern shake, and fear consumed him as he witnessed what Spiritual Energy could do. Dust covered his vision for a few seconds, but he could still hear the sounds of battle.

Green Spiritual Light illuminated the chamber as the insectoid sent a barrage of condensed energy bolts in Viran's direction. The man continued to dodge them, but the strain was visible on his face. Red could see blood starting to drip once more from his bandaged stomach.

The creature didn't use the blade of light again, simply relying on shooting small projectiles from its hand to put pressure on its opponent. The monster was in no hurry to push its offensive either, seemingly aware of Viran's deteriorating condition. Even now, it kept its distance, repositioning itself every time he tried to move close enough to attack.

Red ducked behind some rocks to avoid being hit by any stray bolts. His eyes could barely keep up with their movements. He didn't know the capabilities of a creature that had opened its Spiritual Sea, but there were no signs of it running out of energy. It was a dangerous situation for Viran, and the man knew it.

He redoubled his efforts, but the insectoid was too fast, dancing around the chamber while shooting Spiritual Bolts at him. Eventually, the warrior failed to dodge a bolt in time, and it pierced straight through his thigh. Viran's steps faltered, and the insectoid saw an opening.

Spiritual Energy gathered in the monster's hand, and, not willing to waste its attack again, it closed the distance to its opponent. The creature's right arm charged up while Viran did his best to move out of the way—when suddenly a shadow moved from the corner of its vision.

Red approached the foe from the flank, chopping at the insectoid's side with his cleaver. The monster seemed surprised, but it was still able to react, its left hand shooting back to slap the weapon away. The cleaver shot out from Red's grasp with incredible force, and his body followed its momentum, falling to the ground.

The insectoid didn't even spare him another moment, turning back towards what it considered to be the real threat.

It turned just in time to get the side of its skull smashed by Viran's scythe. The monster's body soared from the force of the blow as shards of broken carapace scattered on the ground.

Viran glared at Red and shouted, "Get up, you fucking moron! I didn't give you my signal yet!"

"You were going to die..." Red said, but Viran was already off.

The insectoid cradled its head with one hand, green blood flowing between its claws. Even after taking a heavy blow directly to the side of its skull, the creature still stood without losing its balance. But that didn't change the fact that the monstrosity had suffered its first actual injury of the battle.

Viran crossed the distance between them quickly, even with his wounded leg. The creature, still stunned, could only raise its arms in a feeble attempt to shield itself as the scythe came crashing down upon it. With renewed fury, the man relentlessly smashed his weapon against the monster.

Viran's overwhelming blows pushed it into the stone floor, cracking the ground beneath them. Red heard more sounds of shattering carapace over the thunder of clashing strikes. The man had forced the insect into a terrible position. Not even its sturdy defenses would last much longer under this kind of assault.

Until a sudden premonition of danger came over Red.

His hands shot up to block his ears, but it was too late.

"TCHREEEEEE!"

The deafening sound crashed against his mind, and he collapsed onto his knees, his vision darkening. The scream was shorter this time, but it still brought Red to the brink of unconsciousness. By the time he recovered, he heard blood splattering against the ground.

His eyes shot back to the battle. Viran had five deep claw marks running across his chest from where the insectoid had slashed him. The man stepped back unsteadily, still recovering from the screech and having suffered a grievous blow. The insectoid, however, was merciless.

In a frenzied state, the monster jumped at the man, slashing with its claws. Viran barely had enough time to raise his weapon to block the attack. Scratching and clashing sounds echoed in the cavern as the insectoid unsparingly struck the scythe, forcing its opponent back step after step.

Eventually, another shattering sound was heard, but this time it came from Viran's blade. The weapon snapped in half, and one of the monster's claws dug into his already wounded side. Viran gritted his teeth and struck at the creature's head with what remained of the scythe. The insectoid was sent back stumbling as another piece of its carapace cracked and fell from its skull.

This time, Viran didn't push his advantage and instead limped back. His wounds were mounting, and his movements had noticeably slowed since the battle began. Heavy and raspy breaths came from his figure, a noise Red recognized very well. The gasps of a dying man.

Seeing his dire situation, Red tried to run forward.

"Stay there!" Viran held his hand up. "You still have your part to play..."

The man fished around in his pouch before taking out a white, glassy rock. The insectoid, which was still recovering from its wounds, froze as it saw the object in his hand.

Red felt it before he even laid eyes on it. The Spiritual Stone.

Viran tossed aside the broken remnant of the scythe and reached down towards his ruined bandages, tearing them off his body. The gaping wound was exposed to the air once again, blood pouring out at a much faster rate than before.

"Well, then... I guess I'll have to gamble a bit more." With that, Viran shoved the stone into his punctured abdomen.

A white glow covered the wound. The light spread through his body, lighting up veins under his skin, like roots spreading through the warrior's frame. Red's first thought was that they were blood vessels. However, he remembered something.

The wall of the cave where he had trained so many times.

Then, a realization hit him.

The Twelve Spiritual Veins on Viran's body glowed with energy. The man's roar echoed throughout the whole underground.

CHAPTER 20
POWER EXPLOSION

An enormous pressure surged from Viran, even stronger than that of the insectoid at the start of the battle. The man's body trembled for a moment as his muscles spasmed under the burden of the Spiritual Energy crawling beneath his skin. Finally, the glow of the stone diminished.

Viran removed his hand from the wound. The rock he held was now covered in crimson blood, and its radiance had dissipated. The warrior squeezed it in his grasp and the stone crumbled into dust. Red's Spiritual Veins shivered from the energy emitted by the man's body.

The creature likewise became wary at Viran's transformation. However, it didn't deign to leave its opponent any more time to prepare. The monster's hand glowed, and a barrage of green Spiritual Bolts shot out in Viran's direction. This time, he didn't dodge the attack.

Viran charged straight at the projectiles. They impacted but simply exploded upon contact with his skin, leaving behind minimal damage. The monster seemed shocked, but it didn't have time to think before Viran was upon it.

Another crack rang out as an uppercut smashed the creature's body into the ceiling. It tried to recover, but a thunderous kick sent it flying once more. Red had to quickly move out of the way as the insectoid bounced against the floor, leaving behind a trail of green blood.

Viran's feet dug into the ground, and he shot forward in pursuit. Before the monster could even hit the other side of the chamber, another blow struck it down. The creature's shell fractured under the bombardment of attacks.

Whenever Viran moved, Red could see a white mist leaking from his skin. The flow of the mist was fast and intense, yet the energetic glow in Viran's Spiritual Veins didn't dissipate.

The old soldier threw a barrage of punches at the downed insectoid. Even without his weapon, it seemed as if the sudden injection of Spiritual Energy had given his body a boost in strength. The man's fists rang like hammers as they clashed against the monster's frame.

Its armored torso splintered with a loud snap. The creature tried to protect itself with its arms, but even the limbs that had once served as shields failed it. Frantically, the insectoid reared its head back, Spiritual Energy gathering in its throat.

"TCHREE—"

The sound died as a punch hit it square in the face. The monster's head bounced against the stone floor in a daze, and Viran continued his relentless assault.

However, his pace slowed as the effort took its toll on his physique.

Red didn't know how Viran had injected so much Spiritual Energy directly into his body. Still, he guessed it didn't come without its consequences, or else Viran wouldn't have waited until he almost died before using it.

Even as he slowed down, Viran didn't give the insectoid a second to breathe. While his fists were not as effective as his weapon, the man's increased strength more than made up for it. More fractures appeared in the monster's exoskeleton as its struggling diminished.

Just as Viran seemed to have the battle under his control, Red noticed something.

In his peripheral vision, he saw a faint trail of green mist taking form, soundlessly moving towards the combatants. Red had to squint to even notice it. He traced it back and saw the mist originated from the moonstone he had dropped on the floor when the battle began.

Before he could even process what it meant, he noticed more of these trails traveling from the connecting tunnels into the chamber. Ten, thirty, fifty, a hundred of them. They were faint on their own, but as they gathered together, the light became brilliant.

They took on the same color as the Spiritual Energy of the insectoid.

Red tried to warn Viran. "Something's happening!"

The number of strands continued to increase. Viran seemed to have noticed the phenomenon, but he didn't stop attacking. Instead, he redoubled his efforts. Soon, the first mist trails reached the two combatants, and they were absorbed into the insectoid's body.

Into its eyes.

The two outer eyes shone, but a second later they went dark.

Viran's eyes widened in shock. With no wind-up, a small bolt of energy pierced straight through his gut. He stumbled back, staring at the monster's right hand which had just shot him.

Earlier in their fight, the technique had taken more time to prepare, the gathering of Spiritual Energy slower and more deliberate. That was how Viran had managed to dodge them. This time, before the man could even react, the creature had fired a Spiritual Projectile.

As both he and Red looked at the gathering green mist, the reason for the sudden change became obvious.

Red was reminded of what Viran had taught him earlier—that the moonstones contained some traces of Spiritual Energy and that he should keep them close by during his practice. Despite following his instructions, Red never felt a marked improvement in his acupoint opening speed, even with the presence of dozens of moonstones.

It seemed, however, that the creature could somehow absorb all that energy into itself. Perhaps one or two moonstones wouldn't have made a difference, but who knew how many were in the mine and from how far away the monster could call upon them?

Viran must have noticed the same thing, but now it was too late.

Light gathered in the insectoid's eyes, this time in the middle pair. Viran did his best to move out of the way, but the tears in his stomach made the task difficult.

The brightness in the creature's eyes peaked and went dark a moment later. Green light covered its raised arm. A blade of light formed out of thin air, ready to cut Viran in half.

At the last moment, Red's weight crashed into the monster's frame. The power behind his charge was small, but he managed to knock the insectoid's arm ever so slightly out of its path.

The blade of light, however, still shot out.

Another deafening boom rang out, a cloud of dust enveloping the chamber.

Red looked over at Viran. He lay gasping to the side, having successfully dodged the attack. It seemed like Red's interference had paid off.

But as he observed him, he noticed something was wrong.

It wasn't until a thudding sound caught his attention that he saw it. Viran's left arm had fallen a few meters away, severed at the elbow. It was the price he'd paid to escape the attack with his life.

Red's gaze moved back to Viran. To his surprise, their eyes met, and the man's expression twisted.

"Watch out!"

On instinct, Red ducked down, just in time for one of the insectoid's claws to miss his skull. He dashed back, trying to put some distance between himself and the monster. But the creature didn't chase him. It simply stared at the boy with its two final glowing eyes. It pointed one of its claws towards him.

Red saw death flash before his eyes, but he wasn't nearly as fast as Viran. The green bolt hit him square in the chest and he was thrown against the rock wall.

"FUCKER!"

The creature turned around just in time for a fist to send it stumbling back. However, the glow in Viran's skin had diminished considerably. With his body battered and wounded, he couldn't gather the same strength as before.

That didn't deter him, though. With his one remaining hand, the warrior hammered down on the creature's head. Blocking its opponent's desperate attacks with its raised arms, the monster bided its time as more green mist flowed into its body.

Viran raised his hand once more, but the monster moved first. Its leg whipped around to hit the man's side. He saw it coming and grabbed its ankle, trapping the monster's leg against his body.

The monster panicked and tried to free itself, but to no avail. Even in his current state, Viran's strength was still greater than the insectoid's. He swung the creature around and hit it furiously against a wall, again and again. The weight of the monster seemed negligible under his rage.

Finally, the man threw the monster at the wall, lunging forward to finish it off. The insectoid managed to put up both of its arms to block the attack.

Viran didn't let up and pressured his opponent to give way, hammering it with his fist.

The creature slowly lost ground and was forced to kneel, its carapace cracking under the attacks. There was some hesitation in the insectoid's actions, but then the mist flowed into its two remaining glowing eyes at a much faster rate, making them shine like lanterns.

A second later, the brilliance reached its peak, and its last pair of eyes went dark. The monster's hand lit up, and it lowered its guard to attack. That was when the insectoid's face was met with a wave of glowing blood full of concentrated Spiritual Energy. The crimson fluid exploded on contact.

The shot went wide, and the creature fell back, its eyes burning from the blood Viran had spewed. Another crushing blow flung the insectoid's head down onto the floor.

"I'll show you, you fucking bug—"

Another punch.

"Why they call me—"

Another crack.

"THE FUCKING RED HEART!"

The back of the monster's skull started to fracture, leaking green fluid. In a desperate attempt to protect itself, it gathered Spiritual Energy in its throat and made another screeching attack.

"TCHREEE!"

The scream was very short and not even half as effective as before. But Viran, having lost liters of blood, still suffered as his senses were assaulted. For a moment, he stumbled on his feet.

His opponent didn't let the chance slip away. Its claw shot out and stabbed into the man's midsection. This time, however, it didn't pierce all the way through. The jolt of pain snapped Viran out of his confusion and he swung his fist down against the creature's head.

But the insectoid was prepared for it. Its other hand grabbed the man's wrist, halting the attack midway. Viran struggled to free himself, but his strength waned. His eyes burned with fury, and with the only weapon available to him, the warrior headbutted the monster right between its six eyes.

More shattering noises echoed through the cavern. The monster's head reeled back, but this time, it was the one who refused to let go.

Viran headbutted it again, and the creature's grip weakened. Blood flowed down his forehead and into his eyes, but he didn't stop. Right as he was about to go for the third headbutt, the man jolted, seemingly feeling a sharp pain shoot up his body. His opponent pressed its claw deeper into his midsection.

The insectoid took the opportunity and opened its mandibles wide, biting into Viran's clavicle. It tore into flesh and bone, gripping tightly to its foe. At that point, the pain didn't even seem to register in Viran's mind as he struggled to get free.

A river of blood poured down from the man's body. Life slowly slipped from his figure as his strength left him, but the fire in his eyes didn't diminish. Suddenly, he noticed something, and a wide smile spread across his face.

He laughed, blood spilling from his lips.

"Ha... haha. It's time to play your part, kid..."

CHAPTER 21
CLOSING MOMENTS

THE INSECTOID HEARD the soft footsteps approaching it from behind. Frantically, it released the grip of its mandibles and tried to turn to look at its hidden assailant. This time, Viran didn't allow it to let go. As soon as the insectoid tried to pull away, the man headbutted the creature.

It was dazed, and by the time it recovered, Red was already upon it. His cleaver moved soundlessly, severing the monster's arm with a single motion. Then, before his newfound strength left him, Red had already retreated from the two combatants.

His thought process was simple: he wasn't sure if he could kill the monster, even under the effects of the drug Viran had given him. So instead, Red freed the one person he knew could finish it off.

The monster didn't have any time to react. With his remaining arm now free from its restraints, Viran's fist came crashing down. Another crack rang out as more of the insectoid's skull fractured. Viran, however, didn't raise his hand for another strike.

His fingers dug down into the creature's exoskeleton and whatever organ or flesh was beneath it. The monstrosity shrieked as green fluid dropped from the holes in its head. Perhaps for the first time in the fight, it felt the pain directly. Viran didn't let go, even as the insectoid's one remaining set of claws dug deeper into his body.

It seemed the man was lacking the strength to pierce any further into the monster's head. What he had done wasn't enough to kill it, evidenced by the beast's increasingly desperate struggle.

"Should've just stuck to hunting defenseless slaves, bug."

What remained of the gleaming Spiritual Energy under Viran's skin flooded towards his arm. The light reached his hand, where it radiated a bright glow. The insectoid felt the gathering energy on its head and fought even harder. It tried biting and kicking Viran, but all to no avail.

Its angry shrieks turned fearful as the monster saw what was about to happen. Viran just smiled.

The energy in the man's hand reached a crescendo. Something threatened to burst from under his skin, when suddenly a roaring boom resounded.

Red had to protect his eyes from the light of the explosion. He felt droplets of blood and gore pepper his whole body. It was only after a few seconds that his vision finally recovered.

Viran's remaining hand had disappeared, and half of the insectoid's head was gone along with it. The man used his stump to remove the creature's limp claw from his stomach. Its corpse fell lifeless to the floor, and the green mist around the room dissipated.

The battle was over.

"Somehow it worked, huh?" Viran said as he looked at Red.

He smiled.

Red was already experiencing the aftereffects of the drug. His body felt as if it had just undergone an hour-long training session against the old soldier, but he didn't sit down to rest. In Red's chest, where the Spiritual Bolt should've struck, a green light was glowing under his skin. Slowly, the brightness of the energy faded, and a painful sensation throbbed in his Spinal Vein.

"It did," Red said. He saw the man's legs tremble. "You—"

"Not now." Viran shook his head. "Help me sit down."

Red did as he was told. The man put his arm—or what remained of it—around the boy's shoulder, and Red felt a tremendous weight on him as Viran struggled to remain standing. Before they both collapsed to the floor, Red brought them near the cave wall, and Viran sat down and leaned against it.

Red examined the man's wounds. There was so much blood covering his body that it was hard to tell how many injuries he had received. Red frowned.

"What are you standing around for?" Viran asked, his voice much weaker than before. "Go look inside that thing's head. There should be a crystal there."

With some reluctance, Red walked over to the insectoid's corpse. Sure enough, searching through its partially destroyed skull, beneath the bits and pieces of insect meat, he found a crystal lodged inside what looked like the creature's brain. It had a green color mixed with vivid streaks of blood red. He had to use his iron knife to cut it out. The gem was smaller than his fist, and it looked jagged and rough at the edges, like the minerals the slaves would find in the caves.

Returning to Viran, he showed him the crystal.

"Red? That's strange..." The man seemed confused. Pressed for time, however, he had no choice but to throw his bewilderment away. "That is the equivalent of hundreds and hundreds of moonstones, kid. It'll make opening your special acupoints much easier... but this one is a little odd. I would investigate it for you, but I'm in no condition to do so. If you find anything strange about it, do not hesitate to throw it away." Viran then pointed at the ground in front of him with his stump. "Now, sit. We need to talk about some things."

Red hesitated after seeing the man's bleeding wounds. It seemed as if Viran's will alone was keeping him alive at this point.

"Ha, nothing down here can patch this up, kid."

"We could ask the guards."

"Even if they had the right medicine, the only thing I could use to trade for it is gone. Besides, even if you went up, you probably wouldn't make it back in time." Viran pointed at the ground in front of him again. "Come on, sit down, before..."

His voice trailed off. Finally, Red did as he was told.

"Good," Viran said. "You know, if I knew all this shit was gonna happen, I wouldn't have been so stingy with my lessons to you."

"Did you know *this* was going to happen?" Red asked, pointing at his glowing chest.

When he was hit by the Spiritual Bolt, he felt immediate pain, but the blood he'd expected to explode from his chest hadn't come. Instead, the energy seemed to flow into his body, and he swore that the attack had rein-vigorated him instead.

"Well, I hoped so, but I wasn't too keen on testing it against a powerful creature like that." Viran spat a glob of blood towards the corpse of the monster. "That thing employed the same kind of Spiritual Energy that's present all over these moonstones. That was how you survived. Your special acupoints were supposed to diffuse that kind of power, but with only one of them open, I thought..."

The man's voice trailed off and he smiled.

"Thankfully, either my method was far more effective than I thought, or the monster didn't use its full strength with that bolt—or else both of us would be dead."

Red was about to inquire further, but Viran cut him off.

"You must have a lot of questions in your mind, kid. But there are more important things to talk about while we still can," he said. "You need to leave."

"I haven't even finished opening my second Spiritual Vein," Red protested.

"Heh, don't I know that. But after they learn about what happened here, the guards will probably collapse this entrance for good. No more food or supplies for whatever is left alive down here. And besides, where there's one of those insects, there will probably be more."

Red felt startled. He thought that with the main culprit eliminated, he could stay in the mine and slowly open his Spiritual Veins until he was ready to escape.

"How do I get past the guards?" Red asked. He'd had minimal contact with the people overseeing the mine entrance, so he wasn't sure how he would go about staying hidden from view.

"Get past them?! Haha—ugh..." A jolt of pain cut off his laughter. "No, kid, you're not getting past them. They have a way of knowing about every-thing that leaves this place. Besides, even if you could kill them all and leave, you would definitely be hunted afterwards. No, the only way to escape is..."

Red had a bad feeling about Viran's next words.

"Down."

"I'll die," Red said with certainty.

"You probably will. But it's the only way to go about it."

Red felt conflicted, but between one sure way to die and the other, there was not much difference in the end.

"How do I do it?"

"I have a map," Viran said. "I managed to explore much deeper than you might think. There are signs of a tributary..."

The old soldier stared at Red silently, as if expecting something.

Red was confused for a second before understanding dawned on him. He had almost forgotten who he was dealing with.

"Even in this situation, you still want to act like a bastard?" he asked.

Viran smiled. "Maybe, but then again, you're not the one who's dying. So?"

"What do you want me to do?"

"Two things. Two wishes of mine, if you can call them that," Viran said. "The first one is for your own benefit. There's a forest very far away from here, called Autumn's Hearth. A native tribe lives there. Go meet with their chief, his name is Aksvale, and tell him that 'The One who Burns the Brightest' sends his disciple to collect what is his. It'll be a shame if my trove collects dust for eternity, or even worse, ends up in the hands of those savages. So, if you ever make it out of here, make sure to go there as soon as you can. Do you understand?"

"I do." Red memorized the strange words. Whatever could benefit him in opening his Spiritual Veins and Sea, he wouldn't refuse. This, however, didn't seem like the arduous task he was expecting in exchange for his life.

"The next wish of mine..." His words grew faint, and it was like the atmosphere in the chamber had changed. Viran seemed to recall something. The smile faded from his face, and an expression of hatred came over him.

"The one who hunted me, the one who took everything I had... the one that put me in this state." His voice trembled in anger, as if simply remembering this individual were enough to make him go mad. "If... when you leave this place, I need you to kill him."

This time, Red hesitated. He didn't know why, but somehow, he could feel the weight behind the man's words. Like this wish of his would have further ramifications than Red could judge right now. But in his mind, anything was better than rotting in these caves.

"I'll do it."

"That's not good enough!" Viran gritted his teeth. "I need you to promise it."

Another moment of silence passed.

"I promise."

"Good." Viran seemed relieved, and the tension left his body. "His name is Bernard, but most people know him as the Silver Knight. Remember that well."

Red wasn't going to forget that name anytime soon.

"Now, reach for my waist. My knife should still be there."

Red followed the instructions. He found the weapon still strapped to the man's belt, covered in blood.

"Break the handle," Viran said.

Red stared at him, confused.

"Do as you're told. Just make sure you're careful."

Red picked up his cleaver and delicately cut into the knife's wooden handle. The brittle material quickly gave way, and he noticed it was hollow inside. Carefully splitting the wood apart, he saw a folded-up paper hidden within.

After unfurling it, Red was surprised to find a detailed map of the cavern system spread before his eyes.

"You can use that to escape," Viran said. "It's not complete, but it's better than nothing. I jotted down the areas you should avoid and the place you should look for—the stream."

"I can't read," Red said. The layout seemed familiar, but the words were gibberish to him.

Viran frowned. "Just make sure you stay away from the bad-looking symbols."

Red nodded and folded the map again before storing it in his pouch. Finally, he turned to the soldier, waiting for his next orders.

"Then... that's it, you can go."

Red didn't move.

"Nothing more for you here, kid," he said when he saw the boy still hadn't moved. "I told you all you need to know right now. If by some miracle you do manage to make it out of here, then you can learn the rest by yourself."

Red still didn't budge.

Viran laughed. "Want to squeeze me dry of everything I have? My hideout is still open. You can go look for stuff there, but you already have my most prized possession, so don't hold your breath."

Red continued to stare at him impassively.

"Feeling some sympathy, huh?" Viran snorted. "No need for it, kid. You know, when I embarked on this journey, I knew I could die at any moment. But I would be lying if I didn't see myself going out with a bit more of a bang. You know, a memorable battle against my most hated rival with the entire world as a witness."

Viran lifted his handless arm.

"Instead, I get to die with a dark fucking cave as my grave, killed by a fucking bug I could have crushed like an ant in the past. And on top of that, I even ended up playing the hero and saving a little brat like you... Ha!"

He laughed before coughing up even more blood.

"... How they would laugh at me if they knew."

Viran laid his head back against the cave wall and closed his eyes, a smile on his face.

"Now, go! Leave a man to spend his last moments in peace. If you don't end up in some insect's stomach, one day you'll understand how I feel."

Red finally broke his silence. "You deserved a better end."

"Hmm..." Viran hummed in agreement, his eyes still closed. "I guess I can't complain. It's better than what many people get."

"I'll make sure you're not forgotten."

"I hope so. A man is only worth as much as his word."

Viran stopped talking. His breathing became labored, and the pool of blood beneath him grew.

Red decided to grant him his wish.

He turned and walked away into the dark tunnel. He didn't look back.

CHAPTER 22

DEPARTURE

THE CAVES WERE EERILY QUIET, more so than usual. As Red walked through the tunnels, he saw the slaves' living chambers empty of life, their previous inhabitants never to return. He collected whatever he thought could be useful for his journey down below, which wasn't much.

His lack of supplies worried him. He didn't know for how long he would have to travel, and not even Viran's map, in its incomplete state, could tell him.

According to the drawing, Viran had found a stream far below the tunnels most slaves explored. As Red thought further, he realized this could have been the result of heavy rain draining into the caves. The mine was full of small holes and channels into which no human could fit, so rainwater flowing down here to form small currents wasn't a rare sight. It was the reason they hadn't died from thirst, after all.

There must have been some other reason why Viran believed the stream was special. It was a tributary, he claimed. Red didn't know what the word meant, but he knew what a river was. Those only existed on the surface, as he had heard, and sometimes branched out into smaller streams. So, following this stream would lead him out. Or so he assumed.

It didn't take long for Red to arrive at Viran's hideout. He rummaged for supplies for his trip, and since the man had given him permission, he didn't hold back. He searched mostly for food that wouldn't perish quickly, like bread. There was quite a lot of stored away, seemingly enough to make a venture of unknown length into a dangerous land. Viran had clearly been preparing for his escape.

He sorted whatever food he could find into a bag.

I hope this is enough.

His most urgent goal completed, Red scanned the room for any other useful items. There were quite a few torches, but he never liked to use them while wandering the tunnels. They were too bright and would attract too much attention.

He would rather use the moonstones. Their light was weaker, but they also weren't as likely to get him noticed and eaten by the giant insects.

Other than that, most of what Red found were insect parts and a lot of notes. Red had no use for the former, but the latter might be helpful to him when he finally reached the surface and learned how to read. Perhaps they would offer some insight into whatever Viran had been working on down here. With that in mind, he stuffed as many of the yellowed pages as he could find into a pouch.

He also looked for the medicine and bandages he had used earlier to patch up Viran. The pot of medicine was almost empty, but there was still enough for at least one application. As for the wound dressings, there were enough to cover a small child, which would come in handy when he was inevitably injured.

After gathering everything, Red tested the weight of his bag. It was much heavier with all the food, but he knew that if a monster noticed him, he probably couldn't outrun it either way. His running speed wouldn't be as crucial as his ability to stay out of sight.

Finally, Red stepped back and took one last look at the wall. More specifically, at the drawing of the Spiritual Veins.

Much of his last few weeks had been spent in this place, being beaten to a pulp by Viran. They were painful memories, but he didn't regret any of it. In the end, Red found that there was some truth in his mentor's words.

Experience was the best teacher. Right now, he didn't think he'd still be alive if Viran had spent their training handholding him. Red didn't know what to expect in his future, but he felt certain there wouldn't be anyone teaching him what he needed to do. He would have to rely on himself to adapt and improvise as quickly as he could. Although Red could have become more skillful if Viran had given him more advice, he wouldn't have been as confident in fighting against the unexpected.

Granted, he wasn't very confident he would survive the journey at all, but his situation could've been even worse. He tied the sack around his chest in preparation for the trip. In one hand, he carried a moonstone, and in the other, his cleaver.

He left the room. His first stop, however, wasn't the unknown trail. He would look for a place to sleep.

So much had happened in a short amount of time. Red had gone from a fight against a giant insect armed with scythes to a life-or-death struggle against the insectoid. Not to mention, the effects of Viran's drug weighed heavily on his body. If Red tried to press forward like this, then he would definitely be killed.

But he didn't dare sleep in this place. He remembered Viran's words. Who knew what other monsters would crawl out of the cracks? The only part of the cave Red felt confident enough to hide and rest in was the one where his... dark friend lived. Red hesitated every time he approached those tunnels, but he'd found it to be one of the safest places to hide during insect attacks.

Most monsters avoided that part of the mine, and he could guess why. Besides, it was one of the few passages that remained unblocked, and the one Red was the most familiar with. It wasn't a safe bet by any means, but it was still the most reliable option he had.

As Red walked through the tunnels, he could hear the distant noises of insects hissing and fighting against each other beyond the blocked passageways. He guessed that since the insectoid had died, their peaceful coexistence had ended.

There was still an unblocked passage in the main tunnel of the mine, where the wind flowed towards the depths. Once the monsters smelled the fresh blood, who knew how many would come swarming?

Red wasn't keen on getting in the middle of that.

He sped up despite his exhaustion. But it wasn't too long before his head throbbed and his senses dulled from the effort. Rather than simple exhaustion, Red felt a sickness coming over him. His eyelids were getting heavier, and his ears and nose seemed clogged.

The effects of the drug.

That was the best guess he could come up with.

After what felt like hours of walking, Red saw the familiar tunnel. There, he knew where all the best hiding spots were, as well as where the moonstones grew.

This was the place he felt the safest.

However, Red didn't relax. He examined the ground to make sure there were no insect tracks. Much to his relief, he found nothing but the footsteps of slaves in the dust of the rock floor. At least for now, he didn't need to worry about being attacked from behind.

After wandering further down, Red found one of his designated sleeping spots. Hidden in between a few stone pillars was a hole that was barely visible in the dark caves. It was small even for a child, but he would take an uncomfortable rest over being ambushed while sleeping.

He untied the bag from his shoulder, eager to finally lie down.

Then, a tremendous force hit him on the side. Red was sent flying from the impact before crashing to the ground. He tried to sense what was happening, but the only thing he heard was the sound of approaching steps.

Though Red tried to react in time, his whole body felt sluggish. In any other situation, he wouldn't have been taken by surprise like this.

He was tired, but he had let his guard down. He'd assumed he was the only slave left alive. It was clear now that this wasn't the case.

A large hand wrapped around his throat. Red was lifted into the air before his head slammed against the wall.

The air escaped his lungs. His hands shot out in desperation, trying to free himself from the vicelike grip on his neck. It was a pointless effort.

"You abandoned us... YOU KILLED THEM!"

It took a few seconds for him to recognize the voice. Gruff.

The darkness at the edges of his vision retreated for a second, allowing him to take in the image before him. Gruff was covered in dried blood, his face completely twisted in rage.

And somehow, still alive.

Red's surprise didn't last long. He supposed that if any slave other than Viran and Red could have survived the insectoid's scream, it would've been the giant. Perhaps the monster had ignored him just like it had Red, judging him simply unworthy of death while its main prey ran away. Or maybe keeping Gruff alive was its revenge from beyond the grave?

Such thoughts flashed through Red's mind as the grip around his throat tightened. Gruff had a crazed look on his face, his singular goal to take the life of the boy in his hands. Red kept trying to pull the hand off, but he quickly learned it was futile. Even after having opened two Spiritual Veins, he couldn't match strength against someone of the giant's size.

It was then that panic took over. He struck and scratched, but Gruff's grip was like steel, the man's hateful eyes boring into his head. Red saw the world go black. In desperation, one of his hands dropped to his side, hoping to find anything to help him.

His fingers brushed against something cold.

The knife!

With one swift motion, he pulled out the weapon and stabbed it into Gruff's wrist.

"ARGH!"

Gruff recoiled in pain as the knife lodged into his arm, dropping Red onto the ground.

As soon as he was free, Red fell into a coughing fit. In his panic, he had forgotten about his weapon. Thankfully, he'd remembered it just in time.

Time he didn't have much of right now.

"I'LL BURY YOU HERE WITH THEM!"

Gruff jumped at him. While Red was trying to catch his breath, the man had dislodged the knife from his arm and now held it in his hand. Red rolled away at the last moment, his movements sluggish but just fast enough to avoid the wild lunge.

Unfortunately, it wasn't enough to escape Gruff's reach.

"THIS IS ALL YOUR FAULT!"

Red felt a hand wrap around his leg. Dragged backward, he turned around just in time to see the knife stab into his thigh. He gritted his teeth as Gruff twisted the weapon inside his leg.

"I'LL MAKE YOU FEEL A FRACTION OF THE PAIN YOU MADE US GO THROUGH!"

The words didn't even register in his mind as his consciousness slipped bit by bit. Yet he refused to just give up.

What do I do?

Gruff had his weapon, and Red couldn't hurt him with his bare hands. He needed something. Something...

He looked around, spotting the gleam of a dark metallic blade.

Red grabbed it just in time. In the next moment, he felt his body leave the ground. Gruff held him upside-down by the ankle with his free hand.

With a furious grunt, he tore the knife out of Red's thigh, ripping through his flesh.

"Now... I'll split you in half!"

His weapon was just about to skewer him again when Gruff suddenly lost his balance. A jolt of pain shot up the man's left leg. He dropped the boy and fell onto his back. Looking down, he saw his limb had been cut off cleanly just below the knee.

Blood poured out incessantly from his new stump.

"You... you..."

His voice dwindled away in shock. Red didn't hesitate, though. He crawled over, dark cleaver in hand, and swung it down against his assailant's head. Gruff barely had time to put his arms up to block.

His forearm was sliced through, unable to stop the cleaver which lodged itself deep in his rib cage. A desperate look came over Gruff as he struggled with his remaining hand to pull the weapon from his chest. Red tried to yank the cleaver from between the bones to finish the job, but the blade was stuck tight. He instead opted to push the weapon further in.

"Argh!"

Gruff spewed a shower of blood in Red's face. The crimson fluid pooled around the giant's chest and lips, and his efforts grew weaker. Only after seeing that Gruff was dying did Red let go of the weapon. He slid off the top of the man's body, collapsing onto the ground by his side.

His eyelids were too heavy to keep them open. His vision darkened.

"You... you cursed us..."

It was the last thing Red heard before he fell unconscious.

CHAPTER 23

GAMBLE

"The Holy Priest has said the last word on this matter, Abraham. We'll hold the wall and fight to the death if need be."

A commanding voice shook Red from his oblivion. In front of him, he saw a pale, desolate sea of sand, extending far beyond what his eyes could perceive. The golden sky was lit by rays that had no point of origin. It was a world that defied description and logic.

A place he recognized.

I'm here again.

This time, however, Red wasn't standing on the wall. He looked down in confusion, only to feel a wave of nausea rush through him. There was nothing below his feet. He was standing on air.

I'm flying.

There was no sign of the wall around him, only the endless white desert. Red's throat tightened, but even after many seconds had passed, he didn't fall.

"Abraham, do you understand your orders?"

The same voice that had awakened him spoke again. Red turned to face its source. A middle-aged man sporting a fine beard and long black hair stared at him sternly. His frame was burly and exuded an immense pressure. The warrior wore intricately decorated plate armor, which Red recognized from his previous dreams. Upon closer inspection, though, he noticed something different. What he'd thought were simple accessories on the protective gear brimmed with a power that flowed out of the confines of the armor.

A powerful figure—more powerful than he could even measure. And this individual was staring at him.

What now?

Red thought back to how his dreams ended. He always died.

He examined his surroundings. There was no mysterious entity, no battle, nothing else that could threaten him.

Only him and this person.

Realization hit him.

"You're going to kill me," he said in a voice that wasn't his own.

The man's face contorted in shock. His eyes narrowed and killing intent flowed from his body. The formless aura pressed down on Red, making it difficult to even move his head.

"How did you know?" the warrior asked.

It took Red a few seconds to register what had happened. He'd spoken, and the man in front of him had heard his words. The simple exchange shocked him to no end. His actions in his dreams had always been very limited. At most he would move around a little before being killed.

Most of his dreams took place in catastrophic scenarios where conversations weren't commonplace. Red had always thought the independence he had to look around and act in these scenarios was simply an illusion, inconsequential to the result of the dream. Nothing would change, no matter how hard he tried to change the outcome.

He had concluded that talking to others would also be impossible, but this was clearly not the case. Here he was communicating with someone, something that should've been impossible in a dream.

Red forgot for a moment that the man still wanted to kill him. There was so much he wanted to know—where he was, what was happening here, how they could simply stand on air. Soon, his curiosities settled down and Red recovered some of the composure that had kept him alive all this time.

Would this man believe him if he said he wasn't the person whose body he now occupied? Unlikely, and even if he did, would the man keep him alive? It all depended on how much this warrior wanted to kill him, which at the moment looked like a fair amount. Perhaps escaping death was impossible, but this wasn't his first dream and he doubted it would be the last.

The most important thing right now, rather than avoiding death, was to obtain information. The man was unlikely to answer his most pressing and mundane questions, so Red had no choice but to play along.

"I asked you a question!" The warrior glared at him, impatience clear in his words. "How did you find out?"

"How do you think?" Red asked, once again in the unfamiliar voice.

"Hmph!" The man's eyes narrowed. "So there are more rats sneaking around the Temple, huh? We dug you out and we'll dig out those remaining, no matter how well they think they can hide!"

Rats? I'm a spy?

"Even if you know, tell me—what was your plan in still coming along?" the warrior asked, looking around. "There's no one nearby to help you, I made sure of it. Did you really think you could stop me from killing you all by yourself?"

The otherworldly pressure on Red increased. Every inch of his body felt weighed down, and he struggled to even get out a word.

The man snorted. "Very arrogant on your part, traitor. I carved my name into the totem before you were even born. I could have killed you back then with one hand. But now?"

A golden mist of energy covered the warrior.

"I don't even need to move to do it..."

The shining curtain of energy expanded until it reached Red's body.

"Wait—"

He couldn't finish his words before darkness surrounded him once more.

How unreasonable...

That was the first thing Red thought as he woke up. Right after, a massive headache hit him. Then another terrible pain bloomed in his lower body. It took a few seconds for his vision to adjust to the darkness.

He peered to his side. He saw Gruff's face, wide-eyed and motionless. Even in death, his expression seemed twisted, staring at him in hatred. Slowly, Red recalled what happened before he passed out.

My leg...

Red reached down, his hand touching something slick and warm. He saw a small puddle of blood gathered beneath the cut in his thigh. He didn't know for how long he had slept here. Thankfully, it seemed like Gruff hadn't hit an artery, or else Red would have already bled out in his sleep.

It didn't mean the wound was any less painful or serious, especially in these caves. He needed to stop the bleeding immediately, or else he would still die. Red tried to get up, only to tumble down again. He could barely put weight on his left leg, and his whole body was still aching. Whatever rest he had caught while unconscious had not helped his recovery.

He crawled over to his bag and searched for the medicine inside. After some effort, he pulled out both the medicinal paste and bandages. Leaning against a wall, he pulled up his pant leg to check the wound. The knife had entered above his knee, and with Gruff twisting the weapon, it had done plenty of damage.

After cleaning his leg as much as he could, Red smeared his hand with the paste and applied it over the wound. A stinging pain spread over his thigh, much more intense than when he had used the medicine on his ribs. However, he saw the effects of the substance very quickly. About half a minute later, the bleeding had decreased substantially as the paste adhered to the open wound.

Red then used the bandage to cover the wound and tied a tight knot to apply some pressure on the cut. It was a method he had learned from Viran. Apparently, you were supposed to suture wounds like this closed so they could heal faster. The slaves, however, didn't have any line or needle to do the job. Viran said the paste would be just as efficient in closing an injury.

Red had seen the effectiveness of the medicine, so he didn't doubt it would work. The problem was how long it would take for the cut to heal, and if he would have enough paste to last until then. Right now, Red needed to move away from this place as fast as he could. Monsters were attracted by the smell of blood, and he didn't want to be caught with a bad leg.

He tried to get up again, but weakness shot up his left leg and he fell to the ground. With a grunt of pain, Red repeated his efforts, only to fail once more. Finally, on the third try, and after a minute of catching his breath, he managed to get up with the support of a rock pillar.

Red learned his lesson and didn't immediately try to walk. He looked down at his leg. Above all else, he feared the effort would cause the wound to worsen and bleed once again. Still, considering his situation, what other option did he have?

Would Red risk bleeding out from walking or chance being eaten by giant insects by staying put? He laid against the wall and sighed.

I'm going to die here, aren't I?

It was the obvious conclusion. It was a fact mostly left unsaid when Viran left him with his last words. This cave was full of horrible things that Red didn't have the slightest chance of killing on his own. As he'd heard countless times from the other slaves, the deeper one went, the stronger and scarier the creatures became.

He thought back to his encounter with the insectoid. Would the lower levels of the cave have monsters as strong as that? If Red found another one, he would have no other choice than to accept his death. His brilliant plan, from the beginning, had been to rely on his stealth to pass unnoticed. It was his strongest weapon, but with a wounded leg, what else could he do?

Even in his best condition, Red knew how hard that would have been. And now, with his mobility compromised? He would die.

It was one thing to brave danger when you had skills you could rely on, no matter how difficult the task proved to be. It was another to do so while completely deprived of every advantage you once had.

Red felt disheartened. Should he take his chances up here trying to recover, hiding while the monsters ate the corpses of the slaves? Even if he went unnoticed, would he ever get another opportunity to escape this place again? Once his supplies ran low and the insects reclaimed the area, would he still be able to escape? It was just another gamble, perhaps less immediately dangerous than descending into the mines, but it wouldn't bring him closer to his goals.

Red wanted to escape. He wanted to leave this cursed place behind. He wanted to explore the world he had heard so much about. To see the sun, the stars. The moon. It was all he ever desired and dreamed about while fighting to survive down here. And after everything, his goal seemed as far away as it ever did.

It was then that he felt it, a strange sensation. A tingling in the back of his mind. He never felt this before, yet somehow could decipher what it meant by instinct.

His friend, whom Red hadn't visited in more than a month, was calling to him. Hungry.

He looked back. If he walked further down the tunnel, he would find the entrance to its lair. Then his gaze returned to the corpse of the giant man in front of him.

Red sighed once more.

If he was going to take a gamble, he would always choose the option that gave him the biggest chance of success.

No matter the risk.

CHAPTER 24

FORCEFUL BREAKTHROUGH

RED KNEW Gruff's body wouldn't fit through the tunnel leading to the blob. It would need to be hacked apart if he wanted to transport it. It was a cruel fate, even for someone who'd tried to murder him.

He didn't like the idea of what he was about to do. To him, it was one thing to cut down someone who was trying to kill you, but to butcher them like an animal after they were dead? It reminded Red of all those slaves who'd resorted to savagery and cannibalism to keep themselves alive. However, he couldn't let his conscience get in the way of his escape.

Most people who died down here ended up eaten by a monster regardless, so Red was just going to expedite the process. At least that was how he rationalized it.

He hobbled over to Gruff's corpse and tried to pull his cleaver free. The weapon had sunk deep into the man's rib cage, and it looked like it would take some effort to loosen it. Still, with patience and a lot of wiggling, Red finally pulled it free.

He gave the cleaver a once-over and was relieved to see no damage on its edge. It would still be useful against the monsters, but next time he needed to be more strategic with his attacks. Gruff was a human, and the wound had been enough to kill him, but the giant insects were far bigger and sturdier. If Red got his weapon stuck in their body and they didn't die, it would be a very unfortunate situation.

He also realized that both his clothes and blade were covered in blood. The monsters down here were sensitive to all manner of smells. If Red wanted to sneak through their nests, then he would need to get some new clothes or clean the ones he was wearing. But not yet.

The dirty work still wasn't done.

Red took a deep breath and started hacking away with his cleaver.

Unsurprisingly, the task took a long time. By the end of it, Red's body was almost completely covered in blood. Still, that was the easy part of the job. Now, he needed to bring it all over to the other side of the tunnel while walking on a bad leg.

It took more than an hour for Red to crawl through the small tunnel with every piece of flesh. He had to be especially careful not to scrape his wounded thigh on the stone floor, which made the process take even longer.

He eventually had to give up on the giant's torso. It was too big to go through the tunnel while allowing Red to move at the same time. Not to mention, he wasn't about to bisect the man's chest and carry all his organs and guts one by one, either. Time was of the essence, and he felt that would be going too far, even for him.

Once Red brought everything else to the other side of the tunnel, he felt as if he had just gone through a battle with another monster. But there was no time to rest. He tied up the remaining pieces of flesh and hobbled down the last stretch of the cave.

Comfortable purple light greeted him, and Red swore it seemed brighter than he remembered. The position of the strange creature and its tentacles remained the same, however. As soon as he entered the chamber, a mouth formed at the heart of the blob, and Red heard its voice echo in his mind.

"Where have you been?"

The tone of the creature seemed no different from usual, but a shiver ran down his spine when he heard it.

"... Occupied," Red said.

"With what?" the blob asked.

He pointed at his wounded leg. "Monsters."

"Ah, I see." It seemed satisfied with Red's brief explanation.

He wasn't lying, either. He had been occupied because of the monsters, but that wasn't the reason he hadn't visited. Still, since it believed him, there was no point in pressing the issue further.

"Did you bring food?" it asked.

"Yes." Red threw the tied-up body parts forward. "I brought meat."

"Really?" It sounded like it didn't believe the words it was hearing.

"Yes, it's for you."

As soon as he finished talking, the blob's tongue shot forward. It wrapped around the pieces of flesh and brought them towards its mouth with extreme eagerness. Red wondered how it was going to eat it all, but its mouth suddenly grew much bigger, covering almost the entirety of its body.

It swallowed everything into a dark abyss before the mouth returned to its normal size.

Then it chewed. Sickening crunching sounds of tearing flesh and breaking bones echoed in the chamber. The blob's teeth crushed the corpse with little effort.

To Red's surprise, its size didn't increase despite the creature swallowing so much flesh.

For a second, he was too distracted by the noises to do anything else. Seeing as the blob was paying him no mind, he started his training exercises, though it was a hard task to accomplish with his bad leg. As Viran had explained it, the movements were designed to stimulate the body to an optimal state. Even if Red couldn't execute them perfectly, it was enough to complete the routine, no matter how long it took.

After five minutes of stumbling through his steps, a numbing feeling spread over his spine and upper arms. He fell onto the ground in a sitting position, his body drenched in sweat and trembling from the effort.

He looked at the blob, only to find it still chewing away.

"I need the energy," Red insisted.

The munching got faster. After a while, the being finally opened its mouth. What came out of it, however, was something Red had never seen before. A vast purple mist mixed with traces of red spread over the chamber, its vivid color obscuring his vision.

The Spiritual Energy forced its way into his body before Red even had the chance to absorb it. An aching pain spread through his acupoints as the energy swept across his Spinal Vein and towards his Upper Arm Veins. He felt like he was on the verge of passing out as the force swept through his insides, and he struggled to stay lucid as black spots formed in his vision.

Red did his best to direct the energy towards his unopened acupoints, but he could barely control the brutal wave of power sweeping over him. It sought the path of least resistance and was soon knocking against the edges of his Upper Arm Vein. Following an excruciating burst, his acupoint opened. But the energy wasn't finished, and it continued attacking the vein.

Minutes passed, and soon Red felt another one of his arm's acupoints open.

"ARRGH!"

The pain was even worse this time, but he refused to let himself fall unconscious.

"Can't you handle it?"

The words barely registered in his mind. As the energy battered against his Spiritual Vein, Red felt a small degree of control return over his body. From what he could tell, the ten standard upper arm acupoints had opened. The vein could be considered completed, but he knew there were still two more he needed to open with Viran's special technique.

Red was also aware he would need to direct the process himself for those acupoints. They wouldn't open on their own like the previous ones.

Surprisingly, as he struggled to gain control over the energy inside him, he felt another type of energy flow in from an object within his pouch. He looked down and saw a green mist seeping into his body.

"Hmm? That's interesting," the blob said.

Red didn't understand what was happening. He felt two quick pops in his arm, the pain far milder this time around, and he knew the two special acupoints had been opened. The Spiritual Energy inside his body lessened significantly, but it was still strong enough to ravage his veins.

The concentration of mist in the room diminished, and Red could once again see his surroundings. Having recovered from his initial shock, he directed the remaining energy towards his legs. More accurately, his left leg.

This had been Red's plan from the beginning. He'd hoped to skip his arm completely and concentrate on opening one side of his Upper Leg Vein. Viran had explained to him in the past that doing something like this would be very unwise. Targeting two separate veins, like the legs and the arms at the same time, would create an imbalance within the body, causing the Spiritual Energy to split and dissipate into the two incomplete veins. Opening acupoints in either vein would therefore become twice as hard.

However, Red had not only planned to do that, but he'd also wanted to focus only on one of his legs, specifically the wounded one. Viran hadn't mentioned any adverse effects of focusing on one limb only. Still, Red was sure this probably wasn't a wise course of action in the long-term. His goal for now was simply to strengthen the leg and improve its healing.

It wouldn't make an immediate difference, but perhaps it would be enough to speed up his recovery and allow Red to ignore the injury. He had seen Viran power through some very heavy injuries with his twelve opened veins, so he hoped opening the leg vein would make a difference.

Of course, his entire plan had gone south when the Spiritual Energy had ravaged his insides. He couldn't control the raging force, and it had naturally flowed into his arms.

What remained of the energy, Red intended to use to open his Upper Leg Vein and increase his chances of escaping.

He focused on his left leg and felt the faint existence of a closed pathway connected to his Spinal Vein. With some effort, he used his partial control over the energy to direct it towards that point. The power battered against the vein, and after another minute, Red sensed a pop inside his body.

His left leg spasmed. Red had to bite his lip so as not to pass out from the sheer agony that spread through his thigh. The remaining energy, having found a new channel to flow into, smashed into the vein's next acupoint in his right thigh.

This wasn't Red's plan, though. He forcefully directed the Spiritual Energy towards his left leg and into the next point in that limb. Doing this would be equivalent to opening the third or fourth acupoint in his Upper Leg Vein, which would increase the difficulty substantially. Still, Red was set on seeing the task through.

Minutes passed as he steered the power towards his left thigh. The pain Red felt was debilitating. The rest of his body ached from exhaustion, and at times he considered simply letting go of the energy. However, his desire to survive and escape kept him going through pure will.

Right as the Spiritual Energy was about to run out, he felt another pop. The acupoint opened, but this time he couldn't hold on.

This again, huh?

The last thing Red saw was the blob, seemingly staring at him even without eyes. Then there was only darkness.

CHAPTER 25

OFFER

THIS TIME RED didn't dream. There was only the endless dark of unconsciousness. He didn't know how long he stayed in that state, but soon awareness slowly returned to him.

Red opened his eyes and was greeted by a cave ceiling lit with a soft purple glow. As he moved his body, the excruciating pain he'd been expecting didn't come. Red still felt aches and pains in most of his body, but the agonizing sensation of opening his acupoints had disappeared.

His hand reached down to touch his wounded leg. The cut was still there, his fingers dampening with blood and medicine. However, the pain from the injury had lessened substantially. Red was eager to try moving it again, but then he remembered where he was. Such concerns could be addressed later.

He sat up and looked at the dark blob. The creature's mouth was still present, and he once again felt all its attention directed towards him. Red kept staring at the being for a long time before he finally broke the silence.

"You almost killed me."

"Hardly," the blob said. Although its voice still seemed to belong to a child, its tone was far more serious than usual. "I kept my end of the deal and provided you with more Spiritual Energy than usual in exchange for meat. Any other practitioner would have killed to train under such conditions. It's not my fault your body couldn't take it."

Red didn't believe its words, but he felt suspicious about another matter. Something had changed in the way the being spoke, but he couldn't tell exactly what.

"I'm leaving," he said.

"So it seems." From the tone of the blob's voice, it didn't seem surprised.

Another long silence prevailed over the cave.

"Are you not going to eat me?" Red asked.

"Eat you?" The dark being sounded amused at the question. "You don't seem to understand. Not even the corpses of all the humans in this hole are enough to fill the gaps between my teeth. As for you? The energy I would spend chewing you up wouldn't be worth what I would gain from it."

Red's suspicion grew.

"Then what was the point of all of this?" he asked. "The food, our deal... If it was never any help for your recovery, was it all just a joke?"

"Not at all. It served a purpose, just not the one you might think."

A low, eerie sound echoed through the cave walls as the creature's tentacles slithered around the room. Smaller appendages sprouted from the bigger ones, like the branches of a tree. The expansion continued until every surface in the room was covered by the blob's tentacles, even the exit. The feeble purple light became a dazzling spectacle, and Red had to block his eyes as they struggled to adjust.

The tentacles stopped just short of him, leaving Red isolated on his own island of rock. He was alarmed by the sudden transformation, but he didn't panic or try to escape. After a long day witnessing some truly strong beings and monsters, Red could tell when he was completely outmatched. He could only stand still as the tentacles surrounded him.

"We are very similar and yet very different, human," the blob said. "We both seek our freedom from these shackles the world has put on us... but I have the power to grasp it, while you do not."

"If you were truly capable, you would have escaped this place a long time ago," Red said. "I might not be as powerful as you, but nothing is tying me down here or looking to kill me out there."

"Oh, human, how pitiful..." Its voice filled with sadness. "Your prison is far bigger than just this cave."

Red's eyes narrowed in puzzlement. "What do you mean?"

"This is not something a lowly mortal like you can fathom," the creature said. "Whoever put you down here was intent on doing good for you, but they unknowingly exchanged one evil for another far worse than they could imagine... You're not a prisoner of this cave, you're a prisoner to your own fate, human."

"Speak plainly." Red's face remained impassive, but his concern was growing.

The dark being's words didn't make much sense, but this was the closest he'd ever come to learning about his forgotten past.

"How can one speak plainly about matters the listener cannot understand?" It sounded frustrated. "You are cursed by powers beyond your comprehension, human. Even if you escape these caves, what awaits you on the surface is more suffering and despair. The life you are expecting to find up there does not exist. Nothing you do will change that, not even practicing with Spiritual Energy. This idea, of grasping your own fate with both hands, is merely an illusion. So many times you will think you're close to being free from this curse, only to be proven wrong, again and again..."

The blob sighed.

"The moment you set foot in this place, your destiny ceased to belong to you. It's what happens to every being down here."

Silence returned to the chamber. Red stared at the blob, trying to process what it had said. It was almost too much to take in at once, and he didn't dare accept whatever the thing said at face value, either. Still, the back of his mind kept reminding him of certain memories. The day he awakened in this place. His strange dreams. The conversation he'd had with Viran. Gruff's last words.

No matter how much Red disbelieved it, he couldn't discount the possibility of a curse. He thought back to the technique Viran had taught him. The man had always been much stronger than Red would probably ever be, so what did he need the help of a child for? Just to counter the green Spiritual Energy? That didn't seem likely. Even if Red had many more veins open, he doubted he could take on a monster that had opened its Spiritual Sea.

Viran had told him he would learn the rest by himself once he reached the surface. Was this curse what he was referring to?

As possibilities mounted in Red's mind, he addressed the blob again. "Why are you telling me this?"

"Didn't I say already? I have the power to free you from your shackles, human."

The tentacles around the room slithered with renewed vigor, their purple glow intensifying.

"I can give you the strength to resist your fate. You will dominate this world and fight against gods and devils alike. Nothing will stand in the way of your ascension, not even the strongest curse your enemies can throw at you." As it spoke, the blob's voice had changed from a child's to something dark and dangerous.

"And what do you gain from it?" Red's cautious nature wouldn't let him put his guard down just because of a tempting offer.

"It's simple. After a thousand years, your body and mind will be mine to control, and the being known as Red will be no more. Both of us will get our freedom this way."

Suddenly, the blob's intentions became clear to Red.

"If you want my body, then why didn't you just take it?"

"How do you think I ended up like this, human?" The creature gritted its teeth. "I tried to break the rules of this world once and paid the price for it. Now, tell me your answer."

Red still felt baffled by the blob's explanations, but he understood the essence of it. It couldn't force him to accept the deal. One thousand years of being possibly the most powerful being in this world in exchange for giving his body to this strange alien once his time was over.

It was a very good deal. Red couldn't care less about whatever the blob did with his body after his mind was wiped out from existence. He didn't even know if he was going to survive the next day, so how much better would one thousand years be compared to that? To explore the surface and do as he wanted. To train his Spiritual Energy and fulfill his promises to Viran. To find his purpose in this world.

Still, he didn't find himself nearly as delighted as he'd expected.

Purpose.

Red was reminded of when he started training with Viran. The feeling of grappling with opening his acupoints. The sparring sessions with the old soldier. The life-or-death fights against the bloodthirsty underground monsters. There'd been so many failures, so much struggle. But then there was the sense of accomplishment at every victory or breakthrough, no matter how small. His successes were all earned through his own blood and sweat.

Luck might have played a part in it. However, if he hadn't been as smart or hadn't worked as hard as he had, he would never have made it this far. Being a slave, it was the only life Red knew. The constant struggle for improvement and survival.

While others older and stronger than him died, he was still alive. What he achieved, no matter how insignificant, he'd achieved with his own two hands.

And that was the best feeling he had ever experienced. It was the only thing that gave him any amount of joy in his life.

Freedom.

"I refuse."

There was a prolonged silence after he made his decision.

"Why?" the blob asked, confused.

"I want to do this on my own," Red said. "Getting out of here, fighting against this curse. I want to prove to myself that I don't need any shortcuts to accomplish the things I want." He looked up at the blob. "If it's not through my own efforts, it holds no meaning. Even if I die, that is the kind of life I want to live."

"There are fates worse than death, human."

"You may be right," Red agreed. "But both the failures and successes will all belong to me. That's all I could ever ask for."

The creature was silent for a long time. Suddenly, all the tentacles around the room slithered over each other, slowly headed in his direction.

"Foolish creature, you'd rather have a brief life of suffering than one thousand years living like a god?!"

Its voice was furious, echoing inside Red's mind. His eyes continued to stare directly at the blob's heart.

He was resigned to his fate. In front of such an otherworldly being, no amount of struggle would make any difference.

At the very least, Red had remained true to himself to the very end.

"No," the blob said. Just as abruptly as the tentacles had started to move, they began to retract.

The purple light in the chamber diminished. The many branching appendages retracted into the larger tentacles, and a few moments later the cave looked exactly like it had a few minutes ago.

"I admire you, human." The creature's voice returned to a childlike tone once more. "Foolish as it may be, this is what makes mortals different from us..."

Red didn't stand up immediately. "You're not going to kill me?"

"For what reason?" the blob said. "Our fates were tied together from the moment you were brought here. If you don't die here, one day you will learn that my words were true. That no amount of pride or freedom is worth the suffering this curse will inflict upon you. When that day comes, remember this..."

It smiled.

"The deal still stands."

A flash of purple light erupted inside the chamber. Red was blinded momentarily and had to shield his vision.

When he opened his eyes again, the blob was gone.

CHAPTER 26
INTO THE DEPTHS

RED LOOKED AROUND THE CHAMBER. Not a single trace of the being's existence remained. For a moment, he wondered whether the whole exchange had been nothing more than a dream. However, his opened acupoints were still there, and that was evidence enough.

He examined the room for any other exits but found nothing. Nowhere the blob could have escaped to. Its expansive body and tentacles would never fit through the way Red had entered, either.

He shook his head in resignation. His time would be better spent preparing rather than trying to understand every mystery in this place.

The first thing Red checked was his left leg. His injury was still there, but the pain was nowhere near as debilitating as before. The two opened acupoints had been effective in speeding up the limb's recovery. The muscles in his thigh were reinforced by a substantial increase in strength, and he could walk normally again. Of course, he needed to be careful not to exert the leg too much and risk opening his wound, but at least Red wouldn't have to hobble through the rest of his journey.

Not willing to spend any more time in the chamber, he traveled back the way he came. No longer burdened by Gruff's corpse, the return trip was much shorter.

Some twenty minutes later, Red arrived back in the main cave.

He checked to make sure no insects or resentful slaves were waiting in ambush before leaving the passage. Now that the blob was gone, Red assumed the unnatural pressure that kept most monsters away from this area had also disappeared. If that was the case, he had no way of knowing when the giant insects would start flooding into this part of the cave.

He needed to be quick.

First, his clothes. The smell of dried blood was almost overwhelming—he couldn't walk around like this. His pants could still be spared, since Red could cut away the stained lower legs, but his shirt was a lost cause. It was completely covered in blood, and he could feel the added weight of the cloth dragging him down.

With no hesitation, he pulled the shirt over his head and threw it to the ground. Thankfully, the temperature in the caves wasn't too low, so the slaves didn't have to fear freezing to death due to lack of proper clothing. It was scarce comfort, since you would still rather have even a torn piece of cloth between you and the chilly stone floor while you slept.

Most of Red's clothes were too large for him, as the guards didn't have child-sized clothing to trade, but he made do by cutting and tying whatever he was given into a usable state. He walked over to his travel bag and pulled out another ragged white shirt he'd taken from the slave camp. He then used his knife to adjust it to a wearable size before also cutting his pants above the knees.

The clothes weren't comfortable by any means, but they were preferable to walking around naked. He scrubbed his hands and face clean of blood with the leftover rags.

Then, after double-checking his equipment, Red used the map to determine his general location. The drawing was impressively detailed, which was a surprising fact considering who'd drawn it—Viran had only lived in the caves for a relatively short amount of time. It took only a few moments before he found his current location.

Upon a closer look, something else caught his eye.

Red looked back at the tunnel leading to the blob and compared it to the map. A path corresponding to the same entrance was drawn there, too. However, this path was only half-finished, with a big red skull painted over it. Some words were written right next to the marking, but he couldn't understand them. It still told him one thing.

Viran had found the passage and made sure to mark it as dangerous.

Red wasn't surprised the man had found out about the blob. But it brought up a few questions. The old soldier couldn't fit inside the passage, which was likely why it looked unfinished on the map. However, if Viran couldn't reach the other side, why would he mark the entrance as dangerous? Was it just out of an abundance of caution?

Red shook his head. Perhaps if, or when, he learned how to read, the words next to the symbol would explain the reason. Right now, he had bigger problems to deal with.

The next thing he did was determine his route. Unsurprisingly, there were many tunnels and chambers in between him and his destination—the stream Viran had marked in the depths of the mine. Some of the passages looked bigger than others, but he had a hard time telling if these were to scale.

Immediately, Red excluded any path with a skull over it. This eliminated more than half of the paths he could take. Those remaining were roundabout routes and still passed through some dangerous-looking symbols, but at least they didn't mean certain death.

Of course, Red had to keep in mind that Viran hadn't drawn this map for him. What might have been a manageable situation for the soldier could mean certain death for a child. For instance, if Red encountered another one of the monsters with scythe-like arms, he would most likely be killed. This meant Red would need to avoid as many of those insect nests as possible.

After these considerations, he decided on his path. It would pass through a big centipede nest, if the drawing was anything to go by, but these were the creatures he was most familiar with. His cleaver would have a hard time against the thick body of a horned beetle, for instance, but a centipede was another story. They might be very long, but they were still relatively thin. If he could land a blow, he felt confident he could cut one in two.

But there was still one more concern in Red's mind. Between him and his destination, there was a danger he seemingly couldn't avoid, no matter what path he took. A large skull and a drawing of an eight-legged monster.

Spiders.

The slaves rarely encountered them, and Red himself had only seen two in the years he could remember. As Viran explained to him once, spiders weren't wandering monsters, and they preferred to ambush their prey. However, of all the creatures he had encountered, excluding the insectoid, they were still the most fearsome.

Red remembered how many slaves had died to a single spider that had encroached on their living quarters. The monster had been set on creating a nest. Thankfully, they hunted it down with Viran's help. But that took the effort of the entire camp.

What could he do by himself?

A concern for another time.

If he tried to think through every possibility, he would never begin. He put the map away and re-tied the bag around his shoulder and set off towards the unknown.

The passages beyond his usual territory quickly became harder to traverse. They weren't adapted for human use, so Red faced sheer drops and squeezed through narrow gaps. It made a trip of a few hundred meters take the better part of an hour.

It was a frustrating experience. Still, he didn't have any choice but to forge ahead.

By now, Red was in foreign territory. The number of moonstones on the walls increased substantially the further he descended. Some parts of the cave were well-lit, and he found other kinds of minerals too. He couldn't judge their value, but he hadn't brought the equipment to mine them either way.

Red hadn't seen any signs of monsters, but he doubted it would stay that way. Sure enough, a few hours later, he came across the first few traces. Footprints, pieces of exoskeleton, and even human bones were strewn around the tunnel.

Then came the noises.

It didn't take long for Red to reach trouble. From the chamber ahead came loud hisses and the sounds of legs clattering against the floor. Red slowed his pace and approached the scene slowly, clutching his cleaver.

Soon, he saw the source of the ruckus—a group of centipedes currently engaged in a fight against a large beetle. This one didn't have a horn, instead sporting a giant set of serrated mandibles. The many-legged creatures wrapped around its carapace, but the beetle was far too bulky and strong for them to hold onto for long.

Around them lay the mutilated corpses of two centipedes that hadn't been fast enough to dodge the beetle's jaws. The others kept attacking, their mandibles clamping down on the beetle's carapace. But the beast had a very sturdy exoskeleton, and it seemed capable of shrugging off the attacks.

It had still sustained some wounds, though. Two of its legs were missing, and the monster's mobility suffered for it.

Red did his best to stay hidden while observing the battle from afar.

The beetle reared up for another attack, and one of the centipedes wasn't fast enough to move out of the way.

Its carapace broke as the beetle bit down. The centipede was bisected, its halves twitching in its death throes. But while the beetle was distracted, its two siblings seized on the opportunity.

One of them dashed behind the monster and, with a clasp of its mandibles, severed another of its legs. The beetle stumbled and tried to turn around, but it had grown far too slow and unbalanced. The centipedes could easily avoid its dangerous mandibles with their faster, sinuous movements. Another one of the beetle's limbs snapped off, rendering it nearly immobile. Instead, it shook itself from side to side to throw off its opponents.

The centipedes, however, were no closer to piercing the beast's carapace. Their persistence might have paid off eventually—if Red hadn't decided to intervene.

The monsters were too embroiled in their fight to hear his approach. As another centipede was thrown off, he took his chance to strike. The creature was about to return to the fray when something struck its back.

It shrieked. Looking back, the insect saw Red dash away. A third of its body had been severed by the cleaver, but it didn't die immediately. The centipede snapped around in a frenzy, aiming for Red.

With its movements slowed by the loss of almost half its legs, he easily dodged its lunge. Then, taking advantage of the centipede's overextension, he brought down the cleaver on the monster's head.

With a crunch, the weapon dug deep into its skull. He hit its brain, and the centipede shook with spasms. Not willing to risk injury, Red pulled out his weapon and ran away.

The other centipede noticed the thrashing of its companion. It hissed and jumped off the beetle's back to seek revenge.

However, something stopped it.

With a jolt, it turned to see a pair of mandibles chop off a section of its body. The centipede dashed away with its remaining legs before the beetle could follow up its attack.

It was enough of a distraction for Red, who charged towards the centipede.

With one swift motion, he chopped off its head. The rest of the monster's body fell limply to ground, where it flailed around. He gave it a wide berth, watching the two centipedes slowly die off.

It took half a minute for the creatures to stop moving, but eventually, the room grew calm once more.

Now only one monster remained.

Red looked at the immobile beetle. Both of them stood completely still, and a strange atmosphere enveloped the chamber. Red nodded towards the insect.

"They did quite a number on you." He sheathed his cleaver. "I suppose there's no reason to kill you, though. Whether you live or die now will be entirely up to you."

He turned and wandered to another tunnel. He swore he felt the beetle's gaze on his back as he walked away.

CHAPTER 27

DISCOVERED

Over the next few hours, Red's progress slowed down further. The environment became even more difficult to traverse, and he had to be careful so as not to lose his step. Traces of bigger and scarier creatures began to appear on the tunnel floor, and he did his best to avoid these beasts.

The map also proved to be less useful than Red would have hoped. It was clear after a few hours of travel that the underground was in a state of upheaval. The havoc wreaked by the insectoid had greater ramifications than Viran could have predicted, extending deep into the caves.

The monsters were fighting each other for territory, almost as if in a frenzy. Their bodies littered every corner of the caves now. The sheer noise of their battles, as well as the long distances the echoes traveled, made it easy for Red to avoid them and sneak by. Though it also meant he had to switch routes multiple times.

Eventually, his senses failed him and he caught sight of an enormous monster. It had two giant claws and a tail adorned with a wicked-looking stinger at its tip. Red watched in horror as it feasted on the corpse of its prey. It was even bigger than the scythe-armed monster he had fought before, and he didn't hesitate to turn back immediately.

Unfortunately, Red was running out of viable options, even after making many detours. It was clear that the further down he went, the more common the obstacles became. If he still wanted to avoid the dangerous nesting areas of the monsters, then he would eventually have to take a risk and try to sneak past some insects.

Definitely not that one, though.

Red considered moving forward a bit more, but he'd already been walking for a long time. He was becoming hungry, and his body was taxed from traversing the difficult terrain. Viran had marked what he thought were safe areas in the tunnels, but considering the recent upheavals, he just couldn't trust the symbols anymore.

Red stopped at an intersection and studied the tunnel ahead. The path led down and the ground was steep and difficult to stand on. After a close examination, he found a hole in the soil blocked by a few rocks. When he moved them out of the way, he was surprised to find a small chamber. It was filled with what looked like empty egg sacks, each roughly the size of a human head.

The surface of the broken white shells was shiny, with some mucus still inside of them. Red, however, wasn't too interested in the eggs. Instead, he examined the hidden space. It was the perfect place for him to sleep. There were still insect tracks inside, just like the rest of the caves, but these were faint and told him that monsters didn't travel by here too often. Or at least no big ones did.

It was far from ideal, but it was the safest choice Red could make if he wanted to rest. He examined the eggshells and considered whether he should throw them away. Even with the shells, there was still enough space for him, but he worried their smell could attract predators. Disposing of the eggs wouldn't necessarily help, but it would at least prevent any creatures from being led directly to his hiding place.

He weighed his options before deciding to dump the eggshells some-where. They were surprisingly heavy despite their brittle appearance, so it took a few trips to throw away all seven of them.

While he was making his last trip, he felt a warm sensation at his waist. Red jolted, looking down in alarm.

He expected to see a bleeding wound he hadn't noticed, but he found nothing other than a warm, red glow coming from the pouch tied around his waist.

Red had a realization. He opened the small bag before fishing out the crimson core he'd extracted from the insectoid earlier. Ominously, its glow had intensified.

He recalled Viran's words, warning him about the core.

Should I throw it away?

Almost as soon as the thought came to him, the glow of the core diminished. Red frowned in suspicion, but he stowed away the core for now. He could examine it later in a safe place.

With the eggs disposed of, he entered the hideout and blocked the exit with the stones that had previously concealed it. He sat against the wall and took out a few moonstones to light up the small burrow. Red couldn't stand up, but at least he could stretch his legs while he slept.

It was far more than he could say for most of the resting places he'd sheltered in.

Examining his equipment, he checked the condition of his bag. It wasn't uncommon for it to tear; sharp jagged rocks and poor-quality cloth weren't a good match. Thankfully, Red was being careful during his travel to make sure this didn't happen.

After verifying everything was fine, Red wolfed down a piece of dried insect meat. The texture was tough and leathery, and the taste wasn't much better. Still, it was about as nutritious of a meal as a slave could get down here. After finishing his food, he double-checked his hiding space to make sure there was nothing he had missed.

He took out the crimson core, examining it. There was nothing amiss about it, and the glow from earlier hadn't returned. Red was still somewhat wary, but knowing the value of the item, he wasn't going to just throw it away.

He stowed it back in his pouch, and only then did he lie down to rest. He had no issue using the cold stone floor as a bed, especially given his exhaustion.

Soon enough, darkness overtook his consciousness, and Red fell asleep.

A hissing noise echoed in the cave.

Red snapped awake. He grabbed the cleaver by his side, and his head swiveled to the entrance of his hideout.

The stones were still there, and nothing had entered while he slept. But he didn't relax.

The shrieking sounds of insects reached his ear, and this time they seemed closer than before. He recognized the calls—centipedes, and more than one by the sound of it.

Red still struggled to judge how far they were from inside his nest. Noises in the tunnels could travel for several kilometers, so assessing their distance was always hard.

He approached the entrance of the hideout and put his ear to the stones.

The hissing continued, but other than that, Red didn't hear any other sounds. At the very least, it didn't seem like any centipedes were waiting right outside the entrance. But this was hardly a comfort, since the roars were still approaching his position. He tried to count how many distinct screeches he heard.

At least three... No, four.

It was difficult to count them, but Red was certain of one thing. That was at least three too many for him to take on. He considered running away before they got here, but he didn't feel confident he could outrun them. The centipedes were fast and accustomed to traversing the tunnels, while Red needed to be worried about twisting his ankle and falling down the steep passages.

His safest bet was to remain hidden, as uncomfortable as it was having his back against a wall. Red crawled away from the blocked entrance and gripped his cleaver with both hands, ready for anything.

Soon enough, the furious hissing grew even closer, and he heard the creatures' many legs clattering against the stone from afar.

There were more beasts in this group than he'd previously thought. Alarm grew in Red's mind as he considered what could've made the centipedes this agitated. Was it the shells he threw away? He didn't know what monster eggs looked like, but he felt this burrow was too small for a centipede nest.

Were they hunting? That seemed more likely, but what kind of prey could require such a large group to move together? It was a strange situation, and not one he was eager to uncover.

Soon, Red could feel the vibrations through the earth. They were close, almost on top of him.

He held his breath.

The incessant hissing reached its peak, and the stampede of centipedes ran over his hideout. At one point, the shaking knocked a few rocks from the opening, revealing a glimpse of the monsters.

Red's heartbeat quickened, and he gripped his cleaver even tighter, waiting for the wave to pass. Thankfully, the creatures were in a rush, and they didn't stop to look around as they ran past. Otherwise, considering how many of them he saw, there was no way he would have lived.

Soon, the vibrations and noises diminished. Red let out a sigh of relief. Even finding a safe place to sleep down here was a monumental challenge.

Red prepared to exit his hideout and run as far away from the area as he could. Just the thought of facing that many centipedes at once sent a shiver down his spine. Even Viran might not have escaped with his life.

And yet he considered the centipede's nest the safest to pass through...

Perhaps that was the case when the man had explored the area himself, but things had changed between then and now. Regardless, it was probably time for Red to reevaluate his route. With a sigh, he crawled towards the exit.

However, the entrance suddenly opened, and a shadow flashed in front of his eyes. Red froze.

An insect revealed itself to him. It had two slender antennae, six legs, and a meter-long body that tapered towards the back of its abdomen. In its mandibles, it carried a round white egg identical to the ones Red had found in his hideout. Except this one was not broken.

Both the human and the monster seemed surprised to encounter the other face-to-face. They stared at each other for a few seconds, eye to compound eye. Suddenly, the insect's antennae shook, and Red had an awful premonition.

"KREEEEEE!"

An extremely shrill noise came from the insect. Red's ears rang in pain. Only after a few seconds did he recover his senses, but when he looked back at the entrance of the hideout, the monster was no longer there. He stood up and looked down the tunnels, finding no sign of the insect.

At his feet, he saw the same egg it had carried, only now it had a clear crack where mucus poured out. The whole situation with the centipedes and the eggs became clearer to Red. But when the ringing finally left his ears, he heard something else.

He had no time to process the situation before the hissing sounds returned. They weren't moving away anymore.

They were coming right for him.

CHAPTER 28

COLLISION

RED LOOKED DOWN at the broken egg in front of him. An explanation for the centipedes' frenzied behavior dawned on him. His hideout was compromised, and he needed to leave as quickly as possible.

Red had to abandon caution for speed as he ran up the slope. His left leg still hadn't completely recovered, but with the two acupoints he'd opened, he could push himself farther with every step. However, there was still an imbalance between his two legs. This made his pace feel awkward, but Red didn't have the time to worry about it right now.

As he reached the tunnel's crest, the hissing horde was quickly gaining on him. His plan right now was to get far away from this area and find another hiding spot before the centipedes could catch up. Red needed to keep an eye out for that other insect too, lest his position be revealed once more.

The beast was most likely the culprit of all of this. It had stolen one of the centipedes' eggs and sent the monsters into a frenzy. When Red thought back, he realized the burrow was most likely where it nested. It brought its food there, including the eggs, and lived unnoticed by the larger predators of the caves. That would explain why Red found all those cracked shells.

His conclusion led him to believe that the creature was extremely sneaky. Even now, with the centipedes out in force and intent on hunting it down, the insect had managed to stay unnoticed and returned to its nest. Of course, that was when it found out its home was occupied by a human.

Red wouldn't have reacted well in the monster's place either, but now all its troubles had fallen in his lap.

While the smaller beast was quite adept at sneaking around, Red wasn't nearly as confident in his own abilities. He dashed down the tunnel, hoping to get as far from the nest as possible.

A few moments later, the hissing noises intensified.

They found it.

They had come across the broken egg, evident as their frenzied sounds approached him even faster. They might not even have been hunting for Red specifically, but in their rage, they would kill anything they came across.

Red used his memory of the map to trace a route. Soon enough, he came to an intersection in the passage and promptly took the side tunnel. He didn't know how well the centipedes could track him, but Red would do everything he could to throw them off his trail.

A few moments later he could still hear their approach. He couldn't tell by their sounds if any of them had gone to search the wrong passage. As long as the number of monsters was higher than one, though, the risk of death remained the same.

Red was forced to take a few turns down unfamiliar paths to avoid getting caught. While some of the noise decreased, the centipedes possibly thrown off by his maneuvers, a substantial number remained in pursuit. By now, his breathing was heavy from running, climbing, and crawling through the tunnels.

It wouldn't be long before they caught up.

After turning a corner, he came across a large damp chamber. The floor was wet and rock growths littered the room. Red looked around and saw a large group of stalagmites on one side of the cave. Without hesitation, he dove into their midst and tried to position himself out of the centipedes' view.

It took only a few moments for the tide of monsters to arrive. They spread over the entire chamber like a liquid, their hundreds of legs clicking against the stone floor. Red didn't dare stick his head out to assess their numbers.

Still, he heard something nearing his hiding place. The long silhouette of a centipede suddenly rushed across the ceiling, climbing over stalactites while its antennae waved in the air, searching for the smell of its prey. Red lay on his belly close to the ground and held his breath. What felt like an eternity passed as he watched the beast weave through the spikes of rock.

Thankfully, the monster didn't stay there for long. As quickly as it had arrived, it ran off to join the rest of its siblings, who were already leaving through the next tunnel.

Their frenzy worked once more to Red's advantage. The creatures, it seemed, weren't smart enough to thoroughly search everything in their path, looking only to kill something as quickly as possible in revenge.

Just as Red thought he could relax, he felt something touch his foot.

He froze and his breath caught in his throat. Looking over his shoulder, he saw an antenna brushing against his feet. Promptly, the rest of the centipede's head appeared.

It froze, processing the smell it had just caught. Red watched the monster arch its body back, realization hitting them both at the same time.

His cleaver swung around and cut into its eyes. From his awkward position, Red couldn't deliver a powerful strike. The centipede arched back in pain and retreated outside of his reach. He rushed forward to finish it off, but it was too late.

"HISSSSSS!"

The noise echoed down the tunnels. A chain reaction followed, and the hisses of countless distant centipedes answered.

Red felt his blood run cold, but adrenaline guided his actions. Before the monster in front of him could attack, he had already taken off, weaving through the stalagmites as he ran towards one of the chamber's exits.

However, something lunged at him from above before he could make it out. Red stumbled, ducking just in time as a centipede's mandibles crashed into the stone above his head.

He climbed to his feet and kept running. He could see the vague forms of centipedes rushing in his direction, at least five of them, with more joining the fray.

Death was approaching.

As he made towards the exit, another centipede lunged at him. Red gathered strength in his left leg's acupoints, planted his foot, and pushed off.

The monster bit down empty air, and before it could even react, he was already past it.

The benefits of having opened his Upper Leg Vein were made evident, but Red had no time to gloat. Having outpaced his pursuers, he dove into a different tunnel.

The centipedes kept chasing him, but he'd bought himself some precious seconds. Now he had time to think.

How do I escape this alive?

Red discarded the idea of fighting the centipedes—he simply couldn't kill them all. With that option gone, he was left with only a single course of action, which was to lose the monsters.

It was, of course, more easily said than done.

The boost his left leg afforded him was a provisional solution. It would buy him time, but he doubted the creatures would tire before he did. Not to mention, his leg was still wounded and Red feared it would give out if he pushed it too hard.

Hiding? It was the best solution, but it wasn't simple either. The centipedes could probably identify his smell by now, and it would be hard finding a good hiding spot while on the run. Viran's map had been very detailed, but it couldn't depict every nook and cranny of the massive cave system on a piece of paper. The man had only marked the major tunnels and chambers he could find, as well as some landmarks, to orient himself in the maze of passages.

Landmarks... That chamber!

Red had an idea.

But at that moment, he heard something approaching him from the side. Without hesitation, he rolled forward, avoiding the mandibles of a centipede which had appeared out of nowhere.

He looked back and saw even more creatures pouring out from another passage. The calls of their siblings had attracted the rest directly to him, but their numbers seemed irrelevant at this point.

He gathered strength in his left leg again and shot away. The distance between them increased once more, but he felt something wet rolling down his left thigh. He didn't need to look to know his wound had opened again.

It was a minor risk when his life was on the line.

Ahead, the tunnel split into two paths. There was some hesitation in his eyes, but it lasted for only a second before he rushed into the left passage, the group of centipedes furiously chasing in pursuit.

By now, their shrieks must have alerted the whole monster population nearby, which was exactly what Red wanted.

His limbs tired, the incessant tide of centipedes slowly gaining ground. Right as he questioned whether he'd made a wise choice, he heard something up ahead. It emitted almost no noise compared to the centipedes, but he could sense its heavy steps quickly approaching his position.

An enormous scorpion appeared at the other end of the tunnel, occupying most of the passage. It charged forward with impressive speed.

They were on a collision course.

Instead of slowing down, Red once more gathered strength in his wounded leg. His eyes narrowed, his heart raced and his whole body tensed, ready to explode into motion—his next move would decide between his life and death.

As he entered the monster's range, the scorpion's tail shot towards him like lightning. Red dove forward with all the power in his Upper Leg Vein, ducking under the blow.

He heard a ripping sound.

Something tore as the scorpion's tail scraped against his back. Red didn't know what the creature had hit, but all he could think about at that moment was the fact that he still wasn't dead. His momentum sent him crashing to the ground, sliding beneath the monster's abdomen.

The giant insect seemed confused for a second, but it didn't have the time to search for its missing prey.

The centipedes were still charging forward, undeterred by the sight of the terrible beast in their frenzy. Intent on killing anything they came across, the monsters focused their rage on the huge scorpion blocking their path.

The eight-legged beast didn't seem afraid either. It attacked, having found much more worthwhile prey compared to the small human that had slipped by.

With the opportunity presenting itself, Red got up and ran. He heard the familiar sounds of shattering exoskeletons and splattering blood behind him, but he didn't look back.

He kept running.

He ran to the point of exhaustion. Only a few minutes later, when he couldn't hear the sounds of combat, did Red stop.

He collapsed in a heap against the cave wall, struggling to catch his breath. His bare feet burned and bled from scraping against the rock floor and, checking his left leg, Red also noticed that the cut had opened.

It wasn't as severe as before, but it needed to be addressed; otherwise, he could risk passing out from blood loss in a few hours. Red pulled the bag from his back, but his pack seemed much lighter than before.

A chill ran down his spine as he examined the bag.

A tear had ripped through the cloth.

His food, medicine, bandages—they were all gone.

It was completely empty.

CHAPTER 29
CENTIPEDE NEST

RED LOOKED in the direction he had just come from. Further down the tunnel, he saw a single yellow page filled with Viran's writing, the only thing within his reach to recover.

He walked over and grabbed the paper. The idea of going back to look for his supplies crossed his mind, but he dismissed the thought. There was no way he could fight against the scorpion, or whoever the survivors from that battle turned out to be. Even if he returned, all of his food would have most likely already been eaten.

Red had been careful not to let his bag tear open, but it was to no avail in the end. The only things he had left were his cleaver and the items in his pouch: the map, the insectoid core, and his iron knife. No food to eat for the rest of his journey and no bandages to patch himself up.

There was also no time to complain, though. With his leg bleeding and a group of bloodthirsty monsters nearby, Red needed to escape. After applying some pressure to stop the bleeding, he changed his bandages, using a strip of cloth from the ruined bag as a replacement. It wasn't ideal, but it was the cleanest thing he could find at the moment.

After that, Red took out his map to locate his position. He couldn't determine his precise location, but considering how close he was to the scorpion nest, he could make an educated guess. Right now, he urgently needed to find a place to rest.

Thankfully for him, it seemed the other insects weren't too keen on stepping out of their lairs to face an angry tide of centipedes. After walking for about an hour, Red found a relatively small and reclusive chamber.

As he neared the point of exhaustion, he hid behind some stone pillars and lay down. Before long, his body slackened, and sleep overcame him.

Red woke up alarmed.

He looked around in distress before remembering where he was. The last few hours had been so stressful and charged with adrenaline that his memories of the events were rather fuzzy. He'd been so tired he hadn't even paid attention to his safety in this clearing, sleeping in the open air.

Thankfully, no monsters had attacked him during his sleep, so Red supposed his instincts still worked, or he was just lucky. The difference between the two had become tenuous these past few days.

Now that he was awake, and with no giant insects chasing him, he had time to think.

He had no more food.

Red had gone without eating before, but this wasn't about merely dying of hunger. To survive the caves' monsters and insects, he needed to be in top condition. Without consistent nourishment, his physical abilities would diminish considerably after a day or two. Red wasn't even at the hardest part of his journey, so how could he still have a chance at freedom?

He would need to forage for food.

He considered hunting insects for their meat but quickly dismissed the idea. Even if he were successful, he had no means to make a fire, and uncooked flesh was more likely to get him sick. The only remaining option was to look for edible mosses and mushrooms. However, while there were quite a lot growing in the caves, only a rare few were safe for human consumption.

The majority were toxic, and what remained for the slaves to eat was not nearly enough to sate their hunger. But Red was only a child and didn't need as much to sustain himself. Still, he wasn't sure if he would find sufficient food through foraging.

Whatever came out of this plan, his lack of supplies meant he would need to hasten his escape.

He checked his leg, his hand smearing with coagulated blood. The bleeding had stopped. The rest of his body was still sore, but he was used to the feeling. At the very least, it would work for the foreseeable future.

Red pulled out his map and, now devoid of proper illumination, grabbed the crimson crystal for light. When he grasped the insectoid core, he felt a strange, warm sensation.

He let go of the crystal in shock. Like before, the core emitted a warm glow, which Red was certain hadn't been there moments before. He looked down at his hand, half-expecting to find some kind of wound.

Instead, Red saw his rough but clean skin.

Wait, clean?

He winced. Weren't his hands bloody from tying up his wound earlier?

Red looked down at the crystal core, noticing its glow and warmth were already gone. A possibility came to him, but he hesitated to test it.

A few seconds later, he let out a sigh.

Do I have the luxury of choice here?

The answer was obvious.

He grabbed the core and held it to the blood around his leg, careful not to make direct contact with his wound. Like he'd imagined, the fluid was sucked into the crystal, disappearing without a trace, and in its wake the crimson core glowed with a warm light.

The light, however, was very fleeting, and the core soon returned to normal.

Red wasn't sure what was happening, and he didn't know if he should try to find out. Still, with death so close at the moment, he made use of the core and cleaned his body of the blood splatters that had dirtied him. This way, monsters would have a harder time tracking his scent.

The crystal glowed for a moment before returning to normal. Red frowned in concern. He felt completely bewildered by the item. Viran's warning about the strange things down in the caves once more crossed his mind.

He was unsure if the core was a curse or a blessing. However, on the off chance it could help him, it was worth keeping, even if just to stay alive a moment longer.

Maybe it can help me later...

Red decided to hold on to it for now. He'd spent too long in one place already, and there were more pressing concerns than figuring out the secret behind the crystal.

He opened the map and used the faint light of the insectoid core to read it. The chase from the previous day had taken him off track, and he was now uncomfortably close to the centipedes' main nest. Their large lair was connected to multiple tunnels, and he wanted to take a route which passed through the territory as quickly as possible.

Unfortunately, with his way back blocked by a huge scorpion and his supplies gone, Red couldn't afford to make any more detours in his escape. He would need to take a risk and sneak straight through the monsters' nest. With a sigh, he put the map away and moved forward.

Over the next few hours, traces of the centipedes' presence appeared all around him. Dozens of their footprints and the broken carapaces of their prey littered this part of the caves. Red even saw more of the monsters skittering through the tunnels.

To his luck, they traveled alone or in pairs, and he sneaked past them with relative ease. Red expected to see more of the centipedes as he neared their nest, but that wasn't the case. At some points, he even wondered whether he was going the correct way, but the evidence around the tunnel said otherwise.

Are they outside their base hunting for the egg stealer?

It was possible, but Red didn't lower his guard either way.

After another hour of walking, the passage rose up in front of him, and Red knew he was approaching the nest. He reached the crest of the rise shortly.

The passage led to an overlook that allowed him to observe the large chamber below. What he saw took his breath away.

The clearing was enormous, far larger than Viran's map had indicated. It measured roughly one hundred and fifty meters across, with a ceiling that reached over ten meters in height. Dozens of moonstone veins grew all around the cave, illuminating the room with their green glow. The ground was filled with large holes where the centipedes burrowed to create their nests. Dozens of them slithered around while others rested together in groups, forming horrifying balls of legs and mandibles. But even that wasn't the most surprising thing.

In the center of the chamber, a huge centipede slept. It was much larger than the ones Red had seen, easily surpassing ten meters in length and boasting a width thicker than an adult's torso. Its antennae waved around as even its siblings gave the creature a wide berth. Its eyes, though, presented him with another shock.

They were green, a similar hue to the insectoid eyes Red had seen before. A formless pressure emanated from the monster's body that he could feel even from afar.

Another beast that's opened its Spiritual Sea.

Red wanted to curse Viran, but the man was already dead. Did the old soldier really consider *this* path to be the easiest one to take? What would the others even look like if the centipedes' nest was already this dangerous?

Red felt the situation was curious. Even Viran would have a hard time dealing with this kind of creature, considering his fight against the insectoid. So why wouldn't he mark the area as deadly on the map? Perhaps the creature had appeared after he created his map? Or was it just an elaborate way he'd come up with to get Red killed?

Whatever the case, it proved one thing—the map wasn't perfectly reliable. Things had changed since the insectoid emerged, and Viran's information had more than once proven to be outdated. But there was no way his mentor could have predicted this, and Red was still much better off with the help of the map.

Yet he still faced a hard decision.

The tunnel leading to his destination lay on the other side of the chamber. However, a colossal beast, as well as an army of its smaller but still dangerous siblings, stood between him and his target.

Sneaking through a nest full of centipedes was already a difficult task, and now one of them had even opened its Spiritual Sea. Who knew how improved its senses were? Red doubted he could outrun it, considering the speed of its lesser counterparts.

On the other hand, if he avoided the chamber, he would need to backtrack and choose a completely different path. Not to mention, he still needed to go through some other monster nests, which likely had creatures just as strong as this one. With no supplies to make such a roundabout trip, Red would struggle to even reach another nest.

His first option was the best and only one he had—sneak through the enemy's base and make it out unnoticed. More easily said than done, but Red was set on his decision.

Still, he had no intention of rushing. He hid behind some rocks near the tunnel's entrance and observed the behavior of the centipedes and their leader. He hoped the monster would leave the chamber or enter one of the burrows.

Over the next few hours, Red observed them in silence. Centipedes left and entered the room, some even bringing new prey. None used his tunnel, luckily, so he remained unnoticed the whole time.

Unfortunately, the giant creature had barely moved at all. If it hadn't been for its antennae waving every so often, Red would have thought the centipede was dead.

Just as he considered making a dangerous move, he noticed something shifting through the outer area of the chamber. Red looked over, but the only things he saw were rocks strewn across the stone floor. Just as he was wondering whether he'd been hallucinating, he perceived movement again.

It came from a long rock.

He blinked, doubting his own eyes, but a few seconds later, the object walked forward again. It slowly approached the centipedes' burrows. When Red examined it further, he noticed small legs jutting out from under the rock and recognized the shape of the well camouflaged insect.

The egg-stealer. It had come back for more.

CHAPTER 30

DISTRACTION

THE INSECT SNEAKED UNNOTICED towards the centipedes' burrow. At many points, the other monsters walked right by, even waving their antennae over it. Yet at no point did they suspect that the gray-colored beast was anything other than a simple rock.

Red was surprised. He knew most of the monsters in the caves had poor eyesight and relied on their other senses to hunt. Some of them didn't even have eyes.

The fact they couldn't distinguish the little creature from a normal rock was not surprising—even Red had to pay very close attention to notice it. But for the beast's scent to go completely unnoticed was even more shocking.

It proved an invaluable opportunity for Red.

He moved without hesitation.

Red stuck to the edge of the chamber, keeping his eyes trained on the monster. He dropped from the ledge, his bare feet making no sound against the coarse rock floor, and ducked unnoticed from cover to cover. Red got within thirty meters of the little creature but had to stop moving, as he risked discovery if he came any closer.

The egg-stealer still crawled slowly towards the entrance of a burrow. At some point, centipedes even slithered over its body, but it remained undetected. After five minutes of slow but constant progress, it reached one of the holes, diving inside in search of its prey.

This gave Red the time to develop a plan. He didn't know how often the creature came into the nest to search for food, so he couldn't afford to wait for the next opportunity to make his move.

His plan was rather simple. Get the insect noticed and, once the centipedes went on high alert chasing after it, run through the chamber towards his destination. A few things needed to go well for his idea to work, though.

First, he had to remain undetected. There was no point to any of this if the centipedes started chasing after him.

Second, he needed the bigger monster out of the way too. If only a few of the beasts noticed him, Red would still have a chance to escape or kill them in the tunnels. But if their leader went after him, then he would most likely die.

There was no way for him to guarantee either of those conditions, but he reminded himself of Viran's advice. The most important part of any plan was being able to adapt. Red couldn't account for any unforeseen occurrences, but he could do his best to be ready for them.

In preparation, he gathered up a pile of rocks. After getting sufficient ammunition, he started tossing them next to the centipedes to see what kinds of reactions he could garner. The monsters were quick to react, turning towards the sudden sounds and menacingly waving their antennae, ready to strike. However, as soon as they found no strange smells and no movement, they would return to their tasks.

Red tried throwing the stones farther away from the creatures, but even if they turned towards the sound, they wouldn't go out of their way to investigate it.

This made sense to him. The nest was busy, so the centipedes didn't bother looking into every noise that happened around them. It would be hard to draw their attention.

Red came to this conclusion after three minutes of testing. He looked at the hole the egg thief had disappeared into, but he saw no signs of it. The underground burrows were probably even more crowded with centipedes, so it made sense that the creature would take longer to sneak around.

Red's only worry was that the monster would choose a different burrow to leave from. If that happened, perhaps he wouldn't have enough time to enact his plan.

Then Red came up with a different idea. He tore off a piece of the slightly bloody bandage tied around his leg and wrapped it around a rock. Aiming carefully, he hurled it at a wandering centipede.

The stone landed right by its side, and the monster turned around in surprise. This time, its antennae seemed to pick up a strange smell. It touched the cloth tied to the rock, probing it curiously, and waved its antennae as it searched for movement. There was nothing there, but that didn't discourage the centipede. It became alert, and it searched its general surroundings.

Its behavior even affected some of its siblings, who joined in hunting the possible intruder. At one point, Red wondered whether he'd made a mistake, as one centipede neared his hiding place, but he let out a sigh of relief as it passed by without noticing him. After searching their nest with no success, the centipedes gave up and returned to their normal routine.

It seems to work.

Red was glad to see the results of his experiment. Over the next few minutes, a few other centipedes also examined the unfamiliar smell that had appeared near the small rock, but they too gave up after some time. Red found the tactic wasn't enough to put the nest on high alert, but it would make the centipedes nearby more attentive to potential intruders. It would be a vital part of his plan.

He tied pieces of his bloody bandage to a few additional rocks and prepared for the right moment when the egg thief would appear again.

Some time passed, though, and he saw nothing.

Did I miss it?

It was possible. Maybe the insect had chosen another burrow to leave through, in which case Red would most likely not have noticed it. Still, he decided not to give up yet.

He waited... and waited.

Just as he feared he'd missed his chance, something moved. At the entrance of the burrow, the same strange rock-like creature appeared. It seemed even slower this time around. Only when the rest of its body crested the edge of the hole did Red understand why.

Somehow its midsection had swollen to almost twice its normal size. The insect's diminutive legs were spread apart even further as it dragged itself along much more carefully than it had on its way in.

Did it... swallow the eggs?

Red couldn't claim to know much about animal physiology, but he thought this kind of behavior was absurd. The goal of the thief was to get in and get out without being noticed. If it carried the egg in its mouth, the centipedes would likely see that something was wrong with the inconspicuous rock. In a way, the behavior made sense.

But how could it also eat the shell? From what Red had seen in its lair, it didn't consume that part. Did it simply use its stomach to store the egg and then barf it all out for later consumption? How could it fit something that big through its small mouth?

This is... fascinating.

And sure enough, its strategy seemed to be paying off. Despite its larger size, the insect walked unnoticed past the centipedes. To them, it was only a slightly larger rock to walk over.

After being engrossed for the better part of a minute watching the creature, Red's sense returned to him. As interesting as observing the monster was, it wasn't as important as escaping the caves. He grabbed one of his bloodied rocks and threw it right next to a centipede.

The creature's reaction was much the same as what he'd seen in his earlier tests. It immediately became alert when it detected the sudden sound and unfamiliar smell, beginning to search its surroundings. But Red didn't stop there.

He grabbed the rest of his rocks and threw them at every centipede surrounding the egg thief. Soon enough, all the nearby beasts were communicating with each other and scouring the area in search of the origin of the smell. The frenzy even spread to other parts of the nest, and more centipedes joined them.

Red was impressed that his small action could cause such a commotion. He moved back so as not to be discovered and continued to observe the camouflaged insect from farther away.

Much to his dismay, the creature remained in the same place, staying completely still. Many centipedes even crawled over it repeatedly, but none gave the rock a second glance. Red questioned how the beast had been chased through the tunnels earlier if it was this hard to detect. However, at that very moment, he spotted movement near the center of the chamber.

The giant centipede stirred from its rest, roused by the sudden alarm in the cave. For the first time since Red had entered the chamber, the monster moved. It didn't seem to be in a hurry, but its enormous body allowed it to cover a substantial distance in just a few seconds.

As its oppressive aura drew closer, Red felt cold sweat run down his back, much like when he first saw the insectoid. The lesser centipedes scrambled to move out of the way of their leader. One of them wasn't fast enough, and the monster walked over it, casually crushing its body and carapace under the weight of its legs.

Red's breathing became heavier as the creature strode forward. The enormous centipede stopped as it neared the area of the commotion, and its antennae quivered, detecting the unfamiliar smell. Just as Red wondered whether his plan would backfire, the monster suddenly froze and shifted its head to stare in another direction.

The same place where the egg thief was hiding.

A low, grave hiss came from the creature's mouth, the vibrations making Red's body shake. All the other centipedes froze, and as soon as that happened, the camouflaged insect seemed to notice something was wrong.

Before anyone could react, it shot forward at an incredible speed. The giant centipede howled and rushed after in pursuit, while all its lesser siblings joined in its roar and followed behind it. Red feared he would go deaf and had to block his eardrums while the nest erupted into a frenzy.

He sneaked farther away, staying hidden for a while longer as dozens of centipedes scurried towards the tunnel the thief had escaped down. Only once the hissing grew faint did Red come out of hiding.

The nest, which had been so full of life, was now only occupied by a few centipedes, stragglers that remained behind to care for the eggs.

The way forward was finally open.

CHAPTER 31

REPRIEVE

RED MADE his way around the edge of the chamber towards his goal. Although the diversion had worked better than he'd expected, there were still centipedes roaming around the burrows. Even so, none of them wandered far from their nests.

Soon, Red arrived in a part of the chamber without much cover. From here to the entrance of the tunnel, he still had to traverse almost half of the chamber's length, with no other means to aid his stealthy passage. The remaining centipedes would most likely notice him, but he'd already created as good of an opportunity as he could hope for. He wouldn't let it slip by.

Still in a crouched position, Red walked into plain sight. He moved forward step by step, making minimal noise and trying to steer clear of the centipedes. He was halfway to his target before a centipede wandered past, its antennae weaving through the air in front of it.

It froze, detecting a foreign scent.

Before it could even screech, Red shot ahead. More and more centipedes noticed the intruder running through the middle of their nest, and hisses of alarm echoed in the wide chamber. Dozens of monsters surfaced from their burrows, giving chase.

Red didn't look back.

After pushing himself further, he arrived at the tunnel, prepared to lose the insects in the passages. The screeching of centipedes accompanied him for half a minute before growing distant.

A moment passed, and Red couldn't hear them anymore. Only then did he slow down and look back.

Red was surprised. He'd expected the centipedes to pursue him for much longer. He waited, half-expecting to hear their approaching shrieks, but a minute went by and he heard nothing.

They're guarding the nest.

It was the only reasonable explanation Red could come up with. Since they stayed behind while dozens of their siblings joined the hunt, their role must have been an important one, such as guarding the eggs and infants. If that was the case, they wouldn't run after a human who didn't appear to pose an immediate threat.

I guess I'm lucky.

Red didn't intend to wait around, though. He traveled down the tunnel, putting as much distance between the centipede lair and himself as possible.

Only an hour later did he decide to stop and rest. He sat down against a wall, allowing his muscles to relax. Physically, he hadn't been taxed too much this time around, but he felt mentally exhausted.

His constant brushes with death and need to maintain extreme awareness of his surroundings was taking a lot out of Red. At least back in the upper caves, he'd had his hideouts and didn't have to worry about giant insects lurking behind every corner. He'd been familiar with that place and could run away if he encountered danger.

But here? Not only was this completely unfamiliar territory, but it was also inhabited by creatures that Red couldn't outrun if he was noticed. The extreme pressure, the awareness that any mistake could be his last, drained him.

In fact, even just sitting down to rest was a big risk. Yet it was necessary if he wanted to succeed in the long run.

Red took out his map to check his progress. Now that he'd made it past the centipedes, he wouldn't need to worry about any other large monster nests before he arrived in spider territory. Of course, Red had learned not to fully trust the map. It showed no large, insect-infested chambers for the next leg of his journey, so he hoped whatever threats awaited him could be avoided.

Maybe I should be worried about something other than the monsters, though...
He needed nutrition.

Red wondered how Viran would have dealt with the situation. As he recalled, the man could easily go days without food or water, most likely because he'd opened his Stomach Vein. Red couldn't help but think how convenient it would be to have something like that right now.

With a sigh, he stood up. He needed to find food before anything else, or he wouldn't even have to worry about the spiders.

Another day went by in the underground world.

Red didn't have much success in his foraging. This part of the tunnel network was desolate, and he found little in the way of edible mosses or mushrooms. Almost no water flowed down from the surface either, so his thirst became another concern.

Due to the barren domain, Red also hadn't met any monsters during the past day of travel, which was scant comfort.

Physical effort became more taxing, and he had to take additional breaks to conserve energy. The map also became less specific the farther down he went, as Viran hadn't explored the areas closer to the underground river in full.

Red often found passages that weren't marked on the map, forcing him to backtrack to find the proper landmarks and ensure he was on the right path. His progress slowed, and Red wasn't sure how long it would take to pass through this section of his journey. Not to mention, there was nothing good waiting for him on the other side.

After all, the most dangerous part of the journey still awaited him further ahead.

It wasn't until another day passed that Red witnessed a change in the environment. Monster tracks became more frequent, and he started coming across beasts again.

The tunnels became wider, with the occasional large chamber, too. More moonstones and strange ores appeared, encrusted within the stone. Red swore that if he'd had access to this much material to exchange with the guards, he would never go hungry again.

Down here, the insect variety changed. He saw many kinds of odd beasts wandering the chambers and tunnels, and it seemed the ones that inhabited this area were smaller and far less aggressive than the ones in the upper caves.

Red saw monsters similar to the egg-stealer, all of which fled upon noticing his presence. Another had a long, thin body and hid against the cave walls, causing him to almost stumble over it, but the monster didn't seem interested in or bothered by his presence. One creature he found even resembled the centipedes, except it had even more legs and moved far more slowly.

The sudden change in behavior of the beasts gave Red some space to relax, but it raised other concerns in his mind. This was an undisturbed habitat of prey for the monsters above to hunt, so why didn't he see any of them in the area? Nothing on Viran's map told him to expect this either, and he wondered whether it was another recent change to the underground.

Red considered killing a few of the creatures for food, but he thought better of it. Despite behaving peacefully, some of them still looked extremely tough, and he didn't fancy his chances against them in his current condition.

Instead, another plan came to mind. Since the monsters weren't acting like predators, it was likely they fed on something other than meat to stay alive down here.

Red reckoned following them to their feeding grounds was a safer move.

Sure enough, after another hour of travel, he came upon a large chamber. The place was partially illuminated, like most parts of the caverns, with glowing moonstone veins inlaid along the rock. The ceiling was full of deep holes, and in the center of the room was a pond bigger than any body of water Red had seen before. In the walls of the cave, green-looking tufts grew in large quantities. They almost went unnoticed by Red in the dim light, but a group of feeding insects brought his attention to them.

Moss. And water, too.

Red wondered whether he was hallucinating. He blinked, but the scenario remained, in all its natural beauty. The inhabitants of the area didn't fight over the food either, and none seemed to acknowledge the human's arrival. The environment came as a shock to him, but Red's cautious nature didn't allow him to lower his guard.

He watched the chamber carefully, almost expecting some horrible predator to be waiting in ambush. Even after five minutes of observation, Red still couldn't notice anything out of the ordinary. Only then did he set foot in the chamber.

The first thing he did was approach the pond in the center of the room. The water was clear and Red could see the bottom of the pool. To his relief, no monsters were waiting within it. He scooped up some of the liquid with his hand and brought it to his nose, but he couldn't smell anything off about it.

Red still hesitated, but he knew that this was probably the only source of water he would find for a good while. He first tasted some of the liquid by licking his finger, but with no adverse effects in the subsequent minutes, he drank the water with big scoops.

Only after his thirst was quenched did he turn his attention toward the moss. Some insects latched onto the wall were devouring the green tufts, but there seemed to be plenty to go around. This time, Red was a bit more cautious.

All living creatures drank water. That was something he knew. As for the food they could eat, it differed greatly from being to being. The giant monsters Red had encountered could eat raw meat, for instance, but if he tried to do the same, he would likely get sick. He didn't know enough about the moss or these creatures to determine if the same logic applied in this scenario. He had no choice but to test it.

Red plucked a tiny tuft off the green growth and brought it up to his nose. There was no abnormal smell. Finally, using the same approach as with the water, he ingested a small piece of the moss. There was no taste to speak of, and the texture was soft and slimy—not comfortable to chew in the slightest.

After a few minutes of anticipation, Red was relieved to see his body had no adverse reactions to the food. No longer hesitating, he tore large tufts of moss from the wall and ate greedily. He didn't know how nutritious this stuff was, but it was better than walking around on an empty stomach.

Just as Red finished eating, he noticed some strange movement nearby. A round insect, about a meter long, was struggling with all its might. It was stuck in place, right by a patch of moss in the ceiling on the other side of the chamber. Red was confused for a moment before he noticed something else.

More movement, this time from the holes above the pond. And not just one creature.

Red blinked. Long, hairy legs crawled slowly out from the crevices.

His blood ran cold.

Three large spiders revealed themselves, fangs glistening in the low light.

CHAPTER 32

SPIDER TERRITORY

THE EIGHT-LEGGED monsters studied the room. From limb to limb, they were over five meters long. One of them approached the smaller insect stuck in its near-invisible web, ending its life with the bone-crunching bite of its fangs. The sudden attack startled the other creatures in the chamber, and they ran for their lives.

The two other spiders immediately burst into action, moving with tremendous speed for monsters of their size. Before Red could process the situation, they pounced on their prey, a beetle and another creature resembling a centipede.

There was no fight to speak of. The prey were much slower than the spiders, and their carapaces gave almost no resistance. Sharp fangs pierced deep into their exoskeletons, green blood oozing from the punctures. Their struggle lasted for ten seconds before they went still.

Red crouched down in alarm. He crept around a corner of the chamber, hoping to remain unnoticed. He considered running away while the monsters were occupied with their victims, but he chose to hide instead.

His decision was validated in the next moment, as it seemed the spiders weren't done hunting.

Their fangs retracted from their dead prey, still clutching it with their pedipalps, and they chased after the remaining insects. Their explosive speed was jarring to witness. Red had never seen anything move so quickly, and the sight was unnatural and terrifying. If he'd been the target of their attacks, there would have been no way for him to avoid capture.

Nothing escaped their grasp. Soon the three spiders had each chased down and seized another insect with their fangs, but even then, the monsters weren't sated. One of them looked over in Red's direction. Its eight emotionless eyes stared directly at him, and Red swore he could see his own reflection in them.

He froze.

At that moment, a bigger insect ran past him, and the spider's attention was diverted. It retracted its legs and leaped across the chamber to land atop the creature, biting down with unerring accuracy.

Red watched on with his breath caught in his throat. He gripped his cleaver tighter and slowly stepped away from the monster. The beast, however, turned in his direction when the prey in its grip finally died.

Red's chest tightened. His muscles screamed as he prepared to run.

But it didn't move toward him. Instead, the monster turned around and climbed the wall, back towards its nest, holding three different insect corpses by its pedipalps. It seemed like it couldn't carry anything else.

Red looked around the chamber and saw the other two spiders also returning, each carrying its own collection of prey back to their resting hole in the ceiling. The remaining insects had dispersed from the pond into the connecting tunnels in a panic. Red stood motionless, watching the large bodies of the arachnids squeeze into the crevices in the rock, disappearing inside the darkness as quickly as they had emerged.

Red fell to the ground and let out the breath he had been holding for far too long. His cleaver fell from his grip as he tried to recompose himself.

He had faced death before, but never had it come so close as right now.

These spiders didn't rely on direct confrontation to kill their opponents like the other monsters he'd met in the underground. Instead, they lay in wait for the best opportunity to strike, ending the battle in a single blow with their extreme speed—before their prey even understood what had happened.

What scared Red most wasn't their strength. Rather, it was that despite examining the entire chamber, he hadn't noticed any signs of the creatures. Even now, he couldn't spot the spiders' web from his position.

Cold sweat ran down his back. Red understood why Viran had said this was the most dangerous territory of the caves, as no amount of conventional combat experience could have prepared him to deal with the spiders. He couldn't dodge their explosive attacks, and now he knew he couldn't detect them reliably, either.

Red was beyond ill-equipped. Still, he got up and grabbed his weapon. He shuffled towards the other side of the pond, his eyes alternating between the crevices above him and the path ahead in search of webs.

Red found he could only spot the threads once within arm's reach, and he was surprised to find them thicker than he expected.

There was something special about these webs, but he didn't dare touch them to investigate. As sneakily as he could, Red made his way past the spiders' lair and out of the chamber.

Red had a lot to consider, and he stopped to think as soon as he found a relatively safe area in the tunnels.

He had witnessed the fearsome nature of the spiders. Even one of them would prove a deadly enemy, and there was a nest full of them up ahead, not to mention the ones on this path. How many awaited him? Probably fewer than the centipedes, but even just one was enough to kill him. Not to mention, Red also had to consider the possibility of a spider that had opened its Spiritual Sea in their midst.

He immediately discarded the idea of direct confrontation, but that was probably not even a valid scenario. The spiders were ambushers, not active hunters. With their invisible webs, they could catch anything unawares, including Red by the looks of it, and the possibility of sneaking by them seemed even more hopeless when he considered that fact.

He sighed.

No, there has to be a way.

After some consideration, he came to a few conclusions. Since these spiders were ambushers, they probably only inhabited places where they could hide. Those three from before, for instance, had all made their lair in a chamber with holes they could use for cover against prey. This meant Red was unlikely to find any wandering around narrow tunnels or blocking passages.

However, thinking further on it, he still wasn't confident about his assumption. What if there were more than one type of spider in the territory? Not to mention, hadn't they also found their way up to the slaves' living area? The spiders might not be as stationary as Red wished. But even if that was the case, he could hopefully see or hear a creature of such a large size approaching and avoid it. The threat of ambushes remained the fundamental problem.

He looked at the map again. There were many chambers between him and the river, including the vast room where the main nest was located. He needed a way to avoid the webs, but the only way he could figure that out was through experimentation.

He steeled his nerves and took a deep breath.

Red walked ahead on the path of no return.

It didn't take long for him to come upon another large chamber.

He examined it from afar. The space was seemingly empty, the green glow illuminating the rock floor and showing no signs of movement. From this distance, though, Red couldn't see many of the details of the room.

Cautiously, he approached the cave chamber, and more revealed itself to him. It was smaller compared to the room with the pond, but it was still bigger than most of the caves closer to the surface. Stalactites and stalagmites covered most of the area, but in the middle of the stone spikes on the ceiling, Red could see a dark crevice.

It seemed too small to fit a creature the size of a giant spider, but Red stopped either way. He looked for signs of an invisible web, but even after a few minutes, he didn't discover anything nearby.

Next Red examined the ground for tracks. Most were similar to those of the herbivore insects he'd seen this deep in the caves, but he couldn't discern anything else from the marks.

Despite all his findings, he still refused to move forward. Only an abundance of caution would give him a chance to make it through with his life.

After some more thought, Red had an idea. He grabbed a small rock and threw it at the area around the dark pit.

The stone drew an arc in the air and hit the opposite wall of the chamber. Red waited for a reaction, but nothing happened. Still not satisfied, he picked up another rock and repeated the same process, this time aiming at a different area.

Still, no sound or movement came from the hole in the ceiling. Instead of being relieved, though, he became more nervous. It didn't make him think the chamber was safe to cross, but that he might've missed the webs and was about to walk right into a spider's trap. Viran would've probably called him paranoid, but Red could never have enough caution when it came to his own life.

For the following minute, Red continued throwing rocks into the chamber, but he hit nothing. Just as he was about to give up, however, he noticed something.

A small pebble suddenly changed its trajectory midair, as if it had hit something. The shift in direction was slight and easy to miss if one wasn't paying attention, but this was exactly the sign Red had been looking for. To confirm his suspicions, he continued throwing stones in that specific area, hoping to witness the same thing.

After a few more tries, one rock seemed to crash straight into an invisible obstacle in the air and bounced back to the ground. Red saw a faint, blurry line vibrating from the rebound force.

Then he heard it.

A scratching noise inside the hole in the ceiling. A furry leg came into view, and soon the dark head of a spider emerged through the opening. Red didn't stay to see the rest.

He turned back and ran. Only when he couldn't see the green light from the chamber did he dare to stop and rest.

Between heavy breaths, Red sat down once more, slumped against the wall. It was a scene that had become commonplace these last few days.

That's one way blocked...

CHAPTER 33

SCOUTING

RED WASN'T surprised when he found more paths infested with spiders. Wherever there was a hole big enough for the monsters to hide, there would be at least one of them, no exception. In fact, it wasn't uncommon for Red to find two or three sharing the same crevice.

When these spiders made their way up to the surface caves, they were always alone. Down here, they lived together with no apparent conflict. Red used the same strategy with the rocks and learned some curious information about how the creatures worked.

The first was how they detected prey. Their webs were very sticky, and whenever the spiders identified something disturbing their lines, they would come out of hiding to investigate. This wasn't the limit of their senses, though. The monsters still had keen eyesight, hearing, and smell to capture fleeing prey, as they had done back in the chamber with the pond. Even if Red avoided their traps, he could still attract their attention if he wasn't careful.

They also seemed to share their "web-senses." That is to say, if Red hit a single thread with a rock, then all the spiders in the vicinity would be alerted, no matter how far away. He supposed that all their webs must be interconnected, so there was no way of alerting one spider without alerting the rest.

The third thing Red tested was the thread density of their webs. As far as he could tell, they were evenly interspersed through the chambers the spiders inhabited. The monsters had spread them across key points where their prey was likely to walk through, such as tunnel entrances, while other areas were free of webs. He couldn't tell exactly how densely the threads were packed without close observation, but he was confident in his conclusion after extensive testing at a distance.

Red could theoretically sneak by the spiders without touching their webs, but he wasn't confident. If he was noticed midway through a monsters' nest, for instance, then how would he run away with invisible threads surrounding him? It was a journey with no return, and one he wouldn't choose until he'd exhausted all his options.

However, it didn't seem like he would have a choice.

After the better part of a day spent scouting the area, Red found that every path he could take was at some point blocked by spiders.

I have to sneak through.

After coming to his conclusion, Red found a place to sleep first so he could face the task ahead in prime condition. Or at least the best condition he could manage in this hellish place.

The time spent lying down had relieved Red of some tension and allowed him to think with a clearer mind.

While he needed to sneak past the spiders no matter which passage he took, he would choose the safest path possible.

The potential passages weren't straight paths leading towards the river. Many of them were interconnected according to the map, and some led to unmarked locations. The worst thing he could do was take a roundabout route that went through multiple ambush points on the way to his destination. However, some chambers only had a single spider, while others had three or more.

It was a matter of weighing risk and benefit.

In the end, after considering all his options, Red settled on a path.

He retraced his steps to the first chamber he'd tested with rocks. There was a single spider here, and he could use the rock formations to hide. While the chambers it led to were more dangerous, altogether it was one of the most straightforward routes.

Red had accomplished the easiest part, the planning, but now came the execution.

Careful not to make any noise, he crouched down and approached the chamber. He more or less remembered where the thread he'd found before was located, so he tried to avoid that area. Soon, he was inside the lair, farther in than he'd dared to go before.

Red looked around but saw no signs of the spider or any of its webbing. If he hadn't seen the creature wander out of its hole, he might've assumed the chamber was safe to walk through. He knew better, though.

He studied the rift in the ceiling, making sure nothing was coming out, and only after a few minutes had passed did Red feel composed enough to take his first steps forward.

One... two... three... four...

He stopped and looked around again. He stuck close to the walls, keeping the stalagmites between himself and the spider lair, and decided he wouldn't walk more than a few steps at a time before checking for any webs in his path.

Sure enough, right in front of him, he saw a shimmer. He squinted, and the image of a long line became clear, horizontally connecting a stalagmite to a wall. It stood right in his way, at the level of his abdomen—too high to step over.

Red took a quick breath, crouched down and moved forward. At a snail's pace, he moved closer to the thread. As he looked past it, he could see even more transparent lines waiting for him up ahead, but for the moment, he wasn't at risk of touching any.

Red moved underneath the thread, passing by without much trouble, but still paranoid that any sudden movement would disturb it. He looked around to assess his surroundings, and only then did he sit up again.

No movement.

Along the edge of the room, the number of webs increased significantly. He could probably still sneak through them, but it was better to look for another way.

He found a far less cluttered path along the rock spikes. The spider hadn't bothered setting up any webs amid the stalagmites, since the space between them was too small for its usual prey to pass through. Red, however, could squeeze by with some difficulty. He wasn't about to let this opportunity go to waste and crept towards the exit of the chamber via his new path.

Soon, his cover grew thinner, and he had to try his luck against the threads that waited for him ahead. Red maintained careful control over his entire body to not make sudden noises or bump into the threads. Fortunately, his effort was paying off.

It took nearly ten minutes of careful weaving between rock cover and open space for him to approach the tunnel opening. But much to his dismay, what he saw there crushed his hopes.

The entire passage was covered with crisscross threads blocking his way forward. They were not dense enough to see from the entrance of the chamber, but as he came closer, their existence became all too evident.

Red gritted his teeth. There was no way he could sneak through without disturbing any of them.

Perhaps this was yet another lesson he needed to keep in mind. Always expect the worst.

Red shook his head. He couldn't allow his spirit to be crushed, not now. He had come too far for that. Conviction came to him as a plan formed in his mind.

He picked up a pebble. He scanned the chamber, searching for a place he recalled was dense with webbing. After examining his target for a few seconds, Red threw the rock, hoping to hit the invisible line.

The projectile hit the opposite wall of the room. A miss.

Not discouraged, he picked up another stone and adjusted his aim. The rock sailed through the air until it collided with an unseen obstacle. The flickering and blurred image of a thread appeared, shaking from the rebound and alerting the owner of the nest.

Red took cover, knowing what came next.

Large hairy legs surged over the edge of the hole, and soon the entire body of the spider appeared. The creature examined the room with its eight eyes before directing its attention to the still-quivering thread. It shuffled forward, feelers and front legs examining the web in search of prey. It found nothing.

But Red wasn't about to let it lose interest.

He peered around his cover, doing his best to not be noticed. Then he picked up another stone and eyed the opposite side of the chamber. This time, he gathered all his strength in his Upper Arm Vein and, with a heave, hurled the pebble towards the tunnel he had just come from.

The stone clattered against the hard surface, splintering into shards. This time, the noise wasn't subtle.

The spider immediately moved with that same suddenness and speed that had terrified Red, charging towards the sound. Nothing was there to greet it, though. It stood in place, searching the area, at least one leg always connected to the invisible thread in the air. It looked curious, perhaps wondering where its prey was hiding.

It was then that Red moved.

He drew his cleaver and charged towards the blocked exit, swinging the blade against the webs in his way. They offered little resistance against the edge of his weapon, and the passage opened to Red, who didn't hesitate to run through it.

A second later, he heard something heavy moving through the air.

Red immediately threw himself forward in desperation, falling onto his hands and knees.

Something brushed against his leg. He scrambled away and looked back.

The spider had crossed the entire chamber in a split second and almost reached Red in a single jump. Its feelers stretched through the opening in the web, trying to grab him. Something seemed to have stopped its momentum, though, and it took him a second to notice what it was.

Ironically, the same net of webbing it had raised to stop prey from escaping now held it in place. But the taut threads wouldn't keep it tied for long, as more and more lines snapped under the monster's strength.

Red didn't stay to watch. He pushed himself up and ran away.

More tearing noises and the sound of shuffling feet came from behind him. He redoubled his efforts to gain some distance from the beast, but he knew it was in vain. He needed to hide.

As Red turned around a bend, he heard the spider approaching him from behind. Frantically, he examined his immediate surroundings for cover or anything else useful.

The monster got even closer, the distance between them diminishing in a matter of seconds. Red was fully expecting the creature to jump at his back, but then he found what he was looking for. Protruding rocks, forming a small alcove where Red could crawl inside. It was fairly shallow, though, and he wasn't sure it would keep the spider from reaching him.

Abruptly, the footsteps ceased, and then came the sound of stirring wind as something heavy sped through the air.

Red threw himself towards the cover, slamming against the rocky wall.

Behind him, another thud came as the spider's body landed not an instant later. Red felt something rubbing against his back and pulling him by his shirt with tremendous force. He crawled away and tore the shirt from his body. Thankfully, the poor-quality fabric helped him, and Red found himself free of the clothing as he dashed into the corner of the alcove.

He turned around and saw the spider's feelers grabbing his shirt as the creature's menacing fangs dug into it. It thought for a second it had caught its prey. Red saw his opportunity and swung down on one of the monster's appendages with the cleaver.

The beast reared back from the pain as its pedipalp was bisected. It hissed before angrily reaching for its prey again. Red met it with another slash, which damaged its other pedipalp and forced the spider back once more. He could hear its shuffling legs as he cowered in the corner of the small alcove.

Soon, no other sounds came from outside.

A minute went by in complete silence. Then five minutes.

And then half an hour had gone by, in which Red neither saw nor heard anything from the spider. He still didn't dare to leave his cover.

Finally, when almost an hour had passed, he heard the heavy shuffling of the spider's eight legs. It seemed to be leaving the chamber.

Red didn't come out.

Not until another hour went by.

CHAPTER 34

BAIT

RED PEEKED out of his hiding spot to confirm the spider was gone. It took a lot for him to convince himself to leave the alcove, though, and he had to force his body to move. And move he did.

He ran, and only after he was far away from his previous location did he decide to stop and collect himself.

With a thud, he sat down on the cold rock floor.

I'm alive.

There was no sense of victory in his mind, only dread. It consumed him, growing from the pit in his stomach after he'd come so close to death once more. He knew that if there hadn't been a hole to hide in or if he'd been one step slower, that would have been his end. Perhaps he should have been celebrating, but the longer he was forced to rely on luck, the more powerless he felt.

How did Viran do it?

Red now had firsthand experience with trying to dodge the spiders. His conclusion was simple—he couldn't do it. If the webs hadn't stopped the spider's charge for a few seconds, he would have died. And yet, not only had Viran made it to this point, he'd even gotten past their nest and found the river.

Perhaps the man was outstanding at stealth, or maybe he could just kill everything that tried to stop him. It didn't matter. It was all far beyond Red's capabilities. Not to mention that there was no guarantee of success, that following the map would lead to escaping the mines. Viran hadn't been sure the river went to the surface, and what if even worse things than these spiders awaited him?

Red had shown determination in front of Viran and the strange blob, saying that he would persevere no matter what, even if death was his ultimate end. However, only this far into the journey did he understand the weight of his words.

I wonder how I sounded to them...

In retrospect, it was laughable for someone as weak and insignificant as him to be making such grand claims. Still, could he turn back now? Or better yet, would he turn back if he were given the opportunity? He had asked himself that question many times during his journey, yet never as seriously as he did now.

No matter what happened, when Red searched deep within himself, the answer remained the same.

I have to keep going.

He stood and continued moving towards the spiders' nest.

The tunnels following the chamber split even more frequently, and Red once more scouted the way ahead. He found multiple caves and passageways with the same holes in the ceiling, but this time around, he didn't waste his time checking if spiders lived inside. At no point had he come across a room with a lair that wasn't occupied, so he spared himself the effort of blindly throwing rocks to verify their existence.

As he walked through the tunnels, though, he noticed something that caught his attention.

Something reflected the green light from the moonstones, covering a stone pillar further ahead. It was camouflaged very well, but he had learned how to spot things hidden in plain sight over the last few days. It was something big.

Or so he thought. The mass shimmered when it heard his approach, and Red had the opportunity to study what he was seeing more clearly.

It was an insect.

No, that's not right.

It was more than one insect. There were many of them.

It took a second for him to identify what exactly the creatures were. A group of meter-long round insects, like the ones he'd found in the pond room, had gathered by the dozens around a large stone pillar. Their black, glossy carapaces blended with their surroundings, and they barely moved.

One could mistake them for dead.

Red frowned, raising his guard. Although he'd met these creatures before and they hadn't attacked him, there hadn't been so many of them gathered in one place.

He wouldn't push his luck. Using his most reliable method, he picked up a small rock and threw it towards the pile of beasts.

It struck one of the insects head-on.

The monster shrieked in panic, and like wildfire, alarm spread to the rest of the group. With surprising speed, the creatures dispersed every which way through the tunnel, some even heading in Red's direction.

He had little time to react before a few reached him. He stepped out of the way, but the monsters weren't interested in his presence. In fact, they actively avoided him. They ran towards the other side of the tunnel, seemingly into the rock surface and out of his sight.

He noticed the rest of the insects had vanished too, leaving the passage empty. Perplexed, Red walked towards a spot where he'd seen some of the monsters disappear.

He was surprised to find a small hole hidden in the rock surface. It was just big enough for the creatures with their flat bodies to fit into, and when he tried examining the inside with a moonstone, he saw that the passage curved out of sight.

Red then searched the rest of the tunnel. Sure enough, he found similar holes all around the area. The stone pillar the monsters had been attached to was full of a green-colored moss. The monsters had been feeding before being interrupted by Red's presence.

He grimaced, reflecting on his discovery.

After passing the chamber where he'd met the spiders the first time, Red hadn't found any other type of creature. This made him question how the arachnids kept themselves fed. Now, it seemed, an answer had been presented to him.

Over the next hour, Red explored the rest of the connecting tunnels. He found more of the round insects, as well as their burrows, but nowhere near as many as there'd been on the stone pillar. They were skittish and ran away as soon as Red got too close. At the very least, he didn't need to worry about being attacked by them.

However, their presence made him consider several possibilities. He still needed to cross more spider chambers, and he didn't feel like he would be as lucky the next time around.

Maybe I could use them...

Red wasn't sure if his line of thinking would pay off, but it was something worth exploring.

He tested some ideas. First, he sneaked around several of the creatures' nests and waited for them to emerge again. It took a few mind-numbing hours, but one monster eventually wandered out of its burrow and examined the surrounding area. After a few minutes, it returned to its lair once more.

Soon enough, more emerged. Not only from that hole, but from the surrounding ones, too. After half an hour, they gathered around the pillar again, recreating the same scene as before.

Red guessed that the first insect to come out was some kind of scout checking to see if the threat had disappeared. After finding no predators, the monster must have returned to the nest to tell the rest of its siblings, who came out to feed on the moss again.

What confused him was the fact that the creatures reemerged from all the holes in the vicinity—not just from the one the scout had come from. Did this mean the nests were interconnected beneath the rock surface?

He counted the number of insects as they appeared—thirty-two of them exactly. Then he once more startled the group into escaping, and they again disappeared into their burrows. When they were all finally gone, Red began to work.

He plugged the holes shut with rocks of all sizes and checked them multiple times to make sure the insects couldn't push them open, leaving only a few of them unblocked. After that, Red once again hid further away and waited.

Another hour of silent waiting passed, but he didn't mind the monotony. One insect came out at that point and the same scene repeated. It returned to its nest, and shortly after, the entire group emerged in full, feasting upon the moss again.

At one point, he saw some rocks shaking in the holes he had blocked, but the movement soon stopped. As the monsters came out, Red counted them slowly in his mind until the final one left its burrow.

Thirty-two insects in total.

Red was pleased. He didn't need the number to be exact, but for what he had planned, the more insects, the better.

It was time to put his plan into motion.

Red waited behind a rock cover. He had blocked all holes but one and scouted the tunnel thoroughly, making sure there was nowhere the insects could go but forward. It was tiring work, but nothing compared to what he'd gone through over the last few days.

Finally, the creatures poured out of the last remaining hole, the one furthest from the stone pillar. Red counted their number and noticed there were slightly less this time around. It would have to be enough.

After they gathered in their bunches and started to feed again, Red crept towards the last open entrance to their burrow and plugged it with more stones, completely blocking any passage in or out.

His task accomplished, he moved back, getting ready to put the next part of his plan into motion.

Red still wasn't sure how well this would turn out. Realistically, the insects could probably just run around him in the other direction, but he hoped to project a menacing image to prevent this.

After preparing, Red came out of hiding and screamed at the top of his lungs.

"AAAAAAAAAAAH!"

He flailed his cleaver wildly in the air while trying to spread his limbs and make his figure as big as possible. Or at least as big as a ten-year-old kid could be.

The effect was immediate. The insects scrambled and tried to run back into their holes. Unfortunately for them, there was no getting inside their burrows anymore.

They panicked, checking every entrance to no avail. At that point, Red charged.

"AAAAAH!"

He didn't stop screaming, swinging his weapon at the closest creature in range. He hit it, cleaving into its carapace as the insect shrieked in pain. All its siblings reeled and ran for their lives.

They all moved exactly where Red wanted them to go.

Towards a chamber full of spiders.

CHAPTER 35
APPROACHING DOOM

RED RAN close behind the insects. For creatures with such small legs, they were shockingly fast, and he had to push himself to keep up.

As they sprinted through the tunnel's twists and turns, some of the insects tried to get around him and return the way they'd come. He couldn't stop all of them, but most of the creatures were frightened enough by his display of intimidation to continue running down the path he had prepared.

After a long chase, he could see his destination ahead. An irregular chamber, decorated with large moonstone veins encrusted along its walls. It was mostly empty, except for a few stone pillars and three large cracks in the ceiling. Even with all the noise he was making, the spiders still weren't coming out of their hiding spots. That was all about to change.

The insects didn't seem to understand what awaited them ahead. Many of the beasts even sped up as they saw some semblance of cover to hide from the mad human chasing them. Soon enough, the first creature made its way into the chamber. It ran for a few meters before it suddenly clashed with an invisible obstacle.

It bounced back while the web attached itself to its carapace. The creature struggled to free itself, to no avail. Its siblings, who were not even a second behind, didn't have the time to process what had happened. They swarmed the chamber.

Red stopped running as he observed the results from afar. Most of the creatures got tangled in the threads near the entrance of the room, but some made it further in before suffering a similar fate. A few still ran along the sides of the chamber, lucky enough not to get caught in the trap.

The amount of vibration coming from the webs alerted the spiders. Neither slow nor deliberate gestures were seen once they emerged from their holes. First, they turned their heads towards the corner of the room, seeing the large number of prey that had fallen for their ambush.

They almost seemed confused, but that didn't last long before instinct took over. Each one pounced on the closest insect, their fangs sinking in and putting an abrupt stop to the prey's struggle. Even then, there were still many more of the small beasts caught in the chamber. The spiders held the dead prey between their pedipalps before charging at their next targets.

They repeated this process a few times, but it seemed the arachnids had far too much food to eat all at once. Their fangs had already claimed most of the smaller monsters, and they were struggling to add any more to the bundles held together by their pedipalps. The number of creatures still struggling against their webs was quite substantial, and the spiders seemed uncertain about how they should deal with the unusual situation.

They had likely never experienced such a windfall.

This was what Red had been waiting for. While the spiders wandered the chamber, he made his way through, but this time he was in a hurry. He did his best to avoid the threads, but as soon as he saw an obstacle that seemed difficult to pass, Red didn't hesitate to slice through the web with his cleaver.

The spiders felt a few of their taut webs split apart and were quick to spot the human figure, but Red didn't bother trying to be stealthy. With urgency, he cut apart any string that appeared in front of him, making his way to the chamber's exit.

The monsters weren't happy with his actions and approached him. They didn't seem to be rushing, but Red didn't dare spend a moment more than was necessary in the chamber.

As he arrived at the exit, he found another similar blockade of threads. Without hesitation, he swung his cleaver against the webs and cut them apart like they were nothing. He jumped through the opening, and a second later felt something push against his back.

Red fell hard, but he was quick to get back up and continue running. He heard nothing chasing behind him, though, and looking back, he noticed a spider staring at his distant figure. As it had more food than it knew what to do with, the monster didn't seem concerned about pursuing its prey. The spider turned back and continued to deal with the situation inside the chamber.

Red kept running down the tunnel for a few more minutes while the spiders feasted on the meal he had so graciously delivered to their doorstep. After covering enough ground, he sat down against the stone wall to rest in a scene he was quickly becoming familiar with. However, his mood this time around was quite different.

Red was pleased.

Perhaps for the first time in this stretch of the journey, Red felt his imagination had played a pivotal goal in crossing an obstacle. He didn't get complacent, but it was a good boost to his suffering confidence. Maybe in the end, he didn't need to be as strong as Viran to make his way out of this place.

Red took a moment to assess his situation. His left leg still was in the process of recovering, but he hadn't been involved in any long chases over the last few days, so at least his situation hadn't worsened. Hunger had become less of a problem. The moss wasn't a very nutritious meal, but it did enough to keep his stomach filled, and he'd even stored a few tufts in his pouch.

As for his thirst, Red was parched, but not to a debilitating degree. He could still hold on for a while more, and if he could cross the spider territory, then it wouldn't take long for him to reach the river. If he failed instead, then there was no point in worrying about water.

More immediate matters required his attention, though. Red didn't know for how long he'd been awake, but his mind and body felt worn down. Sleep would soon overtake him, and he was better off finding a safe spot before it did.

He wandered off further into the tunnel in search of a small hole in the rock that he could call home for the next few hours.

This is it, then?

Red checked his surroundings. According to the map, there were no more ambushes to worry about, and he had verified as much over the past few hours.

There was only one thing left. This tunnel was a straight and long path leading up to the last obstacle between Red and the river—the spiders' main nest.

If the scale of the drawing was even vaguely accurate, then this chamber was even larger than the centipedes' den. Merely thinking about the size of the room gave Red a preemptive headache. This lair connected to several other parts of the caves, and all routes to the tributary passed through it. Viran had checked this thoroughly, since many other areas on the map were left empty, the end of each path marked with a large red X.

As he walked, Red also looked for creatures similar to the ones he'd used earlier as bait. There were many of them, and scores of other insects he was unfamiliar with, but he didn't know if his strategy would work again. The tunnel had become far wider, and the beasts had too many burrows that were completely out of his reach to block. Not to mention, if the chamber up ahead was as big as it seemed, then who knew how many insects Red would need to agitate to pass unnoticed?

Either way, their presence was still worth noting.

After walking for another hour, he noticed the green glow intensify around him. The passage widened, and the number of moonstone veins laced within the stone increased. Finally, he came around a bend where the tunnel opened up and led into another chamber.

Red paused.

A feeling of imminent dread came over him. It wasn't the threat of being ambushed. No, his instincts told him that he shouldn't go forward, that whatever he was about to see was an existential danger.

He hesitated.

Red trusted his instincts. They were what had kept him alive all these years, and they never lied to him. At the same time, what he wanted and what they told him to do weren't always the same. If Red had listened to them every time, then he would have run from the insectoid and left Viran to die alone. He wouldn't have risked his life against terrifying monsters while searching for a way to escape. He would have taken the blob's deal instead of choosing the harder way out.

His instincts kept him safe, but it wasn't safety that Red was seeking. He steeled himself and turned the corner.

A cave chamber larger than he could ever imagine revealed itself before his eyes. Moonstones encrusted almost every surface of the room. The ghastly green veins joined together, forming an extensive network of interconnected radiance that spread like roots all over the chamber. Their joint brilliance was stronger than any single seam in the underground, and they bathed the vast space with a magical and overwhelming light. Enormous rock pillars were spread along the cave's boundaries, as if holding up the ceiling. Smaller stone spikes and growths spread around them, forming what looked like a forest around the room.

For a second, Red thought he'd arrived on the surface. However, as he looked up towards the ceiling, the illusion was shattered.

Pits of all sizes and shapes littered the cave roof. More than a hundred of them. Too many to count.

But that wasn't all.

Spiders silently hung on the threads around these holes, looking at everything and nothing at the same time. They didn't bother hiding. And in their midst, there was something bigger.

Another spider, twice the size of the normal ones and with glowing green eyes, motionlessly hung from the ceiling. But there wasn't just one of them.

When Red was done counting, he found four of the massive spiders. There might have been even more hiding in the large pits, judging from what looked like the reflections of their bright eyes.

The concentration of the previously invisible threads was so high that they became clear to Red. The webs stretched from the ceiling down to the ground below, reaching every corner of the room and forming an impenetrable prison.

Red couldn't help but laugh at himself.

There had never been any hope in the first place.

CHAPTER 36

IMPASSABLE

RED SILENTLY WATCHED the spider colony. On the rare occasion the spiders moved, it was just one diving in or out of their holes. They remained still, doing nothing as their soulless eyes stared blankly into space.

No, that's not it...

They were waiting for something, and Red had a good guess as to what it was.

A few minutes later, he saw a flurry of movement in one area of the colony, and several spiders crawled down their webs. Activity spread across the nest as others went over to check. Five spiders had descended—a mere fraction of their numbers, but still a terrifying scene for whoever had to face the monsters.

Red's gaze followed their moving figures as they reached the ground and disappeared amidst the rocks and webs. He could not see what was happening, but soon, the spiders made their way back up. One of them carried a large round insect clasped between its mandibles. It resembled the beasts he'd herded through the tunnels, but he couldn't confirm it from his vantage point.

The spider disappeared into one of the holes in the ceiling, and peace once more returned to the arachnids. The process happened several times while Red studied them, but in different sections of the chamber. Something would alert the creatures in an area, and a handful of them would climb down to check things out, always bringing back some kind of smaller prey in their fangs.

Red sat down and took it all in. None of the bigger spiders moved much, and whenever they did, it always sent some kind of alarm to the rest of their colony. The lesser members moved out of their way as fast as they could to accommodate whatever space the enormous beings required.

What now?

Red waited and waited, as if something would eventually change the scene before him. Something that would give him a glimpse of hope or opportunity. But nothing happened.

What am I doing?

He did not know. Throughout his journey, his difficulties had gotten consistently worse. Yet through luck and ingenuity, he'd persevered and always found out how to live through them. But this? This was beyond his abilities. It wasn't fair. Then again, it was never meant to be.

Red wondered how many people had reached this point in their escape, only to have their hopes ultimately dashed. Viran couldn't have been the only one with opened Spiritual Veins to end up down here. Maybe this was why none of the slaves had ever heard of anyone escaping the caves.

There was nothing that made him special compared to the old soldier, or those who came before him and failed all the same. In fact, Red started to further doubt Viran's map. Red had seen the man fight against a creature that had opened its Spiritual Sea and, although he'd won, he'd paid an enormous price. Even though Viran was far stronger than him, he had a hard time believing the man had gotten past this chamber alive and verified the existence of a river on the other side.

Besides, why hadn't he just kept going after locating the tributary? What was it that had stopped him? Red couldn't think of any reasonable explanation beyond Viran's enigmatic words about needing help to escape. Perhaps the story about a route to the surface was all just a lie to give him some hope.

That doesn't sound like him at all...

Viran had always been blunt and honest with his words. He'd never hesitated to crush Red's hopes before, so why would he lie to him just before his death? They had both acknowledged that the task would be impossibly hard, so he just couldn't see the need for Viran to deceive him.

Red snapped out of his daze.

There's no point in sulking. Maybe there's something I missed.

If Viran had made it past this chamber, then it was not by brute force, so Red decided to look for clues.

The chamber wasn't completely covered in webs. There was a relatively large perimeter right outside his entrance that the spiders hadn't occupied, and Red examined this area first. The first thing he discovered was more tunnels leading into the room. Like the map showed, the path he'd traveled wasn't the only one leading to the monster lair.

Not useful information.

After that, Red looked for footprints. He found a few of them, but they were mostly near the entrances of the nearby tunnels. None of them led through the forest of webs, and Red wasn't particularly surprised. Insects and beasts possessed an excellent sense of smell, and while they might miss one or two spiders lying in ambush, there was no way they wouldn't notice a chamber full of monsters.

However, this raised another question. How did the spiders keep themselves fed? From his last hour of observation, Red had seen them hunt for prey located inside the room, but if the prey hadn't come from outside the chamber, then did that mean they were living in here?

It seemed impossible with all the webs blocking their way, but Red remembered the round creatures he'd found before. They were one meter long and had flat bodies, occupying little space compared to most other giant monsters, so it wasn't an outlandish idea that they could have a nest in this chamber. The skittish insects lived in large groups, and even in a small tunnel, Red had found over thirty. What about in a chamber of this size? How many could fit in here? Hundreds, maybe more than a thousand? It would be enough to keep the spiders fed, considering he'd learned from Viran they could go a long time without food.

Red thought about employing the same distraction tactic again, but it didn't seem possible in this scenario. First, he would need to navigate through the webs without getting noticed to locate a large enough group of insects. If he could sneak by the obstacles unnoticed, what would he need the bait for, anyway? Second, he would need to make enough noise to alarm the creatures, and that was as likely to have him discovered by the spiders as simply bumping into their webs. There were many other problems with the idea, but those two alone made it impossible.

It was a dead end, so Red explored further into the chamber, walking along the cave's wall. He found similar holes to the ones he'd seen in the past, with signs of insect tracks around them. However, the burrows were far too small for even a child to fit through, so they weren't of much use to him.

With his options exhausted in this corner of the cave, Red had no choice but to investigate the area near the web forest. He sneaked closer to the threads, keeping an eye on the spiders in the ceiling. Although they were relatively far away from him, he didn't dare let his guard down.

After he arrived at the edge of the glimmering forest, Red circled the perimeter and examined the blockade. Unsurprisingly, there were no blind spots he could see even this close. The creatures had done a good job of covering everything, and the netting only got sparser towards the ceiling where they lived. Although the spiders didn't seem to get stuck in their own threads, Red imagined it could still prove annoying to move around with the threads blocking their large bodies. Unfortunately, he didn't have any way of flying or climbing the walls, or else the task would have been much easier. He also searched for some kind of hole that Viran might've dug near the barrier, but he found nothing of the sort.

Another thing of note was the coloration of the webs. When by itself, each thread looked almost invisible. However, with so many bunched together and the bright illumination of the moonstone veins, their appearance became clearer to Red from far away, and he knew it was possible for him to cross through some of them. There might've even been enough space to move ahead, but not in a straight path. In fact, there was no path at all. He couldn't even see the other side of the chamber.

The sheer amount of webbing made scouting a route a difficult task. The threads crisscrossed in irregular ways, and he would need to weave through them on the fly, sometimes crawling, sometimes jumping. And that was only for what he could see. It would require extreme care and precision, things he wasn't confident he possessed—all of this, just to avoid bumping into anything. But even then, how would he know what awaited him? What if there was another section that had been webbed shut, like the ones he'd found before? It was an extremely risky plan.

Unfortunately for him, he found nothing else. He checked the chamber again, hoping to stumble upon something he'd missed on his first pass.

Nothing.

He tried again, this time spending almost an hour in search of a hidden passage or anything else that would help him reach the other side.

Still nothing.

Red thought about trying again, but he knew he was wasting his time. Slumping down against a rock wall, he reflected on everything he'd seen up to this point.

What am I missing?

Was he not perceptive enough to spot some trick or secret tunnel Viran had used? Was it possible he really sneaked his way through the web forest unnoticed?

This is ridiculous... How can I even pretend to know what he could or couldn't do?

Red remembered how the man hadn't been detected by the insectoid until the moment he attacked. Who knew what other tricks and abilities the soldier had up his sleeve? Red understood little about him, and it was presumptuous on his part to guess.

But coming to this conclusion didn't bring him any comfort. It only meant that the toughest option was the only option.

Red closed his eyes and took a deep breath. There was no going back. The only way was forward.

If that's the case, what's the point of hesitating?

He was tired and spent, both physically and mentally, but he felt as if he had done his best. He'd gotten this far already. Who would have even believed a malnourished child slave could do it? Not even Red had been confident in his chances when his journey started. Yet here he was. Above all, Red had proven himself wrong, and if this was the way it had to end, then he wouldn't feel sad.

Viran was at peace with his own death... If there's anything I can hope to match him in, it's my attitude.

He opened his eyes and got up, ready to face his own destiny.

CHAPTER 37
VALLEY OF DEATH

RED FELT COMPELLED to leave a carved message on the stone wall for whoever passed through this place in the future. It would serve as some kind of legacy to show how far he'd gone, as little as it would matter in the end. He couldn't read nor write, but he could still copy whatever scribbles Viran had written on the yellowed paper he still had.

He took out the old and dirty page and considered which of the weird symbols would be the best to leave behind. Since he couldn't tell what any of them meant, he chose the one that seemed the most interesting. A bunch of lines at different angles connected to form a sleek figure that Red thought was pleasing to look at. He could only hope it wasn't some kind of insult.

He etched the lines into the cave wall near the tunnel entrance with his cleaver. The weapon wasn't meant for this kind of task, but he completed the drawing with some effort.

Red stepped back and admired his work.

It looked horrible, but it was indeed a very faithful copy.

I wonder if anyone will ever see this...

Red doubted any humans would ever pass through this place again, but that wasn't the point. Viran had wanted to leave some kind of legacy after his death, so Red thought it was only natural for him to do the same. This was his limit, but maybe hundreds of years in the future, when someone stumbled upon this chamber, they would know a slave had braved all kinds of dangers to reach the surface. Maybe they would admire his tenacity then.

Actually, Red wasn't sure this drawing would still be here after one hundred years, but he'd wasted enough time with pointless thoughts. None of the spiders seemed to have noticed his presence, but he didn't want to push his luck. He walked towards the webs, holding his cleaver in one hand. He didn't know if he would have the time or space to draw the weapon from his back, so it was best to hold it ready at all times, for all the good that it would do him.

Red assessed the outer edge of the blockade of threads and decided to start his trip from a path near the wall. His primary aim was to reach the large rock pillars where several stone spikes grew from the ground. He knew from experience that the spiders couldn't navigate the tight spaces between the stalagmites, nor spin their webs through them, so he hoped that by reaching the rock formations he could avoid most of the threads. It was a dubious plan, since Red couldn't see the way ahead through all the webbing, but it was the only idea he could come up with.

When he got within arm's reach of the webs, Red stopped. He tried to calm his nerves and control his body. There was no room for mistakes anymore. If he wanted to succeed, he needed to be perfect.

Finally, after a few minutes had passed, he took the plunge.

The initial obstacles were rather dispersed, as the concentration of threads waned towards the edge of the chamber. He could even stand up beneath the lines and walk normally if he wanted to, but he kept his body as low as possible. Even if there was enough space to move freely, this would rapidly change up ahead, and he saw no reason to risk it.

As Red took his first steps, he felt a formless pressure in the atmosphere weighing down on him. For a moment, he panicked and thought that he'd been found out, but after a few seconds, no spiders approached him. Soon, he noticed the strange pressure was coming from the webs around him. Some kind of force flowed through them that he hadn't felt from afar.

He guessed it was Spiritual Energy. This kind of power hadn't been present in the webs he'd examined in the earlier chambers, so it might be the handiwork of the bigger spiders. However, he didn't have the faintest idea of what his discovery could imply. Maybe the threads were better at detecting intruders such that the prey didn't even need to touch one to alert the spiders? That would be a horrible development, but Red hadn't been swarmed by monsters, so he thought it unlikely.

Either way, it didn't change his plans.

He walked at a snail's pace, and soon the space around him grew tighter. No longer could he stand up without bumping into a thread.

Red stopped and searched for what path to take. Only then did the severity of his situation make itself apparent.

Sure, Red could have rationalized and planned all he wanted when looking in from outside, but when the time for action came, it was an entirely different matter. Threads surrounded him, blocking his vision in all directions, and if he extended his arms, he could easily touch one. There was less than a meter separating him and certain death. No path to retreat to or hole to hide in.

The webs were so close that Red was afraid of even breathing too hard in case the air disturbed them.

Why did I stop to think?

He had failed to consider the human factor in his task. Red wasn't emotionless, as much as he might act the part. He was still afraid of dying, and that fear would inhibit his actions. The longer he spent considering his next move, the worse his nerves became, so Red let his instincts take over.

Potential routes and paths appeared in his vision, and he didn't let hesitation hinder his steps. He crawled below a thread that almost brushed against his back. Then, when the path was too narrow to squirm under, he tiptoed over the web. At some points, when the obstacles were bunched up too close together, he had no choice but to backtrack the way he had just come.

Almost in a trance, Red repeated the same process over the next half an hour. He didn't stop to think about how close he was to bumping against the threads at every moment. As soon as he walked over one web, his thoughts turned to how to proceed past the next. His body and mind functioned in unison to keep him going.

It was the only way he had found not to let panic take over, and it was working.

His progress was extremely slow, and although he couldn't place his exact position in the chamber, he knew he wasn't even halfway through the room. But Red still hadn't been noticed by the spiders, and that was all that mattered.

After what felt like an eternity, he neared the center of the room, where the stone pillars rose through the forest of threads. However, the webs became more cluttered the closer he got. Red backtracked and approached the area from different angles, but no matter how much he circled it, there was no clear path forward. The spiders had done their best to block off this section of the chamber, and although there were gaps in the webs, they were too small. Even if he could've passed through them, it would have been almost impossible to not bump into any other threads.

Red's already slow progress ground to a halt. The pressure he'd ignored until now started to weigh on him like an unstoppable tide, and with it came the awareness of his condition.

Pain and dread returned.

His body was covered in a cold sweat, as if he'd just gone through a dozen battles against the insectoid. His muscles burned, tense and cramped from navigating the grueling obstacle course. A throbbing headache spread through his skull. All the exhaustion and aches he'd put his body through over the last few days finally caught up to him, and they arrived with interest.

Every time he blinked, Red felt as if his consciousness would slip away into darkness. He was tired—too tired to keep going. Even the veins he'd opened made no difference. This was his limit.

Not now...

Red resisted while his body threatened to shut down. His efforts were barely enough to keep him from collapsing, and he didn't know what would happen if he tried to move forward.

Suddenly, he heard hissing from above. A jolt of adrenaline surged up his spine. Red looked up.

The monsters were moving. Not towards him, but to something else nearby. For all his efforts not to touch their webs, he'd forgotten that the spiders could still notice him if they climbed down to collect their prey. The forms of the arachnids became increasingly visible among the webs. He couldn't see how many there were, but they quickly approached.

Red shivered.

He looked ahead, only to find the same wall of webs blocking his way forward. His eyes wandered towards the biggest gap he could find, which was barely half a meter wide and too high for him to climb. If he wanted to reach it, he needed to jump.

No, there's not enough space to run.

Leaping over it required him to gather momentum, but Red was still surrounded by threads. There was simply no way he could reach it from his position.

He tried to think of another way. Seconds passed, and the spiders grew closer.

I need to hide.

But there was no cover. Red could only crawl under a few threads, hoping they would block the spiders' vision.

The monsters reached the ground, unimpeded by the webs. Some of them landed no farther than five meters from him.

Red felt his throat tighten up, his heart ready to burst from his chest.

He heard the familiar sound of fangs digging into insect flesh. A short and loud shriek accompanied it.

Then there was silence.

The spider who'd dealt the killing blow started to climb back up. The others examined the area for other prey. One of them wandered closer to Red.

He tightened his grip around the cleaver.

The monster's feelers waved in the air as it roamed. Suddenly, the creature stopped. Its appendages moved over a certain thread. It felt something. The spider slowly turned around, its pitch-black eyes eventually landing on Red's small figure.

His heart sank.

The spider walked over slowly, one of its legs reaching out to seize the human. Red didn't freeze. His cleaver swung up, cutting off the monster's limb.

The spider hissed in pain, and the sound echoed through the entire cave.

He felt hundreds of eyes turn in his direction.

CHAPTER 38

LAST STAND

IT'S OVER.

That was Red's first thought as the entire spider colony was alerted to his presence. However, his body had already reacted before his brain could fully process the information. His cover was blown, so there was no longer need for subtlety.

With a jolt, he cut the threads in front of him and ran, the sound of the spider's crawling limbs already approaching him from behind. His legs struggled to keep up, and he knew that even in peak conditions he couldn't outrun the spiders.

Red rushed towards the webs blocking his way to the stone pillar. It was the only chance he had of losing the monsters, and so he slashed the barrier with his cleaver. His strength was lacking, though, and the threads were woven tightly around the area. One blow of the blade was not enough to open a wide enough path for him.

He twisted his upper body through the gap and threw himself in. He fell onto the ground hard, but still managed to get past the webs. Stalagmites rose from the ground in front of him, offering cover and only a few strings woven between them. He tried getting up, but something suddenly gripped his leg.

Red looked back in alarm and saw a piece of thread wrapped around his right foot, holding him in place. The spiders were closing in. The one he'd maimed reached its feelers through the same hole Red had opened, and he felt its appendages trying to drag him away.

He leaned over and swung his cleaver at the arachnid. Unfortunately, it had become wise to the danger of his weapon and dodged just in time. But Red's target was never the creature in the first place.

With a swift motion, he split the web stuck to his feet and dashed towards the rock spikes. As he turned to run, Red saw the spiders break through the dense threads and charge frantically towards him. He had made it between two stalagmites, just as a tremendous force hit him from behind.

Red crashed against the rock with a loud impact. Behind him, he saw countless legs and fangs grasping for him. They couldn't reach the stone cover he was in, though. At least not from this position.

The spiders quickly figured as much. They climbed over the tall stalagmites, hoping to grab him from above, but Red wouldn't give them the opportunity. He drew in quick breaths, ignoring his pain, and ran deeper into the maze of rock spikes.

A thin black shadow lunged at him from above, and he could barely raise his cleaver to block it. Another impact struck, and he was thrown against the wall once more. A sharp pain ran up his spine, but he didn't stop, using the impulse to push himself away from his pursuers.

Red couldn't outrun them, and more spiders approached from above. Thankfully, the number of rocky spikes also grew, and they had a hard time reaching him while he kept low to the ground.

But they didn't give up their pursuit. Red could see that their numbers were increasing, and they soon had him surrounded. They blocked almost all light from the veins in the cavern wall, and he had to bring out his own insectoid core to illuminate the way forward.

Even in his precarious condition, Red avoided any wandering arachnid limbs trying to catch him and continued towards one of the large stone pillars, spotting some of the small round bugs running through the stalagmites. Spider legs kept brushing against his head and shoulders, but they couldn't get a firm grip on him.

The monsters all hissed and watched his movements, not keen on giving up on the invader.

After a minute of running, Red finally arrived at the pillar. Many stalagmites and other natural stone structures blocked the spiders from approaching him, and the arachnids could only watch as he slumped to the ground.

Red looked up and shivered. He couldn't count how many of the creatures were staring at him with their menacing eyes, all eager to sink their dripping fangs into his flesh. They studied him from every direction, their grasping legs forming a writhing prison. Red was shrouded in the shadow cast by their large bodies, only the light of his crystal illuminating the horror of the scene.

A few minutes passed, and although the spiders still seemed eager to kill him, he confirmed they couldn't get any closer, no matter how hard they tried. At that point, Red allowed himself to relax, even as terrifying monster limbs waved in front of him. His body almost collapsed on the spot.

Somehow, I did it.

He wondered whether he could just sleep here and wait until the arachnids gave up. However, he wasn't confident they would retreat. From experience, he knew the monsters didn't take kindly to having their den invaded, and they were patient. One spider had waited more than an hour for Red before giving up, and that was when he was outside its nest.

What if they kept watching the entire time? Not to mention, how would he be comfortable sleeping in this place? Although they couldn't reach him now, what if they found a way while he was unconscious? That would mean his death.

Can I lose them here?

It was his best bet. Maybe he could hide somewhere out of their sight and the spiders would give up on pursuing him. After that, he could continue sneaking through their nest. However, Red wasn't familiar with his surroundings and there were too many beasts blocking his way for him to move. If he wasn't careful, he would end up getting snatched, so he decided to not wander around.

Red tried to think of a plan, but it was almost impossible in this situation. His heart was still pounding out of his chest, his breaths were short and ragged, and the only reason he didn't feel more terrified was due to exhaustion.

It was a horrible scenario, but Red had already steeled himself for it. In fact, it was much better than what he'd expected. He'd thought he wouldn't even have a chance to escape if he was noticed, but he'd made it far enough to seek cover among the rocks. Now he'd been granted a second chance, and even if he died of thirst or hunger while trapped here, it would be a better end than being eaten by these monstrosities.

Still, he wasn't ready to give up. The spiders weren't loud creatures, but with so many hissing at him, he had a hard time focusing on his thoughts. Red closed his eyes to consider his next steps while being careful not to fall asleep. But without warning, a strong vibration interrupted his plans.

The hissing noises stopped, and an eerie silence came over the chamber. The spiders ceased their frantic movements and retracted their legs. They retreated like a wave and the shadows cast by their bodies receded. The sudden glow from the cave blinded Red for an instant.

But then the brightness diminished again. Red was confused as a new shadow above him grew larger and larger. He recognized the silhouette of a spider, but somehow it continued to expand beyond its normal size. It took a few seconds for Red's tired mind to register what was happening.

Eight green, glowing orbs looked down at him.

Red's eyes narrowed, and he saw something move. He tried to roll out of the way, but it was too late. The leg of the large monster punched deep into his shoulder like an arrow.

He heard the crunch of shattering bone, and a tide of pain spread through his entire frame. He lost all feeling in his left arm, unable to gather the strength to move it, and dropped the crimson core. It took all his concentration to keep from falling unconscious.

He saw the spider lift its leg and stare at him, perhaps surprised that the small prey had survived its attack. Red stood up to run, but weakness overcame him, and he fell after barely taking a step.

Desperation came over him, and he tried to crawl away, using his one good hand still carrying the cleaver to drag himself forward. Suddenly, though, he felt something touch his back. It stuck to his skin, and slowly he was hoisted into the air, the floor becoming distant.

He struggled, trying to latch onto something, but to no avail. The giant spider's leg lifted him effortlessly, and he was raised past the stalagmites and into the open chamber once more.

As his surroundings brightened, Red could see dozens of motionless, glaring spiders. The creatures stood on the surrounding webs, witnessing the scene from all angles. All of them kept their distance from Red, not daring to move forward, as if they were afraid of him.

No... Not afraid of me.

Red stopped moving. He looked down and saw an enormous spider staring emotionlessly at him.

Its foreleg held onto his back and lifted the small human just above its head. Its eight eyes glowed green, and Red could feel his skin tingling from the Spiritual Energy that emanated from the monster's body. He hadn't been able to tell before due to the distance, but somehow the pressure coming from this beast seemed even stronger than what he'd felt from the insectoid.

He inspected the head of the creature. Its eyes were all different sizes, the center orbs larger than the others. Its giant fangs dripped with venom, and below that, he could see its mouth.

For some reason, Red didn't feel nervous.

"Are you going to eat me?" he asked.

The spider didn't react.

"I probably don't have a lot of meat on my body. You'd be better off looking for something bigger."

It remained silent.

"They say I'm cursed, did you know that? Who knows what will happen to you if you eat me? It would be better if you just let me go."

As if on cue, the spider started to lower Red. Not towards the ground, but its large open mouth.

Well, at least I tried.

The monster didn't seem hurried. It knew the human couldn't escape, so it had nothing to worry about. Red, for his part, measured the gradually closing distance between him and his death.

Four meters. Three meters. Two meters.

"At the very least, I'm glad you're still not that smart," he said.

One meter.

Close enough.

Red's right arm swung with all his accumulated strength. The cleaver he held in his one functioning hand cut into one of the spider's eyes. It etched itself deeply in the beast's flesh, and green, glowing blood splattered all over him as the orb exploded.

The spider hissed in pain and dropped Red from its grip. He fell from the monster's perch, slamming against the side of a rock spike and crashing down near the same place he'd been hiding. His vision blurred, but a second later, he heard the entire nest hiss in fury.

They were coming for him.

This isn't fair.

The large creature's green blood painted his entire body. Red could feel the Spiritual Energy in the fluid burning his skin, but he couldn't deal with it right now.

Maybe Viran would be proud, though.

He closed his eyes, but another light grew in his vision. This one, however, wasn't green like the glow he was used to seeing.

It was crimson.

Red noticed he had fallen right next to the insectoid core he'd dropped earlier, which started to glow on its own.

No, not on its own.

Some droplets from the gush of spider blood had dripped onto it, and it now emitted a glow far stronger than anything Red had seen before. Almost out of instinct, he reached for it with his good arm, wrapping his bloody hand around it.

Then came the reaction.

His hand burned, and the glow intensified, as if the crystal had awakened from a deep sleep. All the blood that covered Red flowed into it like a mist, and something changed in the air.

The radiance of the core grew.

And then the entire world turned crimson.

CHAPTER 39

CRIMSON

RED THOUGHT HE WAS DREAMING. It looked as though the images reaching his sight were filtered through a thick ruby-tinted glass. Everything around him appeared distant, as if separated by a translucent red film, and even his pain and exhaustion disappeared for a moment.

At first, Red thought the problem was his vision, so he closed his eyes. Pure darkness. When Red opened them again, the crimson colors were still there. Not only that, but they had changed. Darker wisps floated past his sight, too fast to examine. His depth perception confirmed this wasn't a hallucination, but something happening in the world around him.

And then the smell came, a sweet and metallic fragrance that invaded his nostrils. It was unassuming at first, but grew stronger until there was nothing else Red could focus on. The scent was so thick and overwhelming he felt he would vomit on the spot—if he could gather enough strength to do so. And yet, under his drowning senses, the odor felt familiar.

Blood...

Not his. Not the spider's either. There was not enough blood in the underground to create a smell this strong. It made Red forget his pain, replacing it with something much more insidious and terrifying.

And then there was the silence.

No noise came from the spiders. For a moment, Red thought he'd been teleported to another place, but looking around, he saw the same rock surface he had become so familiar with. His gaze moved up, and he saw the army of spiders completely frozen in place, including the larger monster.

Beyond the crimson colors, he thought time had come to a standstill. However, his hypothesis was quickly disproven. The giant arachnid who had prepared to eat him started to crawl away, its legs pulling its body up the webs as it distanced itself. Even its blinded eye seemed a lesser concern for the monster.

The movement of the spiders' superior caused a chain reaction. They all retreated to the ceiling, eyes fixed on Red.

Why am I not dead?

Only now did he have enough time to ask himself that. His mind was sluggish, too tired to think deeply, but even then, it didn't take much effort to figure out. His hand clutched the ray of hope that had given him a second chance and seemingly stopped the spiders from killing him.

It was no longer burning, but Red could feel a tingling sensation against his skin as he grasped the stone—Spiritual Energy. Bringing it up to his face, he examined the crystal he'd extracted from the insectoid's brain. The surface of the rough-hewn gem was now completely crimson, free of any green traces, as if the small red threads that previously occupied the object's gleaming surface had taken over and purged all other colors. The darker wisps around him all originated from the stone as well, and when he followed their trajectory with his eyes, he discovered they fizzled out a few meters away.

Red recalled his earlier experiences with the core, and a possible explanation came to mind. But he stopped his train of thought, realizing how pointless it was to consider it right now. The last thing he wanted was to waste this opportunity.

Red raised the stone, and the spiders above hissed in alarm, trying to retreat even faster.

This...

Strangely, it didn't take long for the smell to stop bothering his senses and the prickling feeling to leave his skin. The crimson environment around him remained, though, showing no signs of fading. Red had a strange compulsion to study the stone, but he pushed the feeling aside. Who knew how long the spiders would be intimidated? He pocketed the stone and moved.

Whatever surge of adrenaline the transformation of the core had given him was quickly dissipating. As Red stood, a familiar pain rushed up his right side—a broken rib. Then there was his punctured shoulder, but he took solace in the fact that he didn't need his arm to walk.

He closed his eyes and tried to overcome the pain through deep breaths. It was difficult, even with his experience. If he pushed himself too hard, his body would collapse on the spot. But he couldn't stay here, not now that he'd been given a second chance.

Cold sweat poured over his face as his body burned from strain. He gritted his teeth and gathered his strength. Red recalled the first major injury he'd received in the mines, the broken rib he'd fought through after Viran ordered him to follow. It had taken a matter of minutes to complete a task as simple as getting up, but now he didn't know if he had that long to spare.

Red pushed himself to his knees. He grabbed a stone spike for support and tried to pull himself up. His grip almost slipped, but he didn't let himself fall to the ground. Still, it seemed no matter what he did, he couldn't gather enough strength to move forward.

He fell to his knees once more, his vision darkening.

... Is this a joke? All of that just to pass out here again?

Red refused to accept it. He'd been given a second chance, only to fail because of his wounds. Maybe the blob was right when it said he was cursed. Red thought to try again, but he knew he didn't have the strength in his body to keep going. It was the one thing the crimson core couldn't provide.

Wait, the core...

The memory of Viran during his fight against the insectoid came to mind. More specifically, how he'd used his Spiritual Stone to power himself up. Red didn't have one with him, but he had something even more potent.

He examined the crimson core. He didn't know if Viran had used some special technique to transfer the energy into his body, or what the consequences of such a method might be, but they couldn't be worse than dying. Red only remembered that the man had used the stone and an open wound. He looked at his punctured shoulder, locating the perfect point of insertion.

For a moment, he hesitated.

What if it devours my blood?

Could he take it out before it bled him dry? Or was the core satisfied from its previous meal?

Red realized how stupid his questions were. He couldn't let his hesitation stand in his way.

I hope this works.

With no more delay, Red shoved the stone into his shoulder. A bolt of pain shot through his body as the crystal entered, and he almost passed out again. But other than that, nothing happened.

No sudden drainage of blood, but no miraculous power either.

Red grunted. Perhaps he shouldn't have been surprised that there was more to the process, but he wasn't ready to give up. It just so happened that his left shoulder was part of his Upper Arm Vein, which he'd already completely opened.

Red fought through the agonizing pain and focused on sensing his Spiritual Vein. He recalled the human figure drawn on Viran's hideout wall, pushing the gem further into his flesh until it was where he thought his acupoint was located.

He couldn't judge how close it was, so he plunged it deeper, flesh and bones giving way. Right as he was about to pass out, something flowed into him. It was slow at first, but suddenly, it surged in like a torrent. Another torturous feeling spread through Red's body, but with it strength also came. The energy traveled through his opened veins, pushing away pain and exhaustion and replacing it with power.

Red felt his fatigue being washed away, and the sudden injection of power awakened his tired senses like lightning. He shot up to his feet in a single leap. Crimson-colored energy moved under his skin, following the paths of his opened veins. It was extremely unpleasant, like hundreds of ants crawling under his flesh, but he didn't collapse.

The discomfort disappeared just as quickly. In a daze, Red looked around and noticed the red aura around him had weakened. He hastily removed the stone from his shoulder. The glow of the gem had somewhat waned, but the spiders didn't seem eager to approach again. His wounds hadn't disappeared either, but they no longer hindered his movements. In fact, it was as if his injuries didn't exist.

Is this how Viran felt?

He could move his left arm freely again, and his entire body had seemingly returned to prime condition. Any further investigation would have to wait until Red was past this chamber, though.

Looking around, he was about to continue on his way when he suddenly remembered something.

My cleaver.

How would he cut open the spiders' webs without his weapon? Just the iron knife wouldn't do. But he remembered his cleaver had been embedded in the monster's eye. Red wanted to curse his luck, but he still tried to search for the weapon.

Thankfully, he found it not far away, as the large spider had likely knocked it from its eye socket while wailing in pain. The blade had been corroded by the arachnid's glowing blood, but most of its sharp edge remained. Red could only hope it would be enough to last him the rest of this chamber.

He ran through the stalagmites towards the exit. Eventually, the stone spikes disappeared, and he was faced with the same blockade of webs. This time, he threw caution to the wind. Since the spiders didn't dare to approach him, what was the point in sneaking around?

Red cut the threads in front of him, carving a wide path to the other side. The monsters were alarmed by the invader that dared to barge into their nest, but as soon as they saw the red aura surrounding him, they stopped in their tracks. Red could see more spiders who had opened their Spiritual Seas watching him, but even they seemed afraid of getting closer.

There was no way I was making it through this.

The webs in front of him seemed endless, extending for hundreds of meters. Red couldn't imagine that he would have successfully sneaked through without making a single mistake. Now, though, he didn't need to.

Gradually, the threads in front of him diminished, and the path ahead became clearer. Red heard something else too, a rumbling sound that grew louder the further he advanced.

With one last cut of his cleaver, the web parted, revealing the rest of the chamber. Instead of closing off, the room led to another opening into an even larger space, greater than anything Red could imagine.

But that wasn't what caught his attention.

In the distance, he saw it, reflecting the light of thousands of moonstone veins. It slithered around enormous stone pillars and split the gigantic cave in half. It was rushing water, more than he'd ever seen in his life.

A clear river appeared in his vision. Red had finally reached it.

CHAPTER 40

KINGDOM

ONCE AGAIN, Red thought he'd reached the surface. The chamber was so big he couldn't see the other end. The moonstone veins were so bright and vast that very little of the enormous space was hidden in shadow. It followed a trend he'd noticed—the further down he went, the more moonstones he found.

These stones, however, seemed different compared to what Red had seen before. In such a large quantity and density, they appeared to transform. The color of the veins was more vivid, and the light was far stronger than what could be explained by numbers alone. It was as if the ores were breathing.

It was dizzying to look at. Thankfully, the swirling crimson aura around Red shielded him from the radiance, and he was able to examine the rest of the room.

Enormous rock pillars held up the ceiling of the cavernous kingdom, spreading across the area and separating it into sections. Large mushrooms, fungi, and moss growths decorated the stone. The vegetation wore vibrant colors, which were all painted crimson by his aura, and glowed as brightly as the moonstones, giving the underground a touch of life Red never thought possible before.

The centerpiece of the space was the stream. Red could smell the moist air from afar, even through the blood, and the refreshing sensation cleared his mind. The river was wide, about thirty meters across, and its course stretched across the chamber. The tributary snaked around the rock pillars, with vegetation growing around its banks, seemingly granting life to the hostile underground.

Red followed the course of the stream to the center of the cave, where it flowed down into a massive hole. He couldn't see the bottom of the pit from his position, but the sound of the crashing water was distant enough for him to gaze in awe.

How deep does this place go?

He didn't know, and he didn't feel compelled to find out. Instead, he focused on the space within his reach, the expanse that surrounded this bottomless pit.

As his eyesight adapted to his environment, more details emerged in his vision—giant insects, multitudes of them. Even these enormous monsters seemed small compared to the cave they dwelt in, but Red didn't let himself be fooled. They were immense, many the size of the strongest creatures he'd encountered before—some even bigger—and most possessed glowing, green eyes.

Scorpions with exoskeletons broader than Red was tall, colonies of thousands of small round insects feeding on moss, beetles with vicious horns longer than their bodies. He even saw what looked to be another species of spider, except these were much larger than the ones in the previous chamber.

He found creatures everywhere he looked, some even engaging in combat, their clashes echoing through the cavern. Red eventually gave up on counting, as every second revealed more life forms. They were fascinating sights but also extremely dangerous.

Red realized then why Viran hadn't continued his exploration. It would've been pure suicide.

The Spiritual Energy in the air had become denser, too. It couldn't compare to the amount provided by the mysterious blob, but it was much more substantial than what Red had encountered near the surface. This was probably the deepest any slave had ever ventured underground, yet judging by the bottomless pit in the middle of the cavern, this was merely a fraction of the total expanse of this place.

A morbid curiosity consumed Red. What awaited him further down? What other kinds of monsters existed in these caves? If their size kept increasing, how big would they get?

Red caught himself, remembering Viran's advice. He didn't know how long the energy in his body would last, or even if the crimson aura would protect him against these monsters. He needed to be careful, remain unnoticed and hopefully escape this place as soon as possible.

The stream flowed out from a smaller passage, at least relative to the cave, and Red couldn't see where it would lead him or how far it stretched. However, if Viran was to be believed—and most of his words had been true —this would be his path to the surface.

There was no more time for planning. He needed to move. Even now, Red could see a crimson mist evaporating from his skin, similar to what had happened to Viran. This indicated that the Spiritual Energy was leaving his body, and he didn't know what would happen once it was all gone.

Red moved carefully along the edges of the cave, hoping to stay out of sight while maintaining a steady pace toward his destination. However, his attempt quickly failed. As soon as he walked further into the cave, it was as if he became a beacon of light, signaling his position to every monster nearby.

One insect, which he'd assumed was harmless, screeched in terror as soon as he approached. This alarmed all the other fauna of the cavern, who immediately discovered his presence.

The result was more favorable than he would have guessed. The larger creatures approached but retreated as soon as they caught sight of him. All the monsters strived to keep out of his way, dreading the crimson aura surrounding him. A colony of ants rushed out of his path as they fled from the strange energy. He hoped the effects of the stone would work on every beast he came across, but he didn't want to risk it.

Red saw no more point in sneaking around. He diverted from his original route and made a beeline for the river, pushing his muscles to their limit.

The pain returned, aches spreading over his body. Red didn't even know how long he had to travel, but he needed to use this aura while it was still available.

He swiftly arrived at the edge of the stream, not stopping to examine the water. He turned and followed the tributary upstream. Yet, even after five minutes of running at full speed, he realized he was just over halfway to his goal. The sheer size of this place continued to surprise him, and his initial and hasty estimations had failed him.

To make matters worse, Red felt the strain on his body return and his speed diminished with it. Weakness took over, and every step became heavier than the last. He gritted his teeth and looked down at the stone in his hand. The glow had diminished further over the last few minutes, but at least the monsters weren't any less scared of the aura.

Hesitation crossed Red's mind as he thought about repeating the same infusion process to boost his power. However, he decided against it.

Not yet.

Red had no way of knowing how long this effect would last, and he couldn't risk having it disappear while in the middle of this subterranean jungle. He would crawl if necessary, but he would only borrow the stone's power as a last resort.

In the distance, he noticed monsters staring at him from afar, and beyond them, he saw passages to unexplored parts of the cave and smaller pits leading to strange places. A primal fascination consumed him. It was as if fate was dangling the unexplored and undiscovered in front of him, daring him to stray from his goal.

No, it was more than that.

Something called to him in the depths of this world, its summons silent but still deafening to Red. It was waiting for him. However, just as the sensation appeared, it was gone. Frowning, he shook the strange thoughts from his head.

Still, after evading death's temptation, his situation didn't improve.

His pace diminished further—from a full-blown run to a jog, from a jog to a walk. The river passage was so close, but it felt as if he were approaching an impassable gulf. His body slowed, and the time to use his last resort came earlier than he'd feared.

He looked at the glowing stone. Some of the crimson color had retreated from the gem's surface, the green light again visible along its edges, and the frequency of dark wisps emanating from it had also decreased. Red was too tired to think clearly, but he guessed it wouldn't last up to the river passage.

If he collapsed here, it wouldn't matter if the aura lasted for thirty minutes or three hours; it would be gone by the time he awoke—if something didn't eat him while he slept. The last trace of hesitation disappeared from his eyes, and he shoved the gem into his mangled shoulder.

Red was familiar with the process at this point, but that didn't make it any less painful. He felt the stone pushing apart his flesh, and more blood poured down his body. Eventually, the tingling sensation returned as the glowing core touched his acupoint and the energy transfer began. The jolt of power swiftly rejuvenated Red's strength, and his fatigue was washed away as if it had never existed.

The feeling was almost intoxicating, but Red knew it was too good to be true. There would be a price to pay, eventually, and he dreaded the moment it would arrive.

As soon as Red felt strong enough to continue, he removed the rock from his open wound and surged forward with renewed vigor, crossing the last stretch towards his destination.

The light of the expanse grew faint as he dove into the tunnel. The screams of monsters became distant, replaced by the sound of rushing water from the stream. A whole unexplored world was left behind, perhaps never to be seen again, but it was a sacrifice that Red was willing to make.

There was no telling how much further he needed to go to reach the surface, but it was close, he could feel it. His destiny was quickly approaching, and hope started to burn brightly in his heart.

CHAPTER 41

AZURE

RED DIDN'T KNOW how long he traveled as the Spiritual Energy in his body grew thin. Weakness returned to his steps and his vision blurred, the world around him growing distant.

He examined the core in his hand. The red traces had nearly vanished from its surface, and the aura around him had withdrawn to less than a meter in diameter. For the first time, Red could see what the phenomenon looked like from outside—a formless crimson aura that tapered off into the air without any defined boundaries. The smell of blood had also grown weaker.

This worried him, but he realized how foolish his concern was.

There's no point in extending it.

Red would need to get off his high eventually, and he doubted there was enough Spiritual Energy in the stone to provide him with another significant boost.

Thankfully, since he'd entered the river passage, he hadn't seen or heard any monsters. He wasn't sure whether that was because of his weakened senses failing to spot them or because no creatures lived in this tunnel. Both options worried him in different ways.

Red searched for a place to hide, but even that seemed like an arduous task as lethargy took over. He had hit a wall with his stamina multiple times today, only being able to push past it due to sheer adrenaline or unnatural

218

means. Now, though, it didn't matter how close he was to his goal or how strong his will to move forward—his body was shutting down and he knew there was no delaying it this time.

His legs failed, and with a false step, the world spun around Red as he crashed to the ground. Pain and other sensations grew indistinct, and he had never before felt his consciousness fading so clearly as at that moment. Only one thought came to mind as the world grew dark.

I have to get through this...

Red sensed himself being pulled into a dream. There were no colors, no noises, no warmth, nothing but the feeling of weightlessness as some part of his being was dragged through an endless path. He tried to fight back, to resist its pull, but he couldn't even feel his own body.

There was only a vague awareness, as his thoughts struggled to make sense of something he couldn't possibly understand. He didn't know how long this trip was taking—passage of time was hard to measure in this state —but eventually sensation returned to him.

His senses adapted to his surroundings in mere seconds.

Red found himself in a small square room. The walls seemed worn, made of gray stone brick, with an arched ceiling of red wooden tiles. The place was lit by a handful of candles on the far side of the room, all spread around a simple table, next to a small white slab. Something was written on the surface of the tablet—a line of unfamiliar symbols that Red could only guess formed a word.

Upon closer examination, he recognized a few of the letters from Viran's pages, but his line of thought was interrupted when he felt another presence in the room.

Red turned and saw a man standing in the doorway with his back to him. He sported the type of armor he had become familiar with through his dreams, which announced the man's position as a soldier. This armor, though, looked strikingly similar to that of the burly man he'd met in his last dream, radiating the same pressure that made it hard for Red to breathe.

He thought that maybe he'd met the same person again, but this man was blonde and he didn't look nearly as big. This soldier looked to be far younger, with a clean-shaven face and elegant features, a stark contrast to

Red's killer. If the legends about handsome heroes slaying horrible monsters on the surface were true, then this man would probably be one such protagonist.

Hero or not, Red didn't let his guard down. If his previous experiences had told him anything, this man would be the one to kill him and send him back to the real world. He needed to learn as much as he could before that happened.

The soldier's face looked puzzled as he stared at Red, or whoever the dream was passing him off as at the moment.

Immediately, Red knew something was wrong.

After a few seconds, the man's confusion became undisguised hostility.

"Who are you?" he asked in an authoritative tone. His voice was clear and imposing, as if he expected anyone who heard him to obey his orders. Someone used to command.

It reminded Red of Viran. In fact, he felt strangely compelled to answer his question, like it was only natural. Yet something else snapped him out of it.

Familiarity.

Red didn't know why, but he recognized this voice. He searched his mind, trying to recall where he might've heard it before, but he couldn't remember.

The man's expression contorted in anger at being ignored.

"I asked you a question." His tone grew impatient. "What did you do to my body?"

A golden mist of energy flowed out of him. A second later, though, the man's face twisted in surprise and his aura came to a standstill.

He examined his surroundings with a bewildered gaze. The walls, the white slab, the world outside the windows, even his own hands.

Finally, his eyes came to rest on Red, except this time with apprehension.

"Where are we? How did you bring me here?" he asked.

Red thought about replying, but the sudden turn in the conversation made him cautious. Although these dreams were special, they always seemed disconnected from reality. Yet, for the first time since Red started having these visions, someone had recognized that he didn't belong here—before he'd even said or done anything. Not only that, but this person was also acting strangely, and Red couldn't wrap his head around the meaning of the man's words.

The potential consequences of this interaction made him wary, and he weighed his next words.

"I... don't know. I just appeared here," Red said, deciding against giving out any precise information.

"Just appeared?" His words only angered the man even further. "Then you can only blame fate for what's about to happen."

The golden mist lurched towards him, too fast to follow. Red didn't even have the time to brace himself.

But death didn't come.

Instead, Red felt the energy wrapping around his body and dragging him into the air, towards the soldier. He couldn't move.

"Whatever accursed mortal put you up to this must have thought themselves brilliant to come up with this scheme." The man waved his finger and drew a strange symbol with the golden mist. "But I can reach you even through this illusion."

Red felt alarmed at the threat, but in front of someone this powerful, there was nothing he could do. The incantation shot into his body, and he prepared himself for the worst. Yet, even after a few seconds of silence, nothing happened. At least nothing that Red could feel.

The soldier seemed just as surprised.

"Your soul..." He trailed off.

Red still felt confused, but an unexplainable conviction grew in his mind. The man couldn't touch him in this dream, no matter how powerful he might be.

A moment passed. The soldier stood silent in thought until resolve came over his face. A vertical slit formed in the middle of his forehead, and Red saw something stirring beneath his skin. It forced its way out, and an eye emerged.

It was bigger than the average human eye, with an unnatural pitch-black sclera and dark blue iris. What Red thought was an irregularly shaped pupil at first became a much more terrifying sight. There were countless black dots clumped together, forming a large uneven circle from afar, but the longer one looked into it, the clearer the miniscule boundaries between points became.

It was as if thousands of eyes were staring at him. Red felt dread from the deepest part of his soul, but he couldn't avert his gaze no matter how hard he tried. Silver-colored threads emerged from the man's third eye and made their way forward, seeping into Red's own eyes.

An intrusive sensation reached into his mind. It wasn't painful, but it left him feeling utterly powerless and exposed. However, the feeling disappeared abruptly, and the tendrils extending into his eyes were cut off.

Red could move his gaze again.

The soldier's face slackened with shock as he processed what had just happened. Then his expression twisted, turning into something inhuman. Hatred leaked from every pore of his being, and the golden mist spun faster and faster, expanding until it clashed against the walls of the room. The building offered no resistance and was torn to shreds in an instant.

"Cursed animal!" The man glared at him, and Red felt his body rise higher into the air.

With no roof over his head anymore, he was greeted by a familiar golden sky. Down below, around the room he'd been inside, he could see hundreds of buildings, all intricately constructed and beautiful beyond words. The scene remained only for an instant, however, as even these structures disintegrated as the whirlwind of energy washed over them.

"Your existence is an affront!" The mist changed colors, shifting into the same dark blue as the third eye. "I will find you and the ones responsible for this!"

The cloud of azure destruction expanded into an enormous storm, and the world was drawn into the maelstrom.

"Every one of you will pay for what you've done!"

The mist in front of him cleared somewhat, and Red saw the soldier's figure again.

He had grown larger, far bigger than a human, tearing apart his armor as his skin turned blue. Illusory images beyond Red's comprehension manifested around the man's figure. Creatures were born, lived their entire lives, and were killed in an instant. Empires rose and fell. Worlds were created and destroyed.

A vision of an endless cycle of creation and destruction.

Red tried to resist his restraints with renewed energy.

"You can't escape." The voice was all around him. "Not anymore."

Red looked at the man again. He wasn't even paying attention to him anymore, instead making strange signs with his hand, all three of his eyes closed. Magical symbols appeared out of thin air, built from blue light. They were ever-changing, and any time Red thought he could see their true form, the shapes would transform into something completely different.

He could only watch as the process continued. Soon the sky around them was filled with such symbols. Only after a few minutes had passed did the azure being come to a stop.

He opened his eyes and looked at Red. "I won't allow you to leave, not until I can find you myself—"

His words were cut off as a thunderous boom resounded.

A bolt of energy struck the being's back. Instead of an explosion or injury, the force seemed to be completely absorbed into his body. The man looked confused, as apparently the blow hadn't hurt him.

A second later, though, he roared in agony.

Green radiance appeared under the man's skin, and like snakes, the pale energy spread and coiled around his body. Soon, it reached his head, drawing closer and closer to his third eye.

The man gripped his head in pain, but he swiftly reacted. Azure energy shone from his forehead, and the progress of the invasive force slowed as the two powers clashed. Under extreme strain, he fought against the glowing energy, but it looked like a losing battle. Red could see the green light advance slowly but surely towards the man's center eye.

The symbols around him changed frantically, and the destructive vortex below lost its form, like something was draining its power. Beneath the man's anguished expression, fear appeared.

"C-cursed mortal..." The azure being struggled to get his words out as he glared at Red. "I won't let you succeed..."

The man's body shone. Growths appeared beneath his skin, threatening to burst out, and energy accumulated in the air with the transformed man at the center.

The world went silent. Somehow, Red knew what came next.

An explosion. And then complete darkness.

CHAPTER 42

FINAL STRETCH

AWARENESS SLOWLY RETURNED TO RED. The familiar feeling of waking up from a stupor came to him, but he couldn't even prepare for the blast of pain that followed. This time, the agony came from somewhere else.

It hit his head. A pounding headache that spread through every inch of his skull threatened to throw him right back into unconsciousness. Every one of his senses was overwhelmed by sensations he couldn't parse—unexplainable images flashed in front of his eyes.

The dream... What was...

As soon as Red tried to make sense of his memories, his brain felt like it was about to explode. He could feel organs and other parts of his head squirming beneath his skin and bones—pieces of his body that he didn't even know existed. His flesh seemed to lose the unity that made it work together seamlessly, and every inch of his matter screamed in pain.

Red would have cried out if he could, but the only things he could control at this point were his awareness and his mind—no, not even his mind seemed fully responsive. Images continued to flash past his consciousness, and no matter how hard he tried to forget or divert his attention, they didn't disappear. He sought to grasp something that would let him escape this hell.

He searched for it. Through nightmarish creatures whose forms violated life itself. Through things whose size defied imagination. Through symbols speaking truths that threatened to drive him insane. He searched for something, anything.

And eventually, amidst this chaotic assault of images, he found it.

A white slab. It was blurry at first, but Red could feel it. Something he recognized, something he could anchor himself to.

He held on to that image, and in the end, it paid off. It wasn't the white tablet that caught his attention, but what was written on it. Letters he didn't understand the meaning of, but that he remembered all the same.

Visions continued to flash through his mind, but the same white slab became a constant presence throughout his ordeal. The number of visions diminished as the letters became clearer. Waves of pain cleansed his mind of all impurity, but like a protector, the tablet stood in the center of his every thought.

Red felt an eternity pass before the agony lessened enough for him to function again. The memories now seemed like a bad dream, and he avoided even thinking about what he'd just gone through, fearing it would return. He would rather suffer a thousand broken bones than experience the pain anew.

Control of his senses also returned. The rushing sound and damp smell of the river, the feeling of the cold rock against his skin. When Red opened his eyes, he noticed he was lying face down on the cave floor in a rather awkward position—one of the unfortunate consequences of suddenly falling unconscious.

Other sensations gradually made themselves known. Aches and exhaustion riddled every part of his frame, more so than he was used to. Particularly around his arms and spine, where his opened Spiritual Veins were located.

Red guessed this was the result of the infusion method he'd used with the insectoid core. He didn't know if this was the extent of his resulting injuries, but he was in no condition to examine it further.

The pain he experienced now was distressing, but he welcomed the sensation. Compared to the mental torture he'd just gone through, he guessed that no physical discomfort would ever be as bad.

Now, came the harder part—moving. Red hadn't tried it until now and, considering the circumstances, he guessed it would be an arduous task. First, he tried his extremities. He gathered strength in his legs and arms, and slowly but surely, the muscles responded to him. They trembled and shivered from the effort, but he felt strength return.

What alarmed him, though, was his left arm. Red was aware of the sort of injury he had suffered in his shoulder—it had compromised the movement of the limb—but now it was worse. He could not get his arm to move, no matter the force he put into it. Only the slightest tremble of his fingers and the chilly feeling against his skin told him the limb was still attached to his body.

Troubling possibilities crossed his mind. However, Red pushed those worries away. Everything could be addressed later. What mattered now was to escape this place, and he still had two legs to do it.

The slow process of turning his body over began, but it was interrupted when Red felt a sharp pang of pain in his side. In all his distress, he'd almost forgotten about the broken rib. If he had to guess, it wasn't as bad of a fracture as the one he'd gotten from the centipede, but added to all his other injuries, it was still unpleasant.

The right side of his body felt tender to the touch, and it drained almost all his strength to turn his torso.

Still, that didn't stop Red. After some awkward movement, he rolled over and was now facing the green ceiling. That alone drained almost all his stamina, and he felt tired again, his eyelids growing heavy as sleep threatened to overtake him.

Red felt concerned about resting in the open space, but he knew he didn't have a choice in the matter. His only comforting thought was that since no monsters had eaten him after he fell unconscious the first time, they probably wouldn't the second time either.

That sounds about right...

He tried to convince himself of that as he fell asleep.

Over the next day, Red's progress was slow. Every minor advancement seemed to deplete his entire energy reserves, and he found himself resting more often than moving.

First, it was getting up. He could do it after a few tries, but by the time he succeeded, he'd spent a third of his stamina.

Then he needed to walk. A couple of stumbles later and barely ten meters covered, he nearly gave up again.

Red considered whether it wouldn't be better to wait for his body to recover before proceeding, but he knew that wasn't possible. His left shoulder wasn't bleeding anymore, but it was still an open wound. He didn't know when it might fester with infection, and by then, even if he wanted to, he wouldn't be able to walk.

Not to mention the issue of food. The moss he'd gathered in the tunnels was running out. Red thought himself capable of functioning for a long time without food, but in this wounded state, his hunger became a pressing issue. At least water wasn't a concern with the stream right next to him, but that wasn't enough to sustain his body.

Red kept moving, one slow step at a time, using the cave walls for support. Another few hours passed. This last stretch of his journey ironically seemed destined to become the longest.

The map had become useless, and he couldn't tell how far the stream extended. However, considering how far down he'd traveled, it wouldn't be a brief journey to the surface. His only comfort was the fact that he simply needed to follow the river up.

He came across many other tunnels connecting to the river passage. In some, the stream even branched off into smaller sections, leading towards other depths. The flow seemed endless, and he wondered how there could be so much water in one place.

Red took the time to examine the insectoid stone. Surprisingly, it had returned to the same state he'd found it in, with small red streaks scattered over the bright green gem. No signs of the crimson aura or the bloody smell remained, and it didn't even glow when he fed it some of his blood.

No more protection.

Fungi and moss became common further up the tunnel, but Red didn't dare to eat any, even in his hunger. He didn't know if it was safe, and the absence of any monsters made him even more suspicious. This passage had everything necessary to survive: water, food, and plenty of hiding spaces to nest in. Even one was usually more than enough for insects to inhabit an area. So why weren't there any around?

This feels too easy...

On the surface, having no monsters in his way was a blessing to Red, who could not fight back in his current state. But he was cautious by nature, and even this close to escaping, that part of him was still alert. It left him with a foreboding feeling that persisted, no matter how much progress he made.

As he journeyed, the moonstone veins diminished, and so did their light. The closer he came to his escape, the deeper the darkness seemed to get, and at one point, he had to rely on his own moonstone to light the way ahead. His progress slowed down even further.

I'm close...

Green light no longer shone from the rocks, an indicator that he was ascending higher. However, he didn't know how much longer he could hold on. His food was gone, and Red felt his temperature rise as cold sweat poured down his forehead.

Fever. The harbinger of death.

Other signs would sometimes come with it, but this was always the worst one—the point of no return. Over the last few years, he had seen many slaves develop the same symptoms after being wounded. Almost all of them had died a slow and painful death, and the ones that survived most certainly hadn't been in as bad of a condition as Red.

Not long now...

He knew he couldn't lie down to rest, or he might not get up again. Even if he had to die, he would rather do it while gazing at the sky, something he'd never seen before. People told him it looked blue while the sun was out and black when the moon and stars appeared. It stretched as far as the eye could see, and no matter how high you reached, you could never touch it.

He couldn't conjure the image. The golden sky in his dreams looked too blurry when he tried to recall it, and there was no sun or moon to gaze at. He was curious, but when he asked, he was always met with the same answer.

You'll understand it when you see it.

Suddenly, something caught his attention. Up ahead, he saw it. A flicker, a glow of light.

Red's eyes lit up.

More motes of light appeared closer to him. Round, bright, and brimming with power.

Red's surroundings were bathed in the glow of the small orbs of light, and the source became clearer to him. Six radiant green eyes, a humanoid shape, vicious claws, serrated mandibles, and a dark shining carapace covering its body.

Insectoids.

A dozen of them blocked his way forward.

CHAPTER 43

TIRED

RED FROZE. He dropped his moonstone on the ground and grabbed his cleaver with his healthy right hand, pointing the weapon at his foes. The monsters didn't move, silently staring at him.

This is useless...

His instincts screamed at him to fight, but he knew how stupid the idea was. Every single one of the creatures had glowing green eyes and emitted a pressure similar to the first insectoid he'd seen a few days before. Throughout his journey, Red had learned how to resist the invisible force, thanks to his encounters with the many other strong creatures of the mines, but that didn't mean he felt confident in his chances against a dozen insectoids. Much less so when he could barely walk straight.

Red thought hard, but the inevitability of the situation only became clearer as the seconds passed. Jumping into the stream to escape? If the monsters wanted to, they could catch him before he even got his feet wet, and the water wasn't that deep. Activating the stone again? It wouldn't work without the glowing spider blood, and Red didn't have the power or speed to draw the blood of the insectoids as a replacement.

Run away? He could hardly walk.

Fight his way through? He couldn't even lift his blade properly.

There was no plan to get him out of this, no matter how hard he tried to think of one. Red had expected something of the sort to happen—facing impossible odds, being overwhelmed, and killed—but this close to his destination? It left a bitter taste in his mouth, and even in his hopeless state, he continued to look for a way out.

One thing was certain, though. Cutting his way through the enemies wasn't it.

Red felt the blank eyes of the creatures upon him. They didn't attack immediately, behaving similarly to the first insectoid. The monsters resembled humans in more ways than one, and that included their intelligence. There had to be a reason for them to be here.

Red lowered his weapon and studied the beasts, just as they were studying him. At first glance, the insectoids looked like exact copies of each other, but there were differences. Some varied in size, being a head taller or shorter, while others had longer claws than their companions. Most of them carried old wounds on their bodies, and a handful were missing a few eyes.

Red felt that the monsters resembled Viran in some ways. Compared to the first insectoid, they had more battle scars serving as a testament to their experience, their gazes looked sharper, and even the atmosphere around them seemed more threatening.

Soldiers.

The revelation didn't make his situation any worse than it already was, but it made Red wonder. Why were they waiting here? Had they cleared the tunnel of all insects? What was their connection with the first creature Red had come across? He was missing something, and the reason his escape had started so abruptly in the first place was likely connected to these creatures.

Red didn't know if any of this information mattered, but he couldn't bear to just accept death again, not this close to his goal. He grasped for anything he could cling to, any hope, no matter how slim.

He didn't give up. He *couldn't* give up.

"W-what..." Only now that he was struggling with his words did Red realize how much his throat hurt. Still, he fought through it. "What do you want?"

He knew the insectoids could talk, even if not in the same language, and establishing some sort of communication was the only idea he could come up with at the moment.

The monsters didn't respond. However, for the first time in the encounter, Red saw them move. A slight turn of their heads as the creatures all looked in the same direction. Not at Red, but at one of their own. The insectoid in question stood in the center of the group and kept on staring at him, but Red couldn't discern any emotion or intent behind its gaze.

Their leader?

It was his best guess. There was nothing special about this insectoid that Red could see—it sported the same kinds of scars and looked to be average in height compared to its companions. Looking again, though, Red could tell that its eyes shone brighter compared to the others. As he'd learned during his journey, this was an indicator of strength.

The creature's mandibles moved. Buzzing noises came from its mouth, strange sounds that Red recognized. It was the same language the original insectoid had used, but he wasn't any closer to understanding it now than he was back then.

He shook his head. "I don't understand you."

He wasn't sure if it could comprehend what he was saying either, but its attempt to communicate rather than attack showed it was after something else. Red only hoped he could provide it for them.

The insectoid's eyes flickered, and it muttered something else in its strange language before looking down at the ground, almost as if in thought. Red could only wait for whatever came next.

A few moments later, the creature looked at him again and spoke in its buzzing words once more. Red was about to say he still didn't understand when the sounds shifted in tone. First a letter, then a syllable.

It was trying to speak his language.

Red was taken aback, but the insectoid continued to mouth the sounds. He still had a hard time understanding what it was trying to say, but he made out a familiar word from the creature's attempts.

"Search."

Red's eyes lit up. "You're searching for something?"

There were other ways it could have been interpreted, but with no context, Red made the first connection that came to mind.

The noises from its mouth immediately stopped, and the light in its eyes flickered. He didn't know if this was some sort of confirmation on the insectoid's part, but it once more stared at him in silence. It was waiting for Red to say something else.

"... What are you searching for?" he asked.

The creature sank into thought again. Moments later, it tried to mouth another word with its buzzing voice. This time, Red understood it more quickly.

"Brother."

His heart sank.

The insectoid didn't seem to notice Red's change in expression.

As a possibility came to his mind, Red felt like he had just walked into a beast's nest. In his desperation to survive, he'd forgotten the fact that he was directly responsible for the death of one of the insectoids. Was this why they were here—for revenge? If that was the case, then he'd just dug his own grave.

However, as he contemplated further, he felt nothing had changed from his initial situation.

What do I say?

Red knew that it wasn't a simple matter of lying or not. If he lied and said he didn't know anything about their brother, then his only value to the insectoids would be gone. He didn't know if they would just let him go, especially if they were seeking revenge. Telling the truth was likely just as bad, though, since it would give him away.

"I saw him," he said after some serious consideration.

The insectoid's eyes flickered, stronger than before. It turned towards its siblings and communicated in its strange language. Whatever it conveyed was clearly transmitted to the rest of the group, their eyes flashing in conjunction. Eventually, its gaze came back to rest on him.

This time, Red felt there was something else behind its emotionless eyes. Energy was gathering inside the creature, and although it didn't move, he felt the threat of death looming over him. No, it wasn't as simple as that. It was as if the insectoid were trying to see through him, into the thoughts and intentions hidden behind his words.

Red shivered, a thought crossing his mind. *What if it can tell if I'm lying?*

He had no evidence, but he felt a mystical presence in its eyes. When he met its gaze, his mind buzzed, as if something unseen had passed through it, and his instincts flared in warning.

Yet the insectoid kept staring at him, making no other moves. Red could only assume the worst, assuming it might've seen through his lies.

But between truth and lie, would his outcome change? It was unlikely.

Still, what was he supposed to say now? That he would show them where the monster was? Give them the map and hope they could read it? Would they make him accompany them if they couldn't? Would they let him go when they found out their "brother" was dead? He thought about buying time to come up with a plan, but he didn't have time to spare.

He might collapse and die before then.

Dozens of similar questions crossed his mind in an instant, but Red knew that none of it mattered in the end. He didn't think he would make it through another day in his condition. Whatever roundabout plan he could come up with would take too long and be too risky to accomplish, and he was too tired to think of one either way.

He was too tired to think. Too close to his goal to come up short. Too close to his death to wait any longer. And, perhaps most important of all, he was too fed up with this place. The monsters, the green lights, the cold cave walls, the disgusting moss.

For most of his life, survival had been the only thing that mattered. He had no dreams, no goals—only led by his instincts to live to see another day. He was careful, stayed out of trouble, and scavenged for food. Stories about the surface he heard from other slaves seemed like nothing but distant dreams to him, things he could only imagine but never see for himself.

And then Viran had appeared. The man had shown him how to get stronger by harnessing Spiritual Energy, and his overwhelming power proved that it could work. The obstacles had still seemed almost insurmountable for Red, but for the first time, he felt hope in his heart. He felt ambition and yearning, the desire to see the world that had been stripped from him.

He had something to look forward to, to live for.

The underground—which hadn't bothered him before—grew unpleasant to look at. His dreams became more frequent and his imagination more active. He became impatient, reckless, willing to put his life on the line, all for the mere possibility of seeing the surface one day. It was only now that these changes became clear to Red.

Maybe Viran had noticed it. Maybe it was why he'd decided to train him after his fight with the centipede. Viran's thoughts and actions had always puzzled Red. How he seemed so reckless and impatient while still carefully planning his escape. It was a contradiction, and Red thought he would never understand it.

He was wrong. Now he felt he cared about something more than just surviving.

I want to see it.

He wouldn't turn back, no matter what.

"I saw your brother," Red said, "and I killed him myself."

CHAPTER 44

INFECTION

THE INSECTOID'S glowing eyes flared with renewed intensity at Red's confession. He guessed this was what passed for an emotional reaction from the creatures, though he couldn't tell what kind of emotion.

Silence reigned.

The insectoid didn't fly into a rage like he'd expected. It remained still, examining him, and Red didn't avert his gaze either. He felt that same unnatural feeling flash through his mind, this time more intensely.

At one point, the wordless confrontation was interrupted by a buzz. A creature by the leader's side said something. It sounded eager. The leader finally broke eye contact with Red and replied with incomprehensible words of its own. At that, a ripple seemed to pass through the other monsters, and one by one they turned to look at Red.

He felt the pressure on him increase, but he still couldn't tell whether there was killing intent behind their eyes. A few of them engaged in energetic discussion. There were different intonations here and there, maybe indicating disagreement. He could gather the topic was serious from the intensity with which they spoke.

It was pressing enough that the discussion went on for minutes, and they ignored Red throughout. The main insectoid barely said anything the whole time, but it was with its own command that the debate came to a stop. The other monsters didn't speak further, and all turned back to stare at the human.

The leader, whose eyes hadn't left Red the whole time, mouthed some words again.

"Weak... Liar."

Red understood the meaning. It thought he was lying about killing their companion because he was too weak to do it.

To his surprise, Red, who didn't mean to lie, realized he'd told them a half-truth. He hadn't been the one that ultimately killed the insectoid, but he'd played a part in its death.

What interested him, though, was that while the monsters spoke animatedly during their discussion, they never seemed angry, and had remained calm after learning of the death of their sibling. Perhaps they didn't feel emotion the same way humans did.

"You're right, I had help," Red said. "But your brother is dead... I saw him die."

At that, the leader exchanged a few buzzes with the other insectoids before regarding him again. It raised its claws, and Red flinched, expecting to be struck by a bolt of energy. However, the blow didn't come. Instead, the creature brought one of its sharp fingers up and pointed at its triangular head. It tapped at the space between its six eyes, the center of its forehead.

Red quickly figured out what the insectoid was referring to. It was asking about the core he'd harvested from their companion's brain.

He hesitated.

He knew there was little chance of him surviving if any kind of fight broke out, but the crystal was still his last line of defense. Since he'd come this far communicating with the insectoids, though, there was no point in hesitating. He would give up ten cores if it meant he could escape with his life.

He fumbled around in his cloth pouch while the insectoids watched in anticipation. Then he grabbed the strange glowing stone and lifted it up, showing it to the creatures.

Their reaction was instant. The monsters' eyes flickered in unison, and Red saw the Spiritual Energy within their bodies flow outwards. Green light gathered in their claws as if prepared to strike. But they didn't move forward. All of them took a few steps back and raised their guard. Only the leader maintained its composure, but even then, Red could see its exposed muscle tense up.

It was the first reaction Red could clearly recognize since he'd met the creatures—fear. His first thought was that this might be an effect of the crimson aura, but its distinctive glow was nowhere to be seen.

No, it wasn't because of the stone's effects. It was what the core and its crimson marks symbolized.

Red recalled how Viran had told him the crimson streaks weren't normal, and that if anything strange happened with the item, he should throw it away. However, that same weird phenomenon was what had saved his life. Red would never part with such a useful item.

He considered threatening them with it, but by then most of the party seemed to have recovered from the shock, and the creatures still had Spiritual Energy flowing through their claws. Their fear must've been a reflex.

"What is this stone?" he asked.

His words were ignored. Another bout of discussions began within the insectoid group while they closely eyed Red—or rather, the stone in his hand. This time, the debate was far more vigorous. Were they afraid? Concerned? Red couldn't tell, but he guessed the creatures were discussing what they should do next.

None of them stepped forward to take the object from him. The mere fact that they didn't immediately attack gave Red some hope.

Still, the discussion didn't show any signs of stopping. Their buzzing voices grew louder, some of them sounding angry. The situation had become far more complicated than Red could've predicted, yet he had no choice but to wait.

Just as Red thought the insectoids were about to come to blows, the leader interrupted them with a shriek. Right away, the argument stopped, and all the creatures turned to their leader, awaiting its orders.

Its attention shifted from the stone to the human.

Red repeated his question. "What is this?"

The insectoid deliberated for a few seconds before pointing at itself. "Power."

So it's connected to their abilities?

This was something he'd already guessed. It was likely each of them had a similar core in their heads, but it would be impossible to get more specific information from the creature's limited vocabulary.

"And these red lines?" He pointed at the streaks, which he thought was the source of their fear. "What are they?"

This time the insectoid took longer to respond.

"Danger..." it said. "Disease."

Red had already figured the lines were dangerous from the creature's reaction, but the second word disturbed him. Were these red lines evidence of an infectious disease? It would explain why they were so afraid of the stone. Yet, when Red thought about it, the insectoid that had carried the tainted crystal didn't seem any different from the ones standing before him.

No, that's not right.

Why had it been alone? What was it doing near the prisoner's quarters in the first place? Why did it attack the slaves? What could it have sought to gain in that part of the mine, which was scarce in moonstones to consume for power and insects for food?

But Red knew that wasn't the most pressing issue. He'd directly injected the power of the crimson crystal into his Spiritual Veins. If it really was a disease, what kinds of effects would it inflict on him?

"What... what do you mean by 'disease'?" he asked, his voice trembling from exhaustion. "What does it do?"

"Spread," the insectoid said. "Transform. Control. Recover."

A shiver ran up his spine. It explained the insectoid's erratic behavior while also raising other questions—none that he felt compelled to ask right now.

He'd been in constant contact with the core. In fact, he'd injected its energy directly into his body.

"Am I infected?" he asked.

"... Unsure. Early." The insectoid pointed at him. "Human. Weak."

It wasn't comforting. He would've preferred a definitive answer, even if it confirmed his fears, as the uncertainty would eat him from the inside.

However, this also meant that he couldn't give up hope yet. Getting out alive remained his priority. The insectoid's willingness to answer his questions hadn't gone unnoticed, and an idea formed in his head.

"I can take the stone away," Red offered. "To the surface."

The leader showed no reaction. Red imagined the possibility had crossed their minds already. With the arguments the creatures had, the willingness to talk to this weak and wounded human, perhaps they were figuring out how to deal with this infectious crystal.

They were afraid, and they didn't know what to do. Or perhaps they did, but some of them weren't willing to do it.

Red didn't know how this crimson virus could infect other living beings. But if it was as dangerous as the insectoid made it sound, then it was reasonable that they didn't want to interact with it. Destroying it probably wouldn't work either, or else it would be an easy choice. Perhaps they needed to contain it at risk of infection to themselves.

It didn't matter. What did matter was that at least some of the insectoids weren't eager to put their own lives on the line. Not when a far better solution stood before them.

The leader looked at its subordinates, conveying something in its language. They all were focused on their leader, but none of them spoke.

At this moment, everything hung on the insectoid's decision. The group might've been divided, but the final say would come from their leader.

Eventually, the insectoid's gaze came to rest on him again. "Why. Escape."

Red was taken aback by the question. For the first time, the creature was asking him something personal. He'd never told the monster what he wanted to do, but it could guess his goal. It was simple to figure out, considering where this route led, but the fact the insectoid was giving thought to this surprised Red.

The answer, however, was never profound.

"... I want to see what it looks like."

It was that simple. He had no deep reasons, no grand quest he wanted to undertake. He was curious to see the sights he'd heard so much about, and that curiosity had driven him on his journey of no return. It was what spurred him forward, through broken bones, through monsters he had no hope of winning against. Even if he'd been forced by circumstance, it didn't matter. Red knew that even without Viran's death, one day he would've traced the same steps, undergone the same risks, and maybe still failed in the end.

It was what he wanted to do, and any struggle he suffered through would one day be worth it.

It was the insectoid's turn to be taken aback.

"Surface. Danger," it said. "Pain."

Red shook his head. "I am already in pain."

Whatever awaited him there, he doubted it could be any worse than the underground.

At that, the insectoid didn't respond. It turned to its companions and said something in its buzzing voice. This was met by a cacophony of replies, but they were cut short by the leader's authoritative shriek.

The insectoid looked around at the other monsters and any protest immediately died.

Then the creatures moved out of the way at their leader's behest. Some of them hesitated, but they all moved.

Red stared at the insectoid.

"Go," it said. "No. Return."

Red looked ahead, further up the tunnel.

The path forward was finally clear.

CHAPTER 45

FREEDOM

RED WATCHED THE INSECTOIDS, and they met his gaze silently. He stowed away the core and moved forward, one slow step at a time.

None of the creatures moved to stop him from walking along the riverbank, and a few moments later, he was past them. Red could feel their eyes on his back as he trudged away, but he didn't look back.

He walked.

And walked.

And soon he couldn't feel their presence anymore.

As he wandered through the empty tunnel following the stream, Red's thoughts strayed.

He remembered when he'd taken the first step of this trip. The true difficulty of the journey hadn't become clear to him until halfway through.

He remembered Viran's advice, to not let himself be distracted by his dreams, but he hadn't listened, and hopelessness had threatened to consume him at every new obstacle. However, he'd persevered, no matter the difficulty. Red had made peace with his own death at several points, but he never gave up, no matter how slight his chances of success. Even when he knew he would almost surely fail, it didn't deter him from pushing forward.

All for a simple dream and nothing else.

At first, Red had wanted to prove to himself that he could do it with his own strength. Now he knew, though, that his skills would never have been enough to make it through the underground. Could he have made it through the spider's nest with his own power? Would he have made it through the enormous expanse after that?

It was a silly thought, and maybe Viran had always known that, but not once had the man been any less driven about escaping. In that sense, Red could only recognize his own inferiority. And yet, here he was, while the old soldier had died without ever having the opportunity to put his plan into motion.

It was unfair, but nothing about their situation had ever been fair. Red accepted that there were levels of strength that no amount of cleverness or cunning could make up for.

That was why he didn't feel disappointed that his own power had proven insufficient for the journey. It was why he'd accepted his lucky chances. He had done the best he could at every moment, so perhaps fate had decided to reward him. Or perhaps this had all been preordained.

The strange blob's figure flashed in his mind.

It didn't matter. Now Red was through it all. He had achieved his goal. Now he could seek a fair beginning, he could explore the world and not have to rely on luck anymore. It was all he could ask for.

A few hours later, Red sensed it. A chilly breeze striking his face. He had only ever felt it when he approached the exchange point with the guards.

The air of the surface.

He was near.

He was going to make it.

With his luck, Red expected something to pop up and bar his way forward. Yet nothing appeared.

His mind wandered again, thinking back to the very first day he'd awakened in these caves. Covered in unfamiliar clothing, alone, with nothing but a moonstone by his side illuminating the darkness. The first thing he remembered feeling wasn't fear. It wasn't anger. It wasn't joy, either.

It was emptiness. Like something had been taken from him, leaving an enormous vacuum he had no means to fill. His memories of those early days were fuzzy. He didn't remember how he'd survived, how he'd met the other slaves, or how he'd lost his original clothes.

Red often thought that his lack of recollection from those initial days was a side effect of his sudden awakening. For all he knew, it was indeed the case, but as he approached the surface, certain things came back to him. Not complete memories, but flickers here and there, images showing what had happened.

There was a man. An old man. He had taken care of him when he couldn't do it himself. Red couldn't remember his name or face, but he knew this person was important to him. He recalled a conversation back then when the dying slave asked him for his name, and he had nothing to give.

"We'll call you—"

Red looked up, startled. He examined his surroundings, looking for the source of the voice, but there was nothing. He continued walking, more memories returning to him.

This time it was in another place—a small chamber filled with soft purple light. The old man was still there, and he was showing something to Red. The slave pointed at a spot on the wall and Red saw it. A small dark blob, pulsing like a beating heart.

The man smiled. "There's our salvation."

And then he walked towards the strange being.

It was the last time he ever saw him.

Huh?

Something flashed past his eyes. Not in his memory, but in the real world.

Red caught another glimpse—right in front of him, the image of that same weathered old man, with that same sincere smile persisting on his face no matter the situation. A good person.

He extended a hand towards Red as if offering his help.

Red stopped and closed his eyes for a few seconds. When he opened them again, the figure was still there, but he didn't hesitate any longer. He kept walking forward, straight towards the image.

He didn't stop even as they were about to collide.

The image of the old man dissipated into mist and the path forward was revealed to Red once more.

"Pretend that they aren't there. Pretend that they aren't there. Pretend that they aren't there."

He repeated the old piece of wisdom that Viran had told him under his breath.

Other things also appeared. He saw Viran, covered in blood, sitting against the cave wall. He was smiling at Red, mocking him. Viran knew something that he didn't, and it had always bothered him. It wasn't just about the curse. It was about his origin. He felt compelled to stop and ask the dying figure what it was hiding.

But instead, Red just walked past it, and this image, too, dissolved into mist.

Then there was Gruff's disembodied head, his eyes full of hatred. He remembered how the giant had given him food during the first year he'd been down here. How he, Gruff, and the elder had talked to each other, sharing tales about the surface. Red also remembered Gruff's expression when he learned of the old man's death. It bore a striking resemblance to the one the head wore right now. He felt compelled to ask for forgiveness, to tell him it was not his fault.

He kept walking, and the head disappeared.

The blob was there too, smiling at him with its smug mouth. Red remembered when they had made the deal. He didn't know why he'd returned after the old man's death, but he had either way. He felt angry. Angry at being tricked. He wanted to punch the dark being. It was a foreign feeling.

Yet he kept walking. The blob's figure didn't dissipate into mist, but Red moved past it either way.

He saw other things he didn't understand.

An azure tower from which shining threads extended into the horizon.

A crimson wolf drowning in a river of blood.

A burning black heart that threatened to consume everything in its path.

A golden star that held together the firmament.

A silver sword that flew through the sky for eternity.

A green sphere that depicted the true face of a nightmare.

A purple light that led to another world.

Red felt these things calling to him, as if he'd reached a threshold where everything in the world met. But he didn't answer.

Voices whispered to him. They told him he was cursed, how he would never amount to anything in life, how all his efforts were in vain. But Red knew they were lying.

He'd already made it this far.

The illusions kept trying to drag him back, tempting him, threatening him. But he knew they couldn't stop him.

Because they weren't real.

Ahead, a soft light slowly grew as the tunnel opened up. The stream widened, its surface flashing with a white reflection. Small unfamiliar plants clung to the riverbed and the cave walls, and the ground beneath his bare feet changed into brownish moist clumps. Fresh air he'd never breathed before entered his lungs.

At first, he thought they were more illusions, but as he walked through, they didn't dissipate. Red gradually felt as if all the exhaustion and pain in his body ceased to exist, and his steps hastened.

Ahead, a large opening was blocked by growing vines, but he could see glimpses of the world beyond through the gaps. Red let go of the cave wall and moved forward on his own. Before he knew it, he was shoving the plants aside and opening a way forward.

Then he saw it.

A body of water that extended well beyond anything he'd ever witnessed before, flowing downstream. The rivulet was merely a small arm of a vast river containing so much clear water that he thought his old knowledge of the world's size was laughable.

When Red looked closely, he saw something floating on the undisturbed surface of the river. No, it wasn't floating. It was reflecting on it, shimmering. Flecks of light, more than Red could count, and then a large circle in the middle of it all.

He looked up.

A dark, endless sky appeared before his eyes. But it wasn't all darkness.

Countless stars of various colors painted the firmament, swimming amidst a blue nebula that split the heavens in half.

But there was something brighter.

A white disc larger than everything else in the night sky. Red recognized it instinctively.

The moon.

His hand reached up, trying to touch it, but it was too far. The illusions had long since dissipated, and at that point, Red knew.

He was finally free.

CHAPTER 46

ENCOUNTER

A FEW MINUTES LATER, Red had still barely left the cave's entrance. He held a clump of leaves between his fingers, taking in their fresh and earthy scent. He didn't take a bite out of it, even though he felt compelled to do so. While Red had heard the surface was nowhere near as dangerous as the underground, what if he just so happened to pick up something poisonous?

However, even his hunger was pushed to the back of his mind as he examined the plants. They were unlike the moss and fungi Red knew from the underground—they had roots, stems, leaves, and fragrant flowers.

And there were more further ahead. On the other side of the river, Red could see towering vegetation, dozens of thick trunks with branches and leaves, towering far above him.

Trees.

This was where the wood the slaves used came from. They looked much bigger than he'd imagined, and with so many of them clustered together, Red could hardly distinguish one from the other. But there was still the deep, rushing river he had to cross first.

Curious, Red crouched down by the river and submerged his hand. The cold liquid flowed around his fingers. Although the surface of the water looked calm, what he felt told a different story. He could only imagine the force this river could muster against a person caught in its current.

Crossing it was obviously not a good idea.

Only now did Red bother to examine the area he'd come from. The mouth of the cave was almost completely covered by vines and other hanging plants, and the opening blended into the rocky hill face that rose high above. Red examined his surroundings and found a path curving around the contours of the cliff, covered by shrubs.

He couldn't see where the route led, but right now, it was his only option. With the natural light of the moon, the few moonstones he still had provided little in the way of illumination, so he stored them in his pouch and made his way forward.

Red kept an eye out for any creatures waiting in ambush. He'd heard the surface wasn't as treacherous as the underground, but there were still things that could kill you if you weren't careful. He used his cleaver to hack his way through the undergrowth, but thankfully, there didn't seem to be any monsters hiding among the leaves.

Soon enough, the cliff wall sloped down, providing a way to climb the hill. He ascended the path, using his weapon as a crutch, until he reached the ridge.

It seemed Red had underestimated the scope of his surroundings. There were trees as far as the eye could see, and a series of hills blocked off his view of the horizon. Wherever he looked, he was met by an endless sea of greenery.

The color was nothing like the moonstones, though. These greens were darker, and Red could sense an abundance of life flowing from everything. When he looked down, he also saw how big the river truly was. It extended into the distance before it snaked behind some large hills.

For a second, Red just closed his eyes. He could feel it in every breath, the taste of nature—of life—flooding into his lungs. It was so different from anything he'd ever felt before. The images, the smell, the noise—

The noise?

Red was momentarily startled by the sound in his ears but understanding quickly dawned on him. These noises had always been there, beneath the loud roar of the river. And there were so many of them.

Some faint, others loud. Some constant, others irregular.

All around him, Red could hear them. Animal life, present in every corner of the forest. So many unfamiliar calls, and more of them joining with every passing second. It was almost deafening at first, but eventually, it started to feel relaxing.

He was baffled and excited at the same time.

When he scanned the forest, though, he couldn't find any animals. But they were there, buried beneath the sea of trees. Red could only imagine what was hiding in the thicket, what kinds of strange animals lived on the surface.

Red climbed down the ridge, relishing the feeling of grass under his bare feet. It didn't take long for him to arrive at the foot of the hill, where a few isolated trees grew. Red walked up to the closest one, touching its large trunk and examining the nooks in its bark.

It looked and felt old, its surface coarse to the touch. Above, the main body of the plant split into branches that diverged into even smaller offshoots. Green leaves grew from the arms of the tree, blotting out the star-studded sky. A bed of leaves lay around the roots, some of them brown and wrinkled. These were their dead counterparts, Red reasoned.

Questions came to his mind, but as he got up, Red saw so much more to explore. He decided not to waste too much time on a single thing.

No farther than twenty meters away, the number of trees multiplied, creating a dense forest. There was more space to walk between them than he would've guessed from afar, but the canopy blocked the moonlight from the forest floor. The way ahead looked much darker than it had from on top of the hill, and Red hesitated for a second.

In the end, he made his way in, using a moonstone to guide him. He hadn't walked farther than a few steps when he saw something in the corner of his vision. He froze and twirled around to face it.

At first glance, he couldn't see anything. However, as he kept peering through the dark, he recognized a shape.

What is that?

A small creature was hiding in the grass. It had pristine white fur—which resembled the fur Viran used on his bed—and oversized ears that stood upright from the sides of its head. It held something within its small paws that it nibbled at with its large incisors. And then there were the eyes—blood-red, unblinking and, unlike any other animal Red had ever seen before, with dark pupils.

The creature didn't seem dangerous, but its appearance was so bizarre that he couldn't help but be taken by surprise. Curiosity came over him, and Red tried to retreat unnoticed to observe from a safe spot. But in his astonishment, he didn't notice where he was walking.

A twig snapped under his foot with a crack.

The creature looked at him, and for a split second, his breath caught in his throat. Then the small beast turned around and bolted in the other direction.

Red watched as the monster fled, when suddenly something swooped down from the sky. A winged beast almost the size of Red dove and grabbed the smaller creature within its talons. He heard a shriek from the prey before it was promptly silenced.

Red barely had enough time to look over the predator before it flew off into the air, carrying the white animal within its grip. He tried to follow it, but it soared into the tree canopy and disappeared.

Red didn't know how long he stood frozen in place. Eventually, he snapped out of his daze and walked towards the spot where the smaller creature had been caught. After brushing past some grass, he saw a dark, viscous fluid had dripped onto the surrounding plants.

He rubbed the liquid between his fingers and brought it closer to his face, examining it under the moonlight.

Crimson.

Red held it under his nose. A familiar scent greeted him, sweet and metallic.

Blood.

Not the insect kind, but something similar in color and smell to human blood.

The revelation excited Red. With no further hesitation, he investigated the sea of trees and walked into its embrace.

In less than ten minutes, Red saw more kinds of life than he'd seen in two years underground. Birds of all sizes and feathers perched in the tree canopy above his head. Small critters, like the one he'd seen before, made their burrows along the roots of the trees. Even bigger animals, with large tails and human-sized bodies, roamed the forest floor.

None seemed too keen on bothering Red, though, and it made sense. Although some of them looked dangerous, with vicious claws and teeth, Red didn't feel the same sense of danger as he'd felt from the giant insects in the underground. Fortunately, it seemed he had emerged in a relatively safe area, but he didn't lower his guard.

He also found a few clearings within the thicket of trees. Those hadn't been apparent when he looked at the forest from above, and they were more common than he'd expected.

They allowed him to look at the sky, and it was from one that he noticed something unexpected.

It was a smoke trail, rising straight into the sky.

He had seen this kind of thing before. The slaves sometimes made bonfires that emitted smoke in the caves, too.

That means...

People.

Red hesitated. This wasn't necessarily good news. In fact, during most of his life in the underground, he had avoided any human contact for his own safety. He'd been told that people weren't as vicious on the surface, and that might be true, but it was hard for Red to let go of his caution.

Still, he knew that eventually he would need to get out of this forest and find civilization. He had no idea where he was, and this might be the only opportunity he might come across in days. He couldn't let it pass by.

However, he first took some precautions. He found a spot he could easily remember and buried all his belongings in the dirt. The insectoid crystal, the map, the cleaver, the moonstones—everything. If he was carrying nothing on his person, then people would have no reason to rob him and might help him instead. Not to mention, he wasn't aware of the situation on the surface, and it would be dangerous to reveal any clues about his status as a slave in the moonstone mines.

After that was done, he moved toward the trail of smoke. It took longer than he expected, but eventually Red saw the bright-orange glow of a bonfire in the middle of a clearing. Three figures were standing around it, but from his distance, he couldn't make out many details.

He sneaked towards them under heavy cover, intent on observing before making contact.

But when he was within fifty meters, one of the figures turned in his direction and raised something in their hands. Red felt a premonition of danger and dove behind a tree.

With a thunk, something pierced deeply into the bark, wood splinters flying everywhere. Red felt his heart beating out of his chest and didn't dare to move.

"Who's there?" an angry female voice called from the bonfire's direction.

"I'm... I mean no harm," Red said, his voice shivering from the effort.

A response didn't come immediately, but he could hear whispers of hushed conversation.

"... a child?"

"... doing here...?"

The quiet voices started to sound distant, and Red looked down at his bleeding shoulder as if he'd suddenly remembered something important. Was it his pain, his fever, his exhaustion? Did he suddenly get healed? No, that wasn't it.

His injuries were still there. As if his body was suddenly reminded of them, the adrenaline and curiosity of achieving his lifelong dream disappeared, and his injuries and exhaustion hit him all at once.

That's right, I'm dying...

"... what are you doing here?"

Red couldn't hear the voice clearly anymore.

"I'm... I'm..." He tried to get his words out, but the world around him dissolved into black.

"What... say?"

Red couldn't gather the strength to reply. He collapsed to the ground with a thud and fell unconscious.

CHAPTER 47

PEOPLE

RED FELT A WARM, soft sensation against his back. He recognized it. He'd felt it before, when he'd awakened in Viran's tent. A cushiony fur and a fluffy material.

Bedding.

For the first time in what felt like forever, Red was sleeping on something other than cold stone. While he wanted nothing more than to relish the feeling, the situation filled him with alarm.

What happened?

Red tried to open his eyes, but he was met with a brightness that nearly blinded him. He squinted, blocking the light, as his vision adapted to his surroundings.

A clear blue sky appeared, with no sign of the stars or the darkness of the night. The vivid, unfamiliar color sent him into a daze, and he almost forgot about his situation.

"... doing in the middle of nowhere?"

Snippets of conversation dragged him out of his reverie. Red recognized the voice—it was the woman who'd screamed at him as he approached the camp.

"But didn't you check him already, Miss Valt?" someone else said—another female voice.

"Don't play dumb with me, girl! Just because I didn't find anything wrong with him doesn't mean he's safe."

Unless another stranger had wandered into their camp while he was unconscious, Red guessed they were talking about him. He shifted around, trying to turn toward the two women, but instead saw someone sitting and staring at him.

A man sat cross-legged by his side. He had sharp features and an unkempt appearance, grime and coal coating his skin. A large and messy beard covered his face, even bigger than Viran's, and long black hair flowed down his back. He wore leather armor and a black cloak draped over his shoulders.

His hands were currently cutting an apple up into pieces and shoving them into his mouth. However, his keen gaze never wandered from Red, who couldn't discern anything other than seriousness from his expression. Red chose not to avert his eyes either, and a silent staring contest started between them as the conversation continued in the background.

The angry woman continued to berate her companion in an authoritative tone. "This is a risk we don't have to take, no matter how much sympathy you may feel for—"

The man cut her off. "He's awake."

The discussion immediately stopped.

"What?" the same woman asked.

"He's awake," he repeated.

Footsteps approached, and another figure appeared behind the man. A tall woman sporting stern features, with bronze skin and a powerful physique, glared at Red. Her brown hair was tied in a long braid that reached her waist. She wore a similar armor to her associate, except it consisted of more leather layers held together by metal pins.

She crossed her arms and stared down at him. "Well, how long are you going to lie there? We need to ask you some questions."

Red didn't respond. Instead, he looked at his left shoulder. The wound had been closed and patched up with a bandage, and although he still couldn't move his arm properly, the pain had diminished substantially. His right hand touched his previously broken ribs, where he found a similar dressing tied around his chest.

He still felt weak, but sitting up didn't prove too difficult. Red tried to stand, but a hand held him down.

"You're still injured. You don't have to get up," another voice said from behind him.

Red twisted around. A young woman with short black hair smiled at him sincerely, making him feel at ease. Unlike her companions, she wasn't wearing any armor. Instead, she was dressed in loose robes tied at the waist by a black sash.

However, he could sense remarkable strength from her hand that gripped his shoulder. Not enough to hurt, but enough to hold him in place. Instantly, his ease turned into caution.

For the first time since he'd awakened, he spoke. "I'm fine."

"Are you sure?" the young woman asked with concern.

He nodded, but she hesitated.

"You heard him," the armored woman said. "Now, stop holding him and let's get this over with so we can get back on the road."

Her kind companion shook her head. "Fine." She turned to Red. "But if you feel too much pain, don't hesitate to tell us." With that, she let go of his shoulder.

Red nodded. He braced himself with his one good arm and sat up fully, getting a clearer look at the encampment. Ahead, he could see the ashes of the night's bonfire, as well as a handful of large bags stuffed with supplies. What caught his attention, though, were the weapons lying against the packs —a large steel saber, a wooden bow and a quiver full of arrows, and six knives all sheathed in holsters.

In the mines, it would've been a trove of treasures that any slave would kill for.

As Red scanned the weapons, he heard the armored woman clearing her throat. "What are you staring at, kid?"

"Nothing," Red said.

She gave him a suspicious look but didn't press him further. "What were you doing alone in this forest?"

The bluntness of the question caught Red off guard. As he was thinking about how to answer, the younger woman interjected.

"You've scared him." She gave her companion a disapproving look.

"Scared him?" The warrior looked offended. "He's the one who almost scared us shitless last night! He's lucky Rog didn't shoot him dead!"

"You're not helping. Let me talk to him." She crouched down, facing him at eye level with a smile on her calm face. "My name's Eiwin." She extended her right hand in greeting. "What's your name?"

She was trying to be friendly, but it had an adverse effect on Red. He'd never met someone so kind before, and he felt suspicious about her intentions, though he kept his expression blank.

"Red."

A snort came from behind him. "That's not a name, that's just a word!" the armored woman said. "What, did they just decide to call you that because of your hair?"

Red looked at her and nodded.

"Uh—" The woman was taken aback. "Right. Listen, Red, we're quite curious about what a kid your age is doing in the middle of nowhere with all those injuries."

He didn't answer, sinking into thought instead.

The warrior quickly grew impatient. In her eyes, his pauses seemed equivalent to lies. "Listen here, you little—"

"Miss Valt!" Eiwin interrupted, sounding stern for the first time. "Let me handle this."

The tall woman—Miss Valt, apparently—looked like she still wanted to say something, but in the end, she just grunted and walked away. Red saw her sit on a nearby log, staring daggers at him.

"Red." Eiwin called him, and Red turned to look at her. She wore the same calm smile on her face, and her voice regained its soft tone.

"What Miss Valt wants to know is how someone as young as you ended up in the middle of this forest with such serious injuries."

"That's the same thing I asked—"

The warrior's protests were silenced by an angry glare from Eiwin.

She turned to him again. "So, what happened, Red? Where are your parents right now? Did something attack you while you were all traveling?"

He kept on thinking. Just as the warrior was about to protest again, he answered.

"I don't remember," he said, lying as naturally as he breathed.

"Bullshit!" Miss Valt shouted, promptly getting up from her seat and approaching him.

Eiwin put herself between the warrior and Red. "Miss Valt, please!"

"What, you really believe him, that he just appeared in this place with no memory at all?" She stopped in her tracks, her gaze still trained on Red.

"Why not? We've seen stranger things happen. Having amnesia after a near-death experience isn't far-fetched."

"You know damn well it's not that simple! After all that's happened, this kid just appears out of nowhere and we're supposed to pretend it's not weird?"

Miss Valt pointed at him. "Look at that wound on his shoulder. That's not something a normal animal is capable of—and not something a normal kid could survive!"

Eiwin frowned. "What's your point?"

"That's an attack from a monster, and a damn strong one at that! There haven't been any sightings in this region for months, and now this boy looks like he met one and came out alive! I bet he's even opened some of his Spiritual Veins, or else there's no way he could've survived." Her attention turned back to Eiwin. "Is that not weird to you?"

"It is, but it doesn't mean it's his fault." Eiwin shook her head. "What would you have us do? Abandon him here and sentence him to death?"

"Of course not!" Miss Valt sounded offended. "If he doesn't want to give us answers, that's fine. But he's a liability and we can't risk bringing him with us. We'll give him some food and point the way towards town, and he'll have to fend for himself."

"That's the same as sentencing him to death! With his wounds, how far do you think he'll make it? There might not be any monsters here, but there are still plenty of animals that could hurt him."

"You're letting your feelings get in the way of reason again, Eiwin! We both heard the warnings Hector gave us. How can you just risk everything for a kid you don't even know?"

At that, Eiwin simply closed her eyes and took a deep breath. Red had watched the argument in silence, waiting for the result.

Finally, Eiwin opened her eyes and gazed intently at the warrior. "I call for a vote."

Miss Valt scoffed in disbelief. "You can't be serious. How can this be a matter of concern for the Sect?"

"That's for Hector to judge. We're all elders here, so our votes carry the same weight." She turned to their third companion. "Mister Rog!"

Rog, who had been silently eating his apple during the entire discussion, looked over at Eiwin in confusion.

"Huh?"

"Miss Valt wants us to give food to the boy and let him on his way, while I want to take him back to the Sect. Our votes are tied, so what do you suggest we do?"

Rog took a few moments to think. Throughout the exchange, the man had looked completely uninterested, and now the burden of the decision had suddenly been thrown into his lap.

Miss Valt threw her hands up. "This is stupid—he wasn't even listening! How can he make a decision?"

"These are the rules, Miss Valt, and we have to respect them," Eiwin said. "So, Mister Rog, what is your vote?"

The man didn't reply. Instead, he turned to Red, who was just as confused by the turn of events.

"Do you know how to hunt?" Rog asked.

Red thought for a moment but eventually shook his head.

"Do you know how to shoot a bow and arrow?"

"No."

"Do you know how to set up traps?"

"No."

"Do you know how to forage?"

"No."

"Do you know how to cook?"

"No."

"Do you know how to skin animals?"

"No."

"Do you know how to use a knife?"

Red paused. "Yes."

Rog turned to look at the two women. "We'll take him with us."

CHAPTER 48

FOREST

UNFORTUNATELY, Red wasn't given much time to rest before they set off. Narcha, the given name of the female warrior, insisted they should be on their way, and not even Eiwin's protests could change her mind. The younger women offered to support Red as they walked, but he refused.

His left arm had been secured in a sling, and his fever had disappeared. He was still wounded and weak, but no longer to the point of incapacitation. Besides, even if that had been the case, he still wouldn't have felt comfortable accepting Eiwin's help. Thankfully, they didn't seem to be in a hurry, and Red kept up with their pace.

"I'm gonna go," Rog said, unstrapping the wooden bow from his back.

Narcha, who held the vanguard, grunted in response. Rog seemed to take this as approval and immediately dove into the sea of trees. Red watched him venture off the path, and soon enough, there was no trace of the man.

"He's hunting," Eiwin said.

Red nodded, still following Narcha's steady steps while examining the forest. His curiosity had returned, but he still had a lot on his mind. Suffice it to say, he didn't completely trust these people, but knew he was still alive because of them.

Even if they had some ulterior motive, they had helped him, and the least Red could do was follow them for now. They also knew the way, so it was much safer to travel with them. But that didn't mean he had put his guard down, either.

He spotted a branch with a bulbous, red object hanging from it. Red had learned from the other slaves that some plants on the surface grew edible fruits, and a few were even considered delicacies. He didn't know what they looked like, but the description he recalled matched with the item before him.

It was only then Red remembered his hunger. He didn't want to owe these people even more by asking for food, so he would find some on his own.

At first glance, the red fruit looked out of reach, but that didn't mean he couldn't get it. Red assessed his body's condition, stretching his limbs. His muscles were still sore, but climbing up a tree shouldn't prove to be too challenging for him. Just as he prepared to move, though, he saw a figure fly over him.

Eiwin jumped and plucked the fruit from the branch in one fluid motion, landing in front of him. She turned around and smiled at Red.

"Here," she said, offering him the fruit. "You must be hungry."

Red hesitated for a second but ended up accepting it. He considered examining the fruit to see if it was poisonous, but since Eiwin said nothing, he dug in. With a crunch, his teeth bit into the fruit, a sweet and juicy flavor filling his mouth.

It was a taste Red had never known before, and it didn't take long for him to devour it. Eiwin continued to regard him with her serene and smiling expression, which made him feel uncomfortable. Once finished, he nodded in thanks and turned to follow her companion.

Narcha had already moved down the path, either not noticing that they had stopped or not caring.

"Do you have anything you want to ask?" Eiwin suddenly said from beside him. No matter how hard Red tried, it seemed impossible to avoid the strange woman's curiosity.

"No," he replied curtly, trying to end the conversation before it even started.

Eiwin wasn't dissuaded. "Really? Nothing at all? I noticed how you look at everything around you. Is this the first time you've seen a forest?"

"From what I remember, yes," Red said. Since avoiding the conversation wasn't working, he tried to make her lose interest.

Unfortunately, that didn't work either.

"This entire region is covered in trees, and it's really easy to get lost if you don't know how to navigate it," she said. "We have some experience traveling out here, but if we didn't have Rog with us, then we would probably still get lost now and then."

Red nodded. He didn't understand her intentions, but he had a feeling there was a hidden meaning behind her words.

The underground was also vast, full of tunnels leading to nowhere and everywhere, but it couldn't compare to the surface. Here you had no tunnel to direct you down a path, and if left to his own devices, Red wouldn't know where to start.

"How old are you?" Eiwin asked.

"Ten."

"That's very young. How many Spiritual Veins have you opened?"

Red wasn't startled by this question, considering her warrior companion had already guessed as much. He decided to tell the truth, since he didn't know if they had a way to check.

"Two."

"That's not bad for someone your age," Eiwin said. "Did you have a master, or did your parents teach you?"

"I don't remember," Red told her.

She was probing for information. Perhaps using a softer approach than Narcha, but she was curious all the same. Her help with the apple didn't feel dishonest, but she still had an ulterior motive.

This method of trying to lower his guard made Red even warier of Eiwin. Since she wasn't giving up, he indulged her in conversation to keep her from prodding further.

"What was the name of that thing I ate?" he asked.

"You've never eaten that before?" Eiwin seemed surprised. "It's called a plum. You'll find a lot of those in this region. What did you—"

"What's this called?" Red cut her off, pointing at some white flowers nearby.

"That?" The lady seemed taken aback by his sudden surge of interest. "It's a bloodroot."

"And this tree? Does it have a name?"

"Ah, well, that's just an oak—"

"What about that over there?"

Over the next few minutes, Red bombarded her with questions about the forest and all the things living in it. Since he wanted to learn and she wanted to talk, he found the perfect solution to keep her speaking without asking him tough questions. Although overwhelmed, Eiwin didn't lose her patience and calmly answered his questions. Red even learned the name of the white creature he had seen when he first entered the forest.

Rabbit.

When the slaves told him about the animals on the surface, they spoke about great eagles and fierce wolves, not things like rabbits. However, by the looks of it, the world up here was full of harmless beasts in just as large numbers as dangerous ones.

Red decided to ask about something that had been on his mind for a while. "What about the monsters Narcha was talking about?"

The warrior leading the group stumbled as he said this, but then continued to walk as if nothing had happened.

"Well..." Eiwin thought to herself for a few seconds. "There are some creatures which are naturally stronger than your average animal. They are quite dangerous and most of them are aggressive towards humans, so we call them monsters."

The description matched the giant insects Red had seen underground, so he understood why Narcha was so cautious.

"Is that why you're here? Hunting for monsters?"

"Not quite..." For the first time since they began talking, Eiwin hesitated. "As Miss Valt said, the monsters in this region have been disappearing, and we're trying to find out where they've run off to."

"If they're that dangerous, isn't it good that they're gone?" Red knew it wasn't as simple as that, but he continued to play the role of a naïve child.

"You could say that, but it's not as simple as you might think." She gestured at their surroundings. "You see, as dangerous as these monsters are, they've been part of this forest for thousands and thousands of years. They're an important part of nature, too, as much as a common rabbit or bird. For them to suddenly decide to leave this place, there might be something strange happening in the forest. Do you understand?"

Red nodded but didn't push her with any further questions. The only unusual thing about this forest that he could think of was the entrance into the mines hidden beneath the wall of vines. But there'd been no traces of anything going in or out of the entrance, so he couldn't see a connection. It was worth considering, but he didn't plan on telling Eiwin.

His thoughts were interrupted as he saw something flying above them. A large brown bird, its wingspan almost two meters in length. It looked like the one he'd seen the night before hunting the rabbit. Red watched the creature, bewildered by its ability to soar through the sky so smoothly.

"That's a great eared owl, one of the greatest hunters of the forest," Eiwin said, noticing his rapt gaze. "They can grow even bigger than that, and they're one of the most majestic—"

Suddenly, an arrow shot through the air like a bolt and struck the bird. It made a horrible shriek and fell to the trees below like a broken kite.

"—birds..." Eiwin trailed off, her expression embarrassed.

She put her hand on Red's back to hurry him along, but Rog's rough voice broke out from within the trees.

"We got dinner!"

CHAPTER 49

SKINNING

ROG REJOINED THE GROUP, this time carrying a bird bigger than a child on his back. Eiwin threw the man an ugly look, but seeing as Red didn't seem bothered, she didn't protest. Rather, he was extremely curious about the bow the hunter had used to shoot down the creature, and he couldn't help but examine the weapon from a distance.

"Shoo, kid, this one's mine." Rog frowned at Red as he saw him eyeing his bow.

Red didn't respond, but in his mind, he'd decided he would get his hands on a similar weapon as soon as possible.

For the next couple of hours, the journey was uneventful. Eiwin continued to pester him with questions while Red did his best to divert her attention with questions of his own. Their surroundings didn't change, even though he was sure they had walked countless kilometers. They took some detours because of the rough terrain, but Red felt like they had already covered more ground in a few hours than he had in a day down in the mines.

He felt tired from the effort, but before he said anything, Narcha called for a break.

"We'll rest here," she said.

Narcha, still sulking, walked off to a corner of the clearing and busied herself with her backpack.

Eiwin shook her head at her companion and turned to Red.

"Come," she said, pointing at a spot where Rog was already making himself comfortable. "We'll eat something."

Red followed her as she set a cloth over the grass and began taking all sorts of unfamiliar foods from her bag. But the items were pushed aside as the hunter plopped the large owl corpse on the ground in front of them.

"Rog!" Eiwin glared at him.

"What?" He seemed confused. "It needs skinning, or else how are we gonna cook it?"

"It's an owl, we don't... Never mind." She gestured at Red. "Come, we'll eat somewhere else."

"No, he stays," Rog said. "You're gonna help me skin this."

Red, lost, turned to Eiwin.

"That's ridiculous, Mister Rog. He was so badly hurt yesterday and now you want him to help you butcher an animal?" Despite her reprimanding words, her tone remained respectful. "Not to mention... he's just a kid."

"I learned this stuff when I was his age too. It'll be good for his future, trust me," Rog said. "Besides, that was the condition for me voting in favor of bringing him along."

"You never said that!"

"Wasn't it obvious?"

A loud laugh came from Narcha. Eiwin looked at Red with a troubled expression. Although she still hesitated, it was clear she didn't feel comfortable rejecting Rog's wishes, since he had helped her earlier. Unlike what she might have been expecting, though, Red was actually eager to learn.

"I'll do it," he said. "I've seen dead animals before."

"If... you say so." She shook her head in resignation before looking at the hunter. "Make sure to teach him properly! I'm quite aware of how you like to teach Allen about these things."

"Don't worry, don't worry... Here boy, come." Rog waved Red over, showing him a handful of blades. "I'll let you pick which knife you want to use."

Red examined the tools at his disposal. He didn't know the difference between them but chose the one which looked the most like his knife from the mines. After that, he sat down cross-legged by the man's side.

"Good. Now, first things first, we need to remove the skin before getting to the juicy parts." The hunter turned the bird over, placing it belly-up. "You see, the feathers of an animal like this are quite valuable. Useful for arrow fletchings, and merchants in the city will also buy them to make bedding or quilts, so we have to be careful not to damage them too much."

Rog picked up his own knife and positioned it near the center of the bird's torso.

"Birds have thin skin compared to most other animals, so you don't have to cut too deeply, but it's still good to be careful." With one hand, he pinched a section of the beast's pelt, and with the other, he used the knife to make a small cut. "Now, we want to peel the skin so it's not stuck to the meat. Then, we jam the knife in there and cut our way up to the neck."

Rog squeezed the knife under the incision and hacked his way up through the feathers until he was just short of the creature's head. He peeled the bird's chest skin back and revealed its pink flesh to Red, who had to admit it at least looked more pleasant than insect meat.

"Okay, I made my way up. Now you need to cut all the way down to its legs." He motioned with his knife in the air, showing the path Red should hack through. "It's important to make a straight cut to not damage the skin. Peel it down from the hole I made and keep a firm grip on the knife."

Red didn't move, instead just silently looking at the man.

"What are you waiting for?" Rog asked.

"I can't move my left hand."

The hunter, surprised, examined his injured arm as if noticing the sling for the first time. He winced. "Why did we save you in the first place if you can't even help with this?"

Red shrugged.

"Bah! Just go!" Rog shooed him away. "I'll deal with this myself!"

Red did as he was told, putting the knife down. When he got up, he saw Eiwin looking at him with a helpless expression.

"Don't worry about him," she said as Red approached. "Mister Rog is an... eccentric individual, but once you get to know him, you'll learn he's a good person at heart." She once more laid down her piece of cloth on the ground and set rations on top. "Now, let's eat. It's a long journey ahead, and you need to stay strong to recover from your wounds."

Red examined the food. He recognized the bread and what looked like pieces of dried meat, but there were other unfamiliar things as well.

"We eat rations during the day and only cook during the night, or else we would waste too much time," Eiwin said after noticing Red's questioning gaze. "It's not the best meal, but it should be enough to get you through."

Red obviously couldn't complain. Compared to what he ate in the underground, this was without exaggeration the best meal he'd ever seen. Without delay, he wolfed down the food in front of him like there was no tomorrow.

"Uh, you can slow down," Eiwin said as she watched his hurried munching. "We're not in a hurry and you should be careful not to choke."

Red didn't listen to her. In a matter of a few minutes, he had eaten most of his food, and felt the fullest he'd ever felt. Eiwin looked at him in wonder but decided against saying anything and started to eat.

As Red had nothing to do but wait, he considered his situation. More specifically, his shoulder and the bandages that covered it.

"What did you put on my wounds?" Red asked.

Eiwin was taken aback by the question. "We spread some medicinal paste on your shoulder and ribs. Your wounds, they were..." She paused. "Not good. We gave you some medicine that should help you recover and fight the symptoms, but it's still important for you to get proper treatment once you reach the city, or else it could get worse again."

That's how the fever disappeared, then...

He wondered what kind of medicine they'd used to help him recover so quickly, but he didn't want to snoop around too much. It appeared that even if he was no longer dying, Red still wasn't completely off the hook.

"How long is the journey to the... city?" he asked.

"Two and a half days of travel," Eiwin said. "We intended on going deeper into the forest, but..."

"... But you appeared," Narcha said, completing her sentence. "We could probably make it in two days if we hurried, but of course, we can't do that anymore, can we?"

"Are you in a hurry, Miss Valt?" Eiwin asked, raising her voice slightly.

"Hmph, just because there are no monsters anymore doesn't mean it's safe," Narcha said. "Rog told me he found signs of another camp up north. Now that there are no more man-eating beasts to worry about, this place has turned into a bandit nest."

"We're following the same path we came from, aren't we? If we found nothing on the way over, why should we worry about the way back?"

"You are very optimistic, Eiwin." Narcha snorted. "But there were no bandit tracks here yesterday when we passed through, so I hope you're right. I'm sure a few scoundrels are nothing for you to worry about, but you can't say the same for the kid."

Eiwin smiled. "I'm sure you won't let any of them get through you and hurt us, Miss Valt."

"Hmph." The warrior didn't rebuke her. "Get up. Rog has finished skinning the bird. I want to be over those hills before the day is done."

With that, Narcha marched off to gather her things.

Eiwin turned to Red. "You don't need to worry about her," she said. "Miss Valt is not the friendliest, but she would never let any of us come in harm's way while she's still standing."

He nodded. As far as Red could remember, every interaction with Narcha was full of veiled and unveiled threats to his life. However, he didn't know her as well as Eiwin, so he would take her word for it.

"Trust me, she's always like that with strangers, but when you get to know her, you'll learn she's a good person at heart."

"Do you say that a lot?" Red asked.

"Huh?" His words gave the woman pause. "I... suppose so, but you must believe me. She was like that when I met her too, but beneath her angry, obstinate and indifferent persona, she's a very kind person, and one of the only people in this world I would entrust with my life."

Her words didn't inspire much confidence in Red.

CHAPTER 50
AGE LIMIT

AFTER SOME DISCUSSION, Eiwin, Narcha and Rog decided that Rog would scout the way ahead. Although Red wasn't part of their conversation, they didn't hide it from him either. The hunter had found the tracks of around a dozen people in the surrounding forest, which alarmed them. That was about the size of Viran's group of strongest fighters, and if they were armed with better weapons, they would prove an enormous threat.

However, not once during the conversation did Red notice any kind of fear or hesitation. He gathered that these people were more powerful than the average slave, but to his surprise they didn't even seem to worry about taking on enemies four times their number. This gave him some reassurance, considering he was in no state to fight.

After they started traveling again, Eiwin approached him.

"You don't need to worry. Rog is just going ahead to make sure the way is safe," she said. "We don't want to fight if we can help it."

"How strong are you guys?" Red asked.

"Strong enough to protect you from anything in this forest, so don't worry." She gave him a reassuring smile, confusing his curiosity for concern.

Red didn't bother correcting her. He could see she had misconceptions about him, but correcting her seemed like more trouble than it was worth.

"What are bandits doing here in the forest?" he asked, changing the subject.

Eiwin's voice became serious. "They're wicked people who have chosen to rely on theft and violence to get by in life. They prey on travelers, robbing them of everything they have, including their lives..."

She trailed off, shaking her head with regret.

"Unfortunately, the disappearance of the monsters in the forest didn't bring us the safety we might have hoped for. Instead, it only replaced one danger with another. Except one is a mindless beast doing things out of instinct and survival, and the other..." She shuddered. "Is an individual who knows that their actions are evil but chooses to do them all the same."

Red could hear uncharacteristic anger behind Eiwin's words. He had touched upon a sensitive topic, and for a moment, she seemed to transform into a different person. Soon after, her expression returned to normal.

"We shouldn't talk about things like this," she said, her bright smile returning. "You're still too young to worry about the evils of the world, so it's best if you just let your seniors handle it."

Red wasn't sure how to answer, so he just nodded. Eiwin was the polar opposite of Viran, and he didn't know what to make of her. At least he wasn't worried she would backstab him.

The trio continued to walk in silence. with the occasional exchange between Red and Eiwin. The forest still held countless surprises, and his curiosity had barely been sated. Time passed quickly, and before he knew it, the sun was close to setting.

Narcha called their march to a stop. She turned to Eiwin. "We need to find somewhere to make camp before nightfall."

"Are we not waiting for Mister Rog?" Eiwin asked.

"How many times has he traveled with us before?" Narcha retorted. "He should know we don't walk after dark, so he's probably coming back soon. He'll find us then. Now, let's hurry—I don't want to trip on anything if I can help it."

With that, she was already walking away.

Eiwin turned towards Red, noticing his puzzled gaze. "She's right. Even with no monsters, it's bad to get caught here in the middle of the night." She motioned him over. "Let's go. We don't want to hear any more of her complaints, do we?"

"I'm still right here, you jerk!" Narcha called back.

Eiwin's grin widened, and she followed her companion with Red in tow.

Since Eiwin and Narcha were familiar with the forest, it didn't take long to find a suitable clearing. Narcha gathered branches and dry leaves for the fire. However, she didn't immediately light it, and instead sat against a tree and waited in silence.

Red stared at her in confusion.

"We're waiting for Rog," Eiwin said. "We need to know if it's safe to light the fire, or else we'll just be telling any bandits our position."

Red understood and also sat down.

An hour later, there was still no sign of the man.

The sun had set, and the starry night sky appeared overhead. Red wasn't bothered by the darkness, as he was too occupied with watching the stars. However, he found it hard to focus when Narcha started to pace around the camp in impatience.

She gritted her teeth. "That idiot is late."

"Do you think he found something?" Eiwin asked.

"How would I know?" Narcha threw her hands up. "Only the gods can guess what goes on in his head."

"Do you want to go look for him?"

"Hm..." Narcha hesitated. "No. I'm more likely to get lost and end up needing his help."

Red noticed the pair seemed relatively calm. "Aren't you worried?" he asked.

Narcha looked at him with a confused expression. "About what?"

"About your friend. What if something bad happened to him?"

"Something bad happening to Rog?" Narcha snorted. "If anything in this forest can hurt him, then I can guarantee you that we won't make it out alive—"

"What she means to say, Red," Eiwin said, cutting her off, "is that Rog is a very experienced hunter. He spent decades living in this forest. There's probably no one in the world who knows it better than him, so he'll be alright."

If that was indeed the case, there really was nothing to worry about. Red hadn't seen any surface monsters yet, but if they were as dangerous as those beneath the surface, then the man was truly capable.

Sure enough, half an hour later, a low whistle from the nearby foliage startled them.

"He's here," Narcha said, looking in the sound's direction.

Rog walked out from behind a tree trunk, carrying the bow on his back. The man had been twenty meters from them, yet they hadn't noticed him until he made his presence known. The hunter looked none the worse for wear.

"Where were you?" Narcha snapped.

"Was out scouting," Rog said.

"I know what you were doing! I mean, why did you take so long?"

"Oh. Found bandits camped up ahead."

Red perked up at the man's words, and Narcha's face turned serious.

"Did they see you?" she asked.

"No. At least I think not. Had to drop the bird so they didn't smell it, though, so no cooked owl for us tonight."

"How many?" Eiwin asked.

"Ten initially, thirteen by the time I left," Rog said. "More might have joined since then, but I couldn't tell you. I saw them snooping around the place where we camped a few days ago."

Narcha's expression worsened.

"Can we avoid them?" Eiwin asked.

The man scratched his chin. "It's possible, but we'd need to make quite a detour."

"We'll do that then—right, Miss Valt?" Eiwin asked, staring at her companion.

Narcha didn't respond immediately, occupied with her own thoughts. Finally, she turned to Rog and broke her silence. "How strong are they?"

"Miss Valt—"

Eiwin tried to interject, but Narcha raised her hand and cut her off.

"How strong, Rog?" she asked again.

"Run of the mill. Probably a few with opened veins, but nothing too tough..." The hunter paused, before grinning with a wicked smile. "Do you want to kill them?"

Narcha paused, but eventually nodded her head. "... Yes, we'll do it."

"Miss Valt, we have—"

"I know, I know. We have orders, priorities, and everything else, but think about this, Eiwin."

She pointed at the path they had been traveling.

"These people already have our trail. The next time we pass through this place, they could be waiting in ambush. Isn't it best to take them out while we still have the element of surprise?" She came closer to Eiwin. "I mean, what if they kill more innocent people after we let them go? Isn't it our responsibility to get rid of this evil?"

At that, Eiwin couldn't help but wince. Red noticed her throw a quick glance at him.

Narcha noticed as well. "You don't need to come, Me and Rog are more than capable of dealing with a few scoundrels. In the meantime, you can look after your new little brother."

"You..." For a moment, Eiwin's voice filled with anger, but she caught herself. "Very well, but be careful."

The warrior smiled. "We will." Narcha walked over to her bag, picking up her large steel saber. "Come on, Rog, lead the way!"

The man smiled. He tossed his bag aside, picked up his bow and quiver, and dove into the trees with Narcha in tow.

Soon, Red couldn't hear their steps anymore.

"I'm sorry you had to listen to that, but she is right." Eiwin sat down across from him. "These bandits are a blight on this land, and if we don't get rid of them, there's no telling who they might hurt next."

Red, however, had other concerns on his mind. "Can't we go watch?"

"Excuse me?" Eiwin stared at him in surprise.

"I mean..." Red tried thinking of a way to rephrase his question. "I want to see Narcha and Rog fight against the bandits. They look really strong."

"Oh." She sighed. "I don't think that's a good idea. Those two are... very violent when they fight. Even I find it hard to watch sometimes. Besides, it would be hard for you to keep up with their pace. By the time we arrived, it might already be over."

Red couldn't help but recall the scene he'd witnessed when the giant insects had ambushed the slaves near the mine's exit. But he wouldn't tell Eiwin about that, and she still had a point with their difference in strength.

The conversation created an excellent opportunity for him to ask something that had been on his mind. "How many veins have they opened?"

"All of them," Eiwin said, more than willing to sate his curiosity. "Both of them have already opened all twelve of their Spiritual Veins."

This revelation surprised Red. Were each of them as strong as Viran, then?

"What about you?" he asked.

She smiled. "I have opened eleven veins, so for the time being, they have me beat."

No wonder they're so confident.

"Are they trying to open their Spiritual Seas, then?" Red asked.

"Uh..."

Eiwin's mouth hung open. Had he said something that shouldn't have been said?

"Did your master not teach you about the age limit to open Spiritual Seas?" she asked.

Red shook his head.

"Well, it's a sore spot for many practitioners in the world, so you should be careful about asking these types of questions around them," she said. "The way it works is that the older you get, the harder it becomes to open your Spiritual Sea. Once you reach a certain age, the task becomes so difficult that it's almost impossible to accomplish through training alone. Mister Rog is already far past that age, and Miss Valt is fast approaching it."

"And what is the age limit?" he asked.

"There's no exact number, but the oldest person I've ever heard opening their Spiritual Sea was twenty-six years old."

Great.

On top of all Red's other worries, now he had a time limit.

CHAPTER 51

ILLUSIONARY BARRIER

RED WENT over what he'd just learned. The time limit to open his Spiritual Sea put new pressure on him. Technically, he still had fifteen years to do it, but each Spiritual Vein would get harder to open. Progression would stop being measured in months and instead be counted in years.

However, Red realized he still lacked some crucial information.

"How old is Narcha?" Red asked.

"She's twenty years old," Eiwin replied.

"Is six years not enough to open her Spiritual Sea?"

When she'd told him about the age limit and how Narcha was close to it, Red thought she would be one or two years away, not more than five.

"Unfortunately, it's not that simple," Eiwin said. "You see, opening your Spiritual Sea is not the same as opening your Spiritual Veins. The difficulty of opening each acupoint may differ from person to person, but it's a simple process of accumulation. With a good supply of Spiritual Energy, anyone can open all their veins before they're twenty-six, but that's not the case with the Spiritual Sea... Do you understand?"

Eiwin paused, looking at Red. He was confused by the question but just nodded in response. When Viran had taught him things, he hadn't bothered asking if he understood. Eiwin was clearly more thorough and seemed to enjoy teaching him.

"Good." She smiled. "Basically, pure energy alone can't open your Spiritual Sea. Well, that's not technically true, but the results wouldn't be ideal... Anyways, that's beside the point—you can't just throw energy at it and expect to succeed as you can with a Vein Opening Technique. Here, I'll show you."

With that, Eiwin stood. She picked up a branch and drew a large circle in the dirt.

"Think of this as your Spiritual Sea. It's an organ inside of your body just like your heart and brain, and your Spiritual Veins too. However, it has a property that makes it very special." She looked up at Red, eyes shining with enthusiasm. "It doesn't actually have a form."

Eiwin stared at him earnestly, as if expecting something.

"How so?" Red asked, his voice and expression remaining as flat as usual.

"Oh..." Eiwin looked disappointed but didn't let it deter her. "Well, it's hard to explain, but this organ technically exists in a different dimension from our own, one we can't see with the naked eye. However, certain parts of the Spiritual Sea can interact with the material world, like this..."

With her stick, she made small gaps at the boundary of the circle.

"These spaces indicate areas you can use to reach into your Spiritual Sea. The gaps are tiny, and they exist between real and illusory states, so you can't touch them with your hands. But there is something that you can use to interact with these gaps. A special substance that is the foundation of how everything works in this world..." She trailed off, waiting for Red to finish her sentence.

"Spiritual Energy?" he asked.

"Yes, you got it!"

She acted excited that he had guessed the right answer, but Red felt this was something even a child could figure out.

"Spiritual Energy can not only pass between these gaps, but it can also help widen them once it's through." She erased more of the circle. "As these gaps grow, the barrier separating the Spiritual Sea from the material world starts to disappear, and the organ takes on a real shape and appearance within your body. Once the barrier is gone, then you can say you have truly opened your Spiritual Sea, and a world of possibilities will open before you."

These ideas weren't easy for Red to visualize. Different dimension? Illusionary barrier? None evoked a simple image in one's mind, but he understood the concepts, at least. However, he still had a few doubts.

"You said that opening the Spiritual Sea is different from opening the

Spiritual Veins, but isn't erasing these barriers also a process of accumulation?"

"That's right!" Eiwin said. "That is what I was just about to explain. Unfortunately, the barrier can restore itself extremely quickly. Erasing it is something that must be done all at once, and failure means you have to start your attempt over again."

Red finally understood where the true difficulty came from. This wasn't something you could work on for a long time, but an obstacle you had to get through in one go.

"How hard is it?" he asked. Eiwin had told him what was needed to open the Spiritual Sea, not how people went about it.

She hesitated for a few seconds. "The difficulty depends on two things. One of them is manipulating Spiritual Energy. You need to be able to direct the energy towards the position of your Spiritual Sea and funnel it through the gaps without losing control. It's something that requires extreme precision and a large amount of Spiritual Energy to succeed."

"But don't you need your Spiritual Sea to control Spiritual Energy?" Red asked, perplexed by this contradiction.

"You're correct," Eiwin said. "Technically, one can only completely control it when they open their Spiritual Sea, but once all twelve veins are open, you have a small degree of control over the Spiritual Energy in your body. However, in most people's cases, this control alone is rarely enough to accomplish the task."

"Most people?"

"Yes." A troubled look appeared on her face. "That brings me to the second thing. Talent."

She used her stick to draw another circle into the dirt.

"You see, people have different levels of sensitivity to Spiritual Energy. That sensitivity will not only help you open your Spiritual Veins, but it can also assist you with your Spiritual Sea too."

"So talent will help with controlling the Spiritual Energy and breaking apart the barrier?" Red asked.

When he thought about it that way, it made sense. If one was more sensitive to the energy in their body, they would obviously have an easier time controlling it.

"Yes, but that's not all..."

Red wondered why Eiwin hesitated this time. Was she worried about how this information would affect him? Even if it was depressing, Viran had already crushed his expectations many times. Red doubted anything he learned would put more of a damper on his expectations.

"Please, continue," Red said, trying to reassure her.

"... Alright," Eiwin said. She made a few gaps along the circle again. "The amount of natural gaps in this barrier also differs from person to person. An average individual might only have a few tiny gaps that she has to find and use to open her Spiritual Sea. But for someone more talented..."

She erased more parts of the circle until it was full of holes. The original shape was almost completely gone.

"The barrier might barely exist at all, making the whole ordeal of opening their Spiritual Sea much easier."

Red stared at her drawing, absorbing the information. "So if you're talented, not only are you better prepared to open the Spiritual Sea, but the barrier itself is much easier to break?"

"That's... correct," Eiwin said. "But it's okay, you know. Just because you aren't talented doesn't mean you can't open your Spiritual Sea! Plenty of people have done it before, and there are even pills that can help you."

"Since when do you know how talented I am?" Red asked.

Eiwin didn't know how to respond and blushed. It seemed she'd only been polite earlier when she said his progress was pretty good for his age.

"It's fine," Red said. "I'm aware of my average talent, but I'll still try to open my Spiritual Sea, no matter how hard it may be."

He didn't mean to make her flustered, so he tried to address her concern. But instead of being reassured, Eiwin looked at him strangely.

"Is there a problem?" he asked.

"You're quite mature for your age, aren't you?"

Red fell silent. Had he given away his disguise? He was so caught up in the conversation that he'd completely forgotten to keep up his naïve facade.

"It's okay." She shook her head. "Some kids grow up before their time, much more so when placed under terrible circumstances. I just find you to be a significant contrast to Allen."

Red relaxed after realizing Eiwin didn't intend to question him further. He used the opportunity to change topics. "Who's Allen?"

"He's the apprentice of the Sect Master. You two should meet, I'm sure you would be good friends—"

"Who's ready for a restaurant meal?!"

A familiar roaring voice interrupted their conversation, and they turned around.

Between the trees, Narcha and Rog appeared. They were carrying all kinds of meats and pouches. The duo beamed from ear to ear as they approached the camp, faces radiating a joy Red had never witnessed before.

Rog didn't even greet them before going to light the fire, but Narcha approached both Eiwin and Red, holding out some type of meat.

"Do you see this?" she asked with a laugh. "Venison! And high-quality at that! Who knows who those poor bastards stole it from, but now—"

"What are you doing?" Eiwin shouted.

"What do you mean?" Narcha sounded confused. "I'm just showing you what we have for dinner."

"Miss Valt, look at yourself!"

Narcha did as she was told.

She was completely covered in blood, her leather armor coated in a fine crimson sheen. Her face was also smeared, and not even her hair was spared. Red could see some bits of gore mixed in with the mess, and the smell had grown stronger once she got closer.

"Oh," Narcha realized, "I forgot about that."

"Of course you did!" Eiwin glared at her. "Go wash yourself first before you join the camp."

"Are you kidding me! It's the middle of the night and you want me to go into the river?" Narcha asked, full of indignation. "Is this about the kid again? Look at him, he doesn't even seem scared."

It was true; Red had seen worse.

"It doesn't matter! You stink of blood. I won't let you spend one more second in this camp in that state."

"Fine!" Narcha snorted, dropping her loot to the ground. "But you're cooking!" She spun around and wandered off into the night.

"Hah!"

Rog's voice caught their attention. Turning, Red could see the first sparks of a flame.

"Come here, kid!" Rog called him over. "Make yourself useful for something and watch the fire, will you?"

That was certainly something Red could do.

CHAPTER 52
WOUNDS

ROG WENT to prepare the food while Red watched over the flames. He never told him what he should actually do—other than just observe the campfire —but eventually, Eiwin came over and instructed him. Red learned he had to add more wood to keep the fire burning at an appropriate temperature, not too hot and not too cold.

It was a strangely laborious task at first, not knowing how the flames would react as more fuel was added, but he managed.

Ten minutes later, Rog came over to the fire with an iron pan holding a large piece of seasoned meat. He put the pan over the campfire, setting it atop a couple of thick branches. At that point, Red was relieved of his duty and told to sit and wait. He could already smell the aroma of cooked meat and spice rising, and his mouth watered.

Narcha rejoined the group soon after, her armor and hair still dripping wet. Once she saw the meat was almost ready, she rushed over to her bag, grabbing a dark glass bottle from within.

"Guess what else we found?" she asked with a smile.

With a popping noise, she uncorked the bottle with her hands and took a large swig. Red liquid spilled over the sides of her mouth. With a satisfied sigh, she wiped her face with her arm and laughed.

"I wonder how a bunch of bandits managed to get their hands on wine from the goddamn Empire." She tossed the bottle at Rog.

He eagerly took a swig of his own. If Red thought Narcha was a sloppy drinker, then he didn't know what to call the hunter.

Rog savored the taste. "Ha, it's been years since I've had a drink this good."

A moment later, Rog noticed Red looking at him curiously. He was quite interested in what they were drinking, and the man easily read his intentions.

"Want some, kid?" he asked with an ugly smile. "Here, take it!"

Rog threw the bottle at Red. Just as he was about to grab it, though, someone else snatched it in midair before it could reach him.

Eiwin, clutching the bottle one-handed, glared at her two companions.

"Oh, you want some too, Eiwin?" Rog said unashamedly. "You just needed to ask!"

Unlike the hunter, Narcha's expression was suddenly laced with worry. "Wait, Eiwin, just pass the bottle here—"

With a crunch, the glass shattered as Eiwin squeezed it between her fingers. The remaining red liquid spilled to the ground.

"No!" both Narcha and Rog bellowed, but it was already too late.

Eiwin wiped her wet hands on her clothes before sitting down by Red's side as if nothing had happened. He frowned, confused by the sudden turn of events.

"That liquid contains a poison," she said with a serene smile. "It's an addictive substance that inhibits clear thought and messes with your senses. You should never drink it."

When she put it like that, Red realized she had indeed done him a favor. He would never willingly put poison into his body. Strangely enough, her two companions didn't seem to share his opinion.

"You—you..." Narcha stared at Eiwin. "Do you know how expensive that was?"

Rog sorted through the shards of glass, as if hoping to gather its remains. "If you didn't want it, you could have just given it back!"

Eiwin was unfazed. "One should refrain from drinking alcohol, for it is the cause of heedlessness." She pointed at the fire. "The meat is burning."

"Agh!" Rog fumbled to his feet and rushed to the iron pan.

Red's confidence in the group's abilities diminished by the second.

After Red had stuffed himself with his most delicious meal yet, Eiwin approached him again.

"We need to change your bandages and apply the medicine," she said, showing the items in her hand.

Red squinted. "Medicine?"

"Yes, for your infection."

He'd almost forgotten about that. "Give it to me. I can do it myself."

"Are you sure? The paste hurts a fair bit, and you can't even move your other arm. Wouldn't it be easier for me to help?"

"It's fine. I can do it."

Eiwin, however, still seemed to doubt him.

"If he thinks he can do it, let him do it," Narcha said from the side, polishing her steel saber. "Kid needs to learn the price of being stubborn."

Eiwin hesitated, but once she saw Red's unflinching gaze, she relented. "Fine, but if it hurts too much, ask for help immediately."

With that, she handed him the bandage and a wooden container. Red examined the paste, comparing it with what Viran had given him in the mines. Aside from the consistency and uncomfortable smell, there weren't many similarities between them. He untied the loosely wrapped bandages around his ribs first.

The injury still looked purple from the bruising, but Red had been so absorbed in other concerns during the day that the pain had barely bothered him. Whenever he breathed too deeply, though, the discomfort was still there, and the area felt tender to the touch. He smeared the paste over the injury. Sure enough, a sharp, burning pain surged around his skin, but it wasn't anything he wasn't used to. Next, he bit into one end of the fresh bandage and grabbed the other with his functioning hand, wrapping it around his chest.

The process was awkward, and he could only wrap it loosely, but Red knew the dressing shouldn't be too tight anyway. After fumbling around for a bit, he managed to bandage the injury.

Next was the hardest part—his shoulder. This wound was nowhere near as painful as his ribs, but the absence of pain concerned him, as he still had limited feeling in his left arm. Still, there was nothing he could do right now other than treat it.

He removed the bandage and was greeted by a gnarly sight. The area around the wound had swelled, and there were bloody scabs and yellowish pus where the shattered bone fragments had pierced through the skin. Red had seen worse injuries on others, but this was the worst he'd ever sustained. Looking at it jarred him, but he fought through the feeling.

Careful not to pop the abscesses, he spread the paste over the wounded areas. The pain was immediate, and he had to stop as some feeling returned to his shoulder. The sensation was agonizing.

Through gritted teeth, Red continued to smear the medicine on the wound until he was sure he had covered it completely. Then he wrapped the bandage around his shoulder, repeating the same process from before. With some difficulty, he finished the dressing with a tight knot.

Sighing in relief, Red leaned back, but he noticed Eiwin and Narcha looking at him, bewildered.

"Have... you done this before?" Narcha asked.

"A few times," Red replied. "Never something this bad, though."

Another prolonged moment of silence.

Narcha grimaced. "Kid, what the fuck have you been doing?"

"Miss Valt!" Eiwin stood up. "That's beside the point. What matters is that he knows the basics of healing and first aid. Isn't that right, Red?"

"I suppose." He shrugged.

Eiwin smiled at that. "Well then, it's getting quite late, isn't it? We should get ready to sleep." She went over to her bag and picked up a large roll of brown cloth. "Here, you can use my bedroll tonight," she said, stretching the thick blanket in a nearby spot in the clearing. "You don't need to worry about me. I'll be taking the first watch and using Narcha's bed once she takes over for me."

"Hey, I didn't agree to that!"

"What, would you have me sleep on the ground?"

Narcha hesitated. "What about Rog?" She looked over at the hunter.

To their surprise, he was already lying on top of his bedroll with his hood pulled over his head. The faint sound of snoring could be heard.

Narcha gritted her teeth. "Fine! But that's just for today."

Eiwin smiled. "Great! You should be going to sleep as soon as you can, Red. It's important for your recovery."

He stared at her. This was the first time he would go to sleep in the presence of others by choice, and the prospect made him uncomfortable. But he had no other option.

"Okay." He went over to the bedroll and tucked himself in.

Eiwin seemed taken aback by his compliance and looked at Narcha, who just shrugged. The two of them stared at Red as he closed his eyes. They waited in silence, busying themselves by organizing the camp.

Once Red had been "asleep" for a while, Narcha spoke again. "I told you there was something strange about him."

Eiwin shushed her. "Quiet... If you want to have this conversation, how about doing it somewhere where we won't wake him up?"

"Fine."

Red heard both women distance themselves from the campfire's embers, moving to the other side of the clearing.

A few seconds later, he opened his eyes, wide awake. He could hear some murmurs of conversation, but they were too far for him to make out. He didn't intend to sneak over, so he could only lie in bed and pretend to sleep.

Ten minutes later, they returned to camp. Narcha went to her bedroll while Eiwin took watch as promised.

A few hours passed, during which Red monitored the group, listening for anything suspicious. However, Narcha and Rog seemed to be truly asleep, and Eiwin didn't approach him.

Only then did Red allow himself to relax. He did not show it, but he was truly tired after a whole day of walking. At the very least, it didn't seem like he needed to worry about being murdered in his slumber.

With that, Red let sleep overtake his consciousness.

CHAPTER 53

ARRIVAL

AT THE CRACK OF DAWN, bright rays of sunlight shone through Red's eyelids and stirred him from his sleep. He blinked rapidly, shielding his face with his hand. It would take some time for him to be comfortable with the sharp contrast of night and day. He looked around and saw his companions were already waking up.

Narcha was finishing her watch, and it wasn't long before the other two were up. A few minutes later, the trio were already talking and packing up the rest of the camp while Red was still waking up. Under Narcha's prompting, though, he got ready quickly.

After a short breakfast, the group hit the road as if they'd never stopped. Red struggled to keep up, but at least Narcha didn't press them to walk any faster, something he was aware the others could do with ease.

The following hours were uneventful. Eiwin was as talkative as yesterday, although beneath her words he could detect something else, as if her remarks were laced with... worry? He couldn't quite tell, but the way she addressed him had changed. It was likely the product of the conversation between her and Narcha during the night.

It made him somewhat wary, but her positive attitude towards him hadn't changed, from what he could tell. So Red continued to engage her in conversation as usual, ignoring her worry.

"What's the Empire?" he asked once their chat turned towards his usual barrage of questions.

Narcha had mentioned it yesterday. He remembered some slaves referring to it in passing conversation, but in the mines, they rarely discussed much of the world outside—they had more pressing matters. He could never tell what this "Empire" was, other than some kind of powerful organization.

His innocuous question gave Eiwin some pause. "It's... difficult to explain."

"Are they strong?" Red asked.

"Yes, they're a very powerful nation."

He frowned. "That's it?"

"Well..." Her gaze turned uneasy, and she cast a glance at Narcha up ahead.

Red kept staring at her, waiting for her to continue.

"Listen Red, it's a complicated subject to talk about right now," she said. "Just know that they're—"

"They're our enemies."

Eiwin was interrupted by a voice dripping with intense hatred.

It was Narcha.

"The Empire wants to destroy our way of life," the warrior went on. "They hide their true intentions and cruel nature behind a mask of order and harmony, but the only thing they want is more slaves and sacrifices to serve their Celestial Gods." She spat on the ground in disgust. "If they only wanted to take our lives, I would respect them more. Instead, they want to take our freedom and the only way people like us can change our fate. They're less than human and worse than monsters."

Narcha fell silent once more. Red was caught off guard by her sudden outburst, but just when he was about to ask another question, Eiwin put a hand on his shoulder.

"Not now." She shook her head solemnly and pointed at Narcha with her eyes.

Red saw that she had already walked far ahead, not even caring if they were still following. Soon, they could barely see her through the tree trunks.

"It's a sensitive topic for her," Eiwin said. "Well, not only for her, but for everyone who lives around here. We can talk about it later when she's not around, if that's okay with you?"

"I see," Red said.

This was the second time he had inadvertently caused tension within the group, and he doubted it would be the last. Now he had to consider the impact of his words on those around him. It was strange, but Red supposed that at least it wasn't as dangerous as watching out for his own safety every second. Or so he hoped.

"They're fucking crazy, kid," Rog said from behind. "Batshit insane, believing that people live above the sky or something." He pointed up. "Look, do you see anyone up there?"

Red looked up as he was told. He was only met with the clear blue sky and the sun beating down on their heads.

"No," he said.

"See? As I said, all crazy. There are no gods up there." With that, the man walked past them, hurrying to catch up with their leader.

Red continued to stare at the sky. He felt something awakening within his memories, and the world around him shifted.

The sky turned golden, as if illusion and reality had merged into one.

The air shimmered.

Enormous cracks appeared in the sky, breaching through the very fabric of reality. Something pushed through them, and space contracted and expanded to accept their form.

The rifts gradually opened and gigantic disembodied orbs surged from within them, floating aimlessly through the sky. The spheres rotated in place as if searching for something.

The speed of their revolutions was so great that Red saw them as blurs. Abruptly, they all stopped and turned to stare in his direction. That was when he recognized them.

Eyes.

Countless eyes, looking at him.

They each had a pitch-black sclera, a dark blue iris, and myriad dots that formed irregularly shaped pupils. The world froze as Red suddenly felt a terrifying sense of familiarity reach into his mind.

He shivered.

"Red?"

A voice broke through the illusion. He blinked, and the strange scene disappeared, receding into the calming blue sky. For some reason, he couldn't remember what he had just been looking at.

"Are you okay?" Eiwin asked.

Red looked over, noticing the woman's hand on his shoulder.

"I'm fine."

"Okay..." Eiwin didn't look convinced, but she retracted her hand. "We should hurry, or else they'll leave us behind."

Red nodded and followed.

The rest of the day was uneventful. Rog scouted ahead for them again, but there were no bandit camps nearby. Red was told that this was because they were nearing the city, and outlaws avoided more densely populated areas.

Throughout their journey, they had followed the river's course, never straying too far from it. However, their path suddenly diverged from the river, and they started to walk away from it.

Just before nightfall, they came across a peculiar sight. A stretch of smoothed terrain appeared right in the middle of the forest, clear of any trees or plants. It extended on either side before twisting behind the tree line, out of sight.

"This is a road," Eiwin said. "People build these to make traveling between settlements easier."

"How long is it?" Red asked.

"This one runs well over a hundred kilometers, and it joins up with an even larger road past the forest. It can take days to travel the entire length, but we're not going that way, thankfully."

Red couldn't help but marvel at the road, how much effort and time it must've taken to carve it through such a thick forest. And there was an even bigger road it was connected to? Just thinking about it filled him with the urge to explore.

"We'll keep going for a bit more. There's a clearing by the roadside we can camp in." Narcha turned to Rog. "Any trails?"

"A couple. A few days old. A cart too." He crouched to examine the ground. "Doesn't look like it's seen much movement."

"That little?" Narcha frowned. "Is there a reason for that?"

He shrugged. "Bandits? Maybe trade crisis? Who knows."

"Something must be going on past the river," Eiwin said. "Things weren't this bad even when there were monsters around."

"We've barely left town for a week!" Narcha said, exasperated. "I hope Rimold's been making himself useful and knows something about this."

Red, completely unaware of what they were discussing, listened to the conversation silently.

"Do you think...?" Eiwin trailed off.

"Another war?" Narcha's frown deepened. "Even if that's the case, it shouldn't affect things this far east, but we can't dismiss the possibility."

Eiwin shook her head. "I don't want to spend another minute more than necessary here, so let's just be on our way."

The group started moving again.

An hour later, when night had already settled, they arrived in a clearing and made camp. Red partook of another meal of roasted venison, this one of a lesser quality than the previous, but still among the best things he had ever eaten.

As the night grew darker, the group prepared to sleep. This time, Rog took charge of the watch for the entire night, completely foregoing his rest. Red thought this was strange, but he was told that once you opened certain veins, you could easily go many days without sleep.

After changing his bandages, he took his borrowed bedroll and found a corner to sleep. This time there was no secret discussion between his travel companions, but only after an hour did Red feel comfortable letting himself rest.

If Narcha's previous predictions had been correct, they would arrive in town tomorrow. He had no idea what awaited him there, but the recent tenor of the group's conversations suggested that he may have ended up in a more troublesome region than he would have preferred.

The next day came without interruptions, and the group continued to make their way, following the road. Some semblance of strength had returned to Red with the paste's help, and he almost wanted to practice then and there. He thought better of it, though.

Soon, they arrived at a crossroads that split into three paths. Wooden signs shaped like arrows stood in the middle, pointing in different directions, but he couldn't read what they said.

"We're almost there," Eiwin said. "Just a few more hours of travel."

"Yeah, and then we can see what Hector says we should do with you, kid," Narcha said, earning herself an ugly look from her companion.

These last few days had almost made Red forget the warrior had been quite adamant about leaving him to die in the forest. But he didn't blame her —he would've probably done the same in her place. After all, he wouldn't like to hang around someone who was both cursed and possibly infected with some sort of virus.

A few hours later, Red saw shapes appear on the horizon. Ruins and dilapidated stone, with wooden constructions built around them creating an odd contrast.

Red turned to Eiwin. "Is that...?"

She nodded. "That's Fordham-Bestrem, home to our Water Dragon Sect."

CHAPTER 54
NEWS AT THE GATE

THE FIRST THING Red noticed was how large the town seemed. They were still a few kilometers away, but even from here, he could tell the town stretched far from side to side. It sat on an incline, sprawling out the further downhill it went. Red made out buildings of all shapes and sizes decorating the hillside, but he had a hard time seeing finer details from a distance.

"How many people live there?" he asked.

"Around ten thousand," Eiwin said.

Red was in disbelief, yet he saw no dishonesty in the woman's expression. "How?"

"How what?" Eiwin seemed confused.

"How can there be so many people in there?"

Up ahead, Narcha chuckled. "You'll be surprised at how many people can fit inside a town if you pack them tight enough. But this is nothing, kid. It's even small compared to the capital. That one has more than one hundred thousand people all crammed way tighter than in our little shire here."

Red had a hard time wrapping his mind around those numbers. In the mines, he'd never seen more than fifty slaves at one time. This town held hundreds of times that amount, and it wasn't even on the high end for the surface. How could they even find enough food for everyone?

"Come on." Eiwin put a hand behind his back, hurrying him along. "It looks even better from up close."

Red soon found out she wasn't lying.

As the trees and vegetation grew sparser, more of the town was revealed to him. The city had no walls, and most of the buildings were built from wood and stone. But what caught his attention were the ruins that stood in the middle of the settlement.

The remains of the grand and elaborate buildings stood out like a sore thumb. Red couldn't imagine what they'd looked like in the past. The town seemed to have grown up around the ruins, with some parts even used in the newer buildings. At the top of the hill, for instance, there was a large castle patched up with different materials. It was by far the largest building in the town, and the best-conserved ruin of what had once stood.

It all made for a bizarre but intriguing sight for Red. It was as if two different towns existed simultaneously in the same place.

"People built this town on top of long-destroyed ruins," Eiwin explained. "No one really knows for sure what was here before, but some assume it was a temple built to honor the old gods."

"Is that why you haven't torn them down?"

"Well, partly," she said. "Some people have tried in the past. But no one was able to break down what was left of the structures."

"What do you mean?" From what Red could see, the ruins were made of normal stone, if a bit darker.

"The material of the ruins is actually enchanted. People have tried to use all kinds of methods, but none work. Not even Spiritual Practitioners can leave a dent in the stones."

"How did it get to that state in the first place, then?" Red asked.

But Eiwin simply shook her head. "That's another thing we don't know. Whether it was a natural disaster or a monster, they must have been extremely powerful... But you don't need to worry." She seemed to suddenly notice how foreboding her words were. "This town has been here for over two hundred years, right around the time we began settling in these lands, and nothing bad has happened since then."

Her explanation only brought more questions to Red's mind, but he noticed something else. A group of people was escorting two horse-drawn wagons. Some of them were equipped with armor and weapons, and the party moved down the dirt road straight toward Red's group. In total, there were about twenty of them guiding the wheeled caravan. Although there were still a few hundred meters between them, Red couldn't help but look questioningly at Eiwin.

However, it was Rog that answered first.

He squinted. "Looks like Gustav's group."

"Great." Narcha snorted. "Is the man himself there?"

"No," Rog said. "Reinhart is, though."

Narcha looked even more displeased. "Let's just get this over with, shall we?" With that, she walked past them and towards the wagons.

Red started to worry about whether a fight was about to break out, but Eiwin just patted his back.

"Just stay behind me, okay?" she said.

Red was planning to do that anyway.

The caravan was a hundred meters away when it came to a stop. A man in intricate scale armor and a longsword strapped to his side stepped down from the wagon and approached Red's group. His brown hair was tied back in a ponytail, a short beard covering his face. Red thought the man's features resembled those of a noble more than a warrior.

"Good afternoon, Narcha." He smiled and extended his hand. "How fortunate to meet you on this fine day."

The warrior winced and made no motion to accept his handshake. Instead, she looked past the man, at the rest of the caravan. Unlike their leader, they all glared at Narcha and her companions with scowling faces, their hands hovering over the hilts of their weapons.

"Hm?" The man noticed her strange expression and looked back at his subordinates. "You morons, you weren't supposed to give it away! How are we supposed to take her by surprise when you guys can't even pretend to be friendly?"

His subordinates stared at him in confusion, but he had already turned back to Narcha.

"Sorry, can we just pretend that didn't happen?" The same smug smile returned to his face. "So, how are you doing today, Narcha?"

"I was doing pretty well until a few minutes ago," she said, not taking her eyes off his subordinates. "What, do you really want to fight right outside of town, Reinhart?"

"Never!" he said, feigning shock at her question. "We aren't quite at that level of hostility yet. It's just that my men have been a bit jumpy ever since we received some news from the plains..."

"What do you mean?" Narcha asked.

Reinhart hesitated. "Well... I would like to tell you, but it's confidential information, unfortunately—"

"Stop fucking around. Tell me what you want."

"Hm, you see..." He was about to continue, but he suddenly caught sight of Red, who was hiding behind the others. "What do we have here? Another stray to join your party?"

Red didn't know how to respond, but he felt Eiwin's body tense in front of him.

She glared at the man. "None of your business, mongrel!"

At that, Reinhart's subordinates stirred into movement, their hateful eyes focused on Eiwin. She didn't back off. In fact, she stepped forward as if ready to meet them in combat. This gave the soldiers some pause, but none stepped back.

"That's enough!" Reinhart raised his arm, stopping his subordinates. "I apologize, Eiwin. I forgot this is a sore spot for you."

She didn't seem to believe him, but under Narcha's gaze, she stepped back. Narcha sighed, before turning back to Reinhart.

"What do you want?" she asked again.

"You see, I was about to ask you what you'd learned from your recent visit to the forest, but suddenly I find myself more interested in something else." Reinhart's gaze settled on Red. "Tell me how you found this kid. Last I heard, you weren't planning on visiting any villages."

"We found him alone in the forest," Narcha said.

For the first time, the man showed some annoyance. "What, that's it?"

"That's it," she said. "I wish I could say I was hiding something on purpose to upset you, but that's all that happened."

Reinhart stared at her for a few more seconds, seemingly hoping to see a crack in her expression. But nothing changed, so he just shook his head.

"I assume you found out nothing about the monsters?" he asked.

"What do you think? Now, tell me, what news did you hear?"

"Normally I would say that what you gave me isn't worth it, but I'm sure some people in your Sect will tell you when you get there," he said. "We received news from the plains a day after you left town... They say there's an incoming monster tide from the Skycrown Mountains."

Narcha's frown deepened, and seconds passed in silence. Red glanced at Eiwin for an explanation, but she appeared to be preoccupied with processing the news as well.

"How long until it begins?" Eiwin asked, her voice tinged with concern.

"You never know with these things, but they say that it could happen anytime from a month to a year from now." Reinhart shrugged. "Depends on how eager the horde is to find new territory."

"Is it gonna reach here?"

"The Sects say it's a manageable number this time around, but we've both had our hands full with hordes in the past," he said. "They might hold the bulk of it at the border, but there's always plenty that slip through the cracks. We can only hope it's something we can handle."

Narcha didn't respond, silent in thought.

"Now, if you'll excuse me." Reinhart moved back towards his carriage. "Mister Gustav is intent on securing his sales on the plains before everything goes to shit, so I have to be on my way."

Narcha glared at them. "I hope you get caught in the middle of it."

"Now, wouldn't that be something?" The man smiled. "Unfortunately for you, I've survived worse."

Reinhart whipped the horses into action, leading the caravan forward with his subordinates following. Red moved out of the way, staring at the large animals and the armored guards throwing him ugly glances as they walked by.

Reinhart smiled at him.

"Watch out for Hector, buddy," he said. "He's not one to be trusted."

Eiwin had already put herself between him and Reinhart before he could respond, throwing the man an icy glare. A minute later, they had all passed by the group.

Eiwin turned to Red with a concerned expression. "Don't listen to him, okay?" she said. "He's not a good person, and Hector has always taken care of us."

Red nodded. But deep down, he knew he hadn't needed the man's warning in the first place.

He never took anyone at face value.

CHAPTER 55

THE TOWN

THE GROUP RESUMED their journey to the city gates. Both Narcha and Eiwin wore grave expressions, their previous eagerness to return home nowhere to be found. Rog didn't seem affected by the news, but Red had never seen the man worry about anything before.

"What were they talking about?" he asked Eiwin.

Red had considered staying silent, but if there was something he needed to watch out for in the future, then he would like to learn more as soon as possible.

"Remember when we talked about what caused the destruction of these ruins?" she said. "A monster horde is considered the most credible explanation. Countless monsters all driven into a frenzy and obliterating everything in their path... There's nothing quite as destructive."

Her words didn't bode well.

"Didn't that man say they would be held back in the mountains?" Red asked.

"That's the hope, but there's no way the Sects can guarantee none will breach through." Eiwin shook her head. "If a powerful monster slips past and reaches us, then..."

She caught herself.

"Sorry, I said too much." She looked at Red apologetically. "This is not the first horde this town has faced, and despite how dangerous they are, we're still here. You're too young to worry about this. Just focus on growing up strong while your seniors handle this kind of stuff."

She smiled.

"It's our duty, after all."

Her words were no comfort to Red, but he put it at the back of his mind for now. They were nearing the town, and he could discern more details in the landscape.

On the outskirts were wide fields full of unfamiliar plants. The farmland circled the base of the hill, curving around the corner and out of his sight.

Amid the fields, there stood a few grazing animals that Red likewise didn't recognize. Farmers tended to the farmland with metal tools, and some even greeted them as they passed. They were unarmed and looked far weaker than the mercenaries from before. Red couldn't help but think he'd gotten the wrong impression of what to expect in the town.

They soon reached the sea of buildings that was the town proper. The more Red saw, the more he realized that the layout and size of the stone-and-brick buildings were defined by the ruined foundations beneath them. The mishmash of materials looked crude, lending to the town's disordered appearance. Yet it was still the greatest display of human ingenuity Red had ever seen.

Human activity increased as they wandered further into town. Dozens of people moved about frantically, most either ignoring or not noticing their presence. Their clothes were, unsurprisingly, an upgrade when compared to the slaves' clothing in the mines. Men wore laced tunics overlaid with vests, baggy breeches, and leather boots, while most women had in long dresses that reached their ankles. Some even sported straw hats or woolen caps.

A select few seemed better off, wearing more intricately designed clothes made of fur and expensive fabrics, such as satin and silk. There were also many people sporting leather armor and carrying all kinds of weapons, including uniformed guards who watched the streets with bored expressions. The commotion and hubbub of conversation were almost too much for Red, and he felt himself getting dizzy from trying to process it all.

Things only got worse farther ahead.

Eiwin noticed his hesitation. "It can be a bit overwhelming at first, but you'll eventually get used to it."

Red nodded, but he couldn't see himself ever adapting to a place like this.

The dirt road beneath them eventually gave way to dark stone pavement built of the same material as the ruins. As they walked, the noises became even louder. Red could smell the aroma of food and spices, making his belly rumble.

"Got a new shipment of goods, straight from the Empire!" a man dressed in fancy clothes shouted at the top of his lungs.

Red paused in front of a large stall with all kinds of fruits and meats on the counter. People gathered around it, haggling with the merchant and his workers. He wanted to get a closer look, but Narcha was in a hurry, and he was already struggling to keep up with her long strides.

The road ahead widened, and many other stalls lined the street. All sorts of items were on offer: cloth, cooking utensils, even weapons and armor. The ones that attracted Red the most, though, were the food stands. The smells wafting in the air were even more mouthwatering than what Rog had cooked a few days ago, and he couldn't resist stealing a longing glance.

"I'd buy you some, but I'm not carrying any money." Eiwin smiled apologetically.

"Money?" Red asked, confused.

"It's..." She hesitated, before abruptly pointing forward. "Look, it's the town square!"

Further ahead the road became a large plaza, where the bustle of the city reached a crescendo. More than a dozen stalls, even bigger than the ones Red had seen, filled the space. Crowds of people gathered around, and more joined by the second, coming from other roads. City guards were present here too, directing the throngs of people and watching for any troublemakers.

What caught Red's attention, though, was a large rectangular pillar in the middle of the square. It stood three meters tall and was broken at the top, indicating it had been even taller in the past. Symbols and drawings were etched on the surface of the dark structure, but he had a hard time making them out from afar. Not to mention, the area seemed sealed off by the guards, who encircled the column as they watched the square.

Red felt a faint familiarity with the pillar, but the thought vanished as quickly as it had appeared. He wanted to ask Eiwin about it, but holding any sort of conversation in the plaza without shouting was virtually impossible. Thankfully for him, they were only passing through.

Narcha weaved through the crowd and shoved those who blocked the way, earning herself quite a few curses. When her victims turned their eyes on her, though, none of them pursued the matter.

Soon they were past the square and on a road leading up the hill. While there were still people around, it was much more manageable to walk, and Red could hear his own thoughts again.

Up the road, he saw a large building which served as another center of frenetic activity. People with all kinds of armor and weapons walked in and out, happily carrying heavy bags. Red couldn't quite see what was happening inside, but he could hear loud laughter, and an overwhelming smell filled his nostrils. Although the atmosphere radiating from the building unsettled Red somewhat, he could see that each person hanging around appeared and carried themselves like a warrior.

A possibility came to his mind. "Is that your Sect?" He looked at Eiwin, questioningly.

She wasn't the one that responded, though.

"Our Sect?" Narcha scoffed. "That place is full of weaklings who can't even hold a candle to us!"

She didn't bother lowering her voice, which earned her many hostile glares from a group nearby. Narcha seemed unbothered and met their eyes directly, as if challenging them to do something about it. None of them stepped forward.

Does she have any friends in this place?

As they passed the building, even Red received some unfriendly looks, and he couldn't help but question Narcha's methods. She might be strong enough to intimidate them, but what about him? If they thought he was associated with her and decided to create problems for him instead, there was no way he could take them on. However, Eiwin and Rog didn't seem too worried, and soon enough, they were far away and turning onto another road.

By now, the crowds had lessened substantially. In fact, there were so few people Red wondered whether they were still in the same town. Even the number of buildings had diminished. He looked around incredulously, but confirmed they were still in the center of the town.

"Master Hector doesn't like to live near other people," Eiwin said. "He says it's too noisy."

"I never thought there would be such a quiet place in the middle of everything," Red said.

"There isn't" Rog said. "Hector just kicked everyone out and made it like this. You had to be there, it was very—"

"Look!" Eiwin exclaimed, cutting him off. "We're here!"

Red looked where she was pointing. There was a tall wooden fence that had seen better days, and through the cracks, Red caught glimpses of a large yard and a set of rundown buildings. The place was huge, and a few of the buildings were tall enough to peek over the fence.

Despite the distance, the faint sounds of conversation and metal striking against metal reached their ears, but it was nearly silent compared to the rest of the city. Narcha walked up to the wooden gate and swung it open with all her strength.

"Hector!" she said, announcing her entrance with gusto. "We're back—"

A large iron utensil shot out from within the courtyard with lightning speed, hitting her in the forehead. Narcha reeled back from the impact and clutched her head in pain.

"STOP SCREAMING, DAMN BRAT!"

CHAPTER 56
THE SECT

"WHY—"

Narcha started to scream back but caught herself midway. Her protests died down into a grumble as she picked up the object that had just struck her head.

Red could see now that it was an iron spoon, lacking any sharp edges or prongs. If the woman had been struck by an actual weapon—with that kind of force, there was no way she would have survived.

He looked past Narcha, expecting to see whoever had just thrown the spoon, but there didn't seem to be anyone in the courtyard. Even the sounds of conversation and clinging metal had ceased upon their arrival.

"Bloody old fart..." Narcha muttered under her breath, looking back at the rest of the group.

More specifically, she scowled at Eiwin.

"You've brought this problem along with us, so I hope you're ready to abide by whatever Hector decides."

"I..." Eiwin tensed up, but after a few seconds, she nodded. "I will respect his decision."

The atmosphere between the women changed, as if they were about to face a terrible enemy. Red didn't like how they were talking about something directly related to him without even asking for his input. Even though he doubted they would hurt him, he still wasn't sure what Eiwin hoped to accomplish by bringing him to their Sect.

"Very well. Rog, since you voted for it, you'll have to come too..." Narcha turned around to look at the man. "Rog?"

The group of four had stealthily been reduced to a group of three. Rog was nowhere to be seen, and none of them had noticed his disappearance.

"That bastard—" Narcha choked back the enraged shout rising in her throat. She sighed. "I don't care anymore. Let's just get this over with."

"Miss Valt, would you give me one second to talk with Red before we go in?" Eiwin said before her companion could walk away.

"Do what you want, Eiwin. I'll be waiting inside." She waved her hand before walking inside, entering the main building in the courtyard.

Complete silence descended over their surroundings. Eiwin turned to Red with a smile and crouched down to his eye level.

"I can see that this is all very new for you." She patted the dust off his shoulders. "I can't imagine the things you must have gone through before we met, but it's not important at this point. All you need to know is that you're safe right now, and it doesn't matter what anyone inside that hall says. At the end of the day, I promise you'll be taken care of. Do you understand?"

Red would have liked to claim he did, but her words carried a certain weight that made him wary. However, he simply nodded.

"Good." Her smile widened. "Just stay behind me and listen to what I say, and everything will be alright."

He didn't plan on doing anything else. With that, Eiwin stood and walked into the stone building with Red in tow.

Like the rest of the lot, this house also was in disrepair, with broken and uneven windows and construction materials strewn about. The door was open, and a wide room greeted them.

The walls didn't look much different on the inside, but they were decorated with parchments and skins which were covered with words and drawings Red couldn't make out. What caught his attention, though, was the long wooden table in the center of the room. All kinds of things were spread haphazardly on top, like books and cooking utensils, and it was lined on both sides by several chairs. Four people were already sitting down, staring at him and Eiwin.

He recognized one of the figures—Narcha. Across from her were two people. One of them was a boy sporting short blonde hair, bright features, and elegant blue clothes. He was bigger and older than Red. The other one was a man who looked about Rog's age. He had a finely trimmed beard and wavy black hair, which stopped just short of his shoulders, and wore a dark coat. The expression on his face was placid and blank, which Red had difficulty reading.

And then there was one other person. An old man, bald and with a bushy white beard. His long white robe was grimy and full of holes, and, for a second, Red wondered whether this was an escaped slave like himself, but his seat at the head of the table indicated he was the leader of the group. He was currently scooping some soup out of a bowl with a look of anger frozen on his face.

It reminded Red of Viran.

Eiwin came to a stop at the other end of the table. Red moved behind her, cautiously scrutinizing the people in front of him.

"Master Hector, we need to seek your decision on an important matter," Eiwin said to the old man in a respectful tone Red had never heard her use before.

"Important?" Hector snorted, putting his bowl down. "Is it about that dirty brat you brought along?"

"You're one to talk..." Narcha said underneath her breath.

"What's that?" The old man pointed his iron spoon in her direction. "Did you say something?"

"No... I mean, yes. I said I can talk—about what happened, that is."

"Well, then... go on, I love a good story while I'm eating." He picked up his bowl again. "Eiwin, sit over here and bring that brat over. I don't want to have to shout to talk to you."

She did as she was told, guiding Red along until she sat by Narcha's side. Curiously, she didn't offer a seat to him, simply instructing him to stand next to her. Up close, he could feel the scrutiny from the others intensify.

The black-haired man, still as relaxed as ever, smiled when he saw Red look in his direction. The other kid, however, had eyes burning with curiosity that had followed him since the moment he'd entered the building. Red averted his gaze and looked at Narcha, who was preparing to speak.

"It was night, and we were in the middle of the forest, at least two days from any settlement," she began. "When suddenly we saw someone sneaking up to our camp. Rog shot a... warning arrow. We tried to talk to whoever it was, but after we got no response, we went closer and found this little brat almost dead."

She nodded at Red.

"Tons of bruises, broken rib, shattered shoulder, and an infection to boot. Not normal injuries, especially the one on the shoulder, which looked monster-inflicted. He was lucky to have found us, or else he would have died. Either way, we patched him up and waited until he woke up so we could ask him how the hell he ended up in the middle of nowhere and in his sorry state. But guess what?" The warrior snorted. "Just so happens he conveniently couldn't remember a thing!"

Eiwin grimaced. "We've both seen what a traumatic situation does to people, much more to someone his age," she protested. "Amnesia is nothing strange in these cases."

"We both know that's not the only issue with him. He was clearly lying!" Narcha cried.

"How would you know? You didn't even try to talk to him!"

"Not only are there no monsters in that region, but he also knew how to bandage himself! How was he *not* lying—"

"The rest of the story, please!" Hector cut them off. "I need to know how all of this is of any concern to me."

"Right, let Eiwin explain why we're here, then." Narcha crossed her arms and leaned back.

Everyone turned to the younger woman, who nodded.

"Miss Valt was too angry and suspicious to be reasonable and wanted to send him off on his own to the nearest village with some supplies," Eiwin continued. "I argued that this would be a death sentence, but she didn't budge, so... I ended up calling an elders' vote."

At that, the mood around the table changed. Even the black-haired man looked dumbfounded. "Eiwin," he said amicably. "You do know that it's against the rules to use that kind of privilege lightly, right?"

"I told her that!" Narcha threw her hands up. "But she still went ahead."

"Enough!" Hector raised his hand, stopping another conversation from erupting. "Since you called a vote for such a stupid matter, why is the boy still here?"

Eiwin looked away in embarrassment.

The old man squinted. "What's the problem?"

"... Rog was there," Narcha said.

"Fucking moron!" He slammed his bowl down on the table, visibly shaking in anger. It took a few seconds before he finally calmed down.

"I'm disappointed in you, Eiwin." Hector shook his head, reprimanding her as a parent would. "I trusted you with that privilege only for matters of survival. I thought you, of all people, would know better than to betray my trust."

"But it was a matter of survival, just not ours." Despite being berated, everyone at the table turning against her, Eiwin held her position. "Miss Valt would've left him to die out of pure paranoia, and Mister Rog didn't even care to begin with. If I had left him to die knowing I could have done more to save him, I wouldn't be able to forgive myself..."

"We all know why you really did that," Narcha said. "Just can't help but try to be a saint at every opportunity you get."

"You—" Once more, Eiwin almost lost her temper before Hector interrupted them with a wave of his hand.

"Stop acting like children!" He glared at them. "Even the kids are more well-behaved than the two of you."

His words gave the women pause, and they leaned back into their seats in silence, staring daggers at each other.

"We'll discuss what to do about your abuse of position later, Eiwin," the old man said. "But since you won the vote, we'll respect the rules as I established them. Now tell me, why did you bring him here?"

"I wanted Master Hector to take a look at his wounds and help him recover," Eiwin said, pointing at Red's shoulder.

"Hmm, I can do that much, I suppose..."

"... and I also want you to accept him into the Sect."

Everyone looked at her in surprise.

Including Red.

CHAPTER 57

MEETING

NARCHA SLAMMED her hands on the table, glaring at her companion in disbelief. "No way!"

This time, Hector didn't stop her outburst.

"Was this what you had planned all along?" she asked, getting up from her seat. "Gods, I should've known. I should never have let you bring him with us!"

Eiwin didn't reply, calmly waiting until Narcha was done screaming. Her silence, however, only seemed to anger the warrior even more.

"Do you even know anything about this kid? Haven't you heard about all the strange things happening in that forest lately!" she raged. "This isn't even the first orphan we've come across during our travels. Are you planning on having all one of them join the Sect, too?"

"Narcha, please," the man sitting across from her interjected. "How about you give Eiwin some space to breathe so she may explain herself?"

"We shouldn't even need to hear her!" Narcha gritted her teeth. "She's always been like this, too naïve for her own good. We all put up with it until now because it never got in the way of business—but look at where that got us!"

She waved her hand at Red.

"I mean, look at him! Look at his wounds... his eyes! I've never seen such dead eyes on an adult, much less a child. They're not normal! *He's* not normal!"

"Not normal?" The man smiled. "As opposed to the rest of us?"

"Look... you know what I mean. Let's say that despite everything about him, he just so happens to be a normal child—it still doesn't mean we should just take him in!"

"We are getting ahead of ourselves, Narcha," he said. "The final decision still falls on Hector, and he won't choose without hearing both sides. Let Eiwin explain herself first."

"But—" She looked over at the old man, seeking his support, but Hector's eyes were closed in thought. She could only throw her hands up in frustration. "Fine, then! Let her speak."

The warrior sat back down. The entire room's attention shifted to Eiwin, who seemed as serene as ever.

"Thank you for your help, Mister Domeron." She nodded at the man sitting across from her. "Unlike what Miss Valt would like you to believe, I didn't make this decision lightly. In fact, I was just planning on having him healed by Master Hector, but I changed my mind midway through our journey."

Narcha tilted her head skeptically.

"At first, I thought of him as an innocent child who had survived a terrible accident, in dire need of comfort," Eiwin said. "But I was quite wrong. Despite his wounds and terrible situation, not once did Red become discouraged or even complain. He was never dragged down by his condition and was quite eager to explore and learn about a world that he was seeing for the first time."

She looked at Red and smiled.

"I thought that perhaps it was just the ignorance of a child too young to be aware of his terrible circumstances." Eiwin shook her head. "But I was wrong again. He knew about his situation, about his injuries, and it probably wasn't even the first time he's gone through something like this. Despite that, he fought on and survived to tell the tale, more mature and determined than most people I've ever met.

"When I looked at him again, I didn't see his lifeless eyes. Rather, I saw a gaze of resolve. Of someone who wasn't just eager to survive, but to live, to experience a life that he probably never had a chance to see. Maybe he's not normal, but the same strangeness that might make him a threat, as Miss

Narcha seems to believe, might make him special and helpful to us. Who can say they know which is the case?"

She met the eyes of each person at the table, one by one, as she continued.

"We are not the strongest, neither are we the most talented, but none of us have ever lacked the resolve or character to see our duties through. That is what makes a good Spiritual Practitioner, and what made our Sect what it is today."

She paused at Narcha.

"Wouldn't someone like that make for an exemplary member of our group, Miss Valt?"

Eiwin's speech made her hesitate, but Narcha still held some doubt and anger in her expression.

"All that sounds very poetic and convincing," she replied. "But isn't the real reason you want him in the Sect because he reminds you of someone?"

Eiwin pounded her fist on the table in fury and was about to lunge at the other woman, but at that moment, the old man opened his eyes.

"Enough!"

Eiwin and Narcha glared at each other but settled into their seats once more.

"Before we move on... Domeron, do you have anything to add?" Hector turned to the dark-haired man.

"I'll respect your decision, Grand Elder Hector." Domeron smiled at him. "You won't throw this responsibility onto my shoulders."

The elder cursed under his breath before turning to look at Red. "Well, then... Here's what I have to say—"

A child's voice cut him off. "What about me?"

Everyone turned to look at the boy sitting by Hector's side who had remained silent throughout the entire discussion. And all of them frowned.

"What about you, Allen?" Hector asked.

The kid grinned. "Aren't you going to ask my opinion?"

"I don't think that's necessary—"

"I think it would be great if he joined us," Allen said. "I mean, it's really boring with only adults around. All you do is train and talk about uninteresting stuff! Even Eiwin doesn't want to play with me anymore!"

He turned to Red. "With him here, I'd finally have someone my age around! So, I think he should join us. My vote is yes!"

Hector grimaced. "This is not up for a vote."

"Why not?"

"Because I'm the one who has the final say on everything in this Sect."

"That's not fair!" Allen jabbed a finger toward him. "Why do we have to put up with your tyranny?"

Without warning, a metal spoon hit the boy on the forehead.

"Get out of here, you brat!" Hector glared at him, waving a second utensil in the air.

Allen cradled his head, tears swelling in his eyes. "What did you hit me—"

Another smack.

"I said get out!"

He stumbled out of his seat, running outside with all the speed he could muster. Everyone around the table acted as if they hadn't seen what had just happened.

"That little shit!" The old man gritted his teeth, his chest heaving in anger. "I'll show him who's the tyrant..."

It took a few seconds for Hector to calm down before he turned to Eiwin and Narcha again.

"I've heard what the two of you have said, and you both make good points." He looked at Eiwin first. "While what you said about temperament is true, this is still a Sect at the end of the day, and a small one. We don't just recruit anyone with a courageous personality. Everyone in this Sect is either talented enough to warrant investing in or extremely skilled in their own specialties to be useful for us."

Narcha looked at her companion with a smug smile.

"But he's still just a child," Eiwin said. "His talent for Spiritual Practice might not be good, but what if he's talented in something else instead?"

"Hmm..." The old man looked Red up and down. "I'm not in the habit of recruiting kids based on anything other than their talent for cultivation."

"Please, at least give him a chance to prove himself."

Hector fell into deep, sincere thought, and Narcha's smile disappeared.

"Come here, kid." The elder waved Red over.

Red hesitated, remembering how violent the man had acted before.

"It's okay." Eiwin patted him on the shoulder. "He's just going to examine you."

This didn't make Red feel any more comfortable. Would Hector find traces of the crimson energy inside his Spiritual Veins? He considered refusing, but he could see the impatience on Hector's face as he hesitated. Red didn't think he could run away, so in the end, he just did as he was told.

Hector gazed into his eyes for a moment before extending his hands and grabbing his wrist. Red considered resisting, but despite how frail the elder looked, his grip felt like steel clamps locking down his arm. Thankfully, Hector wasn't trying to hurt him, so Red simply stood in place.

Abruptly, something flowed into his arm. It gave him a tingling sensation that he was very familiar with.

Spiritual Energy.

Red could see a faint white glow around his wrist. Not only that, but it came directly out of Hector's hands. When the realization hit him, Red looked up at the elder.

"You've opened your Spiritual Sea?"

"Hmm?" The old man seemed surprised at the question. "Just be still, brat. I need to finish examining you."

Red followed his orders. He wondered why he didn't feel the same pressure emanating from Hector he'd felt coming from the insectoids and other monsters underground, but then something else grabbed his attention.

He could feel the thread of Spiritual Energy flowing through his flesh and into his opened Spiritual Veins. It felt different from what he'd absorbed before, which was chaotic and hard to control. This energy was refined and seemed to have a will of its own. Curious, Red tried to direct it like he did when opening his acupoints.

A bony hand slapped the top of his head.

"I told you to be still!" Hector glared at him. "Do you want my energy to go out of control and cripple your veins?"

Red rubbed the spot that had just been hit, feeling a dull ache swelling. He nodded and chose to truly remain still this time.

"Good," the elder said. "Now, then, let's see..."

Red felt the energy creep around his opened Spiritual Veins, passing through every acupoint of his arm. The thread stopped at each of them, flowing around it for a second before moving onto the next one.

"Hmm? You've opened special acupoints? Interesting!"

Hector's energy stopped in front of the acupoints Red had opened with Viran's help. His curiosity only continued to grow, however, as the energy moved forward. It once more came to a stop, snaking around his injured shoulder.

"Huh?" This time he looked truly shocked.

Red felt his blood run cold.

Does he know?

The strand of energy wandered around the area a few more times, and a frown slowly formed on Hector's face. Eventually, he let go of Red's wrist and stared at him with a strange look.

"Kid, who the hell taught you that?"

CHAPTER 58
ELDER'S COUNCIL

"Taught me what?" Red asked, although he had an inkling about what the old man was referring to.

By the look on Hector's face, Red's act wasn't fooling him.

"You know damn well what I'm talking about." The elder pointed at his wounded shoulder. "Busted up acupoint, swelling vein—all signs of force-fully injecting energy into your body."

Red hadn't expected Hector to accurately guess the root of the problem, and he hesitated. Fortunately for him, someone else was eager to step in.

"What do you mean, old man?" Narcha asked, staring at Red.

"It's an outdated and wasteful method to get a quick boost in strength for people who have yet to open their Spiritual Sea," Hector said. "You need a Spiritual Stone and an open wound, preferably one that connects to a Spiritual Vein. Then you have to force the stone in until it touches one of your acupoints. That way, the energy will flow into your body and give you a momentary increase in strength."

Narcha frowned and turned away. "That's insane. There's no way it can be that simple!"

"It's not," the elder said. "You risk losing control of the energy inside your body, making your organs explode. Not to mention, this method causes extreme injuries to the acupoint and permanent crippling of the vein."

Red wasn't surprised to learn this. It was, in fact, just about what he was expecting would happen from all he'd learned from Viran. However, it didn't tell him about his own present condition. Someone else took the initiative.

"What about him? Is he okay?" Eiwin asked.

"Oh, definitely not okay," Hector said. "He'll live, but his shoulder acupoint is completely ruined, and that's already getting off lightly from using such a dangerous method." He turned to Red again. "Do you even know the consequences of what you did?"

Red shrugged. "It's better than dying."

Hector laughed. "Hah! I suppose you're not wrong... but you still haven't answered my first question."

He regarded Red curiously. "The method you used was outdated when I was a kid. Now we have pills that can do the exact same thing much more efficiently, without having to cut yourself up. I haven't even seen anyone talk about this kind of technique for decades!" The old man shook his head. "So, tell me, who taught you this?"

Red hesitated again. Eiwin was about to interject, but an ugly look from Hector was all it took to stop her. Seeing as he couldn't escape the situation, Red had to give an answer.

"No one taught me. I just saw someone doing it and tried it myself."

He wasn't lying. Viran had never specifically taught him the technique.

Hector grimaced. "You know what I'm asking, kid. I have to deal with people who think they're smarter than me on a daily basis, so stop trying to act clever. I don't care if you saw it or someone else taught it to you. I just want to know who that person was."

Just as he'd feared, there was no getting himself out of this. But the old man's display of authority didn't scare him after everything Red had gone through.

"I can't tell you," he replied.

He was being honest, just not in a way that seemed to please Hector.

"... Why not?" His frown deepened.

"Master Hector, is this really necessary—"

Eiwin's protests were cut short by a wave of the elder's hand. A formless force shoved her back into her seat and left her looking shocked.

"You brought him to me, so this is none of your concern anymore, Eiwin!" he said. "Don't forget your place in this Sect!"

This display of authority completely silenced her, and she gazed at Red with concern.

"So, why can't you tell me, brat?" Hector asked him once more.

What now?

He didn't want to tell them about Viran. Not only would it invite more questions, but it might expose his background as a slave in the moonstone mines. According to Viran, the guards made sure nothing ever got out, so if word of it somehow got back to them, Red was truly afraid of what could happen.

He could feel Hector's body exuding a sense of danger that froze him in place. But what was the old man compared to a nest full of spiders and a dozen insectoids? Could he still kill him? Probably, but Red was sick of feeling intimidated. He hadn't survived all those challenges and powerful monsters just so he could cower before powerful people on the surface.

For some reason, he thought back to when they'd just arrived at the courtyard, to something Narcha had said. He felt it was an appropriate response now.

"Because I don't want to, you old fart."

Hector's eyebrows twitched as his eyes widened in fury. Eiwin's mouth hung open, seemingly at a loss for words, and even Narcha stared at him in shock. A silence settled over the room while Hector looked as if he were about to erupt like a volcano.

But then a laugh broke the tension. The sound made Hector even angrier, and he turned toward the culprit.

"You think this is funny, Domeron?" Hector asked, foaming at the mouth. "I oughta slap you two dead and throw you out on the street."

"We both know you'd never do that, old man." Domeron shook his head with a smile. "I'm too useful, and he's one of the few people in this town that dares insult you to your face. That's reason enough for him to join our Sect!"

"Absolutely not! I am the Grand Elder, and I have the final say!"

"I never said I wanted to—" Red tried to interject.

"Quiet, you brat! You think you're clever? Insulting me just because you know I won't hurt you? Well, then here's what you get for your cleverness— while I'm alive, you'll never be a member of this Sect!"

"That's the same thing you said about Narcha," Domeron said, causing Narcha to look away in embarrassment.

"Shut up!" Hector pointed a trembling finger at the man. "If you like this kid so much, then you may as well leave this place with him!"

"Alright." Domeron got up from his seat and turned to the exit.

"No, wait!"

The man turned back with a grin, which only made the elder angrier.

"He's a talentless brat!" Hector said. "We can probably pick up an orphan off the street with better prospects than him."

"We both know that's not true, Hector," Domeron said. "Look at him, the boy's a survivor! He did something a lot of practitioners would hesitate to do in his place, all just so he could live another day. Besides, we haven't even tested any of his skills, so how can you know how useful he'll be?"

"We don't need anyone else in the Sect. Much less a brat like him!"

"Hector, we only have eight members."

"Not just eight members, but eight masters of their craft!"

Domeron sighed. "Do you really want me to do this?"

"Do what?" Hector's face slackened.

Domeron fished around in his pouch and picked out a necklace with the symbol of a fish, throwing it onto the table. "I want to call for an Elder's Council meeting."

"Domeron!" Narcha and Hector shouted at the same time.

Eiwin looked surprised too, but her lips soon spread into a bright smile.

"First Eiwin and now you!" The old man was shaking. "How are the rules of the Sect something you can just play around with? Are you planning on starting a rebellion?"

"Stop being delusional, old man!" Domeron said. "It's been eight years since we last took in a member because no one is ever good enough for you. And now that we have a promising prospect, you just want to throw him away?"

"But he could be dangerous, Domeron!" Narcha said. "We know nothing about him or how he appeared in that forest. There's definitely something strange about him."

"So what? Did we turn away Rimold because of everything in his past?" Domeron asked.

"Rimold is... different."

"Not at all, Narcha. He was a risk we were all aware of when we took him in, but in the end, that risk paid off and benefitted all of us." He pointed at Red. "In comparison, this boy is much less of a gamble."

Despite all of that, Narcha still didn't seem any more convinced, and the man simply backed off in disappointment.

"It's okay if you don't agree. This is what the council is for."

"You only have Eiwin with you. There's no way you can win with just her vote," Narcha pointed out.

"I also have Allen."

"You— Why do we even give a vote to that brat?" She glared at him. "That's still only three votes. Hector's vote counts for two, and with mine, we already have three. There's no way the others will support you!"

"Really?" He smirked. "I can't vouch for Rimold, but what about Rog and Goulth?"

Narcha didn't seem convinced. "Why would they want another kid to join us?"

"Wasn't Rog the one complaining about wanting someone to help him with hunting? Wasn't Goulth begging Hector for an actual disciple for years?"

Narcha froze, realizing her situation.

"I never agreed—" Red tried to speak up again, but the man talked over him.

"That's five votes against three, dear Narcha, and I'm sure I could convince Rimold, too."

Narcha was at a loss for words. She looked to Hector, searching for support, but his face was already sober with recognition. He had already understood the situation before Domeron even explained it.

"... Why are you doing this?" Hector asked.

"Because you're too stubborn for your own good," Domeron said. "Do you want to regale us with the story about how you ended up here in the first place?"

"Enough!" The old man waved his hand in defeat. "I get your point."

"Master Hector—" Narcha was about to say something, but she was silenced by a stern look from the old man.

She could only sit down in frustration while Eiwin beamed at her. Red, during all of this, was still standing behind Hector, with no idea what to think or do. Hector, however, turned to face him.

"It seems you have quite a few supporters, little bastard," he said through gritted teeth. "If it was up to me, I'd have already kicked you to the streets."

Red just stared back in silence.

"Don't get confused, though. Once you join the Sect, you'll also have to pay your respects to *me*, or you will be punished! You will have duties, obligations towards the Sect and its members that you will need to see through. You have to defend the Sect with your life! Do you understand?"

Red made to speak but hesitated.

"What is it now?" Hector glared at him. "Out with it, but be aware that if you insult me again, I won't let you get away with just a warning!"

"What do *you* do?" Red asked.

"What do you mean?"

"I mean, what does the grand elder do besides sit at a table and give orders? I thought this was supposed to be different."

Hector's eyebrows twitched. "Different?"

"Yes, I thought you were supposed to be like a gang or a guild or—"

A lightning-quick slap hit him on the side of the head.

"DON'T DARE INSULT OUR SECT, YOU BRAT!"

CHAPTER 59

JOINING THE SECT

RED RUBBED the sore spot on his head.

"Listen, kid. We are a Sect, do you understand? A *Sect.*"

"What's the difference?" Red asked.

He could see that he had struck a nerve, but he decided to take the opportunity to learn more about the subject.

"The difference? Everything about it is different!" Hector said with indignation. "A guild is a band of greedy, good-for-nothing mercenaries whose only interest is making money! They don't stand for anything, and more often than not, they're just a bunch of rogues and thieves who made their criminal ways legal."

"What about your Water Dragon Sect?"

Hector smiled proudly. "Our Sect is a noble institution, full of like-minded people who all work together to elevate the organization while on their journey of Spiritual Cultivation and pursuit of enlightenment!"

"Really?" Red was skeptical. "It doesn't look like you stand for—"

He was suddenly interrupted by a hand on his shoulder.

"Thank you for accepting him, Master Hector." Eiwin stepped forward and bowed towards the elder. "You will not regret this decision."

"Hmph, you have the gall to say that after forcing my hand?" He snorted. "I will respect the Sect rules, but this kid better be worth the trouble. Since both you and Domeron seem so keen on taking him in, you will be responsible for teaching him. I'll be closely monitoring his progress in these next few months and if I find him lacking, I won't hesitate to throw him out of the Sect!"

Eiwin nodded. "You do not need to worry, Master Hector. However, could I ask you about the situation of his wounds?"

"His shoulder should recover in a few weeks, so his left arm will be fully usable by then," he said. "However, his shoulder acupoint is an entirely different matter, and critical if he wants to open his Spiritual Sea."

"Is there a way to heal it?"

"There are certain medicines that can help, but they're all very rare and we most certainly don't have any of them here." He shook his head. "The boy made his choice, so he has to live with it now. As he said, it's much better than being dead."

Hector headed towards a set of stairs at the back of the meeting room.

"Go ask Goulth for some medicine. Since the boy already knows a special technique for opening his veins, there's no need to give him the Sect's manual." He waved his hands in dismissal. "Don't bother appearing in front of me again until you have something to show for yourself, brat."

He was already halfway up the stairs and soon disappeared from view. Red, still quite confused about what had just happened, looked around for guidance.

"Congratulations, Red," Domeron said. "It's best that you rest while you can for today. If you want to stay in this Sect, then you won't have any time to spare starting tomorrow—wounded or not. Eiwin will assign you a place to sleep. We'll see each other tomorrow." With a nod, he walked out of the hall.

Now only Red, Eiwin, and a brooding Narcha remained at the table.

Eiwin looked at her companion with hesitation. "Miss Valt..."

"Enough. You won, alright?" Narcha said. "Whatever you see in this boy... whatever troubles he'll bring us... I hope it's all worth it." She got up from her seat and moved towards the exit.

Then there were only two.

"Miss Eiwin." Red looked up at the woman. "You never told me anything about joining a Sect?"

Eiwin gave him an embarrassed smile. "I'm sorry for keeping that from you, but I had to keep it from Miss Valt, or else she wouldn't have even let you enter the courtyard. Besides, you told me you wanted to open your Spiritual Sea, right?"

"I did."

"Then this is the best place to do it. Or did you have any other options?"

"I... guess you're right. But from what Hector told me, those benefits don't seem to come for free."

"You're right, but Master Hector often exaggerates when discussing the Sect. We more or less work like a guild—taking on client requests to deal with monsters or gathering materials for money, and a bunch of other things. It's the way we manage to get by. We're far from comparable to a proper Sect."

"Then why does he insist on calling you a Sect?"

"That's because he wants us to be a Sect. Master Hector was part of a large Sect when he was younger, but it was destroyed by the Empire. He was one of the few survivors we know of."

"So he's trying to revive it?"

"More or less, and he's put all of his hopes in us. But more specifically on little Allen, the boy you saw earlier," she said. "He's the son of Master Hector's friends who were also part of the same Sect, and he hopes that one day Allen can take over his position and bring our group to greater heights."

"How many veins has he opened?" Red asked.

"Seven veins." Eiwin had learned not to worry about undermining his confidence, so she didn't hesitate to answer as she had in the past.

"And how old is he?"

"He just turned eleven a few months ago," she said, gauging his reaction.

Red wasn't affected by the news, though, and simply nodded. "I guess I have a lot of catching up to do."

"That's the right mentality," Eiwin said. "Now, let's get out of here and take you to your room. I assume you're still very tired after all those days of sleeping on the ground."

Red had never actually slept anywhere other than the ground, but he wasn't about to correct her. He followed her outside to the courtyard. There were quite a few buildings in total, with the hall they had just left at the center of everything.

Red saw a fenced-off area where a flock of chickens wandered about in the grass. Another building puffed clouds of black smoke from its chimney, with junk and tools gathered in a messy pile by the entrance. He even saw Allen sitting atop a box right outside the hall, ears pressed to the wall to listen in. His face brightened once he saw Red, and he dashed inside the main building in a hurry.

There was still so much more that Red didn't have time to examine before they stood face-to-face with a small wooden house towards the back of the courtyard.

Eiwin opened the door. "This is my room. You can sleep in here today, and tomorrow we'll find a room that you can call your own."

Red wandered inside behind her. He was greeted by a cozy bedroom with an actual bed, a table, a chair, and a small wardrobe. Eiwin moved around the room, cleaning up and stuffing some items on the floor into her backpack. From what Red could see, she barely had any possessions.

She turned to Red. "Right, as Domeron said, you should rest for now. If you want anything, I'll be in the courtyard cleaning things up. If you decide to stay here, I'll come to wake you up at dinnertime. Is that alright?"

"Alright," Red agreed without much thought.

Eiwin nodded but didn't leave the room. Instead, she continued to gaze at Red with a serene smile on her face. Some moments passed in silence, and Red grew uncomfortable under Eiwin's stare.

"Is there a problem?" he asked.

"Not at all," she said. "I'm just glad you're here with us, Red. Regardless of what Miss Valt and Master Hector may think, I still believe I made the right choice in bringing you here. I'm sure you won't disappoint us in the future."

That's unnecessary pressure.

"I'll do my best."

Red thought about rebuking her, but her words seemed genuine. Some of what Narcha had said today indicated another reason why Eiwin treated him so well, but there was nothing malicious about it, as far as he could tell. It wouldn't be wise to refuse someone who was doing nothing but helping him.

"Then I'll leave you to it." With that, she left the room, closing the door behind her, and Red was suddenly left alone for the first time in what felt like an eternity.

He hopped onto the mattress, relishing the incredible softness and comfort. However, when he looked at the walls, he didn't feel any warmth. Only uncertainty.

He examined his shoulder, slowly unwrapping its bandage. There was nothing different about the wound, which was still scabbed over and in the process of healing. At the very least, it seemed the old man hadn't done anything to his body that he had failed to notice. He put the bandages back and sat cross-legged on the bed.

There was so much Red needed to think about that he barely knew where to start.

The last few days since he'd reached the surface felt like a fever dream. Meeting strangers in the middle of nowhere who weren't keen on killing him was a first for Red, not to mention one who wanted to help him out of the kindness of her heart. He hadn't believed it at first, but no matter how hard he looked for the slightest crack in Eiwin's mask, he never found one.

But that didn't bring him any comfort either. He didn't understand her. Well, he didn't understand any of these people, but he felt that in every interaction he was more capable of comprehending the reasoning behind Narcha's actions than Eiwin's, even though the former was clearly against him.

Underground, everyone's primary concern was their own survival. There was no space for kindness, as it was more likely to get you killed than be repaid in kind. But these people didn't operate on the same principles, which left Red stumped on how to interpret their actions.

He didn't trust any of them, not even Eiwin. Suspicion was in his nature. It was how he had stayed alive for this long. Even if someone proved time and time again not to have ill intentions, he couldn't bring himself to lower his guard. He remembered the slaves that had tried to trick him with sweet words and promises.

He remembered the blob.

One mistake was all it took to lose one's life in this world, and even if it was safer on the surface, that principle didn't change. These people were far stronger than him, and Red would never feel comfortable sleeping in their vicinity.

So that brought him to one crucial question.

Should I stay?

CHAPTER 60

FIEND

BEING CONSTRICTED to one place wasn't the life Red had been looking for on the surface. That being said, he needed time to recover and adapt to his new and unfamiliar world. It just so happened these people offered him a wonderful opportunity to do so, though Red wasn't yet sure if—and how much—this opportunity would cost him.

Narcha's display in the street told him this Sect wasn't particularly well-liked by certain groups, and on top of that, there was a monster horde heading in their direction with a chance of making it to the town. All of that, as well as his still unknown responsibilities inside the Sect, made Red hesitant.

What if he was unknowingly dragged into a dispute? From the looks of it, it might already be too late to worry about that.

However, Red also didn't take this chance for granted. Whatever these people had in store for him, they'd still saved Red's life. What would Viran think if he decided to abandon them without repaying them for everything they'd done? It just didn't sit right with him.

I guess there's no choice, then...

In the end, he chose to stay in the Sect, at least for the time being. In the future, once he felt he had repaid his debt and was healthy, then he would consider his next steps. By then, it wouldn't matter if they didn't want him to go, since Red could slip away into this maze of a town and easily disappear.

He sighed, tension escaping his body. Arriving at a decision about his immediate future took much of the pressure off his mind, but his wounds and fatigue still weighed heavily. Although it was the middle of the day, he was in dire need of rest.

Red still didn't feel comfortable sleeping here, but the quiet room and the fluffy bed compelled him to drop his guard, if only for a moment, and to get as much rest as he could. Yet, before he did that, there was something he had been waiting a long time to try.

Red stepped down onto the wooden floor and assumed the boxing stance Viran had taught him. He'd never tried the exercise with just one hand, but he didn't expect it to pose a problem. He performed the movements by heart, entering the training trance he'd become so used to.

Although his tired body ached and protested, Red pushed through it. Then a familiar sensation surged across the surface of his skin. He sat down cross-legged on the bed and felt for the Spiritual Energy. It took a few seconds, but sure enough, as the intangible power flowed into his Spiritual Veins he couldn't help but be ecstatic.

The density and quality of the energy seemed far greater on the surface compared to the mines. Although still somewhat below what the blob had provided him, it was like Red could finally swim after being stuck in a puddle for so long.

He savored the feeling. He soon let the energy disperse, though, as he knew better than to cultivate while exhausted and injured. Besides, he didn't have any moonstones, so he wasn't sure how effective Viran's technique would be.

Red recalled the stash he'd hidden in the forest before meeting the group. His weapon, the insectoid crystal, the underground map, and an assortment of moonstones were all there. He still remembered how the clearing looked, so if he happened upon it again, he would definitely recognize it.

The one thing he didn't know was how to get back. Regardless, Red would need to wait until he was completely recovered and more acquainted with his environment before trying to retrieve his items. In the meantime, he could only hope no one would stumble upon his cache.

Maybe they have moonstones in town...

Just as Red was wondering how to ask that question without arousing suspicion, he heard a knock at the door.

What is that sound supposed to mean?

Another set of knocks, this time more frantic. Red remained silent. The sound didn't repeat, and he thought he was finally free to relax. As he laid down to sleep, though, he heard someone fumbling outside. He was wondering whether he should go out to investigate, when something caught his attention.

"Psst. Over here."

Red looked up. High up on the wall, at the small strip of a window in the otherwise completely closed-off cabin, he saw a face. A child's face he recognized from the meeting hall. For a moment, Red was too confused to speak.

"Hey, I thought you were sleeping!" Allen said. "How come you didn't answer the door?"

Red frowned. "What do you mean?"

"Look, it doesn't matter. Just open the door before Eiwin notices!"

The face disappeared from the window, and Red heard more fumbling. He didn't move from the bed, though. Soon there was another set of knocks on the door.

"Come on, open it already... Look, I have something really cool to show you!"

"Can't you just open it yourself?" Red asked.

"Oh."

The doorknob turned, and Allen hurried inside. He smiled at Red and extended his hand to him.

"My name is Allen! I'm the Sect Master of the Water Dragon Sect!"

Red didn't move to accept his handshake, staring at Allen in confusion.

"I thought Hector was the Master."

"What?" Allen looked indignant. "No, that old geezer is just the Grand Elder. I'm the actual Sect Master!"

"But wasn't he the one giving orders?"

"That's just because he's a dictator! He says that just because I'm too young, I'm not allowed to rule the Sect yet... but Rimold told me the truth!" Allen grunted, hitting his open palm with his fist. "He's trying to usurp me!"

"Usurp?" Red was unfamiliar with the word.

"Yeah, it means he wants to steal my power or something like that," Allen said, though he didn't sound confident. "He wants to take everything that belongs to me for himself!"

"You mean the Sect?" Red asked.

"Yes!" Allen looked angry. "And all the buildings and treasures in this courtyard, too!"

"That's great." Red had a hard time believing him, but more than anything, he simply didn't care.

"No, it's not great!" Allen's eyes widened in shock. "Have you not been listening?"

"I have. But why are you telling me this?"

"Because I need your help!" Allen said with a smile. "I want to recruit you as my supporter."

Red's frown deepened. "You need my help for what?"

"To overthrow that old man, of course." Allen put on a serious expression. "I've tried to talk about this with everyone else, but none of them seem to believe me! They've all been taken in by Hector's lies. He probably cast a spell of obedience on them!"

"Does something like that exist?"

"Yes, Rimold told me he uses it all the time on the townswomen. But that's not what matters," Allen said. "What does matter is that we need to do something about Hector before he ends up destroying the Sect! And you're going to be my right-hand man for the task."

"I don't—"

"It's okay." Allen raised his hand to cut him off. "I know you're tired, so we don't need to do anything right now. The old man is too smart anyways, so we'll need to come up with a good plan for this."

Allen approached and patted him on the shoulder. "You should rest and recover for now while I try to think of something. You're now my brother-in-arms, and together we'll take down that old man even if it's the last thing we do."

Red didn't bother responding. Allen walked towards the door after giving him what he must've thought was a motivating look.

"Oh yeah, I forgot." He stopped right as he touched the handle. "What's your name, brother?"

"... Red."

"Red? That's not a name, that's just a word!" Allen shook his head. "We'll have to think of a more fitting name for you, like Allan or Allyn. Don't worry about it, I'll help you come up with it. Rest well!"

He slipped through the door, closing it with a thud and leaving Red in silence. He heaved a sigh of relief before laying down in bed.

What a bother.

As sleep took him, the last thing Red thought about was how he could tell Hector about Allen's plan to gain his trust.

Here I am again.

Red could tell that he was in a dream before his senses could even adapt. After leaving the underground, he'd wondered whether the visions would persist, but now he had his answer.

As sensation returned, Red felt something strange. His entire body was heavier than normal—even opening his eyes was arduous. Eventually, he succeeded. Yet what he saw was nothing like his old dreams.

He was in the middle of an endless desert. But the sand wasn't pale gray, instead composed of pitch-black grains. All around him, mounds of bones pierced the dark wasteland, rising like mountains across the otherwise flat horizon. The sky was also different. The golden color had been replaced by a crimson red, and at the center of it all was a sphere.

This sun, however, was dark and surrounded by a burning crimson corona.

Red felt like something was terribly wrong. It was as if the firmament itself were sinking, heaven and earth merging into one. The terror of imminent slaughter and carnage consumed him, and he found himself longing for the eternal golden sky of his previous dreams.

Then, things changed.

In the distance, he spotted something. A shape stirred beneath the earth, rising out from the sea of black sand. The desert and the sky grew distant as the emerging force shifted the world around it. An endless tide of black sand flowed down its colossal shape, and the source of the upheaval was revealed to Red.

The head of a crimson fiend emerged. It was extremely far away, but even so, the creature seemed impossibly large. Its elongated head looked reptilian, and two horns protruded from the sides, though one was partly broken off.

Red knew that the creature was wounded, though he didn't know where this conviction came from.

The demon opened its maw, revealing fangs bigger than mountains, and raised its head towards the dark sun. Something stirred in its abyssal gullet, and it took a few seconds before the noise finally reached Red.

A roar. One that wasn't heard by his ears, but that reached directly into his soul.

For a moment, Red felt he understood the creature. Its cry wasn't one of anger.

It was one of grief.

It was the eternal agony that had accumulated inside a suffering and lonely soul as old as time itself.

It was a cry for help.

Suddenly, everything went dark.

CHAPTER 61

DISCIPLE

RED WOKE UP. As he opened his eyes, he found himself staring at the wooden ceiling of the cabin. He couldn't tell how much time had passed, but the scant sunlight streaming in through the narrow window looked red. He sat up and tried to recall his dream.

Unlike his previous visions, Red could actually remember this one quite clearly. The black desert, the mounds of bones—the crimson sky, the dark star, and the fiendish creature that rose from beneath the dunes. Most important of all was the feeling he'd been left with after the roar, an anguished grief that made him question why a living being had to suffer so. Red felt strangely compelled to help this monster, to do anything to reach it, even if he didn't know where to start.

However, a minute later this odd emotion dissipated, as if it were never there. Red shuddered. Why had this irrational thought appeared in his mind? Had the creature done something to him inside the dream? If he included the visions during his escape from the mines, this was the second time Red had experienced strange side effects from his dreams.

In the past, he'd often looked forward to his dreams. They offered him an opportunity to experience something other than the monotony of the mines, a chance to imagine the outside world. But now, it seemed, he had to be wary of them.

Was this all part of the supposed curse?

A few minutes went by as Red reflected on everything he'd seen, the differences between this dream and the previous ones. However, his thoughts were cut short by a knocking at the door.

At first, Red didn't respond, but then he remembered Allen's complaints.

"Who is it?" he asked from the bed.

"It's me, Red," Eiwin said from behind the door. "May I come in?"

Red didn't understand the need for the question. "It's your room."

The handle turned, and the woman entered, carrying a few things in her arms. The first thing Red noticed was the bright lantern that illuminated the room and made his eyes squint in pain.

"Ah, sorry, I forgot you were inside all day." She fiddled with the lantern, and its brightness magically decreased until Red could see comfortably again. After setting her items on the table, she smiled at Red. "How are you feeling?"

"Better," he answered. Actually, aside from his wounds, he'd never felt more well-rested.

"Good," Eiwin said. "You almost slept through the entire day, so I can imagine how tired you must've been. Unfortunately, I had to wake you up so we could apply the medicine and change your bandages."

"It's okay. I don't feel tired anymore."

"That's good, because then you can come with me and grab something to eat. I brought you some clothes, but..." She looked at Red and his disheveled state. "It's best that you take a bath first before you change."

"A bath?"

"Yes, so you can wash away all the grime and dirt from your body, and so we can properly apply the medicinal paste. But you can do that after you eat." She grabbed all her things from the table again. "Come with me. There's someone who's been quite eager to meet you."

Red winced. He wasn't sure if he was supposed to take this as a good or bad sign.

"Who?" he asked.

Eiwin grinned. "You'll find out."

Red didn't feel like any more surprises, but he sensed it would be strange to argue about it. He got out of bed and followed her outside into the night air.

The courtyard was well-lit, with lamps similar to the one Eiwin carried. In fact, looking downhill, most of the city was also shining, glowing in the darkness in an otherworldly way. It wasn't the warm, orange light of a torch, but a different, whiter light.

Red looked at the object in Eiwin's hand. "What's that thing?" he asked.

"This?" She lifted it. "It's a lantern."

"I know what it is. I mean, what's creating the light inside of it?"

"Oh!" Eiwin smiled in embarrassment. "It's flarestone. The town runs a mining operation in the canyon for this material and we export these to cities all over the world."

At the mention of mining, Red's heart beat faster. He did his best to maintain his composure, and Eiwin didn't seem to notice anything strange.

"Do you mine anything else in that...?" Red trailed off.

"Canyon? We do. There are lots of useful ores and precious gems down there, but flarestone is the most common. The area is actually infested with monsters, too, so there's still a lot of it we haven't explored. There are lots of books I could show you on the subject, but that'll have to wait until tomorrow. For now you should focus on eating and recovering."

Red nodded and didn't push the subject further. Internally, though, his mind was concerned. Could it be that these mines were also the ones he'd been imprisoned in, or were at least linked to them? Given his background, that could be dangerous. It was a priority for Red to find out more, but he still needed to gather this information carefully.

If he was too eager to ask specific questions, he would arouse suspicion. More than he already had, that is.

Eiwin's voice interrupted his thoughts. "We're here."

Red looked up. In front of him stood another large stone house, the second-biggest in the courtyard. He recognized it as the place where he'd heard the clanging metal earlier.

He gave Eiwin a questioning glance.

"Be warned that Goulth's attitude can be a bit..." She struggled to pick the right words. "Too much, when you first meet him. However, he's truly excited about the prospect of having someone study under him, so... be nice, okay?"

Red didn't know what he had done to warrant this kind of warning, but he simply nodded. He recognized the name from earlier in the day, but he didn't know what to expect.

Eiwin knocked on the door. "Master Goulth, I'm here!"

Silence.

"Master Goulth!"

"Come in, come in!" a deep voice said from within the house. "I'm at my forge!"

They entered.

Unlike the outside, the house was illuminated by a soft, orange glow Red was used to. The first thing he noticed was the mess. Materials and tools of all kinds were spread around the room—an assortment of hammers, planks, plates, and other objects Red was unfamiliar with. The pair had to step around them to make their way inside. Along the way, Red even saw a few weapons in varied states of disrepair.

There was also a sulfuric smell lingering in the air. It was over-whelming at first, but Red had smelled worse and quickly adjusted to it. As they entered another room, he came face to face with the so-called Master Goulth. He sat next to a burning furnace and tended to a pot placed over it, which emitted a pleasant smell. Goulth was a large, bald, middle-aged man, almost as big as Gruff but a bit overweight. He wore an apron and baggy clothes that were as dirty with coal and grime as the slaves in the mines.

As soon as they entered, the man turned to greet them.

His voice was deep. "I thought you would never arrive, Eiwin. The food is almost ready..."

He trailed off as his gaze settled on Red. He blinked. Shock came over his expression, and he turned to stare at Eiwin.

"Is that...?"

"Yes." Eiwin patted Red's shoulder. "Red, meet Master Goulth, Master Goulth, meet—"

The large man shot to his feet before she could finish and approached them in a sprint. Red's survival instincts activated, but before he could do anything, the giant was already upon him.

He froze.

But Goulth stopped right in front of him, crouching down. He examined Red with a curious gaze.

Red, confused, looked over at Eiwin, but she only shook her head in resignation.

"Calm and collected attitude... Looks young, maybe around ten?" Goulth said as if he were studying a weapon. "Good age to teach, though. Any older and they're already too set in their ways to ingrain good habits. A bit dirty, but nothing a bath can't solve."

Red thought about rebuking the man's evident hypocrisy, but he remembered Eiwin's advice.

Goulth's gaze came to a stop over his shoulder. "Very serious wounds, it seems. Here, let me see your hand."

Red hesitated, remembering his earlier experience with Hector.

"It's fine." Eiwin patted his shoulder.

You said the same thing about Hector...

In the end, Red supposed he didn't have any more secrets to keep about his wounds. He extended his good hand, and the man gripped it, inspecting his palm.

"Perfect!" Goulth said. "These are the hands of someone who hasn't led a pampered life like that good-for-nothing Young Master. You're a bit on the malnourished side, but a good diet is bound to solve it..."

The man set both big hands on his shoulders. Red almost yelled in pain, but upon seeing Goulth's expression, he stopped himself. Goulth had a huge smile on his face, and he could almost swear he saw tears welling in his eyes.

"My disciple! You've finally come home!"

With that, he embraced Red with a hug that took all the air out of his lungs. Red felt his still-recovering rib creak in pain, and tried to struggle out of the man's bearlike grip, to no avail.

"Master Goulth!" Eiwin cried. "He's still injured!"

"Oh, I forgot!"

The giant of a man let go of Red who promptly fell to his knees, trying to catch his breath. However, Goulth's hands hoisted him back to his feet.

"Sorry about that." He did not look sorry. "Here, I actually have something for you."

The large man wandered off to a cluttered desk nearby and, after sorting through the mayhem, retrieved a vial. He returned to Red and offered him the glass container. There was a dark-brown liquid inside.

"You can consider this a gift from your new master!" Goulth said proudly.

Eiwin looked surprised. "Is that...?"

"It is," he said. "But you better not tell the old man about it, girl!"

She smiled and shook her head. Red hesitated, but a look of encouragement from Eiwin made him accept the vial. He examined it with confusion.

"Drink it, kid!" Goulth urged. "The results will surprise you!"

It didn't look very appetizing, but he had eaten worse-looking things before. He uncorked the vial with his teeth and an acrid smell overwhelmed his senses.

I'm supposed to drink this?

Red paused again. With Goulth's expectant gaze trained on him, though, he didn't falter again.

In a single gulp, the liquid went down his throat. The taste wasn't any better than the smell, and Red was on the verge of vomiting out its contents. However, a few seconds later, he felt a gentle warmth in his stomach. A familiar tingling feeling spread throughout his body, but he soon felt it accumulate around his shoulder and bruised rib.

Suddenly, more pain appeared around his injuries, but it was nothing beyond what he was used to dealing with. Somehow, Red could feel the flesh under his skin moving. Before long, about a minute later, the feeling was gone.

Red felt different, though he wasn't sure why. He was about to ask the man what the purpose of the liquid was, but then he felt something new. A slight movement of his left arm. He tried to move it again, and the limb responded as strength slowly but surely returned to it.

Goulth laughed. "There we go! Can't have my disciple running around with only one functioning arm, right?"

CHAPTER 62

BLACKSMITH

"HOW DID YOU DO THAT?" Red asked, gazing in bewilderment at his newly healed arm.

"It's Spiritual Medicine, kid," Goulth said. "If you have the right materials, you can make something that can cure even worse wounds. Some can even help you with your practice."

Red recalled his conversations with Viran. He had mentioned something like that, but seeing it in action was a completely different experience.

"Mind you, this isn't enough to heal your crippled acupoint." Goulth hung his head in resignation. "That kind of damage can't be repaired by common Spiritual Medicine. But enough talk!" He pulled two chairs over from the other side of the room. "Let's sit down and enjoy the meal! Have you ever had chicken stew, kid?"

Red sat and shook his head.

"Hah, great! It's my specialty!"

Goulth used a ladle to scoop the stew from the pot into a bowl, filling it up to the brim. He passed it over to Red, who couldn't help but stare at it in wonder. He'd never been served so much food in one go, but he didn't even think about complaining. Before Goulth was finished serving Eiwin, Red was already stuffing himself.

"Good appetite!" Goulth said. "You truly don't disappoint."

Red didn't even lift his head. Iron spoons clanking against bowls were all that could be heard in the house over the next few minutes. Before Red was done with his first serving, Goulth was already well underway with his second one.

As the man noticed Red's first helping was almost finished, he picked up his ladle again.

"Here, eat more!" He scooped up another serving, filling Red's bowl to the brim again.

The two of them continued to eat like voracious beasts—Eiwin didn't seem nearly as rushed. Red couldn't match up to the large man's stomach, though. When Goulth was on his fourth serving, Red was finishing his second bowl and getting full.

"Want some more?" Goulth asked him.

Red hesitated, but in the end, he shook his head. He had to fight against his instincts to deny any food that was offered to him, but he felt truly stuffed.

"Well, don't mind me, then."

Goulth continued to eat. Both Red and Eiwin had finished, so they waited until the man ladled himself the rest of the pot. A few minutes later, he set his bowl aside with a satisfied sigh.

"Ah, that's the stuff!" Goulth patted his belly in satisfaction. "Did you know you can also train by eating food, kid?"

"How?" Red asked, skeptical.

"It's true! The Sects do it all the time! The meat of strong monsters is actually full of Spiritual Energy, and eating it can aid you in practicing," Goulth said, animated. "Of course, you can't just eat it raw. That would be no different from eating poison. But there are people who specialize in cooking monster meat, turning it into consumable food, and once in that state, these meals can prove invaluable to a cultivator's training."

"So... it's like Spiritual Medicine?"

"Hmm, you can think of it that way," Goulth said. "But medicines are substantially more powerful. They have concentrated essences that make their effect much stronger than just a normal spiritual meal, but they also have their downsides."

Red listened eagerly while Eiwin observed from the side, smiling in silence.

"Spiritual Medicine may also contain toxins that are harmful to the body," Goulth said. "So if you take too much at once, you'll suffer some serious side effects. This isn't the case with monster meals, though. While they're far less effective, they can be eaten more often and serve as a supplement to a cultivator's training."

"Were there toxins in the thing I drank?" Red cringed. If he had known that before, he wouldn't have drunk the vial.

"Of course there was!" Goulth said with a laugh. "But for medicine of that level, there's generally not many toxins, and in a few weeks your body will naturally expel them."

That easy?

The trade-off was certainly worth it in Red's mind. He also couldn't help but marvel at how the liquid was considered "low-level" among Spiritual Medicines. What was considered the bottom of the barrel could heal what would've taken weeks for Red to recover from naturally.

"Is that what you do here?" he asked. "Make these medicines?"

"Bah!" Goulth snorted. "No, I'm not an alchemist! I'm a blacksmith!"

These words sounded foreign to Red, and he looked to Eiwin for clarification.

"Alchemists are people who make Spiritual Medicines," she said. "A blacksmith is someone who makes equipment and items using metal, such as weapons and tools."

Considering the materials spread around the house, this made more sense to Red.

"So who made the medicine I took?" he asked.

Goulth frowned. "I made it."

"But I thought..."

"You don't get it, kid!" Goulth became annoyed. "When I joined the Sect, I became the Master-Crafter, responsible for all matters of crafting, including medicine. Do you know how ridiculous that title is?"

Red shook his head.

"Listen, kid, there are so many types of crafting that to claim someone is a master of them all is just about the most absurd thing in the world!" He got angrier. "Even in blacksmithing there are all kinds of different specializations I can't claim to be a master of. But Hector decided that just because I knew more than the others, I would be in charge of crafting everything in this Sect!"

His rant didn't show any sign of stopping. "Medicine, weapons, talismans, buildings... even formations! Each of these subjects require more than a lifetime of studying to master." Goulth's eyes widened. "I'm so over-whelmed I barely have time to focus on my projects!"

"Doesn't anyone else help you?" Red asked.

"That Allen brat is too dumb to know which way to hold a hammer, and everyone else is always giving me excuses!" He glared at Eiwin as he said this.

She gave him an apologetic smile. "We've talked about this before, Master Goulth. We're all too busy on missions for the Sect, and the last time I offered my help, you ran me out of your forge."

"You screwed up the quenching and shattered my weapon!"

"But I asked you to teach me before..."

"What's the point if you're gonna screw everything up anyways! But you don't need to worry about that now. My new apprentice is much more talented than the lot of you and wouldn't fail at such a simple task."

Red felt the pressure on him had unfairly increased. Still, he was inter-ested in learning how to craft, despite the risk of angering his teacher.

"So, where do we begin?" Red asked.

"Huh?" Goulth looked surprised. "What do you mean?"

"Didn't you want to teach me? Why don't we begin right now?"

"I'm not sure that's a good idea, Red," Eiwin interjected. "It's the middle of the night, and Master Goulth has had a pretty long day—"

"Yes!" Her words were interrupted by a shout of eagerness from the giant. "That's the attitude I was talking about!" Goulth approached Red and patted him on the shoulders. "A good apprentice must be eager to learn, no matter the time of the day. Here, I have something else to give you!"

The man ran off, sorting through the mess on one of his worktables, while Red patiently waited. Eiwin could only stare helplessly at the two of them. In the end, she simply stood aside and observed.

Goulth returned carrying a leather-bound book.

"This is the accumulation of all my work!" he explained excitedly. "It belonged to my master before me, and to his master before that. This contains some of the forging philosophies of the long-destroyed Amber Saber Sect, and it's something every blacksmith should read!"

Goulth offered the book to Red.

"I'm letting you borrow this, for now," he said with a smile. "Read it and learn what it means to be a blacksmith. Once you've proven yourself to me, I'll let you keep it and pass it on to your own disciple later in your life."

Red held the book as if touching a delicate treasure. Carefully, he unlatched the string binding the item shut and opened it to the first page. It was clear the man wasn't lying about how old the book was. Red was afraid he would destroy the paper if he handled it carelessly.

However, when he was greeted with the symbols on the page, he remembered something. He looked up at Goulth.

"What is it?" the man asked.

"I can't read."

"You... what?" Goulth looked astonished.

"I never learned how to read," he said.

Goulth blinked and looked over at Eiwin. She looked just as shocked.

"Red, you never told me this," she said.

"You never asked." Red shrugged. "Besides, I didn't have to read anything before, anyway."

Goulth sat down and put his head in his hands. "This... this is a disaster."

He seemed about to cry. Red was confused.

"What's the problem?" he asked. "Can't I just learn now?"

"Of course you can," Goulth said. "But how long will that take? A year? Maybe more? That book doesn't use simple language, either, so who knows when you'll be able to understand it."

"It's okay, Master Goulth." Eiwin put a comforting hand on his shoulder. "Red is one of the smartest kids I've ever met, so it shouldn't take that long for him to learn. Besides, can't you just teach him what's in the book yourself anyways?"

"I suppose, but... Ah, what am I talking about!" Goulth's face changed into one of determination, and he slapped himself a few times. "Who ever said teaching was a simple task? Since my disciple is eager to learn despite his shortcomings, I, as his master, should do my best to teach him!"

He got up and approached Red, gazing at the boy intently.

"Kid," he said, "I don't know what you've been through, but you've clearly gotten the short end of the stick in life! Not knowing how to read, being all skinny and wounded, I can't even begin to imagine how many things you still have to learn. So, know this..."

Goulth crouched down to Red's level.

"You can't afford to slack off! Hard work is the bare minimum, but if you truly want to make something of yourself in this world, you must be willing to sacrifice everything in the name of improving yourself! That means no breaks, no time for playing, nothing but fully devoting your heart and soul to learning! Do you understand?"

Red felt overwhelmed by the sudden speech, but he knew everything the man said was true. Only after hearing it being put into words and acknowledged by others, though, did the weight of the task ahead become clear to him.

In the end, he simply nodded, not averting his gaze.

"Good!" Goulth smiled at his determination. "Then let's start!"

"Not now!" Eiwin cut them off. "Tomorrow."

CHAPTER 63

SPIRIT KEY

BEFORE THEY COULD START HAMMERING AWAY in the middle of the night, Eiwin dragged Red out of the forge, despite Goulth's objections. Red found himself in the courtyard again, Eiwin leading him to another building.

"I've prepared a bath for you," she said. "Your new clothes are inside."

Eiwin left him alone inside a room furnished with a large wooden tub filled with hot water. Towels were hanging on a rack, his new clothes were neatly folded on a table, and on a nearby stand, there were all kinds of toiletries, including a few bars of soap and some pleasant-smelling bottled liquids; the purpose of which Red had no clue about.

He didn't know where to start, but he was above asking for help with this kind of task.

Ten minutes later, Red exited the bathhouse wearing his new clothing—a long-sleeved black shirt and black pants. They were a bit too big on his body, but they were by far the most comfortable clothes he ever remembered wearing. He could get used to them.

But then there were the shoes.

Red had never worn anything on his feet, so getting used to having them completely covered by a thick material was difficult for him. However, since everyone else in town seemed to wear shoes, he thought it was worth trying to fit in.

Further ahead, he saw Eiwin on a chair, calmly waiting for him. As he approached, she studied him up and down, observing his transformed appearance.

She glowed. "Now you look like a proper young man. These clothes fit you very well."

"Not really. They're actually a bit too large for me."

"I meant..." Eiwin was at a loss for words. "We'll buy you better-fitting ones, eventually."

Red nodded. "What now?" he asked.

"Hm, I didn't think about that." Eiwin looked up at the night sky. "Are you tired?"

Red shook his head. He'd only woken up an hour ago, after all.

"Uh... I didn't think about this too much." Eiwin was struggling. "Do you want to visit the library?"

"What's that?"

"It's where we keep the Sect books," she said. "You might not be able to read yet, but I can summarize a few of them for you if you'd like."

"That sounds interesting."

There was still so much he wanted to learn about, and waiting until he could read wasn't an option for his plans.

Eiwin led him to the other side of the courtyard and into a closed-off stone house. She opened the door and held up her lantern, illuminating the interior.

A cramped room greeted Red as a wave of musty air hit him directly in the face. Bookshelves lined the library from wall to wall, holding hundreds of books in various conditions. Some looked as old as the one Goulth had offered to him, while others were nothing more than piles of paper bound together with string.

Red had to be careful as he walked between the shelves, fearful that even the slightest touch might turn their contents into dust. Thankfully, Eiwin led them to an open space where they could breathe.

A large table stood in the middle of this room, with books and papers scattered across its surface. Eiwin cleared a space to set down her lantern and pulled up two chairs.

She took a seat. "Here, sit down." Eiwin pointed to the chair at her side. "I have something I'd like to show you."

Red sat and observed Eiwin as she sorted through the pile of books. Eventually, she found what she was looking for. She put a book in front of them, which looked to be in far better condition than the rest of the collection.

"Have you ever seen this book before?" Eiwin asked.

Red felt compelled to say he'd never actually seen a book before today, but in the end, he just shook his head.

"This is one of the oldest known books in the history of humanity," she said. "It's widely available these days, and it has had so many versions that no one knows what the original one looked like—or who wrote it, for that matter. The message remains, though."

She pointed at the book cover.

"It's called *Spirit Key*. It's the first recorded document about Spiritual Cultivation, back when humans were still in the process of figuring out how they could use Spiritual Energy to their benefit."

Red's interest was piqued. "What's written in it?"

"All the basics you need to know about Spiritual Cultivation." Eiwin opened the book and turned to a certain page. "Here, do you know what this is?"

Red studied the page and saw a familiar illustration. It was an outline of a human body depicting the twelve Spiritual Veins, their acupoints, and the Spiritual Sea. It seemed far more detailed than the drawing in Viran's hideout, but Red noticed the picture contained only the ninety-nine basic acupoints and none of the special ones the man had mentioned to him.

"I recognize it," he said. "It's the Spiritual Veins and the Spiritual Sea."

"That's right. Not only does this book explain the special organs required for cultivation, but it also depicts the most common method for opening acupoints and the Spiritual Sea. These techniques are nothing special compared to those some factions have, but the simple act of spreading this knowledge increased humanity's strength as a whole."

Seeing Eiwin's passion for the topic, Red felt as if she had forgotten he was even in the room.

"This book was written during a time when cultivation wasn't a tightly kept secret, and when humanity was united against one common enemy," she went on. "Things have changed since then. Humans fight against humans now, and every faction keeps their knowledge of Spiritual Practice a secret from the world..."

She looked down in dejection.

"I wish I could rebuke them, but they do what they must to survive." Eiwin pointed at the book. "All the same, they couldn't keep this knowledge from spreading even if they tried."

"What were they fighting?" Red asked before she could move on. "Humanity, I mean."

"... Monsters." She looked conflicted. "Before humanity discovered the secrets of cultivation, powerful creatures ruled and dominated the world. Humans only survived by hiding from them, and because they were of no threat to the true rulers of the continent. This all changed one day, of course, but that's a topic for another time..."

Eiwin rifled through the pages of the book before settling on another page. This one didn't have any technical illustrations but vividly depicted a swordsman in the middle of a forest.

"This book talks about more than just plain cultivation. So, tell me, Red." She turned to him again. "What do you know about Spiritual Energy?"

Red felt this was a trick question, but he didn't see any reason not to answer.

"It's a formless energy that's present in the air, and that we can use to unlock the true potential of our bodies." Red tried to put what he remembered from Viran's explanation as simply as he could.

Eiwin grinned, a little smugly, as if she already knew his answer would be wrong and was happy to display her knowledge to correct him.

"That's partially correct, but there's a lot more to it than just that. Have you ever wondered why they call it 'Spiritual' Energy?"

Red shook his head. The thought had never even entered his mind.

"It's because the energy has a will of its own," she said. "It's capable of influencing its surroundings and, at the same time, it can be influenced *by* its surroundings. That is to say, it has a spirit of its own, hence the name."

Red frowned, confused. "Does that mean it can think and make decisions like a human?"

"Not quite like that," Eiwin said. "It's still energy, not a person, but it's a powerful reflection of the world it lives in and is capable of telling us things we can't see with the naked eye. In other words, Spiritual Energy can take various forms and attributes depending on where it's located."

Red recalled the different colors he had seen the energy display. There was the pure white from Viran's Spirit Stone, the green from the insectoid's attacks, and the crimson that had protected him from the spiders.

"An easy way to think about it is by using the elemental classification," Eiwin continued. "Different schools of thought have different opinions on how to categorize these elements, so I'll mention all the agreed-upon ones: Fire, Water, Air, Earth, Metal, Wood, and Lightning—these are all types of elemental attributes that Spiritual Energy can take.

"So, for instance, in the forest where we found you, there's an abundance of Wood and Earth Spiritual Energy. Near the river, though, there was more Water Spiritual Energy. But that can change, too. If you set fire to the forest, the Wood Spiritual Energy would transform into Fire Spiritual Energy. However, the energy can change the material world the same way the material world can change the energy. As an example, if you could somehow capture lots of Fire Spiritual Energy from somewhere else and throw it into the forest, then the trees would catch on fire without you having to produce a spark. Do you understand?"

Red nodded. In his mind, he wondered which attribute the insectoid's green energy had belonged to.

"That is actually one of the most important principles behind the Spiritual Arts once one opens their Spiritual Sea. But these aren't mentioned in this book," she said, to Red's dismay. "Of course, it's also important to know that this energy is rarely found in its pure form in nature. A single strand of Spiritual Energy in the forest will have mixed attributes between Earth and Wood, but also small trace amounts of Water, Air, and sometimes even Fire."

"But there's no fire in there...?"

"There are different theories to explain that," Eiwin said. "Some say that all life, including plants, is made up of different elements, hence the presence of Fire Energy in the middle of a forest. Other people say it's because of the warmth of the sun beating down on our world, which is associated with fire. No one truly knows for sure, but what is important is that one shouldn't speak in absolutes when discussing the properties of Spiritual Energy. Some techniques require very pure amounts of a certain type of Spiritual Energy, while others require a precise mixture of different elements. The special method you're using to open your Spiritual Veins probably has its own set of requirements too, doesn't it?"

Red nodded but refused to comment any further.

"You keep calling it Spiritual Energy, but it sounds more appropriate to call it Elemental Energy," he said. Her explanation seemed to revolve entirely around natural elements.

"That's a good catch," Eiwin said. "People actually used to call it that at one point, but then they made an important discovery."

She paused, relishing Red's anticipation.

"That energy is influenced not only by nature, but also by people and their actions. Emotions, martial arts, craftsmanship, and even more abstract concepts, such as life and death, fate, law, and order. Absolutely everything in this world can influence the shape and attributes of Spiritual Energy!"

This time, Red didn't understand at all.

CHAPTER 64

DEMONIFICATION

"But those things aren't..." Red struggled to find the right words.

"Physical? Material?" Eiwin completed his sentence for him. "You're right, and that is exactly what makes Spiritual Energy so special."

"How does it manifest? I can imagine what Fire Energy can do, but what about... Emotional Energy? Martial Arts Energy?"

"There's actually a story in this book explaining the discovery of this."

She pointed at the illustration of the swordsman and the forest.

"A long time ago, when humans were still figuring out the specifics of Spiritual Cultivation, there was a group of warriors who stood at the very vanguard of humanity's war against monsters. The preferred weapons of this group were swords, which they used to cut through the thick hides of their enemies. They practiced their swordsmanship in a forest valley where the density of Spiritual Energy was very high. Every technique, every tactic, every breakthrough in their cultivation—it was all developed in that place.

"Thousands of disciples came and went, great heroes who could call that forest home. Then one realized that something had changed in the valley. It wasn't an immediate transformation, but a gradual one that happened over centuries. The Spiritual Energy in that place had changed..."

"Changed how?" Red asked.

"It had taken on a new attribute," Eiwin said. "Wood Energy was still abundant there, but some of it had evolved into something you couldn't find anywhere else. They noticed that when they used the Spiritual Energy of that valley to practice, their Sword Arts would be much stronger. The accepted explanation was that after centuries of people practicing and developing their swordsmanship in that valley, the Spiritual Energy there was influenced by their spirit. It became something never before seen in the world: Sword Spiritual Energy."

"And I assume that's not the only type of energy they discovered?" The explanation cleared Red's doubts, but he still had many questions about the process.

"Not at all," Eiwin said. "That was just the first one. After that, cultivators discovered many types of Spiritual Energy. Some had always been around, but people only noticed when they looked at them with a new perspective. For instance, a dying person would emit Death Spiritual Energy, while a newborn baby would be full of Life Spiritual Energy. Turbulent Spiritual Energy would fill a battlefield between armies, influenced by the fervor of thousands of soldiers fighting to the death. On the other hand, a hallowed academy of scholars would be saturated with an orderly and wise Spiritual Energy.

"They understood that just as nature could influence Spiritual Energy, so could human actions and emotions, and they learned to manipulate that aspect to their own benefit."

"From what you're saying, though, these transformations take hundreds of years to happen. Isn't that far too slow?" Red asked.

"Indeed, but through a lot of experimentation, they found ways to induce those transformations far more quickly. One of them is by using an organ of vital importance in Spiritual Cultivation..."

"The Spiritual Veins," Red said. He recalled Viran's explanation in the mines.

"Correct!" she said with a smile. "By circulating Spiritual Energy through our veins and acupoints in different patterns, we can force it to change at a much greater speed. Of course, there are also limits to our transformation capabilities. For instance, if you tried to transform Water Energy into Fire Energy, the process would be much harder, and you would end up wasting most of the energy. Therefore, the original attributes of the Spiritual Energy you absorb are still of vital importance to cultivators."

"But all this is only possible after opening the Spiritual Sea, right?"

"Yes. The Spiritual Sea allows you not only to manipulate Spiritual

Energy but also to keep it within yourself. Those are two things you can't do with just Spiritual Veins."

Red stopped asking questions and tried to absorb the information. His understanding of Spiritual Energy was more incomplete than he first assumed, but even though the subject was fascinating, he could only interact with it after he opened his Spiritual Sea. And who knew how long that would take?

The eagerness was eating him from the inside, but he recalled Viran's advice to not bite off more than he could chew. He still had many veins to open, so it would be counterproductive to focus on a future that was still out of his reach.

Red changed the subject. "What about the valley? Does it still exist?"

"It does," Eiwin said. "It's considered a holy site for Spiritual Cultivation, and it's home to one of the oldest and more powerful Sects in the world— the Hallowed Valley Sect."

It was yet another unfamiliar name to add to Red's growing list of powerful organizations.

"I assume these Sects are quite... different from our own, right?" Red tried to approach the question without offending her as he had Hector.

"They are much more powerful." Eiwin confirmed his suspicions with a helpless smile. "It's impossible to even begin to compare the two, especially when our name is so often mocked by others."

"So why does Hector call it the Water Dragon Sect?"

Eiwin sighed, some sadness behind her eyes. "Master Hector is one of the few survivors of a now-extinct Sect. He considers it his responsibility to make sure the name of the Sect lives on to the next generation. For that, he chose the lot of us to be responsible for it."

"What happened to his Sect?"

"The Empire... happened." Her voice became bitter. "We shouldn't change topics, though. You'll learn about all that eventually, and there's still something important you should know about Spiritual Energy."

Although Red was still curious, he agreed with her. Rushing to learn about these things was pointless.

"I explained to you why it's called Spiritual Energy, right?" she asked.

"Because it can both influence and be influenced by its surroundings," Red repeated.

"That's right. And in the same way humans can influence Spiritual Energy, they can also be influenced by it."

Red's eyes narrowed. "In what ways?"

Eiwin closed the book and looked at him seriously.

"Red, it's important to know that Spiritual Energy can be influenced by absolutely everything humans do. Both good things and evil things. Intense emotions, like pain, fear, rage, greed—these will convert Spiritual Energy into a wicked and twisted form. More often than not, these negative emotions will be more intense than positive ones. Once the Spiritual Energy transformation reaches a certain level, it will also change people who come into contact with it."

She paused.

"That corruption process is called demonification."

For some reason, Red shuddered.

"What happens then?" he asked, although he felt he somehow already knew the answer.

"The first stage of demonification is merely a change in temper," Eiwin said. "Someone's personality will become twisted over time, and they'll start acting on their baser instincts, depending on the type of corruption that has affected them. After that comes the second stage, where a person's body is transformed into... something horrible to witness. The third stage completes the process, where the original individual is completely gone and, in their place, only a demonic monstrosity remains."

Red felt his blood run cold. But Eiwin didn't seem to notice this and continued.

"You see, it's important for Spiritual Cultivators to know about this. They are in constant contact with Spiritual Energy, and compared to normal people, they are far more sensitive to its changes. This corruption may happen because of external influences, but it can also happen from the inside. If a cultivator loses themselves to their emotions, then the corruption process starts from within, and the Spiritual Energy inside their body slowly becomes twisted..."

She paused, finally noticing Red's silence.

"I don't mean to scare you by telling you this," she said, trying to comfort him. "But it's important to always have your emotions in check if you choose to continue cultivating. This doesn't mean you should be emotionless, but you should never become lost in your feelings or let them cloud your judgment and reasoning. Many heroes fell into this same trap and ended up unleashing disaster upon the world. Their downfall serves as a cautionary tale for future generations."

Eiwin tapped her temple. "While there are plenty of external threats to worry about out there, never forget the danger from within..." Her serious expression dropped, and a smile returned to her face. "I'm sorry that we have to end today's lesson with such a grim topic, but it's something every Spiritual Cultivator should know."

"I understand," Red answered, but he was lost in his own thoughts. "Is that all for today?"

"Yes. As much as I would love to keep talking, it's important to let you reflect on what you just learned. I can see you have a lot of things to think about."

He didn't respond.

After a long silence, he asked, "Can... I go to my room?"

"Sure. You don't need to ask for permission." Eiwin laughed. "I still haven't prepared your room, so you can continue using mine. I'll be here for a little while organizing this..." She waved at the books and scrolls spread around the table. "Mess."

Red nodded but didn't immediately leave.

"Is there something else?" Eiwin asked, confused. "Do you need me to bring you there?"

"Not really."

"Then... aren't you gonna go?"

"I suppose so."

Red stood from his chair and left the library under Eiwin's inquisitive gaze, closing the door behind him. He wandered through the courtyard toward his temporary bedroom, but his mind wandered as he looked up at the starry night sky.

The moon was different today. The bright section had diminished compared to when he first saw it a few days ago, and its light had decreased.

Red slowed down until he finally came to a pause in front of his room. He remembered something Eiwin had just mentioned.

It's called demonification.

His mind wandered further back to his encounter with the insectoids when he was close to escaping the underground.

Disease.

Red shivered. He recalled the feeling of the crimson aura, the overwhelming smell of blood. It hadn't invoked any negative emotions within him at the time, but that didn't mean he was safe.

Had his temper changed? Not that Red could recall, but this kind of corruption was insidious and slow, as Eiwin had explained it. Although no changes had happened yet, he couldn't guarantee they wouldn't come to pass one day.

Besides, that wasn't the only thing he had to worry about. The blob had also spoken of a curse, and he didn't think it was referring to the core. What if that was yet another source of corruption that was actively influencing Red?

Now that immediate death was no longer a concern, Red faced an uncertain future. However, not everything was hopeless.

There were the special acupoints he had opened. Viran had told him he would understand their use once he left the underground, but Red hadn't noticed anything special about them. He didn't think the man would have lied, though, and he expected their true purpose would eventually be revealed.

The best he could do right now was open as many acupoints as he could, as soon as possible, and walk further down the path of a Spiritual Cultivator. Then possibilities and opportunities would present themselves.

Red now knew for sure. It was only by seeking this power that he would become truly free to do as he pleased.

CHAPTER 65

OBSTACLES

RED WASN'T keen on getting more sleep. He had rested for most of the day already and was eager to continue his training. While the rest of the Sect were in their beds, he practiced his Vein Opening Technique and approached the third acupoint of his Upper Leg Vein.

It was only now that the consequences of his earlier choice hit him. Back in the underground, Red had opened two acupoints on his left leg because of his injury, leaving his right leg untouched, and this had created an imbalance in his Spiritual Veins. He could feel the Spiritual Energy being pulled in two directions.

This next acupoint would be especially hard to open, but Red could solve the issue once he cleared this obstacle. He couldn't guess how long it would take, but there was no other option but to keep at it until the acupoint gave way.

After finishing his training, Red lay down and got a few hours of sleep before morning arrived. A rooster's crowing foretold the imminent sunrise, and a few minutes later, he heard the first signs of activity within the Sect. He debated whether to wait until he was called upon, but after almost half an hour passed, he tired of staring at the wooden ceiling.

Red left the bedroom and looked around the courtyard. There, he saw a man rocking in a chair while sipping on a steaming mug. His attention was fixed on watching the chicken coop in front of him. It was Domeron.

Red hesitated but decided to approach him.

As he arrived by his side, the man didn't react. Red thought about making his presence known, but then he noticed something strange about Domeron's appearance.

"You're missing an arm," he said.

He hadn't noticed it in the meeting hall because of the large coat the man was wearing. Now, though, Red could see the empty sleeve where his right arm should have been.

Domeron scoffed, not turning to look at him. "Really? How did you notice?"

"Because of your empty sleeve. It's quite obvious when you look at it."

The rocking of the chair stopped, resuming a few seconds later.

"How did it happen?" Red asked.

"It got cut off," Domeron said. "Listen, Red, it's early in the morning and I like to enjoy my quiet time before Goulth starts banging on his forge. What is it you want?"

"I want to train."

"Can't do that with only one functioning arm," Domeron said. "Best you focus on recovering for now."

"Both my arms are working now."

"Hm?"

At that, the man finally turned to look at him. Red waved his left arm around to back up his claim. The bandages were also gone, and all that remained of the shoulder wound was a dull, aching pain and a nasty scar.

"Did Goulth give you any special medicine?" Domeron asked, cutting straight to the heart of the matter.

Red nodded.

"I see... That girl is far more cunning than she lets on." The man looked away and smiled. He pointed to an area of the courtyard in front of him. "First, go ahead and show me the routine you used to open your veins."

Red hesitated for a second, but still went along with it. As far as he was aware, there was nothing special about the exercise itself, so he had no reason to hide it. He entered his training posture, legs apart and slightly bent, fists held at his waist. And then he started.

Like always, the exercise consisted of a mix of punches and low kicks that gradually increased in intensity and speed. In the past, Red could only keep up the routine for a minute before his body was exhausted, but now he could comfortably surpass that mark. According to Viran, the longer you could last, the better prepared your body would be to absorb Spiritual Energy.

The previous night, he had discovered that his limit was just below two minutes, but he pushed himself harder this time around. Finally, he barely crossed the threshold before his body was spent and a familiar tingling sensation came over him.

Red sat down cross-legged and started to attack the acupoint in his right leg. The barrier barely gave way, but he was already used to this kind of result. Opening veins was a matter of accumulation, and true progress would only come after weeks of training. A few minutes later, he finished the process and looked up at Domeron.

The man was frowning, looking quite displeased, which left Red confused.

"I only meant for you to show me the basics of your movements, not to plop down in the middle of the courtyard and start cultivating," Domeron said.

Red shrugged.

"It doesn't matter." Domeron massaged his temples. "I assume the person who taught you this routine is the same one who taught you how to inject yourself with a Spiritual Stone?"

There was no reply, but his silence was enough confirmation for the man.

"This is actually a very old set of army exercises people used to practice up north. That is, before the cultivation community up there was wiped out by the Empire," Domeron said. "There's nothing wrong with the method, but it's not ideal for a child's body to be practicing it."

From that alone, Domeron seemed to have figured out more about Viran's background than Red himself knew. Still, he doubted it was enough to pin down his mentor's true identity.

"I'm used to it by now," he said.

Domeron sighed, his expression troubled. "Either your mentor wasn't very good at teaching, or he didn't care enough about you to do it properly. What else did he teach you?"

Red gave it some thought. "Footwork. And also knives. Kind of."

"That's it?"

Red nodded.

"Alright." Domeron got up from his chair. "Follow me."

He led him to the other end of the courtyard, behind a few houses. Getting there, Red saw a large fenced-off area that hadn't been visible when he first entered the Sect. Wooden and metal dummies, sparring weapons, swinging bag obstacles, and other kinds of training equipment were all lined up in the outdoor arena.

As they approached, he noticed that many of the tools showed signs of wear and tear. It was apparent that at least someone in the Sect used this training space quite often.

Domeron opened the gate and went over to the weapons rack. He picked up a wooden longsword for himself and threw a small wooden baton over to Red.

He caught it, face wrinkled with confusion.

"Sorry, it's the closest thing we've got to a fake knife here." Domeron shrugged. "It's not my favorite kind of weapon."

"Are we not going to use the real thing?"

The man laughed. "What, did your master train you with real knives, too?"

But his laughter eventually trailed off as he saw the serious expression on Red's face.

"What kind of maniac did you have for a teacher, anyways?" Domeron shook his head in resignation. "We are here to train, not to cut ourselves bloody while you try to figure out the basics. In the future, once you've shown a certain level of proficiency, then we can certainly raise the stakes and use real weapons."

Red nodded in understanding. "So what do we do?"

"Now you show me your footwork," Domeron said. "Over here."

Domeron led him to the obstacle course: a circle of tall wooden arches from which sandbags hung by ropes.

"Stand in the middle."

Red did as he was told. Now he was surrounded by obstacles.

"What now?" he asked.

"Now you stay in the circle and dodge."

Domeron's sword flashed and struck one of the sandbags. The heavy sack flew towards Red, and he stumbled back in an attempt to dodge it, narrowly getting out of its way. While he was still recovering his balance, though, another bag hurtled towards him from a different direction.

This time, Red was more prepared. He dove to the side, completely avoiding the hit. But that was when he noticed he'd just put himself in the path of two other bags swinging for him. His mind turned, and he worked out another path to safety.

Unfortunately for him, Domeron seemed to have predicted his move. This time, three bags came at him from different angles, and Red could only throw himself on the ground to avoid being hit. He looked up and noticed that in his prone position, the heavy sandbags flew over his head harmlessly.

"What are you doing, you little smartass?" Domeron glared at him as the swinging obstacles eventually came to a stop. "I told you we were testing your footwork! If the goal was simply getting out of the way of the bags, then you could just step outside the circle!"

"You caught me by surprise." Red got up, patting the dust off his clothes and removing his shoes. "I'm ready now."

The man snorted. "You better not have interrupted my morning routine just for this."

He swung his sword and sent another bag flying forward. This time, Red adopted a different dodging strategy. He took a quick step to the side and ducked out of the way. Then, with a swift assessment of his immediate surroundings, he sidestepped into a different spot where fewer bags were moving. Sure enough, his change in tactics paid off, and he didn't feel nearly as pressed a few seconds in.

He'd noticed that his desperate dives would often take him into the path of another obstacle. These large jumps were a habit he had developed after fighting against giant monsters who could kill you in a single strike, when the only thing that mattered was getting out of the way and not where you ended up afterwards. However, it wasn't appropriate in this situation, where Domeron had more than enough time to predict his movements and set a trap for him.

Red realized that moving in short and explosive steps made his actions harder to read. He also had to constantly consider his position, so that he wouldn't end up trapped between two incoming obstacles.

This new strategy worked, but eventually, Domeron increased his speed. Red's reflexes were pushed to the limit, and his mind went into overdrive figuring out the next correct move at every split second.

He couldn't rely on quick thinking and was forced to lean on his ingrained instincts to dodge.

The bags got closer and closer every second, and some of them even scraped his clothing. Red didn't know how much time had passed, but his body started to feel spent from the sheer effort. He had to rely on more desperate moves to get out of the way, but ultimately, even that was not enough.

Red didn't even see the bag coming. He felt a heavy impact against his back throw him to the ground, and after that, he knew it was over. The obstacles swung overhead until they stopped, signaling the end of their exercise.

Red lay on his back, trying to catch his breath, but a voice interrupted his rest.

"Great work!"

He sat up with some effort and looked over at Domeron. This time, the man had a genuine smile on his face.

"While I can't approve of your teacher's methods, it seems like they really did work!" he said. "Physical prowess and skill leave a bit to be desired, but your adaptability was certainly impressive. You were able to get to the crux of the matter faster than most kids your age."

"But I still failed, didn't I?" Red asked.

"Of course you failed. I was going to keep increasing the intensity until you got hit anyway. It was just a matter of testing your limits before we can start the real training."

Red frowned. "Real training?"

"Indeed." The man cracked a wicked grin. "Now that I know your limits, it's just a matter of pushing past them as often as possible."

Somehow, Red felt that Viran and Domeron weren't so different after all.

CHAPTER 66

FORGING

HALF AN HOUR PASSED before Domeron called for a stop in their training. Red plopped down on the ground, worn out, feeling an aching pain all over his body.

"You did well, Red," Domeron said, smiling down at him. "At the very least, I can say you're a fast learner."

Red looked over at his mentor and noticed he didn't seem the least bit tired. Although Red had arguably done most of the work, Domeron had been constantly swinging the bags at him from all around the circle. Not only that, but the man had also been observing his footwork and correcting it on the spot.

There were more similarities between him and Viran than Red had first noticed. However, he'd also learned more with Domeron in just one quick session. Not only was he offered specific advice on how to improve, but his new mentor also pointed out each of his mistakes. Red hadn't known that the simple act of dodging had such depth and intricacies, and with this alone, his horizons had already expanded considerably.

"How much experience do you have with fighting?" Domeron asked, signaling for him to get up.

"Not... much," Red grunted as he recovered his breath and stepped out of the circle.

The battles he'd fought were rarely straightforward fights, and most of the time, he had just been dodging and running for his life.

"You have the basics of defense more or less figured out. Now you simply need to refine them. Still, that's just half of the footwork," Domeron said. "How you move is also important for attacking, and you have to learn how to flow between dodging and striking."

Red lifted the wooden baton. "Is that why you had me hold a knife?"

"That was just for you to get used to holding a weapon while moving. Holding something in your hands while performing precise movements may hinder your balance, so it must become a habit early on in your training."

"And are you going to teach me how to use it?"

"No."

Red blinked. "Why not?"

"Because I only know how to use a sword."

He was at a loss for words.

"Look, I have one arm, so cut me a break," the man said. "Knife fighting is an extension of hand-to-hand combat, which is something I'll be teaching you too. If you want to specialize in knives, you'll have to figure it out by yourself or ask Rog for help."

Red considered the matter. His gaze wandered over to the weapons rack and the different kinds of armaments it held. There were still many things he needed to try before making this kind of decision.

"Don't feel pressed to make a choice," Domeron said. "You actually don't need to make a choice at all. Many people have their favorite weapon, but they also learn to use different kinds of weaponry, too. In fact, that's the norm. Narcha has her saber, but she also specializes in using all types of heavy armaments. Over the years, you'll eventually learn what you like and dislike and pick something to stick with."

"Then why do you only know how to use a sword?" Red asked.

"That's because I'm a swordsman. I've dedicated my entire life to mastering the sword and becoming one with it. My practice has become more than just fighting and has transformed into a way of life."

Red wasn't convinced. "Isn't dedicating yourself to one weapon better than trying to master many of them?"

"Not always," Domeron said. "You would become very good at that one thing you do, which has its advantages. Though having flexibility and different options to approach combat is also extremely valuable. It all depends on the circumstances."

"Then could someone like Narcha beat you in combat with her skills?"

"She wishes!" Domeron laughed. "I could beat her no matter the weapon she chose."

"But you have one arm."

"One more than what I need to beat up a brat like her."

He couldn't tell whether the man was being serious. But before they could continue their conversation, a voice called out from the other side of the training ground.

"Red, what are you doing?"

He turned around and saw Eiwin walking toward them.

"I see you and Domeron have already started training..." She trailed off as she examined Red's state. "What happened to your clothes?"

He looked down at himself. The clothing he'd been given the previous day was covered in dirt, and there were even a few tears in the fabric.

"I was training," Red answered.

"You're not supposed to wear those clothes for exercising... Where did you even put your shoes?"

She was about to continue questioning him, but instead she just sighed in resignation and turned to Domeron. "You should have known better, Master Domeron."

The man shrugged. "He's the one who rushed me."

"It doesn't matter. I'll fix it later," Eiwin said. "I went by your room, but you weren't there, Red. Master Goulth wants to see you."

Red shook his head. "I'm not finished with training."

"You should go," Domeron said. "Not much you can accomplish when you're tired."

He hesitated. There were still countless questions he wanted to ask.

"He's made breakfast," Eiwin said with a grin.

That was all the convincing he needed.

"Here, have some more!"

Goulth put another serving of scrambled eggs onto Red's plate. He didn't complain and set about devouring the food. A few minutes later, he had stuffed himself full while the blacksmith ate his fourth serving.

He had no other option than to wait in silence until Goulth had set down his bowl. The large man looked at him with a satisfied smile before getting up and walking to his desk. From there, he picked up a hammer and handed it to Red.

"Have a feel for it," Goulth said. "It's important you get used to the weight, since you're gonna be using this a lot."

Red took the hammer. The tool was heavy and not easy to wield, as most of the weight was distributed towards its head.

"Doesn't feel like a very good weapon," he said.

"Who said it's a weapon?" Goulth sounded offended. "Not everything that has a handle is a weapon! That is a forging hammer! It's used to shape metals into different things."

"How does it do that?"

"By hitting the heated metal against an anvil." He pointed at said anvil a few meters away from them.

This, however, didn't make sense to Red. "Isn't metal hard, though? Hitting it with a hammer would just break it."

Goulth sighed in exasperation, struggling to find the right words. "Listen, Red... do you even know anything about forging?"

He shook his head.

"Then let me ask you this—do you think people just find their steel weapons and tools lying around, ready to be used?"

"I... guess not." Red had never considered how weapons were made in the first place.

"It's actually a very complex process." Goulth explained. "First, you need to extract the ore from veins you find in nature. However, most ores are actually a very impure mix of different materials, so next, you need to refine or smelt them to extract the metal. You may also need to mix that metal with other materials to create alloys that have the desired properties. That is already an entire ordeal, and we haven't even gotten into proper forging!"

"And you do all of that here?"

"It depends. If I'm making simple tools, then I'll just buy metal bars from the market. But if I'm making anything important, then it's a must that I control the entire smelting process."

"Why is that?"

"Because I have my own secret recipes, of course!" Goulth's voice swelled with pride. "You see, there are many materials in this world, and they react in all sorts of exquisite ways when mixed. Sometimes, a certain metal by itself may be completely useless, but when it's combined with another metal, it may become the hardest material in the world!"

Red felt fascinated by the prospect. He remembered all the kinds of ores the slaves found in the underground and wondered if any of them fit the blacksmith's description.

"Comprehending these transformations is not only important for a blacksmith but also for all other crafting professions," Goulth continued. "In the same way a blacksmith can transform a useless metal into something valuable, an alchemist can make even the world's deadliest venom into medicine if they know the correct process."

"Is that the kind of information that's in that book?" Red asked.

"That's correct! It has all kinds of recipes for alloys that once belonged to the Amber Saber Sect. But that's just half of the knowledge there. There's also forging, which is the process of shaping metals and alloys into useful weapons and armors."

"You still haven't told me how you do that."

"That's because it's not that simple! You see, temperature can change the properties of certain materials. Metals are very hardy and solid while they're cold, but once you warm them up enough, they become softer and pliable."

Red started to connect the dots. "So after that, you use the hammer to change its shape?"

"Correct!" Goulth said. "But that's only the simplest type of forging. Some metals can only be made into weapons and armor through special methods. That's the other half of the knowledge that's in the book."

It seemed that the book was more useful than Red had first thought.

A shadow fell over Goulth's expression. "Unfortunately, though, most of the information in that book is completely useless to me."

Red was completely taken aback by the sudden shift in mood. "Why is it useless?" he asked.

"I didn't say it was useless. I said it was useless to me." The blacksmith sighed, his voice unusually solemn. "You see, a lot of the methods to smelt and forge these metals require control over Spiritual Energy, and, well... you can probably imagine how that would be an issue for me."

Goulth picked up the book from a nearby desk and opened it.

"It was always my dream to have some of my ancestor's fantastic inventions see the light of day again, but... while this student had the will, he lacked the talent."

Red didn't know how to respond. It seemed Spiritual Energy in this world was not only useful for combat but also for crafting. If you were incapable of opening your Spiritual Sea, it wouldn't matter how much talent you had in other areas, your path forward would still be blocked.

"I'm not any better, you know," Red said. "I don't know if I'll ever be able to open my Spiritual Sea."

"Hah, that's fine, kid!" Goulth's troubled mood disappeared. "I would never choose my disciple based on talent alone. Temperament is the most essential thing in a student, and I would rather let this inheritance be forgotten to time than have it fall in the wrong hands."

He patted Red's shoulder. "Besides, you shouldn't sell yourself short! You're still young and hungry for knowledge, so who knows what you'll accomplish?"

Goulth picked up another hammer from a nearby table and waved at Red.

"Now, come here! I need to teach you how to work the forge!"

CHAPTER 67

ARCANE SCRIPT

OVER THE NEXT couple of hours, Goulth walked Red through every piece of equipment around his workshop. There was the forge, where he heated his metal bars, along with the anvil, which he struck the material against to shape it. Other tools included the tongs and the forging hammer. The process of blacksmithing didn't seem to involve as many items as Red expected, but that wasn't all the man did here.

In the back of his house, Goulth had an even larger furnace. This one, he claimed, was used to smelt raw ores and create the alloys he needed. A blast furnace, as Goulth called it. He used steel as an example and explained to Red how he inserted both iron ore and coal into a blazing furnace and blasted them with air so the ore would melt and mix with the coal, producing the desired alloy. Controlling the temperature of the furnace and the ratio of coal to iron was of extreme importance, a simple mistake rendering the steel useless.

Red realized how complex the man's work was. For instance, how could he measure the temperature of the furnace accurately, and even if he did, how could he make precise adjustments to it? Goulth told him this was a matter of both experience and observation, since different materials would change under different temperatures. At the same time, he also admitted that blacksmiths who had opened their Spiritual Sea had special techniques to better control their furnaces.

In the end, it all came back to Spiritual Energy. Once you could control it, a whole world of possibilities would open before you.

As Goulth's explanation shifted to different ores and materials, Red couldn't help but notice how he had yet to explain most of the equipment in his workshop. There was a cauldron with an acrid smell, a table filled with papers and plates etched with strange symbols, and all other kinds of things he didn't know the use of.

Once Red realized this, he couldn't hold his curiosity back.

"Are those things also part of forging?" he asked.

"Not forging, no." Goulth frowned. "I do all kinds of different things for the Sect: alchemy, formations, talismans, rune carving, just to name a few."

"How do those work?"

"At a very basic level, with my skills." Goulth looked displeased at the change in topic. "For alchemy, I just know how to make a few healing elixirs and medicines, but that's barely scratching the surface of the field. Some of the principles of forging and alchemy are interchangeable, and that's the reason I have some skill in that too. The crafting methods used in those two, though, are very different."

"What about the others?"

"For those, I can't even claim to have scratched the surface. Formations, talismans, runes, and even spells are all different applications of the same subject—the Arcane Script, the language of the world."

Red looked back at the drawings. All he could see were cluttered shapes and strange symbols, and even though he couldn't read yet, none of it looked like any words he knew of.

"A language?" he asked skeptically.

"You heard what I said. You think the world would just speak in perfect human words?"

"How would the world even speak in the first place?"

"It's just a figure of speech!" Goulth glared at him. "Arcane Script is the special set of symbols and line patterns that can be used to represent or induce transformations in Spiritual Energy that interact with the world."

"So, like Spiritual Veins?"

"That's a good comparison, but it's different in principle," Goulth said. "Arcane Script is a series of extremely complex symbols and drawings which can cause immediate reactions in Spiritual Energy. These symbols need to be etched or painted with special materials in order to truly work.

To get the desired effect, you may even need to merge and draw hundreds of these weird shapes in specific patterns to form a larger design. Rather than a language, it would be best to call it an exercise in precision and calculation."

"And do you need Spiritual Energy to draw them?" Red asked, his curiosity increasing.

Goulth hesitated. It seemed he'd never considered the question before. "They are powered by it, but technically you do not need to use any Spiritual Energy to draw or etch them. But no normal human could ever muster the precision and concentration necessary to draw even the most basic of these symbols. Even more than forging and alchemy, fields like formation building, talisman drawing, and rune carving are often the domain of people who have opened their Spiritual Sea."

"... So why are you doing them?"

"Because Hector asked me to! Look at this!" Goulth showed his large and calloused hands to him. "Do these look like the hands of someone who can write Arcane Script?"

Red wouldn't know, but he simply shook his head.

"And yet the old man says that I'm the only one who can do it!" The blacksmith threw his hands up in frustration. "I've been losing nights of sleep trying to nail those sketches, but it's hopeless! It's a waste of my time and talent! Learning Arcane Script is a lifelong ordeal, not to mention trying to master all the different applications. I'm old, I don't have the time or patience for it..."

An awkward silence settled over the room as Goulth grumbled under his breath.

"Can I look at them?" Red asked.

The man waved his hand. "Go ahead. But don't expect too much when you don't even know how to read."

Red walked over and studied the drawings, realizing they were indeed as complicated as Goulth made them sound. Not only was there an enormous amount of detail in each symbol, but some lines were so small that Red barely noticed them at first. And yet, according to Goulth, these were all failures.

He put the papers down.

Maybe later.

He was still interested in this so-called Arcane Script, but trying to comprehend them when he hadn't drawn or written anything in his life was a hopeless task.

"As I said, it's useless to think about it for now," Goulth said. "I intend on testing your talent in different fields, but the only thing I can teach you in depth is forging. If you have interest or potential in these other domains, you might need to look for a different master."

"It's alright." Red shook his head. "I'm in no rush."

His priority was still recovering and learning more about the surface world. He was eventually going to explore all of his options, but he didn't intend to waste the opportunity to learn useful skills from someone like Goulth, a master of his craft.

"That's spirit, kid!" The blacksmith seemed happy to hear this. "It's important to dedicate every second of your life to learning, but if you bite off more than you can chew, then you're bound to learn nothing in the end."

Red wasn't sure how his teacher had taken so much meaning out of such a simple sentence, but he just nodded along with his words.

"Then, where were we?" Goulth scratched his chin. "Oh yeah, come with me. You can help me fire up the forge!"

"What happened to your clothes now?" Eiwin asked with a furrowed brow.

"I was helping Goulth with the forge," Red replied.

His clothing was full of charcoal stains, and one of his sleeves had caught on fire during an accident. Goulth had said that these types of things were part of the learning experience in a forge, and that next time he should wear something with shorter sleeves.

"I... see." Eiwin took a long breath before beckoning Red over. "Come on, it's almost time for lunch."

"But I just ate this morning."

"Don't be silly." She smiled. "Everyone here in the Sect has at least three meals a day, and you're still a child. You have to eat if you want to grow properly."

Red nodded and followed behind her. He wasn't going to complain when offered free food.

"Where are we going to eat?" he asked.

"In the meeting hall."

Red stopped walking. Eiwin looked back.

"What's the problem?" she asked.

"Are you sure that's a good idea? Hector said I shouldn't appear in front of him."

"Master Hector rarely means everything he says. You've seen that yourself," she said in a comforting tone. "You're part of this Sect now, and you'll have to learn how to get along with everyone else. The same goes for them, too."

Being on friendly terms with his companions wasn't a priority for Red—particularly with the ones who didn't have positive opinions about him. He would rather stay out of their way for however long he remained in this place, but he recognized the truth in Eiwin's words. Completely avoiding the others was unrealistic.

"Let's go, then."

Eiwin brightened and led them into the large building. Three people he recognized from yesterday were already there—Hector, Domeron, and Allen —and each of them had a different reaction to his arrival.

Allen grinned in excitement.

Domeron just nodded in greeting before returning to his food.

And Hector's already severe expression grew even worse.

"Little brat, didn't I tell you not to appear before me until you have something to show for yourself?" The elder thumped his bowl down and glared at him.

Eiwin frowned. "Master Hector..."

Red cut her off. "I do have something to show for myself."

Hector was taken aback. "Really?" he asked with a sneer. "What could you have possibly accomplished in just one night?"

The conversation grabbed everyone's attention. Eiwin looked worried, but she didn't interrupt him.

"Here." He lifted his left arm in the air. "I managed to heal myself."

Suddenly, Domeron's loud laughter disrupted the tense atmosphere in the hall.

Hector's face fell. "What medicine did Goulth give you?" he bellowed in anger, ignoring the man's laughter.

"Who said it was a medicine?"

"What, so you just so happened to spontaneously heal yourself?!"

Red shrugged. "Maybe I made the medicine myself."

"Kid, didn't I warn you yesterday not to disrespect me again?"

A dangerous aura spread from Hector's body and enveloped everyone in the room.

Red, however, wasn't moved. "What did I do wrong?" he asked. "I have something to show for myself, as you told me to do."

Hector was at a loss for words. Just as he was about to continue arguing with Red, though, someone else entered the hall.

"G'morning."

A voice he recognized.

Red looked back and saw Rog walking towards the table, the hunter unaware of the tense atmosphere in the room. He picked up a bowl, scooped some food from the pot, and sat down on a free chair across from Domeron and Allen. Just as Rog was about to start eating, he paused and lifted his head.

Everyone in the room was staring at him.

"What?" he asked.

When he didn't get any response, his gaze wandered across the room before finally settling on Red's figure. His eyes widened.

"You're still here?"

Suddenly, a flying spoon hit the man's head.

CHAPTER 68

PREACHER

"IT'S YOUR FAULT!" Hector pointed at Rog in anger. "If you ever bothered thinking before making a decision, we wouldn't be in this situation!"

The hunter cowered to protect his head from any further assaults and silently listened to Hector's rant. At that point, they seemed to have forgotten Red's existence.

Eiwin pushed him along. "Come, let's go sit."

Red joined her. A few minutes later, he and the others were eating again. Throughout the meal, Hector's rampage didn't show any signs of stopping.

"This brat is your responsibility, do you hear me? Yours!"

"What am I supposed to do with him?" Rog asked, looking at Red.

"That's not my problem!"

"Aren't you the leader of the Sect, though?"

Hector lifted his spoon threateningly, and the hunter flinched away.

"Alright!" Rog said. "I'll teach him how to hunt so he can help the Sect!"

The elder nodded in satisfaction, his anger somewhat abated.

"What about me?" Allen asked. "I wanna learn how to hunt too!"

Hector shot him down. "You have other things to worry about."

"That's not fair! You never let me do what I want!"

"Don't pretend to be stupid, you little brat!" Hector glared at Allen. "How many chances did I give you to learn from Rog and Goulth in the past? How many times did I have to hear about how much of a nuisance you were? If

371

you weren't so incompetent in everything other than cultivation, what need would we have for another disciple?!"

The boy didn't look convinced, but Hector's rant silenced his protests for now.

As the rowdy mood in the hall died down, a prolonged silence settled over the dining table, creating an uncomfortable atmosphere. No one spoke, and only the sound of cutlery could be heard in the room.

Red felt Hector's eyes on him the entire time he was eating.

"Where's Miss Valt?" Eiwin asked, finally breaking the silence.

"I saw her leave earlier," Allen said. "She said she wasn't coming back until tonight."

Eiwin looked troubled. "I see." Just as it seemed like the quiet was about to return, though, she turned to Hector. "I need money, Master Hector."

"For what?" he said.

"To buy the necessary supplies for Red," Eiwin said straight out. "We need to get him proper clothing and training supplies, as befits a disciple of our Water Dragon Sect."

Her request was met with silence on Hector's part. As Red was thinking the old man would deny her, though, he nodded instead.

"Domeron, give her the coin for the uniform," Hector said.

"Don't have much more left, old man."

"What, are you saying we don't even have the money to afford proper equipment for one of our disciples?"

"I didn't say that, but we have to watch how we spend our coin. Hunting forest monsters was a big part of our income, and now that they've disappeared, our expenses are draining our coffers. Not to mention, a lot of merchants are eager to get out of this town before the monster tide hits, so requests are bound to get scarce, too."

"Just give her the gold!" Hector waved off his concerns. "I don't need a lecture on our finances every time I decide to spend money on something."

Domeron sighed and reached for a pouch at his waist. With the swift movement of his single arm, he counted the coins inside the bag, putting a handful aside before tossing the pouch to Eiwin.

She caught the pouch midair and smiled in gratitude.

"Thank you, Master Domeron. Thank you, Master Hector." She bowed towards them and then looked at Red. "Now we can go buy you some proper clothes."

Allen's face lit up. "Can I come too?"

"Sure. If Master Hector allows it, that is."

The old man snorted. "Take him. Would make my day more peaceful, at least."

Allen's smile widened. "When are we going?" he asked Eiwin.

"After we finish eat—"

"I'll wait for you at the gate!"

The boy ran from the table, leaving his unfinished food behind. Red stared at his back before turning to Eiwin. "Do I *need* to go?"

She gave him a helpless smile.

The city was no less active than yesterday, with peddlers selling their wares at every corner, but Red wasn't any more used to it. The noise was one thing, but the people were another, and the fact that they walked so close to each other with no regard for their own personal safety baffled him.

What if someone tried to kill them? He didn't see how you could defend yourself in this kind of place. It seemed, however, that he was the only one concerned about it.

"Can we get some cake?" Allen asked.

Eiwin shook her head. "I already told you, Allen, this money is meant to buy Red clothes and supplies. If there's any left over, then I'll consider it."

Allen sighed and looked at Red in search of some sympathy. He was met with a blank expression.

"What kind of clothes are you going to buy, Red?" Allen asked.

He shrugged.

The boy patted his shoulder. "It's not a problem if you don't know. I can help you pick something cool-looking."

"We're buying training clothes for him, Allen," Eiwin interjected.

"Right, right." The young master rolled his eyes. He sidled up to Red and whispered in his ear, "Don't let Eiwin pick your clothing. Do you see what she wears?"

Red looked her over. Her clothes were very plain, a simple shirt and pants tied at the waist with a black belt. The outfit was much better than slave clothing but was also far less intricate compared to the rest of the townspeople.

"What's the problem with it?" Red asked.

"Don't you see it? She's boring," Allen said. "Eiwin is a monk, so she doesn't like expensive or fancy things."

"What's a monk?"

"I don't know. It's like a priest or something, except they only like cheap things and try not to get mad at all."

Red thought about asking what a priest was, but their conversation was abruptly interrupted as Eiwin hurried them along.

He recognized some streets from the previous day. They passed by the same adventurer's guild where Narcha had received some ugly glares, but this time around, Eiwin gave it a wide berth, keen on avoiding any type of conflict.

As they walked downhill and approached the town center, Red could see some commotion ahead. A crowd of people had formed in the plaza around the broken pillar, and even from this far, he could hear agitated voices.

"What's happening?" he asked Eiwin.

She squinted, examining the plaza.

"Members from the Imperial Celestial Church," she said, her face turning grave.

"You mean from the Empire?" Red frowned. "I got the impression they weren't necessarily welcome here."

"Although they often work together, the Celestial Church and the Empire are technically two separate entities," Eiwin explained. "One is a political entity while the other is a religious one. Even here in Fordham-Bestrem, there are quite a few believers in the Celestial Gods. We can stop the Empire's soldiers from invading our town, but their priests are a different matter."

Red was lost. He still didn't know what this Celestial Faith represented, but from Eiwin's tone, she didn't hold a very positive opinion of them.

"What are they doing there?" he asked.

"Probably trying to spread their religion," Eiwin said.

"Can we go listen?"

"I'm... not sure that's a good idea." She hesitated, looking back.

Red followed her gaze. There he saw Allen with a strange expression, a mix of fear and anger twisting his face. He was clenching his fists, and his hands shivered with fury. When he noticed both of his companions looking at him, though, he took a deep breath and tried to relax.

"It's fine, Eiwin," Allen said. "Grandpa Hector told me I have to learn how to deal with them. I can't keep running my entire life."

"Are you sure?" Eiwin asked.

"Yes, I'll be fine."

She sighed. "Fine, then. But we'll remain at a distance. These things have a habit of getting ugly very quickly."

Red felt curious about Allen's sudden shift in demeanor, but this wasn't the time to ask.

Approaching the plaza, they saw a figure standing in the very center of the gathered crowd. It was an old man, dressed in intricate golden clothing and adorned with all kinds of strange jewelry. He cried out to the crowd with a fervent voice.

Red got close enough to make out the man's speech.

"... and look where that got us! Your forests are dying, threatening your livelihood! A monster tide looms on the horizon, threatening your safety! Servants of darkness gather en masse to enter these lands, threatening your soul! The Outsiders threaten this entire world and its inhabitants, and where are your Sects to defend you? Nowhere!"

A wave of grumbles and protests passed through the crowd.

"You know this to be true!" the priest went on. "They hide inside their 'holy lands' while the common folk out here suffer. They have the power to protect and save you from the evils that plague your society, but they choose not to! The only time the Sects ever act is to defend their interests and fight against each other, causing millions of mortal lives to be lost as mere collateral damage!

"Do you think they move to stop this monster horde because they care about your lives? They only do so to protect their own lands and resources! It's in the nature of cultivators—they only act in their self-interest! For thousands of years, the same story keeps repeating, and yet some of you still refuse to open your eyes! Your old gods have abandoned you, and the Sects never cared in the first place!"

More objections erupted from the crowd, but some shouts of approval sounded too.

"In these times of chaos, the Celestial Gods have always offered us comfort! They have granted us protection and strength! In a land once devastated by the greed of Sects, peace finally reigns thanks to their intervention! The common man need not worry about his safety, fear the violent cultivator or the cunning demon! All humans are shielded by the Celestial Light, and order finally reigns supreme!

"So tell me, good folk. When will you stop looking to these aloof Sects and mad cultivators for protection? How many more must die until you finally turn your gaze to ones more worthy of your belief and devotion? Open your eyes, people, and see the truth!"

The priest parted the hair from his forehead. Right there, in the middle of his eyebrows, something bulged out from beneath his skin. A vertical slit appeared, and an orb emerged from the opening.

A third eye.

"Red, are you okay?" Allen's voice came from beside him.

He looked over, confused. "What is it?" he asked.

Eiwin gazed at him with worry. "You're shaking."

Red looked down at his own hands. His fingers had started trembling without his knowledge.

"We shouldn't have come here," Eiwin said. "Come on, let's move on already."

He didn't protest and let himself be dragged along. The priest continued to speak at length to the crowd, and Red looked at him one last time.

There was nothing but plain skin on the priest's forehead, and Red had suddenly forgotten what he'd seen in the first place.

CHAPTER 69

UNIFORM

THEY DISTANCED themselves from the crowd. Red could hear the commotion at the plaza even from a few streets away, though, and it was a topic for gossip among the townsfolk.

He couldn't help but think back on the priest's words.

The man was eloquent and provocative, capable of catching anyone's attention, and Red was no exception. However, Red didn't take the speech at face value or think that the priest only carried "good intentions."

The information from the speech itself, though, was valuable for his understanding of the world. There was still much to reflect on. Eiwin, however, could readily guess the questions on his mind.

"We'll talk about it later," she said. "Cultivators shouldn't have to worry about political conflicts, but that's unfortunately not a privilege we have at the moment."

Red understood her point. With monsters and cultivation to worry about, how could any proper cultivator have the time to bother with politics? Yet the situation on the surface was proving to be more complex by the minute.

The group kept traveling through the streets. Allen, whose mood had been dampened by the event at the plaza, was slowly recovering his cheeriness, bothering Eiwin about food once more. They didn't remain on the road for too long, as Eiwin soon brought them to a stop in front of a large building.

"We're here," she said.

Red examined the store. Like most buildings in this city, the place was a crude amalgamation of stone and wood, but the owner had made up for it with decorations. Large fabric rolls and elegant clothing were displayed in the storefront, and well-dressed folk studied the items while talking with store employees. The store's beauty stood out in the middle of a functional but ugly city.

Red squinted. "Are you sure this is the place?"

Eiwin gave him a knowing smile. "I know what you're thinking,but there's more to this place than meets the eye. Let's go in."

Under the inquiring gazes of the other customers, the clearly out-of-place group entered the store. The interior was even more richly decorated than the outside, and a veritable rainbow of clothing and fabrics greeted Red. An overwhelming smell of perfume hit his nose, and he felt compelled to run away after just a few steps.

"It's okay, Red." Allen patted his back. "These people don't take showers, so they try to disguise their smell with perfumes. You'll get used to it."

This comment earned him several unfriendly looks from other customers. Red nodded along and tried his best to breathe as little as possible. It seemed, however, that their entrance had caught the attention of an employee. A particularly well-dressed man approached them, wearing a frown on his face.

"May I help you, madam?" he asked. His tone was polite, but Red could see displeasure in his expression.

"Yes, I'm looking for Master Frida," Eiwin said.

"Hm." The employee's frown deepened. "And may I ask who is requesting to speak with her?"

"Tell her it's Eiwin."

He looked thoughtful, as if he were searching his memory to determine whether the name carried any weight. A few seconds later, recognition seemed to dawn on him.

"From the Water Dragon Sect?" he asked.

She simply nodded. A murmur passed over the other customers in the store, and their unfriendly gazes slowly disappeared. Instead, it was replaced with a mix of fear and curiosity, and their eyes lingered on Red.

"I'll inform her at once." The clerk disappeared into the back of the store.

Red could hear murmurs as other customers stole sideways glances at the group. Allen puffed out his chest and stared back in defiance while Eiwin ignored them. It seemed the group was used to being the center of attention, but Red didn't feel comfortable being observed.

Soon, the same clerk returned to them. "Please, follow me." He ushered the group towards the back of the store. "Master Frida will meet with you."

They followed the man downstairs into a basement. This place looked completely different from the store proper, with scraps of clothes and fabric strewn about everywhere. In the middle of this sea of merchandise, a middle-aged woman was waiting for them. She wore a long and finely woven red dress, sporting a lengthy ponytail and elegant manners.

"My dear Eiwin, how pleasant to see you again!" She walked forward, embracing Eiwin in a hug.

"Master Frida..." The younger woman looked uncomfortable at first, but she reciprocated. "It is good to see you, too."

Frida stepped back. "You promised to visit more often, but this is the first time you've come in more than a month!"

"I've been occupied with Sect matters." Eiwin sounded embarrassed.

"Isn't that what you always say?" The older woman rolled her eyes. "And who else did you bring along? Is that little Allen?"

"Just Allen, ma'am!" The older boy pouted.

"Right, I forgot! And who else did you bring here?"

The woman approached Red, crouching down to his height.

"What is your name, dear?" Frida asked.

"Red," he said.

"Red?" She frowned. "Just Red?"

He nodded.

"You have beautiful crimson hair, Red. Not something we see in these parts." She extended her hand towards his head, intent on touching his hair.

Red took an abrupt step back and out of her reach.

"Ah, I'm sorry." She smiled before standing back up. "I assume the new clothes are for him?"

Eiwin nodded. "He's the newest member of the Sect."

"A new member?" Frida sounded surprised. "After all this time, Hector stopped being stubborn?"

"It took some convincing, but I can tell you the story another time. As you can see, he started training without having the proper uniform. That's why I'm here."

"And how did he get those burn marks?"

Eiwin hesitated. "He's... Goulth's new disciple."

Frida froze. The atmosphere in the room changed, and Red saw the woman go through dozens of different expressions in a matter of seconds. A few moments later, she sighed, and her dignified composure returned, but the look she gave Red was inscrutable.

"You're the big oaf's disciple?" she asked, her tone icy.

Red blinked. He didn't answer.

"You don't need to worry," Frida said. "My gripe is with him, not you. Although you should watch what you end up learning from that man. If you're not careful, you might end up being too obsessed with your projects to notice what's happening around you."

He didn't know what she meant by that, but he nodded to assuage her concerns.

The pleasant smile returned to her face. "Good. Then you're here for the uniform, Eiwin?"

"Right." Eiwin sounded relieved that the interaction hadn't taken a turn for the worse. "The same fabric, too."

Frida's face fell.

"Is there a problem?" Eiwin asked.

"Demand for spiritweaver thread has increased recently after the news of the incoming monster attack. We have a limited supply."

Eiwin frowned. "Is it enough to make the uniform?"

"Yes, but it's going to be more expensive."

"How much?"

"We have other clients who have placed their requests, too. Some of them have offered almost twice the normal price."

Eiwin's expression soured.

"But you're our friend, right?" Allen cut into the conversation. "Can't you just give us one for free?"

"Allen!"

The boy stared at Eiwin as if he had done nothing wrong.

"I've already explained what my relationship with your Sect would be in the past, little Allen," Frida said, her composure calm. "I've given all of you special treatment for more than a decade, but at the end of the day, this relationship is meant to be mutually beneficial. Giving up on large profits during a time of crisis could lead to my ruin."

"We have no need for charity, Master Frida," Eiwin said. "Since this is a time of crisis, is there anything else we could provide you, other than money?"

The middle-aged woman smiled as if she had been waiting to hear these exact words. "Certainly."

Frida walked off, grabbing a piece of paper from the nearby desk.

"A shipment I ordered from the East is more than a week late. More than a thousand gold coins in merchandise are missing. At first, I thought they might have given up on making the delivery, but after talking to the merchants at the capital, I discovered the shipment had been sent on its way according to schedule. But they were in a hurry to accomplish their delivery before the horde hit—and decided to take an alternative route."

She handed the letter over to Eiwin, who read its contents.

She winced. "They went through the hill trail?"

"That's right. They were so worried about the monsters that they didn't bother scouting their way and lost my entire shipment to some bandits!"

"Weren't they under escort?"

"Ten warriors strong. But I don't need to tell you how treacherous these forests are for someone unfamiliar. An experienced group of bandits could've taken ten times as many soldiers under the right circumstances."

Eiwin sighed. "And I assume you want us to recover this shipment?"

"The merchants promised me a refund, but I can't wait for that," Frida said. "I wouldn't ask this of you if I had any other choice, but there's something very important that was supposed to arrive with that shipment, and you're the only ones I could trust to recover it."

"I understand, but searching for the right bandit group in such a large forest is hard." Eiwin shook her head. "It's going to take a long time, and even if we find them, there's no guarantee your merchandise will still be there."

"That's a risk I'm willing to take. Besides, I assume your Sect must be in search of work, correct? Besides the uniform for the little one, I can offer you four hundred gold coins."

"You put me in a tough spot, Master Frida," Eiwin said. "Master Domeron said that I should never close any contracts by myself."

"I'm not trying to take advantage of you, dear Eiwin. Domeron will know this deal is fair, and if he has any objections, then I'm willing to renegotiate it with him."

Eiwin hesitated and looked to be deep in thought, but she finally nodded. "Fine. But on the condition that you start making Red's uniform right now."

Frida smiled. "That goes without saying, dear," she said. "Now then, shall we take the little one's measurements?"

"Finally!" Allen said, snapping out of his boredom.

Red had been quietly listening to the negotiation, absorbing as much information as he could. When the older woman approached him, though, he stepped back again.

"It's fine, Red," Eiwin said. "She just wants to take your measurements to make your uniform."

He stopped retreating at her words and let Frida get close to him.

"Extend your arms, please," she asked, and Red complied.

The woman got to work with the help of a measuring tape.

"So what kind of clothes do you—"

"His outfit has to look cool!" Allen interjected. "Like the ones wandering swordsmen wear! Kind of like this!" He pointed at his own robes.

"Right. What about your color? Which one do you—"

"Blue! The colors of the Sect! Kind of like mine—"

"Allen!" Eiwin glared.

A few minutes later, they left the store. Frida said the robe would be ready in a week, and Red wondered why it would take so long. In fact, he wondered why they needed to go through all this trouble just for a uniform.

"It's not just a uniform," Eiwin said. "It has something special about it—"

Allen interrupted her. "Hey, isn't that Narcha?"

"What?!"

Eiwin looked where he was pointing. A tall woman seemed to be in a standoff with a group of twelve armed men defending a merchant's store. She carried a large saber on her back, with her hand resting on its handle.

"Yeah, that's definitely her," Allen said. "Wonder what she's doing—"

Eiwin shot toward her, leaving both boys to stare at each other in confusion.

CHAPTER 70

BREAKING AND ENTERING

"What do we do now?" Allen asked, dumbfounded.

Red also hesitated. The brewing battle looked so urgent that Eiwin had dashed off before even telling the two of them what to do.

"We watch from a distance," Red answered once he noticed Allen wasn't about to make any suggestions.

"Right. Good idea," the older boy said. "Uh... Well, follow me, then!"

Allen took off down the street, Red following behind him. They hid behind a stack of large crates, arriving just in time to watch the scene unfold.

Narcha noticed Eiwin approaching before the others. The sudden intrusion surprised the mercenaries, but before they could react, the monk was already in their midst. But Eiwin didn't strike, merely standing by her companion's side.

Narcha didn't look too happy to have her. She snorted. "Been stalking me through town, have you?"

"Stalking you?" Eiwin glared back. "What's the need when you make your presence so obvious, Miss Valt?"

Although their conversation suggested otherwise, the two women were staunchly united against their would-be opponents. There was an unspoken bond of trust and coordination between the pair, and Eiwin hadn't even felt the need to ask about the situation before stepping forward to support her companion.

"Another one of your brigands?" the merchant standing with the warriors bellowed. "I thought your lot stuck to highway robbery! Now you're even trying to extort merchants inside the city?"

"Extort you?" Narcha looked like she was about to explode. "I'll show you extortion, you bastard!"

She advanced, and the mercenaries in front of the store tensed.

"Wait!" Eiwin put a hand in front of her companion. "Miss Valt, what is going on?"

"What do you think?" Narcha glowered at her. "He's lying, of course!"

"Please, explain it to me."

"The pill I ordered months ago! He said he sold it to someone else!"

Eiwin's expression grew conflicted.

Red watched from the hiding spot with rapt attention. "What's she talking about?" he asked Allen.

He had never seen Narcha so angry before, not even during the meeting with Hector the day prior.

"Narcha's trying to open her Spiritual Sea with the help of some pills," Allen whispered. "Goulth can't make the medicines she needs, though, so she has no choice but to search for people outside the Sect to do it."

"Is this pill rare?"

"Very." Allen, too, was scowling. "Narcha put aside a lot of her money for it, always searching for it around the market."

Red winced. It was no wonder she seemed ready to come to blows with the merchant. If his cultivation path was blocked by someone, then maybe he would be just as angry.

"I already told you the decision came from my higher-ups!" the merchant cried. "There's nothing I could do about it!"

"Bullshit!" Narcha pointed at him, her hand trembling in anger. "What about the month-long delay from before? And now the pill is suddenly going to someone else!"

"These types of setbacks are common in alchemy." The man kept his composure. "I've tried to be reasonable with you! I've even offered to put you at the top of the priority list, but you seem keen on making this an issue—"

"I don't care about your damn priority list—I want my wasted time back! I want to know who you sold my pill to!"

At the shift in topic, the merchant's face flashed with consternation. A few moments later, he seemed to have recovered.

He shook his head with a well-practiced, sorrowful look. "It's confidential."

Narcha laughed. "Hah! We both know who you sold the pill to. I bet he paid you good for these delays too, right?"

It was the merchant's turn to be angered. "I won't have my dignity insulted!"

The guards around him responded to his outburst by stepping forward in a display of intimidation. Narcha was all too happy to see it, ready to meet them head-on.

Eiwin, however, stepped between them again. "Miss Valt, please..."

"God damn it, Eiwin!" Narcha glared at her companion. "We both know what they're doing!"

"I know. But we have our orders. The time is not right."

"'The time is not right'?! When will it ever be right? The only reason Gustav keeps doing this is because we don't do anything in return!"

"Miss Valt..."

"God damn it! You still have your talent and almost a decade to open your Spiritual Sea, but what about me?"

That gave Eiwin pause. She glanced down with a troubled expression, unable to meet Narcha's eyes.

"Red."

A voice interrupted Red's observation. He looked back and saw Allen staring at him resolutely.

"We need to do something."

"Do what?"

"We can't just sit here and do nothing! This is unfair! We have to help both of them!"

Red was at a loss for words.

"They're part of our Sect, Red!" Allen insisted.

"They don't need our help. They're much stronger than the both of us put together."

"Maybe, but are you okay just sitting around here while they steal from Narcha? It's our responsibility as Sect members to help her."

No one told me about this when I joined.

But Allen's words resonated with Red. He didn't feel compelled to help out of a sense of justice, but he recalled what Hector had said about a sect member's obligation to their sect. Since he had agreed to stay and benefit from the Sect, those words weighed on his conscience now. Still, did the old man have this kind of situation in mind when he spoke of responsibility?

Red wasn't too sure.

"What did you have in mind?" he asked.

Allen smiled. "We go and fight them!"

"They have weapons." Red said, shooting the idea down. "They'll kill us."

"We can take them by surprise!"

"We're... not doing that."

"Come on!" Allen looked frustrated. "Okay, then what about..." He scratched his head, observing the group from afar. Suddenly his smile grew. "I got it! We can go and destroy his shop!"

"Why?"

"He's a merchant. He only cares about his shop and his money."

"He's right in front of the store. He would definitely notice if someone started breaking things inside. Besides, how do you propose we get past the guards?"

"Uh... There's a window down that alley!"

"We still have to get past them to reach it."

"Ugh... If only they weren't *right* there."

The plan didn't seem to have any chance of going forward, and Red turned back to the confrontation. However, as he mulled over Allen's suggestion, he got an idea.

"Allen. Tell me, how much do these two care about you?"

"I understand how you're feeling, Miss Valt." Eiwin said solemnly. "But we have to look at the bigger picture."

"Stop speaking like him!" Narcha gritted her teeth. "I have been looking at the bigger picture my whole life—and look where that got me! Just another Sect busybody with no future!"

Her companion grimaced. "You shouldn't speak of our colleagues like that. They've always done their best to help you. You know this isn't their fault."

"Ugh... Damn it!"

Eiwin watched in silence while Narcha paced the street in frustration.

She looked eager to punch the first person she came across, but none of the mercenaries were stupid enough to step forward.

The merchant watched the developments smugly, as if this were the exact scene he'd hoped for. "Now then, if you're done with your childish outburst," he said. "I would appreciate it if you lot left the prem—"

A kid's voice echoed through the street. "GO TO HELL, YOU BASTARD!"

Narcha looked up. "Is that...?"

A small figure charged at the merchant with impressive speed. Everyone in the vicinity was too bewildered to react, including Eiwin and Narcha.

"What the... Ugh!"

The merchant had his breath knocked out of him. Allen's small but surprisingly powerful fist crashed into the man's belly and sent him sprawling to the ground. The boy proudly raised his fist into the air while staring down at his victim.

"This is what you get for messing with our Sect!"

The mercenaries all raised their weapons at the same time. They surrounded Allen, one of them moving forward to strike with his mace.

"You little bastard—"

Before the mercenary could finish his sentence, a fist connected with his jaw and sent him flying into the side of a building a few meters away.

"Don't you dare touch our Young Master!" Eiwin glared at the man, her fist still extended.

The mercenaries turned their weapons at her, but it was clear Allen's display of strength made them hesitate.

"Get them, you fools!" the merchant said, clutching his side. "They were the ones who attacked first!"

At his command, the mercenaries lost some of their fear. They didn't attack immediately, but they surrounded the group in preparation for an assault. Eiwin took this opportunity to get to Allen's side before anyone else could reach him.

The boy smiled at her. "Hey, Eiwin, did you see that?"

Eiwin, however, only responded with a stern face that made him shiver.

Narcha looked at her with indignation. "Hey, I thought we weren't fighting!"

The soldiers had encircled all three of them. Eiwin shifted her stance. "No killing!"

"Ugh, fine!" Narcha walked over to her companion's side. "Gustav always manages to find more fools for these kinds of jobs anyway."

A dangerous smile flashed across her face as she stared down the mercenaries. Narcha moved, and the sounds of battle echoed through the street.

With everyone preoccupied by the fight, Red took the opportunity to slip into the shop through the window. He confirmed there was no one else inside the room before dropping to the ground.

He cautiously scanned the cramped space. The room was cluttered with wooden shelves, stocked with plants, fruits, mushrooms, and other unfamiliar things. The smell inside was strong and unpleasant to the senses, making him wonder what kind of shop this was.

Red hadn't come here to destroy the place like Allen thought. Instead, he was looking for the pill Narcha had bought. That is, if it was still at the shop in the first place. It was a long shot, but still one worth taking.

He had heard the conversation between Eiwin, Narcha and the merchant —he knew their hands were tied. If they tried breaking in, everyone would know, and the reputation of the Sect would fall with them. Red, however, had a knack for sneaking in the shadows, and once he saw the opportunity, he didn't hesitate to take it, no matter what the others would think afterwards. This way, he could help Narcha find the pill and contribute to the Sect.

Of course, he wasn't doing this out of the kindness of his heart. It was in his best interest to contribute to the Sect to make his stay there easier, not to mention he might also gain some interesting items from this foray.

But Red didn't know what he was searching for. Allen hadn't known what the pill looked like. All the information the young master could give him was that pills were kept in glass vials, and that they usually resembled pellets. It wasn't much to go by, but it was better than nothing.

A cursory glance through the shelves was enough to confirm these pills weren't stored here. This room was probably where the merchant sold his common goods, and he would likely never put something so valuable in here. As Red examined the room, he spotted a door behind the counter.

After a moment of deliberation, he headed straight for it.

To his luck, the merchant had left it unlocked in his haste, and Red walked into another corridor that branched off into three more doors. He opened the closest one and entered a storage room full of crates. He didn't have the time to check the boxes one by one, but at a glance, they contained more of what was displayed in the storefront.

He decided to investigate the next room. This one looked like a lounge— a large table, playing cards, and cups full of dark liquid was all Red could find. He closed the door and headed to the next.

After opening it, he saw an office—a wooden desk, chair, papers, and many decorations. There was even a shelf lined with wine bottles similar to the one Red had seen Rog and Narcha drinking, as well as a different window leading into another alley. He saw other miscellaneous items on the desk, but no sign of the glass vials Allen had mentioned.

Are they in the storage? Are they here at all?

Red hesitated, but he knew the man wouldn't just leave such a precious item lying around. He searched through the room in a hurry, and it didn't take long for him to find a target for his suspicions—a drawer in the desk. There was something that kept it fastened in place, though, and no matter how hard he pulled, it wouldn't budge. He considered breaking it open, but to his dismay, it was reinforced by metal plates along its surface.

Red noticed a keyhole at the front of the drawer, but after a quick glance around the room, he couldn't see a key to open it with. Just as he was wondering what to try next, he heard something. The slam of a door and the sound of approaching steps.

"Crazy bitch!"

Red recognized the voice of the merchant, who was heading in his direction.

CHAPTER 71
TOWN GUARD

RED HALTED his search upon hearing the footsteps. In the scant seconds before the merchant arrived, he considered his next move.

Escaping the way he came from was impossible, but there was still the window in the back of the room. But he had yet to find what he came here for, so he hesitated.

Red considered hiding. Would the merchant hurt him if he were discovered?

Rather, could he?

He recalled how a child half the man's size had knocked him down with a punch. Red might be weaker than Allen, but he didn't feel he had much to fear, so he made a split-second decision.

Hastily, Red crouched and hid below the desk. The door to the office swung open.

"Fucking bitch!"

The merchant continued to shout obscenities, throwing items in anger. Red heard glass shattering.

There goes the wine.

He raged for a bit longer. Eventually, it died down, and Red could only hear the merchant muttering curses under his breath.

"I'll show her... I'll show her! I'll cook her alive!"

The man walked toward the desk, and Red tensed. He heard more fumbling as piles of paper fell to the ground. When the merchant walked around the table, Red could now see his lower body only a meter away. Thankfully, at this angle, he remained unseen.

The footsteps stopped in front of the drawers. Red couldn't see what the merchant was doing, but after another bout of curses, he began to search his pockets. Red saw the man's shaking hands patting around his pants before fishing something out. Before he could see what the item was, it left his line of sight.

Then there were scratching noises around the drawer, and Red's eyes narrowed.

Is he...?

He bent over to get a better view. Sure enough, the merchant was trying to open the locked drawer.

"I need to... Shit!"

The object fell to the ground, bouncing a few times before finally coming to a stop by Red's side, shining brightly. He didn't have time to examine it, though, as the merchant stooped down in search of the item he had just dropped.

"Damn it! Where did it..." The man's words died in his throat as he came face-to-face with the skinny kid hiding below his desk. He blinked in disbelief. "What the—"

Red didn't give him the time to recover from the shock. His fist connected with the merchant's nose, and the man reeled back in pain.

"Agh! You little—"

The merchant couldn't even finish his curse before Red pushed him off balance. He hit his head against the wall with a heavy thud and was left staggered once more.

Blood poured down his nose, but Red didn't leave him space to breathe. He threw another punch.

"Ugh!"

The man moaned in pain as the small fist connected with his face, but he didn't seem any closer to unconsciousness. In fact, he was recovering his composure.

Not enough.

Red looked around for a weapon. His gaze settled on the shelf on the other side of the room—more specifically, on the wine bottles. He dashed over and grabbed one of them.

"You little shit..." The merchant gritted his teeth as he tried to get up again with the help of a chair. "I'm going to kill y—"

Glass shattered over his head and dark-red liquid splattered all over the room. The merchant stumbled again and hit the ground face down. Red stepped back, drenched in wine and holding what was left of the bottle in his hand.

He examined the man's body for any movement, but other than a few twitches and a groan of pain, he didn't get up again. Red took this as confirmation that he was unconscious and returned to the task at hand.

He dropped the broken glass and hurried to grab the key from the ground. At first, Red wasn't sure how to unlock the drawer. He hadn't used a key before, only heard about them, and all he knew was that it needed to fit perfectly into the lock. However, after a few twists and jerks, he heard a click.

He slid the drawer open and was finally treated to its contents—a small ornate box, an intricate red symbol drawn on a yellowish slip of paper, and lots of documents. There were no pill vials. Red tried to open the ornate box, but it was locked, and the drawer key didn't fit into its hole.

He looked over at the unconscious merchant and started to search his clothes for another key, but there was nothing except for a bag of coins and some jewelry. Red hesitated and wondered where the man might have hidden this kind of key. The muffled sounds of fighting outside were already diminishing—he didn't have much longer.

Then, he heard a shout.

"In the name of the Baron, stop this madness this instant!"

Red froze. It wasn't until a few moments later that he noticed the bellow came from outside. The noise of the fighting came to a stop.

He didn't know what was happening, but he needed to hurry. He picked up the box, the slip of paper, the documents, and the coin bag, but then he noticed he didn't have a pouch to carry his spoils.

Red looked down at the merchant and had an idea. He took off the man's vest and used it as an improvised bag, putting all the items inside.

That was when the same voice called from outside. "Darus, you bastard, come out here right now!"

Red stood up and threw the window open. Behind him, he heard a door open, but he didn't stay to greet the new visitor. He dove off into the alley and ran.

"I dare you to try to arrest me!" Narcha roared as town guards surrounded her and her companions. Around them, the results of the battle were clear. Out of the twelve initial mercenaries, five of them were out cold while the rest could barely stay on their feet. Eiwin, Narcha and Allen, however, showed no signs of any damage.

"Miss Valt, please!" Eiwin put a hand on her companion's shoulder. "Let's not make this any worse than it has to be."

Narcha snorted and refused to back down, even as the town guards reached twenty in number.

On arrival, they had immediately broken up the fight. The mercenaries hadn't resisted, allowing themselves to be detained. However, Narcha had stood her ground and threatened everyone who dared to touch her or her companions.

These guards weren't as afraid as the mercenaries. They were better-equipped, and although they still sized up Narcha carefully, they didn't back down.

"Men, that's enough!" someone called from behind the group.

From within the store, a tall man stepped out. He was middle-aged, with slick hair and a finely trimmed beard which both held traces of gray. He sported well-fitted metal armor similar to the other town guards, but his chest plate bore a symbol—an indication of his rank. A halberd stood straight in his grip, which he kept upright even as he walked.

The man carried himself authoritatively and fearlessly, and even Narcha looked wary as he approached.

"Captain Orvin, we can explain how all of this happened," Eiwin said, trying to defuse the situation before her companion made it any worse.

"He's unconscious," the captain said.

"What do you mean?"

"The merchant's unconscious. Looks like someone took advantage of the fight out here, knocked him unconscious and robbed the store."

The group was shocked.

"Who did it?" Narcha asked.

The captain shook his head, his expression sullen. "I was hoping you could tell me."

"What do you mean by that? You think we stole from him!"

"You're certainly the prime suspects," he said, unbothered by her anger. "A fight goes down in front of a store, and while everyone's distracted, someone sneaks in and steals whatever they want. Seems like a straightforward and effective plan."

Narcha didn't look convinced. "Anyone could have done that! Besides, it's just the three of us here. There was no one else!"

Behind her, Allen tensed up. His expression changed. The shift didn't go unnoticed by the captain.

"Is that true?" Orvin asked, his attention turning towards Allen. He narrowed his eyes. "Was there no one else with you?"

"I..."

Allen was about to say something, but a hand came to rest on his shoulder.

"There was no one else with us, Captain Orvin," Eiwin said serenely. "All our members are at the Sect, and Rimold is out of town. You can check, if you so please."

"Hmm." The suspicion in his eyes didn't decrease.

But Eiwin didn't give away any signs that she was lying. Eventually, the man gave up and decided to move on.

"Then, to the matter at hand," Orvin said. "What happened here?"

Narcha perked up. "These fuckers were—"

"What Miss Valt wants to say," Eiwin interrupted, "is that these people tried to attack Young Master Allen. We had to defend him."

"Bullshit!" one of the mercenaries on the ground interjected. "The kid attacked first."

The captain frowned at Eiwin before looking back at Allen. The embarrassment on the boy's face was all he needed to confirm the mercenary's story.

"So, you attacked first. And tell me, why did you do that?"

"Because they were trying to screw me over, like they always do!" Narcha said. "We were just tired of taking it lying down and did something about it!"

Eiwin cringed, but the situation was already out of her hands.

"I see." The man nodded. "You know the law, don't you, girl?"

Narcha glared at him. "Screw the law! What good has it done me? It only serves to protect those fat, corrupt merchants!"

"It's because of people like you that the law exists!" The captain met her gaze and tone, not to be outmatched. "It's exactly because of little brats like you who wish to solve everything through strength that there are rules! If you had it your way, we would still be beating each other up over our disputes!"

The man's words and intensity gave Narcha's temper some pause, but she still looked as if she were about to erupt.

"Go ahead!" The man waved her over with a smile. "Attack me! Don't you like to solve everything with strength? See what happens when you're not fighting small fry!"

The warrior gritted her teeth. She was about to take up the challenge when Eiwin stepped forward and held her back. Narcha turned and saw her companion shaking her head gravely.

With much hesitation in her eyes, Narcha eventually stepped back and took a deep breath.

Orvin snorted in contempt. "At least one of you is smart. The Baron and your Sect Master made a deal precisely so that children like you wouldn't make a mess out of this town. It seems, however, that toddlers always find a way to screw things up." The man signaled the other guards. "Take them away."

"What?!" Narcha's eyes widened.

"You heard me. I'll get someone to fetch Domeron, and I'll keep the lot of you in a cell until we sort this mess out."

"This is not—"

"Miss Valt!" Eiwin interrupted her once again.

Narcha grunted in anger, but the weight of their predicament started to dawn on her as she stared at the guards surrounding them.

"Fine!" She threw her hands up. "But you're not taking my saber!"

"Like you would be able to do anything with it," the man huffed, much to her displeasure. He turned to Eiwin. "The kid has to come too. He should stay with you two rather than being left in the street—for his own protection."

Eiwin nodded, but she looked hesitant.

"Is there a problem, girl?" Orvin frowned.

"No. Let's be on our way."

"Good. Someone go fetch that slob from inside. I need to talk to him, too."

Red watched from a distance as the guards took his fellow Sect members away. He couldn't hear everything that was said and didn't know what had happened. In the end, he could only look down at the bag he was carrying.

What now?

CHAPTER 72

LOOT

THE SITUATION HAD DEVELOPED in a way Red hadn't expected. Narcha and the rest had beaten up the mercenaries as he predicted, but he hadn't planned for a third party to get involved. He'd seen a few guards spread throughout the town, but never twenty of them in one place.

Although they weren't treating his fellow Sect members as roughly as the mercenaries, it was still clear Eiwin and Narcha had no intention of resisting their escort. Not to mention, they were also bringing the unconscious merchant along. What if they figured out Red was behind the robbery? Would they come looking for him?

The merchant might not know who Red was, but what about his companions? Eiwin was not aware of his plan, but she would definitely suspect him. Allen was the real issue, though. The older boy merely needed to connect the dots using their earlier conversation to figure out Red was responsible. Would they give him up if the guards pressed them?

Red would have liked to think they wouldn't, but it was hard for him to rely on people he had barely known for a few days. If he'd known things would develop like this, he would've thought twice before trying to steal from the merchant.

Although when Red looked at the precious items he was carrying, he found it hard to regret his decision.

Finding the item Narcha had ordered had been his primary objective, but he wasn't exactly selfless. When Allen had mentioned pills to him, Red had hoped to find something that would benefit his cultivation, too. He'd found no medicine, but the heavy coin purse alone was more than worth it, if Eiwin and Hector's previous conversation was any indication.

Should I escape?

Running away from the town was the first idea that came to mind. However, Red left it as a last resort. It would be an extreme reaction, much more so given that he still had so much to learn and hadn't exactly repaid the Sect for helping him.

Should I return the items?

That was even more absurd. They could be of great help in his cultivation, and it would be unwise to give them up. Besides, Red doubted the merchant and the guards would just let him go.

I need more information.

Red sighed. That was the root of the problem. He didn't know how much trouble he was in, and making a decision without being fully informed would be stupid on his part. Yet, he had limited options when it came to asking for help. In fact, there was only one person in the Sect who had a positive opinion of him, other than Eiwin and Allen.

It's gotta be him, then...

The walk back to the Sect was one of the most stressful journeys Red had ever made. He didn't have trouble navigating the streets—he had memorized the path, made easier by his experience underground. The real problem was the people.

Most of the townsfolk didn't even spare him a glance, but whenever Red noticed someone eye him, his heart leaped in fear. Still, their interest was merely passing, and no one tried to stop him. He also did his best to stay away from the guards, giving anyone with a uniform and weapons a wide berth. Luckily, they didn't seem to be looking for him in the first place.

Eventually, after no small number of false alarms, Red found himself on the street leading up to the Sect. He observed the place from afar, in case anyone might've been waiting for his arrival. The road, though, was just as deserted as it had been the previous day.

Red felt ill at ease as he approached the courtyard. He was fully expecting someone to jump from behind one of the abandoned buildings and announce his arrest. Thankfully, he arrived at the Sect's gate without incident.

At the courtyard fence, Red stared through the cracks in case anyone was outside. Seeing no one, he carefully opened the gate and slipped inside, trying to make as little noise as possible.

Hopefully he's still there...

He made haste towards Goulth's workshop. There were no sounds of hammering coming from inside the house, but as Red approached, the smell of burning fuel hit him. He neared the door and imitated something he'd learned just yesterday.

He knocked.

Ten seconds later, there was still no response.

He knocked again, harder this time.

"Come in!" Goulth's voice welcomed him from inside.

Red opened the door and stepped into the workshop. The blacksmith wasn't in the first room, so he followed the corridor to the forge. There he saw the giant man bent over his desk, focused on drawing something on a large scroll using a quill. Goulth raised his head as he heard Red enter.

"Apprentice!" He greeted him with a smile. "I thought you had other lessons to attend to."

"I did... I need your help." He saw no point in beating around the bush.

"Hm?" Goulth put down his pen. "What happened?"

Red felt it was best to show the man rather than try to explain it. He untied the improvised bag from around his neck and handed it over to the blacksmith.

"What is this?" Goulth picked up the sack and sniffed it. "It kind of smells like wine."

"Open it."

He did as much. He put the scroll he was working on aside and spread the bag open over the table.

"Hm, this looks like a jewelry box. Is this a bag of coins? And trade documents?" Goulth squinted. "Where did you even get this? And what's this..."

The man trailed off as he picked up the slip of paper. He examined the item closely. Suddenly his eyes widened, and his breath became ragged.

For a second, Red thought the man might be having a heart attack.

"A talisman!" Goulth stared at him. "Kid, where did you even get this?"

"What's a talisman?"

"It's like a portable spell, except it can— Wait, you didn't answer my question! This is an extremely expensive item, Red. How did you even buy it?"

"I didn't buy it. I took it from someone."

"Huh?" Goulth frowned. The shock of the discovery was starting to wear off, and his eyes wavered back to the documents. "Did you steal this?"

"Yes." Since Red had decided to come to Goulth for help, he would be honest. Even if he tried to lie at this point, he doubted the man would've believed him.

"Kid, that's not a very nice thing to do." Goulth shook his head in disapproval, but Red didn't feel his reaction was very genuine. "Tell me what happened."

"A merchant sold Narcha's Spiritual Medicine to someone else. While she and Eiwin were fighting against his men, I snuck in and stole what he had."

"What a bastard! She put aside almost a year of her salary for that!"

"That's not all," Red said. "The merchant caught me in his office. I took him by surprise and managed to knock him out."

"That's dangerous, too dangerous! Did he see your face?"

"I think so. But it all happened very fast."

"Well, it should still be okay in the end... You're new in town, so I doubt rumors about you have had time to spread. You should avoid going out until this all blows over, though."

"That's not all..."

"There's more?"

"The guards arrived and arrested Narcha, Eiwin, and Allen, as well as the merchant and his subordinates."

"Ugh..." Goulth looked even more troubled. "Was the captain there? Tall, middle-aged, looks very tough?"

Red nodded. "There was someone that fit that description."

The blacksmith sighed. "Did you guys have this fight in the middle of the street?"

Red nodded again.

"That makes things slightly more complicated," Goulth said. "Did you get the name of the merchant?"

"I think they called him Darus."

"That guy?" Goulth winced. "To think we had him as one of the safe people to do trade with, too..."

A silence settled in the room as the man fell into thought.

"Listen, Red, the merchant might have deserved it, but what you did was not right." Goulth looked at him sternly. "More importantly, it was dangerous. You might not be aware, but the situation in town is more complicated than it seems. Our Water Dragon Sect is one of the strongest factions in this place, but even we can't do as we please. There are still people here that can hurt us if we're not careful."

"Then... we have to give this back?"

The man laughed. "Give it back? No, we do not. Although we're not invincible, we aren't the type to take offenses lying down. Since that guy decided it would be a good idea to make an enemy of us, it's only appropriate that you taught him a lesson."

"But what about the guards? Aren't they going to come looking for me?"

"They might make a token effort, but once they learn you're related to us, they'll just have to let it go," Goulth said. "Besides, our Sect has done a lot to help this town. The Baron does not take kindly to those who mess with us, and Gustav has already been giving him plenty of trouble."

There's that name again.

"What about Narcha and the others?" Red asked. "They looked like they were in trouble."

"They'll be fine. It's not the first time they've fought someone in the middle of town, and it's always against people who deserve it, anyway. After they're released, they'll probably get lectured by Domeron and Hector, but that's about it. As for you, try to remain inside the Sect until things die down."

It seemed Red had overestimated the severity of things. Although this place had laws, strength still mattered the most, and the Water Dragon Sect didn't lack it.

"What about the things I took? Won't the others be mad at what I did?"

"Not really," Goulth said. "Hector might pretend to be mad, but he would do much worse things himself if someone disrespected our Sect to his face. Besides, you'll have to donate some of what you've stolen to the Sect, too. After all, you're still using our name for protection."

Red winced, but he had seen this coming. In the end, he couldn't help but accept the reasoning. After all, it was still much better than having it all taken away. Speaking with Goulth had given him more confidence in the power of this Sect, and confirmed that he had made the right choice by joining.

"Don't worry, Hector has always been fair when it comes to contributions." The man patted Red's shoulders, then pointed at the box. "Anyways, isn't there something you're forgetting?"

"Can you unlock it?" Red asked.

He smiled. "It'll take a bit of work, but it can be done. These types of lockboxes are sometimes booby-trapped, so it's a delicate process. I was wondering what might be inside, but now that I know who the merchant was... Aren't you curious to see what kinds of pills are in this?"

CHAPTER 73

IMITATION

"How are you gonna open it?" Red asked.

"I've picked up a bit of locksmithing over the years too," Goulth said. "I'm not as good as Rimold, but it should be enough to open a simple box."

"Is he a locksmith?"

"No, he's just a thief." He pointed at another table in the room. "Go fetch my tools."

Goulth elaborated about which of his instruments he was referring to. After a few attempts, Red finally brought back the right set of tools, and the blacksmith began his work.

"Locksmithing is just as much about opening locks as it is about making them." Goulth picked out a small set of pins, each one with a hook at the end. "It's a more specific field than blacksmithing—and not as useful to Spiritual Cultivators."

"Why is that?" Red asked.

"Well, locks rely on mechanisms. You need the right key to open one, but that in itself is just ineffective against cultivators, since they can use their Spiritual Energy to unlock the mechanism. What genuine cultivators use to keep precious items locked away are magical restrictions."

"You never mentioned restrictions to me before."

"'Restrictions' is the name we use for formations used to keep things locked away."

"You didn't tell me what formations are either."

"Listen, kid, I'm trying to focus here!"

"But you're the one who..." Red trailed off as the man gave him an angry look.

Goulth turned back towards the task at hand. Using the pins that hardly suited his large hands, he started to fiddle with the lock. Over the next minute, the box clicked now and then. Red didn't know what was happening, but after one final click, the man leaned back with a proud smile.

"It's done."

"Already?" Red was skeptical.

"What can I say? I'm pretty skilled."

"Didn't you say you weren't—"

"Now to the next part! Checking for traps. Apart from the lock, there might be some hidden mechanism that could destroy the contents of the box if it's not dealt with properly. This box looks too small to have anything of the sort, but it's better to be safe than sorry."

He examined the box again, lightly pressing and weighing different parts of the ornate casing. Upon discovering nothing out of the ordinary, he lifted the lid ever so slightly with one of his pins. He then jammed the tool inside to keep the lid halfway open.

He noticed Red studying his motions. "Some traps only trigger once you open the lid," Goulth explained. "So you need to search the gap for any mechanisms before flipping it open."

He moved the pin around beneath the lid, searching for any resistance. After a full lap around the box, he removed the pin and grinned at Red.

"Seems safe, but you should take a step back, just in case."

Red readily took his advice and went to the other side of the room. Goulth then put both of his hands on the lid, took a deep breath, and in one swift motion, flipped the box open.

The blacksmith flinched back and half covered his face in fear. No explosion happened, though.

"Can I approach again?" Red asked, eager to see the contents of the box.

"Sure." Goulth waved him over. "Seems like we were worried about nothing."

Red actually appreciated his teacher's caution, but he was too distracted to praise the man. He neared the opened box. What he saw inside made his heart skip a beat.

"Is that...?"

"Yes!" Goulth nodded with a wide smile. "Spiritual Medicine!"

Inside were three glass vials containing pills, resting on top of a soft cloth. The vial on the left had three small black-blue pellets, the one in the middle held a dark-green pill, and the one on the right contained four bright-yellow pellets.

"You struck a gold mine this time around, kid! These are pills that not even I could make with confidence, and it would take me months to get this many of them!"

"How do you know what they are?" Red asked.

"It's the coloration and the markings," Goulth said. "Look closely."

Red leaned over to examine the pills closely. They were about the size of his fingernails, and he had to get extremely close to notice anything, but sure enough, there were faint patterns on their surfaces that formed strange symbols.

"What do they do?"

"These can help you open your Spiritual Veins," Goulth said, pointing at the dark-blue pills. "They're called Vein Opening Pills."

Red recognized the name from a conversation with Viran that might as well have happened a lifetime ago.

"These ones," the man said, indicating the yellow pills, "are Blood Revival Pills. They can stop bleeding and heal superficial wounds. Good for when you're in the middle of combat, since you can ingest many of them in a row. As for the last one..."

Goulth picked up the vial containing the single dark-green pill.

"... it's a fake Parting Sea Pill."

"Fake?" Red frowned. "What does it do?"

"It's meant to help you open your Spiritual Sea. However, this is merely an imitation of the real thing. Its effects are nowhere near as good as the legitimate product."

Red had a sudden realization. "Is that the pill Narcha was looking for?"

Goulth sighed, his smile fading. "Very likely. That girl is very foolish to be spending her money on this..."

"Why do you say that?" Red asked, noticing the change in the man's mood.

"This is not the first time she's bought something like this. Unfortunately, it's just an imitation at the end of the day. It provides minimal help in opening the Spiritual Sea and has some dangerous side effects. On top of that, it's also very expensive. The only reason it's still sold is because sometimes one cultivator out of ten thousand gets lucky enough to open their Sea with it."

"Can't she get more money to buy the real thing?"

"I wish it were that simple," Goulth said. "Production of these pills is controlled by the Sects and other factions. They put up a limited amount of them for sale every year, and each pill is more expensive than what our Sect makes in an entire year."

Red had no idea what the number could be, but he felt the weight behind Goulth's words.

"Are they that rare?"

"Not rare. Sects can produce plenty of them. But for a cultivator, they are priceless. They might allow someone who has no chance of opening their Spiritual Sea to have a glimpse of hope. Sadly, they're even beyond the means of cultivators who have already opened their Spiritual Sea, not to mention people like us."

Goulth's gaze fell, then shifted to Red.

"This is the sad truth of this world, Red. The Sects and other great powers don't want everyone to be running around with the secret to opening their Spiritual Sea. For that, they maintain a monopoly on the production of these pills and limit their availability to the outside world. That way, not only can they prevent the rise of rival powers, but they can also compel cultivators to join their organizations.

"People like Narcha, who are stuck at this bottleneck, search desperately for any aid they can find, no matter how small or dangerous it may prove to be. This obsession hardly ever pays off, though, and at the end of the day, it's more likely to just get her killed..." Goulth sighed, a distant look in his eyes. "I worry about her."

Red didn't respond, not sure what he should say.

"Sorry, kid, I shouldn't be putting so many bad thoughts in your head," the man said. "Although getting a genuine Parting Sea pill is difficult, it's not impossible. For now, though..."

Goulth handed him the vial with the green pill.

"You can give Narcha this yourself. I'll take the other items to Hector and explain the situation to him. Unless you want to do it yourself?"

Red promptly shook his head.

Goulth gave him a hearty laugh. "Haha! It's fine, kid. As your master, I would never allow you to get the short end of the stick."

He closed the ornate box and picked up both the talisman and the bag of coins.

"You can wait here while I talk to Hector and Domeron. Make yourself comfortable... but don't steal anything!" he warned before leaving the forge.

Red looked down at the glass vial, eyes narrowed.

He had a lot to think about.

Goulth didn't return for the next hour. Red couldn't hear any sounds of shouting coming from the hall, but the wait made him anxious about what might have happened. Could the blacksmith have been mistaken about how Hector would react? Was the elder thinking about expelling him from the Sect?

Such thoughts kept crossing Red's mind as he waited in the forge by himself. Eventually, though, he heard the front door open and looked up to find that Goulth had returned.

"It went well," he said. "A bit too well, if you ask me."

"What does that mean?" Red asked.

"Hector was mad as expected, but that's just about normal for him." Goulth shrugged. "The Town Guard actually appeared at our front gate while we were in the middle of our discussion, and Domeron went with them to pick up the brats."

"Did Hector say anything about what I did?"

"No, actually." The man looked puzzled. "I expected to have to argue with him, but he was pretty accepting of the terms I put forward. He did have one condition, though... He wants to meet with you alone after dinner."

Red frowned.

"Look, I know what you're thinking, kid." Goulth said. "Hector is not that kind of person, though. If he wanted to kill you, he would never go through so many hoops."

"That doesn't make me feel any better."

"I know. If you want to, I can go with you. I won't be able to stop Hector if he decides to do something, but I can probably hold him back long enough to give you a head start in your escape."

Red couldn't tell if he was being serious.

"Look, I know it's difficult to put your trust in people you've barely known for a few days," Goulth said. "But I'd like to think we've been pretty genuine with you, right? In the end, our actions speak louder than any words I could use to convince you."

The man could guess what concerned Red. Things were moving too fast for him to keep up, and he didn't know when or if he would ever get used to living around these people. But in the end, he had already taken plenty of risks. Meeting with Hector alone was hardly more dangerous than insulting the belligerent elder to his face in front of other people.

"I'll go," Red decided.

"Good." Goulth seemed satisfied. "Those folks should be back in a bit, too..."

He had barely finished speaking when a wave of loud sounds spilled over from outside. Their source was a single rude warrior.

"I'm gonna murder that fat pig even if it's the last thing I—ugh!"

Narcha's tirade was suddenly interrupted as she yelled in pain.

"STOP SCREAMING AND GET INSIDE THE HALL RIGHT NOW!"

Hector's even louder voice drowned everything out, and Red could almost feel the rage emanating from his words.

He winced and looked at Goulth. "You said he wasn't mad."

The blacksmith shrugged.

CHAPTER 74

DEBT

"You should stay here until they're done," Goulth said.

"How long will it take?"

"Not sure." He shrugged. "Probably only an hour."

Red could hear more shouting from within the hall. He took the man's advice and remained inside the forge.

It took just about as much time as Goulth had suggested for the sounds of uproar, then discussion, to die down. Red was about to ask whether he should finally go when they heard knocking at the door.

"Come in!" Goulth shouted.

Red heard a door open and close from the other room, and a few moments later, Eiwin appeared in front of them.

"How did it go, girl?" Goulth asked. "Did the old captain give you any trouble?"

"Not any more than usual," she said. "However, he seemed more on edge than I remember."

"Might have to do with the monster horde. But then again, there might be more happening than we know of."

"Isn't that always the case, Master Goulth." Her attention shifted to Red. "I actually came looking for you... We need to talk about what happened."

An awkward silence settled in the room. Goulth seemed oblivious to it, though, and continued his work as if he were alone.

"Did Allen tell on me?" Red asked in his monotone voice.

"No, he didn't," she said. "He refused to, even in front of Hector. He said he told you to run back to the Sect and get help while he stayed behind to fight... Unfortunately, he's always been a terrible liar."

That Allen would refuse to tell on him surprised Red. He didn't think Allen was an untrustworthy person, but he was still immature and seemed likely to yield under pressure.

"Did the merchant say something?"

"He was raving about being attacked by a child when he returned to his shop," Eiwin said. "The guards thought he was talking about Allen, but he was outside the entire time."

With these kinds of clues, it would have been weird if she hadn't guessed Red was involved.

"You shouldn't have done that." Her words sounded like an admonishment, but the calm tone of her voice made it difficult for Red to take it as such.

"He was trying to steal from Narcha, so I thought it would be fair to do the same to him," he said, trying to explain.

"I know, but we don't measure the evil of our deeds by the person we do it to," Eiwin said. "That merchant may be an awful person, but it is still wrong to steal. Though life is not always so simple, ideally his unjust conduct should have been punished lawfully. If we all were to take justice into our own hands, the only result would be chaos."

"It just seemed right at the time. Besides, I don't really make a habit out of stealing."

Red wasn't lying. He'd never stolen back in the underground, though that was mostly because there wasn't much to steal.

Eiwin looked conflicted. She knew Red had tried to help the Sect and her friends, but at the end of the day, she seemed to have a hard time justifying his actions.

"Give the kid a break, Eiwin," Goulth interjected. "If he hadn't snuck in, then something bad might have happened."

"What do you mean?" she asked.

410

Both of them looked at the blacksmith in confusion.

"The merchant was carrying a talisman." Goulth said, holding up the slip of paper from earlier.

"What?!"

Red suddenly remembered the existence of the item. He had been so absorbed by the Spiritual Medicines that he'd forgotten to ask Goulth about its use.

"What is that talisman for?" he asked.

"It's a portable spell." Goulth said. "It's equivalent to a strike from someone who has already opened their Spiritual Sea. This one is a fireball Spiritual Art. It could have easily wounded or even killed Narcha and Eiwin if they were caught by surprise."

Red winced as he recalled the merchant's threatening words. Something about cooking Narcha alive. "Can anyone use it?"

The blacksmith nodded. "Yes, as long as they know how to activate it, even a normal person can use a talisman. They're very hard to make, but their ease of use is why they're so dangerous."

It suddenly became clear to Red how close to death the group had been at that moment.

"That's not normal," Eiwin said as she recovered from the shock. "A talisman is not the kind of thing a merchant like him could get his hands on."

"That was my thought too." Goulth gently put down the slip of paper. "The only talisman maker I know of lives in the capital, and his items are way beyond what anyone in this town can afford."

"Were there any markings?" she asked.

"Not any I could recognize."

Red was confused again. "What do you mean by markings?"

"Remember what I told you about the pills?" Goulth told him. "Those markings on their surface also serve as a signature of the person or faction that produced them. The same goes for talismans, except this one had no signature."

"Could it be fake?" Eiwin asked.

"Not at all. It was carved on quality monster skin, and it was painted with genuine Spiritual Ink. Looks like it was produced by a true master of their craft."

Eiwin's expression grew even more troubled.

"The kid also brought some trade documents from the merchant's office." Goulth pointed towards a pile of papers on his desk. "I looked through them but couldn't find anything out of the ordinary. Maybe you'll have better luck, though."

"I will take a look at them, Master Goulth." Eiwin gathered the files.

She turned to Red. "I can't agree with your decision, Red, but I recognize how much help you were to us," she said, sounding genuine. "I also don't agree with lots of things Miss Valt does, but she always has the Sect's best interest in mind. In the future, though, I'd like you to be more careful... Things could have turned out much worse."

Red nodded. The next time he stole something, he needed to be careful about these talismans, too.

"It's unfortunate he'd already sold Miss Valt's pill, though." Eiwin shook her head in resignation.

"We have it," Red said.

"Huh?" She perked up. "What do you mean?"

"Here." He took the glass vial out of his pocket and showed it to her.

"That's..." Eiwin narrowed her eyes as she examined the green pill. Eventually, she let out a sigh. "So it turns out he didn't sell it to anyone else. I suppose Gustav could have just paid the merchant enough to not deliver this to Miss Valt. Either way, that's just more evidence that he didn't have any good intentions..."

She looked at Red with a smile.

"You should give it to her. She'll be very happy."

Red hesitated, but still nodded in the end. Wasn't this the reason he'd stolen the pill in the first place?

"Do you know where she is?" he asked.

"I saw her walking towards the training field. Do you want me to come too?"

"It's fine." Red shook his head. "I can handle it."

Eiwin was always eager to help, but if he wanted to establish some kind of amicable relationship with the others, he would need to interact with them on his own.

With that, Red stood from his seat and walked out. Eiwin watched his back with a conflicted expression while Goulth let out a laugh.

"He is really direct, huh?"

Sure enough, Red found the warrior on the training field, whaling on a wooden target with a large practice blade. There was no rhythm or skill behind her blows, Narcha simply letting out her anger more than anything.

He paused after seeing the scene, but still approached. As he got closer, he noticed plenty of cracks in the training weapon.

"Fucking old man..."

Another strike.

"Fucking merchant..."

Another hit. More wooden splinters flew off from the impact.

"I'll show them!"

With one final blow, Narcha completely shattered her weapon against the target. An explosion of splinters hit her face and chest, but she didn't flinch.

"Fuck!"

She flung the ruined weapon to the ground.

Narcha turned around abruptly, striding toward the weapons rack. Suddenly, she froze upon noticing Red silently standing there.

She glared at him. "What do you want, brat?"

He was worried she would hit him if he wasn't careful with his words.

"Here." Red didn't beat around the bush. "Your pill."

He threw the glass vial over to her. She caught it but hadn't registered his words until she examined the object in her hands. Her furious expression was replaced by bewilderment.

"This... My pill!"

She blinked, having a hard time accepting the sight before her. Eventually, realization crossed her face.

"It was you! You stole from that bastard!"

"Yes."

Narcha was at a loss for words. A few seconds later, she frowned. "Are you hoping to buy my trust with this?"

"Yes."

"Uh..." She didn't know how to respond. "At least you're honest, I suppose."

Narcha pocketed the vial and regarded him closely. They both stared at each other in silence, seemingly forever.

She finally broke the silence. "I owe you one, kid. I intend on fully repaying this debt, but I want you to know that this doesn't change my thoughts about you."

Red would've been suspicious if she'd claimed otherwise.

"I can see you're resilient," she continued. "But I know you're hiding something. We all are, but I don't think your secrets are as simple as ours. I really want to be wrong about you... I wish that you'd be just another normal member of our Sect and contribute like the others. But I have the feeling that one day, your past will catch up to you and get all of us involved, too."

Red didn't respond.

Narcha laughed. "It sounds stupid when I put it like that, huh? But it's the truth. For some reason, I've been having terrible dreams ever since we found you that night. Some might call it superstition, but once you understand enough about the mysteries of this world, you'll learn not to ignore any signs you receive... When you add that to all the weird shit that's been happening in the forest, how can I just pretend everything's normal?"

"I... understand." In fact, he understood her all too well.

"Good," she said. "I don't actually hate you, kid. I hope you know that. In fact, I kind of admire you. When I was your age, I didn't have my shit together like you. Maybe I still don't. But these people... They're too important for me to take this matter lightly."

"Is that why you're risking it?" Red asked. "With the pill, I mean."

"That big oaf has been talking too much," Narcha said. "But yes. That's one of the reasons I want to open my Spiritual Sea. That, and for revenge..."

She went silent, as if she'd said too much.

"What if it doesn't work?"

"I've been trying for years. I've failed more times than I can be bothered to count." She shook her head. "But I have no other option than to keep trying. I have to succeed... I will succeed, no matter the cost."

Red could feel the absolute resolve behind her words. It bordered on madness, a desire that was consuming her being.

But maybe this is just what's required if one wants to walk this path...

"Alright," Red said. "I'll think of a way you can repay me."

Narcha scowled. "Hey, I didn't say I was going to do just anything!"

"I thought this pill was very important to you. Isn't it?"

"Well... yeah."

"And you said you were going to repay your debt, right?"

414

"That's... Yes."

"Then you would need to help me with something really important, too. It's only fair, right?"

She nodded, somewhat begrudgingly.

"Then I'll think of something when the time comes," Red concluded. He walked off, leaving behind a brooding Narcha who couldn't help but grumble to herself.

CHAPTER 75

PROMOTION

A FEW HOURS LATER, Red was called to dinner at the main hall, and when he arrived, everyone but Goulth was in the room. Allen's face lit up at his entrance, and the boy pointed to a free seat by his side.

Red hesitated but took the seat. As he scooped food onto his plate, he couldn't help but notice the awkward atmosphere around the table.

No one spoke. Eiwin looked worried, Narcha and Hector were trading unfriendly gazes—only Domeron and Rog acted unconcerned. Only the sounds of cutlery and chewing could be heard in the hall, and Red didn't have any intention of speaking up either.

That is, until he felt a nudge at his side. He turned to Allen, who was leaning towards him and whispering in his ear.

"Hey, I didn't tell anyone about what we did."

Red froze for a moment, but then continued to eat his food like he hadn't heard. At the head of the table, Hector's expression twitched, but Allen didn't seem to notice.

"What even happened in there, anyway?" he asked in a hushed voice.

Red remained silent. However, the older boy continued to stare at him expectantly.

He shook his head. "Not now."

"Uh... right." Allen leaned back and looked around the table.

Much to his luck, no one was looking in their direction. The silent atmosphere returned, but Red could tell that Allen was growing fidgety in his seat. He considered trying to calm him down, but he just went back to eating.

"Wonder what happened inside that shop, huh?" Allen said, breaking the silence in the meeting hall.

Everyone's eyes turned towards him, but he just smiled in a carefree way.

"I mean... wonder who could have robbed that guy without anyone even noticing, huh? I'm sure whoever did it must've had help from some very capable companions."

Hector's expression darkened, and the rest of the table regarded him strangely. But Allen seemed oblivious to their reaction.

"Stealing is wrong, though." His face looked pinched. "But the merchant definitely deserved it... I just wish I could meet whoever came up with this plan and shake their hand— Ugh!"

A metal spoon hit the boy right on the forehead.

"GET OUT!" Hector pointed at the door.

"But I didn't even—"

"OUT!"

"Tyrant!"

Allen ran off, screaming. A few moments later, everyone returned to their meals as if nothing had happened.

Eventually, people finished their food and started to leave the table. Only Eiwin, Red, and Hector were left in the meeting hall. Eiwin looked at Red oddly, noticing he'd long since finished his meal and was just sitting there.

"Let's go, Red," she said with a smile. "I plan to teach you some letters today."

"I can't right now. I have to speak with Hector first."

"What do you mean?" Her face fell as she looked over at the old man.

Hector didn't respond, meeting her gaze with serenity.

"It's fine, Eiwin," he said. "Goulth already spoke to him about it."

"I see..."

Eiwin relaxed a bit, but worry was still evident in her expression. She hesitated, but eventually stood and nodded at him.

"I'll be waiting for you outside when you're done."

She gave him one last glance before walking out of the hall and closing the door behind her, leaving only Red and Hector inside. Silence reigned for a few seconds before the elder snorted.

"Hmph, does she believe you're so innocent she needs to stand up for you like so?"

"I think the more important question is why she needs to be worried about you in the first place," Red answered.

The old man frowned but didn't reply to his remark. "Did Goulth already tell you about the deal?"

"He didn't tell me any specifics," Red said.

"I see. First of all, I need you to understand something. I approve of your actions today."

Red looked up at the elder in surprise. This conversation already wasn't going the way he'd expected.

"You might not have known this before you acted, but a Sect should never allow itself to be pushed around," Hector said. "Our enemies should never think they can safely hide behind laws and politics. A Sect and its cultivators must never be tied down by these conventions."

"Then why did you scold Narcha and the others?"

"Because, unlike you, they were stupid and decided to violate the law in front of the entire town. We are strong, but not strong enough to do as we please and ignore the town's laws. As long as that remains the case, we have to compromise with the Baron and his people... We have to be smart about how we act."

"Then are these laws just an inconvenience for you?"

"They are," Hector said, his face as stern as ever. "You might think this kind of reasoning is immoral, but we are cultivators, not mortals. Strength is still the most important thing in this world, and to think otherwise is just willful ignorance."

He spoke like this was a matter of fact.

"The Empire and other kingdoms justify their laws as protecting the common people, but that's a bunch of nonsense. These rules and systems are just another aspect of strength, a method they use to make others obey their authority and act in their interest."

Red felt like he understood this reasoning. It seemed that even on the surface, people acted with self-interest in mind. They just didn't make their motives so overt.

"If the Baron didn't have the strength to back up his authority, no one would obey his rule," Hector said. "But let me ask you this—do you think these laws apply to everyone equally?"

Red recalled how the mercenaries were treated compared to Narcha and the others. It was clear that the guards didn't dare to handle the Sect members as harshly as the others, no matter the tough front they displayed.

"That's the point, kid. Strength is still what matters the most." Hector gave him an intense stare. "It defines how you'll be treated in this world, laws or not. Do you think that if the Baron committed a crime, he would suffer any consequences?"

"Isn't he the one who makes the laws? Who's going to punish him?" Red asked, confused.

The elder smiled, satisfied with his answer. "Precisely. There is no one to punish those in power for violating the laws they made themselves! This is all just a way for nobles to keep those weaker than them under their thumb. The laws don't apply to them, even if they may claim otherwise to the public. Maybe some of them believe in their own words, but most of them are just hypocrites."

This was something Red hadn't considered. The situation on the surface was far more complicated than he'd first thought.

"Sects are at least more honest about how they act—they just take what they want by force! Of course, I'm making Sects sound more villainous than they actually are. Most of the time, they simply avoid contact with the common folk, and our interests rarely intersect."

Things were becoming clearer to Red, but there was still so much he didn't understand.

"But which way of acting is better? I mean... which benefits cultivators the most?" he asked.

"That's not a simple question to answer." Hector sounded troubled for the first time during their conversation. "It's more of a matter of philosophy than of simple gains. To put it plainly, most Sects believe that the cultivator world and the secular world should remain two completely separate entities. The Imperial practitioners, though, believe they must rule and guide mortals."

"And what's the problem with the way the Empire does things?"

He couldn't find any apparent issue with their way of thinking. If they could govern and use normal humans to their benefit, why wouldn't they do it?

"Cultivators should focus on cultivation, kid, not mortal matters," Hector said. "Besides, there's a reason Sects don't get involved with the common folk, and it's because they tried it in the past. It never ends well."

Red recalled the priest's words at the plaza and weighed them against Hector's explanation. They each were biased to their own factions, and it was hard to take what either of them were saying at face value without knowing how both groups worked. However, he felt Hector's words resonated more with his own way of thinking.

Of course, Red still intended to learn more about the situation from other sources.

"Did you call me here to explain this?" Red asked.

Hector shook his head. "That's just meant to sate your curiosity. You might have acted with your own self-interest in mind too, but you wouldn't be the first cultivator in history to do so. As long as the Sect benefits at the end of the day, your original intent doesn't matter. In a way, I feel as if you have more of a cultivator's spirit than a lot of people in this Sect..."

Hector said these last words with an exasperated sigh before grabbing something from his pocket and throwing it at Red.

He caught the item and examined it. It was the glass vial with the Vein Opening Pills, all three still contained within.

"You can keep those," Hector said.

Red was taken by surprise. "Don't other people need to use any?"

"Other than Allen and Eiwin, everyone else in this Sect has already opened all twelve of their veins. But their talents are much better than yours, and you'll benefit from these pills more."

Red was aware of Allen's talent, but he hadn't known Eiwin was also superior to him.

"Of course, that's just what you earned on your own," Hector said. "The talisman and the Blood Revival Pills will go to the Sect vault and will only be taken out when necessary, so you can't have those. As for the money, it'll be used for other Sect expenses. However, I'll be providing you with more Vein Opening Pills and other medicines in the future due to your contribution to the Sect."

Red's eyes lit up.

"You can consider yourself an inner disciple of our Sect now," Hector explained. "There are more rewards coming your way, but I'll need to discuss it with the other elders first. In the future, you may also ask for guidance from me in cultivation matters."

"Was my contribution that vital?"

"The talisman alone was of extreme importance, but you can also think of this as an investment. You've proven me wrong over the course of one day, and now I can see the value Eiwin saw in you in the first place. You might not be able to open your Spiritual Sea, but in the future, you can still be a useful asset for the Sect." The old man grimaced. "Why? Is there a problem with this arrangement?"

Red shrugged. "I thought it would take more than this."

"Hmph, don't think of me as an ingrate, you brat. A Sect is supposed to work on a system of contributions. The more you help the Sect, the more the Sect helps you. Of course, I hope you don't intend on slacking off, or else I'll immediately take back your benefits!"

Red shook his head. "I won't."

"Great." Hector nodded, satisfied. "Vein Opening Pills are meant to be consumed when you encounter difficulties in opening your acupoints, so be careful about when you use them. They can't be used back-to-back, or else their effects will be reduced, and you risk crippling your Spiritual Vein."

Red nodded in understanding.

"Then you may go." Hector waved him away. "Just make sure that if you have any questions, you come to visit during the daytime."

Red didn't get up, staring at Hector in silence.

The Grand Elder frowned. "What is it?"

"Should I consume the pill if there's an imbalance in my Spiritual Veins?"

"What do you mean?" Hector sounded confused. "Come here!"

Red did as he was told. Hector grabbed his hand and yanked him over before injecting Spiritual Energy into his veins. Red felt a strand traveling past his shoulder, where it had stopped the last time, before wandering down his spine and into his newly opened Upper Leg Spiritual Vein.

The energy froze once it wandered past his left leg, and Hector's expression fell.

"Moron, what did you do?"

Just as Hector raised his voice, the doors of the hall burst open and Eiwin and Goulth stormed in.

"Master Hector, please be calm!" Eiwin pleaded.

Goulth ran in right behind her. "Old man, don't do anything you'll regret!" he threatened.

Hector was taken off guard by the sudden intrusion, but his expression promptly twisted into an angry glare.

CHAPTER 76
WRITING

AFTER BERATING Eiwin and Goulth for interrupting him, Hector instructed Red on how he should proceed with his cultivation. The elder was still mad that he had created this predicament with his Spiritual Veins, but it was an easily solvable problem.

"You should consume one of your pills as soon as possible," Hector said. "Although some of the medicinal power might be wasted, it's best to solve an imbalance as fast as you can."

Red agreed with his solution, and after Hector dismissed them, he, Goulth and Eiwin exited the hall. It was already night, and the moon was high in the star-filled sky.

"I'm gonna go back, Red," Goulth said, smiling. "I told you there was nothing to worry about with Hector."

He felt like the Goulth's actions suggested otherwise, but he didn't comment on it. As the man walked off, only Eiwin and Red remained in the courtyard.

"I didn't expect Master Hector to change his attitude this quickly," she said, breaking the calm silence. "It seems even I underestimated you."

"Isn't it dangerous to trust me like this?" Red asked. "He's barely known me for a few days."

"Why? Do you intend to escape?" she joked.

Red shook his head.

"Master Hector has always been a good judge of character," Eiwin said. "Besides, even if you run away tonight, your contributions to the Sect are still there. You earned yourself a reward, and I bet the pills weren't the only thing he promised you."

She was right. Hector had promised to sponsor his future growth if Red kept contributing to the Sect. He knew this was a lure for him to remain in the Sect and keep adding to their efforts—but he didn't mind. As long as he maintained steady progress in cultivation for the near future, he felt this was a fair trade.

Something still bothered him, though. "Can't Allen and you use the pills?" he asked.

"They would be of minimal help to me. The power in these pills wouldn't bring me much closer to opening my next acupoint, and Allen has no need for them with his training speed."

"But you helped me. Isn't it unfair if only I get rewarded?"

He had always been on the receiving end of bad luck in the past. Now that he'd been rewarded while the others were punished, he didn't quite know what to think.

Eiwin, however, looked unconcerned.

"We also started a fight in broad daylight. In the end, I'd say our rewards and punishments cancel each other out. You can ask Allen about it if you'd like. He'll say the same thing."

"Alright..." Although Red still felt confused, he decided to let the matter go. "Are you going to teach me how to read?"

The question caught Eiwin off guard. "Right, I did say that, didn't I? Although it's better to study during the day, just a quick session shouldn't hurt. Let's go to the library."

Red followed Eiwin into the building with her white lantern lighting the way. The library was just as disorganized as last time, but she had made good on her promise and cleaned off the table. She told him to wait there while she went about the bookshelves.

A few minutes later, she returned carrying a handful of books and sat down across from him.

"I forgot to ask you. How much do you know about reading or writing?"

"Nothing at all," Red answered.

"Really? Do you at least know a few letters?"

He was about to deny it again, but then hesitated. There was indeed the symbol he recalled drawing at the spider's nest, but he wasn't sure if asking what it meant was a good idea. What if it gave something away about his origins?

"Do you remember something?" Eiwin asked, noticing his hesitation.

Red nodded at last. "I do."

In the end, he guessed he might have been overthinking it. Back then, he'd only picked out a small, random symbol out of hundreds, and he couldn't see a situation where his background would be exposed from that alone.

"Great!" Eiwin gave him a smile. "Do you know what it means?"

Red shook his head.

She looked puzzled. "Do you at least know how to write it?"

This time, he nodded. At his confirmation, Eiwin got up and looked through the library again. She brought back some paper, a quill, and a small ink bowl.

"Here." She spread the items on the table. "I'll show you how to use them."

She provided a demonstration by submerging the tip of the quill into the ink and drawing a strange symbol on the paper.

"Now you try it."

Red hadn't held such a delicate tool before, but the process itself seemed simple. He tried to recall all the details of the symbol and drew it on a fresh sheet of paper. Due to it being his first time writing, however, it went poorly —a bit more poorly than he had expected.

He looked down at the symbol in disappointment. What Eiwin had written looked far crisper and more intelligible.

"It's fine. I can still read it."

But when Eiwin spun the paper around and looked down, an awkward, alarming expression formed on her face. Red thought back to his earlier fears about revealing the symbol.

"Is there a problem?" he asked.

"No, not really." Eiwin shook her head with an embarrassed smile. "I can still read it, but... are you sure this is all you remember with this word?"

"More or less."

Memorizing what was written on Viran's papers was hardly a priority back then.

"Well, you see, there's nothing wrong with what you wrote," she said. "But it looks incomplete, like it's a part of a bigger word."

"What does it say?"

"It just says 'mo.'"

Red felt disheartened. Didn't he write this in the spider lair? Was his inspirational message, the testament of his journey, just a bunch of gibberish?

"Look, when a letter is by itself, it might mean nothing." Eiwin picked up the quill and started to write. "But when you put it together with something else, it can form a word."

She turned the paper around. Red could see a few new symbols had been added next to the one he'd written.

"What does it say now?" he asked.

"It says 'moon.'"

A wave of realization hit Red. Was this the entire word that Viran had written? He didn't remember, but he felt compelled to return to the spot where he'd left his items to check right away.

"This is just an example," Eiwin said. "The first thing we'll do is learn the alphabet and how to write it. It might be hard at first, but it'll get easier with practice."

Red agreed, and the two of them began their lesson.

Red was instructed to copy the entire alphabet multiple times, with Eiwin correcting his mistakes along the way.

Although the task was repetitive, he found himself enjoying it—how the quill felt in his hand, how random lines and shapes would come together to form a letter. It was like Red was experiencing an entirely new world of creation, and even an hour into his task, he was still absorbed in the exercises.

Although he still made mistakes, it didn't take him long to memorize most of the letters and how they were pronounced.

Eiwin, however, eventually put a stop to their lessons.

"That's enough for today."

Red lifted the quill, looking down at his penmanship and the mess of paper spread across the table.

"I can still do more," he said.

"There's no need." Eiwin gave him a strange look. "I think... You're already done with the basics."

"Already?" Red had expected this to take much longer.

Eiwin nodded. "If I didn't have proof of your progress here, I would've thought you were lying about being illiterate."

She picked up the papers and showed them to Red. At first, his writing was barely recognizable scribbles. However, as she sifted through the other writings, they became more intelligible.

"Most people take weeks to show this kind of improvement. They have to become accustomed to the quill and how to coordinate their hand movement. But you were using the quill as if you already had years of experience."

Red didn't respond. The pen felt natural in his hand, and he'd found little difficulty in copying the letters from the book.

"My assessment of you was not wrong," Eiwin said, her voice filled with pride. "It'll take far less time to teach you how to read and write. I'm sure Master Goulth will be pleased."

"So we're done for today?" Red asked.

"With learning how to read and write? Yes. But I can also answer some of your questions about other subjects if you so desire."

Red had been waiting to hear those words. There was still so much he wanted to know, but one important matter in particular stood out.

"Who's Gustav?" he asked.

"Gustav?" Eiwin seemed taken aback by the question. "He's the most powerful merchant in the city. He has many people working under him, and we've had a lot of problems dealing with him."

"What kinds of problems?"

"Well, Gustav is a very dishonest individual. He's extorted townsfolk in the past, and he sells a bunch of illegal merchandise."

Red was confused. "Illegal?"

"Yes. There are certain businesses the Baron prohibits from operating in his town. Like selling harmful drugs and other... questionable practices."

"If they know Gustav is doing it, why don't they arrest him?"

"I wish it was as simple as that." Eiwin shook her head in resignation. "But Gustav is too smart. He makes sure none of these crimes can be traced back to him, and even if the guards find clues, it's rarely anything substantial."

Red, however, didn't think the explanation was that straightforward.

"It can't be that simple. He has to be very powerful for the guards to ignore his involvement, right?"

Eiwin looked surprised that he had figured this out. "You're right... Not only does he have money and powerful subordinates, but he's also part of a powerful faction of merchants from the capital. Moving against him is bound to get a host of important people involved."

Hector's cynical words from earlier were starting to make more and more sense to Red.

"Is there a reason our Sect is fighting with him?" he asked.

"Gustav manages an adventurer's guild in this town, and he sees us as competition. We often end up working on the same contracts, and our Sect is far more capable than common mercenaries, so we complete the requests first. Not to mention, we've also put a stop to some of his shady practices in the past."

Red had expected a deeper reason for their conflict, but it was simply a matter of resources.

"Did you ever fight each other?"

"Sometimes, like earlier." Eiwin sounded ashamed. "But we try to avoid spilling blood in the town. Outside, though... that's another matter."

She didn't elaborate any further.

"Isn't Gustav afraid of Hector?" Red asked.

"He is," she said. "Which is why he doesn't act against us directly. However, Master Hector isn't the only person in town who has opened his Spiritual Sea. In fact, Gustav has two subordinates who are also at that level."

Red had neglected to consider this possibility, and the revelation surprised him.

"If he has two Spiritual Sea cultivators on his side, why is he afraid? Doesn't that make him stronger?"

"It's not that simple, Red," Eiwin said. "There's also a difference in strength between people who have opened their Spiritual Seas. In fact, opening your Spiritual Sea is merely the first step in one's cultivation journey."

Red was shocked into silence.

CHAPTER 77

CULTIVATION REALMS

"First step? What do you mean by that?" he asked.

"It's just as it sounds," Eiwin said. "Opening your Spiritual Sea is merely the initial foundation for cultivation. In fact, Cultivation Sects only consider an individual a real cultivator after they've opened their Spiritual Sea."

What the woman said made sense. Red had been so focused on the task of opening his Spiritual Sea he hadn't even considered what might come next, or that there would even be a next step.

"What's there to do after you've opened the Spiritual Sea? Can't you already control Spiritual Energy at that point?"

"You give too little credit to cultivators, Red." Eiwin shook her head with a grin. "Just because they can control Spiritual Energy doesn't mean that there's no longer any room for improvement. For one, their control isn't perfect, and they're limited in how quickly and skillfully they can manipulate that energy. And there's also the fact they can only use the energy inside their Spiritual Sea. Depending on how much they have, there's a limit to the power of their Spiritual Arts."

Red understood the principle of improving control—proficiency came with practice. Yet, something still puzzled him.

"You said they use the Spiritual Energy inside their bodies for their Spiritual Arts, right? If that's the case, once they expend everything, won't they have to cultivate all over again?"

"That's a common misunderstanding. To comprehend this, you have to understand what Spiritual Cultivation is in the first place."

Eiwin reached for a pile of books and picked out a volume Red recognized. *Spirit Key*.

"So, you already know that once you open your Spiritual Sea, you can both store and control Spiritual Energy, right?" she asked.

Red nodded.

"One thing you need to understand, though, is that the Spiritual Sea is not an immutable organ. In fact, cultivators have found a way to constantly improve and transform the Spiritual Sea using Spiritual Energy. By doing that, they can increase not only the amount of energy they can store in their bodies, but also its quality and density. The Spiritual Sea has a limit on how much energy it can contain, and absorbing more is not only ineffective but also dangerous. As an example, imagine someone just opened their core, and their capacity at that point is ten strands of Spiritual Energy. Once they spend all that energy, they can still recover their reserves after some time. The true difficulty doesn't lie in replenishing your Spiritual Sea, but rather in increasing how much energy your Spiritual Sea can contain."

She stopped, giving him time to absorb her explanation.

"Cultivation proper is focused on improving your Spiritual Sea, not merely on accumulating Spiritual Energy. Is that clear?"

Red nodded again, but the revelation was still shocking.

"Is improving your Spiritual Sea difficult too?" he asked. If opening the Spiritual Sea was already this hard, how challenging would it be to develop it further? He couldn't help but feel that he'd underestimated how complex cultivation was.

"That... depends on the way you see it," Eiwin said after some consideration. "Unlike opening it, improving the Spiritual Sea is a process of accumulation. Your progress will remain after each cultivation session, but it will be quite slow."

Red's eyes lit up. "Then it's like opening your Spiritual Veins?"

"Yes, but much harder and slower." She gave him a feeble smile.

These words dampened his enthusiasm. If opening all Spiritual Veins could take more than a decade, how long would it take to improve the Spiritual Sea? Red didn't even want to ask.

He changed topics. "Is there a limit to how much you can improve your Spiritual Sea?"

"Technically, no, but there are some hard obstacles you need to cross to progress, and you may need to rely on different cultivation methods," Eiwin said.

"Are there levels to it like with the Spiritual Veins?"

"Yes, we call them Cultivation Realms." She pointed at *Spirit Key*. "It's what I wanted to show you today, actually."

Eiwin leafed through the pages. She finally came to a stop on a specific figure—an outline of a person sitting cross-legged on the ground. Inside was an orb representing the Spiritual Sea, and within the orb, mist-like strands floated around.

"This is called the Lesser Ring Realm. It's the first realm one arrives at after opening the Spiritual Sea. The Spiritual Energy at this level is limited and exists inside the Sea in a gaseous state. As you know, in this realm, one gains control over the energy and can execute Spiritual Arts."

She turned the page. There was an identical figure there, but the energy inside the Spiritual Sea now looked like water.

"At some point, you will arrive at your first bottleneck. You'll need to force your Spiritual Sea to undergo a great change, and once you succeed, you'll enter the second realm." She pointed at the drawing. "The Greater Ring Realm. At this level, you'll be able to condense Spiritual Energy into a liquid state. The amount of energy available to you will increase substantially, and so will your power."

"Liquid state?" Red frowned. "I thought Spiritual Energy was meant to be intangible." Every time he had seen the energy in its pure form, it was always elusive and misty.

"It is still intangible," Eiwin said. "It's hard to find liquid Spiritual Energy in nature, but using our Spiritual Seas, we can create it. In fact, the first three realms are all based on the three physical states of matter. Are you familiar with them?"

Red shook his head.

"Well, the three states are gaseous, liquid, and solid. The matter is denser in each following state. You can think of it as..." Eiwin struggled to find the right words. "More matter occupying a smaller space. Does that make sense?"

He understood the principle, but still felt confused by the specifics. In the end, though, he just nodded.

"Good." Eiwin smiled. "The same principle applies to Spiritual Energy.

We could say that one strand of liquid Spiritual Energy is equivalent to ten strands of gaseous Spiritual Energy in power. In this case, though, one liquid and one gaseous strand occupy the same space inside the Spiritual Sea. So, you can see how it would be more efficient to store Spiritual Energy as a liquid, right?"

This example gave him a better idea. Red had never needed to consider these kinds of things when he was in the mine, but now his eyes were opening to the complexities of the world.

"Then does that mean someone at the Greater Ring would have ten times as much energy as someone in the Lesser Ring?" he asked.

"That measurement depends on a lot of things, but you're more or less correct."

"That means the third realm must have to do with solid Spiritual Energy, right?"

"Exactly!"

She turned the page again. Red looked down and saw another similar figure, but this time with a small sphere inside its Spiritual Sea.

"It's called the Spirit Core Realm," Eiwin said. "However, the principle for transforming Spiritual Energy into a solid state is far more complicated than the previous ones. You need to form something called a core inside your Spiritual Sea, which will require special methods and rituals. In some cases, you may even need to use some rare ingredients to induce the transformation!"

Red creased his brow, unsure of how ingredients could help in a ritual. "Is it harder than opening the Spiritual Sea?"

"Much harder. However, once you progress to that stage, you'll also be better equipped to deal with such challenges. When you reach the second realm, for instance, you'll even be capable of flying!"

Flying?

Red remembered some of his dreams. Weren't there people flying in them? Had they all reached that realm? Then how strong were they?

Or maybe...

"Is that the limit for cultivation?" he asked.

"Not at all," Eiwin said. "There are realms above that, but information on them is scarce and not available in this book. In those realms, the focus on cultivation shifts quite heavily. One will start cultivating things like their soul and spirit too, but unfortunately, even I don't know the specifics."

432

Red was disappointed, but he let the matter go.

"What realm is Hector in?"

"He's in the Lesser Ring Realm, but even within the same realm, there are different stages. Master Hector is at the peak of the first realm, while the experts under Gustav are in the initial and middle stages. They can't measure up to our Grand Elder's strength. In fact, no one in our town is stronger than Master Hector."

She looked proud as she said this, and Red could now understand the confidence behind the Sect's actions. Though they might have few members, they were stronger than the average cultivator.

However, there was still another topic that puzzled him.

"I was wondering... You told me how humans cultivate, but aren't monsters also capable of opening their Spiritual Seas? How do they cultivate?"

"Well..." Eiwin scratched her head in thought. "Monsters actually don't cultivate at all."

"What do you mean?"

"Monsters don't need to cultivate to get stronger. They simply inherit their strength through their progenitors. We call this phenomenon blood-line power. Basically, the strength of a monster is defined by how strong its parents are. It grows in power naturally as it ages, without having to do anything until it finally hits maturity."

"Isn't that much easier than cultivation?" Red was stunned. It hardly seemed fair how much struggle humans had to go through compared to beasts.

"It is, but it has its downsides, too," Eiwin said. "A monster's power is defined by its bloodline, but it is also limited by it. Other than some rare mutations, it's exceedingly difficult for a monster to grow stronger than what its lineage allows. As such, it's not so much they don't need to cultivate, but that even if they wanted to, it wouldn't be possible."

"Aren't humans limited too, by their talent?"

Eiwin looked taken aback, as if she'd never considered this perspective before.

"Well... they are, but they can surpass it. There are plenty of untalented people who managed to advance further than what their talent would normally allow."

Her words seemed genuine, but Red could tell that there was something left unsaid. For every person that succeeded, how many others had failed? And even for those that did succeed, didn't they eventually hit their limit, too? He didn't voice these doubts, though.

"So do monsters have realms too?" he asked.

"They do. These realms are more or less equivalent to cultivation realms, but they are defined by something other than Spiritual Energy density."

"Like what?"

"These monsters still use their Spiritual Seas as their center of power. But once a monster opens their Spiritual Sea, the bloodline power naturally accumulates Spiritual Energy inside their body and gives it a crystalline shape."

Her description sounded familiar.

"These things are called monster cores, and they're some of the most sought-after goods for cultivators!"

Red recalled the crystal he'd taken from the insectoid's head.

CHAPTER 78
CONSUMING THE PILL

RED TRIED to remember every detail about the insectoid core. Viran told him that the stone was equivalent to hundreds of moonstones, and now he could understand that it represented the monster's cultivation realm. However, this still didn't explain the crimson lines. Was it even possible for something like a core to be infected?

Eiwin noticed his prolonged silence. "Is there a problem?"

Red looked up at her and hesitated. In the end, he simply shook his head.

"Alright." She didn't linger on the topic. "I think this is enough information for today. Unless you still have something you want to ask?"

"It's fine."

He obviously still had many things he wanted to know, but he held back for now.

"Is there anything else I can do today?" Red asked as he got up from his chair.

"You've already had lessons with Master Goulth and Master Domeron, right? It's best if you take this time to rest and absorb what you've learned. In fact, most cultivators choose to use this time of the night to open their acupoints. Maybe you should try using one of the Vein Opening Pills, if you feel up for it."

"Right." Red had been learning so much in the last few days that he'd forgotten some of his time was supposed to be spent in cultivation, too. Without further delay, he turned around and abruptly began to walk out of the library.

"Hey!" she called after him.

Red stopped at the door and looked back. "Hm?"

"Uh... Have a good night!" she said sheepishly.

He frowned in confusion but nodded in acknowledgement before walking out.

He heard Eiwin sigh as he left.

A few minutes later, Red found himself back in his room. Well, it wasn't his, but it was the one he was using right now. He fished around in his pocket and grabbed the glass vial containing the pills, examining them.

At first, he'd had no clue how these were meant to be consumed, but from Hector's explanation, he'd found out the process was as simple as just swallowing them whole. Yet there were still some things he had to be mindful of.

First of all, Red couldn't consume more than one Vein Opening Pill at a time. Goulth had already explained that these medicines contained toxins, but Hector had provided further context. The Spiritual Energy contained in one of these pills would still strain a person's Spiritual Veins, and consuming multiple in a row could do more harm than good. Then there was the matter of resistance, where the body would eventually reject the medicinal power of the pill, reducing its effectiveness.

These were just a few reasons why even rich cultivators couldn't simply rely on medicines to open their veins.

Hector had also mentioned that even if these problems could be circumvented, it wasn't wise to be reliant on pills, since as one cultivated, the power of the medicine required to assist them would increase, and the stronger the pill, the harder it was to find. The experience of cultivating with no external help would prove invaluable once one happened upon a bottleneck, too.

Red could see the old man's logic. However, could someone with inadequate talent afford to adhere to that line of thought? After all, experience alone wasn't helping Narcha. He would try not to worry about it right now, taking whatever advantages would help him in the short term without crippling him.

The other instruction he'd received was to treat this as a normal cultivation session. That meant Red should go through all the warm-up exercises and only consume the pill once he was ready to attack his acupoint.

Hector had refused to provide any further instructions, saying that it was best if he experienced the effects of the pill for himself. Red was hesitant at first, but there was no reason to doubt the elder on that point. If there was no substantial risk, he would prefer to figure these things out by himself.

Red set the glass vial aside and started to perform the exercises Viran had taught him. After a few minutes, he began feeling the familiar tingling sensation, though this time he decided not to push himself past his usual limit, so he didn't hurt his concentration.

He sat down cross-legged, feeling the Spiritual Energy enter his veins. The vial was already in his hands, uncorked, and Red found himself staring at it in a moment of hesitation. It didn't last long, though.

He tipped the vial, letting a pill fall in his hand before popping it into his mouth and swallowing it whole.

At first, Red felt nothing other than the pellet making its way down his throat. A moment later, however, a strange sensation rose in his stomach. A warmth that spread through his whole body, intensifying until he felt a fire burning him from the inside.

It was a sudden and intense pain, but Red had been expecting it, and endured the sensation through gritted teeth. Strangely enough, this warmth disappeared as quickly as it came. He was confused at first, before he sensed something moving within his Spinal Spiritual Vein.

Red recognized the feeling.

Spiritual Energy.

And a lot of it. It was a sudden tide that invaded his body and roamed through his veins. But for some reason, it felt different compared to the sudden injection of energy he'd used to practice with in the past. There was no pain, and the flow felt more peaceful and slower.

Red tried to confirm his suspicions by directing the current towards his legs and found, to his surprise, that the Spiritual Energy was remarkably responsive, moving according to his will. It soon arrived at his partially opened Upper Leg Spiritual Vein. He barely had to direct it before it started to hit the closed acupoint of its own volition.

But here Red quickly noticed a problem. Although he directed the energy towards his right leg, some of it split off and moved into his left leg instead.

The imbalance.

The Spiritual Energy seemed eager to intensify his predicament rather than solve it. Of course, although he'd detected the problem, he could do nothing other than try to make sure the energy stayed on the right path. There was no solution to this other than opening the acupoints he had neglected until now.

To his joy, he could physically feel the acupoint in his right thigh giving way. Half a minute later, the unmistakable and uncomfortable feeling of a Spiritual Vein opening spread in his leg.

The third acupoint of the Upper Leg Vein had opened.

Almost immediately, there was a change in the behavior of the remaining energy. The runaway strands stopped moving towards his left leg and returned to the path Red was directing them to. Surprisingly enough, there was still a substantial amount of Spiritual Energy left in his body. He didn't let it go to waste, attacking the next acupoint in his right thigh.

A minute later, just as Red had made some progress in clearing that hurdle, the energy finally ran out. He guessed that if some of the power hadn't been wasted earlier due to his imbalance problem, he could have probably opened another acupoint.

Still, there was hardly any reason for him to be angry. The medicine had proved to be effective beyond his imagination, sparing him weeks of training, and Red could only sigh in amazement.

It's no wonder they're so expensive.

With the two remaining pills, he assumed he could open the rest of his Upper Leg Vein in less than a month, but he would follow Hector's advice and wait before consuming the next one. Not to mention, he still needed to recover his stash with the moonstones and insectoid crystal, or else he wouldn't be able to open the two special acupoints.

How can I go back there?

Red hesitated to ask for help. The items were related to his background, and he wouldn't reveal them unless he had to. In fact, he worried he'd already exposed too much about himself these last few days, and this was why he was reluctant to ask Eiwin more specific questions.

For the most part, the information Red had revealed up until now was inconsequential. But what if he told them more about his past, or about the stash? Even if it wouldn't be enough to give away his background, it could arouse the suspicion of his fellow Sect members—and Narcha was already set against him.

The Sect might not get any answers from him, but what if they investigated on their own? Could he guarantee they wouldn't find anything?

Red wasn't familiar with the surface yet, so he couldn't be confident of anything. His main concern was still the mine guards, who surely worked in the region, and might even be working for someone within the town. There was no way to be sure, but for now, he had to be careful about what kinds of questions he asked.

Just as Red was trying to come up with a plan, he heard knocking at his door. Having learned how to respond yesterday, Red walked up and opened the door.

He was surprised to find Rog on the other side.

"What is it?" Red asked.

"We're going to hunt," the man said.

This made him frown. "Now?"

"Yeah."

Red hesitated, thinking for a moment. Finally, he nodded. "Alright." He closed the door behind him and stepped outside.

"Follow me." Rog walked away.

He led him to another wooden house on the other side of the courtyard. Red still hadn't visited most of the houses, but he guessed this must be where Rog slept. By the entrance were two large backpacks, a pair of wooden bows, and two quivers full of arrows.

Rog pointed at the items. "Get one of each."

"Are we going to travel?" Red noticed the bedrolls.

"We're gonna spend the night out. Gonna be back tomorrow."

This journey seemed rather abrupt, but he didn't complain. He was always eager to improve his survival and combat skills, and the hunter had much to teach him. It was late, but he wasn't groggy. If Rog was only going to show up whenever he pleased, then it was up to Red to use his visits to their fullest.

He tried to follow Rog's example and strapped the equipment around his body, but he quickly noticed a problem. Everything was too big for a ten-year-old child. Both the bow and the bag were almost as tall as him, and Red had difficulty walking around with the unwieldy equipment.

Only now did Rog seem to realize this. "Oh, I forgot you're just a child. Give me a second."

The hunter unstrapped some sacks and items from Red's bag before putting them on his own.

Rog stepped back. "What about now?"

Red immediately felt how much easier it was to walk around, but just taking off these items didn't change the fact that the bag and bow were still much too big. In the end, though, he just nodded.

"Good." Rog looked contented. "Let's go, then."

He walked off, and Red followed in tow. Curiously, he noticed they weren't taking the same route he'd become used to these last few days.

"Is there a reason we're taking this path?" Red asked. "Actually, why are we going out during the night? Isn't it easier to hunt during the day?"

"It's easier, yeah," Rog said, scratching his scraggly beard. "But we go during the night so that we're not followed by anyone. Plenty of times I needed to dodge some people who were keen on killing and robbing me out there. Then they started to follow me during the night too, so I took a different route... It's very annoying."

"Did you... tell anyone else you were leaving?"

Rog squinted at him. "Huh? Why would I tell them?"

Red started to have a bad feeling about this trip.

CHAPTER 79
BOW AND ARROW

"Does anyone else in the Sect know we're hunting?" Red asked.

"Eh, no need." Rog shrugged. "If there are too many bandits, I'll just lose them in the forest. If it's just a small group, I can teach them a lesson."

"You sound confident, but what if Gustav sent someone at the Lesser Ring Realm after you?"

"Huh?" Rog stopped walking and looked back in shock. "Why would he do that?"

"I mean, if he really wanted to get rid of you, that would be a good way to do it. No one would be there to see it, and they could hide all the evidence."

Rog looked appalled. Apparently, he'd never considered the possibility. But a few seconds later, his expression returned to normal, and he shook his head.

"They wouldn't do that," Rog said. "I could still lose someone like that with some luck. And if Hector suspected I was dead, he would definitely attack Gustav's people first."

"Is he really that strong?" Red asked.

"Stronger than you can imagine. Come, we don't want anyone to spot us."

Unfortunately for Red, Rog didn't seem interested in elaborating, so he didn't insist on it. He followed behind the man as they sneaked through the town.

Surprisingly, there were still a few people walking the streets at this hour of the night. In the distance, he could even hear murmurs activity, but Rog made a point of avoiding any human contact along the way.

They weaved through alleys, waiting until townsfolk or guards passed by before moving on. From the way Rog acted, Red had the impression that they were doing something illegal. He knew this wasn't the case, but he supposed it was necessary if they wanted to avoid being followed.

Much to his surprise, they managed to get to the edge of town unnoticed. Just when Red thought he could relax, though, Rog put a hand on his shoulder.

"This is the most dangerous part," he said, voice hushed.

Red's brows creased in concern. "How so?"

"They might be in wait, kid. My pursuers might not know which way I'm taking, but they definitely know where I'm going. Look, it's all open space."

Rog gestured down the hill, and Red quickly understood. Although the town was shrouded in darkness, a vast swathe of open space and farmland stretched up to the tree line. In fact, he even spotted a few farmers walking down the road, lanterns in hand.

"So, what do we do?" he asked.

"See those cornfields?" Rog pointed to a different area, a large plot right outside of town.

"I see it."

"We run through them," Rog said.

"Through them?"

"Yeah, that way they won't notice us."

This situation was absurd to him, but he couldn't find fault with the man's logic. "Alright."

"Then... go!" With a sudden shout, Rog shot downhill in a sprint.

Red watched his figure move away with a confused look.

Why did he scream if we're trying to go unnoticed?

When he finally decided to run after him, the man was almost a hundred meters away. With no other option, Red pushed himself to catch up. Thankfully, his newly opened acupoint helped, as he was much faster than before.

But it still wasn't enough to catch up to Rog. The hunter disappeared into the cornfields, and Red had no other choice than to follow blindly, shoving the stalks aside to make way. Traveling through the field took far longer than he had expected. He did his best to stay in a straight line, but he wasn't sure how successful he was.

When Red finally made it to the other side, he saw no signs of Rog. He walked out a bit further, examining his surroundings, when he heard a voice call to him.

"Psst, kid. Here."

Red looked in the direction of the sound and spotted Rog's crouched figure hiding behind a stone fence. He waved at him.

When Red approached, he saw Rog was carrying a handful of corn in his arms.

"What's that?"

"Corn," Rog said matter-of-factly. "Didn't you get any?"

"Was I supposed to?"

"You're not eating any of mine."

Red didn't know how to respond, and Rog didn't give him the opportunity either, getting up.

"Come on, we have to hurry. The farmer's dog might sniff us out if we stay for too long."

"Dog? I thought we were hiding from..."

Before Red could even complete his sentence, Rog ran off.

He could only sigh and give chase.

It didn't take long to reach the tree line. Rog continued to cut through the farmland, grabbing whatever he pleased, and Red raced after him through it all. Surprisingly, the pair wasn't discovered. Just as Red was growing tired from the punishing pace, the hunter finally slowed down.

"We can relax a bit," Rog said. "No one's following us, for now."

Somehow, that surprised Red. "What do we do now?"

"We hunt." Rog began moving carefully through the underbrush.

Red followed behind. "I meant... what exactly do we do now?" he asked.

"Well, we need to walk further into the forest. Most game doesn't hang out this close to town."

"What are we hunting?"

Rog shrugged. "Anything we can get our hands on feral hogs, bucks, rabbits, birds. After monsters disappeared from the region, there's nothing too valuable or dangerous to hunt here. Perfect place for you to learn."

Red got curious. "Did you hunt monsters before?"

"Yeah. They're tough bastards, but a well-placed shot can still kill them in one hit."

"What kinds of monsters were there?" Red noticed that once the subject shifted to hunting, Rog seemed more eager to talk, so he tried to take advantage of this to learn more.

"Too many to count. Steel-horned owls, fireleaf deer, tree-bark bears. Some of them had opened Spiritual Seas too, but that was rare around here."

"What about insect monsters?"

"You might have found the odd few in the past, but they're rare in this region."

Red had no way of knowing if those insects were the same as what he'd seen underground. He considered asking Rog for more details but thought better of it. Although Rog had never shown suspicion towards him, he didn't want to risk it.

The two of them walked through the trees for the next hour. Red tried to learn more about what they were doing, but Rog's answers were evasive. One would have suspected he was acting strangely to test his patience, but Red had seen his interactions in the Sect and knew that Rog acted like this with everyone.

Their journey passed in almost complete silence, save for the rare few moments Rog stopped to explain something. Soon, they came upon a clearing illuminated by the moonlight, and he ordered a stop.

"Are we camping already?"

Rog shook his head. "Just gotta teach you some things first."

With that, Rog put down his backpack and picked up his bow and quiver. He looked over at Red expectantly.

The boy frowned. "Are you going to shoot me?"

"What?" Rog seemed confused. "Why would I do that?"

"I don't know. This just looks like the perfect opportunity to get rid of me, now that I think about it."

"I wouldn't go through so much trouble just to kill you. Could've just done it inside an abandoned building in town, and no one would've known."

He didn't look like he was lying.

"Anyway, I want to teach you how to use a bow."

Red finally understood. He eagerly dropped his backpack and picked up his own bow and quiver, imitating Rog's actions.

"What now?" he asked.

"Now watch."

Rog walked to the other side of the clearing and nocked an arrow into his bow. Red stepped aside, just in case, studying Rog as he pulled back the string and raised the bow. Then, a few seconds later, he released it with a twang.

Red couldn't follow the trajectory of the arrow, but an instant later, he heard a thud on the other side of the clearing. The arrow had pierced halfway through a tree.

The sheer power of the weapon impressed him.

"Was that what you wanted to hit?"

"What? Of course it was." Rog scratched his beard. "I suppose I didn't call my shot beforehand."

He seemed genuinely puzzled for a moment.

"Now you do the same." Rog pointed at the tree. "Stand here and shoot an arrow at that."

"Just like that?"

Rog nodded and refused to elaborate.

With no other choice, Red walked over to the same spot. He tried to replicate what he'd seen, but right away, he was faced with problems. The bow, for one, was too big for him, and he had to tilt it so it wouldn't scrape the ground. Although he could see the tree's outline, it was still a considerable distance away. Now that he had the weapon in hand, he didn't feel nearly as confident in his aim as Rog had seemed.

Still, Red saw no point in hesitating. He nocked an arrow and pulled the string back. With a twang, he released it. The projectile flew off into the sea of trees and missed its intended target by a considerable distance.

Rog watched this with a displeased look. "That was awful. You didn't even shoot it straight. I mean, were you even trying to hit the tree?"

Red just stared at the man.

"Have you ever shot a bow before?" Rog shook his head. "Here, you need to keep the arrow straight. One finger over it and two below. Do it again."

Red refrained from responding and nocked another arrow.

"Pull the string back further, kid," Rog instructed.

"I can't."

"Why not?"

"My arms aren't big enough."

"Oh, right." Rog seemed to realize once again that he was dealing with a child. "Anyways, make sure to always keep your arm straight. You have to memorize the correct stance so you can be consistent with your shots."

He continued to give instructions. Finally, when Red felt somewhat confident, he let loose his second shot. It flew wide again, but this time by a smaller distance.

To his surprise, with a few corrections from Rog, his improvement was already evident.

"Damn, you're really bad at this." The man scratched his beard in worry. "I wonder if we have enough arrows."

Not to Rog, apparently.

They continued to train for the next hour. Red repeated the same movements until his arms were sore. His shots became more consistent towards the end of the session, and he managed to hit the target a few times.

Rog, however, became stricter, giving him smaller targets to hit. Just as Red gained some confidence, he realized how challenging it was to master the bow. What Rog could hit with no difficulty from this distance, Red struggled to even get close to.

"It's fine." Rog shrugged. "Maybe if we find some injured prey that can't run, walk, or roll over—you can get close enough to hit your shot."

With that, the man walked off, leading the way further into the forest. Red could only follow behind him with a sigh.

The hunt had just begun.

CHAPTER 80

BOAR

"Look!" Rog pointed at the ground beneath his feet. "Right here. Can you see it?"

Red crouched down alongside him to examine whatever had caught his attention. But when he stared at the ground, he saw nothing.

Rog pointed again. "Here, kid. Can't you smell this?"

"Smell what?"

"Fresh droppings."

"Droppings?"

"Poop."

"Oh. Why is this relevant?"

"It's a trail," Rog said. "When you're hunting, you need to look for these types of signs. They tell you whether an animal is hanging around the area. Now, look around—do you see anything else?"

Red followed his instructions. It was very dark, and his vision wasn't as good as Rog's, but he eventually found something.

"Tracks." Red pointed out a set of heavy footprints marked on the leaves littering the ground.

"Good." Rog didn't sound surprised at his discovery. "This looks like a hooved animal—the easy type to track, since they leave deep footprints wherever they go. This one looks like a boar—a big one, too."

"Is it dangerous?"

"For normal people, sure. But it's no monster," Rog said, unconcerned. "Now, let's follow the trail. Make sure you watch where you're stepping."

The pair continued to travel through the forest. Red had been surprised multiple times by how well Rog could see in the darkness. While he had to get very close to identify any footprints, the man could spot details from far away, all while teaching him about tracking.

"Depending on what kind of animal you're hunting, you need to look for certain signs," Rog said. "Different animals eat different foods, so you can find them hanging around specific areas of the forest."

"What does a boar eat?" Red asked.

"Just about anything, really. Fruits, nuts, even small critters."

"But that's not specific."

"Oh, well. Thankfully, they're not very sneaky, so we shouldn't have a hard time finding them."

Sure enough, some ten minutes later, the hunter called their march to a stop. He crouched down and pointed into the distance.

"There," Rog said quietly. "A few hundred meters or so ahead. Do you see it?"

Red crouched by the man's side and looked where he was pointing. All he saw were trees and shadows.

"I see nothing," he said. "I haven't opened my Five Senses Vein yet."

"Oh, right." Rog nodded in realization. "It's the boar. Looks to be eating off a berry bush."

Red squinted, and for a moment, he thought he saw the shadowy silhouette of an animal between the trees. It was hard to be sure, though.

"What do we do now?" he asked.

"Hm..." Rog scratched his beard in thought. "Can you shoot it from here?"

Red didn't need to double-check to know the answer. "No."

"Then we need to get closer," Rog said. "When you get close to prey, you have to be careful so the wind isn't blowing at your back. Animals have very good noses, and if they smell you, they'll run away before you can shoot."

Red understood that principle. The giant insects in the underground could smell blood from kilometers away, and although this boar wasn't a monster, its sense of smell was probably still better than a human's.

"How do I approach it?"

"You can figure it out on your own." Rog sounded untroubled. "Just make sure you have a clear shot and try not to make any noise."

Since the man wasn't placing any pressure on him, Red decided to do what seemed natural. After checking the direction of the wind, he approached the boar. He didn't move in a straight line, instead circling the animal while slowly closing in, letting the trees cover his advance.

Once Red got near enough, the boar became clearer in the low light. It was a large furry creature, much bigger than him, with two tusks protruding from the sides of its head. He looked back at Rog, who had been following close behind him.

"Are you sure that's not a monster?" he asked in a whisper.

"Positive. Well, it's not like there's an official monster definition, but I can tell you that boar is just about normal."

Red was still skeptical, but he focused on the task at hand. He tried to measure the distance between them.

"Do you think you can hit it from here?" Rog asked.

"No," Red said without hesitation. The shot could probably reach that far, but he doubted it would find its mark.

"Then you need to get closer," Rog said. "A boar is a very tough animal, and it can survive a shot that misses its vital organs."

"Where do I aim?"

"If it's facing you, go for the head. If it's sideways, go for the spine or the heart. The spine is right behind the ears, and the heart is immediately above and behind the shoulder. Also, make sure you have your arrow nocked before getting too close."

Red nodded and continued his approach, watching his steps in hopes of avoiding any twigs or dry leaves. He drew closer until he had a clear view of the prey.

At that moment, the boar perked up.

Red froze. The creature looked around in suspicion, but after a beat, it resumed eating the berries. He let out a sigh of relief. However, he also knew that if he tried to get closer, it would probably end up alerting his prey.

Rog was right behind him but said nothing this time around. Seeing that no complaint or snarky comment was forthcoming, Red prepared his shot.

He first tried to visualize the targets Rog had described to him. The boar was faced sideways, so Red decided to aim for the spine. He pulled back his nocked arrow, trying to recall the correct stance and the anchor point Rog had taught him earlier. Then, before his arms started to tremble under the effort, he released it.

He heard a thud, followed by a shriek.

The arrow had hit the animal, but it didn't bring the boar down. The animal ran away in a frenzy, faster than Red had thought such a stocky creature could move. Right as he got up to give chase, he heard a twang from behind him.

An arrow flew over his head and hit the boar in the spine. The beast fell utterly still in an instant, and no more shrieks were heard. He looked back just in time to see Rog lowering his own bow.

"Let's go see the damage, then," the hunter said.

Red followed. As they approached, he was once more surprised by the sheer size of the beast. Unsurprisingly, it was no longer breathing.

"You had the right idea... but poor aim." Rog pointed at the boar's leg.

Red's arrow was sticking out of the creature's thigh. It didn't look like it had penetrated too deeply.

"Now, look at my own."

The hunter's arrow had hit exactly behind the prey's ears, where he'd told him to aim. It was buried deep into the boar's body.

"You see, hitting this kind of prey in the spine is almost an instant kill. It can immobilize it and make it go into shock. The heart is easier to hit and is also an almost guaranteed kill, but the boar would probably run for a bit before falling dead."

Red nodded in understanding.

"So, how did it feel?" Rog asked.

"What do you mean?"

"How did it feel to shoot the boar?"

"Was I supposed to feel anything?"

"I guess not." Rog shrugged. "Some people have different reactions when they kill their first prey. Anger, sadness, happiness, and everything in between."

This wasn't the first time Red had killed someone or something, but he didn't remember being emotionally affected by it, even back then.

"What about you?" he asked. "What did you feel?"

"Me?" Rog hadn't expected the question to be turned back to him. "I suppose that at first, I felt a bit of sadness. Still do."

That was the reply Red had least anticipated. "Sadness? Why?"

"I mean, aren't these beasts amazing?" Rog said. "The things they can do out of instinct alone, it's beyond human understanding. I enjoy watching them living their lives in nature—even the monsters."

Red remembered how he felt watching the egg-stealer in the centipede nest. Strangely, he couldn't help but agree with Rog.

"If you like them so much, why do you hunt them?" he asked.

"It's what I'm good at, and I need to make a living. Besides, some of these animals, like the boars, are pests to the farmland. They need to be killed, and as much as I like them, they're not as important as my well-being."

Once again, Rog's words took Red by surprise. He'd never thought that beneath his brusque exterior, the man considered things so deeply.

"Now, no more time for talking," Rog said, interrupting his thoughts. "Come help me. We need to get it tied up."

"Aren't we going to skin it?"

"Skin it? In the middle of the forest?" Rog looked at him like he was stupid. "Skinning animals like this is very messy. Besides, we're not going to cook it, we're gonna sell it. Now, shut up and come help me."

He did as he was told. Once they were done, Rog put the hog on his shoulders, and the two of them began traveling deeper into the forest.

Another hour passed by in silence.

"Are we still hunting for something?" Red finally asked.

"Not really," Rog said. "A boar this big is already a nice haul, and it's not like we can carry too many things on our backs. I expected we would need to spend the entire night here before we found something good."

"Then why aren't we heading back to town?"

"Because we're being followed."

Red froze.

"Just keep walking, kid," Rog said in his usual, calm tone.

He nodded and kept walking.

"How close are they?" Red asked.

"Almost a kilometer back. They're afraid of being discovered, so they're just following our tracks."

"But didn't you just notice them?"

"Yeah, but that's because my eyes are better than most."

"And how many are there?"

"I saw two or three, but there might be more. One of them might have even gone to get reinforcements. Bandits like overwhelming people with numbers."

"Bandits? How do you know they're bandits?" Red asked.

"Just a guess. These guys act like bandits and clearly know what they're doing. If I wasn't careful earlier, I might have missed them. I just didn't expect to find them so close to town."

This time, Red was truly worried. From Rog's evaluation, these people were professionals. "What do we do?"

"We lose them in the forest."

"What if we can't lose them?"

Rog didn't immediately respond, scratching his beard in thought. A few seconds later, he looked back at Red with a wide smile on his face.

"How do you feel about live target practice?"

CHAPTER 81

AMBUSH

As they walked along, Red had a hard time pretending everything was normal. Rog had to tell him off about turning to look back in search of their pursuers several times.

"Even if you looked, you wouldn't find them," he said.

Red knew the hunter was right, but it was an ordeal to fight against his instincts. They continued to move at a slow pace for the next five minutes, and Rog didn't speak at all during that time. Red thought this behavior was strange, but he chose to say nothing.

After five more minutes passed, though, he spoke up.

"Are you sure we can lose them like this?" Red asked.

"Not really," Rog said. "I was just changing my path to see how insistent they are about stalking us. Turns out they're still on our trail."

Red was surprised by his words. Rog had acted naturally in his eyes over the last ten minutes, and Red was unsure when he would have gotten an opportunity to look back at their pursuers.

"So, how are we going to escape?" he asked.

"I'm still thinking," Rog said. "With this boar on my shoulders, it's gonna be hard to hide my tracks."

Red had almost forgotten about the prey. The man didn't look weighed down from carrying it, but Red knew the boar was probably heavier than the average adult. Sure enough, looking back at Rog's footprints, he could see how deep they were.

"Shouldn't we drop the boar, then?"

"And give up on this good haul?" Rog sounded offended. "No way!"

"Then do we just wait until they decide to ambush us?" Although it wasn't apparent in Red's neutral voice, he was growing worried about their passivity.

"Hm, I should be able to see them coming." Rog scratched his beard, unconcerned. "But you're right. It's not good to just be waiting around."

"Do you have a plan?"

"Yeah, let's ambush them before they can ambush us."

Red frowned. Although he wasn't too keen on picking a fight, it was better than just waiting around. "How do you plan to do it?"

"We can circle around one of these hills and lie in wait." Rog pointed ahead. "Once they get to that bend, we shoot them."

"What if they notice something's wrong?"

"Then we improvise."

Red didn't feel comfortable with the plan. Perhaps Rog had little to worry about with his strength, but it was another matter for him, and he didn't think the hunter was accounting for that.

"What if we use the boar as bait?" he suggested.

"How so?" Rog asked, his voice intrigued.

"We can pretend that we just found out we're being followed and dropped the boar to run. But instead of escaping, we'll just hide behind the trees in ambush. When they're distracted examining the boar, we shoot."

"That's..." Rog's eyes widened. "A great idea, kid! I knew it was smart bringing you along. We'll do as you say!"

"Good, then when are we..."

"Now!"

Red didn't have the time to finish his sentence before Rog dropped the boar and set off in a sprint. He cursed the man in his mind before running off to hide.

A few minutes later, six men approached the area, all of them wearing leather armor and carrying weapons. Although their equipment was worn and in disrepair, the group still looked menacing and capable. Anyone would recognize these people upon laying their eyes on them.

A group of bandits.

The one in front—a tall middle-aged man carrying a bow—frowned as he looked over the abandoned boar corpse.

One of his travel companions approached his side. "Woah, why did they leave this behind?" he asked, awestruck.

The rest of the bandits were right behind him, just as thrilled at the discovery. The leader of the group, however, examined the footprints in the area. A few moments later, he turned to the others.

"They noticed us and ran."

The others looked surprised at the revelation.

"How?" asked the one carrying a hatchet in his hand. "We were tracking them from hundreds of meters away."

"How am I supposed to fucking know?" The leader gritted his teeth. "We picked a clever target this time around. Maybe a hunter who came here to teach his apprentice?" He trailed off, pondering the situation.

"What do we do now, boss?" another bandit asked.

"We chase them, of course. We can't let them run back to the town and tell others about us." The leader walked around the footprints, determining their direction. "Well, at least they're escaping deeper into the forest. We can try to catch them there." He turned to one of his subordinates. "Morrick, go warn the others. Have them encircle our target from the north."

"Alright." The bandit named Morrick walked off.

"The rest of you, get ready to give chase," the leader said.

"What about the boar?" someone asked.

"The boar's not going anywhere. We can—"

"UGH!"

All the bandits heard a scream of pain and turned around. They looked just in time to see Morrick fall to the ground with an arrow through his throat.

The leader's reaction was almost immediate. "Get to cover!" he shouted, already diving behind a tree.

But the other bandits were slower to react. They stumbled over themselves searching for the nearest cover, and another arrow flew out from the trees before they could reach it. Another man fell to the ground with a thud.

An arrow jutted out of his chest, and the bandit struggled briefly before falling still.

The rest of them found cover just in time, and no more arrows came. Gradually, an eerie silence settled over the forest, and only the bandits' labored breaths could be heard.

Just like that, there were only four left.

The leader looked over at the corpse of one of his subordinates and grimaced. The arrow had pierced the man's heart and burst through the other side. Not only was the shot extremely precise, but it had to have carried a lot of strength to puncture both the armor and the chest of the bandit.

"Boss, what do we do?" a low voice asked from a few meters away.

The leader stared at his remaining followers, who were all crouched low behind the trees with uneasy expressions. However, even with two of their comrades dead, they didn't panic. In fact, they had even managed to identify the direction of the shots and chose their cover accordingly.

"The shots came from the hill," another bandit said from his prone position. "He has the high ground."

"Do you think you can see him?" the leader asked.

"I don't know. I can try approaching from a different angle."

"Do it. He might be moving."

His subordinate gave a grunt of affirmation. The bandit started to crawl along the ground, using the plants as cover. The rest of the group watched their companion's progress with bated breath, afraid that another arrow would fly out at any moment.

It didn't come, though. Soon enough, the sneaking bandit had crawled away and crouched behind a different tree. He turned around towards his leader, looking for confirmation. The man nodded back, and the bandit peeked past the tree in the direction of the shots.

He didn't have the chance to scream. An arrow pierced through his eye and out the back of his skull, and the bandit immediately fell dead. The rest of his companions gaped at his corpse in shock.

"Fuck!" one of them screamed in fear.

The leader felt a cold shiver run down his spine. His group was experienced and accustomed to death—it was why they didn't panic after the ambush. They had robbed heavily guarded caravans before and even killed monsters in the forest. They had seen their share of strong and well-armed men, but with their skills and knowledge of the land, they had always come out on top.

It was clear now, though, that they were dealing with someone stronger than anyone they'd ever faced before.

When Red had suggested his ambush idea, he'd forgotten to consider an essential factor. He had just learned how to shoot a bow a few hours earlier, so how could he possibly hit a person with one?

Only when the bandits finally appeared did he realize the issue. He was still considering what to do when Rog let loose the first shot from a different direction.

Red considered helping the hunter with some shots of his own. However, before he could even take aim, Rog had already killed another one. He realized he had overestimated how much he could contribute to this plan.

He had little choice but to quietly watch the situation. The bandits had managed to find cover, and not even Rog could shoot what he couldn't see. A few moments later, though, even Red spotted one of them crawling out and changing cover. He considered warning Rog, but he needn't have worried. The sneaking bandit was shot dead as soon as he tried peeking from behind the tree.

Red couldn't help but admire the hunter's strength.

After that, none of the other bandits dared to move. Another minute went by before one of them spoke up.

"Listen, we can negotiate!"

The voice came from a tall man carrying a bow of his own, one set apart from the rest.

"We clearly messed with the wrong guy, and you already killed three of us! Just let us go!"

Rog didn't respond.

"We can leave all our belongings behind! We have plenty of gold with us!"

Still no response. Red could see the bandits becoming restless.

"Look, we're part of Rickard's band!" the man pleaded, seemingly changing tactics. "You know him, right? If you let us go, he might reward you! But if he found out you killed his subordinates—"

This time, a response came in the form of an arrow. It splintered against the tree the bandit leader was hiding behind, and he crouched lower to the ground in fright.

"You motherfucker!" he cursed, abandoning all attempts at diplomacy. "You better hope none of us gets out of this alive, or we'll hunt you down!"

Red couldn't help but wince at those words. Why did he always find himself new enemies wherever he went? Still, this problem had an easy solution. They just had to make sure none of the bandits survived.

He took the opportunity to act while the bandits were focused on Rog and sneaked around, seeking a clearer view of the leader. The man was whispering to his subordinates, clearly planning something. Red wouldn't give them the chance.

He nocked an arrow into his oversized bow and took aim at the bandit leader. They were too far away for him to be confident that he would kill in one shot, but he didn't need to hit them. He just needed to scare them.

Red let loose, and the arrow flew towards his target. The man whirled around as he heard the projectile, but it was too fast for him to react. It pierced his thigh, and he let out a scream of pain.

"There's another one!"

That was all it took to send the group into a panic. They immediately sprinted off, desperate to escape.

Rog didn't let the opportunity pass him by, raining hell upon the bandits.

CHAPTER 82

SKILL

THE FIRST BANDIT who left cover made himself an immediate target, as Rog's arrow punched through his chest before he could take two steps. The man didn't even let out a scream of pain before his death.

The next bandit was luckier, since Rog couldn't shoot two arrows at once. He went in the opposite direction of his companion and covered a long distance in a scant few seconds. Unfortunately for him, he didn't leave the hunter's range.

Another shrill sound and a shriek. This bandit, too, fell dead with an arrow through his back.

It all happened so fast Red barely had any time to process the situation. He still wasn't sure where Rog was hiding until several seconds after the last death, spotting his shadowed figure kneeling behind a tree. Eventually, the sobering realization of the hunter's prowess dawned on him. With Rog's skill as an archer and familiarity with the forest...

These bandits never had a chance.

But the leader was still alive. Unlike his subordinates, he didn't immediately move after the first attack, despite having the opportunity, even after being shot in the leg. Perhaps he knew Rog's strength? Red wasn't sure, but just as he was prepared to shoot again, he saw the leader look in his direction.

He had a bad feeling about this, and sure enough, the man shot into a sprint towards him. The wound on his thigh seemed almost immaterial, the bandit managing to move with incredible speed. Red realized this was a powerful individual, and he reacted just as quickly.

He gave up on the idea of trying to hit a moving target. Instead, he ran into the open, where Rog could clearly see him. By that point, the bandit had already crossed half the distance between them, but when he saw Red's latest move, an ugly look crossed his face.

The man didn't continue the chase. Instead, he zigzagged through the trees. A moment later, an arrow shot through the spot where he'd just been. He'd avoided the hit.

Red, now taking cover, couldn't help but marvel at the bandit's swift movements. Unfortunately for him, it was Rog he was up against.

Another shrill, whistling sound cut through the forest. The leader immediately dove to the side, dodging the shot. However, before he'd gotten back to his feet, another arrow stuck into his spine out of nowhere. The man stumbled with a disbelieving look on his face.

"What...?" A croaking noise of incredulity came from his throat.

He didn't seem to understand what had happened, even as his death approached. The bandit took a few more uneasy steps before falling to the ground, unmoving.

Red slowly emerged, walked over, and stared at the corpse. Even from an outsider's perspective, he still wasn't too sure what he'd witnessed. Apparently, not only did Rog shoot two arrows in the blink of an eye, but he'd even predicted which direction his target would dodge. He couldn't wrap his head around how someone could be so precise.

"Whew!" Rog said loudly. "That worked out well."

Red looked over and saw the man leisurely walking towards one of the bodies. There were no signs of exertion on his face. No one would have guessed he'd just killed six people by himself.

"Help me pick up the arrows," he said.

There was a lot Red wanted to ask, but he did as he was told first. He neared the leader's corpse and tugged on the arrow that was lodged in the man's spine. Unfortunately, the task proved more difficult than he'd at first imagined.

"I don't think I can pull it out without breaking it," he said.

"That's fine," Rog said. "Just make sure you don't leave any pieces behind."

Seeing as Rog wasn't bothered by it, he took out a knife from his equipment and got to work.

It took them a while to gather all the arrows, including the ones that had missed their targets. Only two were still in usable condition, and one of those was the one Red had shot.

"You must go through lots of arrows," he said.

Rog shrugged. "Have to make do with cheap material."

Red wasn't sure this was the material's fault.

They also used the opportunity to loot the bandits. Sadly, other than rations, they weren't carrying anything valuable, despite their earlier claims. However, Red did find something interesting in the leader's pocket.

It was a map depicting a place he didn't recognize, but from the sketches of trees, he could make an educated guess.

"Do you recognize this?" He showed the map to Rog.

"Hm, looks like a map of the region. Doesn't have any written information, though." He pointed at certain symbols. "Do you see these X's? From their location, I'd be willing to bet these are the bandits' hideouts."

"Are they far?"

"Several days away," Rog said. "This isn't very valuable, though. Everyone knows the bandits live between the hills. The real problem is going out there and dealing with them."

Red nodded, but he still decided to keep the map.

"What about that person he mentioned?" he asked. "Rickard, I think. Should we be worried?"

"If we were facing him directly, then sure. He's already opened his Spiritual Sea. He's the reason why the town hasn't eliminated these bandit nests."

The revelation concerned Red. "Will he find out that we killed his men?"

"Can't imagine how. Not like we left a lot of evidence, and I took my arrows back on the off chance he could trace them back to Goulth."

"What about the corpses? Shouldn't we hide them?"

Rog laughed at his suggestion. "Hide them... how? Are you planning on digging a ditch for six people? Even if we did manage to dig a hole that big, any experienced tracker could find it. Not to mention that animals might even dig them up and eat the corpses."

"So... do we just leave them here?" The prospect left Red uneasy.

"There's no need to worry, kid. Bandits under Rickard die every day in this forest, and he doesn't investigate each death," Rog said, trying to assuage his concerns. "That guy is strong, but he isn't that smart. Else, he wouldn't be a bandit."

Red would've preferred to hide all the evidence, but he knew the idea wasn't practical. While he was lost in thought, Rog had already walked up to the boar.

"Aren't they going to track our footprints?"

"We're going back to town, so we don't need to worry." The hunter lifted the boar onto his shoulders. "Too risky out here right now, and we already got a nice haul."

Red nodded. If they were going back to a settlement with thousands of people, the bandits obviously couldn't track them down. As Rog walked away, he realized there was really nothing else to do here.

Just like that, six people had died, the matter treated as a triviality. Red didn't feel pity for these men, but he couldn't help but think about them.

It seems like human life is just as cheap on the surface.

On the journey back, Red took the opportunity to clarify one of his doubts.

"How did you do that thing with the arrows?" he asked.

"What thing?"

"You shot two arrows at the same time at the leader."

"I didn't do that. I just shot them really quickly."

Red frowned. It seemed absurd that someone could do the entire routine of nocking an arrow and shooting it two times in less than a second. However, Rog had no reason to lie to him.

"If you could shoot that fast, why did you wait until then to do it?"

"Can't keep that rhythm up for long. Would tire me out eventually."

Red examined Rog's countenance. He didn't look tired at all. Of course, there was also another issue on his mind.

"You shot the two arrows before he even dodged, right?"

Rog nodded.

"How did you know he was going to dodge that way?"

"I didn't." The man shrugged. "It was just a guess."

Red was unconvinced.

"Look, I'm not lying," Rog said. "The first arrow was to urge him to dodge in a particular direction, and the second one was to hit him where I thought he would land. He might have reacted in some other way, and then both shots would have been useless. It was just a bet that turned out well."

Red understood his reasoning, but he was also convinced this wasn't a mere gamble. Every shot Rog took was fast and precise, and the fact he could make these kinds of decisions in the heat of battle was a testament to his skill.

"You're very strong," he said. Red wholeheartedly admired the man's strength.

Rog just shrugged, though. "When you can't advance any more in cultivation, you focus on other things. I ended up choosing archery and hunting, but what I achieved is nothing impressive, really."

"It can't be that simple. I doubt every archer is as good as you."

"You're right, I guess." He scratched his beard. "I suppose it's why Hector chose to recruit me. But there are some things no amount of skill will let you do. Spirit, cultivation, and talent are still the most important things at the end of the day."

Red didn't detect any regret in Rog's voice, but the bluntness of his words still surprised him.

"This Sect is just a bunch of has-beens with no future, who dedicated their lives to learning a trade," Rog said. "We might be better than the average person, but compared to true cultivators, we're no better than dirt. After all, if we were that good, we wouldn't be stuck at the same obstacle for our entire lives, right?"

Red didn't respond.

"Don't take us for an example, kid. What we can achieve is just scraping the bottom of the barrel. You'll have to be better than us if you want to make anything out of yourself in this world."

Their conversation died down, and silence trailed their footsteps as they continued on their way to the town.

Red wasn't sure how much time had passed since they'd left. It was still the middle of the night, and almost no one could be seen on the streets. Rog didn't bother with sneaking this time around, as it was unlikely he could go unnoticed while carrying a giant boar on his shoulders.

It earned them some strange looks from a few patrolling guards, and Red worried they would arrest him for his earlier crimes. But no one stood in their way, and the pair peacefully made their way back to the Sect.

As they approached, though, they overheard a commotion in the courtyard. From afar, Red could hear two women arguing behind the gate.

"He wouldn't just leave like that!" Eiwin said with concern. "I just spoke with him earlier. Something must have happened!"

"We've not even known him for a week!" Narcha said, unconvinced. "How can you claim to know him that well?"

"It doesn't matter! I'm going to look for him. Are you coming or not?"

"Ugh... Fine!"

With Narcha's agreement, the gate swung open. As they walked out, they saw Rog and Red approaching from down the street.

Both women froze in place, surprise painted on their faces.

"Oh, yeah," the hunter realized. "I forgot to tell you I was taking the boy along."

Narcha seemed to understand what had happened. She let out a loud peal of laughter. "Hah! There they are! No need to be worried, right, Eiwin? ...Eiwin?"

Eiwin stared silently at both hunters, and Red felt a shiver run down his spine.

CHAPTER 83

RESEARCH

EIWIN ADMONISHED them for over ten minutes. Red thought about arguing that this wasn't his idea in the first place, but once he saw her expression, he changed his mind. Not to mention that she brought up good points, like how dangerous it was to leave without notice. He couldn't help but agree with her, especially considering their encounter with the bandits. Rog, on the other hand, had an exaggerated look of regret on his face.

At Narcha's insistence, Eiwin finally calmed down and took notice of the boar on Rog's shoulders.

"It seems you got lucky," she said as a serene smile returned to her face. "Did you learn something, Red?"

"Yeah, I learned how to shoot a bow. Rog planned to stay longer, but we couldn't because of the bandits."

Eiwin's grin vanished as suddenly as it appeared. "Bandits?" She turned to Rog, expecting an explanation.

"Yeah, uh..." He scratched his beard in embarrassment. "We ended up being stalked by some bandits."

"This close to town?" Narcha sounded surprised.

"I thought it was weird, too. Can only imagine they were there for something else, but thought they found some easy prey."

"Are they dead?" she asked.

"All the ones we encountered, yeah. But they probably had others in the region too. I didn't stick around to look for them, though."

Narcha gritted her teeth. "These guys are getting too ballsy. What gives them the confidence to mess with our town?"

No one answered her. Now Eiwin looked to be in deep thought, and Red also considered what could happen next.

"We'll talk about this with Master Hector tomorrow," Eiwin decided. "We still have the mission Master Frida gave us to consider. Perhaps we can tackle all these matters in one go." She turned to Red. "You should probably get some rest. None of your teachers will give you a break tomorrow."

He nodded before looking to Rog. "Can I keep the bow?" he asked.

Rog frowned. "What for?"

"For shooting things."

"Oh. Yeah, sure."

With this confirmation, Red wandered off towards his room. The two women stared at Rog in silence, with judgmental looks on their faces.

"What did I do now?"

The rest of the night passed by uneventfully, and Red slept peacefully. As ever, the rooster's crow foretold the arrival of sunrise, and he got out of bed. When he walked outside, he was met with a familiar scene.

Domeron was sitting in his rocking chair, sipping from a mug while watching the chicken coop. Red watched him for a moment before deciding to approach.

He didn't hide or quiet his footsteps. Domeron, however, didn't turn to look at him, pretending he wasn't there.

"You're a swordsman, right?" Red asked.

Domeron gave a grumble of confirmation.

"Where's your sword, then?"

The rocking chair stopped, and the man turned to Red with a stern look on his face.

"Do you like bothering people?" he asked.

"Not particularly."

"I see." Domeron resumed the chair's swaying. "I have a sword. I just don't carry it with me inside the Sect."

"Shouldn't a swordsman carry his sword at all times?"

The man scoffed. "Is that what qualifies someone as a swordsman?"

Red supposed there was no rule saying that. His mind quickly moved on from this matter, and he thought back to the previous night in the forest.

"Could you beat Rog in a fight?"

"Depends." Domeron gazed at him with curiosity. "What prompted this line of questioning?"

"I saw him shoot down some bandits yesterday," Red said. "He was really skilled."

"Bandits?" The man winced. "Well, under the right circumstances, Rog could definitely be considered the strongest person in the Sect—other than Hector. No common equipment can block the power behind his arrows, and if he has a clear shot on you, then you're probably dead."

"Could you block them?"

"I have some tricks up my sleeve, but I'm not completely confident they would work," Domeron said. "Only chance I would have of winning is if I got close enough."

"Even with only one arm?"

"What? Do you want to spar with me to check it?" Domeron tensed, narrowing his eyes.

Red shook his head. He wasn't stupid.

"What are we training for today?" he asked, changing the subject.

"More footwork." Domeron got up. "We'll be doing that for a while until I feel you're skilled enough."

"I thought you said my footwork was good?"

"It's decent, but there's always room for improvement. Not even the strongest people in this world can claim to have mastered everything there is to know about a skill, much less a child. In cultivation, simple proficiency is barely even the start."

Red nodded in understanding. He was eager to learn how to wield weapons, but he knew he had just barely begun training. The best decision was to defer to the one with more experience and knowledge.

The two of them walked to the field to begin another day of training.

An hour later, Red finished his training session. The improvements in his footwork from yesterday were small, but they were still there. Domeron explained that substantial change would only come over weeks and months, but Red was already used to that and wasn't in any particular hurry.

After they were done, Red didn't wait for Eiwin to come looking for him. He walked up to Goulth's workshop, where sounds of activity could already be heard. He knocked on the door.

"Come in!"

Red entered the house he'd become so familiar with over the last few days. In the next room, the blacksmith was already preparing breakfast, and he smiled once he saw Red come in.

"Come on, we need to start the day with a good meal!" Goulth said, pulling out another bowl.

Red didn't stand on ceremony.

After they were done eating, the two of them began to work the forge. Red followed Goulth's instructions, and soon the furnace was ablaze. Goulth went through more of his explanations, this time about handling metal bars, and Red got to have a more hands-on experience.

"Here, use the tongs to hold the bar over the anvil." The man handed the tools over. "I'll be hammering it down."

Red did as he was told, focused on keeping the tongs steady. However, he soon found the task was not nearly as easy as he'd expected. When Goulth's hammer came down, a shockwave ran up his arms from the sheer force of the blow, and the ringing tongs nearly escaped his hands.

"Hold steady!" Goulth glared at him.

With no complaints, Red recomposed himself and tried to use the strength of his Upper Arm Vein. The second blow came down, and he felt the force travel up his arms again, but this time, he held steady through the trembling.

"Good!" Goulth praised. "Now turn it over!"

Red used the tongs to awkwardly flip the metal bar. The tools were unwieldy, making it hard to handle the material with precision. Once he'd positioned it correctly, Goulth told him to stop moving before his hammer came down again.

They continued this process for the next few minutes until Goulth finally called for a stop. Red was exhausted, a dull pain spreading through his arms. The simple task of holding the metal bar still while the blacksmith shaped it with hammer blows took more out of him than most training he'd gone through in the past.

"Good work, kid." Goulth patted his shoulders. "Look at what you've created."

Red had barely any chances to examine the object on the anvil while focusing on his task. When he looked over now, though, he only saw a misshapen piece of metal.

He frowned. "Was it supposed to come out like this?"

"Oh, not at all." Goulth shook his head with a smile. "It's completely useless."

"What was the point of all that, then?"

"To get you accustomed to handling the tongs. Most blacksmiths just have their apprentices handle the hammer, but I like to have you involved in every process of creation."

Red understood the man's intentions, but felt like he hadn't been able to learn much while fighting for his life holding the tongs.

"Anyways, go rest a little bit." Goulth pointed to a chair. "I'm gonna melt this piece into something usable again. Next, you'll handle the hammer, and we'll actually make something."

Red didn't know how much more strength he could gather, but he simply nodded. As Goulth was occupied preparing the material, a question flowed into his mind. He hesitated for a while but still decided to speak up.

"Do you only use metals to forge equipment?" Red asked.

Goulth nodded. "It's what I specialize in. But it's honestly not that simple. Often there are more things than metal that are needed for a finished product."

"What about monster parts? Can you use them to make things?"

"Depends on the part of the monster. But generally, body parts are obviously not as easy to transform as metal. If we're talking about solid components like bones or horns, I can still do something with them. Hides and softer things are not my specialty, though."

"I see. Is that why the Sect orders the uniforms from somewhere else?"

When he mentioned that, Goulth froze. His expression went through a sea of changes in a matter of moments before returning to normal.

"Yeah. I'm not good at making those things."

The change didn't go unnoticed by Red. He recalled how Frida had reacted at the mention of his master's name. It was clear this was a sore spot for both of them. He didn't dare to probe further, though, since he'd found the answer he wanted.

He changed topics. "Do you also work with stones?"

"Not really. That's more masonwork," Goulth said. "Besides, stones are not as easy to shape and forge as ores."

This troubled Red. It wasn't what he wanted to hear, but it also wasn't the end of the world for him. It merely meant he would need to get his moonstones from another source.

"Is there something you want to know?" Goulth asked.

The question made Red's blood run cold. Did the man suspect something? But he quickly calmed himself down. It wasn't weird that Goulth would ask if there was a purpose behind his apprentice's curiosity. As far as Red could tell, it was a harmless question, but it still made him reluctant to continue.

Should he finally ask the one thing that had been on his mind the entire time? Despite everything he'd gone through, he still found it hard to take that last step, as if there would be no turning back afterwards. Yet it was obvious his silence had unintentionally given rise to more suspicion on Goulth's part.

"It's fine if you don't want to tell me," the blacksmith said. "There are also things I don't feel comfortable telling you. Just know that whatever you tell me doesn't go out to anyone else if you don't want to."

Red couldn't help but blame his indecision for his predicament. If he hadn't taken so long to reply and had played it off as mere curiosity, then Goulth probably wouldn't have suspected anything. However, he also found his concerns to be somewhat pointless. If even a hothead like Narcha suspected he was hiding something already, how could his master not suspect it either? What mattered more, in the end, was what they did with that suspicion.

If Red didn't feel secure asking his question directly, perhaps there was another way.

"Do you have a book on common materials?"

CHAPTER 84

MAP

GOULTH LAUGHED AT HIS QUESTION.

"Common materials? There are way too many to count. There are different books in the library on metals, plants, and all other types of materials. But do you even know how to read yet?"

"Don't they have illustrations?" Red asked, recalling the *Spirit Key* book Eiwin had shown him.

The blacksmith was taken aback. "Uh, I guess there might be. But I wouldn't count on it."

Red's face fell. It seemed like this information would be out of his reach until he learned how to read.

"Can you show them to me?"

"You can ask Eiwin." Goulth shrugged. "I don't really visit the library that much."

Red nodded. Right as he was wondering how to approach that subject, he was interrupted by a sizzling noise. Red jumped in surprise. Goulth had brought the metal piece over to the forge and was in the process of heating it up.

"Don't get distracted!" he cried. "You have to focus while you're in this workshop. Get the hammer!"

Red followed his instructions, and the pair got lost in their work.

After Red left the workshop, he felt like he had gone through an excruciating workout. His arms ached, and his ears rang from the clanging sounds of metal against metal. Goulth not only asked for precision with his hammer strikes, but also required Red to strike as hard as he could with every blow.

He had lost count of how many times he had repeated the same overhead swing over the last hour, and still, the blacksmith was unhappy with his strength. Some metals required great force to bend into shape even after being heated—force which Red obviously lacked. At the end of the day, though, there wasn't much he could do other than keep training. After he finished opening his Upper Leg Vein, the Lower Arm Vein would be next, and perhaps by then, he would have the required strength.

Now was the time for another lesson, though. Right as Red was about to look for Eiwin, he saw the woman waiting for him nearby. She smiled and waved him over.

"Now that it's still daytime, we'll have an easier time with your lessons," Eiwin said. "Let's go to the library."

Red followed along. As they entered the room, he saw that Eiwin had already set aside books and papers. She sat on one side of the table and pointed to the other chair. He took her cue and sat down.

"We're going to be reviewing what we learned yesterday." Eiwin pointed at the paper in front of him. "Do you still remember everything?"

Red nodded and picked up the quill, dipping it in ink. He proceeded to write out the entire alphabet, trying to recollect the shapes. After he was done, he set the quill aside and looked up at Eiwin. She wore a strange expression on her face.

"Did I do something wrong?" he asked.

"No. I was just surprised you remembered everything so well."

Red had paid strict attention to the letters yesterday. Even as he'd gone to sleep, he had imagined their shapes in his head, so he didn't think it was odd that he'd remembered them.

"I thought we might have to repeat the same lesson, but it seems I was being overly concerned," Eiwin said. "Now we can move on to smaller words and how they're read."

Red listened intently to the lesson, eager to learn.

As he'd imagined, there were many intricacies to language, and the same letters put together in specific orders could be read in completely different ways. At first, Red was confused by the rules, but Eiwin's explanations were clear, and he quickly grasped them.

By the end of the lesson, he had memorized a handful of words and how to write them. In fact, Red could even decipher some words by himself. Eiwin once more looked at him strangely.

"Are you sure you don't know how to read?" she asked.

He nodded, but even he didn't feel so confident about his reply. It was clear that his learning speed was abnormal, and he couldn't think of a reason as to why. While Red had paid close attention to the lessons, he'd had a weird feeling as he worked. It was as if he weren't just absorbing the knowledge, but uncovering something he already knew.

Maybe this had to do with his life before the underground, but Red wouldn't mention that to Eiwin.

"I just feel like it's very easy," he said.

"Maybe you have a talent for words. Pretty soon, you'll be able to read everything in the library by yourself, and you won't have to ask me for help."

That would certainly make things less awkward, but for now, Red still had to rely on her.

"Do you have a book on common crafting materials?" he asked.

"We have a few. However, they are all very technical. I don't think you'll be able to read them just yet."

Her response didn't surprise him, so he tried another way in. "Do they have illustrations?"

"A few of them do, I think, but most are just writing. Is there something specific you're looking for? I could look it up for you."

Red seriously considered her offer, but in the end, he simply shook his head.

He settled on a half-truth. "I was just hoping to learn more, since I'm working on blacksmithing now."

"That makes sense," Eiwin said. "Maybe I can teach you about the surrounding areas and the materials we extract from them? Would that be useful?"

Red nodded, his interest piqued.

Eiwin smiled and got up to search the bookshelves. When she returned, she brought a yellowed paper to unfold over the table. Red could immediately recognize it as a large map because of its detailed drawings of roads and terrain. Unlike the bandit's map, this one seemed stuffed with all kinds of information.

"This is a map of Fordham-Bestrem and the surrounding areas." She pointed at a specific spot. "This is our town."

Red looked over and recognized the relatively small circle on the map representing the settlement. "That's very small."

"This is just to scale. Relative to the rest of the world, it is quite small, and yet it can hold more than ten thousand people. Can you imagine if it was bigger than this?"

Red, in fact, could not even begin to imagine it.

"As you can see, we live in the middle of a large forest." She pointed at the surrounding drawings of trees. "We appropriately call it Bestrem Forest. It encompasses this whole region, as well as a few other settlements."

The forest occupied almost half of the map. In the middle were a few other villages that looked even smaller than their town.

"You used to hunt monsters here, right?" he asked.

"Yes, it was an important venture for the town." She shook her head in resignation. "However, monsters aren't the only thing in this forest. You might not have had the opportunity to see them, but there are plenty of Spiritual Plants that grow there. Iron-bark wood, for instance, is a rare spiritual material that's native to this forest..."

She went over some of the other things that could be found in the region, but there was never any mention of moonstones, to Red's dismay. The next thing that caught his attention was the vast river cutting the forest in half.

He noticed it extended past the map. "How long is this river?"

"Extremely long," Eiwin said. "It begins in the Skycrown Mountains to the east and ends in the Imperial lands to the west. It almost crosses the entire continent, and it gets much bigger than this at certain points."

"Is there something special about this river?"

"There is. In certain sections, the river is overflowing with Spiritual Energy, making it a perfect place to cultivate. A lot of cities and Sects are built close to it because of that."

"What is it called?"

"Crystal River. They say the founder of the Crystal Sky Sect was the one that created it."

Red was confused by this. "How do you create a river?"

"I'm not sure, but when someone is powerful enough, there is little they can't do in this world." It seemed Eiwin had no more knowledge on the subject, so he could only suppress his curiosity.

"What about this?" Red pointed at another landmark on the map.

To the west of the town, there was an odd depression. While the forest occupied more than half of the map, these strange rocky symbols filled the remaining terrain.

"That's the canyon I told you about before," Eiwin said. "It's called the Great Serpent Canyon. But what you are seeing here is just a corner of it. The whole canyon occupies an incredibly vast area that borders multiple countries, and all kinds of monsters and rare materials can be found there."

"Like flarestone?"

"Exactly." She smiled. "But that's not even among the rare materials that can be found there. Black Iron and other kinds of Spiritual Ores are mainly extracted from within this canyon."

Eiwin went into more detail about the materials that came from the canyon. However, once again, there was no mention of moonstones.

Red tried to approach his question from a different perspective. "What about the monsters?"

"There are all kinds of monsters in there. They're more powerful and more numerous than those in the forest. The further into the canyon you go, the stronger they get," Eiwin said. "There are a bunch of reptiles, like lizards and serpents, and they have some of the deadliest venom in the world. But there are also monstrous mountain lions, foxes, birds, and even insects like scorpions and spiders."

At the mention of insects, Red's eyes lit up, but he hid his curiosity behind his blank face. Just because there were insects didn't mean they were the same dark ones from the moonstone mines.

Red tried to keep his next question on topic. "Do you guys have lots of mines in there?"

"Our city has dozens of them, and that's actually a small amount compared to some other cities. The canyon itself has an immense network of tunnels that contain precious materials. However, all kinds of monsters also live down there, so it's dangerous to explore them."

His curiosity about the canyon increased. "And does the Sect ever have missions there?"

"Rarely. The canyon is far more dangerous than the forest," Eiwin said.

"Many monsters who have already opened their Spiritual Seas live in that place. If we ever do something there, then it needs to be worth the risk."

Worth the risk?

"Do you think I could explore the canyon one day?" Red asked.

After some hesitation, Eiwin said, "Maybe when you're stronger. But even for people who have opened all twelve of their veins, exploring that place is a risk. Perhaps only Master Hector could move around safely, and not even he would risk going too deep into the canyon."

Red understood her. If even Hector could be in danger in that place, how would he fare?

CHAPTER 85

THE MOON

EIWIN CONTINUED her explanation of the region, but moonstones never came up. The information was still helpful to Red, as he now felt he had a clearer understanding of how large the surface world was. The underground and its tunnels could not even begin to compare in size.

"I assume there's a lot more than just this region." He pointed at the edges of the map.

"This doesn't even begin to cover it," Eiwin said. "It's just a province in a larger kingdom."

"Kingdom? I thought we lived under a baron."

"We do, but the Baron is a noble serving under the true ruler of these lands—the King. There's a fealty contract these nobles sign with each other that lasts for generations. I could explain it to you, but it's a complicated topic. Most of it might not make sense to you without proper context."

"I understand." Red was interested, but learning about the intricacies of the ruling class wasn't his priority.

Eiwin folded up the map and looked at him with an expectant smile.

"Did my explanation help you?" she asked. "There are many other materials we import into the city, but the ones I mentioned are native to our barony."

"It was helpful." Although he hadn't found what he was looking for, learning about his immediate surroundings would help him achieve his goals.

"Do you think I could still have that book on materials?" he asked.

"Sure!"

Eiwin went to look through the bookshelves. This search, however, took her longer than Red expected. When she returned, she brought three books to spread on the table.

"So, these are the ones we have," Eiwin said. "There are many different kinds of materials in the world, but they're more commonly divided into three classes: minerals, plants, and animals—animal parts, that is." She pointed at each book in turn.

"There are other materials that might not fit into any of these categories, but they're extremely rare. In any case, these books have a lot of words you probably won't recognize, but it might be good practice. Besides, there are also a few illustrations that could help you."

She opened the rightmost book, revealing a depiction of a terrible winged beast gorging on the entrails of a smaller animal.

"Uh... Yeah, parts of it are unnecessarily descriptive." Eiwin gave him an awkward smile. "But it's nothing someone as mature as you can't deal with."

Red picked up the books. "Can I bring them to my room?"

"Master Hector says we aren't allowed to..." Eiwin frowned. "But I honestly can't recall the last time he ever bothered visiting our library, so go ahead. Just make sure you return them."

He nodded, running off with the items in his arms, leaving behind a speechless Eiwin.

"Be careful with them!"

By the time Red was done with his lessons, night was fast approaching. He almost wondered how he was supposed to be reading these books in the dark, but then he recalled the lantern Eiwin had shown him before. To his luck, there were dozens hanging around buildings and poles in the courtyard.

Rather unceremoniously, he picked up a lantern that had already been lit close by and returned to his room. Once inside, he set the light and the books on the table.

It was time he did his own research.

Of course, Red knew that what he was looking for was probably a mineral. That eliminated two books from the get-go. The book on minerals seemed to have over two hundred pages, and he couldn't help but wonder how he should sort through it.

Just by opening it, Red understood Eiwin's earlier warnings. Unlike the other books he'd seen before, this one was written with small letters crammed into endless paragraphs. The authors were perhaps eager to fit as much information as they could into the pages.

Red leafed through the book and found out, to his dismay, a distinct lack of illustrations. There were a handful, but none looked particularly well-drawn. When he finished skimming the pages, he concluded there was nothing resembling a moonstone in the pictures.

He didn't panic, though. There was still a word he knew that could help in his search.

Moon.

He remembered Eiwin's explanation of how the word was written, so maybe if he looked through the book again, he could find it. It would be a strenuous task, but not one Red was unwilling to try.

Unfortunately, even after two hours of arduous searching, he couldn't find any sign of the word "moon." Red tried to look for it in the chapter titles, in the large blocks of text and everywhere else, but there was no sign of the word.

He considered doing another search but decided against it. It seemed moonstones were either rare enough to not be considered a common mineral, or they were kept a secret from the public. Neither of these possibilities made much sense to Red.

There was an unending supply of them underground, and as far as he could tell, they had no particular use. It didn't make sense to keep them hidden. If these stones were so important, they wouldn't rely on malnourished slaves to scavenge for them.

From what Red had learned from Viran, the guards were put there to make sure nothing left the mine. But if that was their only use, why not collapse the mine entrance? That way, nothing would get out.

There's something I'm missing.

It was of the utmost importance for Red to uncover everything behind those mines. Too much still lay shrouded in mystery, and just because he'd escaped the underground, that didn't mean that place couldn't affect his life again. There was the curse the blob had mentioned, the guards who might be looking for him, and also Viran's special Vein Opening Technique. It wasn't just a matter of curiosity. This concerned his own safety. Any of these matters might blow up in Red's face without warning.

But in the end, he could only sigh in resignation. Without guidance and considering his lack of knowledge, it was unlikely he would find an answer anytime soon. Would he be forced into revealing his hand?

Not yet.

Red wouldn't do it until he'd exhausted all other options. Not to mention, he'd been on the surface for almost a week, and nothing serious had happened for him to rush his decision.

Maybe nothing bad will happen.

These words, however, sounded uncertain even inside his own mind.

Just as Red was reflecting on his choices, something caught his attention. Out of the corner of his eye, he saw a wisp. It was ethereal, almost invisible. Once he focused his vision, though, he saw it more clearly.

It was a misty green strand.

Red recognized it. He squinted and felt his blood run cold.

Trying to keep himself calm, he examined the green mist. It was identical to the strands he'd seen in the fight with the insectoid, no matter how much he tried to convince himself otherwise. He struggled to determine its trajectory with the bright lantern in the room. He threw a thick blanket over the light and had another look.

In the darkness, the green strands became clearer. There were three of them, and they were all coming from the window.

No, that's not right...

They weren't coming in. The strands were leaving through the window.

Red shuddered and followed the green energy to its origin.

The strands were coming out of his body—two strands from his upper arms and one of them from his spine. Even in his apprehension, he could immediately tell these were the positions of his special acupoints.

He was confused, but he knew something bad must be happening. Red felt nothing strange within his body, but how could he ignore these signs? He walked over to the window. Unfortunately, due to how high the opening was, he couldn't see where the strands led.

Red narrowed his eyes and wondered.

Can the others see it?

The strands were faint, and even now in the middle of the night, Red still had to focus to keep them in sight. Yet someone like Rog, with opened acupoints aiding their vision, could likely see them at a glance. However, whether or not others could see them, what could he possibly do about it? That was out of his control, and it shouldn't be his priority right now.

He needed to understand what was happening.

No longer hesitating, Red walked out of the room. Strangely, the green strands connected to his body broke off as soon as he closed the door. But more energy continued to leak from his body and float upwards, uniting with the severed strands.

Red looked up, trying to see their path. As he followed their traces, he eventually lost track of them in the night sky. They seemed to float up forever, and he could only watch on helplessly, unaware of their destination.

Eventually, his eyes caught something curious. The moon was dark tonight—all of its light was entirely gone, something he hadn't seen before on the surface. Although the white illumination was gone, the outline of the celestial sphere was still visible in the starlit sky.

For some reason, Red felt his gaze being drawn to it. His eyes adapted to the darkness, and more details of the moon's irregular surface came to view before his eyes.

And that was when he saw it.

Something moved.

Red blinked in disbelief.

And yet it was still there.

Movement. Something was moving on the surface of the moon. Red couldn't see it clearly, but the faint outlines of an indescribable stirring shape were there. Eventually, the movement came to a stop, but he could still see a silhouette that had been hidden from him until a few seconds ago.

Something was on the moon.

Suddenly, Red felt a gaze set upon him, and he was plunged into an icy nightmare. He felt horror and apprehension spread to every part of his body and mind, and yet, he couldn't move or avert his eyes.

That "thing" was looking at him. It had noticed him.

A sharp pain entered his body. The green strands started to escape him even faster, and his acupoints strained under the unnatural pressure. Soon enough, all the green energy had been drained out of him as the strands dissolved, and yet the siphoning pain didn't disappear.

It wasn't satisfied.

Something else started to leave his body too. Red didn't know what it was, but he felt a pain attacking parts of his body he didn't even know existed, and he was helpless to stop it.

After what could have been hours, the feeling disappeared, and he collapsed to his knees.

The gaze moved away from him.

Finally, Red could move his body again, and he braced himself for the wave of weakness. It didn't come, though. He tentatively moved his body in confusion, only to find it seemed as strong as before.

He couldn't help but wince.

Another illusion?

Red recalled the feeling of horror that somehow felt different from what he'd experienced in visions before. Doubt filled his mind, but he realized there was perhaps an easier way to tell if what had happened was real.

He hesitated, but there was no other way to be sure. After steeling himself with a deep breath, his eyes moved up again, to the moon in the sky.

His blood ran cold.

The shape was still there, as clear as day, and at that moment, Red could feel it.

It was looking at him, too.

CHAPTER 86

AFTERMATH

THE STRANGE BEING on the moon was still there, slithering, pulsating.

Red closed his eyes, taking a deep breath.

It's just an illusion... It's not real.

He kept repeating the sentence under his breath. It took the better part of a minute for his heart rate and breathing to return to normal, and when he finally calmed down, he opened his eyes again.

His mind was shaken anew. The thing was still there on the dark moon, its gaze still trained on him. This was no illusion—or at the very least, not one he could escape from. Out of an abundance of caution, Red decided to look away.

However, it didn't seem like averting his eyes worked to divert the being's attention. He could feel it staring at him, weighing on his mind, no matter how much he tried to ignore it.

Why is it still there? Why...

Fear gripped his heart, making it hard for him to even move.

A boy's voice interrupted his thoughts. "Hey, Red! What are you doing here?"

Red looked up and saw Allen sauntering over. The young master was giving the kneeling boy a peculiar look, though once he noticed the strain on Red's face, the expression turned into one of concern.

"Are you okay?" Allen asked.

"It's... it's fine. I just feel a bit dizzy from practice." Red tried to shrug off his worry, struggling to get the words out.

The appearance of a third party hadn't alleviated the pressure of the lunar gaze.

"Here, I'll help you up."

Without waiting for a response, Allen got close and helped him to his feet. Red didn't refuse, trying to find his balance again.

Allen's concern grew deeper when he noticed how pale Red was. "Hang on, I'll call Eiwin!"

"Don't..." Red held him back. "I've already recovered."

"Are you sure?" Allen didn't look convinced.

"Yes, I'm fine."

He backed his words by walking a few steps without help. Allen still looked skeptical, but his concern quickly gave way to curiosity. "Why were you training outside?"

"Just wanted a breath of fresh air." Red couldn't possibly reveal what had just happened to anyone, at least not without understanding it first.

"Ah, I see," Allen said. "I also don't like spending too much time training behind closed doors, but the old man says that you need to be isolated to focus..."

While Allen started going on about his training routine, Red winced in discomfort. It took most of his concentration just to pay attention to Allen's words while resisting the moon's horrible pressure, and his head started to ache.

As he tried to make sense of what was happening, an idea came to his mind.

"Did you look at the moon tonight?" he asked, interrupting Allen's words.

"The moon?" Allen frowned, looking up. He squinted, as if trying to see something, but a few seconds later, he just shook his head. "It's a new moon today, so we can't see it that well."

"A new moon?" Red hadn't heard the term before.

"Yeah, the moon has phases." Allen smiled at the chance to explain. "Basically, it gets brighter at some points and darker at others. When it's completely dark, we call it a new moon. When it's completely bright, we call it a full moon."

When Red thought back on it, he remembered the moon looked quite different from when he'd first arrived at the surface. He never expected there to be names behind the process, though.

"Do you not see anything weird there?" he asked. Red only felt comfortable asking this kind of question because he knew Allen was too naïve to suspect anything.

"Hmm..." The young master looked up again. "I don't see anything. Is there supposed to be something there?"

Red shook his head. "I was just wondering."

He suspected that he was the only one seeing the strange being, which made the situation even more alarming.

"Thanks for your help," Red told his companion. "I'll be going back to my room."

"Are you sure you're fine?" Allen asked, looking worried.

Red's face twitched at the question. Even if Allen was naïve, he still wasn't stupid, so he could only imagine his discomfort was obvious.

"I am," Red said. "I just need some rest to recover."

"Ah, alright."

"Also..." Red paused just as he was about to walk away. "Don't tell the others about this, okay? Eiwin in particular. She worries too much."

This wasn't the only reason Red wanted to keep it a secret.

"Yeah, I know what you mean." Allen patted his chest as a sign of confidence. "Don't worry, I won't tell a soul."

He didn't put much stock in the older boy's ability to keep a secret, but it was better than nothing. With Allen's assurance, he turned and went back to his room.

When Red entered, he almost collapsed on the spot. His body was relatively fine, but the mental strain to stay composed under the strange gaze took a lot out of him. In fact, even with a roof over his head, he could still feel its eyes on him.

He knew that if he went outside, he would still see that being on the moon, and even in the daylight, it would still be there. He had trouble concentrating on anything else, and every time Red tried recalling the specifics of the incident, he could feel his mind trembling.

Yet how could he possibly dismiss this, as he had his other visions? This wasn't an illusion. Even if what he was seeing wasn't real, its effect on his body was very real. He decided to think through everything he'd just witnessed.

First of all, there was the green energy leaving his veins. Red knew it was likely the same moonstone energy the insectoid used in the mines, especially since it flowed out of his special acupoints. However, this raised another issue: where had the energy come from?

As far as Red knew, you couldn't store Spiritual Energy inside your body without opening your Spiritual Sea. Yet energy had quite clearly left his body. Was this a feature of his special acupoints? Storing moonstone energy? He didn't know enough about Viran's technique to be sure.

Then there was the being. Red shivered when he thought back to it, but he tried to fight through the feeling. His first guess was that the energy that left his body all went towards that thing on the moon.

It seemed absurd, but it was the only reasoning that made sense.

He recalled his conversations with Viran, the blob, and the insectoids. Was this the curse they had referred to? If this wasn't the worst of it, Red couldn't bear to imagine what came next.

Still, even under the strange gaze, he had to confirm something. Under heavy strain, Red performed his Vein Opening Technique until he felt the Spiritual Energy entering his body. He concentrated and tried to direct the energy through his Spinal Vein, where one of his special acupoints was located.

It was a difficult task in his current state, but the strands followed the natural path towards his unopened veins, passing through the acupoint. As soon as they touched that area, though, he felt a wave of shock travel up his body. His legs buckled, and he fell to the ground on his knees, the energy inside his body dissipating.

A dull, pulsing pain spread through his spine, and soon it reached his upper arms. He pinpointed the origins of the pain as his special acupoints.

Eventually, the feeling passed, but a strained sensation lingered around those acupoints. They were spent and weak, and moving Spiritual Energy through them almost sent Red into shock. Was this the effect of the disappearance of the moonstone energy?

Red lay down on his bed and closed his eyes. Viran's words came back to him, how he'd said Red's special acupoints would help him escape the underground. He also remembered how the man had wanted to wait until he'd opened three veins before trying to escape.

Had he known this would happen? Maybe he wanted to wait because he knew just three acupoints weren't enough to resist whatever was going to happen.

Midway through the ordeal with the moon being, he had run out of energy and had felt something else being taken from him. He still couldn't identify it, but his instincts told him that whatever it was, it was very important to him. The pain remained clear in his mind, and it reminded him of when he'd awakened from the dream with the azure being.

What would've happened if I didn't have any moonstone energy in my body?

The energy drain couldn't mean anything good for him. It was only conjecture, but it was all Red had to work with.

And what if this happened again? What if the being tried to drain whatever moonstone energy was still left in his body? Judging by the state of his special acupoints, Red could guess there was nothing left at all. Not to mention, even if they were still full of energy, his current level clearly wasn't enough.

Could he even replenish what had been taken?

As these doubts crossed his mind, he couldn't help but feel the weight of the being's gaze grow stronger. He shivered but did his best to remain composed.

With a deep breath, Red tried to focus his thoughts again. What had prompted the transformation? Was it the new moon, as Allen called it? It was the only thing he could think of, but it still didn't give him any assurance. Maybe this would only happen whenever the moon was completely dark, but how could Red bet everything on that? No matter whether the moon was bright or dark, the being could still be there, after all.

The grim reality of his situation was setting in.

What do I do?

Red spent the entire night awake on his bed, pondering under the unyielding gaze of the moon.

Only when the first signs of the sunrise appeared did he feel the pressure diminish. The gaze slowly disappeared, but an unsettling presence lingered in his mind, like a shadow that refused to leave.

It took most of Red's willpower not to immediately fall asleep. There were certain things he needed to do. With a great effort, he got up and left the room. After spending so much time considering his options, he'd arrived at an inevitable conclusion.

He needed moonstones. Red wasn't sure if they would solve his problem, but he knew he needed to prepare himself for the worst-case scenario. For now, there were only two ways to obtain them.

One was by asking someone in the Sect about them, and the other was by trekking out into the forest and finding his hidden stash. Each option presented its own problems.

Searching for his stash by himself would be much riskier. Red had never wandered through the forest alone, and he didn't feel confident fighting off bandits by himself. Not to mention it was at least a three-day trip. At the same time, he also didn't want to risk exposing his background by asking the Sect for help, which led to his dilemma.

However, now that his life was potentially on the line, could he afford to maintain his secrecy? Yet what if this secrecy was the only thing keeping him alive? It was hard to make a decision when he knew so little about his own situation.

I need to think...

Just as he thought that, a voice interrupted him.

"How long are you going to stand there?"

Red looked up and saw Domeron sitting on his rocking chair not too far away.

CHAPTER 87

MOONLIGHT

"I WAS THINKING ABOUT SOMETHING," Red answered.

"Hmm." Domeron nodded and said nothing else.

Silence rose in the courtyard as the man continued to watch the chicken coop. Red, too, was lost in his own thoughts, staring at Domeron in contemplation. Eventually, the man grimaced, giving Red an irritated look.

"What is it, kid?"

"Nothing," Red told him.

"Then why are you staring at me?"

"I was thinking."

Domeron grunted in annoyance before getting up from his chair.

"Come." He waved for him to follow.

"Where?"

"To train, of course." Domeron sounded exasperated. "Isn't that what you wanted?"

With everything that had happened yesterday, Red had almost forgotten. Still, it would be strange for him to deny Domeron now, so he nodded, and the pair walked to the training field.

They at first did the footwork routine like usual, but a few minutes in, Domeron called their training to a stop. Red walked out of the circle, confused about what was happening. The man, however, only regarded him with a judgmental glare.

"Did I do something wrong?" Red asked.

"You're distracted."

Red was indeed distracted, but he didn't see how that was relevant.

"I managed to do all my footwork correctly, though." He had yet to be hit during the quick training session.

"You did, but your heart's not in it," Domeron said.

"What's that supposed to mean?"

"I repeated the same pattern of swings five times in a row, and you didn't notice."

Red was startled. Had that really happened?

"There's no point in training if your heart's not in it." Domeron shook his head. "What I'm teaching you is more than just repeating the same movements. It's about constantly surpassing your limits with time and practice. Being distracted by anything else is not going to cut it."

Red thought about protesting, but he knew Domeron was right. He wasn't in the state of mind to focus on training.

"What should I do, then?" he asked.

Domeron looked at him as if the answer were obvious. "You need to get your problems sorted, of course. Cultivators need focus to train. If you don't have it, then there's no point in practicing."

These words rendered Red silent as he considered them. Domeron, seeing this, couldn't help but sigh.

"The most important thing for a cultivator is their mental state," he explained. "This might not be obvious to you right now, but it'll become more apparent in the future. Even in the face of death, one's attitude can make all the difference."

"I understand. May I go, then?" Red asked.

"Sure," Domeron said. "Just make sure the next time you come to me, you have the right state of mind."

Their odd conversation ended just like that. The man's words were simple and to the point, and their meaning wasn't lost on Red. He didn't feel he would be able to focus before he solved the issue of the being on the moon, but the problem was—could he even solve it?

He wasn't sure, but he knew where he needed to start.

There were no sounds coming from Goulth's workshop, and the chimney wasn't spewing any smoke. Red wasn't sure if the blacksmith was awake, but he didn't feel like waiting any longer. He knocked on the door.

No response.

He knocked again. Still no response.

Just as Red was about to knock a third time, he heard steps from behind him. He turned around and saw Goulth approaching the workshop carrying a large wooden crate.

"What are you doing here this early, kid?" he asked. "I haven't even gotten breakfast ready."

"I was too distracted to train with Domeron," Red said.

"Oh, really?" Goulth looked surprised. "Well, you can help me cook, then. Maybe that'll help you."

Red nodded and followed his master into the workshop. Goulth set the crate down on top of a table before turning to him.

"Go light the furnace while I get everything ready."

He obeyed the instructions. Although he'd only worked at the forge for three days, he felt confident handling such a simple task. After shoveling out the old coal, he added a new batch and lit a flame using the firesteel. As he was getting the coal burning, Goulth returned carrying a large pot.

"Let me look over the fire. You go get the ingredients."

After ten minutes of cutting, peeling, and stirring ingredients inside the pot, the meal was finally underway. He sat in a chair, watching Goulth check the temperature and consistency of the soup. The man nodded with some satisfaction before looking at him.

"So, what's on your mind?" he asked.

Red was taken aback by the sudden question. However, before long, he realized what Goulth was referring to.

"I read a few books Eiwin showed me last night," he said.

"You already know how to read?" Goulth looked shocked.

"Not really. I only learned some small words. I mostly tried looking at the pictures."

The man's expression relaxed. "Ah, I see... Wait!" His face twisted in shock again. "Didn't you only start learning how to read a few days ago?"

Red nodded.

"And you already know how to read some words?"

He nodded again.

"That's... impressive!" Goulth gave him a wide smile. "Eiwin was right! You'll be able to read my book in no time at all!"

Red watched the man jump for joy at the revelation.

"I knew I wasn't wrong about you, kid! But we're getting distracted... What is it you wanted to talk about?"

That question left Red silent. He'd already resolved to ask for help, but now that the time had come, he wasn't sure how to proceed. But thinking about it for any longer wouldn't help him.

"I... was actually looking up a certain material," he said.

"What material?" Goulth sounded interested.

"It's called... moonstone."

Once the word was finally out, it felt like an enormous weight had been taken off his back. Red watched the man's expression for any reaction and braced himself for the worst.

But to his surprise, Goulth had a lost look on his face.

"Moonstone?" He shook his head. "Never heard of it."

For some reason, this answer came as a huge blow to Red. "It's a green stone. It glows in the dark."

"I know plenty of stones that glow in the dark. Some of them are kind of green, too. None of them are called moonstone." The giant shrugged.

Suddenly, Red felt like all his worries and caution over the last few days had been for naught.

Goulth noticed his disciple's quiet disappointment. "What is that stone used for? Maybe I know it under another name."

"I... don't know." Red had actually never figured out why the guards wanted the moonstones.

"Well, let's think, then..." He scratched his head in thought. "A green stone, glows in the dark... There are tree-hearts. They grow below the roots of Spiritual Trees. Does that ring a bell?"

Red shook his head.

"Hmm..." Goulth frowned. "Some unique emeralds glow in the dark, but these aren't really stones... What about Arcane Malachite? It's a special kind of copper, and it glows in the dark too."

"Copper? I don't think so..."

As far as Red knew, there was no metal in the moonstones. Plenty of slaves had tried melting them down, to no avail.

"I'm afraid I'm all out of ideas, then." Goulth said with a defeated sigh.

"This isn't to say that these moonstones don't exist. My knowledge of Spiritual Materials is not exhaustive."

While that might've been true, the blacksmith was still one of the most knowledgeable people in town. If not even he knew about these moonstones, was there a point to asking anyone else?

"Actually, there is something that name reminds me of," Goulth said.

Red's hope returned. "What is it?"

"Well, it's not exactly similar—more like the opposite. I'm talking about sunstones."

"Sunstones?"

"Yeah, those are stones said to contain power similar to that of the sun. They aren't actually formed in our world, but in the sky above us. They say rays of sunlight accumulate at certain points within our atmosphere before gathering into a solid shape. Once that happens, the sunstone falls down like a meteor. It's an extremely rare and powerful material, and factions have gone to war over it in the past."

"Why did that remind you of moonstones?" Red asked, confused.

"Well, they say the moon and the sun are like opposites, right?" Goulth said. "Maybe the same way sunstones can be formed by sunlight, moonstones can be formed by moonlight."

Red was intrigued by this theory, but there were a few problems with it. First of all, moonstones were extracted like any other ore and didn't fall from the sky. There was also the fact that moonstones didn't seem to be nearly as powerful as these so-called sunstones.

But at the same time, Red felt certain that the lunar being had extracted moonstone energy from his body. An undeniable connection existed between the moon and the moonstones, or at least the energy they contained.

"How could that happen if the moon doesn't shine all the time?" Red took this opportunity to ask something that had been on his mind since his conversation with Allen.

"Well, you see, the moon doesn't really shine at all," Goulth said. "Cultivators found out long ago that the moon doesn't emit natural light. Instead, it reflects the light of the sun while it's moving in the sky. It goes through cycles, depending on the time of the year."

Red was startled by this revelation. "If that's the case, wouldn't moonlight be the same as sunlight? Wouldn't its light also form sunstones?"

"Other people thought so too, in the past." Goulth shook his head. "Moonlight, as you might have noticed, is far weaker than sunlight. But that's not all. Cultivators figured out that the Spiritual Energy transmitted by sunlight is different from the energy transmitted by moonlight. It's like once the light from the sun is reflected off the moon, it goes through a transformation."

At these words, Red couldn't help but recall the being on the moon's surface. He quickly pushed away the thought, shuddering. "What kind of transformation?"

"It becomes more ethereal," Goulth said. "Cultivators found that kind of energy was closely connected with a person's soul, they just couldn't say exactly how. Later, they noticed that this Moon Spiritual Energy was also extremely beneficial for certain kinds of creatures."

"What creatures?"

Goulth hesitated. "The bad kind... ones that find life in death, eating the flesh and souls of other living beings. They came from the curse that was unleashed on our world by that damned Queen of the Dead thousands of years ago..."

The man paused. "Ghosts, zombies, ghouls, and other denizens of the Nether Realm. We call them the undead."

CHAPTER 88

REINCARNATION

"UNDEAD." Red had never heard the term before, but Goulth's description was enough to make him shiver. "What exactly do you mean by 'undead'?"

Goulth shrugged. "Well, they're dead, but still alive at the same time."

"That doesn't make it any clearer."

"It's hard to describe..." The giant man struggled to find the right words. "You can think of them as the exact opposite of the living. Humans are full of life essence, and it serves as 'fuel' for us to function and live normally."

Red recalled that Eiwin had given him a similar description of life essence.

"Eventually, when someone is close to death or is dead, that life essence turns into death essence," Goulth went on. "Undead use that death essence as their fuel, and their entire existence is based on it. This way, they manage to find life after death."

"You called it a curse, though. I assume there are side effects to that."

"Of course there are!" Goulth said. "Most undead are no different from monsters, losing all the memories they had before death. Some may still keep some rationality, but their entire existence is a waking nightmare."

"But how do people get this curse?" Red was desperate to know if he was in any danger.

"Well, there are many ways. Generally, undead appear from the bodies of people who died with a lot of grievances. Some undead can also generate more undead by infection, and there are even Spiritual Arts that can create undead at will."

Red reflected on his words. He already had the crimson energy to worry about, so the revelation that even moonstone energy could potentially cause some kind of spiritual infection was concerning.

"Is Moon Energy only useful to the undead?" he asked.

"No, that's just the most well-known use for Moon Energy. Over the years, the undead became intimately associated with the moon. In fact, the connection is so strong that their strength can also change depending on the phase of the moon."

The phase of the moon?

Red latched onto these words. "In what ways can it change?"

"The closer we are to a full moon, the stronger they get. So they're weakest during new moons," Goulth explained.

This explanation only inspired more questions. Red had been trying to draw a connection between what had happened to him and this undead curse, but there wasn't enough information to reach any solid conclusions.

"What I know is just the basics," the man said. "In fact, it's rare even for cultivators to see many undead. There are some organizations out there dedicated to hunting them down, too. Eiwin should know more about it."

"I understand." As curious as he was, learning about the undead wasn't a priority for him. After all, he still had to address the most important issue he was facing.

"Anyway," Goulth said, "if you'd like me to, I can help you by asking about that moonstone of yours. Some merchants I buy stuff from might know more, but no guarantees."

"There's no need. I can find them myself."

Since Goulth didn't know about it, it was unlikely to be available for purchase in town. Even if he could help him acquire it, who knew how long that would take? Not to mention, Red would prefer to keep his interest in the stones a secret. He might be able to trust his master, but could he say the same of the people the man might seek information from?

In the end, there was just one option left for him.

"Well, you sound pretty confident." Goulth seemed surprised by his rejection. "Either way, since you're here already, you might as well assist me. Working the forge clears my mind, so it might help you out too."

Red agreed. After the two were done eating, he attended to the repetitive work under Goulth's instruction. Surprisingly enough, the man wasn't lying. As he immersed himself in his work, he felt some of his agitation dissipate.

A few hours later, Red left the workshop. He was physically tired from working, but for some reason his mind felt more at peace. Now that he knew he couldn't acquire moonstones in town, he was faced with a single, unavoidable fact.

If the being absorbed energy from him again, he would have nothing to give. His stash was more than three days away, and even if he ran the whole way, he obviously wouldn't reach it before nightfall. Not to mention, Red didn't even know how he was supposed to absorb the moonstone energy into his acupoints.

His only hope was that there would be no repeat of last night's events. He felt frustrated having to rely on chance, but there was simply no way he could have predicted this, nor was there a way to immediately address it.

What Red could do was to prepare himself. Even if he could do nothing for tonight, that didn't mean he shouldn't act with urgency. He needed to recover his stash as soon as possible.

"Red, are you finished with your lessons already?"

Red turned and saw Eiwin approach him. She was carrying a few wooden boxes full of books and regarded him curiously.

"Yes, I finished early today."

"I see." Eiwin nodded with a smile. "Would you like to have your lesson with me before lunch, then?"

He gave her question some thought. In the end, he accepted.

The two of them made towards the library. As they got settled, instead of just ink and reams of blank paper, Red also noticed a few books and pages already filled with writing.

"I'd like to try something new today," Eiwin said, noticing his curiosity.

"What is it?"

"You see, so far, I've been treating you as a complete beginner when it comes to literacy," she said. "But you've been surprising me over the last few days. I've never seen someone learn as fast as you did, so I thought... why not try to see how far you can go?"

She handed him the papers covered with all kinds of unfamiliar words, as well as a quill and an inkpot.

"I wrote some more difficult words and simple sentences here," Eiwin said. "I'll guide you on how to read them, and then you'll copy it down on a blank sheet of paper. If you learn what everything means, then maybe you can even try writing your own sentences."

Red was interested in the prospect. Eagerly, he picked up the quill and dipped its tip in the ink. He looked at Eiwin.

"Where do we begin?"

A little over an hour had passed. Red was absorbed in the task at hand, and for a moment, he even managed to forget about his predicament. The words flowed smoothly from quill to paper, and by the end, he could confidently write a few sentences by himself.

Eventually, he didn't even need Eiwin's instructions to continue and started to experiment by himself. Whenever he came across an unfamiliar word, he asked for her help, but he never needed to have something explained to twice.

More time passed as he wrote whatever came to mind, during which Eiwin remained silent. Red was slow to notice this, but when he did, he stopped writing for a moment, only to see Eiwin staring at him with astonishment.

"Are you really sure you didn't know how to read or write?" she asked.

"I'm sure."

"At first, I thought you were just very talented, but this... this is incredible. Maybe you are a reincarnated cultivator."

Her words made him frown. "What do you mean by reincarnated?"

"Well, I wasn't being serious." She gave him an embarrassed smile.

"I know that." Red shook his head. "I've just never heard the term before."

"Ah, I see... Well, they say that when people die, their souls are guided through the Nether Realm. In that realm, some of these souls may find a way to live a second life. They're reborn, and they eventually recover their memories from their previous lives."

"Is that true?"

"Well, no one really knows, and no one has proven it for sure. Some of the people who claimed to be reincarnations turned out to be charlatans. Others, though... well, they may have a better case."

Her words sent Red into thought. His pensive expression seemed to trouble Eiwin.

"I shouldn't have said that earlier," she said. "I demeaned your achievements with my comment about reincarnation. Although your talent is rare, that doesn't mean it's because of someone else's knowledge. I apologize."

Eiwin bowed her head slightly, a remorseful look on her face. Red was taken aback by the gesture, and for a few seconds, he didn't know how to respond.

"It's fine," he said. "I wasn't worried by what you said... I just found it curious."

In fact, what she had said didn't necessarily apply to Red's case. His first memory of this world was as a grown child and not as a newborn, but he still had those strange dreams to consider. He lived different lives in them. He never felt that his memories from these dreams belonged to him, as they didn't change his way of thinking or awaken any hidden knowledge. Whatever the case, his interest in reincarnation was genuine. After all, it might involve his origins.

"I see." Eiwin seemed relieved by his words. "Either way, I feel like our lessons won't last much longer at your rate of improvement." For some reason, she looked sad when she said that. "Soon enough, you'll be able to learn things on your own."

"Maybe. But there are still things I can't learn from a book."

"You're right..." A smile returned to her face. "Speaking of that, is there anything you'd like to ask me?"

There's a lot I'd like to ask...

Obviously, Red couldn't do it, though. He'd already revealed the existence of moonstones to Goulth and hadn't gotten what he had wanted out of it, so there was no point in asking Eiwin about them. There was, however, something else she could help him with.

"Can you show me the map of the region again?" Red asked.

CHAPTER 89

FAVOR

EIWIN BROUGHT THE MAP OUT. "What do you want to know?"

"You said there are lots of bandits around the forest, right?" Red asked. "Where exactly are they located?"

"Well, it's hard to say for sure." Eiwin pointed at part of the forest. "We think they mostly keep to the hills because they have an easier time hiding there. We didn't have to worry much about them in the past, since monsters would block their path. However, now they've been spreading throughout the entire forest."

"I assume it's not normal for them to be so close to the city."

"It's not," she confirmed. "Even if Master Frida hadn't entrusted us with a task, we would still need to investigate this."

This piqued Red's interest. "When exactly are you going to do that?"

"Preferably in a week, after Rimold returns."

That's too long.

He changed topics. "What about the area we met in? Where was that, exactly?"

"That should be..." Eiwin searched across the map before pointing at a spot. "Around here."

Red looked where she pointed. It was near the river, at the very edge of the map. "That's very far from town. What exactly were you searching for down there?"

"Well, you know, we were looking for the reason behind the monsters' disappearance. A hunter said that he saw a large creature in that area, so we went to investigate."

"And did you find anything?"

"Not at all," Eiwin said. "We spent almost two days searching the area, but even with Rog's help, we didn't find any trace of such a creature."

That made Red feel more at ease. He'd more or less gotten the information he wanted, but kept asking more questions in order to conceal his true interests and avoid arousing suspicion. After the lesson was over, he left the library and took some time to consider his own plans.

Unsurprisingly, there were many bandit nests between him and his goal. Red was confident in his sneaking abilities, but he wasn't as familiar with the forest compared to the tunnels. He knew better than to underestimate such a challenge.

I need to be better prepared.

The only problem was that he didn't know how much time he had. However, Red had other pressing matters to worry about first.

After lunch, he secluded himself in his room, excusing himself for cultivation. He continued to work at the next Upper Leg acupoint, and to his surprise, he could feel it giving way. Perhaps in a few days, he could completely open it.

Once he was done with practice, he looked through the book on minerals again.

There were still so many things Red didn't understand inside, but he recognized more words this time around. Unfortunately, even with his newly acquired knowledge, he still didn't find any mention of moonstones. He could only conclude the material was unknown, as Goulth had claimed.

Before he knew it, the sunlight coming through the window grew faint. Night was fast approaching, and with it, Red's fate. Given the circumstances, he could no longer focus on anything else. He decided to patiently await his destiny in his bed.

The sunlight grew fainter, and he closed his eyes in anticipation. Soon enough, a familiar sensation sliced into his mind, and Red could feel the same overpowering gaze from yesterday settling upon him. Its supernatural pressure covered him once more.

It's still there.

This time he was prepared for it, though. Red managed to resist the influence of the gaze, concentrating on detecting any potential changes to his body. Nothing happened in the following minutes, but he didn't let his guard down.

It wasn't until over an hour had passed that he allowed himself to relax.

It's not absorbing anything...

Red felt an enormous weight fall from his shoulders. He didn't have to worry about dying tonight, it seemed.

Once he managed to calm himself down, he got up from his bed and walked outside. He worried that looking at the moon might prompt some reaction from the creature, so he avoided glancing up. Now that he knew the curse was probably not going to strike again so soon, he felt more confident in his plan.

Red walked over to Rog's room and knocked on the door. He heard footsteps from inside before the door opened slightly, the hunter staring at him through the gap.

"What do you want?"

"Do you think I could travel through the forest on my own?" Red asked.

"You're a quick learner and fast on your feet, so you'd probably be fine," Rog said. "But I wouldn't fancy your chances if some bandits got on your trail. You're still too weak to take on a group of them in combat."

"How likely are they to notice me?"

"Depends." He shrugged. "Not all bandits are created equal. But there's a lot of them out there, so chances are pretty high if you go deeper into the forest."

Red had more or less arrived at the same conclusion. Yet hearing it from an experienced hunter like Rog made him confident of his judgment.

"Do you have a smaller bow?" he asked.

"Might have. One second." The man closed the door. Red heard items being shuffled around. A minute later, Rog opened the door again, carrying a bow in his hand.

"Here, a short bow."

He accepted the weapon and examined it. Indeed, compared to the other bow, this one was much easier to handle for someone of his size.

Red frowned. "If you had a smaller bow the entire time, why didn't you give it to me earlier?"

"I forgot it was there. Besides, it's weaker than a longbow. I don't really like using it."

Red understood his point, but he was less concerned with power than accuracy. Compared to a longbow, this weapon was more reliable.

"Do you have knives too?" he asked.

"Yeah, sure." The hunter pulled a few blades from his belt and handed them over.

Red tested their weight before nodding in satisfaction. "Can I keep all of this?"

Rog shrugged, not seeming to care. "Sure, just don't tell Eiwin."

"Alright." Red walked off on his own.

Rog likewise went inside his room and closed the door. The two of them went about their business as if the interaction had never happened.

Red returned to his room and took stock of his newly acquired equipment. He felt confident in his armaments, but he knew weapons alone weren't enough preparation for a trip. He needed rations and medicine, as well as other camping items.

Most important of all, Red still didn't feel confident about his chances. Both Rog and Eiwin had told him about the bandits in the forest. Could he truly sneak the whole way and remain completely unnoticed?

He trusted Rog's assessment, and if the man said he would likely encounter bandits, then that was probably the truth. These bandits were clever, well-armed, and many had opened quite a few veins. If Red were dealing with monsters, he would feel surer of himself, but that wasn't the case here.

If they noticed him, he didn't know whether he could escape or win in a fight. That being said, Red had faced worse odds in the past, and he doubted his task would be as treacherous as sneaking through spider territory. Still, a question remained—did he have to take the risk of going alone? Unlike in the underground, where he had no choice, he had other options now.

Red considered asking someone else to come along, but he was hesitant. Rog, the best option, had no reason to help him, and he was the most unpredictable of the lot. Eiwin and Goulth would probably be willing to help, but Red felt he would need to reveal more of his background in order to convince them. Allen would go without question, but he immediately eliminated him as an option. There was a risk that any of them would reveal his intentions to the others, Allen most of all.

In the end, no option was ideal. Red was seriously considering going alone until he suddenly had an idea.

What about...

The thought gave him pause, but in the end, he decided to give it a try.

Red left his room and began searching for the person he had in mind. He didn't need to look very far. The unmistakable sounds of heavy strikes echoed from their point of origin, the training field.

He approached and saw Narcha hitting a training dummy with a wooden sword. This time, she didn't look nearly as angry compared to when he first saw her.

Interested in learning more about her combat skills, Red watched from afar. She wielded a heavy weapon similar to her iron saber, but it didn't look like the weight had any impact on her movements as she twirled it in her hands. Narcha chained together blow after blow, each one fiercer and faster than the last.

To the untrained eye, it looked as if there were no rhyme or reason behind her strikes, but Red had seen enough fighting to know this wasn't the case. She always struck the training dummy with precision, and every move was made with the next one in mind. Unlike what her hotheaded personality might suggest, Narcha was meticulous in combat.

In fact, Red couldn't help but be reminded of Viran as he watched her practice.

A few minutes later, Narcha concluded her exercise and turned around. Once she saw Red staring at her from behind the fence, her face immediately soured.

"Are you spying on me?" she asked in her usual unfriendly tone.

Red didn't get the question and just shrugged. "I'm not really hiding."

"Ugh, I mean... Never mind!" Narcha shook her head in annoyance. "What are you doing here, kid?"

"I have to ask you for something."

A look of surprise crossed her face, but she promptly remembered their conversation from a few days ago. "Is it about that favor?"

"Yes."

"I thought it would take you a good while longer to come up with something. Well, what do you want? I won't do anything evil for you, and whatever you want has to be within my capabilities."

"It shouldn't be a problem for you," Red said. "But first, you need to promise me not to tell anyone about this."

"Promise you?" Her eyes narrowed. "Is it that serious?"

"Not really, but I would rather no one else knew about it."

She relented. "Fine! I promise not to tell anyone. Is that enough for you?"

It's as good as I'm getting, I guess.

Red nodded.

"Then what do you want me to do?" Narcha repeated.

"I need you to escort me on a trip into the forest."

At that, her glare intensified.

CHAPTER 90
PREPARATIONS

Narcha regarded him with a suspicious gaze. "A trip to the forest? For what?"

"I need to get something I left behind near the place we first met," Red explained.

"You want to go all the way back there?!" The warrior was appalled. "What did you even forget?"

"It's a secret." He wouldn't reveal the items he had hidden, no matter what.

"Ugh, you..." His secrecy clearly bothered Narcha, but she waved him off. "Fine. I'll talk with the others, and over the next few days, we can get a group to set off."

"You can't tell the others," Red insisted. "This is meant to be a secret."

Narcha scoffed. "What, so you just want the two of us going on this trip?" However, once she noticed Red's silence, her expression changed again. "Gods, you're serious?"

"The only reason I'm asking for help is that I'm not confident in setting off on my own," he said. "If you didn't owe me anything, I would have risked it by myself."

Narcha face turned grave. "Are you crazy, kid? Why would you take all these risks!"

"I'm asking you for help, though?"

"But making that kind of trip is dangerous!"

Red frowned. "What, are you not confident you can deal with the bandits?"

"Of course I am!" Narcha seemed offended. "But making that kind of trip into the forest is not that simple. I might have the combat part figured out, but what about scouting? That place can be a maze if you don't know it well enough, and I'm not an experienced hunter like Rog."

"I can handle the scouting."

"You?" She looked skeptical. "You've barely been on a single hunt with Rog. How could you possibly know anything about the forest?"

"I don't know much, but our path isn't complicated. As long as we follow the river, we'll eventually arrive at our destination."

Red still remembered the hill-cave he had exited from, as well as where he'd hidden his stash. If they found the right landmark, then he could retrieve his items.

"That's a very roundabout trip," Narcha said. "It would take us more than three days if we decide to follow the river."

"But it's still doable, right?" he asked.

"It is..." She hesitated, considering the possibility. "We'll probably come across some bandits, but as long as none of them have opened their Spiritual Seas, I can handle it. There is another problem, though..."

"What problem?" Red asked.

"What do you intend to tell the others?"

Red shook his head. "We don't tell them anything. We can leave a message for them to find after we're gone."

"That might cut it with most of them, but it definitely won't work with Eiwin," Narcha pointed out. "Do you remember how worried she was the other day? Even if you say we'll eventually be back, she'll definitely come looking for us. Hells, she'll probably rope Rog into following too."

Red had expected as much. Eiwin was protective of her fellow Sect members, and given the rising bandit problem, he couldn't blame her. Still, this was something that he needed to see through at all costs.

"We might not be able to shake Rog off our trail, but they don't know where we're going," he said. "As long as we remain one step ahead, there'll be nothing to worry about."

He knew the hunter was a highly skilled tracker, but he wasn't a clairvoyant. There was no way he would be able to follow their tracks in such a short amount of time when he didn't even know where they were headed. The forest was vast, after all.

"You put a lot of thought into this, huh?" Narcha raised her eyebrows. "How soon do you need this done?"

"As soon as possible."

In fact, Red hoped to leave tonight, but he knew preparations would take time.

"I need to get more than a week's worth of supplies ready, and if I have to avoid letting anyone know..." She trailed off, thinking through the problem. "Earliest I can do is tomorrow night."

Red nodded. That was the second-best option.

"We can meet here tomorrow night," he said. "I can lead us through the path Rog used to go through town unnoticed."

"Whatever you say, kid." Narcha still looked skeptical but didn't say anything else about it. "Just make sure you're prepared. I can fight off any bandits, but I can't nanny you at the same time."

"As long as you do your part, I'll do mine," Red promised.

With the preparations done, he walked back to his room. Now that everything was set, Red just needed to wait. Unfortunately for him, it didn't seem like he would get much rest under the moon's gaze.

The next day arrived. Red had tried his best to sleep, but the pressure on his mind was unrelenting. Although he fared much better than the previous day, it was impossible to relax under the moon being's presence, and his sleep had been fraught with interruptions.

This wasn't the first time Red had gone without sleep, but it wasn't ideal. Preferably, he wanted to be fully rested before departing on a long journey.

But I can't arouse suspicion. Not right now...

With some effort, Red rose from his bed and went outside, where he found Domeron sitting on his rocking chair as usual. He walked up to him.

The man noticed his approach. "Have you figured it out yet?"

"... Not yet."

"Then why are you here?"

"I think I could use the training either way."

His words made Domeron frown, but his reluctance only lasted for a moment before he got up with a sigh.

"Fine."

The pair walked to the training field. Red stood in the center of the obstacle course, ready. Domeron began throwing the sandbags his way, but soon enough, his lack of sleep became evident.

A sandbag hit him straight in the back and sent Red sprawling to the ground.

Domeron sighed in disappointment. "You're slow." He shook his head. "This is all pointless."

"It's fine." Red got up. "Please, let's continue."

Domeron scoffed. "Why, just so you can get hit again?"

His laugh was met with silence and a determined gaze. For a second, Domeron was taken aback, but he still nodded.

"Fine, but I won't go easy just because you're tired."

They restarted the training. This time, Red fared better, even in his sleep-deprived state. Before long, he passed the twenty-second mark, leaving Domeron stunned. However, the man's expression changed a moment later, as if he'd realized something.

The swinging bags suddenly accelerated, taking Red by surprise. One of them hit him in the face and sent him tumbling.

He held his cheek in pain and looked up at Domeron. "You cheated."

"You're the one who cheated!" The man glared at him.

Red realized what the man was referring to. The reason he'd managed to dodge for so long in his tired state wasn't because of his skill. Over the last couple of days, he had memorized the patterns Domeron used to launch the obstacles, allowing him to predict what was coming next and preemptively dodge the attack. The man had been quick to pick up on this, though, and thrown him a curveball.

"This is not a game to see how long you can last, kid. This is training!" He leveled his wooden sword at him. "It's about learning how to move in combat."

"If an enemy is stupid and just keeps throwing the same attacks at me, shouldn't I take advantage of it?" Red asked.

Domeron looked dumbfounded at his words. But a moment later, a dangerous grin came over his expression, giving Red a bad feeling.

"I underestimated you," Domeron said. "You're smarter than I thought.

And you're right, I need to adapt my training depending on the student. Since this is too simple and stupid for you, I'm sure we can turn up the intensity a bit."

He walked away from the obstacles before standing in the middle of the training field.

"What are we doing now?" Red asked.

"Well, you told me before you used to train with real weapons, right? I can't do that yet, but I think a more direct approach may benefit you." Domeron waved him over with his wooden sword. "We can use wooden weapons. I hit you, and you try to dodge. How does that sound?"

It sounds dangerous.

Red, however, wasn't one to back down from an opportunity to push himself. At least not when his life wasn't on the line. He approached the swordsman, his wooden baton in hand.

Unfortunately for him, he had underestimated Domeron.

The only frame of reference Red had for training was Viran. The soldier had been brutish and fierce during their sparring sessions, not really caring whether he hurt him.

Domeron's attacks weren't as strong, but they were faster and more precise. Every time the wooden sword struck his skin, Red felt a stinging pain, yet he barely had time to process it before the next attack came.

He would have thought that this was a form of punishment if Domeron hadn't instructed him throughout. Even as his weapon struck, the swordsman still barked information at Red, providing accurate assessments and useful feedback on how to improve.

By the end, he was completely spent, his entire body aching. A few welts had even sprouted on his skin.

Domeron stepped back and gave Red a satisfied smile. "So, how did you enjoy today's training? Are you sure you don't want to go back to the obstacle course?"

"I prefer it like this," he said.

"Hah, I thought you would say that—" Domeron caught himself as soon as he registered Red's words. The man was stunned.

"What did you say?" he asked.

"I'd like to do this again," Red said. "I feel like I can improve much faster like this."

Domeron was practically speechless. "You're a weird kid, but I suppose all proper cultivators are a bit weird." He shrugged. "Still, I think it might be too much strain on your body to do this every day."

"As often as possible, then."

"Fine. But you're going to have to convince Eiwin and Goulth about this. They won't be happy."

"What's going on here?!" As if on cue, a woman's voice called out from nearby.

Indeed, Eiwin wasn't very happy about what Red was doing.

Red was ultimately excused from training for the rest of the day. Eiwin was worried about his wounds and chided Domeron for his recklessness. Red, on his part, defended the swordsman, saying he'd approved of the training. In the end, she could only relent and respect his decision.

"You might be eager to improve, but pushing yourself too hard will be detrimental in the long run," Eiwin said. "You're still growing up, and it's important to strike a balance between training and rest with cultivation, too."

Red could see the sense in her words, but she was unaware of his predicament. With the threat of death hanging over his head, he needed to improve as quickly as he could. Some pain and bruises were negligible in comparison.

When he went to Goulth to have his wounds treated, the blacksmith's reaction was much different.

"Is that moron trying to kill my disciple?!" He gritted his teeth. "Is he just jealous? I'm gonna go and beat him up myself!"

Only Eiwin and Red's combined efforts finally calmed him down.

After that, he was excused from practice for the rest of the day. He used this opportunity to catch up on his sleep in preparation for the night's journey.

Red was abruptly woken up by a familiar sensation. The gaze settled upon him again, indicating the arrival of the night as surely as a rooster would crow at the sunrise.

The time to act was upon him.

CHAPTER 91

SETTING OFF

THE FIRST THING Red did was check if anyone was in the courtyard. After confirming it was clear, he left the room carrying his equipment and made his way to the training field. As he approached, he saw Narcha waiting for him. She wore her studded leather armor, as well as the long steel saber. Two large backpacks were at her side, stuffed full of supplies.

"You're punctual," Red commented.

Narcha snorted. "I take my work seriously." She gave him a peculiar look. "What's with the bow?"

"It's for shooting things."

"I know what it's for! I mean, do you even know how to use it?"

"More or less," he said. "I'm not as good as Rog, but I could probably do some damage with it."

"Hm, we'll see about that."

"Did anyone notice you?" Red asked.

Narcha shook her head. "They're used to me wandering off on my own every now and then, so it didn't raise any alarms."

"Good." Red fished a piece of paper out of his pocket and handed it to her. "Can you check if this is written properly?"

She took the note and read it.

"'I be back soon. The big lady is come with me.' What the fuck is this supposed to mean?"

"I just recently learned how to write," Red explained.

"Don't... leave that." Narcha sighed. "Ugh. Anyways, I already wrote my own note. You don't need to leave another one behind."

Red nodded and stowed his note away. As the two of them put on their backpacks, he pointed downhill.

"Follow me."

"What do you mean?" Narcha winced. "Do you even know where you're going?"

"I memorized the way Rog took to the forest," he said. "That way, we can make sure we're not followed. Just follow my lead and make sure to be sneaky."

"I don't need your advice, brat!" She sounded offended. "I know how to sneak if I need to."

Nevertheless, Narcha still followed behind him. Red weaved through the buildings and alleyways of the town, and soon enough, they were on one of the main streets. A few pedestrians were still walking around even this late at night, and some guards were stationed on patrol.

"Now's the important part," Red whispered. "We'll wait until everyone is past, and then we'll quickly make our way across this street."

Narcha spat to the side. "I already told you—I know what I'm doing!"

Her outburst caught the attention of an elderly woman walking nearby. She looked at the alley and noticed the warrior and the small child crouched inside.

Narcha gave her a fierce glare. "Piss off!"

The woman didn't need to hear it twice before she went running. Narcha cursed under her breath before noticing Red's judgmental gaze.

She sheepishly looked away. "That was just an accident..."

Red could only hope this wasn't an indication of how the rest of their trip would fare.

Eventually, they made it past the edge of town and into the farmlands. Red thought to employ the same strategy Rog had taught him by running through the fields, but Narcha shot down the idea. Instead, they settled on sneaking along the road downhill.

Red looked back multiple times to see if they were being followed, but his vision wasn't as good as Narcha's. He asked for her help just as often.

She shrugged. "No one I can see."

Though Red didn't let his guard down, this did give him some confidence.

They eventually reached the tree line. Red told his travel companion to stop.

Narcha was impatient. "What is it now, kid?"

"We can't keep going on the road," he said. "We need to travel through the forest."

"Already?" She frowned. "We're not even past the city limits."

"Last time I came here with Rog, bandits got on our trail pretty quickly. Who knows whether there'll be others watching us? If we just walk on the main road, they'll have a simple time spotting us."

"Bah!" Narcha threw her hands up. "Fine, but don't blame me if we take longer to get to our destination."

Red obviously wanted to travel faster, but not at the cost of his safety. He chose a different path through the forest this time around, avoiding the area where he and Rog had fought the bandits. He wondered if anyone had found the bodies, but it was likely the bandits' companions would be searching around that place.

As they walked through the forest, Red did his best to stave off the pressure of the moon's gaze. His physical capabilities weren't compromised, but the invisible weight made it hard to focus. Thankfully, this wasn't the first time he'd acted under unpleasant conditions.

Compared to what he'd gone through in his escape from the mine, this was much easier.

Although Red wasn't nearly as familiar with the forest environment, his underground experience served him well. He always kept his direction in mind when detouring past obstacles and watched for any signs of footprints or animal tracks.

Throughout the next hour, Narcha didn't say much, silently observing Red in action.

Finally, she broke the silence. "This isn't your first time doing this."

"Yeah, I did it with Rog a few days ago." Red shrugged.

"That's not what I meant. You seem experienced enough to travel through a place you haven't been before—or maybe you know this forest better than you let on. Not to mention, you also act like there might be an ambush waiting for us behind every tree."

Red didn't respond.

"Seems like you had to hide for a living at some point," Narcha said. "Was it from monsters or people?"

"... Both."

"I guess Domeron wasn't lying when he said you were a survivor, huh?" She smiled. "Do you ever get tired of hiding?"

"Sometimes. But my life is the most important thing at the end of the day."

She nodded. "That's a good point. I got tired of hiding a long time ago, though. Unfortunately, I can't say I'm strong enough to do what I want yet."

Narcha seemed pensive as she said this.

"You said you wanted to take revenge, right?" Red asked.

"Yeah, but it's just a dream right now. My targets are way too strong, and I can't even open my Spiritual Sea."

"Did you take the pill?"

She nodded. Red could guess the results from the sour look on her face.

"Are you sure you're fit to fight right now?"

"Fit to fight?" she said, offended. "Just a pill like that can't keep me down! I've fought under worse conditions in the past."

Red quietly reflected on her words. Although Narcha acted fine on the outside, he could tell something was bothering her on the inside. Something obvious.

"Is it that hard to open your Spiritual Sea?" he asked.

"It is," Narcha said. "The first time I tried it, I failed, but it didn't seem that hard. On my next tries, though, I kept falling short at the same point. No matter how I tried to do it or how much more experience I got, nothing changed. It's like this obstacle is so small and weak when I look at it, but no matter how hard I try, I can't break it."

"Is there really no way other than the pill?"

"There probably are, but none that I'd be willing to take."

When she mentioned that, Red couldn't help but recall the deal the blob had offered him. Indeed, there might be other ways to improve, but the price wasn't cheap.

"Maybe we'll find a genuine Parting Sea Pill for you," he said. "And then, later on, you can help me the same way."

This would be a good deal for him, since he would probably find himself in the same situation one day. Narcha, however, laughed at his suggestion.

"Hah, I wish it was that easy. Sadly, I don't have much time left to pull off a breakthrough, and even if I find a pill later, I might be too old at that point."

"Then what do you intend to do?" Red asked.

Although he hadn't known Narcha for long, she didn't seem like the type of person who would give up if there was still hope.

"If the situation gets that bad, then I'll bet the only thing I can bet." She looked at him with a grin. "My own life!"

Red stopped walking and stared back at her.

Narcha met his gaze, perplexed. "What is it?"

"You seem very willing to talk."

"And?"

"I thought you didn't trust me."

"Ugh..." His words seemed to take her by surprise. "Look, do you want me to shut up for the rest of the journey then, you brat?"

"No, this is fine," he said. "I'm sure I can learn something, even from someone like you."

He walked off without waiting for a response.

"Hey, what do you mean by that, you little shit?!" Narcha shouted before following behind him.

The next few hours were uneventful. Red kept his eyes peeled but didn't see any tracks. He had deliberately chosen a roundabout path to avoid meeting other people, and that also meant there wasn't much around to attract people in the first place.

They were already deep into the night when Narcha called for his attention.

"It's getting late," she said. "We should rest for the night."

"Not yet." Red shook his head. "I'd prefer if we traveled during the night and slept during the day."

"Are you sure that's a good idea?" Narcha said. "Although bandits are more active during the day, quite a few still try to ambush campers during the night too. Not to mention that staying still during the day might make us an easy target."

"You're right, but I prefer to move at night."

Of course, the real reason was that he simply couldn't sleep during the night with the moon's gaze on him. He couldn't tell that to Narcha, though.

"We can find a secluded spot in a few hours and camp there," he said. "I'm confident I'll be able to hide us."

"Whatever you say." Although Narcha still seemed skeptical, there wasn't much worry in her expression. Red guessed she didn't need much sleep, since she had opened all twelve Spiritual Veins.

As they continued their walk, Red suddenly caught sight of something.

"Wait." He held his hand up, calling them to a stop.

"What, did you see something?" She scanned their surroundings, her hand grabbing the hilt of her saber.

Red crouched down and studied the ground. After pushing some leaves aside, he saw signs of human tracks—quite a few of them. He pointed it out to the warrior.

"Group of four people, I think." Red made a rough estimate based on the markings.

"People, here?" Narcha frowned. "There's nothing to be found in this part of the forest. Unless..."

"Bandits."

"This close to town? I suppose with what happened to you guys, it's not unexpected."

Red nodded and took an old piece of paper out of his pocket.

"What's that?" Narcha asked.

"It's a map I got from the bandits."

"A map?" She seemed shocked. "Why didn't you tell us about it?"

"Rog said it wasn't important," Red said. "He said it just points out the bandit's hideouts, but everyone knows where they live anyways."

"Ugh, that idiot. Even if it's unimportant, it might help us with our missions at some point... What are you looking for, anyway?"

"According to the map, there are no bandit camps around here." Red pointed at a spot close to town.

"Then you think it's not bandits?"

"Not necessarily," he said. "But if you wanted to start operating closer to town, then wouldn't this kind of isolated area be a perfect place?"

Narcha's expression fell.

CHAPTER 92

DISCOVERY

"YOU THINK the bandits have a camp here?" Narcha asked.

"It would be a good base of operations," Red said after some thought. "No one really travels through this area."

She seemed unconvinced. "They're still too close to the city. There's a high chance someone would notice them, eventually. Once that happens, the Baron won't sit by for long."

"Maybe it's not a permanent camp. Or maybe they aren't worried about getting discovered. It's hard to tell..."

Although Narcha tried to think of a counterargument, it was clear she was genuinely considering the possibility. She had a troubled look on her face.

"These morons are insane. What has gotten into their heads to make them risk provoking the town guard? Aren't they afraid for their own lives?"

"People don't risk their lives for no reason," Red reasoned. "Maybe they have something to rely on, or maybe they have no choice. We can't know for now."

At that, he kept walking.

"Hey!" Narcha followed after him. "Do you really plan to move on just like that?"

"What else do you want to do?" Red asked.

"We need to see if there's really a camp in this area!"

"Are you confident you can take on an entire bandit camp by yourself?"

"I don't plan on fighting anyone," she said. "But we should still check."

"It's too risky. We aren't prepared to deal with that, and neither of us are as good at tracking as Rog. We might just end up getting lost or getting found out."

"Ugh..." Narcha didn't want to admit it, but she seemed to know he was right. "I don't feel comfortable just leaving this up to chance. What if they kill someone just because we didn't act?"

"They would probably never do something like that, if they want to avoid being found out. Besides, if there's a camp, it'll probably still be here when we come back. If it isn't, then these bandits are just passing through, in which case there's no point in chasing them. Or maybe these people aren't even bandits. We can't know."

Of course, Red was more worried about a detour in their mission than anything.

"Fine." Narcha nodded with reluctance. "You really don't act like a child at all. Did you know that?"

You're not the first one to say that.

Red didn't respond and resumed his travel instead. Narcha followed while grumbling at his silence.

They chose to give a wide berth to the area where he'd seen the tracks. That made their path even more roundabout, but Red thought it safer. Along the way, he found more human tracks, making him more convinced of the existence of a bandit camp.

"We might end up being followed," he said, his concern growing.

"It's fine." Narcha still didn't look worried. "It won't be my first time killing bandits in this forest."

Red recalled his second night on the surface, when she and Rog had wiped out a group of bandits by themselves. Her confidence in her strength was definitely warranted.

Thankfully, through luck or not, the pair didn't meet anyone over the next few hours. When the first signs of the sunrise appeared, Red decided to make camp. He picked out a spot covered by heavy vegetation, much to Narcha's dismay.

"We're sleeping here, in the middle of the trees?" she asked.

"Yes, so we stay hidden."

"Ugh. I'm not used to this, but fine." She was quick to concede to him at this point.

"How are we splitting watch duty?" he asked. Of all the impressive and clever things he'd seen the Sect do, he still found watch duty one of the most ingenious.

"You can sleep first," Narcha said. "I can go longer without sleeping than you, anyways."

Red didn't argue with her on that front. He laid out his sleeping bag on an empty spot and tucked himself in. As the sun rose, the moon's gaze faded, and he managed to relax.

He had put on a facade in front of Narcha, but in truth, Red was mentally exhausted. The feeling of being watched had taken a toll on him, and his experience under pressure was the only thing that had kept him functioning.

With such worries on his mind, Red went to sleep as Narcha kept watch over the camp.

"Kid, wake up!"

Her voice immediately woke him up. Red cringed and sat up in a daze. He looked at his surroundings in confusion before spotting the warrior leaning against a tree, grinning at him.

"You must have been exhausted, huh?"

Red was confused by her comment, but then he looked up. The dark tinge of night was already spreading through the sky. Dusk had fallen without his knowledge. He touched his temple, feeling if there was something wrong.

Narcha noticed his strange behavior. "Hey, kid, are you listening to me? Are you alright?"

"I'm okay. I just feel weird."

She frowned. "What do you mean?"

"I don't remember falling asleep."

"Well, that's how sleeping works. You don't really remember the moment you fall asleep."

"No, that's not what I mean..." Red shook his head. "It doesn't matter."

He got up and checked his equipment.

"How long did I sleep for?" he asked. Of course, he had a rough idea from the sky, but he still wanted to confirm it.

"Twelve hours, give or take." Narcha said.

Red winced. He didn't remember ever sleeping that long before, not even when injured or bordering on unconsciousness. He could only blame it on the stress accrued from the moon's gaze, but the feeling he was missing something still lingered.

"Are you sure you're alright?" Narcha asked again.

"I'm fine," Red insisted. "Did you get any sleep?"

She shrugged. "Not really."

"Do you need any sleep?"

"Not right now."

"Then let's keep moving."

At his prompting, the pair continued their eastward march.

According to Narcha's estimate, they would arrive at the river either today or tomorrow. After that, the rest of the journey would consist of following the riverbed as it flowed south.

"The real danger begins there," Narcha said. "Lots of bandits near the hill lands and along the river."

"Why are there so many bandits in this region?" Red asked. Even to someone who didn't know much about the surface world, the number of bandits in this rather desolate region still seemed high.

"There are bandits everywhere in the world, kid," the warrior explained. "But you're right. This region has had a bandit problem over the last few months. Lots of bad things aligned to create the shitstorm we have on our hands now."

"You mean the disappearance of the monsters?"

"That's one of them," Narcha said. "But other things happened too. Most of these bandits are deserters from a neighboring kingdom's army. They disbanded after suffering a defeat at the hand of the Empire, and the kingdom itself was destroyed."

Red was confused. "And the soldiers became bandits, just like that?"

She scoffed. "A lot of them had no choice, or so they would have you believe. They're just pathetic soldiers who weren't brave enough to stay and fight while their country was conquered. I bet the Empire lets them live so they can spread chaos to their neighbors.

"Is Rickard a soldier too?"

Narcha froze mid-step, staring at him. "Where did you hear that name?"

"One of the bandits Rog killed threatened him with that name. Said he was part of Rickard's gang."

"Fucking moron!" Narcha gritted her teeth. "He didn't even mention anything to us!"

Red was taken aback by her explosive reaction. "He said that it wasn't important, and that this Rickard wouldn't find out about it either way."

"He's right about that, but there's more to it than this!" Narcha tried to calm herself down. "If these guys were direct subordinates of Rickard, then the man himself might've sent them here."

"Then, do you mean..."

"There are probably more from his gang in the region! Maybe even Rickard himself."

A Spiritual Sea cultivator running loose would pose a huge problem for their plans. Red shuddered to think how dangerous a human opponent on the level of the awakened centipede or the insectoid could be, but he was in no place to retreat. When he looked at Narcha, he saw he wasn't the only one who understood the threat.

"Fuck, if I knew this, I would have never brought you out here, kid..." Narcha held her head. "Eiwin is going to kill me!"

"Can't you defeat them?" Red asked.

"Of course I can!" She looked offended by the question. "Everyone barring Rickard, that is. The problem is doing it while I'm protecting your ass!"

She paced around, mumbling to herself and cursing Rog under her breath.

"If it makes you feel any better, I would have gone either way," Red said. "With or without your help."

"Bah, you're insane!" Narcha threw up her hands in resignation. "What's even so important for you to risk your life like that?"

He didn't reply.

"But you're right," she said. "I already took you along, either way. Now we have to be even more careful of our surroundings, though."

Red decided not to tell her he was already being as attentive as he could.

They continued traveling, but this time Narcha was wary of everything around her. She annoyed Red by instructing him to search for tracks in certain areas and watch out for traps. He considered telling her off, since as far as he could tell, she didn't seem to know what she was talking about. But as soon as he saw the anger on her face, he decided against it.

As night arrived, Red could feel the lunar gaze on him once more. He'd grown used to the unnatural pressure over the last couple of days. Although the strain was still there, he didn't struggle as much to function.

Eventually, though, Narcha called their march to a stop. "Wait!"

She crouched down and hid behind a tree, and Red followed her actions without hesitation. She looked over at him and pointed forward.

"I think I saw some human shapes up ahead," she said. "They're too far to tell, though."

Red squinted and tried to look where she pointed. He saw no movement, but considering his vision was worse than hers, he didn't doubt her claims. He hurried to come up with a plan.

"I'll flank them from the right," Red whispered. "You can just keep sneaking forward and face them head-on."

She frowned. "You just want me to go straight at them?"

"Isn't that what you're good at? Throwing yourself at a problem?"

"You little... Fine, just make sure you stay hidden!"

Red refrained from saying he was better at stealth and hiding than her. He put aside his backpack, freeing himself from the additional weight, and took out his bow and quiver. As Narcha edged forward, he coordinated his advance with her, sneaking behind trees some distance behind her.

Soon, they had walked far enough that Red could see the shapes she was referring to. They were, however, completely still, and he couldn't help but feel something was wrong.

A gust of wind blew against him, and Red smelled a familiar metallic scent. It immediately put him on alert.

"Fucking hell..." Narcha said, not bothering to lower her voice.

Red saw her stand up and walk directly towards the scene. Since the woman had abandoned any semblance of stealth, he stepped out from behind the trees and followed.

When he arrived at the clearing, the human shapes were revealed to him.

Corpses. And blood.

A scene of absolute carnage.

CHAPTER 93

INVESTIGATING

RED HAD SEEN gore in the past, but nothing quite like this. There were body parts scattered all over the place—limbs, organs, and pieces of flesh, and not one of the corpses was completely intact. He couldn't even tell what some of the body parts were.

"God, this smell..." Not far ahead, Narcha held a hand to her nose, but otherwise seemed unbothered by the scene.

"It's the bandits..." Red said.

She watched his approach, her eyes widening. "Aren't you bothered by this?"

He shook his head. Once one had seen enough blood, one became desensitized to the sight. Red was far beyond that point.

"How do you know it's the bandits?" she said.

"It's their armor," he pointed out. "It looks similar to the bandits that attacked Rog and me."

Leather armor, mismatched pieces of equipment in disrepair and patched together with sloppy technique—all telltale signs of bandit equipment. Apparently, it had offered the men no protection against whatever had attacked them.

"You're right," she agreed. "Uh, how many corpses are here, anyway?"

The fact that it wasn't obvious was a testament to how grim the scene was. Red studied the gore, counting as many heads, limbs, or torsos as he could find.

"Four... I think."

"The same four from those tracks earlier?" Narcha asked.

"Impossible to know."

She nodded and approached the scene, stepping over any puddles of blood.

"We need to examine the bodies, but..." Narcha cringed as she examined the gore. "Ugh, Rog is the one who usually looks into these things."

"I think it's safe to say a monster did this, right?" Red asked.

"I certainly don't think it was a human..." Narcha crouched down and studied a severed torso. A large gash had split it apart from the rest of the body.

"I have never seen a monster be this brutal, though. The corpses don't seem very old, either."

While she was occupied with the corpses, Red searched the rest of the scene for clues. He quickly noticed something peculiar.

"Their corpses are whole," Red said.

"Whole?" Narcha frowned. "Are you sure we're looking at the same thing?"

"I mean, no parts are missing. They're all split apart, sure, but everything is here. Limbs, heads, torsos..."

Narcha was surprised by his words. She double-checked the carnage herself, and sure enough, she found he was telling the truth.

"That's strange," she said, confused. "This is not how a normal monster behaves."

Monsters weren't known for wasting food. Even in the underground, the giant insects only attacked to defend their territory or hunt. Whatever did this had left the corpses untouched.

"Not only that, but this whole scene is weird." Narcha pointed at a torso. "I doubt these bandits would have survived even one of these wounds, but the monster went through the trouble of ripping their bodies apart... And in the end, it didn't even eat them? What kind of monster does that?"

The situation grew stranger by the second.

"Maybe it wasn't a monster?" Red suggested.

"No way. I've seen enough corpses to know these wounds were caused by claws."

"Can you tell what kind of monster could have done it, then?"

"Tree-bark bears have strong claws," Narcha said after some thought. "But there are no bite marks, and they're fond of biting. Not to mention they aren't this brutal with their prey, and they would probably have eaten everything... No, whatever did this is not native to this forest."

Red trusted Narcha's knowledge on this. After all, she had spent years fighting monsters in the region.

"Do you see any tracks?" she asked.

"Not anywhere nearby." It was the first thing he had checked. "I only see the bandits' footprints."

Narcha was unconvinced. "How could that be? Something this strong should be big enough to leave tracks. Not to mention, the claw marks are fairly large, too."

"I can check again. But either it's incredibly light on its feet, or it knows how to hide its tracks."

"A monster that knows how to hide its tracks? If it's that intelligent, it can't even be considered a monster anymore!"

Red recalled the insectoids, who seemed to be as smart as humans. By Narcha's account, did that mean they weren't monsters? Red didn't linger on the topic, since these classifications were purely for human convenience, as far as he could tell.

He suggested another possibility. "Maybe it doesn't move by foot."

"What, did it fly around?" Narcha's eyes narrowed. "Or maybe..." She looked up at the trees.

"Maybe it moved through the branches," he said, following her line of logic.

As soon as the possibility arose, he went to check the tree trunks. At first, he saw no signs, but after climbing one of the trees, he discovered something.

"Claws marks." He waved Narcha over. "Pretty deep ones."

"Really?" She seemed excited. "Do you see where they're headed?"

"How am I supposed to tell?" They weren't like footprints, where you could follow the direction one was walking.

"Bah, this is why we need Rog!" She threw her arms up in frustration. "Check the other trees. See if you can find more claw marks."

Red did as he was told. The forest was dense, though, and it took the better part of an hour for him to find two consistent trails of claw marks. He pointed them out to Narcha.

"So, it either came from the north and headed southeast, or it came from the southeast and headed north," she said. "The first one seems more likely."

"Why is that?" Red asked.

"Well, for one, heading southeast would just bring you deeper into the forest, and we recently confirmed that there are no monsters there. To the north, though, there are still plenty of monsters."

Red understood her rationale, but upon further reflection, he realized a problem. "Aren't we headed southeast?"

The warrior shook her head. "Not directly."

"But we might still end up in the same region, right?"

Narcha smiled at the question. "Definitely."

"Aren't you worried we might meet it?"

"No, I'm excited! It's been a long time since I fought a beast."

"Do you even know what kind of monster this is?"

"No idea."

"Isn't that dangerous?"

"Probably." She seemed unbothered. "But aren't you curious to find out what's behind this kind of carnage?"

Not if it comes at the cost of my own life.

Red could only sigh in resignation. Earlier, Narcha had been worried about having to protect Red from Rickard and his bandits, but now that she had a mystery to explore, she didn't look nearly as concerned.

"But you're right." Narcha nodded solemnly. "My task is still protecting you. But if we happened to come across a monster on our way, then I would have no choice but to kill it, right?"

Red ignored her and turned back to the corpses.

"Hey, what are you doing?" she asked.

"Searching the bodies," he said. "They might have something useful on them."

"Is there even anything left in there?" Narcha asked, skeptical. "Not even their armor is undamaged."

"We'll find out."

Red searched the legs and waists of the bandits, untroubled by the blood, as Narcha watched him curiously from the side. There were a few pouches that carried coins and other miscellaneous items, but all their weapons were still sheathed in their scabbards.

"They didn't take out their weapons," Red realized. "They were taken by surprise."

Narcha laughed. "So, extremely sharp claws, climbs on trees, and also stealthy. Quite a challenge, isn't it?"

He chose to ignore her and continued his search through the bandits' belongings. In the end, he found another blood-soaked map. He couldn't discern many details, but what he could make out was clear enough.

"It's the same map I got from the other bandits."

"Makes sense," Narcha said. "They were probably from the same group."

She leaned back onto a tree with her arms crossed, watching Red work with an indifferent look.

"Are you just gonna stand there and do nothing?" he said.

"What? You're already messing with the dead bodies. Why should I do it too?"

Red sighed and turned back to the task at hand. After a few minutes, he finished his search, finding nothing else of interest.

"They weren't carrying any supplies?" Narcha asked.

Red shook his head.

"Guess they must really have a camp around here..." She sighed. "Well, we should get out of here before their companions find out they're missing."

He agreed. After confirming they hadn't missed anything, the pair started traveling east again, but this time Red carried his short bow in hand as he carefully scanned the trees around him.

"You're weirder than I thought," Narcha said from behind.

He didn't respond, scouting the way ahead.

"I mean, we just saw a bloodbath," she continued. "Even some warriors would puke after seeing that, but you didn't even blink!"

Red shook his head. "Why do you feel the need to say that out loud? You know I won't tell you anything."

Although his voice was still as impassive as ever, he was frustrated with the direction of their conversation.

"I wasn't trying to probe into your background, you little brat!" Narcha glared at him. "It was just a compliment."

He frowned. "How so?"

"I mean, it was a compliment about how you're more collected than many cultivators I've met before."

"Is that supposed to be good for a child?" Red asked.

"How should I know? Ask yourself that, if you're curious!" She took a deep breath, calming herself down. "I'm just trying to make conversation, you know."

"I understand." Red fell into thought. "You're not as dumb as you look."

Narcha froze.

"What's that supposed to mean?" she said in an icy tone.

"It's a compliment." Red said. "I'm just making conversation."

"Do you want to die?!"

The two continued their travel for the rest of the night, and after a few hours, they heard the unmistakable noise of rushing water.

"We're at the Crystal River," Narcha said.

That's halfway there.

"We should find somewhere to sleep." She examined her surroundings. "Probably away from the river. Its noise can drown out other sounds, and we don't want to be caught by surprise."

Red agreed. As they moved through the trees, though, she suddenly froze in place.

"Wait." Narcha pulled him back in alarm.

Red looked at her, confused. "What is it?"

"I hear something."

That immediately put him on alert.

"It's coming from that direction." Narcha pointed to the east.

"From the river?" he asked.

She nodded. "We should see what it is before we decide to camp in this area."

He would have preferred to just avoid the place altogether, but he felt a dire need for sleep after a night under the lunar gaze, and the sun was close to rising.

"Do the same thing you did before," Narcha said. "The flanking thing, I mean."

Red nodded and walked off, bow and arrow in hand. As he got closer to the river, he began hearing the noises too, and looked back at the warrior. She was frowning in confusion, but signaled for him to continue forward.

As he wondered why she was frowning, he came closer, and the sounds grew clearer.

That's... crying?

It wasn't just crying. It was a cry of pain. Narcha cursed under her breath. "Fucking hells..."

As they walked further, the trees cleared and the river was revealed to them. However, what Red saw made him stop in his tracks.

Blood, limbs, gore spread everywhere. Another scene of carnage.

One of the victims, though, lay in the center of the unholy scene, still alive.

CHAPTER 94

REANIMATION

MORE BANDITS...

Neither of them approached the scene immediately. Red had noticed something strange about the carnage before them, and Narcha seemed to share his suspicions.

These bodies were not torn apart like the other bandits. In fact, their cause of death wasn't even evident at first glance. Red counted four corpses, plus the lone survivor on the ground whose cries of pain made it hard to focus on much else.

Narcha looked at him, and they both seemed to have the same idea. She walked forward into plain view, an indication that there was no present danger, so Red followed behind.

As soon as they appeared in view, the survivor's eyes lit up.

"Oh god, please..." He struggled to get the words out. "Help me."

Once Red drew closer, he saw the man's terrible condition. His leg was twisted at an unnatural angle, and he gripped a bleeding wound on his side. Whatever had done this hadn't even bothered to check whether the man was dead.

Red didn't reply to his call for aid, though, and examined the corpses of his companions. They had similar wounds—with broken and twisted limbs, as well as crushed skulls—though they weren't as lucky as their companion and seemed to have died instantly.

"What happened here?" Narcha asked the survivor.

The man looked around in a panic at the question, as if remembering a nightmarish scene.

"It was a monster..." He gritted his teeth in pain. "Oh god, it hurts!"

Narcha winced. It was evident the man was not interested in answering her questions in his state, and she didn't seem to know what to do next. While she was talking to him, though, Red had noticed something.

He called her over. "There's something wrong with these wounds."

"What is it?" Narcha approached.

He was crouched near a corpse with punctured leather armor, blood still flowing out from the wound in its chest. Red pulled apart the armor straps and exposed the bare skin of the corpse.

"Here." He pointed at the body.

The puncture wounds seemed infected, the flesh around it taking a dark-blue color. Even the blood flowing down had an unnaturally dark shade to it. Red thought he recognized the phenomenon from his experiences underground.

"It looks like venom... But there are four puncture wounds, so I don't think it was made by fangs—"

"Get the fuck away from that!" Narcha yanked him away from the corpse in a flash.

Red was so surprised he didn't even have time to resist as he was sent flying away. When he landed, he hurried to get up and looked around, expecting an enemy ambush. Narcha, however, was still just standing over the corpse.

Without hesitation, the woman pulled out her saber and swung down on the corpse. She decapitated it in one swift swing, the head sent rolling away, but that wasn't the end of her attack. With ferocity and precision, she did the same to the other corpses.

Red watched in confusion before she turned to stare at him with the expression of someone who had just survived a close brush with death.

"That's no venom, it's undead infection!" She struggled to catch her breath. "These people were killed by an undead."

A wave of realization hit Red. "Then does that mean..."

"Yeah, they were all probably going to come back as zombies soon enough," Narcha said.

He couldn't help but shiver at the revelation.

To think I was so casual while examining their corpses...

"Does cutting their heads off prevent them from transforming?" Red asked.

"Most of the time. Once they transform, they won't die until almost their entire body is destroyed."

"How long does it take for them to transform?"

"I have no idea," Narcha said. "That's one of the reasons why I took precautions."

Red still found it hard to believe these mutilated and headless bodies could possibly come back to life. However, if the warrior treated it as a serious danger, he wouldn't be careless either.

"Then what about him?" he asked, looking over at the survivor.

The remaining bandit had done nothing but cry out in pain during Narcha's rampage. When he saw the duo looking at him, though, he stared back with pleading eyes.

Narcha sighed. "He's already infected. There's no hope for him."

The bandit didn't seem to register her words, whimpering under his breath.

Red frowned. He didn't particularly care about the man's life, but it seemed he couldn't share much in his current state.

"Give him something for the pain," he said. "At least so we can get him to talk."

Narcha looked conflicted. "It's a waste of supplies... but you're right. We need to know what happened."

She took out a medicine pouch from her bag, approached the bandit and threw the item over.

"Eat that. It'll ease the pain."

The bandit's eyes lit up. With trembling hands, he opened the pouch before pouring its powdery contents down his throat, not bothering to use water to swallow it all. While his arms were raised, Red had the opportunity to examine the man's chest wounds.

Black blood oozed out of it, just like from the corpses.

A few minutes later, the bandit seemed to relax somewhat as the drugs did their work. At that point, he looked around at the bodies of his companions before letting out a laugh full of desperation.

"Fuck me... Why did I decide to be a bandit?" He shook his head.

Narcha snorted. "I wouldn't be too sad. If you didn't die at the hands of some monsters, you would've eventually been killed by us."

The bandit seemed to take in the woman's appearance for the first time, and a smile came to his face. "I would recognize that saber anywhere. Boss did warn us to be careful about you..."

She cut him off. "I know these are your last moments and all, but I'm afraid we don't have time for banter. What was it that attacked you?"

Her words made him grimace.

"We found a body on the riverside..." the man said. "An old peasant, probably drowned in the river and carried downstream. Then... then he got up out of nowhere and attacked us."

"It's a zombie, then..." Narcha nodded to herself. "How strong was it?"

The bandit smiled at the question. "Strong enough to give even the Barbarian some trouble."

"That's for me to judge." She gave him an intense stare, less bothered than challenged by the comment. "Why are bandits moving so close to the city?"

"Come on, girl." The man shook his head. "I might be a bandit, but I'm not so low to sell out my companions before I die."

"What about Rickard? Is he nearby?" Red interjected with a question of his own.

The man just smirked at him.

"If you're such a loyal person, why didn't you die for your country when it actually mattered?" Narcha jeered.

"Don't lecture me," the bandit said. "I did what I needed to do for me and my people to survive. Better than those idiots who decided to die for nothing against the Imperials..."

Narcha scoffed, her expression filling with anger. "Making excuses until the end, huh? Nobody forced you to be a bandit. And now look at where that got you!"

She gestured at the forest and his dead companions. "Dying in the middle of nowhere, where no one will remember you. Was it worth it?"

The bandit went silent.

"... I chose what I chose," he said after a moment. "No matter what you say, you won't make me regret my choices right before I die... Just finish the job while the drugs are still working."

Narcha glared at him. "I could just leave you here to your pain. Probably no worse than how you treated some of your victims."

"What, and risk me turning into a zombie?" the man asked with a pained smile. "You wouldn't do that. I've heard enough about Narcha Valt to know she has some honor to her name."

Narcha's face fell. She sighed, seemingly arriving at a decision. "Have it your way, then."

With that, she swung her heavy saber, decapitating the man in one go. His lifeless body slumped to the ground. Red watched the scene in silence, reflecting on the conversation.

Narcha turned and walked up to the river, washing her weapon of the bandits' foul blood.

"It's important to wash your belongings after interacting with undead," she explained to him, as though nothing of note had happened. "Sometimes, you can get infected just by touching their blood."

Red wondered how she knew so much about this matter, but he felt this wasn't the time to ask. He walked over to the river and thoroughly washed his hands and arms until he felt satisfied. Then, while Narcha was occupied dealing with her equipment, he started to investigate the area for tracks.

A few minutes later, Narcha approached him.

"What did you find?" she asked.

"Bandit tracks leading up there." Red pointed north. "Probably where they came from."

"What about the zombie?"

He shook his head. "There are some very light footprints, but they're too faint to follow. But they were leading to the south...."

The same direction they were supposed to go.

"Great," Narcha said derisively. "If a tree-hopping monster wasn't enough, we're following a zombie's footsteps now too!"

"Can you kill it?" Red asked.

"I... don't know," she said after some thought.

It was the first time Red had seen Narcha unsure if she could handle a fight.

"I've never fought an undead before," she said. "What you need to be asking yourself, though, is whether this little trip is still worth the risk."

Her words made Red go quiet. But his conclusion was still the same.

"I need to," he said.

"God, you're really putting me in a pinch here, kid." Narcha sighed. "Eiwin is definitely going to kill me, but I did make a promise, didn't I? Just make sure you're ready for anything. If shit goes bad, I might not be able to protect you."

Red nodded in understanding.

"Don't bother looking through their belongings." She gestured to the corpses. "You don't really want to touch anything an undead came into contact with."

"Should we continue searching for a place to sleep?" he asked.

"That would be a good idea. Preferably far away from here."

The pair agreed on a course of action and walked back into the forest. The sun was already up at this point, and Red could no longer feel the lunar gaze upon him. For obvious reasons, though, he found himself unable to relax.

Eventually, they found a secluded area to camp some ways away from the river. Red set down his bedroll, but quickly found himself unable to fall asleep. Narcha, who stood on guard not too far away, seemed to notice.

"What, are you too afraid to fall asleep?" she asked him with a mocking smile.

"Of course I'm afraid," Red said, looking over. "It would be stupid not to be afraid."

Narcha looked taken aback at his honesty. "Uh, well... I guess that's true."

"But that's not why I'm not sleeping," he said. "I'm thinking about something."

"Thinking about what?" she asked with some curiosity.

"It's a secret."

"Bah, go to hell, you brat!" She walked away, settling down somewhere nearby.

Red, finally alone with his own thoughts, looked back on the events of the previous night. He recalled what Goulth had told him about Lunar Spiritual Energy and its connection with the undead, and now, it just so happened that he'd come across a zombie not three days later.

Maybe this was all a coincidence, but it made Red wonder. Was this all somehow connected to his stash of moonstones or the insectoid crystal? If so, he would have to clean up his own mess.

CHAPTER 95

TRAIL

RED WOKE up earlier than he had yesterday. The sun was still up, and he found Narcha standing guard not too far from him.

"You can go to sleep if you want," he said.

She scoffed. "What, and risk being ambushed? No offense, but I trust my eyes more."

Considering she had opened her Five Senses Vein, he couldn't blame her.

"Should we continue traveling, then?" he asked.

"Sure," Narcha agreed. "I'm just worried that we might stumble on this zombie if we're too fast."

"We've been in the same place for hours. Shouldn't it be far ahead by now?"

"As far as I know, zombies are very slow. The only time they get energetic is when they see food."

"By food, you mean..."

"Flesh. Human flesh, in particular."

Red narrowed his eyes, noticing yet another issue. "But it didn't eat any of the bandits."

"Indeed, just like that other monster," Narcha said solemnly. "There's something weird going on here. Maybe it has something to do with why the monsters disappeared."

Red had arrived at the same conclusion the night before. Unlike Narcha, though, he had a guess as to a possible cause.

"You told me there are plenty of bandits in the region," he said. "With some luck, the zombie will get tied up with them and let us by without a fight."

"That would be a comforting thought, if not for the fact that every bandit it kills can become another zombie," she said with a resigned smile. "It would be good if we killed it before an undead outbreak spreads through the region."

"... We're not prepared for that kind of fight."

And that is not my priority right now.

Red left the rest of that sentence unspoken. It wasn't that he didn't want to help if the chance presented itself, but his goal was to find a way to survive the moon's curse. Everything else came second.

"You're right, but we might have no choice," Narcha said. "Anyways, let's keep moving, shall we?"

Red concurred, and after he finished picking up his equipment, they resumed their travel.

It didn't take long for Red to notice a curiosity along their path.

"There are a lot of recent tracks around here." He pointed them out at various spots.

"Well, bandits move around this region all the time," Narcha said.

"That's not it," he said. "Some of the earlier tracks were at least somewhat disguised. These people didn't even bother with that."

Narcha frowned at this. "Then you mean..."

"They were in a hurry. Maybe they saw the zombie."

"There are no signs of battle, though." Even Narcha, who had little tracking experience, could tell that much. "If the zombie saw them, it would definitely attack."

"Maybe it was distracted by something else."

"That's... not that absurd, now that I think about it. It even ignored fresh corpses in front of it, so there's precedent for its weird behavior."

As they continued to search the area, Red soon came across another curiosity. He crouched down and examined a patch of grass.

"These plants are all dead."

In fact, it wasn't just a single patch. These dead plants weren't immediately noticeable amidst the leaf litter, but as he continued to search, he found a pattern. A straight line of dead plants leading to the south.

"Was this caused by the zombie?" Red asked.

"From what I understand, it could be," Narcha said. "Technically, undead emit Death Energy, which can slowly kill anything living just by being near them. But..."

She furrowed her brow.

"What is it?" Red asked.

"It's just that, from what I know, these effects take a while to happen. Or that it depends on how much Death Energy an undead has. A normal zombie shouldn't cause this kind of change so quickly."

"Could it be that it's not a zombie?"

"I... don't know." Narcha shook her head. "I'm not as knowledgeable as Eiwin on this subject, but that would make sense. I don't think an average zombie could've killed those bandits so easily, and this might explain its odd behavior."

Her support for his guess made Red even more apprehensive.

"Is this cause for concern?" he asked.

"Of course it is! But I've never fought an undead either way, zombie or not." She shrugged. "Doesn't change much in the end."

Her nonchalant attitude didn't inspire confidence in Red, but he supposed he was the one insisting they continue on this path. He was aware of the risks and could only trust in Narcha's abilities.

They continued moving, and the tracks became more frequent. At some point, Red counted seven different sets of footprints. Eventually, night came, and he braced himself for the moon's gaze.

The inner pressure on his psyche returned, and his mind wrestled against it. For some reason, though, Red felt he wasn't as affected by the gaze this time. At first, he thought it was because of his experience fighting it, but the pressure had decreased so much over the last few days that he figured there was another reason.

Is the gaze getting weaker?

It was the only reasonable explanation Red could find. Of course, once his thoughts traveled in that direction, he remembered his conversation with Goulth about the undead.

He looked over at Narcha. "How's the moon today?"

"What?"

"Can you tell me how the moon is today?"

"Can't you check for yourself?" Narcha asked.

"You have better eyes."

"I suppose that's true—no, wait! That doesn't make any sense!"

"Can you just do it?"

"Ugh, fine." Narcha relented and looked up through the canopy. "Yep, the moon is still there."

"How bright is it?"

"A little bright."

"Would you say it's brighter than yesterday?"

"What kind of question is that?" She gave him an incredulous look. She was only met by silence and Red's blank face.

"Yeah, I suppose it's getting brighter," she said, sighing. That's what the moon does, doesn't it?"

Red nodded in understanding. Although he'd had a feeling this was the case, the confirmation still helped him. It was direct evidence that the phases of the moon were linked to the lunar being and its gaze.

The being was at its strongest during a new moon and was now becoming weaker as the moon grew brighter—the exact opposite of an undead. This also gave Red some reassurance that the absorption process wouldn't happen again anytime soon.

Another piece of the puzzle had fallen into place, and now he was one step closer to understanding his situation. Not to mention, he also had a frame of reference for the being's strength. If Red's theory was correct, it would be at its weakest in ten or so days, during the full moon.

Its strength would also return as the moon waned. It would peak in twenty-five days with the new moon, and at that point, he needed to brace himself for the worst.

Although this didn't mean the end of his problems, his new comprehension helped Red take heart and move forward.

Narcha had noticed his silence. "What are you thinking about?"

"It's a—"

"If you say it's a secret again, I'll just leave you to travel alone."

Red kept quiet. Unfortunately, that didn't seem to appease her either, as she cursed him under her breath and marched ahead.

A few hours later, Red noticed another pattern in the footprints.

"The bandits are all headed south too," he pointed out to Narcha.

"I could've guessed that. Honestly, this is the first time in a long time I've been in the middle of such a mess. Zombies, bandits, monsters... Does that happen often when you're around?"

"We haven't really met any of them, though."

"You're right. Maybe you're not as much of a bad omen as I—" Narcha suddenly froze. "Get down!"

Red, who had learned to trust her instincts, dove behind a tree without hesitation. He fumbled to nock an arrow on his bow, preparing himself for an ambush, but after a few seconds, nothing happened. He looked back at Narcha, who was also hiding not far off.

She shook her head and made a shushing sign with her finger. Red just nodded and waited. Soon enough, he heard voices approaching.

"... haven't seen it yet. Maybe it ran away," a man's voice said.

"And you'd be willing to bet your life on that?" a gruff voice replied. "Just be on the lookout and do as you're told."

Bandits.

Red tensed up but didn't dare peek past his cover.

"I mean, what are we even going to do against something like that?" yet another bandit asked. "Have you seen what it did to Stoyan's group?"

"That's just because it took them by surprise," the gruff voice said. "Besides, we just need to trap it. Once we do, the boss can finish it off."

The voices continued to approach. Red looked over at Narcha and held up three fingers while tilting his head, as if asking a question. She shook her head and replied by holding up five fingers. Red frowned.

The warrior also seemed to be in thought. She met his eyes while her hand slowly came to rest on the hilt of the saber strapped to her back. She smiled and dipped her head in the bandits' direction.

Red shook his head.

Narcha looked disappointed. He rushed to come up with another plan, making a wide circle motion with his hand. She looked confused, but eventually, realization came to her.

He wanted them to sneak around.

Narcha seemed reluctant to accept the plan, but finally she nodded.

Red sighed in relief and considered how to sneak past these bandits without being noticed. Then, an idea came to him. He looked at his feet, searching for a large rock, which was surprisingly difficult to find in the dark.

Narcha watched his actions, baffled. Red didn't know how to explain his plan to her, so he just patted his chest as he'd seen Allen doing in the past. This only confused her more.

But Red, now having found a suitably sized rock, waited until the voices came closer. It was only a matter of time before they walked past their hiding places. When they were just close enough that he could identify their position, he threw the rock with all his strength in another direction.

The stone thudded against a tree, and the footsteps of the bandits all stopped.

"What was that?" one asked, sounding fearful.

"It's the monster! It's waiting to ambush us!"

"Shut up, you moron!" The gruff voice cut him off. "You there, go check what that noise was."

"Me? I don't want to die to that thing!"

"Bah, you bunch of useless cowards! Just keep your weapons at the ready and follow me!"

Their footsteps resumed, and the bandits walked toward the thrown rock. Once Red thought they were far enough away, he nodded at Narcha. That sign she clearly understood, and she began to sneak around the trees while he followed behind.

Red braced himself for Narcha giving their cover away by stepping on a branch or making too much noise. However, she crept through the trees without much difficulty, and the duo left the area without even seeing the bandits.

Maybe she's not so bad at that...

Screams echoed from where they had just come.

Red's blood ran cold. He looked over at Narcha. "We should go."

CHAPTER 96

DEAD PLANTS

"Is that...?" Narcha hesitated once she heard the bloodcurdling screams. Red knew exactly what she was thinking.

"The noise might attract more bandits to the area," he said. "We can't afford to get caught up in a fight."

"I didn't even notice anything waiting in ambush." She solemnly shook her head. "It could have taken us by surprise at any point."

"And yet it chose not to. Maybe it knows better than to attack you. We still need to leave."

The screams and sounds of battle continued to echo from nearby. From another direction, Red could hear loud voices coming closer. Reinforcements, or so he assumed.

The two of them sprinted away. Eventually, Red could no longer hear the sounds of combat, but they only stopped running once Narcha called them to a halt. They gathered themselves, but Narcha continued to look back, towards where they had just left.

"It was that thing," she said with certainty. "The tree-hopping monster."

"We don't know that for sure," Red said. "But its behavior would certainly fit."

"It was too damn close." Narcha gritted her teeth. "It might have been following us."

"Maybe."

"And I didn't even notice it... What if it had attacked?"

"It might have deliberately avoided getting too close for fear of being noticed," Red suggested. "If it tried to attack, maybe you would have discovered it."

"But that's not how monsters act. They're not this smart."

He couldn't refute her—at least not without bringing up the insectoids. But whether a zombie or a monster, the creature wasn't acting according to the norm. It was impossible to predict what it might do next.

"We should hurry, then," he said. "We can keep traveling during the daytime and try to make it to our goal by tomorrow... That is, if you can keep going without sleep."

"I'll be fine," Narcha said. "I can still go for a while. But what about you?"

"I think I'll manage..."

"That doesn't sound very confident, kid."

Of course, Red wasn't confident at all. Although the pressure from the moon had diminished, it was still there, taxing him mentally. Ultimately, he felt it would be much safer if they reached their destination as soon as possible.

"I'll be fine," Red insisted. "You have the bulk of our strength either way."

"Whatever you say." Narcha shrugged. "But tell me if you get tired. I can't look out for dead weight if we're attacked."

He agreed. They kept moving at a brisk pace, knowing the rest of the trip was destined to be turbulent.

Over the next few hours, they came across more signs of increased bandit activity. Mostly fresh tracks, but now and then, they saw the light of lanterns from afar, as well as the sounds of distant conversation.

Thankfully, these bandits weren't too keen on remaining hidden, so Red and Narcha had an easier time sneaking past unnoticed. It also helped that their tracks blended in with the rest, making it difficult for anyone to know they'd even passed through.

Red lost count of how many bandits they came across, but he felt their numbers could rival a small army. Narcha gradually changed her mind on direct confrontation once she realized just how many enemies were in the area.

She swore. "Why the fuck are there so many of them here?"

"Is it because of the zombie?" Red asked.

"Why would they be this concerned about a fucking zombie? It's not like you can get anything valuable from a rotting corpse."

"So, you're telling me even the bandits are acting strangely?"

She frowned. "Well, when you put it that way..."

"Do you think all these odd behaviors are connected?"

"How should I know? What could cause humans, an undead, and a monster to act like this?"

Red once again refrained from voicing his own thoughts.

"There must be something else going on," he said. "Have you noticed any signs of combat recently?"

"Not really," Narcha said.

"And yet we know the zombie was heading in this direction. With so many bandits around, how could they not come across each other?"

"Are you saying the zombie is sneaking past them too?"

"Not necessarily," he said. "The trail of dead plants would be easy to follow if anyone came across it."

One didn't need to have experience tracking to notice the gray, dead plant litter that cut through the forest.

"Then you're saying they're avoiding it?"

"Probably," he said. "Perhaps they also noticed its weird behavior and decided to follow it, or just make sure it leaves on its own."

"Bandits are too stupid to notice something like that," Narcha said. "Besides, this doesn't explain why so many bandits would come here in the first place."

"Maybe they were already here for something else."

"What could have possibly caught the attention of so many bandits? There are no roads to rob, and no hunters come around this part of the forest."

"We can't tell without scouting the region out, but we're not here for that. It's likely we'll be meeting a lot more bandits on the way, though."

Sure enough, Red's words came to pass, yet what they saw wasn't a patrol, but a large bandit camp. A bonfire burned from afar, and boisterous voices could be heard echoing through the forest.

Narcha and Red stopped to examine the place from a safe distance.

"Was this on the map?" she asked.

Red shook his head. "Maybe it's a recent camp... or maybe we were reading the map wrong in the first place."

"Bah, that doesn't help at all." The warrior squinted, examining the encampment. "There might be over ten bandits in there."

"Even if there were only two, we should still avoid combat."

"You don't need to tell me that." She narrowed her eyes at him. "There's lots of activity in there, though."

Even Red could see that. Bandits came and went every few minutes, and there was an air of alarm and tension in their motions.

"With this many people, they shouldn't have had a problem killing a normal zombie," Narcha said.

"But we've already established that wasn't a normal zombie," Red reminded her. "It might be even stronger than we first thought..."

"The only way it could be any stronger than that is if it's..."

"... If it's not a zombie," he said.

They had discussed the possibility before, but now there was more evidence to back it up.

Narcha was still skeptical. "We can't know for sure. Either way, we should get a move on."

By the time they had moved past the bandit camp, the first signs of daylight had emerged. Gradually, Red felt the lunar gaze disappearing. His mind could finally relax.

But he knew the true challenge was just beginning.

"Even if we wanted to camp, we wouldn't be able to," Narcha pointed out. "Now that it's daytime, the bandits could easily find us."

"It's fine," Red told her. "I'm surprised we've managed to avoid confrontation for this long."

In truth, he found that strange. Either these bandits were not as competent as Rog thought, or they were too distracted by something else. In any case, he'd preemptively nocked an arrow into his short bow, prepared to engage at any moment.

To their surprise, the journey over the next couple of hours was uneventful. Red continued to find more bandit tracks leading to the south, but for some reason, they saw no more patrols. In fact, the entire forest seemed unnaturally quiet, with almost no sounds of animals.

Only the rushing river and the crunch of their own footsteps could be heard. Even Narcha had a hard time hiding her unease.

"What the fuck is going on?" she muttered under her breath.

Her attitude put Red on guard. Yet, other than the strange silence, they didn't find anything else as they moved forward.

At least they were getting closer to their goal.

A while later, Narcha said, "We're getting to the hillside." She pointed ahead. "The area we camped in shouldn't be too far."

Red was relieved to hear this. His excitement, however, was short-lived.

The forest's silence didn't disappear as they got closer. If anything, the world seemed to grow more still. Then their surroundings started to change.

It began with a few plants. They were dead and dried-up, much like the ones marking the zombie's trail. At first, they thought this was more of the same, but they were soon proven wrong.

"What the fuck..." Narcha cursed under her breath.

After another kilometer, the death spread to the trees. Everything took on a grayish and sickly appearance, the air heavy and still. Even taking a breath turned into an uncomfortable task. The forest was deathly quiet, and the constant rush of the river seemed stifled under the ghostly atmosphere.

Narcha looked around in a daze.

"This is..." She trailed off, unsure of what to say.

Perhaps for the first time, Red noticed her voice tinged with a hint of fear. He didn't feel any better. Merely standing in this place filled him with a sense of dread.

"Was this caused by an undead?" Red asked.

"An undead causing all of this?" Narcha tried to collect herself. "Maybe, but it would need to be very powerful... and if that's the case, I'm afraid we'll turn into zombies just by standing here."

Red shuddered. "I don't feel like I'm changing, though," he said after examining his body. Other than the sense of wrongness he felt, there was no sign this place was affecting him.

"Same here," Narcha said. "Something else must be happening, then..."

They looked at each other with apprehension, but with no other choice, they kept walking. They had barely traveled any distance when something invaded the pervasive stillness of the world.

Narcha called Red to a stop. "It's the sound of fighting."

"Sound?" He looked around in confusion.

"Right around the area we first met. Try to focus."

Red did as much, and sure enough, he heard something faint. He couldn't distinguish what it was, but he knew something was there.

His worry grew. Now that the forest had changed so much, it would take more time to find his stash. The camp clearing was the closest, clearest landmark he could go off of, but this would also mean walking directly towards the sounds.

"We can try checking it from afar." Narcha pointed at one of the hills. "We can get a better view from higher up."

Red agreed with her idea, and the pair began taking the detour. The sounds of battle grew clearer, and soon he could even hear the bloodcurdling screams of death. As they reached the top of the hill, they could finally see the fight.

And what they saw looked like a fever dream.

"What in the..." Narcha stood staring agape at the scene.

A sickly and half-naked elder danced amid a dozen bandits who all desperately tried to cut him down, to no avail. The old man's skin had a hint of blue to it, and some of his flesh had rotted away. As they watched, it became evident that this was an undead—the zombie.

But it didn't move like one, weaving between the bandits' attacks with skill and grace befitting an experienced fighter. Dodging wasn't all that it did. It actively countered every attack thrown its way with its razor-sharp claws, reaping death amidst its enemies. Already, countless corpses littered the ground, and although the zombie's body was riddled with arrows, it still moved unhindered.

This was not the unthinking beast Red had been expecting.

CHAPTER 97

THE UNDEAD REVEALED

"Is that the zombie?" Red asked.

"I... think so," Narcha said.

"Is it supposed to fight like a human?"

"Don't ask me those kinds of questions! I'm as confused as you are!"

As they spoke, they saw the zombie twist a bandit's neck in a practiced motion. Then it sidestepped an attack, its movements chaining together seamlessly. It wasn't overwhelming its opponents with monstrous strength, but with strategy and speed. Even when hit, it remained unfazed and continued to move as if nothing had happened.

To Red, this was even scarier than a savage beast.

"What do you think?" he said to Narcha.

"I'm not sure." She shook her head. "This is too weird to explain."

"Let's sneak past them while they're occupied, then."

Narcha had a grimace of hesitation on her face. Red could guess she was uncertain about leaving such a threat behind, but after a moment, she nodded.

"You know, if you weren't here, I would've probably already joined the fight. This might be connected to the monsters' disappearance, after all."

Red didn't reply. He didn't think this had anything to do with the monsters' disappearance, but he wasn't going to correct her misconception.

"Let's give that area a wide berth." Narcha pointed in another direction. "Last thing we want is to get involved in that mess."

He agreed with her. Red was just about to turn away from the battle when something odd happened.

As the zombie fought, its gaze shifted away from its opponents and up towards them. For a second, Red could swear their eyes met.

A shiver ran down his spine.

What the...

His entire body tensed, freezing in place. A moment later, the undead disengaged from combat and charged in their direction.

Narcha reacted before him. "He saw us!"

She pulled Red off his feet and ran. It took a second for him to recover from his shock and move on his own two feet.

He couldn't understand how the zombie had noticed them from that distance, or why it would chase after them. He didn't have the chance to think about it, either.

Red pushed his newly opened Upper Leg Vein to its limit. He was already running faster than he ever had before. Even then, he couldn't compare to Narcha. She had to slow down to guard their backs as they retreated.

Narcha looked back to check if their pursuer was keeping up. Her eyes widened. "He's too fast! We need to stand our ground!"

Red knew better than to argue and dove behind a tree for cover. Narcha also came to a stop and unsheathed her saber, ready to face her enemy. Meanwhile, Red prepared his bow and raised it, pointing it in the same direction.

A few seconds later, they heard approaching footsteps, and a shadow came into view. Red held his breath, aiming at the figure.

Once the zombie stepped out, he loosed his arrow. It found its mark and pierced the creature's thigh, causing it to stumble. Narcha didn't waste the opening and charged ahead like a mad bull.

Her saber tore through the air as she sought to split the undead in half. However, at the last second, the zombie spun on its heels and leaned back, narrowly evading the weapon's strike.

In a flash, it jumped away from Narcha.

She looked shocked by the undead's swift movement, and it was already out of her weapon's reach before she could follow up with another swing.

There was a strange pause in their combat as the woman and zombie sized each other up, neither making any moves.

Red could also see its appearance more clearly now. The elderly zombie was unnaturally thin, its blueish skin pulled taut against its bones. It wore only two pieces of ragged and torn white clothing. Its face looked frozen, without a hint of thought behind its white eyes. Small patches of gray hair covered its decaying scalp, and dozens of cuts and festering wounds covered its body.

It was a corpse, and yet it moved with strength and finesse without any sign of breathing or human exhaustion. Red's mind trembled at the strange sight.

"What are you?" Narcha asked.

Red was surprised by her attempt at communication. Could a zombie understand her?

No, that's not right...

This was clearly no ordinary zombie.

As if to prove him right, its face twitched. Facial muscles contracted and twisted into the semblance of a human expression—a twisted grin.

Narcha noticed the mockery behind the smile and snorted. "Go to hell, you bastard!"

With that, she charged.

The zombie, however, was more prepared this time. With nimble steps, it closed the distance between them in an instant, slashing with its claws. Taken by surprise, Narcha was forced to shift her saber up to block its attack.

The sound of scraping metal echoed through the forest as the zombie's nails scratched the saber. Narcha gritted her teeth and tried to push her opponent back with the flat side of her weapon. But the zombie acted with the same swiftness from earlier and used the momentum of her push to jump a safe distance away.

That was when Red shot another arrow.

His target didn't even bother dodging this time. It used its back as a shield against the arrow, which plunged into its flesh with a thud.

The zombie flinched, but the injury didn't seem to hinder its movements.

Narcha sliced forward once more, but her opponent pushed off the ground and circled towards her flank. It didn't give her a moment to breathe and went immediately on the offensive, its claws drawing a swift path towards her throat.

She grunted in anger and used her weapon to block the strike, but the zombie chained its movements into a string of attacks which kept her on the back foot.

Red tried to help her with his arrows. This time, he aimed for the creature's legs, but the zombie was too fast, and he was fearful of accidentally hitting Narcha.

It easily dodged his next few shots.

I can't hit it.

It was a terrible realization. Even if he got closer, his opponent might still dodge all his shots.

At the same time, the zombie increased its pressure on Narcha. The warrior was like a fortress, and none of her opponent's attacks so much as made her arms tremble. Still, she was clearly on the defensive and unable to change her position.

Every time she twirled her saber for an attack, the zombie had already moved out of the way and swiftly counterattacked. Narcha was then forced to parry away its claws, unable to shift the momentum of battle.

No, there's more.

There was a hesitation behind her movements, as if she were reluctant to commit to any attack. It didn't fit Red's image of the warrior.

She doesn't want to get hit.

Of course, it went without saying that one didn't want to get injured in combat. However, one could survive superficial wounds. But no wound was superficial when facing a zombie.

Any scratch on her skin might infect her. Not to mention, they had both seen what the zombie's claws had done to the bandits' armor earlier, so her own armor might not fare any better.

All of this was unfavorable for Narcha's aggressive combat style. She had to be particularly careful, since even if her blows connected, it would still mean her death if the zombie managed to scratch her.

Red struggled to think of a way he could help. Then, he remembered Rog's confrontation with the bandits, and an idea came to him.

"Get some distance and wait for my arrows!" he shouted over the sounds of battle.

Narcha didn't, or couldn't, respond. But a few seconds later, as she parried the zombie, she pushed its claw away and jumped back. It was about to chase after her when an arrow flew towards it.

Red had aimed a shot at its feet, but the zombie simply took a step back, avoiding the projectile with little effort.

That was when Narcha struck, closing the distance and swinging her saber down on its head. Her attack hit nothing but air, though, as the zombie jumped away.

It took a step forward to resume its onslaught, but then another of Red's arrows came for its feet, forcing it to dodge again. Narcha, free of offensive pressure, followed up with another attack, which the zombie barely dodged.

The sequence repeated itself. The tides of battle slowly shifted, as they forced the zombie to continuously dodge their attacks.

It was exactly what Red had planned. He'd gotten that idea when he remembered how Rog had tricked the bandit leader. The hunter had used one arrow to force his target to dodge and another to hit him. Although Red couldn't shoot two arrows in such a brief interval, he had an even better follow-up in the form of Narcha.

He shot another arrow towards the zombie's legs, forcing it to swerve, and then Narcha followed up with her saber an instant later. The zombie needed its mobility both to attack successfully and to dodge. But to avoid the arrow and save its legs, it had to run into Narcha's saber.

This put the zombie in a lose-lose situation.

With the duo's cooperation, it found itself unable to do anything but react, and eventually, it failed to dodge one of their attacks. With a swift strike, Narcha's saber lopped off its right arm at the elbow.

Before she could follow up, the zombie jumped away and began to flee.

"No, you don't!" Narcha glared at it, about to give chase.

However, the sound of approaching footsteps made her freeze in place. From another direction, armed bandits emerged in large numbers. Alarmed, they all pointed their weapons at her.

"Who the fuck are you?" a bandit shouted. "Where's the fucking zombie?"

The group was in a panicked and fidgety state. Red, who was still hidden, could tell that any sudden move might trigger another fight between them. Meanwhile, the zombie had disappeared, and Narcha was scanning the trees furiously.

"I was just fighting it!" She pointed at the severed limb. "It ran away because of you morons!"

The bandits were all taken aback. Some sense seemed to return to them, and they looked questioningly at the man who had spoken. Their leader hesitated.

"We can worry about this woman later," he finally decided, his gaze sweeping over his subordinates. "Finding and killing the zombie is our priority!"

The bandits all nodded. Just as they prepared to leave, though, Red saw a shadow move behind them.

Narcha was a step quicker in warning them. "Behind you!"

Something jumped down from the trees into the center of the group. As it landed, screams rose from their midst, blood and limbs erupting in a blur of death. The bandits, horrified, turned around to retreat. Most wouldn't make it.

When the first whirl of activity settled, there were already five bodies on the ground. In the middle of the gore, a strange creature stood. A humanoid monster with a body covered by crimson red scales, wielding claws as sharp and long as daggers. Two large horns protruded from the sides of its head, which curved forward like a dragon's. Red couldn't help but feel this monster looked like a twisted version of a human.

"It's a demon!" Narcha yelled.

At the same time, the zombie took the opportunity to strike.

CHAPTER 98
CRIMSON WORLD

"BEHIND YOU!" Red shouted.

Narcha was quick to react to his warning, turning to face the zombie. But the creature suddenly changed directions and dashed towards Red instead.

Without hesitation, he turned to retreat. Still, Red knew the zombie was much faster than him. He couldn't hope to outrun it, so he ran towards the bandits instead.

One man almost ended up colliding with Red. Moving away from the demon meant the bandit was unwittingly approaching the zombie. He stopped suddenly, taken aback by the presence of a child.

As the bandit was processing the situation, though, something pierced his back. A skeletal hand burst through his chest, and he didn't even have time to scream before his life was torn from him.

The zombie threw the dying man aside and resumed its chase. Before it could chase after Red, Narcha's saber hacked down, forcing it to jump out of the way.

She glared at the zombie, rage twisting her expression. "You think you can ignore me?"

The zombie dodged again and again as she unleashed a torrent of attacks. Red took this opportunity to put some distance between them, but ahead, another conflict was underway.

The bandits had been sent into a complete panic. The scaled demon dove in between the trees, cutting apart the survivors from its first attack, its sharp claws making short work of the bandits' armor. Some were trying to organize a resistance against the monster.

"Shoot it!"

The three remaining archers followed their leader's order and opened fire on the demon. But the creature was too fast, dodging most of the arrows. When one finally found its mark, it merely bounced off of its scales with a soft ting.

This only served to enrage the demon.

It opened its lizard-like jaws and let out a shriek, revealing hundreds of thin, sharp teeth. It jumped up into a tree and, using it as a platform, leaped at one of the archers. The bandit immediately dropped his bow in retreat, but the demon was even faster than the zombie. The man had barely turned to run before it was upon him.

The demon's claws cut into his flesh like butter. It didn't even seem to care that its victim was already dead, relentlessly slicing apart his body into a pile of gore.

The demon was like the physical embodiment of rage and bloodlust, and Red couldn't help but recall his conversation with Eiwin.

So this is a demon...

He felt something stir within his body.

"Kid, what the fuck are you doing?"

Narcha's voice tore him from his thoughts. He turned and saw that she was standing not too far away, saber raised. She had managed to put herself between him and the zombie, and the two were once more sizing each other up.

"It knows I'm the weak link," he said. "It'll probably continue targeting me."

"I can see that, you brat! Don't just stand there!" Even as she spoke to him, she kept her eyes trained on the zombie.

"What do you want me to do?" he asked. "He might end up hurting you if you focus on defending me."

Narcha snorted. "I know that! You need to go."

"Go?" Red asked, confused. "Go where?"

"Go anywhere! Just run away while I hold it back. That way, I can focus on fighting instead of protecting you."

Red wanted to protest her decision, but he knew she was right. They couldn't shake off the zombie, so they needed to fight it. If he stayed behind, he would just get in her way.

"What about the demon?" he asked.

Not too far away, the crimson creature had already claimed another victim.

"Let's hope it's too distracted by the bandits to do anything," Narcha said.

Red hesitated. Now that the zombie only had one arm, she had a better chance against it, but the presence of the demon could put her at genuine risk.

But what can I do to help?

He didn't let indecision cloud his mind for long. Just standing here wouldn't make him any less helpless.

"I'm going further south to get my things," he said. "You can find me there after you're done."

Narcha laughed. "Hah! Glad to see you're confident. Now, go. It looks like our friend has lost its patience."

The zombie had already noticed the conversation between them, but it didn't approach right away. Perhaps it was wary because of their earlier collaboration? It was impossible to tell from its face, but like Narcha said, it was done waiting and had started inching closer.

Red took the opportunity to run away. The zombie clearly saw what he was doing and tried to chase after him. Before it could lunge, Narcha stepped over and slashed with her saber, forcing it to retreat.

The zombie's attention returned to her, and even in its frozen expression and stiff posture, one could see annoyance.

Narcha laughed and pointed her saber at it. "You're angry now too? Turns out maybe you should've just let us go by, huh?"

She didn't spare any more time on conversation. She charged ahead, and the dance of death between warrior and zombie began anew.

Red quickly put a few hundred meters between himself and the battlefield. Although he hadn't done much in the fight, the sheer concentration and precision required for his earlier shots had taken their toll.

It was clear he was outmatched in this type of fight, and it didn't help that he was using a weapon he'd just picked up a few days before. Red couldn't help but remember his trusty cleaver. With that in his hand, he would have certainly been more confident in a fight against the zombie.

That's right, my hidden stash.

He looked around. As far as he could tell, this was unfamiliar territory. With all the dead trees, relying on the vegetation for landmarks wasn't possible. Thankfully, he still remembered the hills and mounds of the area.

I just need to retrace my steps.

The one thing Red recalled clearly from his first night on the surface was the hill he'd emerged from. It directly bordered the river and had revealed a scene he would never forget, no matter how the plants and trees might've changed.

He used the skills that he'd recently learned from Rog to orient himself and climbed atop a hill in search of something he could recognize. Unfortunately, he didn't see anything.

I need to hurry.

Red knew he didn't have the privilege of taking his time, so he dashed downhill to continue his search. Eventually, he came across some traces he recognized.

A campfire!

He didn't know whether the burnt wood was from the Sect's camp he'd seen on his first night, but this was as good of a clue as he had. Red closed his eyes and tried to recall the direction he had approached their campfire from.

A few moments later, a new idea came to his mind. He dashed in a different direction and soon found what he was looking for—a deep splintered hole in one of the dead trunks.

This is where Rog shot at me.

This not only confirmed he was at the right campfire, but also gave him a direction. Without hesitation, Red dashed in a straight line to the southwest, and sure enough, the terrain soon became familiar.

He was close.

Yet, as he approached his goal, the oppressive atmosphere around him intensified. At first, he thought it was just his imagination, but as he came across scattered animal bones, he knew something was off.

At first, he only saw the skeletons of small critters, strewed in random spots along the forest floor. The further he went, though, more and more bones littered his path, and he had to take care to avoid stepping on them.

Eventually, it wasn't just small bones, but also large animal skeletons half-buried in the dirt, adding to the foreboding atmosphere.

Red found himself slowing down and studying the skeletons. None were missing bones or fractured, which was already odd, but something even stranger stuck out to him.

They were all facing the same direction, towards Red's hidden stash.

What is going on?

His confusion grew, and a sense of dread filled his mind. Before, he'd suspected his stash might have been involved in the changes to the forest, but now he had a confirmation.

The number of skeletons continued to increase as he walked. It was as if all the animals in the forest had gathered here for their death. He couldn't avoid treading on the bones anymore, and with every step came a chilling, cracking sound.

At some point, he saw a glint through the trees. His steps slowed until he froze in place. Red squinted, wondering if what he'd seen was just his imagination. Then came another flicker of light, and this time he saw its color.

A crimson light.

His blood ran cold.

Then, he felt something. A familiar yet strange sensation spread through him, beckoning him forward. Something within him responded, as if resonating with the call.

It squirmed and slithered inside of him, prompting him to go forward, and Red had to fight his body to remain in place. The call suddenly grew stronger, and he felt himself losing control as the feeling spread to his mind.

Sensations and emotions forced themselves into his head, making him feel indescribable things. Fear, anger, despair and sadness grew within him like an unstoppable tide.

Red wanted to run away. He wanted to give up. He wanted to lie down and scream. Yet, as he lost control of his rationality, what remained of his awareness tried to grasp onto something to keep him from descending into this hell.

And it was this part of him that saw a glimmer of hope.

Something like this had happened before. His memory was fuzzy, and he struggled to recall the details, but he knew he wasn't misremembering. When he was leaving the tunnel, waking from a dream, Red had felt his mind on the brink of collapse. Whatever had attacked him back then was not the same thing attacking him now, but their goal was the same.

They wanted to destroy his mind.

Yet something had saved him from that imminent collapse. A specific image. Red had forgotten everything about that dream, but one scene lurking within the depths of his memories now resurfaced.

A white slab, covered with symbols he couldn't understand. Even without knowing what was written, the meaning seemed to come naturally to him at that moment.

We will not yield.

As this understanding came to him, something changed. The words resonated within his mind, and Red felt an inexplicable resolve and resilience swelling from within. The overwhelming feelings, the negative emotions that were trying to destroy him, ceased growing, and he felt as if he could now see them for what they truly were.

Weakness.

To think one would be led astray by such things.

Red had shown weakness. Whatever influence had caused the fear and despair to grow within him couldn't have done it without those feelings being there in the first place. It had merely watered seeds already planted deep in his heart.

His uncertainty, his despair, his fear.

They existed within him, no matter how little they showed through his actions. He wasn't emotionless, and he wasn't immune to the cruelty of the world. He was still human, and that was a part of him. Yet what mattered wasn't the existence of these emotions, but rather what power Red chose to give them.

Once he recognized that, everything was simple to understand.

He wasn't moved by fear.

He wasn't moved by sadness.

He wasn't moved by anger.

The only thing that fueled him was a desire for freedom. To do as he pleased, to go anywhere he wished. Next to that will, his worries seemed insignificant—they couldn't pull him from his path.

As Red had his realization, the strange influence seemed to lose its power over him.

He took a step forward. The negative energy within him surged again, but this time, it couldn't touch him. These feelings nagged at the edge of his psyche, but he faced them head-on and saw them for what they truly were.

Weakness.

It was the sum of everything that had always tried to drag him away from his true path. The solution to this otherworldly force, it seemed, was not some magical technique, but rather resolve and understanding of oneself.

You can't trick me. Not anymore.

Red took another step. And then another. The light grew as he walked, until eventually, he arrived at a clearing and saw its source.

A large dome of crimson energy stood there. It pulsated with flickers of brightness, emanating dark strands of mist that dissipated into the surrounding air. The shimmering surface was too cloudy to see through, but it seemed centered around a scintillating spot on the ground.

Red recognized it. This was the same crimson domain that had allowed him to escape from the underground, except this time, he was looking at it from the outside.

It seemed to have grown far beyond its previous size, its energy much stronger than he remembered. He thought back to the animal skeletons he'd seen, recognizing that they might have served as fuel for the core.

No, beyond that, there's something else...

The entire forest was dead. Could it be that this crimson energy was responsible for that too?

Red cast these thoughts into the back of his mind and continued walking. He had a feeling that hesitation here might spell disaster.

The resonating feeling inside Red increased, but he didn't slow down. Once he arrived at the edge of the energy dome, he stopped and gazed into it, trying to look inside.

The crimson surface pulsed. Somehow, Red felt as if it were responding to his presence. It didn't reply to him with words or intent—but with emotions.

Anger, fear, sadness, despair.

These were the feelings it had fed into his own mind. Yet, beneath it all, Red didn't sense any hate or ill intent directed at him. It was like the crimson presence was simply lashing out in anguish, unaware of what it was doing or who it might hurt.

It was confused, uncertain.

About what? Red didn't know, but he felt it was asking him something.

Perhaps it was seeking guidance, or maybe it sought aid. It was hard to say, but in the end, he felt his answer was the same.

Red stood there in thought, for minutes or hours, before he felt the right words come to him.

"These feelings are all distractions. You can't let them consume you, or you will never find whatever it is you seek," he said, unsure if whatever this being was could understand him.

All he got in response was another stir from the dome and the feelings that accompanied it—confusion, helplessness, uncertainty.

Then there was expectation. It was waiting for his reply.

"I can't teach you how to deal with these feelings, and I don't know what you want." He shook his head. "I'm not even sure if I know where my own path will take me."

The dome shook again with despair.

Red frowned, but another thought came to him. "I can't tell you how to solve this, but... maybe we can help each other."

This time, the dome didn't move immediately. A moment later, it shook again. Red sensed its uncertainty.

"I can't teach you anything," he said. "But if you experience this world yourself, you might learn the answer."

The presence went silent, and its pulses slowed. After a while, it stirred again.

Now Red felt something within his body respond. The same resonance from before, a part of him seeking to rejoin its other half, though this time far milder than before.

At the same time, the dome transmitted an emotion to him. Expectation.

Red had a feeling he understood its intention. It sought a partner. This was how he could help it.

Is this the only way?

He closed his eyes and took a deep breath. He was reluctant at first, but something reassured him. Throughout their interaction, he had felt every-thing the presence felt. It bared its soul to him, and beneath every emotion, every pulse, there was a pervading sensation.

Sincerity.

It didn't lie. It *couldn't* lie. Perhaps, more importantly, there was no reason for it to lie.

If it truly couldn't accomplish what it wanted by its own power, then the only way it could do so was with Red's earnest help.

He exhaled and looked deep into the curtain of energy. "There are certain things I fear more than death... so make sure I won't regret this."

The dome stirred again, as if in understanding. Red then reached forward to touch the shimmering light.

Suddenly, the entire world became crimson.

CHAPTER 99
MERGING

RED'S entire vision was covered in crimson light, and an overwhelming smell of blood flooded his senses. His entire body resonated with the energy, and he felt something worming its way into his veins.

Strands of foreign energy that had lain dormant within his body awakened in response to the sensation. They swam joyfully through his veins before merging with the crimson light.

Red had a sudden realization.

This is...

The infection. It had remained hidden in his body, waiting for the right time to awaken. Red wondered what would've happened had he not found the crystal in time.

Still, the crimson light continued to travel through his blood vessels, gathering all the remnants of infected energy. After it was done, it suddenly changed directions. It headed straight to his heart and burrowed inside.

Red grabbed his chest in agony.

The energy seemed to fuse with the blood traveling into his heart before spreading to different parts of his body. Red felt a transformation happening within his organs, but he couldn't understand it. The process repeated as the energy flowed back and forth through his heart, but after every cycle, he felt less of the energy remaining.

Red could only hold on as the strange sensation continued to assault his insides. Eventually, he couldn't feel any more of the crimson energy in his body. At the same time, the dome in front of him had dissipated into thin air.

He made a cursory examination of his body but couldn't find any abnormalities. At the very least, he hadn't turned into some horrible monster yet.

I need to hurry...

Red knew Narcha was still locked in combat with the monsters, and he couldn't afford to take his time.

He walked over to a spot on the ground—the same place the dome had been centered around. After some digging, he felt the handle of a cold, hard object and pulled it out from the dirt.

Red raised it into the light. It was his improvised cleaver—dirty and damaged from his fight with the spiders, but still as sharp as ever. He was thrilled by the discovery, but he pushed the feeling aside and continued to dig.

The next thing he dug out was his ragged pouch, which he opened in a hurry. What he saw, though, immediately dampened his delight.

His items were still there—the underground map, a page of Viran's diary, the insectoid core, and the moonstones. However, something had changed with the last two items. The insectoid crystal still glowed bright green, but the crimson lines that had once tainted it were gone. Red knew the likely reason why it had happened, but this wasn't what concerned him. Instead, it was the moonstones.

They had completely lost their luster, becoming useless gray lumps of rock. Red squeezed one and watched in shock as it crumbled into dust. It hadn't contained an ounce of energy.

Could this be the work of that moon being?

Red's mind raced with possible theories, but there was little he could do about it. At least he still had the insectoid crystal, which, according to Viran, was worth the energy of hundreds of moonstones. He only hoped it wouldn't suffer the same fate.

As he stored the items in his backpack, something stirred within his body. Alarmed, Red turned towards a set of trees to his left. At a glance, he saw nothing in between the dead trunks, but this didn't assuage his concerns.

The feeling was still there, insistent.

He got up and raised his cleaver in preparation. A few seconds later, a figure walked into view, and he felt his blood run cold.

It was the zombie.

The creature was still missing an arm, but it hadn't lost anything else. It ignored him and examined its surroundings. Eventually, its gaze came to a stop on the hole Red had just dug, and a serious look came over its stony face.

It stared at Red, and he immediately knew what it was looking for. The infected core.

He shrugged. "Someone else took it."

The zombie smiled, and a strange croaking noise came from its throat.

Is that... laughter?

Red couldn't tell, but he decided to take a slow step back. The creature didn't move, staring at him with a mocking smile on its face.

It's not concerned about me running away.

After realizing that running wasn't an option, he changed tactics.

"I thought zombies were supposed to be stupid," he said.

The undead continued to smile. It took a step forward and extended its remaining hand in his direction. A raspy noise came from the creature's throat. Red recognized the word.

"Give..."

He knew what the zombie wanted, but there was no way he would give it up.

"What do you want it for?" he asked.

This time, the zombie's smile disappeared. It had deduced his strategy. Red just wanted to stall for time because he didn't believe Narcha was dead.

He'd seen the undead and the warrior fight before. Back then, they had been closely matched, but Red could still tell Narcha was holding back in fear of getting hit. If the zombie ever managed to wound her, she would never let it go scot-free. The creature would be torn apart in her furious counterattack once she threw caution to the wind.

Red thus concluded that she wasn't dead, and the zombie had just managed to slip by her. His plan was to stall and hope she would come to his rescue. There was, however, no guarantee Narcha could follow their trail, or even arrive in time, for that matter.

And now the zombie was growing impatient. Red tried to think of a plan, when suddenly another question crossed his mind.

Why isn't it attacking me?

It didn't make sense for the creature to not simply take the crystal by force, much less when it was in hostile territory. Still, blindly guessing the reason behind its actions wasn't any help.

"I can't give it to you," he said. "But maybe I can let you borrow it."

The creature grimaced and took another step in his direction.

"Okay, okay!" Red threw his hands up. "I'll give it to you if you let me go!"

The zombie stopped and stared at him, as if in thought. Eventually, it nodded in agreement. But this only made Red more suspicious.

Why is it so cooperative?

He paused, almost compelled to push the subject, but the zombie's grimace worsened once it noticed his hesitation. In the end, he could only pull out his backpack and hunt for some way to prevent the creature from attacking.

Red knew where he'd stored the crystal, but he decided to take his time searching for it. The zombie growled in annoyance.

"I just forgot where I put it," he said.

Another growl, and this time the creature approached him.

"Here, take it!"

He pulled an object out of his backpack and threw it at the zombie. It extended its hand to catch it and looked down at its palm.

It was a piece of rock.

When it looked up, Red was already running away. The zombie didn't wait anymore and shot after him.

Red didn't need to look back to know it was catching up. Any attempts to lose its trail were useless, and the zombie steadily closed the distance between them. He tried to track its pace, focusing on the sound of the footsteps behind him.

He recalled his battle with the scythe-armed monster, and the sheer concentration surviving it had required. Then he remembered the lessons he'd received from Domeron a few days ago. Eventually, his confidence surged. He was ready.

Suddenly, the sound of footsteps behind him ceased.

It lunged!

Red reacted by diving to the side. The zombie's claws missed his body by a few centimeters, striking a tree trunk instead. He could hear splintering wood behind him, but he didn't stop running.

The zombie groaned in anger and continued its chase. Red pushed his Upper Leg Vein to the limit, boosting his speed, but it wasn't nearly enough

to outrun his pursuer. Not to mention, he wasn't confident he could successfully dodge every one of its attacks.

Just as Red wondered whether he should stand and fight, he felt something strange again. It was similar to the sensation that had helped him
discover the zombie earlier, but not identical. Without hesitation, he
changed directions and headed towards where the strange sensation
guided him.

The zombie either didn't notice the change or didn't care, continuing the
chase. A few seconds later, just as it prepared to strike again, a shadow
jumped at it from between the trees.

Red dove out of the way of the dark figure and rolled to the ground.
When he regained his footing, what he saw left him shocked.

The crimson demon had pounced on the zombie. It tore the undead
apart, giving it no chance to react as it ripped off pieces of dead flesh like
paper. In a matter of moments, the zombie was a mangled mess.

Red could still see movement in some of its severed limbs, but soon
enough, even that ceased. He stood dazed for a few seconds before slowly
stepping away from the scene.

A few seconds later, the demon's frenzy came to a stop. It got up again
and turned around, its gaze coming to rest on Red. He suddenly froze, but
rather than fear, he felt something else within his body.

As it looked at him, the monster seemed to calm down. This moment
didn't last long, though, and its murderous nature returned much stronger
than before. It roared at the sky, as if releasing its rage.

Red immediately turned around and ran.

The demon, however, was even faster than the zombie. Red had no hope
of outrunning it and little chance at evading its attacks, so there was only
one option left. He turned back, ready to make his last stand—when he felt
that same strange sensation appear again.

Alongside it came the thunderous noise of air splitting apart. A spinning
saber flew out from the trees, slamming into the side of the demon as it
prepared to pounce on Red.

A panting Narcha appeared between the trees.

"Fucking bastards!" She gritted her teeth. "You're way too fast!"

CHAPTER 100

COALITION

RED LOOKED Narcha over and was relieved to see she wasn't wounded. She looked him over too, frowning.

"I thought you would be dead for sure..." she said. "I gotta say, it was a terrible idea to come— Wait, what's that in your hand?" She pointed at Red's cleaver.

He was just about to answer when a roar interrupted their conversation. They turned toward the fallen demon, noticing it slowly come back to its feet.

"It's still alive?!" Narcha's eyes widened in shock.

Red was also surprised. He could tell how much strength had been in that saber throw—a human would've easily been cleaved in half. As the demon got up, they could see the extent of its damage.

The creature had a large gash on its side that bled profusely. Pieces of broken scales were scattered around the wound, but the saber hadn't penetrated too deeply. It was clear the demon's outer defenses were remarkably sturdy.

For a second, both parties stared at each other, the demon showing some uncharacteristic caution. Suddenly, it turned and ran. Narcha and Red were bewildered by the creature's actions, but the warrior's senses quickly returned.

"Don't let it escape!" she shouted, giving chase. She grabbed her saber from the ground as she ran off.

Red, however, didn't move and simply watched the demon and Narcha disappear within the sea of dead trees. A minute later, she returned with an ugly look on her face.

"Why didn't you follow me?" she asked.

Red shrugged. "It's way too fast. I could never have kept up with you."

"You could've tried to shoot it with your bow."

"If even your saber could barely make a dent, my arrows would never pierce its scales."

Narcha looked like she wanted to argue further, but then she sighed. She recognized the truth in his words.

"So now we have a demon wandering this forest. How great!" Narcha shook her head.

"Maybe this will keep the bandits in check," Red said.

"I wish, but demons are even more of a risk than bandits."

"How so?" Red was aware of how dangerous the demon was, but he couldn't fathom it measuring up to hundreds of bandits.

"Demons can grow in strength too," Narcha explained. "Not by cultivation, but by other... more violent means. A forest full of bandits to slaughter is ideal for a demon to grow. That one looked pretty strong, too, so it might be close to breaking through to Lesser Ring Realm."

Red was surprised by this revelation. "Does it get stronger by killing?"

Narcha nodded. "It's a bit more complicated than that, but you can think about it that way."

Such a concept seemed absurd to him. Now he understood why Narcha wanted to eliminate that threat so much.

"Was that demon a cultivator before?" Red asked.

"Probably. Monsters can also become demons, but from the appearance of that one, it's safe to assume it was a human."

"What about that zombie?" Red pointed at the mutilated corpse nearby.

Narcha stared at what remained of the undead. Wincing, she still regarded it with caution.

"I don't know," she admitted, her concern clear. "But I can tell you it was no normal zombie, that's for sure."

"At least it's dead now."

"You're right, but we'll need to get to the bottom of this once we're back at the Sect."

Narcha sheathed her saber on her back and again eyed the black cleaver in Red's hand. "So, are you going to tell me where you got that from?"

Red shook his head.

"Bah, why do I even bother?" Narcha glared at him. "Did you at least get your things?"

He nodded.

"Then let's get out of here before—"

Her words were cut off by a wave of shouts. They heard voices approaching from the north—a lot of them.

"The bandits are still alive?" Red asked.

"Some of them managed to escape and probably called for reinforcements," Narcha said. "It doesn't matter. We need to get out of here as soon as possible."

He promptly agreed with her suggestion. After he collected his belongings, the pair headed south at a brisk pace, and soon enough, they couldn't hear the bandits. This, however, didn't bring Red any relief.

"They're definitely going to notice our footprints next to the zombie's body," he said. Neither of them had time to cover their tracks while fighting for their lives.

Narcha nodded solemnly. "I know."

"Do you think you can take them all?" Red asked.

"Let's hope it doesn't come to that."

This was telling. It seemed they weren't out of danger just yet.

"We should try hiding, then," he suggested.

Narcha snorted. "At what point did you start thinking I was afraid of them? Besides, they know this forest too well for us to lose them."

"Then what do you propose?"

"We hurry back to the city and hope they know better than to try to chase us."

That was as good a plan as any.

Thankfully, the journey northwest over the next few hours was uneventful. They left the dead zone, and Red began to disguise their tracks again. He didn't know how effective it would be against experienced trackers, but he tried his best.

But there was something bothering him.

The strange feeling that had allowed Red to notice Narcha, the zombie, and the demon hadn't disappeared. In fact, as they returned to the living part of the forest, it flared up constantly, all over his body and at different levels of intensity. Some didn't last more than a few seconds before disappearing. He had trouble identifying where these prickling feelings came from, but he felt them, nonetheless.

Whenever he looked in the direction the sense was pointing him, he saw different things. Sometimes it pointed at birds flying in the canopy. Other times, it pointed right below his feet. Some were so faint that Red had a hard time noticing them.

But there was one sensation stronger than any other in his vicinity.

Red looked up at Narcha.

The feeling she radiated was the strongest by far—not even the demon seemed able to compare. In fact, even if he closed his eyes, he could still pinpoint her exact location.

As if to confirm his theory, he began to change position relative to Narcha. It didn't matter if he was behind, to the side, or in front of her. The strange sense inside his body constantly pointed at her.

"What the fuck are you doing?" Narcha asked once she noticed his odd movements.

"Nothing."

She looked annoyed but let the matter go once Red settled down. He took the opportunity to ponder the change his body had gone through.

After some more observation, he confirmed that the strange sensations seemed to be pointing at living things around him. Not only that, but the strength of the feedback apparently depended on how big said things were. Narcha, for instance, had the strongest flare in his senses, while small creatures were much weaker.

No, that's not right...

Red thought back to his encounter with the zombie. That undead had also triggered his sense, and it definitely wasn't alive. Then there was the demon. It had been bigger than Narcha, but it had felt weaker to his sense. It seemed there were other criteria to how this power worked.

Does it detect strength?

That didn't seem right. The sensation he'd felt from the zombie was much weaker than Narcha's and hadn't matched its strength. Something wasn't adding up, so Red assumed there was more to the puzzle.

As they walked, he tried to think of other possibilities of what his new sense might be reacting to. He considered blood, Spiritual Energy, and even more ephemeral things such as souls or life essence. In the end, Red just couldn't tell for sure what could be causing the sensations without more experimentation.

The source of this new power, though, was evident to his mind.

That crimson thing...

Red didn't feel at ease with its presence inside his body, but he didn't regret his decision either. He was already in deep trouble, and whatever the mist's intentions, they didn't seem detrimental to him.

Red still wasn't sure what the "deal" he'd struck with the crimson energy entailed beyond it just accompanying him. Either way, as long as he got to live another day, there was still hope.

I refused a deal with the blob, only to accept one with a different entity...

The irony wasn't lost on him, and he knew he would have refused the deal under less desperate circumstances, but for some reason, he felt more trusting of this crimson energy. After all, he had discerned its sincerity. It was suffering and in need of help—help that only Red could provide.

As he was lost in his thoughts, Narcha eventually called their march to a stop. He looked up at her in confusion, noticing the serious expression on her face.

"Voices ahead," she said.

"How many?" Red asked.

"Five, probably more."

"Are they looking for us?"

"How would I know? But they're coming in our direction."

"Let's avoid them."

For some reason, Narcha looked reluctant.

"What is it?" he asked. "Do you really want to fight them?"

"That's not it," she said. "I could swear I recognized one of the voices."

"From this distance?" Red was skeptical.

"They're very loud."

Indeed, a few moments later, even Red heard the boisterous voices.

Eventually, recognition flashed across Narcha's face, followed shortly by anger.

"Motherfucker."

Red didn't know what had her upset. "We need to do something," he insisted.

"Right." Narcha nodded, gritting her teeth. "But I need to confirm something."

They decided to hide on top of a small hill nearby, as she insisted on spying on whoever was passing by, and Red could only relent. But when he saw the group of people, even he was surprised.

"Is that..."

"Gustav's cronies," Narcha confirmed.

Red hadn't forgotten their armor from the first day he'd arrived in the city. In the center of the group, he even recognized a figure.

Reinhart—Gustav's direct subordinate.

Not only that, but they were calmly walking amidst the bandits.

CHAPTER 101
REUNITING

RED WAS ABOUT to say something when he saw Reinhart look their way.

"Get down!" Narcha yanked him to the ground.

He didn't resist, and the next moment, the two of them were lying prone behind a bush. He couldn't discern what the men were talking about, but there was no pause in their conversation as they kept walking south. Soon enough, they were out of his range.

At that point, Narcha got up, and Red followed suit. She had a grim look on her face.

"Is Gustav making deals with the bandits?" Red asked.

"Seems to be the case," Narcha said. "But there's something weird going on here."

"What do you mean?"

"Gustav is the biggest merchant in town. His business was hurt the most by the bandits. I can't see a reason as to why he would take the risk of working with them."

"Maybe his subordinates betrayed him."

She shook her head, dismissing the idea. "I doubt the bandits could offer more money than Gustav."

"Then do you want to follow them?"

At this question, Narcha's frown deepened. "... No."

"Are you scared of them?" Red asked.

"Who said I'm scared?" She scowled. "But Gustav's people aren't as easy to deal with as bandits. Not to mention, that Reinhart guy is no slouch. I saw him fight Domeron in the past."

"Really?" Red was surprised by this. "Who won?"

"They didn't get to settle the fight before the guards interrupted," Narcha said. "But the fact that he could keep up with Domeron means he isn't much weaker than me."

Red felt she was downplaying Reinhart's strength. From what Domeron had told him, the swordsman felt confident he could defeat Narcha. If Reinhart could keep up with him, that meant he might be even more powerful than her.

"He looked in our direction," Red said. "Do you think he noticed us?"

"If he did, why would they just keep walking? Either way, we should get out of here just to be safe."

He agreed with her assessment. During their conversation, he had also noted a curious fact. His new sense didn't seem to pick up on the bandits. Red assumed this was likely due to a distance limit on his ability.

The men had been over a hundred meters away, which helped him estimate his range of detection. He couldn't complain—his new sense had already proven useful—but he regretted missing the opportunity to test the power on more people.

Gradually, the pair put some distance between themselves and the bandits. It was then that something dawned on Red.

"Why do you think they were heading in that direction? Back to the dead forest?"

"Who knows?" Narcha shrugged. "Maybe they were also hunting the zombie."

"It didn't look like they were preparing for a fight."

"What do you want me to say?" She narrowed her eyes, annoyed at him. "Unless we follow or question them directly, there's no way we'll know."

Red knew she was right, but the matter still concerned him. "What if they meet up with the other bandits and turn around to chase us?"

"Bah, don't be so pessimistic! We don't even know if the bandits are chasing—"

Suddenly, loud voices came from the place they'd just left. It seemed her question had been answered.

Narcha's face fell, and she shot Red an angry look. "I'm never traveling with you again!"

He didn't know what he had done wrong.

The duo changed course many times over the next couple of hours, trying to lose their pursuers, but no matter what, the bandits simply reappeared from another direction. This told Red they were being chased by multiple groups who had a good grasp of their position and route.

"How the fuck did they find us again so quickly?" Narcha seemed to be in disbelief.

Red was also confused. The bandits were coming from different parts of the forest, far from the first group they'd encountered. Red just couldn't understand how the information about him and Narcha could have spread so far, so quickly.

"Can they communicate over long distances?" he asked.

"They're bandits, for fuck's sake!" She shook her head. "There's no way they could get their hands on something like..."

She trailed off, and Red could imagine where her mind was heading.

"It's that Gustav bastard!" She punched a tree in anger. "Only he could afford communication talismans in this town!"

"Why would he spend so much money to equip the bandits?" Red asked.

"You make a good point," Narcha said. "But other than communication talismans, I don't see how a whole fucking bandit army could be chasing us so soon. Gustav's the only one who could make that happen."

"Maybe there's another explanation." Even as Red said this, he had no idea what it might be.

"Maybe, but it doesn't matter," she replied through gritted teeth. "They might know where we're going, but we're still one step ahead. As long as we keep our pace, we can..."

She went quiet as voices came from farther ahead. More bandits were closing in from multiple angles. Narcha turned around and gave Red a glare.

"Did I do something?" he asked.

"Gah! Let's try to go around them, quick!"

At her command, Red led the way through the trees. However, they could still hear more bandits approaching. Soon enough, sneaking around them would become impossible.

"How the fuck can they pinpoint our location?" Narcha growled.

Red shared her concern. The forest was enormous, and even if the bandits could communicate over long distances, this alone wasn't enough for them to surround the two this perfectly. It was almost as if they had exact knowledge of the duo's whereabouts.

The situation was quickly slipping out of their control.

"What do you wanna do?" Red asked.

"We... try to sneak past them," Narcha said after some thought. "If it doesn't work, we can only fight our way through. Either way, we can't get surrounded."

It was a simple plan, but it was the only one they could devise on the spot. Night was fast approaching, and perhaps that would increase their chances of slipping past the bandits. Just as the two of them were about to head out, though, Red felt something.

His new power, which he had decided to call his crimson sense, detected a strong flare entering his range. It wasn't as strong as Narcha's, but it was still powerful enough to raise his alarm.

"Someone's approaching," he said.

"What?" She stared at him in shock. Still, she didn't try to dispute his claim. "Where?"

Red cautiously pointed behind them. Narcha squinted her eyes and looked between the trees. "I don't see anything," she said, but she didn't lower her guard.

"They stopped moving," Red insisted. "They might have noticed you looking at them."

His crimson sense couldn't tell exactly how far someone was from him, but he could determine whether they were approaching by the increasing intensity of their presence.

Narcha looked awestruck. "How the fuck can you tell that..."

Of course, Red would have preferred to keep his new ability hidden, but he couldn't afford to with their lives on the line.

"I just know," he said.

"You..." Narcha, still annoyed, just sighed and nodded. "Get your bow ready. I'm not gonna have someone tail us while we escape."

"You might alert the other bandits."

"According to you, they might already know where we are, so what's the point?" She winced. "Just get ready and watch my back."

Although the warrior didn't say what she was about to do, Red had a pretty good idea. He prepared his bow, and when she saw he was ready, Narcha sprung into action.

In one swift motion, the warrior shot into a sprint and unsheathed her saber, charging in the direction Red had pointed. All of a sudden, though, an arrow shot at her.

"Shit!"

Narcha cursed before stumbling out of the way to find cover. The arrow, however, didn't even seem to have been aimed at her, striking the ground in front of her feet harmlessly. She was confused for a second before peeking out to examine the arrow.

"Motherfucker." Narcha, shaking her head, walked out from her cover.

Red was alarmed by her reckless actions, but her next words surprised him.

"Rog, what the fuck do you think you're doing?"

A hunter with unkempt clothing and a scraggly beard appeared in clear view. Sure enough, it was Rog, who looked dejectedly at the two of them.

"How did you know I was here?" he asked.

"Is that what you're concerned about?" Narcha scowled at him. "You fucking shot me!"

"I had to stop you before you alarmed the bandits," Rog said. He then turned to Red. "Was it you who found me?"

Red hesitated for a second, but then nodded.

"I was found out by a child..." The man hung his head. "I'm not qualified to be a hunter anymore."

"Hey, you motherfucker!" Narcha hissed, frustrated at being ignored. "How did you even find us?"

"I picked up on your trail the day after you left," Rog said. "Eiwin wanted to follow you, but I told her you guys would always be a step ahead of us anyways. Yesterday, we came across a bunch of bandits moving about, and we decided to follow them. Sure enough, it led us right to you..."

Just as Narcha had predicted, Eiwin really had come looking for them, and Rog had proven to be as skilled as Red expected. However, there was something confusing about Rog's explanation.

Narcha said, "I see—wait, did you say yesterday?"

"Yeah, that's what I said." Rog nodded. "The bandits were all on high alert, and we thought there was a good chance you guys were behind it."

Narcha put on a thoughtful expression.

"We shouldn't talk here," Red interrupted. Even now, bandits were still approaching their location.

"Oh, right!" The hunter perked up as if he'd just remembered something. "I forgot to tell you, but I had to shoot one of them to sneak through."

Narcha froze. "You... what?!"

"Yeah, I mean, it was that or getting noticed..." Rog shrugged. "Either way, they'll probably notice it at any—"

Several shouts suddenly spiked through the forest's silence. The bandits had clearly noticed something was wrong.

"You fucking..." Narcha gritted her teeth and stared daggers at Rog. "Argh! Let's just go!"

Red couldn't agree with her more.

CHAPTER 102

ENCIRCLED

"This way." Rog beckoned Red and Narcha. Now that the hunter was here, the responsibility of leading the way fell to him. Unfortunately, even Rog couldn't keep them hidden for long.

"Hey, I see them!" a bandit called out from behind them.

"Faster!" Rog said, and the group broke into a sprint.

Ahead, Red could already see the silhouettes of bandits rushing towards them. He put away his bow and drew his cleaver, ready for battle, but Narcha was already a step ahead.

"I'll lead the charge!" she said. "You two watch my flanks!"

Rog already had his bow drawn and was aiming ahead. Red felt his crimson sense flare as more people entered its range, and at the same time, the first handful of bandits appeared in clear view.

"They're here—" The bandit couldn't even finish talking, as an arrow pierced his throat.

The other men were startled, and before they could even collect themselves, Narcha had already reached them. With a ferocious swing, she attacked the unlucky bandit who happened to be at the front. Her target tried to raise his shortsword to block, but the saber broke his blade in half and cleaved into his body.

Narcha didn't even stop to keep attacking, rushing past the remaining bandits. The men, perhaps intimidated, didn't give chase, but this didn't spare them from Rog's arrows. He shot another bandit in the chest, who fell to the ground with a groan. One tried to swing at Red as he ran by, but he had no problems dodging past it after all his training and experience.

Just like that, they were past the first blockade with Narcha leading the way. It seemed, however, that they were not in the clear just yet.

"Archers up ahead!" Rog warned.

A handful of bandits armed with bows stood firmly in their path, taking aim at the group. On top of that, even more bandits were rushing to intercept them. Red's crimson sense grew overwhelmed by the dozens of flickers that entered its range.

"From the left!" the hunter called out.

At his warning, Red dove ahead and kept low to the ground. A moment later, the twang of bows sounded. Some arrows hit the place where he'd just been standing while most were blocked by the surrounding trees. Rog and Narcha also dodged without issue, but their sudden change of direction allowed a group of several bandits to approach them.

Narcha, who remained in the lead, just barreled ahead, saber raised. "Keep going!"

Most of their adversaries focused on the intimidating warrior at the front of the group, but a few also went for Rog and Red.

An ugly-faced bandit swung his hatchet in a wide arc, hoping to hit Red. He had no problem sidestepping the attack, but mid-dodge, another bandit tried to stab him with a spear from the other side.

He swung his cleaver up, slicing through the wooden shaft with surprising ease before the weapon could connect, leaving his opponent stunned. But his actions delayed his movement, and the first bandit was already swinging at him again. Red braced himself to block, but an arrow suddenly plunged into the man's chest, instantly dropping him.

"Focus on dodging!" Rog said with uncharacteristic solemnness. "Don't let them slow you down!"

Red noticed that the hunter's opponents had been shot down before they could even approach him. He nodded before dashing ahead, leaving his disarmed opponent clueless as to what he should do.

Narcha had already killed anyone who tried to go up against her, and the remaining bandits kept out of her way, waiting for reinforcements. Still, their enemies had succeeded in slowing the group down.

Rog gave another sudden warning. "From the right!"

More twangs of bows and another wave of arrows came. There were fewer of them this time and were easily dodged. Still, they forced the trio to diverge from their straight path, allowing more bandits to approach.

"This isn't working!" Narcha said as she battered away another opponent. "We need to stay and fight!"

"Not here!" Rog shook his head as he shot another arrow into an approaching bandit. "We'll just get surrounded!"

Red, for his own part, focused on dodging the bandits' attacks and slipping by them. Those who targeted him were frustrated by how slippery he proved to be, unable to even touch the boy. Still, it was clear that as time went on, the task of running past unharmed was proving to be difficult.

"Ahead of us!" Narcha pointed forward.

Red looked up and saw a dozen bandits forming a line to stop their advance.

"How the fuck are there so many of them?!" Narcha gritted her teeth but didn't stop running.

A few of the bandits raised their bows and fired straight at the warrior, who didn't bother to dodge. She raised her saber to block the arrows, and most of them bounced off her steel weapon. A few slipped past her guard, though, and stuck into her leather armor. Yet they either failed to pierce her flesh, or she was unbothered by the wounds, as Narcha's steps didn't slow down for even a second.

Like a mad bull, she charged directly at the bandits, brandishing her saber in a wide arc. A few brave men tried to stand in her way but were thrown aside by the sheer force of her blows. Other bandits flanked her, seeking to stab her with their spears.

"Take her right!" Rog called to Red before shooting at one of her attackers.

Red rushed forward. Thankfully, his first target was distracted by the menacing warrior and didn't notice his approach.

As the bandit got ready to attack, he lost his balance and fell to the ground. Looking down in confusion, he noticed his left leg had been severed at the knee in a smooth cut. He screamed in pain and horror, staring at the escaping child responsible for the wound.

Red didn't even bother finishing him off as Narcha cleared a way through the bandit blockade. However, their opponents had bought more time for their reinforcements, who now approached from both sides.

The waves of bandits seemed endless.

Suddenly, the bandits approaching them from the front froze in place. Screams resounded from the rear of their formation, and they all whirled around in alarm.

Narcha's eyes lit up. "That's our chance!" She sped up.

Rog and Red did their best to keep up, but someone had already started to engage their enemies before they could catch up, literally throwing the bandits around. As the trio approached, the reason behind the sudden commotion was revealed.

"Eiwin!" Narcha's face filled with joy. "Thank god you're here!"

Eiwin didn't immediately respond, too focused on finishing the remaining bandits instead. Red could finally get a glimpse of her fighting style. She was faster and more precise than Narcha, but the strength behind her blows was still staggering.

She grabbed the arm of a bandit in her iron grip and swung him over her shoulder into the ground. Then she followed up with a whiplike kick against another unfortunate man who was too stunned to counter. The bandit was sent flying into a tree, falling limply to the ground.

The quiet that followed was all too brief. "We need to hurry!" Eiwin said.

Indeed, Red could already hear more bandits approaching from several directions.

Narcha shook her head. "We need to fight them! I can stop for a second and take on the next wave."

Eiwin, however, just looked at her with a solemn expression. "We can't. Rickard is here."

Her words heightened the tension in the air, though Rog didn't seem surprised. Red recognized the name of the Bandit Lord who was at the Lesser Ring Realm.

"Fuck!" Narcha gritted her teeth and relented. "Let's go!"

That was all they needed to hear.

"Red, stay in the center," Eiwin said. "I'll bring up the rear."

Red didn't protest her decision. She might have been doing this to protect him, but the truth was that she was far more qualified for the task. The group quickly repositioned themselves and resumed their escape.

Bandits continued chasing them, seemingly unbothered by the recent addition to their numbers. Red thought their bravery was foolish, considering how many of their companions had died at their hands, but now that he knew their leader was nearby, maybe their confidence was justified.

He also took note of Eiwin's presence in his crimson sense. It was on par with Narcha's, perhaps even more powerful, which seemed strange. Still, Red didn't have time to reflect on it.

"More bandits are waiting for us!" Rog pointed up ahead.

"How the fuck can they organize this quickly?" Narcha griped. "Keep course! We'll just punch through them!"

Red could see where Narcha's confidence was coming from, but the whole situation alarmed him. It seemed the bandits were intent on stopping the group no matter the cost, and he just couldn't understand why.

As the group set on an imminent collision course, something entered Red's crimson sense. It was a strong fluctuation, on par with Narcha or Eiwin, and it immediately put him on alert as it steadily approached their location.

"Behind us! Someone strong!" His sudden cry confused the group, but Eiwin was quick to check his claims.

Her eyes flickered. "Narcha, watch out!"

A shrill sound rang out and a spear shot towards Narcha. The warrior was surprised, but she was quick to react too, swinging her saber against the oncoming spear. But the force behind the projectile was greater than she was expecting.

Narcha slid backward, her weapon almost slipping from her hands, but she still managed to deflect the attack successfully. With a grimace on her face, she regarded the spear, which had shattered into pieces upon colliding with her saber. She stared in the direction the weapon had come, but no one stepped out from behind the trees.

Red, however, could still feel a presence with his crimson sense. It had stopped approaching them.

"Let's move!" Narcha brought them out of their momentary pause.

Eiwin frowned at her companion but kept running.

Red felt the flare in his crimson sense weaken as they ran further, until it eventually disappeared. He couldn't help but fear whoever had launched the surprise attack. If the spear had been aimed at him, would he have survived?

He already knew the answer to that question.

"They're retreating!" Narcha called from the front.

Sure enough, the bandit blockade in front of them dispersed, leaving their path free. Almost at the same time, their pursuers had also stopped giving chase. Red was bewildered, but no one in the group had time to question it.

Soon, they were far away from the bandits. Rog didn't call their sprint to a stop until they had changed directions several times to make quite sure they weren't being followed. Red was out of breath from the effort, having to tap into his latent strength to keep up with the rest of his companions.

Narcha, too, didn't seem to be in good condition.

"Fuck!" She spat on the ground and pulled the arrows from her armor.

"Was that Rickard?" Red asked, remembering the ambusher who had almost hit Narcha.

"No. If it was Rickard, I'd already be dead," she said. "It was someone else."

"Why didn't they chase us?" Eiwin wondered.

"I'm not sure," Narcha said. "But I feel like I recognized that spear..."

CHAPTER 103

THE FOREST PROBLEM

"WE SHOULD KEEP MOVING," Rog said. "We aren't in the clear just yet."

"Right," Narcha said. "I just can't shake off a weird feeling about this whole situation..."

Red felt the same way, but the group was not prepared to go against an entire army of bandits just to find out why they'd been so adamant about chasing them. At least not yet.

They continued traveling for a while longer, slowing down to a walk, and night soon arrived. The lunar gaze settled on Red, but this time he was barely affected by it.

It's still getting weaker.

He began to wonder if something special would happen once the full moon arrived. Still, just the fact that the gaze had weakened was enough for now.

Rog had them march for several hours into the night before he felt comfortable setting up a camping spot. He dropped his things on the ground and turned to the rest of the group.

"No campfire tonight. I'll be keeping watch until the morning."

Red was not used to such a serious attitude from Rog, which only went to show how dangerous their earlier encounter had been. No one in the group contested his decision, and soon enough, they had settled down for the night.

"Do you mind telling me what happened?" Eiwin asked. She'd been quiet during the whole trip, but her concern was clear.

"It was his idea!" Narcha pointed at Red.

This was only met with a stern frown from Eiwin.

"She owed me a favor, and I asked for her help with recovering something I lost in the forest," Red said, trying to give a quick explanation.

"Why didn't you ask me?" Eiwin looked troubled. "You know I would have helped you."

"Maybe, but I needed to get it back quickly, and even if you did help me, it might have taken a lot of convincing and time. Whereas with Narcha, I could just force her hand to have her do what I wanted."

"Is that why you chose me, you little brat?!"

Red simply nodded, which only made Narcha angrier.

Eiwin stepped in. "You know that you could have died back there, right, Red?"

"I do." He was obviously aware of that. The mission had turned out to be more dangerous than he expected in the end, but even before he set off, he had already come to terms with the risk.

"And you're fine with risking your life like that?" she asked.

"... If it's for the right reasons, then I don't mind," Red answered after some thought.

Eiwin remained silent for a few seconds. She seemed to be in deep thought but eventually sighed and looked back at Red.

"I understand... However, in the future, I would hope you could put more trust in us."

He didn't respond.

"I don't know what you went through in the past, and I don't know how hard what I'm asking for is, but... Everyone in this Sect is willing to die for each other—all you need to do is ask. Your secrets, your past—as soon as you entered our Sect, we decided to take on all of that too. That's the responsibility we assumed the day we decided you would join. Even the ones that protested"—she looked at Narcha—"will still stand at your side in your hour of need, even if they didn't owe you a favor."

The warrior looked away in embarrassment.

"I'm not asking for the same devotion out of you," Eiwin went on. "But I'm asking you to try considering us from a different perspective. It might take time, and you may find yourself unconvinced, but... When you feel the time is right, I ask this of you: give us a chance, alright?"

Red nodded. Even though he didn't agree with her, he didn't make light of what she was asking of him. In the end, that seemed more than enough to raise her spirits again.

She smiled at him. "Great! Did you find what you were looking for?"

"I did," he said.

"Is it that blade?" Rog asked.

Everyone's attention was drawn to Red's dark cleaver. It was stained with blood, and part of the blade was corroded, but its sharpness was still plainly evident.

"Yes," he said.

This wasn't a lie, though it wasn't the whole truth either.

Narcha glared at him. "Hope that thing was worth having us face a zombie!"

The atmosphere around the camp changed with those words, and Eiwin's newfound peace immediately disappeared.

"What did you say?" she asked.

"Uh, yeah. We found a zombie while we were traveling," Narcha said with an awkward expression. "Not only that, but a demon, too."

Eiwin's frown only deepened.

"No way, a zombie and a demon?" Rog sounded dismayed. "You're telling me I ended up missing all that?"

"... Tell me the story from the beginning," Eiwin ordered.

Narcha, who didn't want to anger her companion, recounted the details of their trip, from the bandit corpses to the dead zone in the forest, all the way to their final confrontation. She skipped many of the gritty details, but still made a point of explaining the oddities they'd found.

"It didn't act like a normal zombie," she said. "I thought the whole dead forest might be related somehow, but I didn't have time to explore it."

"The forest is dying?" Rog asked, wincing. "That's not good."

"Could that be why the monsters disappeared?" Narcha asked the hunter.

"No way," he said. "Monsters can migrate sometimes, but the whole problem with the monsters disappearing is that they left no tracks. They just went, poof, gone, no traces left behind..."

Red, who was keenly aware of the reason behind the dying forest, observed the conversation in silence.

"What you told me about the undead... Are you certain it was a zombie?" Eiwin asked.

"I'm no specialist in undead, but it sure did look like a zombie." Narcha shrugged.

"And yet it was intelligent, as you claim." The younger woman's expression fell. "That can only mean one thing... a Necromancer."

Narcha's expression twisted in horror, surprise. "No way! Wasn't their Sect destroyed?"

"It is, but that doesn't mean survivors weren't left behind," Eiwin said. "Still, they have been extremely secretive ever since. I just can't imagine what might have prompted one to reveal their presence here."

"What's a Necromancer?" Red asked.

"It's someone who cultivates using Death Spiritual Energy," Eiwin explained. "By manipulating said energy, they can create undead and control them freely."

Red was surprised that a person might be behind the monster. "So someone was controlling that zombie?"

"That's the only way an intelligent zombie can exist, but undead thralls can't move too far from their master. You're certain you didn't see anyone else nearby?"

"I'm certain," Narcha said. "But either way, don't they have to be at least in the Lesser Ring Realm to control undead? Someone like that could have easily hidden from us."

"Yet, if they wanted to kill you, why would they need to rely on a weak zombie?" Eiwin shook her head. "There's something we're not seeing here... I'll ask for Master Hector's advice once we return to the Sect."

Red was concerned about the existence of a Necromancer, but he wasn't about to go searching for one in the forest.

"What about the demon, the bandits, the dead forest?" Narcha asked. "There are too many weird things going on here. They have to be connected."

"Maybe. But we can't rush to conclusions," Eiwin said. "We'll likely have to organize some sort of hunting party. Once the Baron learns about what's happening in the forest, he won't stay still either."

"How will he deal with Rickard?" Red asked.

"I'm not sure," she said. "It depends on the stance Rickard takes. There's no doubt that if the Baron really wanted to, he could kill him... The problem is how big of a price he is willing to pay for it."

Red still wasn't too clear on the Baron's strength, but to keep peace in the region, he definitely needed to be powerful.

"There's something else too," Narcha said. "We saw Reinhart and Gustav's men walking with the bandits."

At that revelation, Eiwin looked so stunned she didn't know what expression to assume anymore. "To think he would stoop so low as to cooperate with the bandits... I would like to say that makes matters more complicated, but it might end up simplifying things."

"How so?" Narcha asked in confusion.

"The Baron has always been looking for conclusive evidence against Gustav. If he is in fact working with the bandits, then the Baron could act on the King's authority to arrest him."

Narcha dismissed the thought, her voice tinged with skepticism. "There's no way it's that easy."

"I'm afraid it might be," Eiwin insisted, "which is why looking deeper into this matter is a priority. Unfortunately, there's no way we can explore this region while Rickard is around."

"Wait, that's right!" Narcha jolted, remembering something. "How do you even know Rickard is here?"

Eiwin didn't respond and instead turned to Rog.

The hunter shrugged. "If the way is clear, we can show them tomorrow."

"What do you mean by that?" Narcha frowned.

Rog smiled at her. "You'll see."

Once morning arrived, Rog scouted the way ahead. After confirming everything was safe, he led them towards a clearing.

Narcha was shocked once she saw the scene. "What the hell..."

Before them was a patch of forest that seemed to have undergone a natural disaster. Trees were shredded as if they had exploded from the inside, making the entire area almost devoid of vegetation, and the ground was littered with small craters.

Red approached a tree stump, looking for any signs of what might have caused the destruction. There were no scorch marks, which meant this was no ordinary fire.

"Don't bother, kid," Rog said. "This is a trademark technique of Rickard's. He can cause an explosion of energy at the tip of his spear, blasting everything it comes in contact with."

"Can you even do that with a weapon?" Red asked, fascinated by the possibility.

"That and much more," Rog said.

Nearby, Narcha didn't look nearly as thrilled with this discovery. "Was he fighting someone?" she asked.

"We thought so too, but we couldn't find marks of any other Spiritual Arts," Eiwin said.

"Then what? Was he just destroying these trees for fun?"

Narcha's companion gave her a helpless smile.

"Did you guys find his tracks?" Red asked.

"I tried, but quickly lost them," Rog said. "That guy is smart enough not to leave any obvious trails."

This wasn't unexpected from someone who had broken through to Lesser Ring Realm, Red supposed.

"We shouldn't linger here too long." Eiwin looked around nervously. "The bandits might still be around this region, and the last thing we want is to meet Rickard himself."

The rest of the group promptly agreed, and they continued their journey.

Returning to Fordham-Bestrem still took a few days, but to their surprise, their journey went by without incident. Rog was able to identify several bandit tracks, but it was as if they were all doing their best to stay out of the group's way.

It was a curious matter, but Red wouldn't complain about returning to town without a fight.

The lunar gaze continued to weaken over the next few nights. When he discussed it with Rog, Red was assured the arrival of the full moon would happen soon.

As they entered the town's busy streets, though, Red was suddenly assaulted by dozens of flares in his crimson sense.

CHAPTER 104

NECROMANCER

RED ALMOST COLLAPSED as information overwhelmed his senses. Or, more specifically, his new crimson sense.

"Red, are you okay?" Eiwin asked, noticing his sudden imbalance.

"I'm fine." He shook off her worries, righting himself. "I just stumbled on something."

She looked skeptical but didn't press him. Of course, Red was far from fine, and countless fluctuations continued to attack his crimson sense as they went deeper into the town.

So many people...

Now he had yet another reason to hate crowds, if the previous ones weren't enough. Every person flared in the crimson sense quite clearly, and Red couldn't count how many there were. None were as strong compared to those of his companions, but there were so many that he felt overwhelmed.

Red tried to find some way to "turn off" his crimson sense to no avail, and it became difficult for him to process any visual or auditory information. He could only focus on walking behind his companions.

Thankfully, they soon arrived at the isolated part of town housing their Sect. Most of the flares disappeared, with the only ones that remained belonging to his fellow Sect members. Eiwin kept glancing back at him with concern, having noticed Red's discomfort despite his best attempts to hide it. He only nodded at her, and she refrained from asking any questions.

Once reaching the gate, Red suddenly felt four other fluctuations within the courtyard.

One was remarkably energetic but smaller than the rest of the group—as if it were a spark growing into a flame. The second one was bright, on par with Narcha's flare signature. The third one was also strong, but only once Red noticed it. It was remarkably difficult to pinpoint, requiring focus to confirm its existence.

As for the last one, it was the strongest of them all. It was even beyond Narcha's fluctuation in strength, almost drowning out all the others. However, Red couldn't help but feel there was something else unusual about this signature.

How is this one so different?

Before he could study them further, Narcha turned to speak to him.

"We'll need to report what we saw to Hector," she said.

Red had already braced himself for that, though he didn't know what was to come. Narcha pushed the gate open and entered, but she immediately froze mid-step once she took in the scene ahead.

"You're back!" Allen jumped with joy.

Right by the boy's side, a taciturn Hector stood. The elder had his arms crossed, staring down at the group with his usual sullen expression.

"You knew we were coming?" Narcha asked.

Hector scoffed. "How could I not when you're so damn loud? By the looks on your faces, it seems you have much to tell, huh?"

Narcha was about to talk back, but the attempt was cut short by a wave of the old man's hand.

"We'll talk inside." Hector turned to walk into the hall. "That includes you too, Rog!"

The hunter, who had been trying to sneak off, went totally still.

As the rest of the group filed into the hall, Allen approached Red. "Where did you go?" he asked eagerly. "Master Goulth and Eiwin were so worried!"

"I had to do something in the forest," Red answered.

"Then why didn't you take me? I could've helped you!"

"I don't think Hector would've liked that."

"Well, I suppose you're right," Allen said. He noticed the weapon strapped to Red's back. "Woah, where did you get that?"

"I found it."

"Can I try it?"

"No."

"Oh, come on! Why not?"

"Because I don't want to."

"Ugh..." He went quiet before his face lit up with an idea. "What if I let you try my weapon too?"

Red frowned in confusion. "What do you mean by that?"

"You'll see!" Allen smiled at him before walking into the hall.

Red watched the young master's back with suspicion before also entering the building. Inside, the others were already seated around the table, and to his surprise, Domeron had clearly been there for a while, sipping from a steaming mug.

"Here!" Allen beckoned him over, pointing at a free seat by his side.

Red walked over and sat down. Before the discussion began, he took the opportunity to pin down which flare belonged to each person. The energetic one belonged to Allen, the quiet one belonged to Domeron, and the strongest one belonged to Hector.

When Red looked at Hector, he noticed the old man staring at him with narrowed eyes. He felt a wave of apprehension travel through his body. But maybe it was a coincidence, as Hector eventually turned away to regard the rest of the group.

"So... care to tell me what happened?"

"I asked Narcha to accompany me to the forest." Red spoke first, much to the surprise of everyone around the table.

Hector turned back to him. "For what reason?"

"To get something I forgot there."

"What about those two?" Hector pointed at Rog and Eiwin.

"They were just following us because they were worried."

"Actually, Eiwin made me do it..." Rog interjected, earning himself an angry glare from both Eiwin and Hector.

The elder asked Red, "So, is that it?"

Red hesitated. "Well, there's a lot more that happened, but..."

"But what, brat?" This time, Hector seemed more annoyed.

"Aren't you going to punish us?"

This question was met with silence. A few seconds later, Hector simply laughed. "Hah! Why would I punish you?"

"For abandoning the Sect?" Red said after some thought.

"But you're back here, aren't you?"

"I suppose so."

"Then you didn't really abandon the Sect." Hector shook his head. "I'm not your nanny. Members of the Sect often travel out for other business, so why would I be mad when you were gone for just a week?"

Red was at a loss for words.

"Of course, if you were gone for longer, I would be angry, but as long as there's a reason and you don't get yourself killed, then it doesn't really matter to me."

Red felt foolish. It seemed he had been worried about nothing.

"Then what about me?" Allen asked. "Can I go out too?"

"Absolutely not," Hector said, shooting him down without hesitation.

"Why not?! You let Red do it!"

"You're the young master of our Sect!" he berated the boy, refusing to back down. "Once you've proven to me you can take care of yourself, you can go out as much as you please!"

"But—"

"Enough!" Hector cut him off. "I don't have time for your nonsense right now! If you want to remain here, then you'd better be quiet!"

Allen looked angry, but he just leaned back in silence.

Hector then turned back to Red. "What else happened?"

Red didn't respond, instead waiting expectantly for his travel companion to explain.

"We met a zombie," Narcha said, wincing slightly. "And a demon. And the forest is dying... And the bandits are moving in great numbers, too."

Immediately, the mood in the hall darkened. Both Domeron and Hector stared at Narcha in surprise while Allen looked eager to hear more.

"Explain from the beginning," Hector said.

Narcha did just that. From leaving town to encountering monsters and bandits, and then, finally, the two reuniting with Eiwin and Rog. She also mentioned Gustav's men traveling with the bandits, which didn't seem to surprise Hector. By the end, he had a thoughtful expression on his face.

"You said you didn't feel Death Spiritual Energy in that area of the forest?" Domeron asked.

"At least as far as I could tell, no, there was none," Narcha said. "Whatever caused that, it wasn't undead corruption."

"Then that can only mean one thing," he said. "Life Essence absorption."

The members around the table had expressions of realization. Red and Allen, however, were both confused.

"What does that mean?" the young master asked before Red could do it.

"It's a common demonic practice," Domeron said. "It consists of draining the Life Essence of other living beings to strengthen oneself. Hence why that part of the forest looked dead, and possibly why the demon was attracted to the area. So much concentrated Life Essence could attract demons from miles away."

This explanation confirmed and clarified many things for Red.

"What about the zombie?" Narcha asked. "There wasn't any reason for it to be attracted to that region."

"Unless it was controlled by a Necromancer, as I guessed," Eiwin said. "Rather than being lured over, it might simply have been brought there."

"That still doesn't explain what a Necromancer would want in the first place. Can they directly convert Life Essence Energy?"

Eiwin shook her head. She couldn't answer that.

"Eiwin is right," Hector interjected. "But this matter is more complicated than you might have guessed."

"What do you mean, Master Hector?" Eiwin asked. "I don't understand."

"That's because you lack a deeper understanding of Necromancers," he said. "You see, even if a Necromancer binds an undead to their will, that won't make the undead any more intelligent. A zombie, for instance, can only execute simple orders, no matter what."

"Then how could that zombie talk and perform such complex actions?"

"Because it wasn't being controlled. It was being possessed."

This time, everyone around the table was confused. Only Domeron seemed to recognize the full truth.

"What do you mean by that?" Narcha asked. "How can you even possess something already dead?"

"It takes a higher form of Necromancy," Hector explained. "In most cases, a Necromancer may only give orders to their thralls, not directly control them. This obviously limits an undead's usefulness, since its low intelligence can be a great disadvantage. Possession, however, allows a Necromancer to slip a portion of their consciousness inside their thralls and control their bodies at will."

"Then you mean we were fighting against a cultivator inside a zombie's body?"

"Indeed." Hector nodded. "However, their physical power will still be limited by their host, which is why you were able to get out alive."

Narcha's frown only worsened.

"Isn't there a range for this technique?" Red asked.

"There is, but it depends on the cultivator. The fact they can possess their undead means they're already very powerful, and the strongest Necromancers can control their thralls from the other side of the world."

There was one point Red still didn't understand. "If that Necromancer was so powerful, why did they need to rely on a weak zombie to investigate?"

"Because they're afraid, of course!" Hector said with a smile. "Their entire Sect was hunted to near extinction, and the ones that survived could only live in secrecy. The mere fact a Necromancer this powerful would risk exposure means there must have been something very alluring to them in that forest. In which case, I doubt they will give up on it easily."

Red suddenly had a terrible premonition.

CHAPTER 105

REFORGING

"THERE's no need to be concerned about that Necromancer for now," Hector told the Sect. "Now that they have been exposed, I sincerely doubt they would dare to make an appearance again so soon."

This gave Red some comfort, but it still didn't eliminate the threat in his mind.

"I'll inform the Baron of what we've learned," Domeron said. "Once the Cursebreakers get wind of this, they'll scour the forest in search of this Necromancer."

"Aren't they going to run into the bandits, though?" Red asked.

"Not necessarily," the swordsman said. "As far as their business is concerned, they don't care about anything other than culling undead corruption. If any bandits have been infected, they'll just get rid of them too."

Red didn't know whether they could trace this matter back to him, but keeping everything that had happened in the forest a secret would be next to impossible.

"What about the bandits?" Narcha asked. "Aren't they collaborating with Gustav?"

"That hardly comes as a surprise," Domeron said. "We always suspected that Gustav might be bribing them for safe passage for his caravan. But the fact they were seen together at such an important juncture is certainly concerning."

"This still doesn't explain the way they were acting," Eiwin said. "They seemed to know our exact position within the forest—that level of coordination doesn't belong to lowlife brigands. We considered the fact they might be using communication talismans, but there's no way Gustav could supply so many of them."

Everyone around the table seemed stumped for an answer, and their attention turned hopefully to Hector. The elder, however, was also in deep thought.

"There are other means through which cultivators may communicate over long distances," he said. "However, they are likewise as rare and as expensive as talismans. Whatever the case may be, these bandits have shown they can't be treated as common outlaws. I'm even more certain now that their arrival in the region is connected to the monsters' disappearance..."

At least not everything weird happening is because of me.

"What do you want to do?" Domeron asked.

"This is not something the lot of you can solve by yourselves," Hector said. "I want you to speak with the Baron. Any effort toward stopping these bandits and hunting that demon must be organized by him."

"What about Gustav? Do you want to force his hand?"

Hector scoffed. "Hmph, that little rat isn't stupid enough to be caught like this. He'll likely contribute to the hunt and won't hesitate to throw these bandits to the wolves to clear his own name."

That did seem to fit with what Red knew of the man.

"Then what about Rickard?" Narcha asked. "Do you plan on dealing with him yourself, old man?"

"Hah, why would I need to personally deal with a brat like that? Let the Baron's people lead the charge. If they really can't deal with someone in the middle of the Lesser Ring Realm, then they don't deserve to rule this town."

Red was once more surprised by Hector's attitude. In the end, the levity with which he talked about the situation suggested that he really wasn't that worried.

"We might not be able to accomplish Master Frida's task in these conditions," Eiwin said, looking regretful.

Domeron assuaged her worries. "Frida is a reasonable woman. She'll understand the circumstances in the forest."

"I can only hope she'll still deliver on the uniform."

As the meeting seemed to be concluding, Rog immediately got up from his chair to leave. But Hector waved his hand, and a gust of wind forced the hunter down again.

"I'm not finished yet!" The elder glared at him. "The next matter directly concerns you, Mister Rog!"

"Ugh..." Rog held his head in annoyance. "What do you want from me, old man?"

"I need you to keep scouting the forest," Hector said. "Although we aren't making any moves yet, we still need to be kept informed about the general situation."

"That won't be easy." Rog scratched his beard, thinking. "It depends on how far you want me to go. I can't promise you that I'll escape their detection with how the bandits are acting."

"You don't need to put yourself at risk. Just go as far as you feel comfortable. I need to know if Rickard plans to move against our town before they're at our doorstep."

"Shouldn't be a problem, then..." Rog said. "But what about that demon? Should I try tracking it too?"

"If you can." Hector shrugged, flashing a sly smile. "As long as it sticks to the forest, that only creates more problems for our foes."

Ruthless...

Eiwin's explanation had given Red the impression that demons were the bane of the cultivation world, but Hector didn't look worried in the slightest about one running rampant. It didn't seem to add up.

Sure enough, as he looked at Eiwin, he saw her grimace. Still, she didn't speak up.

"That's all I have to say." Hector stood up. "I might have other tasks for you soon, so don't go running away over the next few weeks."

As Hector brought the meeting to a close, the Sect members started to disperse. Eiwin, however, approached Red before leaving.

"You should go check on Master Goulth," she said. "He was extremely worried when he learned of your disappearance."

Red nodded and walked out of the hall. He still had much to do after returning from this trip, but he decided to follow Eiwin's advice.

Arriving at the blacksmith's workshop, he could feel the man's presence through his crimson sense. The last flare in the Sect belonged to him, its strength about on par with Narcha. After some hesitation, Red knocked on the door.

A shout came from inside. "Come in!"

Red entered the workshop and found Goulth at his usual place. He didn't look up as Red approached.

"You're back, huh?" Goulth said sullenly.

"How could you tell it was me?" Red asked.

"It's the footsteps. I can tell who it is by how their steps sound against the stone..."

The blacksmith trailed off, and an awkward silence settled in the room. Eventually, Red decided to speak.

"I need your help with something."

Goulth snorted. "Hmph, why don't you go ask Narcha for her help? I'm sure she'll probably be more helpful than an old man like me."

Red didn't know how to respond. Instead, he just pulled the cleaver off his back and extended it towards him.

"I found a weapon."

"Where?!" Goulth's sour tone disappeared as he looked over with curiosity. His gaze was drawn to the cleaver in the Red's hand. "That... that's... Let me see it!"

He studied the blade under the sunlight coming from the window. He traced his thumb along the edge of the weapon, and a small trickle of blood dripped off of it.

"Impressive!" Goulth beheld the cleaver in admiration. "Which monstrous insect did you take this from?"

"How can you tell it came from an insect?" Red asked, in awe of the man's knowledge.

"It's the chitin," the blacksmith said. "It's the material most insects' exoskeletons are made of. Although I don't know which monster this came from, I can recognize the material."

"I see... I don't know the name of the insect this came from, though."

Again, Red wasn't lying.

"It's very impressive," Goulth said. "Whatever monster this was, it was probably close to forming a monster core. Unfortunately, it looks like a part of it was damaged. The liquid capable of doing this must have been very corrosive!"

Red recalled the giant spider's glowing, green blood.

"So..." The man lowered the cleaver. "What do you want to do with it?"

"Is there a way to repair it?" Red asked.

"Repair it?" Goulth frowned. "Not possible. The problem with working with animal parts is that you obviously can't replace or repair them as easily as other metals. There is, however, something else we can do with it."

"What is it?" Red perked up.

Goulth smiled. "We can reforge it!"

It seemed the man had completely forgotten he was supposed to be mad at his disciple.

"How so?" Red asked. "You said we can't repair it."

"We can't, but we can use other materials," Goulth said. "We can extract the useful part of this weapon, that being the blade, and use it as the basis for another weapon. Of course, this blade is a bit small, so we can't do anything too big... but it should still work!"

"Can you do it?" Red was excited at the prospect.

"Of course I can! I can make it even better than it is right now, but..." The blacksmith stopped short, a grin crossing his face.

"What is it?" Red asked, confused.

"I'm not doing it!"

"Why not?"

"Because you're the one who's going to do it!"

This stunned Red into silence.

"What? Don't look at me with that face!" Goulth laughed. "I'm sure you'll do a good job!"

"I don't even know how to make a simple dagger yet." Red shook his head. "How can I work on something like this?"

"Well, I'll teach you!" Goulth said. "It might take a while, but when you're ready, you can make this blade into any weapon you want... Don't you feel excited at the prospect of creating something for yourself?"

Now that his master put it that way, this was indeed something that interested Red. His main concern was how long it might take him to be up to the task.

"Is it going to be difficult?" he asked.

"Oh, very much so!" Goulth said. "Dealing with monster parts is completely different from dealing with metals... Any mistakes, and you could shatter this blade and make it completely useless!"

You're not making a compelling argument...

"But this is necessary if you want to craft your own equipment in the future. You can also consider it as a kind of test from me. After all, if you want to pursue blacksmithing in the future, this sort of task can't even be considered a challenge!"

"Okay," Red agreed. "But I can't work right now. I need to rest."

"That's fine." Goulth shrugged, handing him the blade back. "I was occupied anyway."

Red returned his blade to his strap, saying goodbye and heading back to his room. Once inside, he took off his backpack and dumped the items he had recovered from his stash onto the bed.

A bright-green crystal, a yellowed piece of paper covered in writing, a map of the underground, and a shoddy knife. All of his treasures were finally in his possession again.

Now that he finally had time to examine these items, a strange emotion rose inside of him.

He had expected to feel many things. Nostalgia for his life in the underground, fear from remembering his escape, sadness at his mentor's death, relief when he saw the moon for the first time. Yet, none of that was present. Instead, Red felt distant, detached. It was as if all of that happened in another life, to a different person. Like the moment he stepped out of that cave, everything before that point ceased to matter.

Red didn't know if this was a natural reaction, or if something was influencing his feelings. In the end, he decided it didn't matter.

He hadn't changed. His thoughts and his resolve remained his own, of this he was certain. What had changed, though, was his position. He was no longer a slave, no longer someone who had to fight every day for his own survival. No, now he had regained some of his freedom.

Now he was a cultivator, and for the first time in his life, he could see a path for him to walk.

ABOUT THE AUTHOR

Nameless Author is a writer inspired by xianxia, sci-fi, epic fantasy, and just about every genre out there. He enjoys reading, watching movies, and playing RPGs.

About Timeless Wind Publishing

Founded in late 2020 by Lorne Ryburn and Silas Sontag, Timeless Wind Publishing is an up-and-coming indie publishing house. We love sci-fi and fantasy—progression fantasy, power fantasy, LitRPG, time loops, cultivation, system apocalypse—genre fiction of all kinds! We're prolific readers within these genres and endeavor to bring awesome books into the limelight.

We look forward to helping authors (aspiring and published alike) develop and expand an audience of readers who believe in their vision.

Our logo is an exotic cat from a Palmyrene ruin. The word along its back roughly translates to, "Alas!" or "What a shame!" This word is present on all gravestones in Palmyra. It's a recognition that all things come to an end... even the best people and stories. Alas!

We hope our readers will have "alas" moments when they finish our books.

Connect with Timeless Wind Publishing
TimelessWind.com
Facebook.com/timelesswind
Twitter.com/timeless_wind
Instagram.com/timelesswindpub

Made in the USA
Las Vegas, NV
29 November 2024

12863970R00360